SPOILER ALERT!

Before you read this book

read VENGEANCE – Parts 1&2

By the same author

NO CONTRACT

William R Hooper

Copyright © William R Hooper 2023

This story is a work of fiction.

Any resemblance to actual persons is purely co-incidental.

DEDICATION

To my wife, Sue.

With much Love

CONTENTS

INTRODUCTION

NO CONTRACT

EPILOGUE
AUTHOR'S NOTE
JAPANESE PRONUNCIATION

INTRODUCTION

The Caribbean Island of St Margaret is shaped like a banana, or, if you are more romantically inclined, like a crescent moon, with the two ends curving towards the west. The island is laid out on a north to south line and is roughly thirty miles long and eleven miles across at its widest point in the middle. It lies just under fifty miles south-west of the island of St Vincent and is part of the Lesser Antilles group of islands, which are also part of the Windward Islands.

The capital of the island of St Margaret is also called St Margaret and it is on the west coast of the island, just below the middle of the island, and beside a deep-water harbour. The capital is also where the Presidential Mansion is situated; the President of the island is the popular Nigel Ibraheem. He is a big man, being tall and broad-shouldered. He has a bald head and a moustache and he has a tall and elegant wife named Tina. Tina and Nigel have two tall and beautiful daughters; Ola, the eldest, aged twenty-one, and Oyinda, aged nineteen. Together they form the First Family of St Margaret.

St Margaret is also the home of Frank Cross and Tandy Trudeau. Frank, an Englishman, is fifty-four years old and a tall man at six-feet-and-three-inches. He has a handsome clean-shaven face, short black hair that is greying at the temples, a forty-eight-inch chest, muscles and a sun tan. He is ex-British Army, ex-SAS, an ex-Close Protection Police Officer, and an ex-agent in a secret organisation known as the Specialist Operations Unit (SOU), an anonymous part of the British Secret Service. Cross keeps himself strong and fit by working out in his own on-site gym and he is also an expert marksman, who never, ever, misses the target. As well as this, he is also a highly skilled martial arts expert who has been trained on the Japanese island of Kyushu by a Japanese *Sensei,* or Teacher of martial arts; a man called Sensei Nakamura.

As an agent for the SOU, Frank Cross had been their top assassin with a 100% success rate. He is now held in a consultancy capacity as St Margaret's Security Advisor and Anti-Terrorist Training Officer. Frank is also the owner of a photographic shop called Island Photos that is situated in the island's capital, and he also owns a bar that is outside the town of

Nelson which is south of the island's capital. The bar is called The Parrot Shack.

Tandy Trudeau is a native of the Caribbean island of St Lucia, where she was born in the island's capital of Castries. She is 38 years old and she is five-feet-and-nine-inches tall. She is fit and slim and toned and bears a striking and uncanny resemblance to the beautiful Hollywood actress and A-Lister, Halle Berry.

Tandy has been a freelance and internationally infamous assassin known as The Scorpion; she despatched her victims mainly by the use of a lethal injection of a particularly nasty venom extracted from the bodies of a South Sea cone shell. She has also served in the British Army, where she became a sniper, and is extremely accurate with an Accuracy International L96A1 sniper rifle.

Unbeknown to Frank, Tandy had also been working for the Specialist Operations Unit and, as such, she was duped into hunting down Cross by a man by the name of Simon Lancaster. Lancaster was the treacherous chief officer of two sections within that organisation: Recruitment and Training, and Placement and Tracking. Lancaster had been radicalised and recruited into the terrorist organisation known as Intiqam – Intiqam being the Arabic word for Vengeance.

However, Frank was able to discover Tandy's alias and her contract to kill him. As a result - and instead of trying to kill each other - they decided to work together to trace, track and kill both Lancaster and his fellow conspirator: Aarif El-Sayed.

It had been El-Sayed who had adopted the western name of Michael Roblett to avoid suspicion within the British Security Services. This was because he worked within MI5 in an administrative capacity, but was also a deeply hidden operative of Intiqam, working as a one-man terrorist cell.

Working together, Tandy and Frank tracked down and executed Simon Lancaster and Aarif El-Sayed. In hunting down the two men Cross and Trudeau's relationship became closer, until their relationship has eventually turned into an on-going love affair.

Their home on St Margaret is a villa called Cannon Head. Technically this is Frank's villa as he had it built to his own specifications. However, at Frank's invitation, Cannon Head is now Tandy's home as well, although she also keeps a flat in London, England. Frank has a house in London, but Tandy and Frank are thinking of selling both of their London properties and purchasing just one between them, possibly in London's Docklands area.

As they are now both living together at Cannon Head the two properties in England have become superfluous to requirements. However, they both agree that they should maintain a base of operations in London, and they both fancy the idea of something modern and trendy. They have agreed that they would use this London base when they visit the UK and also as a jumping-off point for Europe. However, such a property would never be considered by them as their home because London does not have the same warm sunny climate as St Margaret.

Cannon Head was so named because it occupies the site of what had once been a fort and a gun emplacement back in Lord Nelson's time. The fort and cannons are long gone and only scrub congested the site when Frank applied to buy it. Frank had been given permission to build his villa here after he had saved the lives of the island's President and the First Family from a determined assassin, and a group of Intiqam terrorists, when they hit the president during his inaugural speech as the returning president at the Presidential Mansion, two years ago. And it was at Cannon Head that Frank and Tandy Trudeau took on and defeated another Intiqam death squad that had been sent to kill Cross.

The site that Cannon Head occupies is laid out on the flat top of a high cliff-top promontory that juts out into the Caribbean Sea on the south tip of the island.

The site is at the end of a long driveway that is flanked by tropical trees and plants. At the end of the driveway there are entrance gates that lead onto a broad gravel-covered spoon-shaped parking area which is surrounded by tropical trees and palms and many varieties of shrubs, cacti and flowering plants. As you drive through the entrance gates - and moving clockwise around the perimeter of the parking area - on the immediate left there is a triple garage built of brick and painted white with a pitched roof of terracotta tiles, then a stage built as a *dojo* (a martial arts training area), then a building housing the fully fitted gym, also with white brick walls and a pitched roof of terracotta tiles. This is the gym that Frank and Tandy do their work-outs in. Then there is a swimming pool, and finally the large brick-built white single-storey villa over to the right with the same matching pitched roof and terracotta tiles. The villa has a narrow flowerbed in front of it from which a large flowering passion flower has climbed the front wall and has sprawled across the left-hand side of the roof. The passion flower is being given a run for its money by a younger bright-purple bougainvillea that has been planted in the same bed and which is trying to lay claim to the right-hand end of the roof. Frank Cross had designed it all and it had been constructed by a large team of local building help, and Frank is justifiably proud of his creation.

Frank employs a local lady called Mrs Johnson to clean Cannon Head and deal with the laundry. She comes and goes as she pleases and has the knack of keeping out of sight, so-much-so that Tandy has never actually seen her, and, despite asking Frank numerous times who this woman is, a meeting has never been arranged. And thus, Mrs Johnson has taken on, in Tandy's mind, a kind of paranormal reputation – things get done, but you never see it happen.

The Specialist Operations Unit is situated at the corner of Glasshouse Street off the south end of Regent Street near Piccadilly Circus. The sign etched into the plate-glass front door says that the building is occupied by a company called Amalgamated Exchanges Co Ltd, which is complete tosh.

The SOU works alongside the British Government's Domestic Security Service (MI5) and the Secret Intelligence Service (MI6), but its existence is denied by both of those departments - and if you try and look it up you won't find a trace of it.

To all intents and purposes, it does not exist.

The reason the SOU does not exist is very simple; its singular task is to seek out and assassinate persons and organisations who pose a threat to Britain's National Security - although they are not opposed to also taking off the nation's streets any wrongdoer who poses a threat to society – such as drug traffickers, people traffickers and paedophiles. It does this quietly, efficiently, confidentially, and always terminally.

Because the SOU does not officially exist, it allows Prime Ministers and other Members of Parliament to deny all knowledge of the SOU, thereby allowing the politicians not to lose sleep over it, or worry about its operations and assignments - which the SOU is quite happy about.

The Director of the Specialist Operations Unit is Sir Michael Corrigan. Sir Michael is a shrewd and calculating man; short and stocky with a bull neck and close-cropped greying hair. His face is shaved and he has piercing blue eyes, a wide mouth, and a slightly disjointed nose from an old rugby injury.

The island of St Margaret is not only beautiful it is also a tax haven - and it therefore attracts a lot of international banking business – and, because of this, it has become very rich. This wealth in the island's coffers has allowed Frank the finances to heighten the level of security on the island, and that security protects not only the islanders as a whole but also Frank Cross as an individual, because he has been identified by the media as the man who defeated the attacks on the island by the Intiqam hit squads; although the media could not, and cannot, get any pictures of what he looks like - he literally keeps his head down (or at least behind a pair of Maui Jim sunglasses and under a wide-brimmed hat). And his anonymity with the SOU and his friendship with St Margaret's President looks after the rest.

The security of the island is also supported by the United States of America who have an air base on the north of the island, an air base that rubs shoulders with the Ibraheem International Airport. The island also has two United States patrol boats; these are coastguard cutters, which are highly powered and equipped with twin 50mm deck machineguns. These cutters are called *Shark* and *Eagle Ray* and they patrol the waters up and down the west and east coast of the island. And all of this security is carried out in plain sight and without the islanders being aware of it, so that they can sleep easily in their beds.

Cross, Trudeau, and Sir Michael Corrigan are all hopeful that, following the execution of Lancaster and El-Sayed, the Intiqam threat has been defeated and its forces scattered.

They are soon to find out how wrong they are.

*****

NO CONTRACT

NORTHERN IRAQ
EARLY MAY 2014

Yousuf. The Arabic name means Handsome in English and Yousuf is certainly that. Quite a tall man at five-feet-ten-inches. He has a well-balanced head on broad shoulders and he carries himself with a confident air. His hair and beard are jet black and thick and trimmed short. He has dark eyes below thick black eyebrows and his nose has a hawk-like quality about it. His mouth is wide above a strong chin and he has full lips and good white even teeth. He was always quite a hit with the girls. His full name is Yousuf El-Sayed.

He was dressed in camouflage-pattern army fatigues and he was sitting in a canvas chair just inside the entrance to a large sand-coloured ridge tent. He had his knees apart and was staring down unhappily at the beaten earth between his dusty scuffed desert boots, for he had recently learned of the death of his younger brother.

Yousuf El-Sayed is the leader and commander of an al-Qaeda and ISIS funded terrorist organisation dedicated to bringing down what, in their eyes, is the immoral capitalist and decadent culture of the West. This organisation is Intiqam.

Yousuf's younger brother was Aarif El-Sayed. Yousuf knew that Aarif had been killed by a secret branch of the British Security Services called the Specialist Operations Unit (SOU). Yousuf knew this, and he also knew the name of Aarif's executioner – an agent called Frank Cross. The now dead brother had fed Intiqam information about agent Cross when he had worked for the SOU, and he had fed Intiqam this information in an attempt to track Cross down and have him killed.

What Yousuf El-Sayed did not know was that Cross had been working with a Caribbean lady called Tandy Trudeau and that it had actually been she who had killed his brother. Therefore, Yousuf blamed only Cross, and he did so with an overwhelming, all-consuming, desire for revenge.

Aarif El-Sayed had been the leader of the only Intiqam terrorist training camp which was hidden away in the deserts of northern Iraq. However, following his younger brother's demise, Yousuf had taken over command of the camp. Yousuf was never referred to by his first name, and seldom as El-Sayed. Here, in the camp, and in an organisation, where names were hardly ever used, he had the distinction of being called a different name by his men. Here he was called *al-Makira* – the Cunning.

Al-Makira's Second-in-Command is called Irfan, which means Wisdom. Wise he may be, but he is also cruel and sadistic. Irfan is slightly shorter than his commanding officer. He has thick black wavy hair and his clean-shaven face has been tanned dark by the harsh desert sun. His eyes seem to be set too near each other and this gives him a rather feral-like appearance; an appearance that is enhanced by his sharp canine teeth that show whenever he rarely smiles his thin smile.

Irfan was standing beside his commanding officer and was also dressed in military camouflage fatigues; he had just given his condolences to his leader on the death of his brother.

Al-Makira nodded without looking up. Then he took a deep breath and stood up. "Come with me," he said. "I am going to need your help in killing Frank Cross, the son of a dog bitch who killed my brother." And with that he stepped outside of the tent and spat on the hot ground.

Irfan's eyes gleamed, almost as if he were scenting prey, as he followed his CO out into the bright sunlight. "Then you do have a plan?"

The tent they had just left was one of a number that housed the officers and men. There were other tents for first aid, washrooms, and a couple for administrative purposes and the mess tent. The latrines were the furthest amenities and were simple wooden structures with holes in the ground. They were placed at a distance from the tents because of the stench.

All of this accommodation was strung in a line along the eastern side of a narrow lozenge-shaped hidden valley or *wadi* that was called Wadi Talatah Ma, which roughly translates to the Valley of Three Waters, there being three natural springs in the flat valley floor.

The valley was about four-hundred yards wide and just under a mile in length with each end pinched into a narrow high-walled canyon.

Somewhere in its history the valley had been the course of a river that had run south to north and through those canyons. That river - so old that its name has been long forgotten - was now gone from the surface of the valley, although it still remained some thirty feet down and whose waters were brought up at those three springs by three artesian wells.

The wadi was flanked by one-hundred-foot-high cliffs made of ragged sandstone and was out in the desert and miles from anywhere. It was accessed by Intiqam trucks, some four-wheel-drive vehicles and two helicopters. Two of these trucks, together with two long wheelbase Land Rovers and two Toyota Land Cruisers were parked up on the western side of the camp. The two helicopters were a Bell UH-1 Iroquois (nicknamed the world over as a Huey) and a CH-47 Chinook. These two machines wore matching olive-green paintwork and were sitting on beaten-earth landing pads a few yards in from the northern approach canyon. These aircraft brought in both personnel and supplies. The Chinook is an awkward looking aircraft having two sets of rotor arms, but, by contrast, the Huey is the type of aircraft that looks threatening even when it is powered off and standing still. When it was not moving personnel and supplies the Huey was used by al-Makira as his own personal transport.

Also, on the western side of the valley, but further along from the vehicles, were heaps of old tyres (this rocky ground was not kind to rubber) and large oil and fuel drums, some full and some empty.

In the middle of the valley, and more towards its southern end, was the Intiqam training ground. This was no more than a huge area of flat barren sandy ground that had been beaten flat with sledgehammers and the action of the marching and stamping of many booted feet.

A group of sweating struggling men, wearing the same desert uniform as al-Makira, were running backwards and forwards with assault rifles held over their heads across a marked out square measuring some fifty yards by fifty yards, whilst a sergeant bellowed at them to keep them moving.

Al-Makira and his SiC walked along the line of tents to the mess tent, ducked under the entrance flap, and moved inside, out of sight of any prying spy satellites or high-flying and watching American military aircraft. To their left was a make-shift counter made from two trestle tables pushed end to end and on it were cups and mugs, plates, knives, forks and spoons, pots of coffee and jugs of water. To their right, and in the far corner of the mess tent, was the only other occupant, a man, also in camouflage fatigues. This man sat on his own on a wooden bench seat at a table. He was sitting facing the entrance to the tent so that he could watch who came in. He was hunched forwards with his forearms on the table where they encircled a mug of steaming black coffee.

Al-Makira and his SiC sat down beside each other at a long trestle table just inside the entrance. Like the man in the corner, they were also on wooden bench seats, and they also sat where they could see outside and so that their backs were not facing the entrance. A young man in fatigues came from behind the counter and approached the two men.

"Coffee!" ordered al-Makira and the young man scurried away.

Al-Makira lifted his head towards the man sitting at the corner table and called his name,

"Habib." Al-Makira waved him over. "Come here."

Habib got up. He was a tall handsome man with a close-cropped black beard and a slightly hooded brow over dark hunter's eyes. He was a killer, an assassin, and a trained martial artist; he knew a variety of ways to efficiently kill his target, including poisons, booby-traps and explosives. But he was happier with a knife or a gun. He was Iranian by birth and could trace his ancestral roots back to the area of Alamut, near Tehran.

Alamut had been, centuries ago and at the time of the first crusades, the stronghold of the Hashashin sect, an organisation of highly trained killers. Indeed, the word Assassin is directly derived from the word *Hashashin*.

Habib moved with an easy grace to al-Makira's table and sat down opposite Irfan and his commanding officer, although he was not comfortable with his back to the entrance. He nodded silently to al-Makira, who smiled and nodded back.

Al-Makira sat forwards slightly. "Habib, have you moved the helicopter?" Al-Makira was referring to a Russian Kamov KA-60.

"Yes, al-Makira. I have done as you instructed and moved the chopper from Paris to Marck."

"Good." Al-Makira nodded approval. Intiqam kept a number of aircraft at a number of locations around the globe. The terrorist organisation was well-funded and could afford to buy both the various forms of expensive aircraft and pay for their ground rental fees at airfields. The helicopter that al-Makira was referring to had been based at Le Bourget airport some seven miles north-east of Paris. Le Bourget was the home of a number of private business jets and is the place where they run the Paris Air Show. No-one took any notice of the battle-green livery of the KA-60 helicopter that had been tucked away at one end of the airfield. Why should they? As far as the authorities were concerned it was owned by a respectable millionaire who paid his fees on time. That, of course, was complete fiction. However, under al-Makira's orders, the KA-60 had been moved to Marck just outside of Calais in northern France. From here it was only ninety-five miles to Epping, which was well within the three-hundred-and-fourteen miles range of the helicopter.

Al-Makira, The Cunning, had not informed his Second-in-Command of this move as the Intiqam commander believed in keeping his cards close to his chest. So, the SiC watched the interplay between al-Makira and Habib but said nothing; he had learned that it was not his place to question his CO. However, his curiosity was getting the better of him.

"So," began Irfan, giving one of his nasty rare smiles. "How do you intend to kill this Cross, and will it be soon?"

Al-Makira shook his head and then patted his SiC on the knee; an unusual display of affection. "All in good time, my brother. In fact, it may take a few weeks. I am not going to rush this. I intend to lay my plans very carefully." Al-Makira sat up straight, still smiling. "But I will tell you this, my brothers, it involves abducting Cross's girlfriend as well as a British Member of Parliament...And..." He gave a cruel smile. "And, I am already leaving him a trail of breadcrumbs to follow, to bring him to me."

"Breadcrumbs?" Irfan was puzzled. *What do little bits of bread have to do with this?*

"You will see, my brother." Al-Makira put his right hand on Irfan's shoulder. "All will be revealed." He gave a soft, disconcerting, laugh.

Habib said nothing. He just watched. He listened.

A cockroach appeared on the edge of the table having run up one of the table's legs.

Al-Makira watched it as it scuttled towards him, its long antennae waving as it felt the air.

Irfan slowly shook his head. "I do not understand, my brother. Why don't we just find him and kill him?"

Habib's eyes slid round to look at Irfan. Still he said nothing.

"Because I don't want to," answered al-Makira. His voice had taken on an edge. His hand came down on the cockroach and he trapped the insect under his palm. "I want to enjoy the killing of this dog, and the carrying out of my plans will make his death all the sweeter." Then he pressed down, rather gently. He felt the unfortunate insect's hard carapace crack.

Al-Makira lifted his hand, the cockroach was still alive, as al-Makira had intended it to be. He moved his right index finger and flipped the roach onto its back. It lay there injured and wriggling its legs, waving its antennae.

"No," said al-Makira. "I want Cross to suffer." He reached forward and pulled a leg off the small victim. "I want to have him in front of me, helpless." He pulled another leg off. "I want to inflict pain on him." Another leg. "And then, when I have got him right where I want him, I will kill him very publicly, and with my own bare hands."

Al-Makira balled his fist and brought it down onto the cockroach, smashing it flat.

*****

MID MAY

At night, two men stealthily approached an ancient wooden barn that stood off-centre in a field in Essex, England. The tired old building was surrounded by a crop of tall bright yellow oilseed rape.

The two men, both Iranians, had visited a number of barns like this at night in the Essex area to the north and east of the town of Epping. They had traced a number of barns and farm out-buildings using the Landranger series of Ordnance Survey maps. At each building the two men had inspected the structures for suitability and, if the building met with their approval, the men had then hidden themselves and watched over a period of a couple of days. They had been at this for three weeks and were getting really fed up with it. However, they were under orders, and if they failed in their mission then the price of failure did not bear thinking about. A swift death would be a blessing.

All of the barns, so far, had been of no use to them, being either crammed full of agricultural machinery or in constant use by farmers and farm hands. This latest barn, however, seemed to have an air of desolation about it. So, under the cover of darkness, and using small LED torches, the two men took a turn around the barn and then, coming back to the front of the barn, they pushed one of the huge wooden double-doors open a few inches and slipped inside. The floor was concrete below some ancient dark beams that crossed the span of the barn and which were some fifteen feet above the floor, and above them, there being no ceiling, were the exposed red tiles that formed the sagging roof.

The lower walls of the barn were a double course of red bricks that stood about four feet high into which, at regular intervals, were inserted thick vertical wooden beams. These vertical beams held up the roof. Above the brick courses the spaces between the beams were infilled with rubble and flints that were plastered over.

Opposite the big barn doors, at the other end of the hall-like structure, and up against the wall at the far end of the barn, was an old table with an MDF top and stainless-steel legs. Beside it were a couple of old grey wood and material armchairs and a stack of white, though dirty, plastic patio chairs. All of these items had been here some time and were covered in dust and cobwebs. Apart from these, there was nothing else in the barn. The barn was also not far from the village of North Weald Bassett.

North Weald Bassett is just north of the Essex town of Epping and it has an airfield. It is one of a number of small airfields that are dotted around the countryside on the outskirts of London and a number of these had been identified by Intiqam as places that they could fly into and out of without much trouble, or official interference.

Perfect.

The two men left the barn and headed for a line of trees from where they would watch the barn for a few days.

Three days later and not a farmer or farm hand had come near.

Perfect.

Time to tell al-Makira of their success.

*****

Denise Anderson was a successful Englishwoman. She had blue eyes, long blonde hair and a figure that a lot of men desired and a lot of women envied. She had a nice four bedroomed single-storey house with a swimming pool up on a cliff on the Cote D'Azur in the South of France and she ran a high-end art gallery. Actually, she had a number of such galleries: one along the coast in Cannes, and others in Paris, Madrid, London and New York, and she was getting one soon to be opened in Milan.

Denise had plenty in her bank account.

At 9am, in bare feet and dressed in a long pink fluffy nightgown she went to the front door to collect her mail. There were only two letters; a large brown one and a slim white one; the latter made of good quality paper. She knew the brown one was to do with the new Milan gallery that was soon to be opened amid champagne and celebrities, but the white one was a mystery.

It was postmarked eight days ago and had come from Mosul, in northern Iraq.

Denise held the white one in her left hand and tore it open with the forefinger of her right hand. Her eyes widened in shock, and her right hand went to her mouth as she read the content,

Miss Anderson. Put fifty-six thousand Euros in a black plastic sack and leave it at the end of your driveway on Wednesday night. If you tell the police, or fail to pay the money, some damage will come to you.

It was not signed.
Denise blinked. Then, with shaking hands she read the letter again.
Fifty-six-thousand Euros was about fifty-thousand English pounds.
It had taken the letter eight days to get to her.
It had been delayed in the French postal service.
Today was Thursday.
Her mobile phone rang where she had left it in the dining room. She hurried through to it and picked it up.
"Hello?"
It was the police. Her nice new gallery in Milan had just been blown up.
Denise burst into tears.
Four days later another white letter arrived.
The author wanted more.
Denise began to cry again.

**

10am. The millionaire businessman Rick Duncan, a big muscular guy, barefoot and dressed in jeans and a plain white tee shirt, picked three envelopes up from the front door mat and frowned; two were brown and were obviously bills, but the third was a slim white envelope made of good quality paper.

He carried all three down the wide hall to the back of the house where the spacious kitchen was situated.

Duncan had made his fortune "in computers". What that meant was this: he possessed a mind that could think so logically that he could design websites above and beyond what a customer wanted. It was almost as if he knew more about what the customer wanted and how it should work for them than they did themselves. It was a gift, and he'd cashed in on it. Big time.

Everybody wanted Rick: corporations, banks, oil magnates, Presidencies. You name it.

Rick now lived in an ancient manor house west of Caxton in Cambridgeshire with his wife Paula and their five children. They had bought the house as a dilapidated wreck that had stood boarded up and vacant for forty years and they had completely renovated and refurbished it. With Rick's money they could afford to.

Next to his nice house he had built a double garage in which were parked a Ferrari 458 and a Maserati Gran Turismo. In front of the garage, on the sweeping gravel driveway, sat a Bentley Continental GT.

Rick flipped the bills onto the black granite worktop that went the whole length of a twenty-foot wall but held back the white envelope. It was franked Mosul and it was dated five days ago. Like Denise, he poked his right index finger into one end of the fold-over flap and used it to raggedly slit the envelope open.

He took out the letter inside.

His eyes widened as he read it.

"Shit!"

He was staring at a page of English type:

Mr Duncan. Put fifty-thousand English pounds in a black plastic sack and leave it at the end of your driveway on Friday. If you tell the police or fail to pay the money some damage will come to you.

It was not signed. Obviously.

Rick Duncan picked up the telephone that was hanging on a wall-mount just inside the kitchen door and phoned the police.

An hour later Detective Inspector Sam Orchard arrived on Rick's doorstep and was invited in. He was aged fifty-five and had greying hair and wore glasses on his seen-it-all face that sported a bushy moustache. He wore black trousers and black lace-up shoes and he had a dark grey sports jacket over a light-blue shirt, dark-blue tie. DI Orchard went through to a large front room with Rick. The room had a deep-pile burgundy-coloured carpet and a massive bay window that overlooked a flowerbed and the front drive. They sat down in two button-back dark leather armchairs in the bay.

Rick passed the policeman the envelope with the letter inside.

Detective Inspector Orchard cast his world-weary eyes over the envelope then took out the letter. He read it the once, twitched his moustache and said, "Probably a hoax."

"What if it isn't?"

"Probably is."

Not the help that Rick had expected. "What if it isn't?"

The detective glanced around the room. "Nice house."

"Thank you. What if it isn't?"

Detective Inspector Orchard handed the letter back and took a deep breath. "Mister Duncan, you have a lot of money. Someone else wants some of it. They want you to pay up." There was a pause.

"And?" asked Rick.

"And so, we'll look into it."

Rick was aghast. "And that's it?" He stared at the officer. "What about forensics? What about fingerprints? I mean, this letter has got to be a clue, right?"

"A clue?"

"Yes, a clue. Can't you check out where it came from?"

"We know where it came from, Mister Duncan, it came from Mosul, in Iraq."

"Yes, I know…"

"Mister Duncan, it was posted in Mosul. The paper is of very good quality, so it probably came from Japan. The letter is not handwritten, it is typed, probably on a computer. Now, that may mean that it was written in Iraq and sent from Iraq, but it does not mean that the paper was actually bought in Iraq, or that the writing on it was written in Iraq. It could have been written in Japan, or England or Timbuktu for all I know. And, if someone is being that careful, I doubt whether there are any fingerprints on the actual letter, whereas the envelope will now be covered in them. I would hate to have to arrest the local postman." He watched Rick deflate. "Sorry, Mister Duncan."

Rick held the offending letter in his right hand and ran his left hand over his head. He nodded. "But, can't you at least put someone to watch the end of the driveway on Friday?"

The Inspector raised an eyebrow. "Why? What do you intend to do, Sir?"

"I intend to put a bag of nicely cut newspaper, nicely cut to look like banknotes you understand, out at the end of the driveway for Friday, and when the sender of this letter comes along you can grab him."

The detective nodded. "Yes, that might work."

Rick felt the mild prickle of irritation. "I'm glad you think so."

Detective Inspector Orchard regarded Rick for a few moments. He was working out in his mind who he could spare at the police station for surveillance duty. He came to a decision and said, "Very well, Mister Duncan. We'll put a man on it."

Rick bristled. "A man? Just the one?"

Orchard straightened his back. "As you may have heard, Sir, we are understaffed in the police force. I'm afraid one man, or woman, will have to do."

Rick ran his tongue around the inside of his teeth. "Right. Well, thank you, Detective Inspector. Let's see what happens Saturday."

"Saturday, Sir?"

"Yes, you know, the day after Friday. Let's see if I get shot, shall we?"

Rick did not get shot.

His Bentley was blown up on his driveway instead.

The following Thursday evening Rick put one-hundred-thousand pounds in real banknotes in a black plastic sack at the end of his driveway, having received another white envelope in the post that informed Rick of the error of his ways, and that now the amount of money had doubled.

It was only the start of the demands.

Like a great many other wealthy people, Rick Duncan's troubles were just beginning.

*****

TUESDAY 27TH MAY

On this particular day, Frank Cross walked in the early morning sun and under a clear blue sky, along the private drive that led from Cannon Head to where it met the narrow road that led up from the west coast of the island. This road continued in a wide loop around to the east coast with lush rainforest on the left coming right to the road's edge. On the other side of the road was a narrow border of low flowering bushes in front of the sheer drops into the sea far below.

Frank had left Tandy sleeping in his bed when he had climbed out from under the thin summer-weight duvet to see if Mrs Jones, the post lady, had delivered anything. He was hoping for a cheque.

Tandy had given a little sleepy groan as he had slid naked out of bed. Tandy had her own bedroom at the other end of the villa so that she had her own space. But they often teamed up - in more ways than one – and last night they had shared Frank's bed.

Slipping out of the bed, Frank pulled on a pair of black underpants, shoved his feet into a pair of straw Japanese-style flip-flops, and grabbed his light-blue towelling bathrobe off the back of his bedroom door. He headed through to the dining room where he picked up a battered grey fedora hat and his Maui Jim sunglasses from the dining room table, and headed out into the warm air to go and get the post. He shoved the sunglasses onto his nose and plonked the hat onto his head.

Frank arrived at Cannon Head's very own post box; a large red square steel box on the top of a three-feet-high metal pole by the side of the road. It had a flap door on the front which he dropped open. He took out a spider the size of a fifty pence piece and a sheaf of envelopes. The spider was the reason why Tandy never collected the post; she had an aversion to anything creepy-crawly, all of which she labelled simply Bugs. Frank gently tossed the spider to the grassy floor, knowing that it would be back tomorrow morning, and shuffled through the envelopes. As he closed the box and turned away one of the envelopes immediately caught his attention and he opened it on the spot with a thumbnail. Ahh, there was that cheque.

The cheque was for services rendered by Frank and Tandy's newly formed Close Protection and Rescue Service called Shadows. He glanced at the rest of the envelopes then passed them through his hands like playing cards; one was from his bank, another from the local telephone company and another was hand-written in blue biro from Montmartre, Paris. Frank allowed himself a slight smile; he knew who that one was from and Tandy would not like it, so he tore it in two and shoved the pieces into a pocket on his robe, to be carefully disposed of, unread, later. He turned towards the villa, walked a few steps, then stopped.

Something was wrong.

Frank had spent years in the British Army, part of which had been in the Parachute Regiment and then with the SAS. Following that he had been in the British Police Force and had served as a Close Protection Officer and had operated in the Police Anti-Terrorist Squad. Add to that the years he had spent with Sensei Nakamura honing his senses and you had a man whose survival instincts more than equalled those of a wild animal. If Frank Cross felt there was something wrong with the surroundings, then there was something wrong.

He turned back towards the road and swept his eyes left to right. No traffic; no-one parked up. Then he switched his attention to the dense vegetation that sat either side of the driveway that led back to his villa. After that he turned again and focussed on the opposite side of the road.

Across from him was the profusion of leaves of the island's rainforest; some were the leaves of trailing vines caught up in green tangles and some were leaves as big as Zulu war shields. Amongst them were tall grasses and green fronds, and over them all was a canopy made from the many kinds of trees that grew there.

Frank ran his eyes over the greenery before he shrugged his shoulders, turned, and headed back up the driveway to Cannon Head. But he felt uneasy.

From deep in those green leaves a pair of eyes watched Frank Cross.

When Frank arrived back at Cannon Head Tandy was up out of bed and singing in the shower. Her favourite singer was Rod Stewart and she was giving it large under the stream of water with her renditioning of *Maggie May*. Frank's feeling of unease slowly dissipated.

Tandy was also now employed by the government of St Margaret in their Tourism Department as a film-maker, something that she had studied at college in her late teens and which was something she was exceptionally good at.

However, they had both discovered that running their separate businesses did not have the same buzz attached to them as their former employment as international assassins. Both of them had used their murderous skills to rid the world of criminals; criminals that Frank and Tandy both referred to as "scumbags", and Frank and Tandy had both admitted to each other that they missed the adrenalin rush that came with fulfilling a contract – in other words; killing a scumbag.

And so, they had formed Shadows – a close protection and rescue team.

The name of the company referred to how they would carry out a protection or rescue – they would be there, but you might not necessarily see them – as skilled and silent as the Japanese *ninja*; the Shadow Warriors.

Shadows was already starting to be very successful, as the cheque that Frank was still holding in his hand attested. Shadows also satisfied the need for that buzz. Any threat of danger or physical violence provided the excitement that Tandy and Frank both craved like a drug. The company had been set up only six weeks ago, but, following personal recommendations from President Ibraheem, in the past three weeks they had picked up three Close Protection contracts – bodyguarding.

Shadows consisted of the two owners and three "employees".

The three employees were three guys who the two owners took on with "temporary contracts" - which meant they got paid in cash when the job was done. Those guys were: Thompson "Tommo" Davidson, James "Clonk" Cameron and Roger "T Bone" Collins.

Tommo was a St Margaret islander; he was a huge muscular giant of a man at nearly seven-feet tall with dark brown skin and a completely bald head. He had been in the British Army with Frank and had been in the 1st Battalion, Parachute Regiment, better known as the Paras, with the 1st Battalion being the Special Forces Support Group. Tommo now lived in the accommodation attached to The Parrot Shack bar. This he managed for Frank. Tommo lived there with his wife, Connie, and his daughter, Sandra. Sandra looked after Frank's photographic shop in the island's capital.

When Frank had first thought of recruiting Tommo into Shadows it had been Tandy that had reminded him that although Tommo would jump at the offer of action and possible mayhem, his wife, Connie, would not be enamoured with the idea of her husband risking his life for a few dollars. Which is how Connie would look at it.

Tandy told Frank that they would have to go and see Connie and Tommo, but that Frank could do the talking as Connie scared the hell out of her.

A meeting had been arranged.

Although Tommo was a veritable giant his wife was considerably shorter, even in her very high heels. She was a good-looking firecracker of a woman with a good UK size 12 figure and a very attractive face. She was leaning against the edge of the bar on the public side whilst her husband stood on the business side with his muscles bulging under the thin cotton of the tight T shirt that he was wearing. The T shirt had the logo *The Parrot Shack* emblazoned across the front. There was a young tall slim Caribbean girl standing alongside him; this was not Sandra, as she was at Frank's shop.

At the end of the bar nearest the door was a T shaped perch, and sitting on the perch was a very large macaw, a parrot, which had given the bar its name; the bar was called The Parrot Shack and the parrot was called Captain Morgan.

Captain Morgan was a highly colourful bird and he had his head cocked to one side as he listened. His black beady eyes watched the proceedings as he stood on his left leg and held an unshelled peanut in a gnarled claw at the end of his right.

Frank and Tandy were standing on the customer's side of the bar and in front of Captain Morgan. Tandy was standing behind Frank. If he asked her later why she had been hiding behind him she would tell him she wasn't, she was backing him up.

She wasn't. She was hiding.

Connie was facing Frank.

Connie did not look at all happy and was glaring at Frank from under her long false eyelashes.

"And who's gonna look after this place while he's…(here Connie jabbed the light-blue sparkly nail-varnished thumbnail of her right hand over her shoulder towards Tommo)…off galivantin' aroun' wid'jou?" Her other hand was resting arrogantly on her left hip. If she'd had a gun-belt strapped around her waist she would not have looked out of place in a Western; the saloon owner calling out the bad guy.

"WARK!" said Captain Morgan.

Connie threw the bird a glance that said, *Who asked you?* then said, "I can't look after it." This was because Connie worked full-time as part of the security team at the island's international airport. She continued, "And neither can Sandra, 'cause she's kept busy at your photographic business. So, again…Who's gonna to look after this place?"

Connie had asked a fair question, and one that Frank (usually a very organised and pre-prepared person) hadn't thought of.

"WARK?" said Captain Morgan again and this time Tommo glared at the bird before offering, "Look honey, it'll only be for a short while, won't it Fra…" Tommo's sentence was cut off as Connie's right hand came up, fingers splaying. The nail-varnish sparkled some more, this time off all five tips. Connie was about to say, "Don't you honey me…". But before she could, and before anyone else could speak up (including the parrot) the young girl behind the bar said,

"I can do it."

The girl was Connie and Tommo's niece called Jacinta. Pronounced Ha-seen-ta, it is Spanish for Hyacinth, and Jacinta was as beautiful as that flower.

Connie turned to look across and up at her as Tommo looked down at her. Jacinta smiled sweetly. "Honestly, I can do it."

Jacinta had been with Connie and Tommo for a month. She was taking a few months as a working holiday after finishing with top marks in Business Studies at the island's college. She was twenty-one years old, five-feet-seven-inches tall with long brown hair, brown eyes, full lips, and a wide and happy smile with sparkling white even teeth. She was smiling now.

"Seriously, I can do it. I've been working behind this bar for four weeks now, and it will only be for a few days at a time, won't it Frank?" She was still smiling.

"Absolutely," confirmed Frank. He managed to look serious and keep the grin off his face.

"There you are honey," said Tommo. "You see, it'll only be for a few days at a time…an' I'm sure Jacinta can cope for a few days."

"Sure can," said Jacinta, nodding and smiling some more.

Connie now had both hands on her hips. She puffed some air out from between her lips as her head moved from Jacinta to Tommo to Frank. "Hmm!" she said, tapping her right foot on the floor. "I can see I aint gonna win this one."

"Lovely Connie!" squawked the parrot.

Connie eyed Captain Morgan again and Captain Morgan looked straight back at her. Connie was wondering what he would look like on a plate surrounded by french fries. Then she looked around the group; now everyone was grinning.

Connie, wanting to have the last word, or to have at least managed to get her own ship to go down with a few of her deck guns firing, said, "And where will you sleep my girl? I won't have you travellin' backwards and forwards alone, late at night."

It was another good ploy, because, at the moment, when her bar shift was finished, Tommo drove Jacinta home to her parents' house in St Margaret.

"Oh, I've thought of that," answered Jacinta still smiling sweetly. "I can have Sandra's bedroom here, and Sandra can stop in Frank's flat above Island Photos."

Connie frowned. "And do we know if Sandra will find this arrangement acceptable?"

"Oh yes," smiled Jacinta. "I've already asked her."

With the last deck gun having been fired, Connie's galleon, it's decks awash, slid beneath the waves.

Connie gave up gracefully. "Oh, all right!" She paused and wagged a finger at her enormous towering husband. "But don't you get yourself killed or you'll have me to answer to…" She rounded on Frank and poked the point of a nail-varnished finger into his broad chest. "And that goes for you too!"

Frank raised both hands in surrender. "I'll look after him Connie, I promise."

"You'd better!"

"WARK! Lovely Connie!" said Captain Morgan.

Connie's eyes narrowed as she looked at the bird. Captain Morgan dropped his nut out of his talon and edged along his perch, away from Connie.

With Tommo recruited it only remained for Frank to contact the two other men whom he wanted to make up the personnel of Shadows: James Cameron and Roger Collins. These two men were ex-SAS with whom Frank had served when he had done his stint in the Regiment: James "Clonk" Cameron was a Scotsman who was in his early fifties, five-feet-and-six-inches tall with an untidy shock of fiery ginger hair and a Zee Zee Top beard to match. He was a broad-shouldered stand of muscle. His friends affectionately called him Clonk, due to his habit of using his big hairy fists to end his arguments by knocking-out people who annoyed him. Clonk had never married, but he had a girlfriend with whom he lived in an apartment outside of Malaga in Spain. He was an explosives and demolitions expert.

Roger "T Bone" Collins was an Englishman. Also early fifties. Five-feet-and-eleven-inches tall with a head of quarter-inch shaved stubble, no beard, no moustache. Roger lived in an old cottage in the middle of nowhere in England's Lake District. He was divorced and never saw his ex-wife as she hated his guts and the feeling was mutual. He had one son but never saw him either. T Bone was a communications expert as well as having an almost supernatural understanding about the way mechanical things worked without ever having come across them before. He was also a qualified pilot and could fly anything.

Like most members of the armed forces - who have been taught specific professional skills that cannot be used in the business world, like blowing up bridges or strangling people with a bootlace - when they finally leave the military they are often fish out of water. This particularly applies to members of the Special Forces who, having left their profession, find themselves acting as night-club doormen, or becoming personal trainers, and sometimes getting sucked into a criminal career.

Clonk had set up a small company that used his acquired skills with explosives to be able to level any object or building that you hired him to demolish. T Bone had also been more fortunate than most, having used his communications skills to run his own small business repairing all sorts of communications and listening devices – the sort used in covert surveillance.

When Shadows had first been proposed, Frank had told Tandy that he wanted Tommo, Clonk and T Bone on board. Tandy had already met Tommo a good number of times as they used The Parrot Shack a lot, and Frank played both alto saxophone and electric and acoustic guitars there some nights with the resident band. However, Tandy had never laid eyes on either Clonk or T Bone. So, in order for Tandy to get to know these two new guys – guys that she would have to trust with her life, and vice-versa – a meeting had been arranged and therefore both Clonk and T Bone had been invited to Cannon Head.

T Bone and Clonk had arrived on different flights at St Margaret's Ibraheem International Airport from their separate departure points and T Bone had arrived first at Cannon Head in a taxi. He was dressed in black lace-up shoes, designer jeans and an Armani jacket over a white tee shirt and he had been good manners and charm personified. He had entered the dining room, placed his leather suitcase out of the way in one corner, shook Frank's hand and kissed Tandy's. Clonk had been a different matter. He had also arrived by taxi and was wearing old trainers with no socks, an old pair of cut-down jeans as shorts, and a short-sleeved check shirt that revealed his arm tattoos; mostly snakes, spiders and skulls with some images of chainmail thrown in. He paid off the driver and called out Frank's name.

"In here!" yelled Frank. "Front door's open. Come through!"

Clonk came through the front threshold, through the small hall and in through the double entrance doors to the living room. He was carrying a large hold-all full of his gear which he dumped unceremoniously straight down onto the sealed bare floorboards of the living room floor. He came around the large polished mahogany table that, although it had been renovated, still bore some of the scars obtained during the hit-squad attack on Cannon Head. The table sat in the middle of the room and having moved around it he greeted Frank and T Bone each with a hug that would have done a grizzly bear justice. And then Clonk turned to Tandy who had just entered from outside. She put her sunglasses up onto her head as she scanned him.

"Well…Hel-lo Darlin'," said Clonk in his broad Scottish accent, and he ran his eyes slowly over her body from top to toes and back again. She was wearing a very short pair of bright-yellow shorts and a matching bright-yellow tee shirt. No bra and no footwear. Clonk smiled and said, "Things are lookin' up for me I see."

Tandy did not answer him, but Frank could see her bridle and he thought, *Uh-oh. Here we go! Any second now!*

"This," said Frank, his face betraying nothing, "is Tandy. She's part of the team."

The Scotsman turned to stare at Frank. He was visibly shocked. It wasn't that he was averse to working with women - there are women in the Regiment – but this one, apart from looking stunningly beautiful, he thought should be modelling swimwear, rather than acting as a bodyguard.

"You're joking, right?" asked Clonk. He remained staring at Frank but with a hand outstretched towards Tandy. "I mean she looks very pretty…But you *are* joking?"

"No." Frank shook his head and folded his arms across his chest. "Tandy and I both own Shadows."

Clonk's eyes narrowed a fraction. "Oooo-oooh," he said as he wiggled his right elbow towards Frank. "Partners, eh?" and his voice dripped with suggestiveness.

Never mind what Tandy thought, Frank felt like thumping Clonk right there. But he did not rise to the bait. He knew Clonk of old, and he knew what he was up to. This was what is known as Winding Someone Up. So, Frank kept his arms folded and his face impassive.

Clonk ran his eyes over Tandy again, and said in a very disparaging voice, "Well, as I say, she looks very pretty…" He laughed out loud. "But can she fight?"

"Why don't you try her and find out?" asked Tandy, who never liked being talked about as if she wasn't there.

"Oh, lassie, you must be joking?" Again, with that disparaging tone of voice.

"No, you big hairy bastard, I'm not." Tandy had her hands on her hips, her face had hardened, and her back had straightened.

Clonk's face changed. He didn't like being talked to like that by anybody, let alone this slip of a girl. He turned his head and looked at Frank, who simply raised a quizzical eyebrow, which said, *So, now what are you going to do?*

Clonk was still looking at Frank when he suddenly went for her, hoping to catch her out. He moved fast, reaching out with his left hand to grab her throat. He did not intend to hurt her, just maybe ruffle her feathers a little.

As Clonk's left hand moved, Tandy used *tai-sabaki*, body-shifting. She jerked her body to her right, twisting at the knees and hips, turning her torso and neck away from his thrusting fingers. As fast as a whipcrack she grabbed his left wrist in her left hand and clamped on tight, then she rammed her right forearm into the back of the elbow joint of his left arm and put her right foot across in front of his legs so that his forward momentum tripped him up. She pushed hard with her right forearm into Clonk's elbow joint and, unable to resist the elbow lock and the pull of gravity, Clonk went down heavily. He fell, full length and face first, onto the polished wood of the living room floor.

Tandy went down with him, bending at her knees to keep her balance and to stop his weight from pulling her over. As he landed, Tandy quickly stepped across his body. She still had his left wrist in her grip and she wrenched his arm up his back and sat down on him, straddling his back. Her free right hand went around to the front of his throat and her fingers and thumb went either side of his windpipe, crushing it. The whole defensive move and counter-attack had taken Tandy two seconds.

"Graaach!" spluttered Clonk with the left-hand side of his face pushed into the floorboards.

"Well," said Tandy from her perch on Clonk's broad back. "He's very pretty…But can he fight?"

Clonk tried to get up but Tandy simply eased his left arm further up his back and squeezed some more at his windpipe.

Clonk tried to say something, so Tandy squeezed his throat harder. "Sorry, Mister Cameron?" she asked politely. "Did you say something?"

Clonk put out his right hand and slapped the floor twice – the universal martial arts submission tap, which meant *I Give In.*

Tandy released her choke hold and his arm and stood up. She moved quickly away, balanced, with both fists up in front of her face in a defensive posture and keeping a wary eye on him.

Frank and T Bone were both standing with their arms folded across their chests, watching and smiling broadly.

Clonk rolled over and sat on his bum looking up at her. He nodded his head a couple of times and a smile began to crease his face. Then he rubbed at his throat and gave a small cough.

"Please accept my apologies, lassie. My, but that was some demonstration."

Tandy put her feet apart and her hands back on her hips. "Apology accepted, Mister Cameron."

"My friends call me Clonk." He held out a big right paw. "Friends?"

Tandy smiled at him. She held out her own slim fingers. "Friends."

They shook hands.

Frank breathed a sigh of relief.

It followed that the two new members of the team were even more surprised when they discovered that Tandy was adept in the use of a certain very deadly cone shell venom and had used it in the past to poison her victims, mostly with darts, but sometimes up close with hypodermics. And when Frank also told the two former SAS men that she could shoot the testicles off a spider at a thousand yards Clonk, rather disbelieving, had said that spiders don't have testicles, to which Tandy had replied, "Well, they don't in this house!"

However, Clonk was still sceptical. The record for the longest sniper shot was once held by US Marine Gunnery Sergeant Carlos Hathcock in the Vietnam War and was measured at 2,500 yards or 1.42 miles. That record stood from 1967 to 2002 since when it has been broken a number of times. Clonk simply could not accept that this girl in front of him was capable of pulling off a similar shot – and he told her so.

"Tell him," said Frank.

Tandy folded her arms across her chest, gave Clonk a cherubic smile and said, "Manfred Althaus, Monaco, July, twenty-twelve."

Clonk blinked and his mouth came slowly open. "That was you?"

The cherubic smile stayed in place.

"Man," chimed in T Bone. "That was you? Really?"

"Yes. That was me. Really."

"Well, I'll be buggered," said Clonk. "That was over a thousand yards. Damn! That was one helluva shot!"

"And across a harbour full of ship's masts," added Frank proudly. And it *had* been one hell of a shot. In fact, in the annals of assassination, it had passed into legend: taken from inside a hotel balcony that overlooked the famous South of France harbour, Tandy had fired just the one round. That round had crossed the harbour, avoiding boat masts and ship's rigging, to hit Manfred Althaus in the head whilst he had been reclining on a sun-lounger and reading a book on the sun deck of his motor-yacht. Althaus had been a millionaire German "businessman" who dealt in guns, porn, and people trafficking. Tandy, as The Scorpion, had assassinated him on a contract given to her by the Specialist Operations Unit

"Good God," breathed T Bone, and Frank just stood and smiled broadly at T Bone and Clonk's awe and discomfort. Frank knew just how good Miss Trudeau was at shooting things, and it was a skill that had been acquired by her in the British Army and had been further improved upon (if that was possible) here at Cannon Head under his tutelage. And the fact that she had served in the British Army, as they had, further increased her standing with them.

T Bone and Clonk also discovered why it was that Tandy was a such a very useful martial artist – she had been trained by Frank Cross. You didn't muss with Tandy. As Clonk had found out.

The first two assignments that Shadows picked up had been rock stars; one was a band, and the other was a female singer. President Ibraheem knew the mother of the male who was the lead singer with a heavy metal band called Saint Ud. The name had nothing to do with the Catholic faith and was a deliberate pun, so that when it was written on their posters and tee shirts it came out as StUd.

The lead singer liked to call himself Zak - although his real name was Geoffrey. StUd's manager had already assigned the band four bodyguards from a local security agency, but when Geoffrey – sorry, Zak – demanded further security Shadows had been found on their new website and, because of the Special Forces backgrounds, they were called in to help. In fact, what happened next was that the four members of the security firm handed over control to Frank and his team, bowing to the greater expertise.

Both teams, now working together, had to get the band from their homes in San Luis Obispo, California, to San Francisco where they were giving a concert. They went in convoy up the Californian coastal road through Cambria, Big Sur and Carmel into Monterey, and on to San Francisco where they went through a cordon of screaming fans and into the baseball ground where the concert was to take place. It all went without a hitch.

The other rocker was a solo singer, called Storm - real name Stephanie – a young lady who lived in Coconut Grove, Miami, Florida. She was also appearing in front of an adoring audience at a concert venue, but this one was in Los Angeles. This time the same manager went directly to Shadows and paired them with the same four agency boys.

Shadows got the rock stars to their concerts and home again. No problem. But once home the Shadows team had to leave them, because they could hardly babysit them forever. However, because Frank did not like loose ends, he arranged for the agency guys to do the babysitting and gave them a free crash course in up-close-and-personal close protection work so that they were able to do the babysitting.

The third assignment had been a little harder. There were two people to be protected; an Arab oil magnate and his wife who were living in one of their properties just outside of Paris. The man had received one of those threatening white envelopes with a demand for money and he had refused to pay. As a result, his Rolls-Royce had been blown up on his driveway, and he was now terrified.

The close protection job proved to be a lot tougher, but only because the wife was an overweight, pampered, self-centred bitch who treated everybody like shit. They had received a death threat and were due to go to the l'Opera Garnier in Place de l'Opera, Paris. The death threat was hardly surprising when you considered how the wife behaved.

This time the Shadows team worked alone. The couple were taken to the theatre in a hired Range Rover that had been leased and checked over on receipt by Frank's team. On arrival at the grand opera house the wife insisted on leaving the protection of the group to go to the rest rooms to check her make-up. "Rest room" actually meant toilet and Tandy went with her into the Ladies room. It looked less like a rest room and more like a spa. Along one wall was a polished pink granite surface that was mounted in front of a massive mirror. Set into the pink granite were trendy rectangular white wash basins which were so shallow as to be almost useless – but with their shiny gold taps they looked nice.

Tandy had stood just inside the door, taking up an open-legged well-balanced stance in her laced-up flat black heels, white shirt and dark trouser-suit, her hands clasped together in front of her open black jacket. By standing in this way she could sweep the right-hand side of the jacket to one side with her hand to reveal her Glock 19 semi-automatic pistol that sat on her hip in its supple dark-brown leather holster. The right-hand hip pocket had a small brass weight in it which allowed the material of the jacket to be brushed aside with ease.

"Wait outside," ordered the wife as she leaned forwards and peered at her face in the wall-length mirror.

Tandy didn't move.

The woman paused with an extremely expensive lipstick raised near her mouth and turned just her head. "I said, wait outside!"

Tandy stared at her.

"Get out!"

Tandy took four steps forwards and grabbed the woman's arm above her left elbow and spun her around so that she faced Tandy full-on.

The wife fumbled with and dropped the lipstick. It fell onto the granite, bounced and went into a basin. "How dare..." she began; her colour flushing to her cheek bones.

Tandy grabbed the woman's other arm above the elbow and yanked her forwards and upwards. This woman was soft from over-indulgence and lack of exercise and Tandy had a body that was strong and fit and toned. Tandy worked-out, she lifted weights, she was a martial artist. She held the wife so that she was up on her tip-toes with her heels coming out of her pink Jimmy Choo four-inch-high stiletto high-heel shoes. The woman's mouth was open in alarm and shock as the high colour drained from her face and she stared into Tandy's unflinching eyes.

Tandy growled like a lioness. "Listen to me, you bitch." She jerked the woman's arms. "I am not one of your lackeys, so don't talk to me like that. I am here to protect you, so shut your mouth and let me do my job." Tandy shoved and the woman landed back into her shoes but then nearly fell over.

Scared stiff, pale of face and extremely flustered, the wife grabbed her clutch bag where she had left it on the granite surface, snatched her lipstick out of the washbasin and, speechless, she hurried for the door. As she hustled past Tandy she gave her a look of complete fear, as though Tandy might cuff her around the ear at any second.

Outside the restroom, the wife made it back to her husband as fast as she could.

Had Tandy over-stepped the mark? After all, you were not supposed to rough-up the clients.

However, the evening went along perfectly, with the wife hardly saying a word for fear of being smacked around the head by Tandy.

After the Arab and his wife had been delivered back home safely, Tandy turned to Frank and said,

"We are *not* going to work for this couple again."

Frank looked at her and raised an eyebrow. "Oh, really? Why?"

"Because if someone else does not kill that woman, I will." With the threat in the white envelope Frank knew that there was a high probability that a killing might actually happen. However, he shrugged and deferred to his partner's annoyance and said,

"Yes, she did start out a little difficult. But she did seem to act a little more gracefully not long after we arrived here. In fact, it was just after she went into the washroom with you."

Tandy grinned. "I wonder why?"

Frank stared at her. She looked the picture of innocence.

There was a moment, and then Frank said, "Ohh, don't tell me..." He stopped and began to laugh. "Oh well, I guess we have to strike those two off our list."

And so they did. But only after they got paid. Which was in fact the cheque that Frank had retrieved from his post box.

Two days later the second of the oil magnate's Rolls-Royces got blown up outside their house and the Roll's owner, who now had a very hysterical wife, left a very large bundle of money at a pre-arranged venue in the hope that it would stop the demands.

It didn't.

*****

SATURDAY 31ST MAY

Between assignments for Shadows, Tommo, T Bone and Clonk went their own ways; Tommo went back to the Parrot Shack and the other two either went home or carried out their individual interests elsewhere in the world. However, they all remained on alert; ready to drop whatever they were doing and come if Frank called them.

At the moment they were all between assignments, and Frank was sitting in the sun at a small white wrought-iron table beside Cannon Head's swimming pool. He had finished his breakfast of muesli and fresh mango and was holding a large glass of ice-cold freshly squeezed orange juice in his hand. He was wearing only a pair of bright yellow swimming shorts and his Maui Jim sunglasses. He was sitting back quite relaxed. His muscular arms, chest and legs were tanned from the Caribbean sun and he was watching Tandy.

From where he sat he could see the stage that he had had built when Cannon Head had been constructed. The stage was out in the open and consisted of a surface of smooth and polished wooden planks that were supported two feet above ground height. The stage had been made for the practice of martial arts, but Tandy, who was a highly accomplished gymnast, also practiced her gymnastic moves on it. She was practising now.

She was wearing only a bright fuchsia-pink sleeveless leotard that was cut high at the hips and with a V neckline, and Frank was watching her as she jumped and rolled. She twisted in the air and landed on her hands to pivot and flick up onto her feet before repeating the performance. Eventually she landed on the soles of her neat bare feet with her back towards him. He called out to her and, although she heard him, she gave no acknowledgement, instead choosing to go into another diving roll across the stage and then doing a series of backflips to bring her back to her starting position, again with her back towards Frank. Tandy was not a girl to be hassled.

Finishing with her slim but muscle-toned arms by her side she turned her head to look at Frank. She gave him a dazzling smile and jumped down off the stage, landing as lightly as a breeze. The neckline of her leotard was damp with sweat and little beads of the same substance lined the side of her face and her brow. Frank was both intrigued and delighted by the way that her chest was heaving magnificently with exertion.

Tandy stood perfectly still alongside the stage and took three deep breaths, lifting her arms as she breathed in and lowering them slowly as she breathed out, just as Frank had taught her when he had first started to teach her the martial art of karate. Seconds later she had her breathing under control.

Then she came over to Frank with all the grace of a jungle cat and Frank unashamedly ran his eyes over her perfect body before she reached out and took his glass of orange juice out of his hand. She ran her own eyes over his muscular shoulders and chest then drank down a couple of mouthfuls of the juice before giving it back.

A bananaquit, a small yellow and dark-grey, almost black, finch-like bird fluttered to the table and cocked its head to one side, peering at the table. These birds are common throughout the Caribbean islands and are robbers of anything sugary. In fact, they are so obsessed with sugar that you can teach them to take small pieces of fruit out of your hand. However, this bird, finding nothing to steal on the table, flicked away through the sunlight. Tandy smiled after it then turned to Frank. He had a look on his face. She knew that look. He was thinking.

"What's up, Frank?"

"I've been thinking," began Frank.

"I know what you've been thinking, tiger," she said as she pouted at him and dropped into the other chair alongside Frank. She crossed her legs at her shins and leaned against the hard muscle of his upper right arm. It was like leaning against a carved oak fence post.

"Apart from that," smiled Frank, "I've been thinking…Perhaps we should add to your martial arts skill-set?"

"We?"

"Well, that is…you."

Tandy eyed him suspiciously. "What have you got in mind?" Frank was always dreaming up ways of refining her skill-set; in the past he'd had her balancing on the edges of bricks, standing on the tops of posts, and climbing ropes up the sides of some of the villa's buildings. He'd also had her standing on one leg on the ridge of the roof of the gym and, from time-to-time, he would toss a tennis ball at her for her to catch, testing her reactions.

"Okay…Would you like to go and train with Sensei Nakamura?"

Tandy sat up with her eyes widening. "Would I? Is the Pope catholic?"

Frank laughed. "I take it that's a yes then?"

"I'll say." She took his glass out of his hand again and stole some more juice. "But will he take me? And what about business here, and Shadows?"

"Not a problem, m'dear. As I understand it you haven't got any filming in the pipeline, and you've already done a large body of work for the tourist board, so I'm sure Nigel won't mind you taking some time off."

Nigel was President Nigel Ibraheem and Frank and Tandy not only talked to him on a first name basis, they also considered him, and his family, close friends. Due to her filming skills, Tandy had been offered a job on the St Margaret official Tourist Board by the president to help promote the island. She had accepted, and was carrying out her duties very successfully, and, as a result of her top level films advertising the attractions of St Margaret the tourists were rolling in to the tax-free island.

"Well, if you think so?" offered Tandy.

"I'm sure we can swing it."

"If we can it would be great!" enthused Tandy. "So how do I start? Do I phone Mister Nakamura?"

"Ahh," said Frank. "Two things…He does not have a landline, or a mobile, and you must never call him *Mister* Nakamura. You call him either Sensei, or Master. Oh, and remember…if you meet him, bow…If in doubt, bow!"

Tandy nodded enthusiastically. "Right. Good. So how do I get hold of him to ask if I can train with him?"

"You must write. Not only does he not have a phone, he does not have a computer either. So, you must write him a letter, the old-fashioned way, with a pen, preferably a fountain pen, with black ink. I have the address, although the house doesn't have a number, just a name."

"What's it called?" asked Tandy, and then more eagerly, "I bet it's called something like, Ninja Castle or the Black Pagoda!"

"No," said Frank, shaking his head, "it's not. It's nothing like that."

"Oh." Tandy sounded a little disappointed. "What is it then?"

"It's called *Hagakure*."

"What does that mean?" She frowned. Then her face brightened. "Hang on…I know…it probably means House of Deadly Death!"

"God save us," muttered Frank, shaking his head. "No. It means Hidden Under Leaves."

Tandy's eyes widened. "Hey, that sounds really atmospheric. Is it buried underground? What's it like?" She sat forwards. "Is it covered in ivy and creepers? I bet it's re-ally spooky."

Frank rolled his eyes. "If sensei allows you to go, you'll find out."

"Won't you tell me?"

"No."

Tandy stuck out a petulant lower lip.

"So," continued Frank, ignoring her dramatics, "you will need to write your letter in your bestest handwriting. But," continued Frank as Tandy gave him a puzzled frown, "don't write out your letter like a job application, he won't be interested, and you won't be able to flatter him, he'll just put such a letter in the rubbish bin."

"Blimey."

"And," said Frank, "if you write to him, he'll not reply because he doesn't know you."

"Then how on earth do I get to work with him?"

"I must also write a letter. A letter of introduction."

"Ah. Right. Well then, what should I say?"

"Just *can I come and train with you please, Sensei?*"

Tandy's eyebrows had lifted. "That's all?"

"Oh, you can put *Dear Sensei Nakamura* if you want."

"No *yours sincerely?*"

"No. Just sign it."

"No kisses on the bottom then."

"No, but I can kiss your bottom if you like?"

"Behave."

And so, Tandy had written a letter, and so had Frank, recommending her as a student (with no kisses on the bottom), and they sent them off in the same envelope.

*****

TUESDAY 3ᴿᴰ JUNE

The Chief of MI6, the British Secret Intelligence Service, sat behind his desk with his shirt sleeves rolled up and his elbows resting on the arms of his chair, his hands steepled in front of him. He was going to retire in November of this year and he could have done without this new threat to national security. Because that was what he perceived it to be.

In the last four weeks five people had been abducted, tortured and executed by the terrorist organisation called Intiqam. All of the ghastly tortures and executions had been filmed by the terrorists and placed on the internet. Because British Intelligence monitors this sort of thing, they had picked up on it the moment it hit the web and their computer experts got it removed. Removed from general public viewing it may have been, but MI6 kept copies of it.

Three of the five executed had been men and two were women. Of these, one man was a British journalist, abducted in Iraq's capital, Baghdad. Another was a US Army squaddie, taken in Basra, in southern Iraq, and the third man was a British tourist who was the husband of one of the women; both the husband and wife had been snatched. The second woman was an MI6 agent working undercover as a tourist guide. She had been taken in Mosul, along with the husband and wife.

The odd thing was - and this is what perplexed the Chief of MI6 – the executions had been carried out with no demands; no demands for ransom, or the release of prisoners, or recognition of Intiqam as some form of official organisation. Nothing. Just summary and bloody executions, with the murderer smiling into the camera as he used a length of thin steel wire as a garotte to carry out his grisly business. And at the end of each execution the killer held up his bloody hands, looked into the camera and told his audience that he was al-Makira – the Cunning.

All five of the captives had been executed whilst sitting in a chair with its back to an open window. However, MI6 did not know where the executions were being carried out. All they could glean and assume from the gruesome films were two things: that the filming was being done in an old dilapidated room, and probably on a high floor. The first assumption was based on what the walls either side of the sun-bleached and weathered wooden window frame looked like; they were filthy rough crumbling plaster. The second assumption (that of a high floor) had been made because the camera clearly showed what the view was out of the window behind the execution chair; the ragged straw roofs of village houses and a cliff, or escarpment, in the hazy heat-filled distance. The roofs had the look of an ancient but run-down Arabic village. However, frustratingly, it could be any Arab village anywhere. Because of that it was also assumed that it was probably somewhere in the Middle East. And because the abductions had all taken place in Iraq it was assumed that the village was probably somewhere in that country.

Probably.

The Secret Intelligence Service were trying desperately to keep this all under wraps. God! If the bloody media were to find out about this there would be Hell to pay!

So far MI6 had managed to keep a lid on all of these murders. So far.

And then there were these demands for payment that were starting to crop up all over the world; demands for payment with threats included. Demands on white paper in little white envelopes that had been sent from Mosul. Who was behind these? And were they linked to Intiqam? If there was a connection the Chief of MI6 could not see it; there was not enough intelligence as yet. Had the executed female agent stumbled upon something? Was that why she had been taken? Were the other four deaths a mask to make it seem like the agent's abduction was a coincidence? Was it too much of a coincidence? Did the agent's death have anything to do with the little white envelopes that had been sent out from the same city? If there was, again, the Chief could not see the connection.

The Chief fidgeted his bottom on his seat. He knew that MI6 had another agent in Mosul at the moment, trying to infiltrate Intiqam. But perhaps this was a job for the SOU – send a professional assassin in to kill this al-Makira character. Perhaps.

The Chief knew that the SOU had been responsible for assassinating Aarif El-Sayed, but the Chief of MI6 did not know of the involvement of either Frank Cross or Tandy Trudeau – in fact the only Frank Cross he'd heard of was the Security Advisor and Anti-Terrorist Training Officer of that tiny island out in the Caribbean. The same Frank Cross had recently helped to smash a drugs cartel on the same island. It had made the island's local newspapers. What was the island called? Oh, yes…St Margaret. He knew all of that. He was, however, completely unaware that the Frank Cross on St Margaret had worked for the SOU. And he had never heard of the name Tandy Trudeau, so she did not fall under his suspicion either. The Chief of MI6 did not know of the link between Cross, Trudeau and the SOU because the Director of the SOU deemed that he did not need to know. Sir Michael Corrigan kept his own Department's dirty little secrets to himself.

However, the Chief of MI6 did know who Sir Michael Corrigan was, and he also knew what the Specialist Operations Unit did, and because of that fact the Chief leaned forward and picked up his telephone. His hand held the receiver about six inches above its carriage as he paused and shook his head slightly. Then he put the receiver back on its carriage and reached for his own personal mobile phone – best this went unrecorded.

*****

MONDAY 9TH JUNE

Sensei Nakamura had written back in reply to Tandy. The envelope, a white one of very good quality paper, arrived in the red post box. The letter that the envelope contained was of equally good quality and it bore only two words in black ink and handwritten English; they were, "YES. COME", and he had signed it in the *kanji* form of Japanese script.

Tandy smiled broadly as she read the two words and looked at the signature.

Tandy was going to Japan.

*****

Sir Michael Corrigan was sitting at his desk in the SOU building. Thinking. He spent a lot of time thinking. That was his job; to think, and to out-think everyone else. He picked up and filed away all sorts of information in his incredibly analytical brain; information, large and small, from all over the world from a multitude of sources. He pushed plans and ideas around in his head. He kept some and shelved others. He perused and calculated.

Often these random bits of information clicked together to form a bigger picture which Sir Michael would examine from all sorts of angles before giving voice or action, or even inaction, to them.

Some bits of information were clicking away right now.

It had been a few days since the Chief of MI6 had called him on his own mobile, asking for a favour, and since then there had been media coverage of the rich and famous being sent little white envelopes.

*****

The Right Honourable Lawrence Gainsborough was the Conservative Party Member of Parliament for South West Norfolk, and he lived with his wife in that same county. In the United Kingdom you become a Right Honourable if you are, of have been, in the Government's Cabinet; and Gainsborough was the Government's Secretary of State for The Department of the Environment, Food and Rural Affairs (DEFRA); this post being commonly called the Environment Secretary.

Lawrence's wife called him Larry. He was aged forty-five and stood at six-feet and two-inches tall with light-brown hair and a good-looking clean-shaven face. He had a physique like Superman and was married to Shirley and had five children; four boys and a girl. Despite having five children Shirley had managed to maintain her tall athletic figure that was crowned with a mane of long dark hair.

However, as beautiful as his wife was, Mr Gainsborough MP had a roving eye and it had settled on one Miss Gail Wetton, his Press Secretary, and he kept her under wraps (some would say literally) in a flat that Miss Wetton owned in Epping. Gail Wetton was tall and willowy with long blonde hair, a full bust, and big blue eyes.

The Epping address was handy as Gainsborough could call in on his way through to Westminster from his large detached house just outside of Diss, Norfolk.

Mrs Gainsborough was suspicious of Miss Wetton and, although she suspected the dalliance by her husband, she kept quiet as she particularly enjoyed her house, lifestyle and her Ferrari F430 – all paid for by her husband. She did not even mind when her husband had to go to Europe *for business*.

He was having to go to Europe in the next couple of days. For business.

At least, that's what he told Shirley.

*****

TUESDAY 10TH JUNE

If you are knighted by the reigning monarch of the United Kingdom, or their designated representative, you become a Sir if you are male, and a Dame if you are female. If you become a Sir and you are married then your wife becomes a Lady. However, if a woman gets a knighthood her husband remains as plain old Mister.

Sir Michael Corrigan had received his knighthood at the hands of Her Majesty Queen Elizabeth II some years ago. He had received the honour whilst working for the Government Communications Headquarters (GCHQ) at Cheltenham and he was awarded it for his work in keeping the United Kingdom's secrets safe.

Sir Michael was sitting on his sofa watching the TV at his home near

Hampstead Heath, London, with his left arm around the shoulders of his wife, Maria – Lady Corrigan.

Lady Maria Corrigan is a tall elegant woman who is slim and attractive. She has a mane of very long hair that she dyes a bright red, the colour of a poppy. She started dying her hair this poppy colour when she was a student at an Oxford University and she has been dying it ever since. It is a kind of trademark for her and has earned her the nick-name of Red; even Sir Michael calls her Red... or, Yes Dear.

The room they were in was the living room of their four-bedroom double-fronted detached house in a private road to the west of the Heath. A fake log flame-effect gas fire was burning in the large hearth and their dog, a Giant Schnauzer, was stretched out fast asleep in front of it.

It was just after 10pm and they were watching the ten-o-clock news on the BBC. The news presenter was coming to her next piece; it opened with a long shot of flames tearing through the roof of a beach-side retreat on Grand Bahama. Apparently, it had been the occasional home of a bass guitarist in a very successful rock band called Saint Ud that Sir Michael had never heard of. But what made Sir Michael's mind start to tick over with the precision of a Rolex watch was the fact that the viewing audience were being informed that the bass player had only recently received a threatening letter from Mosul in Iraq. The letter was said to have been demanding a huge (and undisclosed) sum of money.

Sir Michael raised his left eyebrow.

He had heard something like this recently.

He would check it out in the morning.

Time now for another glass of red wine before bed and, hopefully, a good night's sleep.

**

Tandy had already landed in Japan, which was nine hours ahead of the UK in time. She had landed at Tokyo's Narita Airport where she boarded another aeroplane, and she was now on board the flight to Kumamoto on the southern Japanese island of Kyushu.

**

Sir Michael could not sleep, so he rolled gently out of bed so as not to disturb his wife, whom he thought was asleep, and he went into his office just along from his bedroom to think.

*****

WEDNESDAY 11ᵀᴴ JUNE

The flight to Kumamoto took one hour and forty-minutes.

Kyushu is a hilly green warm sub-tropical island. Some of those hills are extinct volcanoes, but fourteen are very much alive and they smoke continuously and sulphurously.

It was mid-day. Tandy was not hungry as she had eaten on the aircraft. She was wearing a light-blue baseball cap, a short grey linen jacket over a dark-blue shirt, skinny-fit jeans, white slipper socks and a pair of white Nike trainers. She was carrying two hold-alls; one had been check-in baggage and the other was cabin baggage. After clearing the usual security, Customs and immigration checks, Tandy had emerged from the air-conditioned arrivals building in Kumamoto airport into the warm 23C sultry air and carrying her hold-alls in each hand – hold-alls that seemed to be getting heavier by the second. She put the bags down and flexed her fingers. Inside the arrivals building a short clean-shaven man with black hair stood with a single small hold-all of his own and watched her through a large plate-glass window.

The man had been following Tandy ever since she had been driven from Cannon Head by Frank to St Margaret's airport. He was the man that had been hiding in the green leaves of the rain forest that bordered the road opposite Frank and Tandy's villa; the man that had put Frank's senses into high alert. Frank had driven Tandy in their open-topped Wrangler Jeep to St Margaret's international airport and the man had followed in a beaten-up Ford something-or-other. Frank had spotted him straight off but had discounted the man in the car as a threat because he was making such a hash of following them. No, he could not possibly be a tail. But, of course, he was.

At the airport the man had disappeared. Frank had kissed Tandy good-bye at the check-in desk and had headed back outside. The man had then re-materialised and boarded the same flight as Tandy. He had sat on the opposite side of the aircraft aisle in Business Class from her and five rows back. Tandy had either her eyes on the entertainment screen in front of her or within the pages of a book, so she never noticed him. When she changed aircraft in Tokyo, he had stuck with her, this time on her side of the aisle and ten rows back; and, again, she never took any notice of him.

The man was a Syrian and a member of Intiqam and he was under orders, orders from al-Makira, waiting for an opportunity to grab Tandy. He'd had a small team behind him on St Margaret but they had been instructed to keep well back from this sole operative who would call them in when he seized Tandy en-route to the airport. However, the intended snatch on St Margaret had been hampered due to the towering presence of Frank Cross and the high level of security that was in place on the island. In the unlikely event that they might have be able to grab and subdue Tandy with Frank around, it was quite another problem to get her off the island. Therefore, the man's instructions had been altered; he must follow her and keep al-Makira appraised of the circumstances as they developed and to try and grab her en route to wherever her destination was.

The Syrian might not have been so casual in his own tracking habits had he known who Tandy was; but then neither he nor al-Makira knew who she was, other than that she was the girlfriend of Frank Cross. Al-Makira did not know that she had a huge range of martial arts skills; did not know that she was also the deadly assassin known as The Scorpion.

Thus far all the Syrian could do was to follow and hope that an opportunity would present itself, and thus far that opportunity had not happened; Tandy was always moving through and staying in very public and crowded places – airports and aircraft. The man had been continually informing al-Makira of Tandy's direction of travel, and, because Intiqam was spread world-wide al-Makira was able to call in the ground troops at the various points of destination. Tandy did not know it but there had been a group waiting for her when her flight landed in Tokyo and there was another, albeit a smaller group, when she landed at Kumamoto, but none had had the opportunity to abduct her.

The Syrian watched Tandy outside on the concourse of Kumamoto airport as she searched for a taxi, and one had pulled up right in front of her as if by magic. He cursed and reached for his mobile phone – the taxi that he had lined up for her had not arrived, and once again she had slipped the net.

With the cab in front of her, Tandy had ducked her head and looked into the cab to inspect the driver.

Like all Japanese taxis and taxi drivers, this one was immaculate inside and the driver was in a dark grey suit with a chauffeur's cap, dark tie and white cotton gloves.

The driver had fairly good English, and although he did not know where Sensei Nakamura's house was, his satnav did (Sensei Nakamura was not at all happy that he had a post code). Tandy got into the taxi. With her hold-alls sitting on the seat beside her she settled back for the ride.

As the taxi pulled away another one pulled up in front of the Syrian who quickly climbed into the back seat. This was the cab that was supposed to have picked up Tandy. Once inside the cab the Syrian gave the driver, a Pakistani, a real tongue-lashing for being late and missing the target. The Syrian then pulled his mobile and called off the second cab – the one that he was supposed to have been following in.

The Syrian's cab moved rapidly away from the kerb and caught up with Tandy's cab, but kept some vehicles between it and Tandy's vehicle as it fell in behind.

Japan is thirteen hours in front of the Caribbean, so it was 2.00pm in Japan but 1.00pm on St Margaret. Tandy had arranged by letter (to which she had received no reply) to Sensei Nakamura that she would arrive at around 4.00pm. "You can be early," Frank had warned her, "but don't be late. And don't forget to bow." For the umpteenth time that morning Tandy checked her watch.

Having driven through and out of Kumamoto Tandy's taxi went south to the town of Yatsushiro. From Yatsushiro the taxi then turned east and up into the heavily wooded hills above the town.

The road twisted and turned and eventually the vehicle pulled up in front of a *torii* gate, a *Shinto* gate.

Torii gates are not gates in the accepted sense of the word; they do not have a barrier that can be opened and closed, and are really simply a tall rectangular arch.

Shinto, *"the Way of the Gods",* is Japan's oldest religion, the belief being that its deities preside over all things in nature, be they living, dead, or inanimate. These deities, or *kami*, are worshipped at thousands of shrines in the hills, forests and waysides throughout the islands that make up Japan. The torii are placed at the entrance to these shrines, but they can also be erected in the front of temples, at paths through hills, by waterfalls, even at sea (as in the case of the Great Torii at Miyajima Island). They can also be placed at the entrances to houses. This torii was the entrance to Hagakure.

This gate, like all the other torii gates in Japan, was painted red and it also conformed to the traditional pattern of a torii gate; it had two round vertical side posts resembling columns that tapered from the ground to the top. It had two cross-pieces across the top, one below the other with the lower one being completely straight but jutting out either side of the columns. The top spar curved up slightly at each end and it also jutted out either side of the columns. Halfway along the lower spar a fitted and jointed piece of wood was set vertically, connecting the bottom spar to the top one. Often there are lengths of folded paper or ropes of twisted rice straw that are attached to the lower spar to ward off evil spirits. This one had the rice straw. The gate led onto a set of stone steps that led upwards.

As the driver parked and applied the handbrake the second taxi overtook them and continued on. Tandy, like her own driver, had noticed it following them, but neither of them were bothered by it; why should they be? Tandy was on a kind of holiday and the driver had a fare, so he had rightly concentrated on his driving on these twisting roads and the comfort of his passenger, and not the car behind. And, anyway, why would they be being followed? Tandy had got all this way in perfect safety. Hadn't she?

Tandy got out of the taxi and then reached in and gathered her bags. She paid off the driver and the taxi pulled away as she turned towards the torii gate, travel bags now in hand and feeling as nervous as a kid entering a new school for the first time. Which, in effect, was exactly what she was. Up until now this whole arrangement had been something of an imagined adventure – now it was suddenly real – and there was no going back. Well, not unless she called for another cab and went all the way back home again. No. That was not going to happen.

Tandy gritted her teeth.

So, here she was, at the entrance to Sensei Nakamura's house because she had asked to be. So, no having second thoughts.

Pull yourself together girl!

The taxi drove away and took a left-hand bend about two hundred yards further on. Having driven out of sight the taxi then went past the car that had been following them which had pulled over and parked. The passenger, the Syrian, in the parked car, took out his mobile phone. He made a brief call and then ordered the driver to drive off.

Tandy had watched her taxi drive away. She gave a little frown and then turned towards the torii gate.

She had received a huge amount of martial arts training from Frank at their home on St Margaret, but she had realised that there was only one way she could learn more of the finer points and fully appreciate the martial arts, and that was to train under the man who had trained and moulded Frank Cross. How long she trained with Sensei Nakamura would be up to Tandy – and also Sensei Nakamura.

Tandy took a deep breath and stepped through the torii, walked a few paces and stopped. In front of her was a steep flight of about forty stone steps that were slightly dished in the middle, worn that way from the passage of many feet. "Steps," said Tandy out loud as she remembered all of the martial arts films she had seen in the past. "Why are there always loads of steps?"

Tandy pulled her mobile phone out of the waist pocket of her jacket and sent Frank a text. It said simply: **have arrived safe @ hagakure xx**. She replaced the phone in her pocket, took another deep breath, lifted her two hold-alls up onto her shoulders by their carrying straps, settled them in place, and then humped the bags up to the top.

The steps led up to a small flat area that was covered in grey gravel chips and surrounded with a thicket of tall thin bamboo stems that were whispering in a light breeze. A path led off to the right with more gravel underfoot and with the thin whispering bamboo forming the walls of a green-walled corridor.

She followed the path until the bamboo ended, at which point she stopped in her tracks and stared at the amazing and beautiful sight that met her eyes. About fifty yards in front of her was Sensei Nakamura's house - a traditional *minka*, a single storey dwelling - set in a very large, well maintained, traditional Japanese garden. All around the house were trees - maples, cherry trees and pines - some of whose boughs overhung the roof, with the branches spreading like enormous open green hands.

Tandy smiled. Hagakure. *Hidden by Leaves.*

At first sight Hagakure appeared to be incredibly fragile with, what appeared to be, fragile white paper walls that were impossibly supporting a red tiled roof. But its appearance was deceptive, because this house had a white painted shell of not paper but cedarwood and, like many other traditional houses in Japan, it could withstand the effects of the many frequent earthquakes that affect this part of the Pacific Rim.

The minka had a high ridge to the red-tiled roof. The tiles swept down with the ceramic heads of dragons mounted at the lower corners. There were no gutters because the roof overhung, by about two feet, the *engawa*, the wooden veranda, that ran right around the outside of the house. The house had no doors in the western style, instead it had *shoji*, sliding screens, and behind these was a narrow corridor that ran parallel with the engawa. On the other side of the corridor was an inner wall made of white shoji which were made of white paper set in wooden frames.

The gravel path that Tandy was treading was lined either side with pieces of weathered stone, about the size of footballs, and they led through an immaculate garden. There was no grass, only a vast carpet of moss that lapped like a green sea around the bases of the trees that had been placed - or left as they had originally grown - in a way that had been specifically designed to look both haphazard and deliberate at the same time. There were no flowers in this part of the garden, only moss and trees, grasses and ferns and Tandy could feel herself relaxing, her nervousness dissipating, as the harmony and beauty of the green place entered her.

A little further on there was a narrow path to her left and one to her right. The paths led to smaller outbuildings, miniatures of the minka – one on her left and two away to her right. She did not know it at the time but the left-hand building was the *onsen*.

Onsens occur all over Japan. They are communal baths that are segregated for the sexes. These baths contain curative minerals and the waters are warmed by the deep underground thermal springs of the volcanic islands of Japan - although in some instances the water is more likely to be heated by a boiler and controlled by a thermostat. They are found most commonly in traveller's accommodations, from *ryokans* to five-star hotels. Ryokans began somewhere around the eighth century as inns for travellers on Japan's ancient highways. There are not as many ryokans as there used to be, but you can still find them easily enough and book a stay in one of these traditional buildings.

The nearest building to the right was Sensei Nakamura's personal wash-house and toilet, and, beyond this, the furthest building was the kitchen - traditional minkas have no interior kitchen; for fear of fire.

As she approached the house a shoji slid open in the end wall of the house which was nearest to her and a small old man appeared. He was dressed in a plain grey cotton *kimono*. Kimono means "the thing worn" and is not the sole preserve of women. Japanese men frequently wear a kimono, most noticeably at their weddings.

Having stepped out onto the engawa, the old man placed his feet in a pair of blue plastic flip-flops. He stood with his arms folded in front of him with the wide sleeves of the kimono hanging down to his small mound of a belly.

This was Sensei Nakamura.

Sensei.

Teacher.

Master.

The man that Frank Cross had once described as being the deadliest martial artist on the planet.

Sensei Nakamura was eighty-four years old and although he did not look his age – he looked more like mid-sixties – he didn't look like a Martial Arts Master either, and he didn't look very deadly. He was short at four-feet-eleven-inches, slightly built but with that little pot belly, and with as much hair on his round head as a billiard ball. He had a clean-shaven, wrinkled and wizened old face and, since he was grinning (which, Frank had warned, did not happen very often), he looked like a good-humoured windfall apple. He had no need of glasses for his eyes and he had all of his own pearly white teeth. Old and wrinkled he may have been, but his eyes watched and saw everything.

Unmoving, he watched Tandy approach.

Apart from the need for punctuality, Tandy had been told by Frank what to expect of Sensei Nakamura. And what *not* to expect.

"Don't expect praise," Frank had informed her. "And if he does praise you then you have done something really really really well. If he gives you praise do not smile, just bow and accept it. Got that?"

"Blimey!"

So, here she was.

She stopped in front of the veranda.

She put her hold-alls down on the ground, took off her baseball cap, and gave a deep bow of respect.

Sensei Nakamura stopped grinning and, now straight-faced, gave a small grunt before returning the bow, although not as deep as Tandy's – she was, after all, to be his student, not his equal.

"Good," he said in a rather gruff voice that seemed to be too deep and too big for his diminutive size. "You on time."

"*Oss*, Sensei," said Tandy bowing again; oss being the standard acknowledgement word of a practitioner of karate. "I had a good flight and the taxi driver…"

"Don't chatter," interrupted the sensei. "You forrow." Like most Japanese he could not pronounce the letter L and pronounced it like the letter R, so *follow* in this instance came out as *forrow*. The sensei turned abruptly on his heel and flip-flopped off along the engawa to Tandy's left, leaving Tandy to shove her cap back onto her head and pick up her hold-alls.

"Well," she muttered under her breath. "And a very good morning to you too."

She did not know it, but Tandy had just passed her first test -Politeness.

Sensei Nakamura walked straight-backed to the end of the engawa and turned right, along what was the front of his house.

Tandy followed him, and as she turned the corner she stopped and stared. "Wow!"

In front of Hagakure was a large pond, about thirty feet long and ten wide with blue irises at the margins and lily pads out in the middle. Halfway along its length was a narrow humpbacked stone bridge that joined the edge of the pond this side across to the edge on the other. The nearest end of the pond started some twelve feet away from her and the long edge ran along the front of the house. There was a gap between the end corner of the house and the end of the pond which allowed pedestrian access to the veranda, there being a path that led up to the veranda. Around and beyond the pond the ground was covered in the same type of moss that she had noticed earlier and which ran away to a barrier of maple trees with low pines in front of them that were only about three feet tall. These pines were growing amongst carefully placed rocks and rounded boulders.

Tandy gathered herself and then followed the sensei along the veranda and, as she walked alongside the pond, she saw one of the lily pads move. The broad back of a large golden koi carp momentarily broke the surface causing oily ripples in the clear water. She looked down into the water as she passed and something else caught her eye.

"Hey!" she called out. "You've got a terrapin in there!"

With his back to Tandy, and still walking, the sensei raised his eyebrows then put them down. "No," he answered without turning. "Is *Nihon Ishigame*…Japanese Stone Turter. Many in pond. Is endemic species."

Tandy blinked. *Turter? Oh, TURTLE.* "Oh, right…Well they're very cute."

"No cute. Is turter. Is damn nuisance."

Well, I think they're cute.

"You forrow."

"This is a beautiful garden, Sensei."

No reply.

Charming!

Tandy huffed and puffed as she lugged her hold-alls along the engawa as she followed along behind Sensei Nakamura. He may have been old but he was moving remarkably fast.

At the far end of the engawa there was a step down to another gravel path which curved around to a long low building over to their right. It was built along the same lines as the Sensei's house: a single storey with white shoji screens, cedarwood support beams, a sloping red tiled roof and a surrounding engawa.

At the end of the path Sensei Nakamura stopped, half turned and offered his left hand towards the building.

"This where you sreep."

Tandy's face registered delight. "Oss, Sensei. It looks grea…" But the sensei was off again before she could finish the sentence. He stepped up onto the engawa, crossed it, and slid open a screen that turned out to be not paper but white painted wood panelling. Before entering the building, he stepped out of his flip-flops and once inside he put on another pair that were just inside the screen.

Tandy made to follow him but he put up a hand. "No. You must take off shoes." He pointed at her trainers. "No wear outside shoes inside."

"Oh, right." Tandy put her bags down and bowed. Then she hopped about on one leg whilst she pulled a trainer off and then started hopping on the other leg to remove the other.

Sensei Nakamura, expressionless, watched her antics and when both trainers were off he pointed at the engawa. "Shoes stay here. No go inside."

"Oss, Sensei," said Tandy. She bowed again. "Are socks okay, Sensei?" She pointed at her feet. She was wearing pink ankle socks that had pictures of teddy bears on them.

Sensei Nakamura looked down at them as if he had never seen socks before. "Hmmm…No probrem."

"Er…What happens if it rains? Won't my trainers get wet? I mean, with them left out here?"

"No get wet." He pointed upwards. "House have big roof." And indeed, the edge of the roof overhung the engawa by an easy twenty-four inches.

The logic was unassailable.

Tandy smiled and bowed.

"Hmm!" grunted the sensei.

They were now in a narrow corridor that led away to Tandy's left. The corridor had a floor of sealed and polished wooden planks and the walls along the right-hand side of the corridor were a series of screens; these were paper. There were obviously a number of rooms along the corridor. Sensei Nakamura stepped across the corridor and slid open the first screen in the line of rooms. "This where you sreep."

Tandy bowed again. "Thank you, Sensei." She bowed once more and stepped into the room.

It was quite a small room and all of the walls were the same white paper screens. The floor was covered in six *tatami* mats made of a composite of straw and rush. These mats are set sizes, although their size varies throughout Japan according to the region they are in. A room is always built to the size of the number of mats that will fill it with no gaps around the edges.

The wall opposite the entrance was divided into three sections. On the left was the *tokonoma*, a wooden floored alcove. Hanging in the tokonoma on the plain white wall above the wooden floor was a long paper scroll that had a simple but beautiful hand-drawn picture of a yellow chrysanthemum on it; the chrysanthemum - along with cherry blossom - being the national flower of Japan. In front of the scroll was a plain white ceramic vase that had been crafted and hand-thrown in the Kyushu village of Arita. Some naturally twisted twigs had been painstakingly arranged in the vase so that they stood in a precise way; to be pleasing to the eye.

To the right of the tokonoma was a section of plain white wall about three feet across. And to the right of this was a set of shelves; some were bare but one shelf had towels and another had a rolled-up *futon* bed. *Futon* is the Japanese word for Bed. A traditional Japanese futon, like the one Tandy was to use, is a very thin mattress with covers and a thin pillow. They had been developed in Japan through lack of living space. When Tandy went to bed she would take the futon off the shelf and lay it out on the floor. When she awoke, she would roll the futon up and place it back on the shelf. No

Mrs Johnson to help out here. There was no other furniture. Not even a chair.

To some people the almost bare room would seem as spartan and unwelcoming as a prison cell; but to Tandy it looked beautiful in its simplicity. She smiled, and Sensei Nakamura noted that smile with some satisfaction, although he did not let it show on his face. Again, she did not know it, but Tandy had just passed another test – Appreciation of Simplicity.

Tandy turned to the sensei. "Please," she asked. "When will I meet the other students?" Tandy had not seen or heard any evidence of anyone else training here, and she had expected the air to be full of the sound of people grunting with effort or shouting *kiais*, possibly even the sound of sticks or swords coming together in combat.

"No-one erse here at present…Onry you."

"Oh! But I thought…"

"What?"

"I thought there'd be others."

"No. Onry you. Now, you unpack. Have wish-wash. You go that way." He pointed through the walls in the opposite direction to his house.

Tandy suppressed a grin, *Wish-Wash?*

Sensei Nakamura lowered his hand. "After wish-wash we have rate runch. Hai?" Yes? It was not a question.

Rate runch? Oh, Late Lunch!

Tandy did not really want another meal so soon after her flight, but as she did not want to offend the old sensei she said,

"Oss, Sensei. Thank you." She bowed.

"At runch you wear kimono. You have kimono?"

Tandy suddenly felt dismayed. She had not known that a kimono would be required of her. She swallowed. She did not want to somehow offend the old man. "No, Sensei. I am sorry. I have no kimono." She rushed on, "But, I have a *gi*, in fact I have three of them…" Tandy was referring to the white uniform of the karate practitioner.

The gi is the standard uniform adopted by many of the Japanese martial arts. It consists of a pair of cotton trousers with a draw-string waist and a jacket that flaps left side over right side.

The jacket is always worn left over right because, in Japan, right over left is the way that bodies are dressed in a kimono, or other wrap, for burial. It is therefore considered very bad luck to dress right over left.

Gis come in set sizes by height only and in various weights of material, with the lightest, at around eight ounces, being usually worn by beginners and fourteen ounces by more experienced practitioners. The gi jacket is worn with a belt, called an *Obi*, which is wrapped around the jacket and tied in place with a traditional knot. These days the belts are made of canvas webbing covered in cotton of the relevant colour but they could be made of anything: silk or linen for example. The belt is not there to hold either the jacket or your stomach in place; it is worn fairly loosely and is a badge of rank because these days people practicing karate (for example) take examinations, called gradings, to see if they are good enough to progress onwards and upwards. Each belt colour from white to brown is called a *Kyu*, or Grade. By custom, these belts start at white for beginner and go up, gradually getting darker, through the colours of yellow (for 9th *Kyu*), orange, red, green, purple, and brown (1st *Kyu*), to finally the coveted black. There are usually two grades within purple and three grades within brown.

All black belts are called *Dan*, or Level. Originally the student went from white to black in one go, but only after many years of training. These days the kyu and dan system has been adopted to give more encouragement to those training, and there are even levels of Dan; *Shodan* (1st Dan) being the lowest, and *Judan* (10th Dan) being the highest.

Tandy had risen to green belt, 6th *Kyu*, some years ago. However, due to her martial arts training with Frank Cross, she was now way beyond that. However, since obtaining her green belt she had never taken an examination for a higher belt. This did not bother Tandy, although it did sometimes make her curious to know as to how well she might measure up in a grading.

Tandy owned both white and black gis, but she had packed only her white ones as white is the more common and traditional colour for a gi. She had brought three with her and as they each weighed fourteen ounces. They had taken up a fair amount of her baggage weight allowance. However, she figured she would not be wearing much else in the way of top clothes as this was to be a training session and not a holiday.

Sensei Nakamura shook his head. "No gi. Wear kimono. Gi onry for training. I get you kimono. Hai?"

"Well, yes." Tandy was now feeling flustered. "Thank you, Sensei. Thank you." Tandy bowed. *Where the hell is he going to get a kimono from?*

"Good. Put on kimono. We have runch in big house…My house."

"Right. Thank you, Sensei." Before she could bow again, Sensei

Nakamura put up a hand.

"No say thank you. Say *arigato*. Means same thing."

Tandy bowed. "Arigato."

Sensei Nakamura returned the bow. "Wercome to my home, Miss Trudeau."

And he left her.

And even though he was on gravel, she could not hear him walking away.

Tandy went back out onto the engawa, retrieved her bags, and began to unpack.

*

With everything stowed away on the spare shelves Tandy decided to have a shower and a change of clothes. So, she dug out some fresh underwear, a clean tee shirt and her black leather toilet bag, all of which she shoved into a plastic carrier bag. Then, clutching the bag to her chest, she went back outside, slipped on her trainers and went for an exploratory walk around Hagakure.

She walked back along the path to Hagakure's engawa, past the turtle pond and the front of the sensei's house and then around to the area where she first met Sensei Nakamura, which was at the south end of the house. She carried on walking along the engawa to the eastern side of the house where, at the end of the engawa, she came up to a solid wooden and locked door in a high brick wall. Tandy surmised correctly that behind the wall was a garden, but she could not see over the door or the wall, even if she jumped up and down.

She stepped off the engawa onto the carpet of moss and walked around the outside of the wall to discover that it was large and rectangular and butted up to the back of the house. She also discovered that here another delight awaited her, for behind the wall was a path made of ancient flat stones that ran beside a large pond that was really a small lake.

Tandy was standing at one end of the lake that, like the smaller pond at the front of the house, had a humpbacked bridge that crossed the lake; in this instance from the west to the east side. At the far end of the lake she could see a small red building, about the size of a garden shed, but much more ornate in the Japanese style.

Tandy walked along the path by the lake. Again, there were blue irises in the margins of the lake and lily pads out in the middle with pink star-shaped water-lilies showing off their vibrant colour between the pads. She stopped and looked out over the lake to enjoy the view and the serenity of the spot. As she stood at the edge, a number of koi carp came over to her and made noisy golloping noises as they lifted their fleshy lips above the surface and sucked, hoping for some tit-bit or morsel, for they were clearly often fed by hand.

Tandy laughed at the greedy fish and turned away. "Not to-day fishes."

Tandy walked away from the koi and headed around the southern edge of the delightful lake. She spotted another three turtles in the water's margins and smiled. *Not turtles, turters!*

Ambling on, she came upon the beautiful little red house that she had spotted earlier, and which was set amongst some clipped pine trees that had been sculptured in the *niwaki*, or *cloud pruning* style. The little house had red cedarwood walls and a red tiled roof. Tandy peered inside one of the open windows. It was a tea ceremony house. Only big enough for two people – the tea drinker and the tea maker - it was built right beside the lake which caught its reflection in its still and silent waters. Tandy moved away from the window in time to see a blue iridescent dragonfly, about two inches long, settle for a moment on the tip of one of the blue irises and then it flipped away with a quiet buzzing noise. Tandy, with her aversion to Bugs, eyed it with caution, but she had to admit that it's colouring was a thing of beauty.

On the other side of the tea house was another path which led to a large building which, like the main house, was aligned north to south. It was another single storey construction, just over forty feet long and about thirty feet wide. It had no windows that Tandy could see and its walls were made of the ubiquitous red cedarwood. Like the main house it had a red tiled roof and, like the main house, the trees around it overhung their branches, as if trying to touch or embrace it.

Tandy was intrigued. What was this building?

She made her way around to the southern end of the building and came upon a door. A door? Not a screen? This was odd. She tried the handle. It turned and the door opened.

It was a *dojo*, the training hall of a martial arts practitioner. *Dojo* means the *Place of the Way*, the Way being the chosen path that the martial arts practitioner has decided to take, be it *karate, judo, kempo, sumo*, or any of the numerous fighting arts. A dojo is usually a training hall; however, it can be an area outside in a field, or a wood, or on the beach, or a car park; it can even be the front room of your house, and wherever the training takes place, that area must be respected by the person training and practicing.

Tandy remained outside as she looked in, respecting the area.

The floor was made of close-fitting and highly polished pinewood planks that were held in place by wooden pegs, sanded flat, so as not to catch the bare feet of anyone training. Three of the walls were plain white but the wall to her left was a set of tall mirrors, like those found in a dance studio. The ceiling was pitched to match the roof and there were great wooden beams spanning the air above Tandy's head. There was a door in the far end wall of the dojo and Tandy could see that it had two small and separate silhouettes of a man and a woman's head. Obviously, the door to the changing rooms. Also, at the far end of the dojo was a large leather kick-bag that was hanging from one of the majestic beams by a chain. The back wall of the dojo, opposite the mirror wall, held racks of weapons: *jo* staffs and *bo* staffs made of white and red oak, *bokkens* (wooden imitations of Japanese *katana* swords), three-pronged steel *sais*, *tonfas* (now used as police riot batons), *kamas* (wooden sickles with a long wooden shaft), two *naginata* (a long pole-weapon with a single blade, much a like a long sword, attached to the business end), and some *nunchaku*, the traditional rice flail, being two short hardwood shafts joined together by either a short length of rope or chain.

It was unusual to see jo and bo staffs standing up, albeit clipped into holders, because they were usually stored flat on the ground to stop them from warping. However, Tandy correctly suspected that these were used so often that they never got the chance to just stand and go out of shape.

Beside these many weapons, and mounted on the wall, were two *daisho*; pairs of Japanese swords – often called *Samurai* swords - made up of a *katana* (the long sword) and a *wakizashi* (the short sword). Frank Cross had a valuable pair of these swords mounted on the wall in the living room of Cannon Head.

So, this was where she was going to have her training. She was both excited and fearful of the prospect. How would the sensei teach her? Would his ancient bones go softly with her? She doubted it. He was probably as tough as old saddle leather.

Tandy quietly closed the door.

She walked away from the front of the dojo and picked up another path that led in a curve away from the training hall and into a circular gravelled area that contained a fabulous collection of *bonsai* trees that were growing in a variety of decorative pots, some ceramic, some terracotta. Tandy stopped for a moment and marvelled at the small trees with their distorted forms that had been deliberately twisted into elaborate and tortured shapes that were very pleasing to the eye. Some of these trees were only twelve inches high, whereas others were nearly three feet tall. Some of them she knew would be over one-hundred years old and worth a fortune.

To the right of the bonsai area was another red roofed building and it differed from the other buildings in that, again, it had a normal door on the front. Tandy approached it and tried the handle. It was locked. Perhaps it was store house? Or the sensei's version of a garden shed?

Moving on, Tandy headed towards yet another red tiled roof that she could see just above the trees. This was the wash-house that Sensei Nakamura had pointed towards. Tandy made her way to it.

Somebody watched her.

*****

John Ketcher was an agent for MI6. He was a tall fit man in his mid-thirties, rather handsome, with grey eyes and light-brown hair that was thinning on the crown of his head. Four days ago, he had been captured in a bar at lunchtime in the city of Mosul. He had been trying to infiltrate Intiqam by pretending to be a radicalised Englishman who wanted to fight for them. But he had been asking too many questions of the wrong sort and he had been staying in a three-star hotel; freedom fighters do not stay in three-star hotels, they inhabit tatty fly-blown rented rooms.

His presence had been reported. The report went to al-Makira who had smiled like a jackal and then given the order that Ketcher be picked up.

Three men in hoodies and jeans had followed Ketcher from his hotel and came in behind him after he entered the bar, they dropped into old wooden chairs at an old wooden table just inside the door. The bar was a run-down seedy-looking place with a stone floor and bare brick walls. There were a few more wooden tables and chairs between the door and the bar at the back of the room. Two old men sat at one of the tables near the bar playing some sort of board game in silence, and a fat man aged about fifty with a grubby shirt, grubby jeans and a balding head was standing slumped against the far side of the bar and was presumably the owner.

The MI6 agent had just ordered and received a beer, after which the owner resumed his slump, when one of the hooded men got up and approached him; his two friends got up and went outside. The hooded man leaned up against the bar alongside Ketcher and away from the owner. He lowered his hoodie down to the nape of his neck and said very quietly,

"I understand you are wanting to fight…for The Cause?"

Ketcher glanced at the bar owner who hadn't moved a muscle. He put his beer glass down on the counter, the contents untouched, and turned to the man. Just as quietly, he answered in fluent Arabic, "That is right, my brother."

The man looked down at the floor, then off to one side, then at Ketcher's face. It was the shiftiest look that Ketcher had ever seen. "Then come with me."

Ketcher hesitated.

"What is wrong?" asked the man, his lips twitching into something resembling a smile. "Don't you trust me?"

Of course Agent Ketcher didn't trust him. He answered, "One must be careful."

"Very true," said the man now nodding serious agreement. "I tell you what…I will leave, and, if you want to, you can meet me outside. The choice is yours."

Ketcher raised an eyebrow and nodded back. The man pushed his hoodie back up, turned and left.

Ketcher, knowing this was his opportunity, took a couple of sips at his beer, put the glass down and followed the man a few seconds later.

The man was waiting for him.

"What's your name?" asked Ketcher. The man did not reply. He began to walk along the broken pavement. Ketcher began to follow. He could feel the heat of the pavement coming up through the soles of his trainers.

A white unmarked van pulled up beside them and a side door slid open.

The man turned to Ketcher. "Get in."

The two other men that had been in the bar earlier were inside the van. Agent Ketcher stepped towards the opening and that was when the man that he had talked to in the bar hit him over the back of the head with a blackjack, a flexible lead-filled truncheon. Arms grabbed Ketcher as he collapsed, and he was hauled into the van.

The door slid shut with a clang.

Agent Ketcher was driven over-land to the village of Qaryat Musawara, Arabic for Walled Village. En route he came around twice and both times he was injected in his left arm.

Eventually Agent Ketcher regained consciousness. His head was lolling to one side as he came around, and as his head cleared and he was able to take stock, albeit somewhat confused, of his situation. Ketcher found that he was still dressed, but that he was tied down on top of a bed by straps around his middle and lower legs. When he tried to move the room spun, the metal-framed bed beneath him rattled rustily, and he felt sick and weak. So, he lay back on the thin mattress.

A man, who was wearing a blue disposable medical mask around the lower half of his face, approached him. Ketcher wanted to demand where he was and what was going on, but waves of nausea kept him quiet and subdued.

The man took Ketcher's pulse, lifted Ketcher's eyelids with his finger and thumb and stared into his eyes. He said something in Arabic to Ketcher then injected him again.

Ketcher slipped back into unconsciousness.

*****

Hagakure's wash-house was yet another single-storey white-walled structure with a red tiled sloping roof, although this building was long and narrow. The walls were cedarwood not paper, presumably because if they had been paper they would not have lasted five minutes, being the walls of a wash-house. The entrance, like the dojo, was through a proper wooden door which was set halfway along the length of the building.

Tandy left her trainers outside and entered barefoot. She found herself in a small passage and confronted by a line of cedarwood doors behind which were small shower-rooms. To her left, and at right angles to the shower-room doors, and at the end of the passage, was a single cedarwood door. On the front of it there had been painted a small picture of a man in a white gi. Tandy turned around to find that at the other end of the passage there was a corresponding door that had a picture of a lady in a pink kimono painted on it.

Ahh. The Ladies and Gents toilets.

Tandy availed herself of the facilities behind the kimono door because by now she was bursting for a pee. She lowered her jeans and knickers and sat her naked buttocks down onto the polished wooden toilet seat, and that was when she noticed the set of buttons on a fixed handset to the right of the seat. She presumed they did something, but did not know what because all of the instructions beside the buttons were in Japanese script.

She pressed a button and music began to play; it was *Morning* from the Peer Gynt Suite by Edward Grieg. In something of surprise and just a little panic Tandy turned it off. She looked around her guiltily, as if she had done something that she was not supposed to. Then she laughed and realised how silly she was being.

She pressed another button and jumped and squealed, because this time a jet of warm water had shot up from underneath her and it had hit her in a very ticklish spot. Then she raised an eyebrow and moved a number of her facial muscles as the water continued to flow and she began to enjoy the experience – then she burst out laughing.

Sensei Nakamura was standing in his kitchen putting together their lunch when he heard first the music, then the squeal, and then the laughing, and the vestige of a smile crossed his face for just an instant as he paused in his preparations with an exceedingly large sharp knife.

Having composed herself, and then having got comfortable and with no further interruptions, Tandy stood up and pulled her jeans and knickers into place as the toilet automatically flushed itself. Tandy looked around as if suspecting that someone had done this for her but then realised it was another example of Japanese toilet-technology at work.

Smiling, Tandy entered a shower-room. There was a space in front of the shower basin where there was a small wooden bench on the left, above which there was fixed to the dividing wall a small white open-fronted cabinet where she could put her clothes. There were a number of large fluffy navy-blue towels sitting in rolls on one end of the bench, and Tandy nodded and smiled in satisfaction. She took out of her plastic bag a clean pair of white Miami-style knickers, a clean white bra, and a clean plain white tee shirt and, as she did not want to get them wet, she put them in the cabinet. She put the leather toilet bag on one end of the bench.

She stripped off her clothes and put these on the bench as well. Then she opened the toilet bag and took out a brand-new bar of soap that was sitting unwrapped in a plastic soap holder. She took the soap out of its container and sniffed at it, enjoying its lavender fragrance and then she stepped into the shower basin and looked at the shower. Two half-inch copper pipes that were fixed to the wall came up from the floor and entered a white plastic box above her head. A chrome pipe protruded from the wall on the end of which was a showerhead about the size of a dinner plate. She was standing directly under it.

Tandy's attention went back to the plastic box; the front of the box had a dial on it about as big as the lid of a jam jar and below that was a small red button. There was no indication as to how the dial worked or what the button was for.

Tandy knew that in England the hot taps were nearly always on the left and the cold on the right. She reached up, turned the dial left, and pressed the button.

Instantly, a heavy spray of freezing cold water struck her naked body like needles of ice.

"Jesus Christ!" Tandy yelped aloud as she dropped the soap and leapt out of the shower. Her knees came together, her arms crossed at her chest and her hands flattened onto her ribcage either side of her breasts. "Jesus Christ!" she shouted again.

In his kitchen Sensei Nakamura gave another of his rare smiles. The newcomers always fell for it.

Check first!

Tandy reached in and turned the dial to the right.

Seconds later the showered water began to steam.

Tandy offered a bare foot into the water stream and, satisfied, she stepped off the edge of the shower basin and under the warm spray. She bent and retrieved the bar of soap and continued with her ablutions.

When she had finished, Tandy towelled off and put the soap back in its box and into the toilet bag. She put the used towels in the middle of the bench. Then she put on the clean underwear and the tee shirt. She pulled on her jeans, collected her toilet bag and put it with her dirty clothes in the plastic bag, and left the shower room.

She exited the wash-house, pulled on her trainers, and headed back to her room.

Tandy stepped barefoot into her little room and stopped. Her eyes widened and her mouth came open.

Hanging from a T-shaped frame in the middle of the room was a cherry-pink silk kimono. It had beautifully hand-embroidered side panels depicting red-crowned cranes - Japanese symbols of happiness and long life. They were on long black legs with their white and black wings just opening and their beaks pointing upwards on the ends of their long black and elegant necks. Tandy walked around the kimono; the back of it was embroidered in the same fashion. Much as she had wondered earlier, *Where the hell did he get this from?*

Sitting on the floor beneath the kimono were a pair of white open-toed flat-soled straw sandals. In Tandy's size.

Tandy resisted the impulse to strip off her old clothes and just chuck them onto the floor because she knew that this would not be the accepted thing. Instead, she took off her jeans and tee shirt, keeping her underwear on, and folded and tidied them with her used clothing onto one of the room's shelves.

Then she tried on the kimono and did a twirl in the middle of the room.

The kimono fitted perfectly and she felt wonderful in it.

She did another twirl.

Yes, it fitted, as did the sandals, and Tandy began to suspect Mr Cross' hand in all of this.

Then she arched an eyebrow. No matter.

With the silk next to her skin, and feeling like a million dollars, Tandy headed for *the big house*, as Sensei Nakamura had put it.

*****

LONDON – THE SAME DAY – 8.30AM

Sir Michael Corrigan reached out and picked up his telephone. Unlike MI6, the Specialist Operations Unit did not have a switchboard; this was deliberate as it therefore made it impossible for anyone to just call them up. After all, they did not exist. If you wanted to speak to someone in the SOU then you had to have their telephone number to start with.

Sir Michael rang a number in the MI6 building at 85 Vauxhall Cross and a man called Brian answered. Sir Michael did not know if Brian was the man's real name, it hardly mattered. What mattered was that Brian was Sir Michael's day-to-day contact. Sir Michael liked to think of him as his own personal MI6 mole.

Brian worked in Intelligence; he gathered it like a spider gathers and wraps up flies: quietly, patiently, deliberately, efficiently.

On paper, Brian was listed as an administrator; he just got on with his job of administrating, pushing paper around, watching computer screens, never making any waves or causing any disruptions. He was so non-descript that not even Brian's manager knew that Brian had been planted in his job years ago by Sir Michael Corrigan. If you were to ask Brian's manager who Sir Michael Corrigan was, she would have replied, "Sir Michael? Sir Michael Corrigan? Never heard of him, have you, Brian?

No.

No notes taken. No records kept. And if Brian's manager did not know of the liaison, then the Chief of MI6 certainly did not know either.

Sir Michael was calling Brian because he needed to know if any of Brian's carefully wrapped flies had revealed anything useful.

"Brian," said Sir Michael affably. "Mike here. Can we do lunch today? Say, twelve-o-clock?"

"Sure, Mike, that sounds good. McDonalds?"

You might think that people who deal in swapping intelligence that could affect the security of the British Isles would meet – as the movies and TV would have you believe – at a Gentlemen's Club, or a top London Restaurant. Not so. Better to meet in public, in full view of everyone, and where everyone is going to ignore you.

"Great. See you there."

*****

Tandy arrived on the engawa of the big house and headed towards the front entrance. She stopped. No bell-push, no knocker. Should she tap on the screens? Probably not. What to do?

The sensei's voice came through the screens. "*Hairu*...Enter."

As she puzzled over how he had known she was there, Tandy fumbled with the edge of a screen and was relieved when it easily slid to one side, revealing a very small room. She stepped in. This was the *doma*, it is the traditional Japanese house version of a western entrance hall. Here the family or visitors can remove their outside footwear before putting on their inside footwear or leaving their feet bare. Tandy closed the screen behind her that she had come through. stepped her bare feet out of her sandals, and paused before yet another set of shoji screens.

"Hairu, hairu," came the sensei's voice.

Tandy slid the screen and her sight took in a room that was beautiful in its simplicity. It was somewhat similar to Tandy's room but larger. It had eight large tatami mats on the floor and a wooden ceiling. The walls were all *shoji* screens and on the wall opposite the entrance was the tokonoma that had a hand-painted scroll hanging on the wall that exquisitely depicted a pink cherry blossom that had burst into flower on its dark twig. In front of the painting was an delightful arrangement of pink chrysanthemums standing in a ceramic pot that had a light-pink glaze.

Sensei Nakamura was sitting cross-legged on the floor with his knees and feet below a very low table. He did not get up, nor did he comment on how beautiful Tandy looked in her kimono. Instead, he put up his left hand.

"Stop!"

Tandy froze on the spot. Had she done something wrong?

"Before you enter room you kneew on froor, sideways on, and open shoji." His words had come out clipped, almost as if he were annoyed, or talking to an idiot. He continued, "Then come in, kneew, and crose shoji. Then you stand and bow." He peered at her from beneath a frown. "Understand?"

Tandy dismissed what she considered to be rudeness on the sensei's part. If anyone else had spoken to her like that she would have told them not to in no uncertain way. However, she was in Japan with its vastly different culture to her own. She reminded herself that she was also at Hagakure, and Frank had forewarned her that the sensei was a man of few words. So, instead of giving Sensei Nakamura a mouthful, she recalled the Japanese for yes, bowed and said, "*Hai.*"

"Good. For now, just sride shoji as you are." He meant standing up and not kneeling.

Tandy slid the screen.

She bowed to the room.

Sensei Nakamura gave a grunt and then beckoned her to the table.

Tandy approached the table and, remembering what Frank had told her *If in doubt, bow*, so she bowed again and sat down cross-legged on the floor opposite the sensei. The table was black and highly polished so that its surface seemed to be made of glass and not wood. Set out in front of Tandy was a tall glass of water and three ceramic bowls of different sizes and colours. The largest bowl held a generous steaming helping of *ramen*;

Chinese noodles in pork broth. There were some thin slices of pork on the surface and the dish included some sliced leeks and spinach. The other two bowls held raw tuna and fluffy white rice respectively.

Sensei Nakamura had not started to eat and Tandy was relieved that she had not been late for the meal. He nodded at her and said, "Eat." He waited until Tandy had picked up her chopsticks (there being no knife, fork or spoon) before he began his own meal. He lifted his ramen bowl to his face and began to slurp the noodles. Following his example, Tandy lifted her own bowl of noodles and began to eat in silence.

After a few noisy mouthfuls, Sensei Nakamura stopped eating and looked at Tandy.

She stopped eating and looked back. "What?"

He lifted the noodle bowl, got some of the contents into his chopsticks, brought it to his mouth, and slurped it all in.

He stopped eating his mouthful and looked at her expectantly.

Tandy blinked.

He looked at her. His eyes unwavering.

Tandy knew that in certain of the Arab parts of the world it was the custom to belch loudly after a meal to show that you had enjoyed it. Perhaps slurping was the done thing here?

She lifted the bowl, picked up some noodles, drew them to her lips and slurped them in; not quite as proficient as the sensei, but good enough to meet the Japanese custom.

Sensei Nakamura gave a nod accompanied by another small grunt and carried on eating; they both tucked in loudly, and with relish, because the food was simply delicious. Sensei Nakamura noted with satisfaction that Tandy could use the chopsticks almost as expertly as he did. She had passed another test.

When they had finished their meal and water Sensei Nakamura stood up.

Tandy got her legs out from under the table with ease and stood up to face him. She bowed. "Thank you for the meal sensei, it was delicious." She bowed again; he nodded.

"Now you begin training. Go and put on gi and come back here." He paused. "Don't forget to take pee."

Tandy forced herself not to laugh. Instead, she bowed again and turned to hurry across the room.

"Stop!" came the sensei's voice.

She stopped.

"Inside house no hurry. Must be carm. Hai?"

Tandy bowed. "Oss, Sensei." She straightened her back and walked slowly to the entrance screen where she knelt down sideways on to the screen, slid it open, and then moved awkwardly across the threshold on her knees and shins. On the other side of the threshold, and still in the kneeling position, she slid the screen closed. Then she stood up, stepped out of the doma, hitched up her kimono, grabbed her sandals and legged it across to the wash-house as fast as her flying feet could carry her.

*

After taking her required pee she sped back to her room and got changed into her gi.

Tandy left her room, not bothering to go through the kneeling-by-the-shoji ritual, and hurried back to Hagakure. Here she did go through the shoji ritual and then stood to face her sensei. He was still in his daily grey kimono. Perhaps he still had to get changed for their martial arts training?

He walked over to her. "Stand up straight. Hands by sides. No move."

Tandy did as she was ordered while he walked around her.

At her waist she wore a white cotton-over-canvas belt and not her green one.

Sensei grunted. "Hmm. Why you wear white obi?"

Tandy remained standing ram-rod straight. She had decided not to pack her green belt as she did not want to seem to be showing off. So she answered, "To show humility, and because I am not a black belt, my Sensei."

"Oh!..Hmmm."

He came to the front of her and stared at her face. She remained impassive under his scrutiny. "Not sho dan?" Not First Level black belt?

"No, sensei."

Sensei Nakamura grunted. Tandy did not know it but Sensei Nakamura only trained those of black belt level, something that Frank had obviously omitted to tell her.

The sensei reached out and took her hands in his. Tandy felt a ripple of surprise run through her, for although he had hands no bigger than a child's she could feel the strength and power in them, just from his touch. She noticed that the middle and forefinger knuckles on each of his hands were calloused from years of striking targets. In karate one never punches with all four knuckles of the hand, only those of the middle and forefinger.

Sensei Nakamura examined her hands. He grunted. Tandy had no such callouses.

He released her hands. "Make fist."

She did so and he seized each of her fists in his own fingers and palms. He squeezed. The pressure built up in her closed fingers. Each of his hands had a grip that could crack a walnut. Tandy did not bat an eyelid. She had often worked-out on a tall leather kick-bag at Cannon Head and the clenching of her fists had strengthened her grip, which had further increased due to holding and lifting weights in Cannon Head's gym

The sensei released her. He gave another grunt. "Come with me."

A screen had been opened on the right-hand side of the room and it led outside. Tandy had to wait as the sensei changed his footwear. Having done so he picked up, what looked like, a plain white paper fan that was open and lying on the floor in front of the open screen. The sensei stepped outside. Tandy followed him along the engawa and away to the left.

At the end of the engawa was the door in the wall that Tandy had seen on her exploration of the grounds. Sensei Nakamura produced a large ornate iron key from the folds of his sleeves and opened the door. The sensei stepped through and Tandy followed.

Her mouth came open and she gasped.

She was staring at a *zen* gravel garden.

There were seventeen stones that had been placed about the large rectangular area; seventeen being the best number that you can have in Japan. Seventeen is called *Ju Nana* and, if you have it, it is believed to bring enormous wealth and prosperity. The stones had been placed in a specific manner, so that you could only see fifteen of them no matter where you stood to view them, and viewing could only be done from the surface of the engawa, which was two feet above the level of the grey gravel.

Some of the stones were quite small, no bigger than a football, whereas others ranged in height and width. The tallest stood just off-centre to the very middle and was about seven feet tall and a foot thick with a flat front about two feet wide that faced the engawa. In contrast to the flat front the back and sides were roughly hewn with ridges and bumps. All the stones had partial coverings of moss and they all stood in a sea of swept gravel which was raked by hand to form patterns of ripples in the stones. They reminded Tandy of the ripples formed on the surface of the ponds by the beautifully coloured koi carp.

Sensei Nakamura brought her in line with the tallest stone and indicated that she should kneel facing it whilst he remained standing beside her. She got down at his feet and tucked her heels under her bottom. Then she sat back onto her calves with her shins and the tops of her feet pressing onto the wood of the engawa. Not very comfortable, but she assumed she would not be expected to kneel like this for very long. She placed the palms of her hands onto the knees of her gi trousers.

"Rook at rock," said the sensei.

Tandy looked at the massive flat-fronted rock and asked, "Is this called *Zazen*?"

Zazen is Japanese word for the correct body position taken up by a person when they are meditating.

"No," said the sensei. "Is cawed rooking at rock."

"Oh."

"Zazen is something erse."

"Oh. Okay."

"Stop chatter. Sit up straight."

She straightened her back.

"Good...Rook at rock." He pointed at the big rock.

"Right. Then what?"

Sensei Nakamura batted her around the back of her head with the opened fan. It turned out that the fan was not made of paper; it was bleached white wood. It was not a hard blow and would not have done any damage, but it made Tandy frown and bridle a little.

"You caw me *Sensei*."

Clang! Thought Tandy.

"Sorry, Sensei...I..."

Sensei Nakamura batted her around the head again. "No chatter. Rook at rock."

Tandy looked at the rock.

After a few minutes she shifted her weight.

Sensei Nakamura, who had not gone away, but who was now standing slightly back from her, batted her once more around her head. "No move. Rook at rock."

Tandy pulled a face, but she looked at the rock.

She stared at the rock.

Why?

She stared harder.

After a few moments Sensei Nakamura interrupted her fractured concentration. "Is not just about rooking at rock. Anyone can do that. You must try to be in the moment. Mind must no wander. When you have achieved state of mind-no-mind then you have achieved Zen. Understand?"

"I think so, my Sensei."

"Ohh, you *think* so?" He sounded almost sarcastic.

Tandy did not answer, she did not really know what to say, and her feet were beginning to hurt.

"Do your feet hurt?"

Tandy blinked. "Yes, my Sensei." She wiggled uncomfortably.

Sensei Nakamura swatted her about the head again. "No move. Ignore pain," he said. "Empty mind. No think of pain in feet. Hai?"

Tandy swallowed hard and gave the sensei a definite-sounding spirited "Hai!"

She stared harder at the rock.

Her feet hurt.

She dare not move.

Her knees hurt.

She stared harder at the rock.

Her lower legs had gone numb.

She stared at the rotten rock.

Her attention started to wander.

She stared at the bloody rotten rock.

She did not know why she was having to do this. She knew this was a zen garden, but what, really, did that mean? She had understood what the sensei had been getting at when he had mentioned mind-no-mind, and she knew that this was supposed to be a place of contemplation and meditation, but how could you do either of those things, or obtain a mind purely concentrating on having an empty mind, whilst kneeling in this awkward position? How could you shut out this pain and achieve mind-no-mind whilst sitting in this damned awkward position that threatened to cut off the feeling in your legs from the hips downwards? Wouldn't it be easier to sit on your bum with your feet crossed in front of you, like you did when you sat in a dojo? So, why must she kneel?

Tandy struggled to keep her back straight. Had Sensei Nakamura left her? She had not heard him leave, but then she had not heard him walk over gravel earlier either.

Not wanting to be struck with the fan again, Tandy held her position for the next fifteen minutes; it seemed like an eternity. At the end of that time her legs felt so numb that she simply could not feel them anymore. The tops of her feet felt like they were on fire, her toes were beginning to cramp and her body was trembling slightly. She was now gritting her teeth so hard that her face had taken on a sickly grin. Without taking her eyes off the stone she listened to the area around her, and when she was sure that the sensei had gone, she shifted her weight.

Sensei Nakamura swatted her around the head again.

"No move…"

"I know, I know…Rook at rock!" she mimicked him. "Je-sus!"

"Jesus not here. Onry me. Rook at rock."

"I'm looking, I'm looking!"

"Caw me *Sensei*." (swat).

"Sensei! Look, I'm sorry…"

"You chatter rike monkey." (swat). "No chatter. Rook at rock."

Tandy stared at the stone. Hating it. Hating the sensei. Hating being here in this place. What was this to do with martial arts? How could this possibly improve her fighting skills? What had she been thinking? This time with the sensei was obviously not going to work out.

She made up her mind to get up, thank the sensei, and go home. Sod all of this!

And then it struck her. Like a lightning bolt cast by the Gods of Japan out of a clear blue sky, it struck her.

This was a test. And with that realisation she understood that Sensei Nakamura had been testing her ever since she arrived. He had not given her a great welcome when she first arrived, seeming almost to ignore her; he had not told her about the toilets or the way the hot and cold dial worked in the wash-house; he had not mentioned how beautiful she looked in the kimono; he had not spoken to her during their meal together and had only given her chopsticks, with no access to a knife and fork. And he had told her the correct way to open and close a shoji screen, speaking to her like he would a child.

This test in front of the stone, like all the others, was about humility and the ability to obey everything that the sensei ordered. It was about not making a fuss and to be able to ignore ignorance. It was also about conquering pain and discomfort. It was about putting up with inconvenience, solving problems and focusing the mind. And it was about the ability to keep completely still and calm under adversity, not moving, being able to be like…like?

Like a rock!

Tandy smiled.

"Ahhh," said Sensei Nakamura as he nodded and watched her face. "Ve-ry go-od."

Tandy kept silent and still. However, the smile stayed in place. He had given her some praise!

She did not move.

"Hai, ve-ry go-od. You may get up."

Tandy struggled to her feet. From her hips down to her toes her bones felt like they were made of jelly. Never-the-less, she turned to the sensei and bowed. "Arigato...My Sensei."

The flicker of a smile crossed the sensei's face. "You understand?"

"Hai, my Sensei. Now I understand."

"Exprain it."

Tandy thought for a few seconds as the sensei watched her face, then she said,

"I must endure."

"Hai! Ve-ry good." He nodded. "No matter how much discomfort you have, whether from someone, or a circum…circums…"

"Circumstance?" offered Tandy.

"Hai. Circumstant. Now matter how awkward your circumstant – in fighting, or debate, or physicaw discomfort, or in rife – you must endure."

"I understand, my Sensei." Tandy bowed.

He returned the bow. "No more training for now."

Tandy limped on both legs as he led her away from the zen garden, past the end of his house and past the wall of his kitchen to a path that she had seen on her arrival. He stopped and pointed at the small building with white walls and a red tiled roof that she had observed earlier. "In there is onsen. You go there now. After, you go to dojo. We train."

Tandy bowed. "What time should I be at the dojo, my Sensei?"

"Come when ready."

"Arigato." She bowed.

Sensei Nakamura went to turn away. Then he paused and turned back. "Be carefur. Onsen very hot water. No stay more than twenty minutes. Heat make you…" He made a circular motion in the air beside his head with his right index finger. "…Make you…" He struggled to find the correct word.

"Dizzy," said Tandy.

"Hai. Dishy." He raised an old white eyebrow then looked intently at her face. "Hai. Very dishy."

Tandy smiled at him. And as gruff as he was, or as gruff as he *appeared* to be, Sensei Nakamura allowed himself a proper smile that crinkled up all of his old face before he silently walked away.

*****

Sir Michael Corrigan arrived at the McDonalds at 291B Oxford Street, London at one minute to twelve noon, having walked there from his office. It was a dry day with some sunshine and the exertion of the walk had made him a little hot in his woollen dark-blue two-piece Saville Row suit. He entered the McDonalds and spotted Brian at a corner table at the back of the fast-food outlet. Brian was also wearing a suit; this one was light-grey, but not Saville Row.

Sir Michael went straight to the counter and ordered and paid for a Big Mac and fries and a medium-sized cup of black coffee no sugar. With his purchase in his hands, he went and sat with Brian and, as he approached, he said in a loud voice, "Hi Brian, how's it going?"

Brian looked up and smiled. "I'm doin' alright mate," he responded. "You?"

"Bloody marvellous."

A few heads turned and then turned back again as Mike and Brian were summarily ignored.

Brian was already halfway through his cheeseburger. He took a gulp of his coffee and then smiled at Mike. In a much quieter voice he asked, "So, Mike. What's up?"

Sir Michael Corrigan said, almost off-hand, "I've been hearing things about little white envelopes coming from Mosul, with demands inside." Sir Michael selected a long french fry in his fingers and munched it down.

"Ahh," smiled Brian. "The little white envelopes. I wondered when they'd get your attention."

"Do we know who's behind them?" Another fry went down.

"Not yet, but we're working on it."

Sir Michael threw an inquisitive glance at Brian who lifted his cheeseburger to his lips and took a bite out of it.

If MI6 were *working on it* then they must have something to work on.

Sir Michael held his Big Mac in front of his face. "The paper is reported to be of superior quality, such as the Japanese make." He took a bite out of his burger.

Brian shook his head. "We think the Japanese connection is a smoke screen."

Sir Michael swallowed his mouthful. "Why?"

"Because of some sand."

"Sand?" Sir Michael tried his coffee. Very nice. He sipped some more.

Brian chomped down the last of his cheeseburger and then wiped his mouth on a paper napkin taken from the steel dispenser in the middle of the table. He leaned forward onto both elbows.

"It's like this. Up until a few days ago all of these letters and envelopes were as clean as a whistle. No fingerprints, no hair, no DNA. And then, a few days ago, a certain Josephine Havers-Whyte, with a hyphen, received one of these letters. The Havers-Whytes live in a bloody great family pile on the borders of Cheshire. They're about two-hundred-and-fifty in line for the throne and spend all day riding and fishing, and shooting anything that moves. Worth a fortune."

Sir Michael fiddled with a fry. Brian saw the fiddle. "Anyway, as I say, Josephine gets a white envelope with a letter demanding money with menaces inside, phones the police and does no more about it. Four days later our Josephine gets up in the morning and goes to check on her horses to find that two of them are lying in their stables with their heads cut off."

"Quite a slant on *The Godfather*," suggested Sir Michael.

Brian smiled briefly at the gallows humour.

"What's this got to do with anything?" asked Sir Michael.

"Ahh, well, the envelope had sand on it?"

"On it you say, not in it?"

"That's right. There were tiny particles of sand found stuck to the sticky strip of glue used to keep the envelope shut and secure."

"That was careless."

"Yes. Forensics think it might have blown onto the paper of the envelope just before it was sealed. The sender probably never noticed."

"I take it that your soil forensics teams have examined the sand?"

"Yes," said Brian, and he smiled again.

Both MI5 and MI6 have access to some of the best forensic scientists in the world, including Soil Forensics. Just by examining particles of soil, or rock, and in this case, sand, the soil forensics people could identify it as coming from any terrain anywhere on the planet to within, in some cases, just a few yards accuracy.

Before Brian could offer an explanation Sir Michael asked, "Could the sand have got onto the envelope after this Josephine lady opened it? I mean, could it have become contaminated evidence? Could it have come from the stables?"

"No." Brian shook his head. "It came from Iraq."

This sudden revelation made Sir Michael pause. Iraq?

Mosul perhaps?

Sir Michael took another sip of coffee and then asked, "Do we know whereabouts in Iraq?" The answer would make Sir Michael sit back in his chair.

"Yes," Brian nodded. "The area around a village called Qaryat Musawara."

*****

The *Onsen* is a particularly Japanese institution. They are, in effect, a communal bath house, except that the sexes are kept strictly segregated.

On entering an onsen the bather must first collect a basket and a towel. The bather then strips naked and places their clothes into the basket and leaves them usually on a shelf to be collected later after towelling dry. It is unusual for a locker to be supplied as this is Japan, and people do not steal other people's belongings that are left out in the open.

Having stripped off, the bather then showers and cleans themselves *before* getting into the hot water of the communal bath. This pre-cleansing act is carried out so as not to contaminate the waters of the onsen with any kind of grime.

Tandy found the onsen to be a wonderful experience (enhanced by the fact that she was on her own and she could splash about to her heart's content), and she had acted on Sensei Nakamura's advice and only spent fifteen minutes in the huge ceramic bath. And yes, it had been hot, and very steamy, but when she climbed out, she was astounded by the fact that the aches and pains she had acquired from kneeling on the engawa had all gone.

Tandy hurriedly towelled herself dry and put her gi back on. Then she headed for the dojo.

Upon entering the dojo, she stopped and bowed, out of respect for the training area. All martial artists do this when entering a dojo.

Sensei Nakamura was already there. He was out in the middle of the dojo and he was wearing a white gi with a black linen belt wrapped around his waist that was tied with the traditional knot. He was performing a *kata.*

Kata are sets of specific moves carried out by the performer to mimic being attacked and defending against that attack. The kata are laid out in a specific pattern and are often referred to in English as *Forms*. The higher up the kyu and dan grades one progresses, the more complicated the form. All of the kata start with a defensive move and then go on through a series of punches, kicks, strikes and blocks as the practitioner turns and moves and alters their direction and balance.

Sensei Nakamura was going through the moves of a kata called *Chinte*, which means *Strange Hands,* and is called this because of the variety of hand techniques this kata uses. Normally a kata is performed at a lively pace to show speed and power, with interludes of slower moves where balance and tension are required. However, Sensei Nakamura was performing all of *Chinte* quite slowly, almost like a Chinese *Tai Chi* exercise. It made the kata that much harder to perform as greater balance and greater control of all the moves was called for.

Tandy sat down on the floor with her legs crossed in front of her and, entranced, she watched the sensei. He may have been old but he moved in a graceful yet powerful way with his body balanced and in harmony.

When he finished, he moved into the *Yoi*, or ready position: feet apart, head, chest and shoulders up, hands as fists, but not tensed, by his sides. Then he put his feet together and bowed to the dojo. Tandy felt like clapping but she stopped herself as she knew that this would not be appreciated by the sensei.

He turned and beckoned Tandy towards him.

She approached, stood before him and bowed.

The sensei returned the bow and said, "You know kata?"

"Hai," affirmed Tandy.

Sensei Nakamura picked a *Shotokan* kata. There are twenty-six different Shotokan katas and each individual kata has its own name, and Tandy had been taught all of them by Frank Cross, although, like most people, some she was better at than others.

Shotokan is the style of karate developed many years ago by Sensei Gichin Funakoshi who is widely accepted as being the founder of modern karate and responsible for bringing it to the masses, and it is practiced world-wide to this day. Sensei Funakoshi was a poet and the name Shotokan is derived from the Sensei's pen-name of *Shoto*, meaning *Waving Pines*. This was the name of the house where he taught his karate to a select few students. *Kan* means house, so Shotokan means *The House of the Waving Pines*.

"Show me *Gankaku*." This was *The Crane on the Rock*, and is meant to represent a crane, or heron, fishing from a rock in a stream. It means that the person performing it has to move about, standing first on one leg and then the other, turning and twisting, bobbing down then stretching up, moving one's arms like wings and stabbing the hands and fists forwards and backwards to mimic the movements of a heron fishing.

Tandy moved into the *yoi*, ready, position.

Sensei Nakamura stood off to one side and gave the command to begin, "*Hajime!*"

Tandy exploded into the kata, pushing hard into the punches and kicks where they were needed and slowing down when tension needed to be applied through her muscles and into a technique. When she had finished, she returned to the yoi position and bowed.

Sensei Nakamura came around to the front of Tandy and looked at her. She stood unmoving, controlling her breathing, staring straight ahead, which meant she was looking over the top of his bald head.

"Re-wax," said the sensei.

Re-Wax? thought Tandy. She'd had her legs done a couple of days before she had left St Margaret. Surely he wasn't interested in what her legs looked like?...*Oh...RELAX!* She struggled to keep a smile off her face.

"Something funny?"

"No, my Sensei."

"Hmmm." He squinted at her through slitted eyes. Tandy's face never moved a twitch. "Okay," said the sensei. "Now do same kata, but not so fast. Do much much show-wer."

Tandy bowed, stood back in the yoi position, and did the kata again. She knew that performing a kata slowly is much harder than doing it fast, and she knew that was why the sensei had told her to do it in such a way. So, she called upon all of her physical and mental resources to get her through to the end.

She finished and moved into yoi.

"Do again," ordered the Sensei. "Do show-wer."

Tandy did not think she could have done it any slower. However, she took a breath and began when she was given the command to start, "Hajime!"

This time Sensei Nakamura walked along beside her as she moved and sometimes he stopped her, altering a foot position here and a hand position there, altering a shoulder and moving a knee. He put his steel-like fingers onto her stomach and pressed inwards to feel her abdominal muscles and pushed the heel of his hand into the tops of her arms, the tops of her legs and across her back. He opened her arms wider when they were supposed to be the heron's wings and pushed at her, checking her balance when she stood on one leg, when she was supposed to be getting ready to strike down or forwards for a fish - like a heron on a rock.

When she had finished, he said, "Do you understand? Heron on rock?"

"Hai, my Sensei."

"Okay. Do again with speed and power! Be heron. Go fish!"

Tandy bowed and once more exploded into the kata. This time she felt the essence of the kata, trying to be the fishing bird; stalking its prey one second and plunging to catch it the next. When she came back to yoi she was tingling with elation. And all this in her first lesson! This man, she realised, was a truly remarkable sensei.

He stood in front of her again and, without smiling, he said, "Ve-ry go-od!"

Wow! More praise!

"Now we fight."

Tandy blinked.

"Something wrong, Miss Trudeau?"

"Umm…No!" She shook her head. "Do we wear fist mitts?"

"What for?"

"For protection." Whenever she had sparred with Frank they had always worn protection mitts and shin guards.

"You think you are going to hurt me?"

"Umm, no."

"Why not? Is karate. Not origami."

"*Oss, Sensei*!" She gave a vigorous bow.

Sensei Nakamura put his hands on her shoulders and pushed her backwards. It was his way of saying, "Move away."

After she had moved back three steps, Tandy's hands came up into fists and she dropped into a fighting stance with her left hand and foot forwards. Sensei Nakamura stood quite calmly with his right foot forwards and his hands by his sides.

Tandy eyed her instructor who wasn't moving.

They stood and looked at each other.

"Are you going to do something soon?" he asked. Not a trace of emotion showed on his wrinkled face.

Tandy could not get out of her head the fact that she was facing a lightly built, very small, old man.

The sensei seemed to read her thoughts.

"Not worry about me! Attack! Attack!"

Well, you asked for this, Buster!

Tandy attacked with spirit, stepping in fast with a lightning-quick right-hand *oi-tsuki* lunge punch to Sensei Nakamura's face – which never landed. As her knuckles shot towards the sensei's head he moved with the speed of a cat. He stepped to the left of Tandy's flying fist and batted it out of the way with the back of his right hand, then he spun on his left foot and turned a full three-hundred-and-sixty degrees and hammered his right elbow into the middle of her right shoulder blade. Tandy yelled out, and no sooner had she yelled than the sensei had turned towards her to strike her in the intercostal muscle between two of her ribs on the left-hand side of her rib cage with the tips of the fingers of his left hand. Tandy went down onto the floor, collapsing onto her knees. With her back towards him the sensei closed in for the kill, but Tandy used her gymnastic skills and she pushed through her feet and sprang upwards, forwards, and away from him. Still moving through the air, she went into a forward roll, twisted out of it and came upright, facing him. She brought her hands up to defend herself.

Sensei Nakamura stood with his hands held open and apart at chest height. He was impressed. He had never seen that move before and he admired the fact that she had come back up into a fighting stance, ready to take him on again. This young lady was turning out to be full of surprises. For the first time, he began to look forward to teaching her; if she carried on like this, she would make a fine student.

The sensei dropped his arms, put his feet together and bowed.

Tandy watched him in astonishment.

"Ve-ry go-od, Miss Trudeau."

Tandy came out of her attacking posture and bowed back. "Arigato, my sensei."

"We go through that again, and I show you where you went wrong. Hai?"

Tandy smiled. "Hai!"

He folded his arms. "But first, must say…" He struggled with the English, "must say that…you showed me what you were going to do…before you did it."

"I did?"

"Hai. You took breath then attacked. No take breath. Keep breathing….how you say?...regurar?"

"Oh, regular?"

"Hai. No show opponent how you breathe. Must have controw. Must controw breathing, body, emotion, mind. No controw, no win fight. Hai?"

"Hai sensei!"

"Good. Attack again and I show you what I do."

And so began Tandy's karate fighting lessons and training.

*****

Sir Michael was back in his office. He had told Vicky, his Personal Assistant, that he was not to be disturbed and he was now sitting back in his comfortable office chair behind his desk with his jacket off and his shirt sleeves rolled up.

He was thinking again.

What he was thinking about was this: his own department had been infiltrated just a few weeks ago by a terrorist organisation called Intiqam. And if it had not been for his best agent – Frank Cross – and a freelance assassin called Tandy Trudeau, the SOU would have collapsed from within and taken the rest of the British Security Service with it, like a man dying from, and spreading, a deadly virus.

Had Intiqam raised its head again? Corrigan suspected it had, that it was like the legendary Hydra - you cut one head off and another sprang into being to take its place. The hydra needed to be stabbed through the heart to make it die, and Cross, the ex-government assassin, was the ideal man to do the stabbing.

However, Cross was now retired and living with Miss Trudeau on their island paradise, and Sir Michael knew that there was no way on this earth that Cross would come and work for the Unit again.

And why did he think that Intiqam was back in business?

The answer was sand.

Sand from the deserts of Iraq.

Sand from a particular part of a particular desert. The village of Qaryat Musawara.

Probably, Sir Michael mused, where the terrorists had their headquarters.

Probably.

Possibly?

So, the hydra needed to be destroyed. And Sir Michael had to figure out a way of doing that, knowing that he could not ask Frank Cross.

What Sir Michael did not know, despite all of his mental manipulations, was the fact that his life was about to be turned upside-down in a way that even he could not imagine.

*****

Sensei Nakamura had been taking Tandy through some intense sparring instruction for almost three hours. She discovered that apart from being fast and strong he was also extremely flexible. All of this had come about through years of martial arts training which he had practiced every day. It was a discipline that he had dedicated his life to and was serving him well in keeping his body fit and his mind alert.

The sparring instruction was not just constant fighting, for no-one can fight constantly for three hours. The sensei broke the sessions up; he explained to Tandy what muscles came into play when she kicked or punched or struck, even those she used when she took a step forward, sideways or back, and how best to use them to get the maximum effect from them. He showed her how she could use her already fantastic sense of balance to even better effect, and how to not only control her breathing but also her mind. To keep relaxed, even when fighting hard. "Keep re-waxed, move faster, more

power. Must be as river." He moved his hands and arms forwards and back.
"How you say?"
"Flowing?" suggested Tandy watching his movements.
"*Hai*. Frowing!"
"I understand, my sensei."
"Good. Attack again!"

*****

THURSDAY 12TH JUNE

Agent Ketcher came back into the world. He was still on the old rusted rattling bed and he still had his old clothes on. He felt dampness at the tops of his legs and was appalled when he realised that he had pissed himself. No-one had bothered to clean him up or change him.

He struggled up onto one elbow and lifted his head. He felt sick and thirsty and weak and he slumped back onto the bed for a few minutes before trying to get up again. He fought the nausea that threatened to engulf him and brought himself back up onto an elbow and slowly looked around. He was in a room; it was a bit gloomy with white drab badly-plastered walls, bare floorboards and a wooden boarded ceiling which were actually the floorboards of the room above. There was a tall window to his left that had wooden shutters that were closed. The light coming through the gaps in the shutters hurt his eyes so he looked away. However, it meant that it was daytime, although he had no idea what day it actually was, or the time.

A door over to his right opened and a man wearing a blue medical mask walked in. Ketcher somehow recognised him, but could not remember why. Perhaps he had imagined seeing him before. The man said something to him in Arabic and then went out again, closing the door behind him. Ketcher tried to call out but his voice was dry and hoarse and came out as a small whisper before he collapsed back on the bed again.

A few moments later the same man came back in with a plate. On it was a hunk of dry grey bread and a slab of sweaty yellow cheese. The man came across to Fletcher and looked down at him from behind his mask. He blinked a few times and then he put the plate down on the dirty floor beside Ketcher's bed then turned and left the room.

Ketcher fell back to sleep staring at the cheese.

*****

In Cannon Head Frank Cross was in the gun room that was off a tunnel underneath the villa. The tunnels had been dug out by naval ratings and marines in Nelson's time and had originally been storage for the explosives for the cannons that had once been on the site. Now Frank used them to store his large collection of arms, ammunition, electronic gadgetry and spare parts for the car and various items of machinery that the villa used for its running. It was Frank's version of a shed – but in this case it was a *real* man cave.

Frank had just cleaned and oiled a Heckler and Koch MP7 assault rifle. He put it upright into a rack with several others, wiped his hands on a section of kitchen roll and smiled as he wondered how Tandy was getting on. He was missing her perhaps more than he thought he would. And he was rather pleased about that.

*****

Errol Moon had set up, developed, and was now running a successful music recording studio on St Margaret. He had been born on the island but had moved away in his early twenties to make his name as a jazz pianist in New Orleans. Although Errol was a good pianist – some said even a great pianist – he had not made the dizzying heights that he had hoped for. But Errol was shrewd. His jazz musicianship allowed him to get gigs with other bands as a side-man - the great musician that you never notice on stage or in the recording studio - who can make all the difference between a good performance and a great performance. And while that was going on Errol watched how they made those recordings of those performances, even offering his services to help out on the technical side when he had gained enough knowledge.

Eventually, with all of that tech know-how stored in his brain, and with his ability to know a good tune - or how to tweak a mediocre one - Errol changed career. He went to work in the recording studios at first for Warner Brothers and then Sony Music. His knowledge expanded. He put away what money he could whilst supporting his family back on St Margaret. He was married with two children, a boy and an older girl, and when he had enough savings, he quit Sony to go home, where he founded his own recording studio. He specialised in helping the struggling musicians of the Caribbean islands and eventually had a string of West Indies hits under his belt. He also had a good reputation; a man to be trusted. He didn't rip you off. His business was thriving.

Errol was now fifty-one years old. He was five-feet-six-inches tall with a bit of a belly. He had a good head of fuzzy grey hair that he had grown long enough to be able to tie into a ponytail at the back, and out front he had a matching grey beard about six inches long. He had a bulbous nose, good straight teeth, and crows-feet laughter wrinkles at his eyes behind round gold-rimmed spectacles,

Of his two children, a son and a daughter, it was his daughter, Diana, who from an early age developed an interest in music – she would sing and dance around the family house where they lived in the small coastal town of Nelson. While the son (Diana's elder brother) went to college to become a Civil Engineer, Diana learned how to play the piano and the guitar. She sang at the local church; first in the choir and then on her own. She had a powerful voice that was full of melody. She had a good sense of rhythm and she had an innate sense of musical timing. In short – she was a natural.

Diana was now twenty-two years old, five-feet-and-eleven-inches tall with a mass of black hair. She had a good figure and a beautiful face that had almond-shaped eyes, high cheek bones and full lips.

She wanted to be a professional singer and dad was helping her. She had already sung in all of St Margaret's major hotels as the evening entertainment for the guests. She had won the island's all-comers singing competition twice, and had wowed them in the big hotels on the islands of St Vincent, Barbados, Antigua and St Lucia. Following this success, and after some string-pulling by her father, she was to sing in one of the restaurant suites at the MGM Grand in Las Vegas in a few days' time. She had already been to the huge hotel for an audition in front of a certain Miss Levin, who was in charge of hiring and firing entertainment for the hotel, and she had passed it with flying colours. She'd been given a six-month contract to sing every evening because Diana was just what Las Vegas wanted; she had the looks, the glamour, the charisma and the voice, and there was no doubting her stage presence. Yes, she was a natural sure enough.

Following the audition, she had been booked into one of the MGM's guest rooms, free of charge, awaiting her big moment. She had phoned her mother and father, and her father was both delighted and proud. His daughter was going to do what he had never managed to do for himself. He was sure that she was going to hit the big time. Diana was so excited, and she also phoned her best friend Ola, who happened to be the eldest daughter of the President of St Margaret.

And then Errol Moon received a plain white envelope with a letter on white paper inside. The envelope was postmarked Mosul and the letter asked for the American dollar equivalent of fifty-thousand English pounds. It told him what bank account to pay the money in to and it told him when. Unfortunately, like the envelope that had been delivered to Denise Anderson, Errol Moon's letter had been held up in the international post. If Errol had paid the money it would not have been in that account for long; it would have been quickly split up and transferred around the world, so as to become untraceable. Errol Moon's letter also came with the warning that if he did not pay the money then he could expect some retribution to come to his family. It also told him not to contact the police.

Being an honest citizen, and believing it to be a scam, Errol ignored the warning and put the letter in the trash bin.

*****

Tandy could see that her days at Hagakure would take on a pattern: in the morning she sat with Sensei Nakamura and ate breakfast with him. This was followed by kata training in the dojo, then a break for lunch and then some sort of combat training in the afternoon. This was followed by a trip to the onsen and then there was a break when Tandy could be by herself.

When she wasn't in her gi she would wear a kimono. She had now been presented with a total of four; the original pink one, a light-blue one that had large white chrysanthemum heads all over it, a white one with a geometric pattern picked out in dark-blue, and a poppy-red kimono that had a huge golden dragon that curled up the back from hem to collar. She was very careful to keep them all neatly tidied away when not in use and she made sure they were kept clean, because she knew how fastidious the Japanese are about cleanliness.

In her rest periods she would change into a kimono and either sit just outside her accommodation and read from her *Kindle* or explore the extensive and beautifully manicured gardens that surrounded the sensei's house. The weather was warm and there had been only a few showers of rain, with the aftermath of the rain only enhancing the garden with its droplets of water that sat like jewels on the leaves of plants and trees, and which lay scattered over the moss beds like tiny diamonds.

Then there would be the evening meal, taken with the sensei. And then there would be more training until finally being dismissed to go to bed.

After this particular day's evening meal had been eaten, and before it had been cleared away, Sensei Nakamura - who was still seated opposite Tandy at the table - looked at her and said, "You remind me of Tomoe Gozen."

Tandy gave a slight shake of her head. "I am sorry, my sensei, but who is Tomoe Gozen?"

"Ahh," said the sensei, putting down his chopsticks on a small ceramic chopstick rest and folding his arms across his chest. "Is from Japanese history. Tomoe Gozen was known as the Beautifur Samurai."

"The beautiful samurai? Really?" Tandy resisted the temptation to touch her hair as the thought went through her head, *Is he actually paying me a compliment...the old rogue!* And then it struck her that the sensei was actually having a conversation with her. This from the man who never spoke much, who kept his speech clipped and only spoke to offer essential information – like "Rook at Rock". This was therefore a rare event, and an honour.

"Hai." Sensei Nakamura gave a quick nod of his head. "Tomoe Gozen fought in the...in the B..." He struggled with the next word. "Batt...Batterer...Batter..."

"Battle?" offered Tandy.

"Hai! Batter. The Batter of Awazu, in ereven-eighty-four." He nodded emphatically and continued. "She was a fearress rider of horses and a great martiar artist, being aber to use both the naginata and the katana. It is said she was worth one thousand warriors in batter!"

Warriors in batter thought Tandy and she smiled – *like cod or do-nuts*, but what she said was, "I thought it was only the men that fought in battles, or as samurai."

"Oh, no." The sensei gave a little shake of his bald head. "Awthough the samurai were a crass of what you might say were warrior knights, high-born women often took part in batters...to defend their cast...caster..."

"Castles?" said Tandy.

"Hai. Casterers. They awso defend their husband and chidren."

"Their family," said Tandy.

"Hai. Famiry. They practice every day the naginata, katana and bow. Especiary naginata. Very fearsome weapon!"

"Tomoe Gozen must have been quite a woman."

Sensei Nakamura looked straight into Tandy's eyes. "Hai," he said. "Quite a woman." Were his eyes twinkling?

Tandy was about to say something when the sensei said, "Now, must crean dishes. Then get changed into gi. Go to dojo."

"Must practice," smiled Tandy.

"Hai!…Every day."

The kitchen was very modern with stainless-steel work surfaces with a large oven, an eight-ring gas hob, a butler sink, a refrigerator and separate freezer and lots of power points, cupboards and drawers.

After the dishes had been cleaned and put away, Tandy did as she was told and went to get changed into her gi. She then went to the dojo, entered, bowed at the threshold and went across to the sensei who was standing by the kick-bag. She expected to have to strike it, instead the sensei pointed at the floor and asked,

"Can you do push-ups?"

"Hai, my sensei." Tandy was not going to boast that she could get fifty out with no problem.

"Good. Give me fifty."

No problem. She kept the smile off her face and went down onto the floor. With her nose almost on the woodwork she could smell the cedar and the polish. She took up the push-ups position with her feet shoulder-width apart and her fingers facing inwards.

"When I say *hajime* you begin. Hai?"

"Hai," answered Tandy and was horrified when Sensei Nakamura put a foot onto her back and pressed down.

"Hajime!"

Not to be beaten, Tandy heaved and grunted and gasped her way through the fifty push-ups with the sensei's foot between her shoulder blades. She finished with runnels of sweat trickling down her face to drip off her chin and her sports bra and knickers were soaked with moisture. However, she had managed to keep her form by holding the length of her body plank-like.

Sensei Nakamura grunted his approval and let her up. "Now strike kick-bag in as many ways as you can, using onry hands and erbows. No kicks. Understand?"

"Hai sensei! I understand."

"Hajime!"

Tandy began to strike the bag. It was filled with sand and was hard and unforgiving and Tandy would not have been surprised if he had told her that the sand had been replaced by concrete. Never-the-less she battered away at it with her elbows, fingers, fists and palms. She used the outer edge of her hands to deliver *shuto*, knife-hand, chopping attacks and the inside edge of her hands by her thumbs to deliver *haito* attacks.

During this work-out Sensei Nakamura watched her intensely, stopping her from time to time to correct a movement or alter the position of a shoulder, a foot or a hip, always improving her.

After an half-an-hour he called a halt. Tandy was just about out on her feet.

"Very go-od. Train hard. Now go to bed."

"Oss, my sensei," and she staggered out of the dojo looking forward to a good night's rest.

Tandy made her way along the path back to her room. The garden was lit by small lamps that were on a timer; Sensei Nakamura may have had traditional Japanese values but he had also embraced Japanese technology. The lamps were set inside lanterns called *Toro* which are shaped like miniature pagodas and made of stone. They cast a warming glow into the surrounding vegetation, enhancing the forms and structures of the leaves and making a false twilight.

As Tandy reached the engawa that led to her room she heard a rustle away to her right. She stopped and peered through the half-light in the direction that the noise had come from. She could see nothing, so she closed her eyes and listened.

Listen and hear.

What was that?

A slight rhythmic whispering sound.

Like breathing perhaps?

It stopped.

Tandy waited a little longer. Nothing.

She opened her eyes and scanned the area again. Nothing.

She shrugged and turned towards her room.

Five minutes later she was in the wash-house shower, and fifteen minutes after that she was back in her room, inside her futon and fast asleep.

**

The man who had tracked Tandy from Cannon Head all the way to Kumamoto airport, and then on to Hagakure, had been lurking around the sensei's house ever since she had arrived. He had silently checked out the area and had been watching Tandy from a distance. He had also managed to get within a few feet of her as she had trained in the dojo, eaten with the sensei and used the onsen and washroom. He had reported all of this back to al-Makira, telling his commanding officer that there had been no opportunity to abduct her, but that he was sure that the opportunity would soon present itself. Al-Makira was not happy with the delay but he understood the need for stealth, and so he cut his operative some slack.

The operative had not been entirely honest in his report; there had been at least three opportunities when he could have grabbed Tandy, and two of them had been just after she had arrived and had been walking around the garden, getting used to the place. Truth was the man rather liked the look of her; she had lovely caramel-coloured skin and she was long-limbed with a good figure and a beautiful face. He had even managed to get a photograph of her naked body when she had gone into the washroom the first time that she'd had a shower. Tandy had been so concerned with the temperature of the water, and it had made such a splashing noise, that she had not seen him or heard him as he had cracked open the door to her shower room. He had risked putting his hand, that was holding a mobile phone, around the edge of the door and taking a shot of her. And, although he had now only seen her naked on the screen of his phone, it was enough to whet his sexual appetite and he wanted to see her body again.

He squatted behind some rocks amongst the trees and shrubs of the sensei's garden and leered at the photograph.

*****

FRIDAY 13TH JUNE

"Can you do box sprits?"

"Box splits? Hai sensei."

"Do now."

Tandy was facing Sensei Nakamura and she put her feet as far apart as she could and then allowed her feet to slide out some more until her bottom touched the floor of the dojo. She had dropped down easily with her legs out to either side and the soles of her feet flat to the floor, parallel to each other and toes pointing forwards. She began to come back up.

"Stop!" ordered the sensei. "Stay down.!

Tandy did as she was told.

A minute later, and still in the same position, Tandy's face was showing that her abductor and adductor muscles, her glutes, hamstrings and groin muscles were under tension and at full stretch – she was grimacing.

"Not bad," said Sensei Nakamura. "But I make better."

"Gaaah," said Tandy.

"No make funny noises. Stay there," ordered the sensei. He walked round behind her and placed his hands on top of her shoulders.

Tandy had a bad feeling concerning what was about to happen.

The sensei pressed down, increasing the tension in her spread muscles.

"OW!"

"No chatter! Re-wax!"

Tandy gritted her teeth.

"Now, sit back into your bottom. Rift feet but keep heews on fror."

Tandy translated the awkward English in her head: *Now lift the soles of your feet but keep your heels on the floor.*

Still standing behind her, the sensei altered the way that he was applying pressure and settled her backwards so that the cheeks of her bottom rested more easily onto the dojo floor. In this position Tandy found that by sitting back just a little more she could move her feet so that her toes were pointing towards the ceiling whilst her heels were on the floor. Even so, it wasn't easy, and she let the air hiss out of her mouth between her teeth.

"No hiss. Sound rike snake!"

Tandy's face was now screwed up in agony, but Sensei Nakamura held her shoulders, keeping her firmly in place with her body upright.

"Sit back into bottom," said the sensei.

"I'm sitting, I'm sitting!" gasped Tandy.

"No chatter. Re-wax."

He let go of her. "There," he said. "Much better. You now in proper box sprits!"

And she was. She was sitting bolt upright with her bottom fully on the floor and with her legs directly out to either side with her toes pointing to the ceiling. She could still feel the pull in her muscles but they had not been torn, or even over-strained. And she had lost the sickly grin off her face. Even the pain had gone.

"This is amazing!" said Tandy.

"Hah!" He actually smiled. "Now get up."

Rather awkwardly, Tandy got to her feet.

He pointed at her. "Hips now open. Hai?"

"Hai!" Tandy wriggled her hips. They sure felt looser.

"Now we do kick training. Hai?"

Bloody hell! "Hai, sensei!"

*****

Agent Ketcher rolled awkwardly onto his back; his hands pinned behind him. A man in a blue medical mask was shining a light into one of his eyes, and then did the other. Then he checked Ketcher's pulse and then strapped on a blood pressure collar around his upper left arm.

The man looked over his shoulder, to someone that Ketcher could not see, and said, "Give him a little water the next time he comes round. Only a little."

The man in the mask then grabbed Ketcher's lower jaw and waggled Ketcher's head left and right a few times before releasing him. Ketcher passed back into blackness.

*****

"You not trying hard enough. Kick me!"

Sensei Nakamura was taking Tandy through kicking practice to see what moves she knew, and to find out how good she was at them.

The Japanese for kick is *Geri* and Tandy was a very good kicker and had mastered mae geri, the front kick, mawashi geri, the roundhouse kick, yoko geri kekomi, the side thrusting kick, and yoko geri keage, the side snapping kick. She could do all of these competently as well as ushiro geri, the reverse kick, ushiro mawashi geri, the reverse roundhouse kick, and boshi geri, the spin kick. Her favourite was the spin kick which she could deliver fast and hard at head height and with a deadly accuracy – striking the target at head height with either her heel or the sole of her kicking foot as it came backwards into her opponent.

Tandy and the sensei were in the dojo and sparring with each other using only kicks. Tandy knew how hard she could kick and had been holding back from kicking the sensei too hard. Her legs were strong and toned with muscle and she could deliver a mae geri, front kick, that could take the average male off his feet and throw him backwards for several paces.

After numerous half-hearted kicks from Tandy the sensei stopped the session and put his hands on his hips and almost shouted aloud, "What you doing? You kick rike duck!" He then began waddling round in circles making quacking noises and kicking his feet and legs out at odd angles. Tandy had never seen anything like it and she struggled to keep her face straight and not laugh out loud.

The sensei stopped his impersonation of a waterfowl and walked up to Tandy.

"Can you kick hard?"

"Hai sensei," said Tandy.

"I ask…Can you kick hard?"

"Hai sensei!" shouted Tandy.

"No hear you!"

"HAI SENSEI!" bellowed Tandy.

"Come here." The sensei walked over to the big leather kick-bag hanging at the far end of the dojo. "Kick bag."

Tandy kicked it with the roundhouse kick; her right foot came up off the floor behind her as she lifted her right knee out to the side and pivoted on the balls of her left foot. This turned her left hip out as she brought her right knee up to her waist height with her right foot trailing behind. Then her right foot lashed around to the front and struck the leather bag with a satisfying thump. She recoiled her kicking foot and placed it back behind her on the floor.

"Too soft!" said Sensei Nakamura. "Do again!"

In fact, the kick would have fractured a skull, smashed ribs or broken an arm or a leg if it had landed on a person, and Sensei Nakamura knew it, but he wasn't going to say so.

Tandy hammered out another kick.

"No good! Harder!"

The sensei made her do this twenty-five times on her right leg and then twenty-five on her left, by which time she was out of breath and her feet hurt.

Sensei Nakamura then moved back out into the middle of the dojo floor. "Now. Kick me!"

Without any warning Tandy drove her roundhouse kick at the sensei's left ear with her right foot. If it had landed it would have taken the old sensei's head off, but it didn't. With the kick only a hair's breadth from his head the sensei stepped forwards and to his right, away from her attacking foot and struck upwards with the fingers of his right hand towards the bottom of her jaw where the flesh is soft in front of the throat. Tandy thought for a moment that his fingers were going to penetrate up into her mouth at the base of her tongue, but then the fingers were removed.

She landed her kicking foot onto the floor and went to turn towards the sensei, to ask that he show her what he had done.

"No stop!" shouted Sensei Nakamura and she immediately obeyed and launched a front kick at him. He dodged that and came back with another counter-attack, a light left-hand punch to her stomach. "No stop! No stop!"

Tandy went for him, she battered kicks at him, twisting into spin kicks, pushing out side-kicks, hammering front kicks at both his chest and head. She kept changing her balance point and her centre of gravity, driving hard, trying to hit her teacher whilst he evaded, twisted and turned as lithe and as pliable as an eel. Not once did he block her with his forearms or palm her away with his hands, he just kept dodging out of the way, and he always came back at her after every kick with a counter attack until eventually he called "*Yame!*" Stop.

Tandy stopped instantly and stepped away from the little man. She put her hands by her sides and bowed and he returned it. She put her hands on her hips and pulled in air through her nose, getting her breathing under control. She noticed that Sensei Nakamura's bald head was glistening and that chest was rising and falling. *He's sweating and he's out of breath! Yes! He's out of breath!*

Very slowly, a smile began to appear on the sensei's face.

"Ve-ry go-od, Tandy. Ve-ry go-od." It was the first time that Sensei Nakamura had used her first name. Tandy picked up on that fact.

She bowed. "Arigato, my sensei."

"And see," he said as he rolled up his sleeves to show his forearms. "No bruises. Not get hurt. If I am not there, you cannot hit or hurt me."

"I understand, my sensei." Tandy bowed. She had just had an advanced combined lesson in kicking and *tai sabaki*, body shifting.

"End of resson."

Tandy bowed again. "Arigato, my sensei." She left the dojo and went to the onsen via her bedroom where she picked up her clean pink kimono. At the onsen she stripped out of her sweat-dampened gi and underwear and washed herself in a shower before slipping into the onsen bath. Then, after a relaxing soak in the rejuvenating waters, she dried herself off and put on her kimono. She then went and sat, cross-legged, in front of the big stone in the zen garden. Here, instead of emptying her mind, she allowed herself to think about her martial arts journey thus far.

*****

Al-Makira was sitting on a wooden chair behind a rough wooden table with his Second-in-Command standing beside him. They were in a room on the ground floor of the house in Qaryat Musawara and al-Makira was eating a leg of cold chicken. He used it to wave a small diminutive man towards him.

The man approached his commanding officer not without a decent measure of fear. The man was aged about fifty. He had a full black beard on a thin face and a balding head and a slightly hooded brow above calculating eyes. He wore round spectacles and a floor-length plain grey djellaba. He was also slightly bent forward and his total demeanour was like that of a rodent. He was clutching a heavy ledger.

This was al-Makira's accountant, Amir Darwish.

Darwish had been abducted in the streets of Baghdad on his way to work in his office. He had been singled out by al-Makira because he was self-employed and successful. And he also had a wife and two young children who could be used against him as leverage. So far they had come to no harm. So far.

"Well, Amir," al-Makira smiled. "How goes the collecting for our funds?" Al-Makira was referring to the demands with menace that had gone out world-wide in little white envelopes.

Intiqam had been funded, until recently, by both al-Qaeda and ISIS. But that monetary support had dried up following the defeat of Intiqam by Frank Cross and the Specialist Operations Unit. Yes, there was still money in the bank, but al-Makira had to be careful how he spent it; it all had to be accounted for, and that was where Amir Darwish came in. Darwish manipulated funds, moved them about the globe, made profits. And he did this under pain of death for himself and his family.

It was true, however, that other money came in privately from Intiqam's supporters, but many of those supporters had crept away like frightened mice following the demise of both Simon Lancaster and El-Sayed. As a result, the money that was now coming in was now only a trickle to what it had been, and al-Makira had a terrorist operation to run and oversee. He had men and women to feed and clothe as well as equipment, arms and ammunition to buy, supplies to obtain, and vehicles and aircraft to maintain. In short, he now had to pay for everything from a toothbrush to a helicopter.

Therefore, al-Makira had been forced to obtain funds by threats.

Darwish bobbed his head. "Things go well, al-Makira. Things go well."

Al-Makira sat forwards. "How well?"

"Through the use of the white letters, we have obtained five-million-nine-hundred-and-fifty-thousand American dollars," said Darwish with a subservient bob. He'd had to convert many different currencies into that of the USA.

"Very good," smiled al-Makira. "I want to spend some of it." He tossed the gnawed chicken bone onto the table top.

The little man's mouth fell open. "Spend it?" he asked in astonishment.

"Yes. Spend it. That is what money is for. What is the problem?"

"It is not available yet, al-Makira."

Al-Makira's eyes hardened. "Why not?"

The accountant's shoulders seemed to shrink inwards. "Banking and then recouping the funds is not as easy as just dealing with a branch on one of the High Streets."

Al-Makira leaned forwards and pointed his right index finger at the accountant's face. "Don't get smart with me, you pen-pushing snivelling little maggot!"

Darwish cringed at the insult. However, he none-the-less gathered enough courage to answer, "B-But al-Makira, the world's banks will shut us down if they suspect that this is money acquired for terrorist purposes." And shut down on them they would. At the first sniff of money laundering the barriers would come down internationally and the accounts would be frozen whilst an investigation was launched by the various world banks, of which there were many involved unwittingly in Intiqam's transactions.

"We must be careful, al-Makira."

"Listen," growled al-Makira, "Al-Qaeda and ISIS have withdrawn funds following the killing of my brother's execution squad on St Margaret by Frank Cross. I need to be able to pay for the operation I am running. I don't care how you get it, or how many risks you have to take." He stood and gripped his right fist tight in the air. "I need that money to bring Frank Cross to me. Understand?"

"Y-Yes al-Makira."

"I doubt if you do. Now, get out!"

Amir Darwish made a movement that was half-way between a curtsey and a bow before scuttling away.

Al-Makira sat down and his Second-in-Command stared down at him. The SiC was horrified at what he had just heard, but he did not want to cross his commanding officer. And so, in a voice that he tried to keep as bland and neutral as possible, he asked,

"Did you really mean that?"

"What?"

"That you are using this money just to bring Frank Cross here?"

Al-Makira looked up at his SiC. "Yes. Does that trouble you, Irfan?"

Irfan took a breath. "Frankly? Yes."

A hard look passed briefly across al-Makira's face before he smiled indulgently. "Why, my friend?"

Irfan had recognised the first look; a threatening look of complete displeasure, but he none-the-less risked it and pressed on, saying,

"It just seems to me to be an awful lot of money to waste on getting just one man."

There was a long drawn-out pause while al-Makira controlled his temper. Then he said, "Irfan, my brother. This is the man that nearly brought down our organisation. The man that made us look incompetent and a laughing stock to our brothers in ISIS and al-Qaeda." He sat back in his chair and looked intently at Irfan. "But I tell you this, my friend…When we get him, I will execute him in front of the world. And then these western pigs will understand our deadly purpose and we can demand even more money for the release of the hostages. And when we have the money for them, I will execute them on television as well." He grinned at his SiC. "And then we will be feared, my friend…and then Intiqam will be feared. And then the funds will flow into our coffers once again."

The SiC grinned now as well. "Excellent! No wonder you are called al-Makira."

The Cunning.

*****

SATURDAY 14th JUNE

Agent Ketcher regained consciousness. This time something had altered.

This time he was totally naked and tied to a straight-backed solid tubular steel-framed chair by a rope around his waist. His hands were tied behind him.

In front of him was a simple wooden table that had a glass and a full jug of water in the middle of it, and on the other side of the table sat a man. The man was sitting forwards with his hands clasped in front of him and his elbows resting on the table. He was wearing army camouflage fatigues and he was watching John Ketcher.

Quite affably the man asked, "What is your name?"

Ketcher, still not quite recovered from all of the anaesthetic that had been pumped into him over the last few days, just gasped and passed out again.

Al-Makira sighed. "Take him back to his bed," he said, standing up. He looked at someone behind where Ketcher was sitting. "Let me know when he comes round again." He went to a door opposite the window and stepped outside onto a bare wooden landing and went down some stairs.

*****

Side-kick training. Yoko geri kekomi, the sideways thrusting kick, and yoko geri keage, the sideways snapping kick. Tandy was proficient at both of them, and with her newly opened hips she felt that they had greatly improved.

The thrusting kick is delivered by the foot thrusting out sideways to the body with the knee and hip pushing the foot, so that the outside edge of the foot lands hard and heavy on the point of impact. The snapping kick is different in that the kicking foot swings upwards and out so that it is the top and outer edge of the kicking foot that strikes the target. However, it is the thrusting kick that benefits more from the ability of the performer to do box splits.

Sensei Nakamura stood in front of Tandy who was in her left-foot-forward fighting stance.

"I want you to step in with right foot and attack me *jo dan* with *mae-geri kekomi.*" A head-level side kick, but delivered to the front. "Understand?"

"Hai!"

"Hajime!"

Tandy stepped in with the kick, turning on the balls of her left foot whilst bringing her right knee up and around to her body before thrusting it out sideways from her hip, but forwards towards the sensei. Sensei Nakamura had his left foot forwards but he stepped back with that foot as the attack came at him. He blocked Tandy's attacking foot with the back of his left hand and then flipped it over her ankle and grabbed it so that he had her ankle and Achille's tendon in his steel-like fingers. He then transferred his weight into his left foot and thrust out his right, whipping it out and up in his own yoko geri kekomi. The edge of his foot landed across Tandy's throat. If it had landed full bore it would have crushed her windpipe and broken her neck. Then, with amazing speed, Sensei Nakamura dropped his kicking foot so that it went behind the back of her legs and, at the same time, he pulled at Tandy's ankle with his left hand. The foot he had kicked with had lightly touched the floor and the sensei then brought this foot back towards him and, with it, he swept Tandy's legs away from underneath her.

Tandy's feet shot forwards but she went down backwards. She hit the floor heavily but managed to get her right hand out in the semblance of a breakfall technique, to take the impact out of the crash. The sensei did not follow her down. Instead, he lifted his right foot and placed it across her throat. If he had pushed with his foot he could have crushed her throat, and if he had lifted his right foot and brought the heel down hard he could have crushed her skull.

He released Tandy's wrist and stepped away from her. She said, "Urhhh."

"Up, up!" said the sensei. "Up, and I show you. Hai?"

"Urhhh."

Sensei Nakamura frowned. "You hit dojo froor too heavy. You okay?"

Tandy picked herself up. Despite her attempt at a breakfall she'd banged her left elbow, shoulder, hip and ankle on the wooden boards when she'd landed. She rubbed her elbow.

"I'll be alright, my sensei."

Sensei Nakamura grunted, nodded, then asked, "Do you know about breakfah?"

Tandy sometimes had trouble understanding his pronunciation of the English language.

Why is he asking me about breakfast? "Breakfah?"

"Hai. Breakfah."

"Ummm…" Then it came to her – *Ahh, he means, Can I break four? Perhaps we are now going to try breaking things.* "No, sensei. I have never tried breaking anything."

A look of puzzlement crossed the sensei's face. "What you tawk about?"

"Sorry my sensei. I have never tried breaking anything before." She made a chopping motion in the air with her right hand.

Sensei Nakamura's bushy white eyebrows went up. "No, no. No *tamishawara*! Breakfah!"

Tamishawara is the ability to be able to break things with parts of your body, principally with your hands or feet, but also with your forehead and elbows. Such things to be broken are usually wood and roofing tiles but can also include blocks of ice, breeze blocks and house bricks. The ability to do this is not to show off, it is to show the person doing the breaking how powerful and strong they have become, and how they must control that power when fighting someone.

Tandy still did not get it. She stared gormlessly at the sensei who frowned back at her.

"Breakfah!" he said. "Breakfah!" And then he slung himself sideways and to his right onto the floor and slapped the wooden boards with his right hand as he landed. Laying on his side he slapped the floor three times and with each slap he said, "Breakfah! Breakfah! Breakfah!"

"Oh!" exclaimed Tandy as the light bulb came on in her head. "You mean BREAKFALL!"

"Hai! Of course! Breakfah!"

Tandy looked down at the master and then started to laugh. She tried not to. She put her right hand over her mouth. But it was no good, she put back her head and guffawed.

Sensei Nakamura's face registered annoyance, then surprise, then humour, and finally he started to laugh as well, until he was laying on his side chuckling aloud.

**

The Syrian who was keeping out of sight in the garden made his way over to the building that Tandy was using to sleep in. He knew that, at the moment, she was in the dojo and had only been in there for about ten minutes, he therefore knew that it would be a couple of hours before she finished her lesson. The Syrian was not bothered that the sensei - whom he regarded as just an old man – might discover him because he was now carrying a semi-automatic pistol, a Glock 17, with seventeen rounds in the magazine. If he was discovered then he would simply shoot the old fool.

His back-up team had passed him the gun on one of the occasions when he'd had to leave the garden – he had to eat, drink and use the toilet after all – and he now had the gun tucked behind his back in the waistband of his trousers. His team wanted to know when they would be able to move in with him and abduct the girl, but he had put them off saying that he was waiting for the right moment. This was not true. What was true was that he wanted to see her naked just once more. He was starting to become infatuated with her in the same way as a stalker follows his victim.

The Syrian entered the building where Tandy was staying and slid aside the shoji screen to Tandy's room and stepped in. He could smell the perfume she used and he gently breathed it in, filling his lungs with it, savouring it.

He went across to the shelving on which she had placed her clothing and delicately picked through the items, coming to a halt when he found her bras, two black lacey balcony bras, two white balcony bras and four black sports bras. He picked up one of the black balcony bras and held it to his nose. Once again, he gently beathed in, imagining her wearing it. He smiled, and for a moment he considered stealing it, but that might alert her, so he carefully, and somewhat reluctantly, put the underwear item back as he had found it.

Then he turned and left the room, sliding the shoji back. Being oh so very careful.

Yes, his time would come.

He disappeared back into the garden.

**

Sensei Nakamura was squatting on the floor of the dojo facing Tandy. His knees were apart and he was holding himself up on just the balls of his feet with his heels touching his bottom. Tandy was kneeling and facing him. He was teaching her how to breakfall.

Frank had not taught this skill to Tandy. Whenever they had sparred, they had nearly always remained standing up, unless Frank took her down to the floor, and then he always did it with control so that she did not hurt herself. Sometimes the take-down to the floor had developed into more than just sparring.

"Sensei, don't we need to do this on padded mats?" she asked eyeing the polished wooden floor that she had already painfully crashed onto.

"Do you have mat with you in street?"

"Ah, no, sensei."

"Do you carry mat around with you?"

"No, sensei."

"So, no have mats to train. Understand?" Again, there was that unassailable logic.

"Hai. Understand."

The sensei grunted and then said, "Watch carefurry." He put his right hand up in the air with his arm at full stretch. Then he reached backwards, still keeping his arm outstretched, and turned his face away to look over his right shoulder. He allowed his weight to take him backwards and he pivoted on the balls of his feet as he fell over. As he went down, he continued to reach behind him with his outstretched arm and then drove his hand down hard to slap the floor with his palm as he fell over. He was now lying on his right side with his head resting on his right arm that was still stretched out and away from him. His tiny feet were tucked up near his bottom.

From his position on the floor the sensei patted the floor with the hand that had slapped the woodwork. "This hand is breakfah. Hai? Understand?"

"Hai, my sensei. I understand?"

"Must breakfah hard with hand. With spirit, or no work."

"Hai."

He pointed at his feet. "Must keep feet up near bum. In this way you keep controw of regs. If attacker comes near you then you can kick. Understand?"

"Hai, my sensei."
"Must breakfah with your hand, not your head. Understand?"
"Hai."
"Good. You try. Do soft. Not fast. Hai?"
"Hai."
Tandy copied what the sensei had just demonstrated. She landed a little awkwardly and went to get up.
"Stay down," said the sensei and he got down onto the floor beside her.
"Feet, regs, body, head," he pointed at them in turn, "are okay. Arm and hand no good. Your hand too near your body. Body weight go straight down arm. Force of body break erbow and break wrist. Must reach out, away from body. Understand?"
She did. Although she had landed slowly and relatively gently, she had felt her elbow and wrist take the strain and weight of her toppling body. If she had landed fast and heavily, she would have broken either her wrist or elbow joints. Possibly both.
"Get up. Do again."
Tandy set herself up and tried again. This time she flung her arm out and slapped her hand down, pulling her feet in towards her bottom as she landed.
"Good. Do again."
After six times on her right side the sensei made her go down on her left.
"Now. Watch." This time Sensei Nakamura did not squat but went into a crouch with his knees bent as if he were about to sit down in a chair. He propelled himself backwards, flung out his hand and arm for the breakfall, stuck the floor with his palm, landed and rolled over.
He got up and straightened his gi. "Now you."
For Tandy this was more disconcerting. For a start she was taller than the sensei, which placed the cheeks of her bottom a lot higher off the floor than his. And because she was taller the floor was further away.
"Don't forget to reach with hand…What you waiting for? Go over!"
Tandy went for it. With a little squeal she collapsed backwards, getting her right hand down fast in a slap to the wood. She remembered to tuck her feet in and, having landed, she rolled over and sprang lithely to her feet.
She found that Sensei Nakamura was staring at her.
"What?" she asked, forgetting to add the word *sensei*.
"How you know how to do that…spring to feet?"
"I don't know, my sensei. It just came naturally, I guess."

"Hmmm," said the sensei somewhat thoughtfully. This was remarkable. "Do again six times. Then other side. And spring to feet."

"Oss, sensei!"

When that exercise had finished, Sensei Nakamura approached her. "So, now, Tandy." This was the second time he had used her first name since she had arrived, and again it did not go unnoticed by her. "I throw you. You breakfah."

With Sensei Nakamura being four-feet-and-eleven inches tall, and Tandy being five-feet-nine-inches, it seemed a bit of a mis-match. However, Tandy was here to learn, so she stood with her right foot forward and balanced herself.

The sensei stood in front of her and took her right wrist in his left hand. Then he took hold of both of the lapels of her gi where they formed a V above her cleavage in his right hand. Suddenly he stepped forwards with his right foot and placed it behind Tandy's right foot and he swiftly turned his body left. He pulled with his left hand and pushed with his right and Tandy came off her feet with a yelp.

With total control the little sensei took her backwards and down to the floor. Tandy swung her left arm out and around so that as she came down the palm of her left hand slapped the dojo floor.

Sensei Nakamura had dropped with her, bending his knees and adjusting his balance as he went into a kneeling position beside her. This put Tandy at a disadvantage because if she tried to get up then the sensei could immediately respond by striking her.

She lay there looking up at him.

"You okay?" he asked. He looked concerned.

A broad smile spread across Tandy's face. "Hai, sensei! That was great! Can we do it again?"

"You want do it again?"

"Hai."

The ghost of a smile flickered across the sensei's old face then disappeared. "Hai," he said. "Okay. But first, you throw me."

"Really?"

"Hai. Very easy. I show you."

For the next hour Tandy Trudeau and Sensei Nakamura - a young woman and an old man - threw each other all around the dojo, and had a lot of fun doing it.

SUNDAY 15th JUNE

NEVADA - USA

Diana Moon had decided to take a walk along Las Vegas Boulevard, the famous "Strip". Like most days in this desert city the sun was out, high and bright in a clear blue sky. She was wearing a red tee shirt with narrow shoulder straps, a pair of calf-length skinny jeans with a tan-coloured leather belt with a large round silver buckle, and a pair of red high heels that put her at over six foot. She had a large tan leather bag held by leather straps over one shoulder, a pair of big blue-framed sunglasses with mirror lenses in front of her eyes, and a big smile on her face. She had recently had extensions put into her dark-brown hair so that it fell lustrously to her shoulders. She looked fabulous, but then she was the sort of woman who could put on an old plastic refuse sack and look like a million dollars. Life was good and getting better. She felt that this chance in the MGM Grand was going to be her big break. She could feel it. She knew it.

She was walking long-limbed and easy along in front of the huge lion that guarded the entrance to the MGM Grand hotel. She was moving in the direction of the traffic, and had just come up to the first turning on the right when a big white van passed her, going in the same direction. She thought that the van was going straight on and so she stepped off the kerb onto the tarmac of the turning.

The van suddenly swung off the Strip and jerked to a halt in front of her. Diana nearly walked into the side of the vehicle.

Then a side door rolled open, two pairs of male arms came out, and Diana was hauled off her feet and into the back of the van. The door rolled shut with a clang and the van was off, rolling back into the main traffic. She hadn't even had time to scream.

A large cotton bag went over her head and then she felt something prick her arm.

She passed out.

**

Diana came around from her drug-induced sleep. She was fully clothed and lying on top of a dirty and uncomfortable single bed in a small badly-lit room that had rough whitewashed walls made of building blocks, a bare floor made of old floorboards, and a single boarded-over window. Thin shafts of bright daylight were spilling through cracks around the board and showing up dust motes in the air so she knew it was daytime, but what time exactly she did not know. She glanced at her left wrist. Her watch had gone. It was an expensive Tag Heuer that her parents had bought her for her twenty-first birthday present.

The bastards have stolen it!

Then she realised that her left wrist was attached to the frame of the bed by steel handcuffs. She moved her other wrist, only to discover that it too was fixed to the bed on the other side also by handcuffs. She started to panic and lifted her head a little, but this made her feel sick so she decided not to try to get up. She tugged at the cuffs and they jangled. Diana would have liked to have rubbed at the top of her right arm because it hurt a little. It was where the needle had gone in to knock her out.

She took a few breaths and then tried to move her legs. No go. Fighting the feeling of nausea Diana craned her head forwards and found that her legs had been tied together at the ankles with a thick plastic cable tie. A single handcuff was clipped around the tie with the other cuff over the far end of the bed and again clamped to the bed frame.

Diana Moon started to cry.

*****

"Push," demanded Sensei Nakamura. "Push."

Tandy was back in the dojo. Sweat was running down her face and chest and she could feel it tickling down her back. She was standing in *zenkutsu dachi*, forward stance; left foot forward and left knee bent at approximately ninety degrees, hips facing forwards and her right leg straight out behind her. She had a one-inch-thick rope in a loop around her waist and the two ends of the rope were being held by the sensei who was standing a few feet behind her. He was urging Tandy to drive forward into the stance whilst he hauled on the rope to pull her backwards. She'd been lunging into the rope for the last fifteen minutes.

"Have feet facing forwards," he advised. "No have feet sticking out rike duck!"

"Hai!" gasped Tandy. She blinked the sweat out of her eyes.

"Too much pressure in ankres, knees and hips if feet stick out rike duck."
What is it with you and ducks?
Tandy made sure that her toes were facing forwards so that she pushed through the balls of her feet and not through her heels.
"Keep moving! Push!"
The object of the exercise was to strengthen Tandy's lower body muscles: her *abdominals*, her *glutes* in her bottom, her *quadriceps* at the front of her thighs and her calf, or the *gastrocnemius* muscles, in her legs, as well as all of the muscles and tendons in her feet. It would give Tandy an even stronger and well-balanced stance to go with her already strong core.
"Now," called the sensei as she drove her right foot forward and the sensei hauled on the rope, "punch with your right hand!"
Tandy shoved out an oi-tsuki.
"Very good. Keep tension in stomach! Must push!"
"Hai, sensei!"
"When finish this I show you brocking."
"Oss, Sensei!"
"Must push!"
I'm pushing, I'm pushing! Bloody hell!

*****

When Ketcher came to again he was back in the tubular steel chair and was still stark naked. The same man as before was sitting there again behind the table; still leaning forwards, still with his hands clasped in front of him.
"What is your name?" The voice was calm, and even pleasant.
Ketcher moved his head. The room seemed to roll. He closed his eyes and swallowed. His mouth was dry and his throat seemed constricted, his tongue too large for his mouth.
"What is your name?"
Ketcher rolled his thick tongue in his dry mouth and said, "K-tchhhh." The effort to pronounce his own name made him feel sick.
Al-Makira nodded at the person behind Ketcher. A man wearing similar combat fatigues came around the side of Ketcher's chair and picked up the glass of water; Ketcher's eyes locked onto it.
"This is my Second-in-Command." Al-Makira introduced the man. "His name is Irfan."

Irfan raised the glass of water, but instead of offering Ketcher the drink he dashed it into his face.

Ketcher ran his swollen tongue over the dribbles that coursed down his face, trying to get some of the precious stuff into his mouth.

The SiC picked up the water jug and filled the glass again. He put the glass and the jug back on the table and Ketcher stared at it. The man remained standing just in front of Ketcher and off to his right.

"What is your name?" asked al-Makira. His voice now had an edge to it.

Ketcher struggled. "K-Ket-cher."

"Is that your first name?"

Ketcher shook his head, which, in his weakened condition came across as a head wobble, and he mumbled, "J-John. J-John K-Ketch-cher."

"Ah, and you would like some water, John Ketcher? Yes?"

"Y-Yesh."

"First you must answer some questions."

Ketcher said nothing. He stared resolutely across the table at al-Makira and firmed his jaw. He was not going to give this son-of-a-bitch any information.

Al-Makira allowed himself a slight smile, then asked, "Who is Frank Cross?"

No answer.

"I asked, who is Frank Cross? Is he a British Agent?"

No answer. Which was not surprising because Ketcher had never heard of Frank Cross.

Al-Makira nodded at his Second-in-Command who slapped Ketcher across his face so hard that it took his head around. Ketcher's nose began to bleed from his left nostril.

"Who is Sir Michael Corrigan?"

Again, the name meant nothing to Ketcher, so he sniffed and scowled at his tormentor.

Al-Makira nodded once more to his SiC who stepped forward and slammed his fist into Ketcher's face, smashing his nose. Ketcher's head went back hard and he went out like a light.

Al-Makira puffed out his cheeks. "I fear you may have hit him too hard, Irfan. Take him away, patch him up and give him some bread and just a little water. Then bring him back at the same time again on Monday. We'll see if he is ready to sing by then."

Irfan answered, "Very well, my brother."

"Is the chopper ready to go?" He was referring to the Bell Huey.

"I can have it ready in a few minutes."

Al-Makira stood up and came around the table. He put his hand on Irfan's shoulder. "We should go and see how the new recruits are shaping up."

"That is a good idea." The SiC cast a look at Ketcher. "I've seen enough of this piece of shit for the time being."

"So have I. Get someone to take it back to its room and we'll leave for the camp."

The SiC called down the stairs and a heavily-built man dressed in camouflage fatigues came up to the room.

"Take this thing back to its room," ordered the SiC.

As Ketcher was dragged out al-Makira watched him with disgust. He knew full well that Agent Ketcher did not know who Agent Frank Cross was, but it amused al-Makira to toy with this man, to show him, as a representative of the decadent west, how weak and puny he was, how insignificant he was to the organisation known as Intiqam. It would show this agent how much the west was hated – and how he could be bent to Intiqam's will, and used.

Al-Makira also knew that Agent Ketcher did not know who Sir Michael Corrigan was; but al-Makira did, because his own brother, Aarif El-Sayed, had been brought into the Specialist Operations Unit. El-Sayed had been recruited by Simon Lancaster. Al-Makira also knew that El-Sayed had replaced Margarita Thorn after she had been killed on Lancaster's orders by the international assassin known as The Scorpion. However, although al-Makira had heard of The Scorpion, he did not know who The Scorpion was. But he did know who Frank Cross was and where he lived and the Arab had recently placed Cross under observation at Cannon Head as part of his plan to kill him. Yes, al-Makira could have sent in another execution squad but, as he had explained to his Second-in-Command, he did not want to just kill him, he wanted Cross to suffer in agony, and then he wanted to kill him personally – to have Cross right where he wanted him; in front of a camera while al-Makira used his garotte on the SOU agent's throat, for al-Makira had wrongly assumed that Frank Cross had carried out the kill on his brother and Lancaster.

As a result of the watch on Cannon Head, al-Makira had discovered that Cross had a girl living with him. The girl was called Tandy Trudeau; a very pretty girl by all accounts. Well, she would not be very pretty after al-

Makira and his men had finished with her – and he would make Cross watch, to add to the man's suffering. The terrorist had never heard of Tandy Trudeau before, he simply did not know who she was, and he did not care; she was just some western whore that was to be used as bait to bring Cross to where al-Makira wanted him. He therefore could not put The Scorpion and Tandy together as the same person, and neither did he know that it was actually The Scorpion that had executed both brother and Lancaster.

However, before his death, Al-Makira's brother had managed to pass a raft of information on to Intiqam, and part of that information was the way that the SOU was set up and organised. Therefore, al-Makira already knew that agent Frank Cross worked for the SOU, although he did not know what he looked like, and he also knew that Sir Michael Corrigan was the SOU Director. And he also knew where Sir Michael lived.

**

Just under an hour later Agent Ketcher came around again. He was back on his filthy stinking bed and his face hurt like hell. Because his nose was broken he could not breathe properly. Blood and snot had run out of his nostrils over his mouth and down his chin to drip onto his chest, and his neck hurt where the force of the blow had pushed his head back. He would have liked to have touched his hands to his face, but he could not because his hands were still tied behind him. He rolled his head around; the pain in his face was immense.

The man in the blue medical mask appeared beside him. He had a bowl of warm water and a cloth and he wiped Ketcher's face which was now swollen and showing the first signs of major bruising. The man worked the cloth gently over Ketcher's eyes and smashed nose.

"Who, who are y-you? Where a-am I?" stuttered Ketcher. Moving his jaws and mouth to ask the two small questions hurt like hell.

The man did not answer, he just carried on his administrations as though he had not heard his patient. The man took the bowl out and came back with some bread and a glass of water. Still not speaking, he helped Ketcher take a few sips and then gently fed him the bread. Then he left and closed the door.

John Ketcher still had his hands tied behind his back.

He tried to move into a more comfortable position but it was useless.

He lay on his left-hand side with his legs pulled up into a foetal position. When was this nightmare going to end?

*****

NEAR LAS VEGAS

The door to Diana Moon's room came open and a short swarthy man came in. He had short curly black hair and a black drooping moustache. He was wearing army boots and sand-coloured army fatigues. He was carrying a tray and he approached the bed. The tray had a tin bowl and a tin mug on it.

"Food and water," he said in a heavy accent. He placed the tray on the floor beside the bed, then he unlocked her left handcuff from the bedframe. Instantly, Diana tried to hit the man but he just swatted her attack away then backhanded her across the face. She cried out as her head went around.

"Try that again," he snarled, "and I'll kill you!"

Diana held her free left hand to her face, it stung like hell.

"Now, eat your food." He lifted the bowl and offered it towards her.

She peered at it. It looked like some sort of meat in a thick oily soup. Diana wrinkled her nose. "What is it?"

"Meat."

"What sort of meat?"

The man shrugged.

"There's no knife or fork."

"Use your fingers." He placed the bowl into her hand then turned and went back to the door.

"Please," she called out, her voice almost failing her, but he left the room and she heard him lock the door.

*****

Another meal had been eaten and Tandy had helped her sensei clear away the bowls and did the washing up in his kitchen. Having dealt with the washing up they were back in the dojo.

"Stand in fighting stance and hord up your hands," instructed Sensei Nakamura.

Tandy moved her feet and got herself balanced, then she lifted her hands so that they were in front of her shoulders.

"When I punch you must use one hand to push punch away. But not hard. How you say…Defrect?"

"Deflect," said Tandy.

"Hai. De-frect. Must de-frect. Understand?"

"Hai."

He threw a light right-handed *gyaku-tsuki*, reverse punch, at her throat. Tandy tapped it away with her open left hand. He threw a left punch. She tapped it away with her right.

"Ah, no," said the sensei shaking his head. "Not just use hands. If brock with reft hand then must turn reft erbow and showder into brock." He put up his left hand to mimic Tandy and moved his left hand, elbow and shoulder in towards the centre of his chest but without pulling his arm in towards him. "Must keep hand away from chest. Brock punch away from chest. Understand?"

"Hai."

"As hand and arm move, hips must move." Again, he demonstrated with his left hand and twisted at the hips at the same time, bringing his left hip forwards and his right hip back. "Remember rope practise we do earier. Hai?"

"Hai, sensei."

"Hips for power. Must drive hips. Understand?"

"I understand, sensei."

"Good. Now we go faster."

Sensei Nakamura went into his fighting stance and rammed a right-hand gyaku-tsuki punch at Tandy's throat. Around came her blocking hand as she brought her elbow and shoulder into play and twisted at her hips. The sensei's attack was palmed away as if it had been no more than a table-tennis ball being tossed at her.

Sensei Nakamura nodded. "Very good, Tandy."

"Arigato, my sensei."

"Now forty times one hand then change. Understand?"

"Oss, sensei."

When the eighty blocks had been carried out Sensei Nakamura then added something else.

"This time, when you brock with hand use it to push attacking hand downwards and out, away from your body. I show you. You punch me, but not with power. Understand?"

Tandy did as she was ordered and jabbed a right-hand gyaku-tsuki punch at about half her normal punching speed. Since a trained martial artist can punch at about 40MPH this put Tandy's punch at around 20MPH. Sensei Nakamura carried out the same block as before but this time he flexed at his left wrist and dropped his blocking left hand over Tandy's wrist. Then, without holding her, and just with his left palm, he steered her arm down and then pushed it out and away to his left. This had the effect of whipping Tandy's attacking hand out to her right and it unbalanced her. Sensei Nakamura finished the demonstration by driving a right-hand *ura-tsuki*, uppercut, in towards her ribs, but he stopped a fraction short of hurting her. He stepped back.

"You try."

Tandy spent the next twenty minutes parrying the sensei's fists using both of her hands as he changed his attacks. Eventually they stopped. They had been standing static in the middle of the room.

"Very Good. Now we try on the move. Hai?"

"Hai!"

For the next hour they moved around the dojo, sometimes at fast speed and sometimes the sensei slowed it down to correct a fault that had crept in on Tandy's technique. They took it in turns to attack and defend and when they were finished Tandy had an even greater respect for the old sensei's remarkable powers of endurance; not many men half his age could keep up this level of training.

When they had finished, they once more headed for their onsens, and it was after Tandy came out of the building refreshed and wearing one of her kimonos that she thought she caught a movement out of the corner of her eye as she was heading along the front of the big house back to her room.

She stopped and stared across the small koi carp pond towards the far trees.

Nothing.

She frowned.

She was sure she had seen something.

Tandy scanned the area again.

Nothing.

She frowned again, then continued on along the engawa to her room.

MONDAY 16TH JUNE

ST MARGARET

Errol Moon was still in bed at 7am when the phone beside his bed rang. Sleepy-eyed he answered it as his wife, Monica, rolled over beside him, away from Errol, grumbling. Seconds later Errol sat up in bed with his eyes now wide-open. "What the Hell?" he shouted.

His wife was also instantly on the alert and she rolled back towards Errol. "What…?"

Errol put his free hand on his wife's arm as a gentle restraint as he tried to take in what the caller was saying.

"But that's not possible…" began Errol.

"What's going on, dear?" asked Monica. Errol lifted his free hand and waved it in the air for her to be quiet. She frowned at this but said nothing as her husband was being clearly disturbed by the content of the call.

"But,,," began Errol again and then he went quiet as he listened. "Right," he said. "Thank you."

The line went dead. Errol stared in horror at the handset.

"Errol," said his wife as she struggled onto her elbows and then came up beside him with the pillows at her back. "What's happening?" There was a touch of panic in her voice. She had never seen Errol's face look like this before.

Errol turned to his wife. "That was the Las Vegas police. They think Diana's been kidnapped!"

Monica Moon's mouth came open as her hands flew to it. Then she feinted.

*****

Al-Makira had arrived at the Intiqam training camp by the Bell UH-1 Iroquois helicopter. He now stood in the desert sun of Iraq and watched as a group of men, new recruits for the Intiqam cause, raced across the hard ground from left to right. They were all wearing army camouflage fatigues, desert boots and carrying AK-47's, the Kalashnikov assault rifle. After a few more yards they flung themselves down onto the sand and dirt and fired rounds at targets that were set up in front of them and fifty yards away and towards the southern canyon. Irfan moved along the line behind the prone figures and barked orders, occasionally stopping to kick a man in the legs.

Under a camouflaged awning some two-hundred yards away from al-Makira and to his right a group of five men, also in camouflage fatigues, were squatting on the ground in front of an easel with a blackboard mounted on it. All of the men were Europeans and all had volunteered to join the beast that was Intiqam. They had all made the journey out to Iraq having given up their families, homes and jobs to come and train and learn how to fight the West. Al-Makira smiled.

Intiqam's existence was not based on any religious or political doctrine, it simply hated the West and all that it stood for, especially capitalism - which was odd, because in order to function Intiqam needed money.

Standing between the men and the blackboard was a petite young woman dressed in the same camouflage fatigues. She had long black hair and skin that had been tanned by the desert sun. She was teaching the men Arabic and wearing a Glock 19 pistol at her hip.

She must have said something funny because the squatting men all laughed out loud together.

Al-Makira let the laughter distract him for a moment and then he felt into the front pocket of his combat trousers and fished out his mobile phone. Nothing. Still no contact from his operative in Japan who was supposed to abduct Frank Cross's girlfriend. When was the man going to make a move?

Al-Makira did not like to admit it but he felt the first slight inclination that his plan was starting to come apart. The girl should have been taken by now. OK, he would give the man another two days and then he would order a mass raid on the house where she was staying. Meanwhile, perhaps he should try something else. He had already had another idea that he had played with in his mind a number of times over the past few days, held back as a kind of plan B. Maybe it was time to put this into operation? His thoughts were interrupted by the shouting of his Second-in-Command and he nodded in satisfaction as he noted that the harsh training regime was bringing the men on nicely.

For The Cause.

*****

Sensei Nakamura and Tandy Trudeau were facing each other.

"You know boshi geri?" asked Sensei Nakamura. He was referring to the spin kick. He and Tandy were back in the dojo.

"Hai, my sensei."

"Show me."

Tandy placed her left foot forward with her right foot behind her and out to the right-hand side. Then she turned to her right on the ball of her left foot and twisted her hips and head around at the same time so that her body was moving in a clockwise direction. She whipped her head around so that she could bring her eyes back fast on her target and kept her foot and hips moving as she lifted her right foot off the floor. She had gained instant speed at take-off and now spun through a full three-hundred-and-sixty degrees with her right leg and foot scything through the air and her head still turning. As Tandy's right foot came around to the front she lifted it so that it swept up and over the sensei's head. Then, with complete control she stopped the movement of the kicking foot so that it hovered over the top of Sensei Nakamura's bald pate.

She pulled her foot back towards her and placed it down on the floor.

Sensei Nakamura had not moved nor batted an eyelid, not even when Tandy's foot had stopped a half-inch away from his scalp. Instead, he gave a small grunt, nodded, and said,

"Not bad."

High praise.

"Do you know Dragon's Tair Whip?"

"Dragon's tail whip? No, sensei."

"Is not Japanese. Is Chinese. Is Kung Fu. Is rike boshi geri, but not same. I show you."

The old sensei put his left foot forward, but instead of turning around he brought his back right foot out and forward and around and up so that it flashed across in front of Tandy's face. But this was a dummy move because the kicking foot continued moving to land on the floor to the sensei's left without striking her. As the dummy foot landed, he spun on the ball of that foot and performed the same boshi geri kick as Tandy had, turning fast through the three-hundred-and-sixty degrees, except that this time it was the left foot that came around and up to strike. Sensei Nakamura's foot stopped directly over the top of Tandy's head. Tandy was amazed; this old sensei was at full stretch with his legs and still he had managed to pull off an incredibly fast and well-controlled kick.

The sensei put his foot to the floor.

Tandy bowed. She realised that the first "dummy" move of the kick was used to add impetus to the following kicking foot, making the actual kicking foot lash through the air, like a dragon's tail. "That was awesome," she said. Sensei Nakamura returned the bow. "Is just practice."

Frank Cross had often said to Tandy that to be good at martial arts, or anything else, the secret was to practice, practice, practice and practice, and when you were fed up of practicing, practice some more.

"Now," said the sensei, and Tandy knew what was coming and what the next three hours would be devoted to. "You try. Then we fight using the dragon's tair. Hai?"

"Hai!"

*****

ST MARGARET

Ola Ibraheem was now Mrs Ola Lewis, having only recently married a Police Officer - Windsor Lewis - who had been promoted to the rank of Captain of the island of St Margaret's police force just before their wedding.

Mr and Mrs Lewis had arranged a hurried meeting with Mr and Mrs Ibraheem, the President and First Lady, at the Presidential Mansion that was situated on the top of a small hill that overlooked the island's capital. They were all sitting out in the sunshine in the gardens of the mansion under a large pink umbrella that was shading a round teak table.

Errol Moon had received another white envelope with a letter now demanding one-hundred-and-fifty-thousand US dollars. It came with the threat that if it was not paid then Errol could expect bits of his daughter to arrive at his house through the post until it was paid. It also told Errol to wait at home for a phone call when he would receive further instructions. The letter and phone call came with the usual warning of not contacting the police.

So, he didn't. Instead, and not surprisingly, he had contacted Ola, because Ola was a friend of his daughter and he knew that Ola was married to a policeman; he was gambling on the fact that the kidnappers did not know that.

They didn't.

Ola was now explaining the situation to her mother and father.

When she finished, she looked at President Ibraheem.

The President kept silent for a few moments as he mulled the problem around in his very incisive mind. He bent slightly forward and said to his daughter,

"I presume that you have discussed this in full with your husband?"

Ola looked at Windsor and then back to her father. "Yes, daddy."

The President turned to his son-in-law. "What do you think…Captain?"

Windsor cleared his throat. "I suggest, Sir, that we contact Frank Cross."

"That's exactly what I was thinking," said the President.

**

Frank was sitting on a sun-lounger beside his swimming pool reading *Heretic* by Bernard Cornwell and sipping a glass of orange juice, when he received a call on his mobile from President Ibraheem. Frank and the President exchanged some brief pleasantries and then the President came to the point,

"Frank, one of Ola's friends has been kidnapped. Will you help please?"

Frank replied immediately. "Of course, Nigel. No problem. What can you tell me?"

"I'll put Ola on to explain better than I can."

Frank put down the glass of juice as he heard the phone being handed across. Then, "Hi Frank, you okay?" She was trying to sound cheerful, but instead her voice held all the fear and worry for her friend.

Frank picked up on it, but he kept upbeat as he said, "Hi Ola, I'm good thanks. What's happened? How can I help?"

Ola explained the problem. "Are you sure you can help, Frank?"

Frank had dealt with hostage rescues on a number of occasions when he was serving in the Special Air Service; he knew how this went.

Of course he could help.

Frank memorised Errol's home landline number and his address and then ended the call. He then rang Tommo.

"Hi Tommo. We've got our first rescue mission." Frank could picture Tommo standing behind the bar of the Parrot Shack, probably polishing a beer glass that did not need polishing, and coming immediately to the alert.

"Oh?" said Tommo. "Who is it?"

"You know Ola? President Ibraheem's daughter?"

Tommo answered, "Yes, of course I do. Jeez...It's not her, is it?" He sounded horrified at the idea. He put the beer glass down onto the bar-top.

"No mate," Frank allayed the big man's fears. "It's one of Ola's friends, in fact it's her best friend. A young girl. She's been kidnapped." He took a pull at his glass of orange juice.

"Frank," said Tommo, now with a chuckle in his deep bass voice, "you're fifty-two years old man, anyone under forty is young accordin' to you."

Frank laughed. "Thanks for the vote of confidence mate, and remember, you're not that far behind me."

Tommo asked, "Does this *young girl* have a name?"

"Diana Moon."

"Oh! I know her. Man, she's a really good singer. We've had her here at the Shack a couple o'times."

"I know, and, in fact, she sang at Ola's wedding, if you remember?"

At the end of the phone line Tommo clicked his fingers. "That's right...So how do we know she's been kidnapped?"

"Her father has received a ransom demand along with the threat of physical violence to Diana if the money's not paid."

"Do we know where she is?"

"No, but we are going to find out."

"Okay Frank. Do you have a plan?"

"Yes," said Frank. "First, you are going to check out the road that Diana's father lives in. Take the Shack's van, park up, and then just take a walk along the road, see if anything strikes you as being out of the ordinary."

"Like people lurkin' in doorways with mobile phones to their ears."

"Exactly. Or, just sitting in cars and not moving. Go and take a look and then wait back in the car until I show up, but don't give any indication that you know me. Just remain watching until I have left the area. Okay?"

Tommo nodded. "Okay."

"In the meantime," continued Frank, "I will call Clonk and T Bone and then get changed into a suit before going to the police station to meet Captain Lewis."

At the end of the line Tommo put his head to one side. "A suit?" he queried.

"Yes, all will be revealed."

"Okay, so when do you want me to start?"

"No time like the present."

"I'm on it."

"Oh, and Tommo?"

"Yes, man?"

"Try and look inconspicuous." For someone who was nearly seven feet high this was literally a tall order. Frank smiled at his own joke; it was Tandy who often referred to Tommo as looking like a brown-skinned version of the Incredible Hulk.

Tommo chuckled. "You gots to be jokin', man."

**

Frank turned Errol's letter and the envelope over in his hands. He was wearing thin blue barrier gloves. He was also wearing a dark-grey two-piece suit with a white shirt and a light-grey tie and he was sitting across the desk from Captain Windsor Lewis in Windsor's office in the police station in St Margaret.

"That," said Windsor, aiming a long finger at the envelope, "is what prompted Errol to contact Ola."

Frank nodded. "And I understand that he has not paid the money?"

"Yes. That's right. When he got the first letter, he thought it was a scam and put it in the trash can, and then he was contacted by phone by the Las Vegas police to inform him that his daughter had been kidnapped. And then this second letter arrived." Windsor pointed at the letter that Frank was holding.

"Hmm," grumbled Frank. "Do we know for sure that it was actually the Vegas police that were calling him?"

"Oh," said Windsor, with his eyes widening.

Frank gave a small smile.

"You mean it could have been the kidnappers?" suggested Windsor.

"More than likely," said Frank. "So now we need to know if Mister Moon's daughter actually has been abducted."

"Right! I'll get right on it." Windsor called out of his office for someone called Annie and a uniformed WPC got up from a desk and came into the room. She was a local islander. She stood at five-feet-four-inches with full hips and she had a mass of black curly hair that surrounded a small face that wore an enormous pair of glasses.

"Annie," said Windsor. "Would you please call the Las Vegas Police

Department and ask them if they have had a report of a Diana Moon being kidnapped in their jurisdiction, and also if they have called her father, Errol Moon, here on St Margaret."

Annie's eyes widened behind her lenses. "You mean the singer, Diana Moon?"

"I do Annie. Do it now, and do it *quietly*. Okay?" Windsor clicked his fingers as a thought struck him. "And then check where she worked, which was the MGM Grand, also in Vegas."

"Yes, Sir." Annie turned, clearly disturbed, but she headed back to her desk, her phone, and her computer console. While they were waiting for those results Captain Lewis set to and made him and Frank some coffee.

Twenty minutes later Annie was back in her Captain's office. "The Las Vegas police know nothing of a Diana Moon being kidnapped. They have not called Errol Moon, and I have personally spoken to the manager of the MGM Grand in Vegas and he confirmed that Diana has not reported for work since Sunday. In fact, the manager was about to file a missing persons report."

"Well done, Annie," said Windsor. "And thank you."

"Yes, Sir." Annie gave a big smile and left.

Windsor looked across his desk at Frank and said, "Now what?"

"We try to find the kidnappers."

"Hmm. But where do we start?"

"Well, since she's gone missing in Las Vegas I'd say that was the pretty obvious place. don't you?"

"Yes," agreed Windsor. "But just cos she was snatched in Vegas doesn't mean to say she's still in Vegas." He thought for a few seconds, then said, "And what has this got to do with these envelopes? They're franked as coming from Mosul, in Iraq."

Frank pushed an empty coffee cup away from him and picked up the envelope and waved it. "This," said Frank as casually as possible, "is not the only white envelope that has been franked as coming from Mosul…There have been others."

"Yes," said Windsor. He was not surprised that Frank knew this. Frank was, after all, the security consultant for the island. Windsor sat forwards. "Police forces have been reporting them turning up all over the world."

"Hmmm," said Frank. He tossed the envelope and letter onto Windsor's desk. "There's not much here to go on, but that doesn't surprise me." He looked across at Windsor.

"How's that, Frank?" asked Lewis with some surprise. "We know the brand of paper, and we know it was posted in Mosul. We can get forensics to analyse the ink and determine what kind of make of printer wrote it. We've dusted it for prints already and we're waiting for the results back, and we can find out where the envelope was made."

Frank shook his head. "All we know from this is that someone knows where to get good quality paper from. It could have been bought anywhere in the world before ending up in Iraq, and I doubt that you will find any useful or identifiable finger prints on the letter, even if there are any, which I also doubt. And since the envelope has travelled internationally it will be smothered in prints and, again, it could have been bought anywhere, and separate to the letter paper. As for the printer; it's probably one of thousands, millions, and could have come from a hotel, or a bank, or stolen out of someone's house or office."

Captain Lewis puffed out his cheeks and sat back. He had received his Captaincy as a result of Frank's recommendation and he had the utmost respect for the man. "So, what do we do, Frank?"

Frank touched the fingers of his left hand to his lips, then said, "Didn't you say that Errol had been told to wait for a phone call?"

"Yes."

"Has he received it yet?"

"Not as far as I am aware. Do you think they'll call?"

"Oh, I'm sure they'll call, they want their money after all and they have to tell Errol where to deliver it. And, if they haven't called him yet it shows that they are hanging this out."

Windsor frowned. "Why would they do that?"

"To play with him. To get him worried. To psych him out."

"Oh, yes, I see."

Frank fished a scrap of paper out of one of the inside pockets of his jacket. He leaned forward and put the paper on the desk in front of Captain Lewis. It had Errol Moon's phone number and address written on it.

"I got that number from Ola," said Frank. "It's Mister Moon's mobile number. I think you had better call it."

"Why me?"

"Because you're the police."

"But the warning in the last phone call said not to call the police."

"Yes, I know, but the kidnappers won't know if he's called the police or not...unless of course they've bugged his house, which I doubt."

"Why?"

"Because the ransom note was sent from Mosul and Diana was taken in Vegas, which suggests...what?"

The question hung in the air for a few seconds and then Windsor said, "It means they are probably not on this island."

"Well done, Captain, you got it. However, they might have an individual watching his house."

"Oh, bugger," said Windsor.

"Not to worry, I have someone watching the road."

"Who?"

"Tommo."

"Oh. Good. Right. Okay."

"Problem?"

"No, no." Despite saying No, Captain Lewis wondered if he should have already thought of that and had a police officer keeping watch on Errol's house.

"Captain," said Frank. "If you had put a uniformed police officer in the road to watch Errol's house you might have done more harm than good. Don't you think?"

Captain Lewis stared at Frank for a moment. Had Frank just read his mind? No, of course he hadn't...Had he? *Damn! He does this to me all the time!* "Ahh, right," said Lewis. He picked up the phone on his desk.

"What are you doing?" asked Frank.

"I was going to call Errol..."

Frank looked at Lewis, who put the phone down. "Gotcha Frank...Don't use the police phone line."

Frank nodded. Captain Lewis picked up his own mobile and punched in Errol's number. Errol must have had his phone right beside him, waiting for the kidnappers to call, because he answered it immediately.

"Errol Moon."

Captain Lewis could hear the fear in just those two words. As softly as he could Captain Lewis said, "Mister Moon, this is Captain Windsor Lewis of the St Margaret police. Have the kidnappers called you yet?"

"No, Captain. Not yet. But I'm not supposed to talk to you."

"It's okay, I assure you," said Lewis. "This is a secure line and they cannot trace this call. Do you understand?"

"Yes, yes. Okay," answered Moon, and this time Lewis could hear some relief in his voice.

"Good," said Lewis. "Listen, we'll be with you in a short while. If the kidnappers call you then let me know straight away on your mobile, not your landline." He gave Errol Moon the number of his mobile then ended the call.

"Right then," said Frank. "Let's go see Errol, shall we?"

"Right," said Lewis and he stood up to his six-foot height.

"But," said Frank running his eyes over Windsor's dark-blue uniform, "do you have a dark suit that you can get changed into first."

Captain Lewis looked down at his uniform. He was justifiably proud of it. "Why? What's wrong with this?"

"Nothing," smiled Frank. "Except you told me that the kidnappers told Errol not to contact the police." Windsor seemed to deflate a little. It would be a bit obvious if he turned up in uniform.

"Bugger," said Windsor.

"Not to worry," said Frank. "You're learning." He smiled benevolently across the desk at his friend and said, "And bring a briefcase. A dark one."

**

Half-an-hour later two tall men in dark suits and clutching dark-coloured briefcases arrived at one end of the street that Errol Moon lived on. It was a short street, just a few back from the waterfront. Tommo was at the other end of that street.

Tommo saw the two men straight-off and he smiled to himself; the two tall men in the suits were Frank and Windsor. Tommo was sitting in his van; a big white job with the words *The Parrot Shack* and with a four-feet-high picture of Captain Morgan, the macaw, painted on both sides.

Tommo had driven into the road, parked up at one end and then got out for a slow stroll down the road and back. The big man knew that he stood out in any crowd so he had made no attempt to hide himself; it would simply not have worked. So, he had put himself in full view of any watchers and had then returned to sit in a van that also stood out in a crowd. Tommo was hiding in plain sight.

On getting back to the van he had got in behind the steering wheel and had been watching the road like a hawk ever since. There had been nothing unusual occurring.

Frank, of course, had spotted Tommo's van straight away and he had completely ignored it, as if treating it as just another white van and of no consequence.

Windsor and Frank knocked on the door of the first house, spoke briefly to the person who opened the door, and then moved on after Frank had called out a loud "Bless you". They did this all the way along one side of the street.

After just under twenty minutes, they came to Errol Moon's house. It was a single storey place, part wood frame and part breeze-block which was covered in wooden feather-edge cladding and painted a light pastel blue with a red tiled roof.

The white guy rang the push-button bell beside the door.

Errol opened first his front door then the fly-screen that was in front of it. He looked as if he had been under pressure for a few days; his face was drawn and his eyes had a haunted look to them.

Frank was standing beside Captain Lewis. Both men were immaculate and sweating in their suits and ties. Errol Moon was wearing a pair of bright-red shorts and an open-fronted flowery shirt, nothing on his feet.

Frank was standing nearer to Mr Moon than Windsor and he could smell alcohol on the father's breath. Not surprising.

Frank smiled at Errol. He said quietly, "Hello, Mister Moon. We are from the police. We've come about Diana. Can we come in please?"

Errol peered at them, squinting up his eyes. He wasn't sure about this. He had been told not to contact the police, and yet, here they were. He nearly stepped back inside to close the door on Frank and Windsor, but then he hesitated and peered some more, and then he poked a finger out at Frank. "I know you; you sometimes play sax at The Parrot Shack."

Frank was not surprised that Errol recognised him; a great many of the islanders knew him by sight as one of the musicians who played in a resident band at The Parrot Shack and the man who owned Island Photos. What they did not know was that he also owned The Parrot Shack.

"That's right, Mister Moon. My name's Frank Cross."

Moon started and his eyes widened, for Frank had been named by the island's President as being an undercover agent - the man that had organised and smashed what the islanders thought was a drugs and arms smuggling ring, when in fact it had been a team of terrorists. Subsequently, Frank had, by reputation, become something of a local hero, although no-one knew what that agent looked like. And it was why he rigorously protected his facial anonymity. Therefore, people never associated the musician at The Parrot Shack and the owner of Island Photos as being the same undercover agent. But Errol Moon just had, and that fact actually impressed Frank, for here was a man who, even under extreme pressure obviously had a very astute mind.

This fact might make Frank's job a lot easier.

However, despite the fact that Errol had accurately unmasked Frank, Frank knew that people only saw what they thought they saw and right now anybody watching would be looking at a couple of salesmen, peddling either double-glazing or religion. They would not see Frank Cross or a Captain of the local police.

Misdirection. And Frank was a master of it.

Frank nodded. "Please call me Frank, and I'm here to help you get Diana back." Before Errol could say anything, Frank asked, "Have the kidnappers called you yet?"

Errol shook his head. "No...not yet."

"Good," said Lewis.

Moon looked from Frank to Windsor and frowned.

"It's okay, Mister Moon," said Frank. "This is a good friend of mine called Windsor Lewis. Windsor is a Captain in the police. He called you earlier."

Windsor smiled a winning smile. "Hello, Mister Moon."

Errol nodded. "I've seen you around," he said.

Moon took his eyes off Windsor and glanced around Frank, checking the road behind them. Clearly ill-at-ease.

Moon nodded. "You'd better come in."

Cross and Lewis stepped inside. Frank's mobile went off in his pocket. It was a text from Tommo. All it read was, "All clear." Frank put his mobile back in his pocket.

The front door led into a tiny hall, but then the house wasn't very big either.

There was a kitchen and bathroom and three small bedrooms out the back and just the one living room at the front.

The three men went into the living room. Across from the entrance door were two old high-backed leather armchairs, and a two-person sofa in front of the front window. The sofa looked as though it had been made from the material left over from making a pair of very loud and lary curtains. Monica

Moon was sitting in one of the leather armchairs, she was gripping part of the hem of the front of her flowery dress in both hands, as if it were wet and she was trying to wring it out. She looked as tired and as worried as her husband.

Beside the two armchairs were some cupboards on which was standing a land-line telephone and a state-of-the-art stereo control system with a pair of big speakers. Above the cupboards the remainder of the wall space was taken up by shelving onto which was racked the biggest collection of twelve-inch vinyl albums that Frank and Windsor had ever seen. There were hundreds of them, and all were in alphabetical order by band or artist.

"Wow!" exclaimed Frank. "That's impressive."

"Thank you, Mister Cross…Frank…A lifetime's obsession." Errol Moon stared at them all; his expression softened and showed that he clearly loved them.

"He don't have to dust 'em," said Monica. It was an attempt at humour and, given the circumstances, Frank could have hugged her for it. She invited Frank and Windsor to sit down on the sofa and Errol plonked down into one of the armchairs, it was positioned within an arm's length of the stereo system.

"So," said Errol, clearly agitated. "You think you can help us, Frank?"

Frank smiled. "Yes Errol, I do." He nodded emphatically and looked at them both. "And I am going to get your daughter back."

Errol sat forwards and asked, "And why do you think you can get our daughter back?"

Frank ignored the implied doubt in Errol's voice and answered, "Because I have done this sort of work before."

Errol frowned. "How come?" he asked.

"Because I used to be in a branch of the British Army's Special Forces."

Errol sat up at that admission and said, "Oh!" He turned and looked at his wife who returned the look of amazement that had just crossed Errol's face.

Frank smiled. "Now, Errol, in order to rescue your daughter, I must ask you some questions. Can I ask those questions?"

Errol returned the smile, even if it was a little feeble. "I'm sorry. We're so worried…"

"I understand, Errol. But, if I may…?"

"Okay…Ask away."

"Thank you. First, you said that the kidnappers have only made contact with you once by phone. Yes?"

"Yes."

"And they haven't called you again?"

"That's right...But waiting for them is driving us both bloody mad!" He made fists of his hands.

"Don't worry," urged Frank. "That means we have some time to play with. The trick about a kidnapping is to get the kidnappers to play the game our way, and not to play it theirs. Now, we have to establish why they've snatched Diana. Have you annoyed anyone that you know of?"

There was a pause as Errol mulled this over, then, "No, I don't think so." He looked at his wife, who shook her head. He turned back to Frank. "But the music business can be a bit cut-throat, so sometimes people get pissed-off over the smallest things."

"Hmmm," hummed Frank. "But not enough to kidnap Diana?"

"No," agreed Errol. "Probably not." His wife shook her head again. She was just about holding it together.

"Okay then, that leaves us with two other possibilities: one, someone in the hotel where Diana is to appear tipped off the kidnappers about a bright young singer, a bit naïve and all alone, whose daddy runs a lucrative recording business - a good target for a kidnapping, and two, this was a completely random snatch."

Windsor spoke up, "Does finding out which one it was help us find Diana?"

"Well," began Frank, "normally, and if the police were handling the case, they would start by checking the hotel, seeing if this has happened before at this hotel, interviewing people who would be involved with employing Diana, finding out who she has made friends with. Then we could check with CCTV cameras and try and find out how the snatch was made and what the snatcher, or snatchers, look like."

Captain Lewis nodded. Police Procedure.

"But," said Frank. "That all takes time. Too much time...and that's not what I'm going to do."

Captain Lewis raised his eyebrows. "It's not?"

"No," said Frank, "it's not." With that, he opened the briefcase that he had been carrying and which was now sitting on the floor beside him, and took out a telephone with a length of white cable attached. He'd picked it up from his workshop in Cannon Head before he had left for his rendezvous with Windsor at the police station. The device had a small state-of-the-art carriage with a speaker system built in so that they could all hear the conversation when the kidnappers called.

Frank got up from his seat and went across the room to where the Moon's telephone was plugged in and swopped the cables over. He placed the replacement phone on the cupboard beside the old one and then went back to sit on the sofa again.

"Okay," said Frank. "Here's what we do…When the phone rings I will answer it…"

Captain Lewis interrupted. "Do you think that's wise?" he asked.

Frank turned to him. "The kidnappers have only made one call, so they won't be that familiar with Errol's voice, so I'll take the call."

Windsor gave a lop-sided smile. "Sorry Frank, but that won't work. You don't sound like Errol, because you're not Caribbean."

Frank looked first at Errol who raised his eyebrows and then back at Windsor.

"Good point, well made," laughed Frank. "Okay Errol, do you want Windsor to do this, or do you want to?"

"I'll do it," said Errol. "She's my daughter."

"Good man," said Frank.

"Problem is," began Captain Lewis. "We don't know when the kidnappers are going to call again."

"True," agreed Frank. "But there's no harm in waiting a while." He wanted to stop and talk to the terrified couple, to boost Mr and Mrs Moon's morale and for them to gain confidence in him and his ability to help.

"Would you like some coffee?" asked Errol's wife.

"Yes please," said Frank. It would give Mrs Moon something to do. She got up and left the room, heading for the kitchen. Frank engaged Errol in a conversation about his record collection.

Half-an-hour later the phone rang.

Frank put a finger to his lips to silence them all and took a notepad and a biro out of an inner pocket of his jacket. He then pushed a button on the front of the speaker device and Errol sat forwards. Frank nodded to him. After they had finished talking about Errol's record collection Frank had briefed him on how to act when the kidnappers called.

"Hello?"

There was a short pause, then, "Mister Moon?" The voice was foggy, muffled, probably talking through a handkerchief or scrap of material.

"Yes, who is this please?"

"You know who I am. Have you contacted the police?"

"No. No, you told me not to. Is my daughter safe?" Frank nodded encouragement at Errol. "... If you've harmed her..."

"Be silent!" snarled the voice on the phone.

"I'm sorry," hurried Errol. "What do you want?"

"Have you got the money?"

Frank was listening intently to the voice coming over the speaker. Not an English voice. Not from the British Isles. Not African or Caribbean. Not American. Western or Central European? No. Eastern Europe? Possibly. Unlikely. Arabic then? Again, possibly; the speech patterns certainly had an underlying guttural touch to them. Something uneasy slid in Frank's mind.

Errol was answering the kidnapper's question. "I've got some of the money, yes, but it's a lot of money that you want. I don't have that kind of money..."

"Be silent!" snapped the kidnapper.

"I'm sorry, sorry." Errol looked at Frank for encouragement. Sweat was forming along the man's brow-line. Frank nodded again and gave Errol the thumbs-up. Monica looked as though she were about to say something, so Frank put his index finger across his mouth again to show her that she must keep quiet; he did not want her blurting something out so that she scared off the caller.

"Listen to me, Mister Moon," said the voice. "We do not care how you get the money, just get it. And you must bring it to Las Vegas..."

"Las Vegas!" blurted Errol, deliberately interrupting. "I can't get to Las Vegas..."

"Be silent!" shouted the voice on the phone.

Good thought Frank. *He's getting rattled. He might make a mistake. Give us a clue.*

"This is where we have your daughter. If you do not get here, we will cut one of her ears off and send it to you! Do you understand me?"

"Yes! Yes, I get you. I'll get to Las Vegas. Just don't hurt Diana." The injection of panic into Errol's voice was not fake. Monica had her head in her hands and was rocking backwards and forwards.

Even so, Frank smiled; he had told Errol to use Diana's name if he could. First names made the victim more human to the kidnapper, not just a bargaining chip.

"Then do as we say," said the voice.

Frank had scribbled something on the notepad and he held it up for Errol to read.

"Okay, okay." Errol glanced at the paper then asked, "Where do I bring the money?"

The voice on the phone came back with the answer. "Come to the parking garage behind the MGM Grand off Tropicana Avenue at ten p.m on Wednesday. We will be waiting for you on the ground floor level."

"Can't you give me some more time to get all the money?" Errol pushed and Frank nodded approvingly. Errol emphasised the shake in his voice. "Can we make it Friday? I'll need time to get to the bank and withdraw the cash."

"No. This Wednesday."

"But that's impossible." Errol added pleading to his voice. "It's not like I'm taking out just a few dollars. Please?"

There was a pause, then the voice said, "Very well. Friday."

"Thank you, thank you." Errol grovelled down the phone. Frank gave him a thumbs up.

"But there's one thing," said Errol.

"What is it?"

"What do you look like? How do I find you?"

Frank looked at Errol. Frank was impressed. Errol Moon was pushing his luck and Frank had been right about how astute this man must be.

"We will find *you* Mister Moon." The voice was laden with threat. "Do not worry, we will find *you*."

"Okay, okay. I understand."

There was a pause then the caller said, "And remember, do not call the police. And come alone…or your daughter dies, piece by piece."

The line went dead.

Errol Moon breathed out heavily as Frank reached out and pressed the button on the device again. Errol's wife had her hands crossed on her chest and she was fighting back tears. Errol took a red handkerchief out of his shorts pocket and offered it to his wife.

"Well done," said Frank.

"Yes, Mister Moon," said Windsor. "Well done. And you too, Mrs Moon. Are you okay?"

Monica Moon looked at the police officer and then Frank. She took a breath and asked, "Do you really think you can rescue our daughter from those…people?"

"Oh yes," answered Frank. "Trust me." He gave her a winning smile. "Okay," he said. "We now know that there's more than one of them because he kept saying We. Also, they are probably amateurs because a professional would know that it takes longer than three or four days to get this kind of money together and they were originally asking for the money to be delivered earlier. So, they are obviously in a hurry, so someone is pushing them. Which means that someone is behind all of this. They also reminded you not to go to the police, so they don't know about Windsor and me, which means they don't have any kind of intelligence network, and they are not bugging your phone or watching your house; they're just going on your say-so that you haven't contacted the police, which is pretty dumb of them, but good for us.

"Also, I think we can also assume that these guys work for the Grand, probably in some menial roll, possibly they park cars."

"How do you know that?" asked Windsor. It was like listening to a real-life Sherlock Holmes.

Frank smiled at him. "Because Diana was staying and working at The MGM when she was snatched just outside, and they have suggested that the money transaction take place in the MGM's parking garage. It's all a bit coincidental, don't you think?"

"That's true," agreed Windsor. "However, there is one thing."

"What's that," asked Frank.

"Why ten p.m.? Why so specific? Why not nine, or eleven?"

"Oh, that's easy," smiled Frank. "They've arranged for the money pick-up for ten because that's probably the slack time for parking, people have usually checked-in to the hotel before ten because they like to arrive, have a shower, unpack and then go for a meal. That means less people around in the parking garage, therefore fewer, if any, witnesses."

Errol joined in. "Doesn't that make it awkward for you, Frank? I mean, it'll be dark outside and they'll probably have the car-park lights on, so there will be lots of shadowy places where they can lie in ambush."

"I'm not worried about that," answered Frank. "I take my own shadows with me." He grinned at his pun on his company name.

Captain Lewis nodded. Frank went on, "There's something else; I can tell from the guy's accent that they are probably of Arabic extraction, so I'd say that they are probably migrant workers in the US on work visas. They probably work in the car-park, probably on short-term contracts, but they have been working there some time. They're certainly not American citizens."

"How so?" asked Windsor.

"Because," said Frank, "they didn't use contractions in their speech."

"Sorry?" said Windsor.

Frank smiled. "A contraction is the use of shortening two words into one; for example, isn't instead of is not, or wouldn't, instead of would not. The guy on the phone never used a contraction, so he wasn't used to doing it. People learning a foreign language seldom use contractions. He used precise speech. Also, he said *be silent*, and he said it three times. An American would have said shut up, or stow it, or be quiet. So, he was probably a foreigner in the country, although he may have been in the US for a little while."

"How so?" asked Errol.

"Well," said Frank. "He pronounced the word *garage* in the American way; Americans pronounce it g'rahge, whereas Brits tend to say it like garridge. It shows he's been in the country and working for the Grand long enough to get used to *some* of the language usage. However, he's not entirely ingrained in the American way." Frank stopped and looked at Errol who, although he was listening, was wringing his hands between his knees. "And," continued Frank, "we also know that Diana is alive and so far, unharmed."

Errol moon stopped wringing his hands. He and his wife zeroed in on the last part,

Errol asked, "How do you know that Diana's okay?"

"Because they threatened to harm her," said Frank and he noted Errol's frown. "Mister Moon, if they had already harmed her they wouldn't be threatening that they *would*. So, she must be alive and well." *And terrified* thought Frank, but he was not going to say that in front of her parents.

"Thank you, Frank." Errol Moon was secretly amazed at how much information Frank Cross had gleaned from just one short phone conversation. "This is very kind of you to get involved." He took a deep breath and hesitatingly asked, "But there is a problem."

"Which is?" asked Frank.

"How am I going to get the kind of money they are demanding?"

"You're not," answered Frank.

Errol raised his eyebrows. "I'm not?"

"No. As our American cousins would say, we aren't going to give them a dime."

Captain Lewis was clearly uncomfortable with this. "If there's no money, Frank," he glanced awkwardly at Monica, "won't they kill her?"

"It won't get that far," said Frank. "I won't let it."

Errol moistened his mouth, stiffened his back and said, "I trust you, Frank. So, what do we do now?"

"You'd better start packing," answered Frank. "You and I are going to Las Vegas."

Errol's eyebrows shot up. "What? Now?"

"No," Frank shook his head. "Not now. Wednesday. I need to pull some strings and contact some people. We are going to need some help with getting your daughter back…And I know just the right people to do that."

*****

TUESDAY 17TH JUNE

VENICE - ITALY

The British Airways Embraer 190 aircraft left London City Airport and landed at Venice's Marco Polo airport just over two hours later at 10am. Lawrence Gainsborough was in a smart light-blue woollen jacket and a white shirt, with dark-blue trousers and black lace-up leather shoes. Gail Wetton was in a pink knee-length dress that was belted at her slim waist. She was also wearing a dark-blue short linen jacket and pink sandals with wedge heels. They were only carrying carry-on baggage so they did not have to delay in the baggage reclaim section and they cleared through customs and passport control with ease. Had there been queues and delays Larry could have played the MP ticket, but he did not need to and he and Gail made it through the arrivals section of the airport terminal without incident.

Larry had been to Venice once before with his wife, but on this occasion, he had left the booking of the hotel to Gail. However, he stipulated that it should not be expensive as high-end hotels attracted paparazzi and he did not want to be spotted with her. She understood, it would not do his political career any good, so she booked a two-star hotel for them. The hotel was called the San Gallo and it was tucked away in a small *piazza* just a few hundred yards from *Piazza San Marco*, St Mark's Square. He had also left the booking of the flights to Gail so as not to arouse too much suspicion with his wife.

They came out onto the public concourse area and, as Larry remembered the layout from his previous visit, they turned towards the water taxi desk.

A dark-haired man wearing cheap trainers, faded jeans and a short black leather jacket over an open-neck checked shirt was standing near a column that was supporting the roof, watching them. He had been on the same flight as the MP and had exited the arrivals hall in front of them. He had not been noticed by either Gainsborough or Wetton – which is exactly what the man wanted.

Larry and Gail exchanged some brief pleasantries in faltering Italian with the lady behind the water taxi desk as they bought their tickets. Having obtained the tickets, and with Gail hanging onto Larry's arm, they headed for the walkway that would transport them to a far escalator which would take them down to the water taxis down on the lagoon.

The man beside the column put his mobile phone to his ear and spoke into it in Arabic. "They are on their way to you." Then he ended the call and followed the couple.

On arriving at the water taxi landing-stage, Larry and Gail could smell the lagoon: old mud, the ooze of time, mixed with the tang of the open sea. There were the cries of unseen seagulls and the sound of water slapping against boats and concrete pilings.

The couple presented their tickets to a man in a square-sided kiosk and he directed them to one of the boats that was tied up and bobbing in its small concrete dock. As they approached the taxi a short elderly man stepped nimbly onto the boat. He was the boat's captain and was wearing a black and white striped jumper, dark trousers and had a weathered cap on his grizzled and suntanned head. The taxi was moored nose-up to the concrete landing stage with the open lagoon behind it. It was a long gleaming black-sided vessel with the decks and cabin being made of strips of wood which were heavily varnished and which shone in the morning light. The skipper helped them aboard.

Larry didn't do boats and he staggered a little as he made it into the aft section where padded bench seats sat out in the open air. The dual baggage he had been carrying hadn't helped much with his boarding and, relieved not to have fallen in the water and embarrassed himself in front of Gail, he put the luggage down and turned to help his mistress on board.

Laughing happily, Gail moved past Larry and plonked herself down onto one of the padded seats. Larry landed beside her, laughing with her at his un-seaworthiness.

The skipper took up his position behind the steering wheel at the front of the craft and started the engine. He turned to them. "We go," he said, and opened the throttle but kept a sedate pace as there are restrictions as to how fast he could drive in this part of the lagoon. The boat headed away from the airport with the sun shining out of a clear blue sky that was flecked with only a few clouds, and the air felt warm. Having motored a few hundred yards, the taxi then hung a left to enter the equivalent of a watery highway whose borders were defined by marker posts. The water beneath the boat was the colour of weak coffee, made that way because it was mixed with the silt of the lagoon.

Once their boat had made the turn they could see, directly in front of them and lying low across the horizon, the City of Venice.

Venetian water taxis are really speedboats and, just like their motoring counterparts, every Italian drives as if he is behind the wheel of a sports car.

The taxi took off, flinging spray.

Gail gazed at the view in wonder and laughed aloud. Larry smiled benevolently at her, pleased that she was enjoying herself.

The island City of Venice is truly unique, being built on a series of low mud banks that are sheltered from the Adriatic within a lagoon that fronts the mainland, known as the Veneto. The city, and the other surrounding islands, regularly floods. Despite this, and despite being built on wooden piles driven into the mud – or perhaps because of it - the city has existed for over four hundred years. At one time it had been the centre of an awesome sea power, but now its revenue is based almost entirely on tourism. Which was fine by Larry and Gail as they were going to enjoy three full days together.

Three hundred yards back from them was another speedboat. Not a taxi. It had five men on board, and four of them were armed.

As the water taxi approached the city, Larry and Gail could make out the top of the towering red *Campanile* that is in front of St Mark's Basilica in St Mark's square on the other side of the island. Gail hugged Larry's left arm as she watched the red brick walls of the city come flying towards her.

They tore past the island of Murano - famed for its glassware - on their left, and then past the high walls of the cemetery island of *San Michele*. The taxi was still heading rapidly forwards, as if to dive into the opening in one of those red walls to gain access to one of the many canals for which Venice is famous. The one right in front of them was the *Rio degli Zecchini*. Suddenly, instead of going into this canal, the skipper put the wheel hard over and they swept around to the left, the bows of the boat throwing up a shower of glittering water at the turn. Gail laughed and cheered at the excitement of it all.

They were now running along the northern side of the island and, looking up, they could see the sides and backs of red-brick houses that were built right up to the edge of the sea. Occasionally they could pick out the fronts of restaurants and bars with sun umbrellas and people sitting at tables, relaxing in the sun, sipping wine. Enjoying the view.

The skipper steered the boat with consummate ease and passed the wall that is the back of the *Ospedale Civile* – Venice's Hospital. A few yards further and the taxi swung right into a canal, the *Rio di Santa Giustina*, where the skipper slowed the boat down to a more leisurely pace so as to not create any wash, which is the curse of the soft bricks that the buildings are made of.

The other speedboat, with the five men, followed.

There are no cars on Venice; its canals are its roads, but alongside its canals are pavements and walkways with a myriad of small bridges which criss-cross the inter-linking waterways. Originally these bridges had no railings on them, making returning home from late night revelry somewhat of a risky practice. Larry and Gail passed under a number of these bridges and negotiated their way along two more canals before they popped out onto the lagoon again, with the entrance to the Grand Canal on their right.

The taxi swung out and around, passing the Bridge of Sighs, the Doge's Palace and the entrance to St Mark's square on their right. The water in front of St Mark's square was clustered with the long sleek shiny black bodies of gondolas for hire and beyond them they caught their first glimpse of the front of St Mark's Basilica with an even closer view of the Campanile.

The skipper guided the boat up to the water taxi rank in front of the Royal Gardens and Larry and Gail disembarked, displaying the same nautical expertise in getting ashore as they had when they had got on board.

The other speedboat had pulled up a few yards back. Four of the men got out leaving the fifth to move the boat.

*****

Agent Ketcher was being kept in solitary confinement, seeing only the man in the medical mask from time to time. He had been fed irregularly so that he could not establish a routine and thereby could not work out what the time of day it was, or even what day it was. He only knew if it was daytime or night-time from the light, or lack of it, that came through the shutters on his room's window.

He'd had his bonds removed so that he could now move freely about the room, such as it was. The only door was locked and he had discovered that the windows were barred on the outside and he could not open the shutters which had been fixed in place. He was now incredibly weak and could hardly stand so he spent much of his time sitting either on his filthy ragged bed or on the floorboards in one of the corners of the room with his back against the crumbling plastered wall. He had received little food and little water, only just enough to keep him alive, and he'd had no use of a toilet, not even a pot, even though he had asked for one, and so he'd had to use one corner of the room that he was in. As a result, the room now stank like a cess pit. And with that had come the flies.

*****

Lawrence Gainsborough MP and Miss Wetton made their way to the entrance of St Mark's Square which is flanked by two columns. One of the columns is topped by the bronze Lion of *San Marco* and the other topped with a marble statue of *San Teodoro*; the latter being the patron saint of Venice before St Mark's relics were smuggled from Alexandria in AD 828. Gail took a picture of both columns with her mobile phone and they headed off across the square to the far end.

St Mark's Square, as usual, was crowded. There were crowds. Crowds and crowds. Business people, shoppers, waiters and waitresses, souvenir vendors, pigeons, and tourists, tourists, tourists, and more tourists. There were three small stages set up; two on one side of the square and one on the other, on which were groups of musicians seated on chairs and wearing formal evening black-tie dress, even though it was nearing mid-day and the square was very warm. St Mark's square is so vast that the music from one cannot be heard from the other due to the distance between them, although when one band is playing the others keep quiet, in a kind of long standing and long-suffering Musician's Agreement. In front of the stages are rows of tables and chairs at which you can sit and have a coffee for the same cost as a family car. There was not an empty spare seat in sight.

Larry and Gail would do all of this tourist bit later. They were headed for the arcades on the far side of the square. As they came up to the north-west corner Larry spotted two elderly tourists sitting on a step eating ice cream from small round plastic containers; the couple were being told to get up and move on by two police officers; one male one female, and both officers were immaculately turned out. It is a by-law that you cannot squat and eat anything in St Mark's square. If you want to eat, then you eat standing up, or you sit in a café.

Larry and Gail entered the arcade and made for an exit that led them to the *Ponte Cavalletto*, the Cavalletto bridge. On crossing this they were on the *Calle Cavalletto*, a narrow street that led out into the small square of *Piazza San Gallo* with its tiny chapel to the same saint, or rather saints, as there are three of them: Saint Gallo of Aosta, Italy, a Bishop who died of natural causes in AD 546; Saint Gallo of Clermont-Ferrand, France, another Bishop who died of natural causes but in AD 551, and Saint Gallo, an Irish hermit who died in Switzerland in AD 630. The chapel - no longer in use to any of its saints - is now used as a gallery to promote local artists and it was immediately to their left as they entered the square. Beyond it, and flanking the whole of the left-hand side of the square, was the Banca Nationale del Lavoro. In front of the bank were some tables and chairs under sun umbrellas with tourists seated beneath them; eating and drinking. To their right, past an ice cream parlour and a pizza shop (the reason for the tables and chairs), was the entrance door to their hotel with a black metal sign hung above it, announcing simply: Hotel San Gallo.

The hotel was in an ancient building that had served in its time as a merchant's house, once as a hospital, twice as a brothel, and now a hotel. As a hotel frontage it was unimpressive, seeming to be just a big dark double wooden door set flat in a long flat wall that had flat windows in it. To the right of the door was a large brass plate with a number of addresses to private apartments. The plate also bore a large brass button below which was the word HOTEL.

Larry winked at Gail who was frowning at the door. It looked more like the entrance to a vault or a mausoleum than a hotel.

They put their baggage down on the floor and Larry pressed the brass button.

They could not hear anything, so they did not know whether the bell was working or not. They stood and stared at the brass plate.

Larry gave a good-humoured shrug. "We'll wait a minute. If no-one appears, we'll try again."

The hotel was actually set within a remarkable and unusual structure of private rooms. Imagine the wards of a hospital, some of which are turned into apartments and you have some idea of the rabbit warren inside the walls that formed the hotel.

Presently they heard a noise behind the door, a lock was moved and the door creaked open a few inches.

They were looking at a man's face. He could have been aged anywhere between thirty and fifty. He had a narrow face with a sallow complexion, a large nose, hooded eyes and a miserable mouth. The door creaked open a little wider and they could then see the whole of him. He was about five-feet ten-inches tall, thin and with unkempt hair. He was hang-shouldered and appeared to be bending slightly forward at the waist.

"Hello," said Larry in English, and as cheerfully as he could. "We are Mister Gainsborough and Miss Wetton. We have a reservation."

After running his eyes over the two travellers, the bell-hop – for that was who this man was - opened the door some more. He had realised from Larry's words that the pair where English, and, in that faltering tongue, but with his own Italian accent, he uttered these words in a deep rasping bass and almost breathless voice,

"Welcome…to-ah the hotel…San Gal-lo."

It was the least welcoming welcome that Larry had ever heard, more like a veiled threat, and Larry wondered what crypt this person had crawled out of. He glanced around at Gail, hoping that she was not about to run screaming from the piazza. But she was smiling broadly. She whispered,

"Perhaps this place is run by the Addams family?"

Larry stifled a laugh. The door creaked open wide.

The man's eyes under his hooded brow did not seem to move, and he did not seem to blink. He asked, in his tombstone voice, "I take-ah your bags. Si?"

Larry was not sure the man had the strength to lift the bags but they were taken from him and the man headed, in a kind of stoop-filled lope, towards a flight of wide stone steps that were over to the left of a large shadowy hallway, steps that went up into the gloom.

As the man moved away, Larry and Gail stepped over the threshold of the front door into the hallway. The man had reached the bottom of the stairs and was going up when the doorway behind them, which they had left open, was suddenly filled by two men who pushed past them.

"Hey!" began Larry. "What do you think…"

One of the men had turned to him and was pointing a pistol - a dark grey 9mm semi-automatic Glock G19 Compact with a suppressor screwed into the end - into Larry's face.

"Shut the fuck up!" hissed the man in a guttural accent that was certainly not Italian. It was the man who had been standing near the column at the airport.

Larry heard a squeal from Gail and he turned to be met with the sight of her being held across the mouth by the other man who was standing behind her. With his other hand he had twisted her right arm up her back.

Before Larry could say anything more, or even react, the man in front of him, who was holding the gun, said, "You are Lawrence Gainsborough, the British MP." Larry gave a start. How did these people know who he was, and that he was here?

The man continued, "You and your girlfriend are coming with us. And if you complain, or struggle, I will shoot you." Larry could not place the accent. The man seemed as if he were picking his words very carefully, as though he had only recently learned how to speak English at evening classes. He turned his attention to Gail. "And I will have no hesitation in also shooting this very pretty girl, but only after we have had some fun with her."

Larry pulled himself up to his full height so that he towered over the gun-man. "You bastard…" he began, but he stopped abruptly as the man's gun came up fast and smacked into the side of Larry's head.

"Do not get tough with me, Mister Gainsborough, or I will kill you."

Larry's head had been turned with the force of the blow and he put a hand up to the left side of his face. The skin beside his eye had split with the force of the strike and blood was trickling in a thin line down and over his cheekbone. He could feel his temper boiling but, because the man was holding a gun, he kept quiet and glowered at him.

Gail's eyes had gone wide as she stared first at Larry and then at the man with the pistol. She tried to say something but her assailant had his right hand firmly across her mouth.

Larry didn't have much choice. "Where are you taking us?"

"You will find out...Oh, and if you think you can outsmart us and run away, know this...We know these passages and streets like the backs of our hands, whereas you do not. So, you will not get far. If you run, I will kill you, both of you, and you will end up dead in a canal, while we simply disappear."

"In broad daylight?" challenged Larry.

"Oh yes, Mister Gainsborough. So much better to be out in the sun, do you not think?" He paused and pushed forwards so that he was close up to Larry's chest and looking up at the bigger man. Then, in lowered tones, he continued, "And make no mistake, Mister Gainsborough, I will happily kill you...and keep the girl...Now, get out of the door!"

Larry thought for one moment about shouting for the help of the hotel guy, who was nearly at the top of the first flight of stairs with his upper body out of view, but then he saw the look in the man's eyes.

Larry looked at Gail. "We'd better do what he says," he said and they all stepped back out into the piazza where they were joined by the other two men from the boat that had been following them. They were all wearing trainers, jeans and a variety of jackets. One of them was even sporting an Olympus Single Lens Reflex camera around his neck – just as if they were a group of sight-seers.

The door was closed behind them and the meet-and-greet man with the bags turned at the top of the stairs as if to say something to the hotel's two new guests – but they were not there. He stood and frowned then put the bags down. Bloody tourists.

Outside, the four men surrounded them as the man's gun with the suppressor slid away out of sight into his jacket and Gail's mouth was released. Should she scream?

She felt something sharp touch her skin through her dress just above her waist.

She looked around at the man with the knife who was tight up behind her and he grinned back. Larry had seen the action and was about to say something to the man when he caught a look from Gail and she gave a slight shake of her head. *Best not.*

The six of them moved off across the piazza, heading away from the chapel and past the tables and chairs and tourists into *Calle San Gallo*, a small street that led away to their left. This street was typical of the many hundreds of tiny throughfares that make up the geography of Venice. In some parts these streets are so narrow that people have to pass each other whilst pushing up against the walls of the houses and the glass panes of the shop fronts. The leader – the man with the gun – turned to Larry and said quietly,

"Behave naturally, as if you are enjoying yourself. If it comes to it, I am not averse to killing other tourists as well as you. Understand?"

Larry nodded and kept quiet as four Japanese tourists came towards them and chattered by.

In front of them was the *Ponte Tron*, a narrow bridge that ended the *Calle San Gallo* and crossed a canal called the *Rio e Bacino Orseolo*. This canal led to a wider basin, the *Bacino Orseolo*, on their left where gondolas were frequently moored up and where the gondoliers plied their lucrative trade from waiting tourists. The basin was named after Doge Pietro Orseolo, who established a hospice for pilgrims here in 977AD.

On the other side of the bridge the street became the narrow alley called *Calle Tron*. They crossed the bridge. Immediately to their left and right a pavement, only some three feet wide, ran alongside the canal and only a couple of feet above its flat murky surface.

The leader turned right onto the pavement and motioned to a small white-hulled rowing boat with a small outboard motor that was tied up alongside the canal. The prow of the boat was pointed away from the bridge – ready for a quick get-away.

"Get in the boat."

Larry and Gail did as they were ordered and clambered awkwardly into the small craft from the stone-clad side of the canal. The boat had three planks of wood fixed across its width to be used as seats: one at the front, one in the middle and one at the back. Gail was placed at the front with Larry on the middle plank, positioned deliberately so that he could see the knife that was still poking into Gail's side. He got the picture.

The man with the gun sat down on Larry's left, his arms folded, but with the Glock held in his left hand and the business end of the suppressor poking out from under his right arm – into the left-hand side of Larry's ribcage. One of the other two men sat at the back whilst the fourth man stood on the pavement and untied the boat. Then he too got into the back of the boat. As he sat down the abductor beside him started up the outboard. They began to move off.

"Where are we going?" asked Gail in a shaky voice; barely concealing her fear and panic.

"Shut up," said the man beside her and he dug with the knife a little more.

"Hey!" shouted Larry. "Leave her alone, you bastard!"

The man with the gun growled, "Keep quiet, both of you. I can easily shoot you here and dump your bodies straight into the canal."

Larry scowled at the man and quietly mouthed the words, "You piece of shit."

The man just smiled at him. And Larry knew that there was nothing he could do about the situation. His indignation was all bravado and he knew he was helpless.

But why were they being abducted? It made no sense. Unless this was just a simple kidnapping? *Yes, that must be it* thought Larry.

He might have thought differently if he had known his captors were members of the organisation known as Intiqam.

Terrorists.

The boat moved forwards into another canal that crossed them at a T junction. Here they turned left into the *Rio Fuseri,* coming up almost immediately to a small bridge. An American tourist in a beanie hat, loud shirt, loud shorts, long tartan socks and open-toed sandals was standing on the bridge with his wife, and he stopped and waved at them.

"Smile and wave back," whispered the man with the gun, and so Larry and Gail, and one of the men at the back, waved and smiled before they passed under the bridge.

A few yards further along they turned again, this time right, into *Rio Di San Luca.* To their right the red brick walls of the *Palazzo Contarini del Bovolo* flanked the tall walls of the narrow canal with less important houses hemming them in along their left side.

The *Palazzo Contarini del Bovolo* is on the list of tourist must-see buildings. It was built as a palace by the Contarini family in the 15th century and is tucked down a dead-end passage. It is famous for its graceful exterior spiral staircase, which is where the word *Bovolo* comes in, being the Venetian for snail shell.

But right now, Lawrence and his mistress cared nothing for this. Had this been a tourist jaunt Larry and Gail would have been quite enjoying themselves. But this was a different ballgame. This was frightening.

The boat puttered along under the power of the small outboard and passed under another three bridges until it emerged into the *Canalazzo*, the famous Grand Canal.

They turned left.

They stayed close to the side of the wide thoroughfare with its merchant's buildings and palaces that lined the busy canal. They continued along, passing the *Sant' Angelo* landing stage for the *vaporetti* or waterbuses. Just past this they swung left between two tall-sided merchant's houses into another narrow canal and travelled a few yards then stopped over on their right. The man at outboard cut the motor. There was a narrow path about three feet above them that ran along the side of a high wall. They had stopped by the side of some small stone steps that were coated in green slimy weed.

The man who had untied the boat from its mooring earlier got out first and tied up the boat. He stood on the path looking down at them.

"Get out," ordered the man with the gun.

The man with the knife made it out first and then Gail followed. The knifeman took up a position to Gail's right and his body language clearly showed that he was to lead the way. The man with the gun poked the barrel of the weapon into Larry's ribs. "Now you. Out."

Larry got up and moved awkwardly out of the boat, putting a foot up onto one of the steps then onto the path. The knifeman looked away to the direction of travel and that was when Larry saw his chance. He brought his right fist around, swinging it past the front of Gail's face to connect with the knifeman's chin. It landed with a satisfying smack and the man hit the wall with his shoulder and went down. Larry grabbed Gail's arm with his right hand to move her away and then pain lanced through Larry's skull as the man with the gun smashed the barrel of the pistol into the side of Larry's head just above his left ear. Larry released his grip on Gail's arm and put out that hand, almost falling against the warm brickwork of the building that towered over them. For a moment Larry thought he was going to pass out as he fought the waves of nausea that swept through him. He was only inches away from the edge of the path and the drop into the canal, and he did not want to fall in. He leaned his right shoulder against the wall and, with his left hand, he felt at the impact site. His fingers came away from his hair and he looked at them. Blood.

Gail was watching in horror with both hands up to her face.

The knifeman got to his feet. His face was red with anger, he still had hold of the knife, and he looked like he was about to use it on Larry.

The man with the Glock grabbed Larry's jacket and hauled him around so that he faced him. He shoved the end of the silencer up under Larry's jaw, digging it into the soft flesh at the base of Larry's mouth.

"Try that again and I will blow your fucking brains out!"

Larry was breathing heavily. He was angry but he was also deflated. What had he been thinking? These guys were killers!

The man with the gun said something in a foreign language to the knifeman and the knifeman snarled before moving away.

The man with the gun shoved Larry. "Move!"

Larry staggered forwards. He caught Gail's eye. *At least I tried.*

She gave him a thin smile.

They moved off along the pathway, passing between high walls that loomed up either side of the canal. The path ended and they were in a broader street with a long narrow modern-looking bridge to their left that was suspended over the canal. The area seemed deserted. They were actually only about two hundred yards from the busy *Campo Santo Stefano*, a huge square with bars, souvenir shops, restaurants and tourists. But Larry and Gail might just as well have been on the surface of the moon for all the activity that was going on in these narrow lanes and backwaters. There was no-one around to see them or hear them.

They crossed the bridge and turned left into the *Calle Del Pestrin*, another narrow street. It was lined either side by the tall fronts of houses with small Juliet balconies, from which hung baskets of flowers along with items of washed clothing which were hanging out to dry and air. Somewhere a canary was singing.

It should have been typically Venetian and utterly enchanting.

Instead, it was completely terrifying.

The six people moved along the street towards the back of a large three storey house whose walls and large untidy garden with its high railings formed the dead end of the street. Larry surmised that the front of the house probably faced the Grand Canal.

He was right.

The railings had an arched seven-feet-tall wrought iron gate set in them. It was locked. The man with the gun produced an ancient key and unlocked it.

They walked into the garden with its old grasses, dead dried flowers and tall dead weeds. Some sort of creeping vine had started to climb the inside of the railings but had given up and expired. There was an old brick path that led from the gate to a big wooden door that was flanked by large, tall, and dirty stone windows; one to the left of the door and two to the right. An ancient yew tree grew in front of the left window.

They approached the door and the man with the gun produced another key and opened the door. Larry and Gail were hustled in. They were in a small room with a paved floor. The air smelled of damp, and heavy dark-red velvet curtains hung at the three windows so that it was relatively dark inside with the only light coming in through the open doorway.

Keeping the Glock aimed at Larry's stomach the man holding the gun reached out with his free hand and flicked a light switch beside the entrance door and then closed the door.

Gail stood still, staring at the floor and hugging herself with her legs bent slightly at her knees. She was also shivering slightly and Larry realised that she was probably in a state of mild shock. Not surprising after what they had just been through, and who knew what was to come?

Larry straightened his back and turned to the man with the gun. "Now what happens?" he asked.

"You continue to do what you are told," answered the man with the gun.

The light from a bare bulb in the centre of the ceiling revealed a room measuring about twenty feet by twenty feet and about ten feet high. The ceiling had dusty black beams running across it and they could clearly see the floorboards of the room above. The walls of the room they were in were white plaster, some of which had blown with the damp and lay in pieces on the floor. The floor was bare wooden floorboards. There was no furniture.

The man with the gun gestured to a door across the room from them and the man who had been at the tiller of the boat opened it. They moved through into a large hall and the tillerman turned another light on. The hall stretched away from them to a pair of ancient blackened wooden doors that resembled barn doors. The doors were secured this side by a heavy bar that was locked horizontally in place on a pair of old metal brackets. The doors clearly exited out onto the Grand Canal, probably to a small landing stage. The old white plastered walls either side of the doors were blackened with mould where the canal's moisture had penetrated.

The hall was as bare, and just as uninviting, with the same décor, as the room they had just come out of. To their right was a large single door and to their left was a rather grand stone staircase that swept up to the next floor; its majestic proportions completely out of character with the bare hall. At some time in its past, with its costly furniture and wall hangings in place, this must have been quite an impressive entrance to a beautiful house.

The man with the gun said, "Upstairs."

Larry turned to the man. "Can I at least have your name?"

"We are not here to make friends." The sentence was delivered flatly and the man's eyes were as cold as those of a fish.

The tillerman led the way up the stairs with Gail and Larry following, with Larry acutely aware that a gun was being aimed at the small of his back. Despite his fear that they may be killed at any second Larry had his right hand on Gail's left arm, to reassure her that everything would be all right, that this was all just some big mistake, that they'd got the wrong guy. But his gut told him the very opposite. These men had known who he was.

At the top of the stairs was a landing. Lights were already turned on up here and they all turned for another flight of stairs; wooden and narrower and far less grand than the flight they had come up.

They kept ascending.

Another landing.

"Wait," ordered the man with the gun. The tillerman went forward and opened another door and they all moved through.

The room measured about thirty feet by thirty feet and was just as bare and smelling of damp as the rest of the house. It looked out over the Grand Canal and, at any other time, the view would have been enjoyable, even magnificent. But there was no view because the windows had been boarded up with big sheets of thick plywood behind iron bars set vertically into the walls top and bottom. To all intents and purposes Gail and Larry had just entered a prison cell.

There was a single cot bed over in the far right corner and an old wooden chair on the far side of a bare table. This was set in front of a large fireplace that was on the opposite side of the room to the entrance door. A man was sitting facing them in the chair at the table.

Because he was sitting down neither Larry nor Gail could tell how tall he was. He had black hair and a close-cropped black beard. His face was swarthy but handsome. He was wearing what looked like an extremely expensive dark-grey jacket over a white tee-shirt. They could see his legs under the table and he was wearing stonewashed jeans and tan-coloured lace-up shoes with black socks.

The door was closed behind them, leaving just Larry, Gail, the man with the gun, the man with the knife, and the stranger at the table in the room.

The stranger had both hands on the table, no rings on his fingers. He lifted his right hand and pointed at Larry. "You are the Right Honourable Lawrence Gainsborough, Member of the British Parliament." His guttural accent, similar to that of the man with the gun, pronounced the word British as *Breeteesh*, and Parliament by its syllables as *Par-lee-ah-ment*. That aside, his English was clear and impeccable. The finger that was pointing at Larry moved to point at Gail. "And you are Miss Gail Wetton, his mistress."

Larry took a pace forwards. "Look," he demanded. "Who are you? What's your name? What's going on here? There must be some mistake."

The stranger's hand that had been pointing splayed the rest of the fingers. He sat back. "So many questions, Mister Gainsborough." But he ignored them all, only saying, "However, I can assure you there is no mistake."

"Well, at least can you explain why we have been abducted?"

"Yes, I can, Mister Gainsborough. You are here as bait."

"Bait?"

"Yes, bait."

"Why? I don't understand."

The stranger gave a smile, showing only a thin line of his even white top teeth. "You are not supposed to understand, Mister Gainsborough. You are supposed to do as you are told." He nodded beyond Larry and the knifeman turned and opened the door; he grabbed Gail's arm. She cried out but he ignored her and shoved her roughly out of the door. Larry started towards her, but the man with the gun lifted the weapon to point it at Larry's face. Larry stopped in his tracks and the door thumped shut, cutting off the sound of Gail's voice.

Larry turned around, all seething indignation. "What are you…?"

The stranger waved his right hand. "Be silent, Mister Gainsborough. Control yourself."

Larry took a deep breath and firmed his chin. "Who the hell are you people? Why should I do anything you say?"

The stranger raised his left eyebrow then nodded at the man with the gun who turned and rapped with his knuckles three times on the door. Seconds later Larry clearly heard two very loud slaps accompanied by the sound of Gail crying out.

Larry's body stiffened and he started to move but the gun came up to his face again and he stopped.

The stranger spoke again. His voice was cold. "Miss Wetton, as you can hear, is my insurance. Do exactly as you are told and no harm will come to her." He paused for effect. "Do you understand me?"

Larry didn't answer. He glared at the man.

"Good," said the man. "I'll take your silence as a yes." He smiled.

Larry forced himself to be calm. This time they had obviously slapped Gail around – *God knows what they'll do to her if I antagonise them further.* Larry's arms were hanging at his sides and he clenched his fists, an action that was more a display of self-control than anything else. "You said I am here as bait. What did you mean? Bait for what?"

"It is quite simple." The man was still smiling at him. "I want someone to come and rescue you."

"What?" Larry shook his head. "Rescue me?" He did not understand.

"That is what I just said."

"But...But who?"

"One of your British Secret Service agents." There was that word Breeteesh again.

Larry shook his head again. He frowned. "Is this some kind of a joke?"

"Hardly, Mister Gainsborough...as your girlfriend has just proved."

In his mind Larry heard Gail's cry of pain again. "Where are you taking her...Gail?"

"Oh, we are going to keep her here. Not in the same room as you of course...but close by, so that you can hear her scream if you disobey us." The stranger watched Larry's face with interest as the MP struggled with almost overwhelming emotions. "She will be perfectly safe, I assure you...as long as you do as you are told. If you do not then..." He let the sentence trail off as he put both of his hands up into the air as if this were all some dreadful inconvenience.

"Very well," said Larry, deflating. "I'll do whatever you want."

"I know you will, Mister Gainsborough."

"Just don't hurt Gail."

"That," said the man as he stood up, "is up to you." Larry could now see that the man was quite tall. He walked past Larry towards the door with all the ease of a predator. "Oh, and by-the-way, do not even think about trying to escape. You will not get out of the windows and the chimney is blocked up. You will have an armed guard outside this door twenty-four-seven. All of my men like to shoot people and, if you did manage to survive being shot, you could afterwards listen to my men *seriously* abuse your girlfriend before you, and she, eventually died."

The man with the gun opened the door and the stranger stepped out followed by the man with the gun. The stranger turned. "I will have some tea and biscuits sent up," he said. "Very British. I am sure you would like that. Yes?" Then, just before the door closed the stranger added, "You asked me earlier what my name is. I am called Habib. I believe that means Beloved in your language."

The door closed.

Lawrence Gainsborough. A Right Honourable Member of Parliament. Captive. Held prisoner. For what? To capture a Secret Service Agent? He stared around the room hopelessly and then his head turned towards the door as he heard Gail's voice outside call out,

"Let go of me! Take your hands off me!" And then he heard a slight squeak, like the first part of a scream, followed by the sound of her shoes scraping against the wooden floorboards as she was dragged away.

*****

"Today," said Sensei Nakamura, "we train for many attacks, coming from different directions. Hai?"

"Hai."

Tandy was standing under what, in effect, was a very large square canopy that measured about ten feet across. It was standing on four substantial legs on the floor of the dojo and the top of the canopy was about ten feet off the wooden floor. Sensei Nakamura had hung ten long strips of red silk, which were each about six inches wide, from the outside edges of the canopy. On each strip of silk the sensei had written a number in black ink, and each number was written in Japanese – from one through to ten. They were not in any order. Tandy knew how to count from one to ten in Japanese but was struggling to remember what the characters for the individual numbers were.

And why silk strips? What were they for?

She put the worry out of her head and instead asked, "Why are we under this canopy, my sensei?"

"Because I not reach beams in roof," he answered.

"Ahh. Right." *What's that got to do with anything?*

"Now, pay attention."

"Oss!" She bowed.

"Take up fighting stance."

Tandy moved into her fighting posture: feet apart, left foot forward and body balanced with both of her hands up in front of her.

"You must keep within area under canopy. No go outside. You must strike a strip with either hand or foot when I caw out number on strip. Understand?"

What good is punching a strip of silk going to do? "I understand, my sensei...However..."

"What?"

She was going to say *What's the point?* but then thought better of it and instead said, "I'm not sure if I remember my written numbers."

"No probrem. You are bright gir. You soon work it out."

Bloody hell!

"Now, stop chatter. Ready?"

No! "Hai!"

"*San!*"

San. Number three!...Oh yes! That's three horizontal lines! That was to her left. She turned and punched at the silk. It wafted gently away from her powerful strike.

"*Hachi!*"

Eight...Like an inverted V. That was behind her. She turned and whipped a spinning kick at it.

"*Ichi!*"

One horizontal line. One! The numbers were coming back to her! *That was in front of me when I started, so now it's behind me.* She spun around, stepped forward and swung her right hand in haito uchi, ridge hand.

"Faster!" shouted the sensei. "No think too much. Move faster!"

"Hai!" yelled Tandy.

The numbers started to be called quicker so that no sooner had Tandy struck one strip of silk than she was told to go after another. In this way she was constantly turning and twisting, altering and finding her position of balance. And in this way Tandy learned how to turn fast and face and attack an opponent. She discovered that the secret of the silk strips was that they made no noise and gave no resistance when you struck them, so you tried to hit them harder. It was a mental trick, and it worked!

After ten minutes the sensei called "Yamae!" Stop!

Tandy opened her arms and sucked in air. She had been taught by Frank Cross never to fold over in the way that runners do at the end of a race, for this closed down your diaphragm and therefore your lung capacity. Better to stand up and thereby get air into you.

Sensei Nakamura allowed Tandy to have some sips of water to replace the sweat that was pouring off her.

"Now. Again," said the sensei. "This time I join in. When you see me step inside awning it mean I am going to attack you. You must brock and counter-attack me. Understand?"

"Oss, sensei."

"Hajime!" Begin.

This time the sensei called out numbers, but every now-and-then he stepped inside the canopy and launched an attack which Tandy sometimes managed to block and counter, and sometimes she did not and got hit. However, even if she took a hit the training did not stop.

Fifteen relentless minutes later the sensei called yamae.

"Very good, Tandy. Have water. Then we do again."

"Oss, Sensei!" *Bloody Hell!*

*****

WEDNESDAY 18TH JUNE

Flying out to Las Vegas had not been a problem. Frank had been to see President Ibraheem the previous day and had asked him if he, Tommo and Errol could use the sleek white Presidential Challenger 650 Business Jet, and could they use the President's Diplomatic Immunity by having the President nominate them as his couriers.

President Ibraheem had puffed out his cheeks and had huffed and puffed a little until Frank reminded the President that it was he, or rather Ola, that had got Frank into this in the first place.

The President relented, and his permission allowed Frank, Errol and Tommo to fly fast and privately. It also allowed Frank to get their weapons into the USA through the process of the Diplomatic Pouch.

Commonly called the Diplomatic Bag the Diplomatic Pouch can be virtually any container whose contents are for the use of the diplomat, or his or her couriers. By international agreement the pouches are never searched, although they are required to be presented to the Border Force of the country they are going into. In fact, international law does not even set any limits on the size, weight or quantity of properly designated Diplomatic Pouches. They are never even X-rayed, as this constitutes opening the pouch for inspection. This system therefore allows visiting dignitaries and representatives of foreign governments to bring into a country just about anything.

Frank was bringing in weapons. These weapons were Frank's Smith and Wesson Revolver, a small round leather pouch that contained *shurikens* (the deadly ninja throwing stars), three Sig Sauer P220 semi-automatic pistols and three Sig Sauer SIG516 assault rifles. These last six were for Tommo, T Bone and Clonk, and all of the guns had suppressors and hollow point ammunition.

Errol felt like he was travelling with a couple of hit-men.

He wasn't far wrong.

*****

"Welcome back," said al-Makira. The voice was now mocking. "Now, are you ready to answer some questions?"

Al-Makira was back in the house in Qaryat Musawara having returned by the same Bell Huey helicopter that had taken him to the training camp with his Second-in-Command. Since being at the camp al-Makira had come up with his plan B; he was going to abduct Sir Michael Corrigan or his wife, or both. He had already issued his orders that they be taken as quickly as possible. He only had to wait. But he did not want to wait long.

Ketcher had been dragged out of his room and was now back in the tubular chair, and once again he was naked and tied to the chair with his hands bound behind him. He lifted his head and looked at al-Makira. Ketcher had been beaten, left in a rank and filthy room, starved and given hardly any water, and now this man in front of him wanted him to answer some questions.

Ketcher could hardly think, let alone speak. He tried to moisten his dry cracked lips with his dry swollen tongue and then croaked, "Yesh."

"Excellent. Are you a British agent?"

"Wha…?"

"I said, are you a British agent, Mister Ketcher?"

A pause. Then, "No." The word came out in a breath, almost as if it were a sexual whisper to a lover.

Al-Makira nodded at his SiC who punched Ketcher in the face again, aiming this time for his right eye.

*****

Frank, Tommo and Errol landed at 9.30am in Las Vegas at McCarran International Airport in the baking sun of the Mojave Desert. As the three men were named as the couriers for President Ibraheem's Diplomatic Pouch, and because they were only carrying carry-on baggage with a change of clothes inside, they passed through Customs and Homeland Security with hardly a pause. They cleared the airport building and hailed a cab which took them to the enormous three-hundred-and-fifty-feet-high pyramid on the Strip called the Luxor Hotel. The hotel is not far from McCarran and so it only took a few minutes to get there, where they checked in.

The weapons and their ammunition were now sitting wrapped up in bath towels, safe and sound at the bottom of the wardrobe in Frank's room. Errol and Tommo were sharing a room next door where they had two single beds, and Tommo was relieved and delighted to find that they were both king-sized, which amazed Errol because it was so big he could get lost in it; whereas Tommo's just about fitted his giant frame.

Apart from the beds, Errol was amazed at the wall which held the windows. Because the Luxor hotel is a pyramid the outside frame slopes inward from the floor to the ceiling and the large windows follow this slope. The room looked out across the flat desert to the hills in the far distance that shimmered in the day's heat.

Frank had given orders for them not to unpack as they would not be in the hotel very long. He did, however, take a shower and afterwards got changed into blue jeans and a plain black tee shirt. Then he sat on the bed and thought about Tandy and wondered how she was getting on.

*****

Time-wise, Tandy was sixteen hours in front of Las Vegas, therefore at Hagakure it was 1.30am on Thursday morning. However, Tandy was not asleep. She had been woken up half-an-hour ago by the sensei who had stood outside her door and barked,
"Get up! Get up! We train!"
Lying in a futon on a tatami floor mat feels a bit like sleeping on hard ground in a sleeping-bag, and it takes a bit of getting used to. Tandy was not quite used to it; she may have been in the British Army at one time but she had always been provided with a bed, no matter how basic the bed had been. And she had never been a Brownie or a Girl Guide, and she had never been camping, so she had never slept in a sleeping bag, and she had never slept on the floor. Tandy preferred hotels.
Bleary-eyed and squinting in the darkness, Tandy had got up out of her futon, moved to the shoji and, still standing, slid it open. She peered at the sensei who was dressed in a gi.
"Do you have any idea what time it is?" She yawned. Then she realised how rude she must be appearing to be. "Oh, I'm sorry my sensei." She bowed.
Sensei Nakamura returned the bow. He was looking at her. In fact, she realised, with not a little surprise, that he had just run his eyes over her. She was dressed only in a burgundy-red light silk chemise that came down to her knees. She widened her eyes and blinked at him.
Without any trace of sarcasm in his voice, and not even the slightest of a smile on his lips, the old sensei said, "Dishy." There was a slight hesitation and then he said, "Now put on gi. We train." He turned and walked away, leaving Tandy with her mouth open. She shut it and smiled, and then under her breath she muttered, "You damned old rogue."

**

Having got changed into her gi, Tandy arrived at and entered the dojo, stopping just inside the door. She bowed. Sensei Nakamura was standing in the middle of the training hall with a jo staff in his hands. Four feet long and about an inch wide the jo is made out of either white or red Japanese oak and is light to hold but as hard as iron.

Tandy bowed again then came and stood in front of the sensei. She bowed again.

"May I ask a question, sensei?"

"What question?"

"Why are we training at just gone one-thirty in the morning?" She stifled another yawn.

Sensei Nakamura spun the jo in his hands. It moved like a propellor blade through the air and made a whirring noise. "Do you think attacks come onry in office hours?" he answered.

"No. No, of course not."

"Then why ask stupid question?"

"Sorry, yes, of course. Sorry sensei." She took a step forward to the sensei's left-hand side.

The jo whirred again, and one end came around to stop on the top of her chest, bringing Tandy to a halt. "Where you go?"

"To get my own stick, sensei."

"Is not stick. Is jo. You not get jo. I have jo."

"Oh."

"Not oh…Jo." He actually smiled at his little verbal joke.

Tandy stepped back.

The jo was now being held in the sensei's left hand with one end up and touching her chest and the other end down and almost touching the floor. Not very threatening.

"Are you ready?" asked the sensei.

"Hai."

Sensei Nakamura smacked Tandy across her right ear with the end of the staff that had been nearest the floor.

"Oww!" Tandy grabbed at her injured ear.

The sensei had spun the jo so that the lowered end had come up from the floor to her head with the speed of a striking snake.

"Sorry," said Sensei Nakamura bowing. "You said you ready."

Tandy rubbed at her ear. It felt hot and it stung.

"First resson when facing man with weapon…Don't say or think you ready when you are not."

"Oss! My sensei!"

"Good. Now. Are you ready?"

Tandy decided that when the end of the jo came at her she would dodge to one side rather than block this hard fast-moving wooden staff and then she would come back with a counter-attack.

"Hai!" She put her hands up in front of her.

The jo whirred through the air again. One end went past her face and before she could move her body and feet to avoid being hit the other end smacked into the side of her left knee.

"Yow!" She dropped her guard. Which was a mistake, because the jo was still moving and it arced through the air and cracked into her left elbow.

"Oww!" She spun from the sensei and limped away holding her arm.

"Sorry," said the sensei, bowing. "I thought you said you ready?"

Tandy didn't know what to rub first, her knee, elbow or ear. "That hurts!" She was almost on the point of tears.

Sensei Nakamura blinked. "Of course it hurts. Is a weapon. Meant to hurt."

He was right of course. Tandy sniffed, swallowed hard and stopped rubbing. This, she realised was yet another test. She stood up straight and bowed to the little master. "I don't know what to do, my sensei."

Humility.

"Ahh, go-od," breathed Sensei Nakamura. "Now I show you."

He walked over to her and gently took hold of her uninjured arm, then he steered her back into the centre of the dojo.

"Just re-wax. Hai?"

"Hai."

"First you must be rike stone outside in garden…Feer no pain. Ignore pain. Pain is onry pain. Pain is there for reason. Hai?"

"Hai."

"Pain there to show you something is wrong. Put pain out of mind, rike kneering in front of stone. Use pain. Worry about reason for pain…after. Understand?"

"Hai my sensei. I understand."

He meant for her to deal with the pain; to ignore the pain and then treat the reason for the pain later.

"Good. Now we fight again. This time you no rook at jo. This time you rook at my hands. Hands move jo, not jo move hands. Understand?"

"Hai."

This time when he attacked, he came at Tandy with the jo moving at half speed. And this time she realised that when he had attacked before she had been watching the staff. This was not possible of course, because the two ends were four feet apart and moving in ever-changing arcs and circles so that it was impossible to keep your eyes on both points at the same time – especially at speed. However, by watching Sensei Nakamura's hands, she was able to see how he was steering and manoeuvring the jo and how to react to the movement. Sure, she still got caught a few times, which made the sensei triumphantly cry out "Aha!", but she kept moving and ignored the impacts of the wood against her body.

As she got more used to the movement of the jo the sensei gradually increased the speed of the jo, so that eventually Tandy was moving like a whirlwind around the floor. After a few more minutes of this high-intensity training the sensei stopped and bowed. Tandy was breathing hard but she stood erect and returned the bow.

Sensei Nakamura brought her back to the middle of the dojo. They bowed to each other again.

"Now you go to bed. Sreep. We train at jo some more in morning."

"It is the morning, my sensei."

"Ahh. So it is. So it is."

*****

Back in Las Vegas, at just after 11am, the hotel's front desk called Frank in his room to tell them that a Mr Cameron had arrived and just over an hour after that Mr Collins checked in.

T Bone Collins had in fact arrived in Vegas some time before Clonk Cameron. T Bone's orders from Frank were that after arrival at McCarran International he was to make his way to any of the many car rental firms that existed on the Strip and rent a large Sports Utility Vehicle. It had to be capable of going off tarmac and into the desert, should this prove necessary.

The first rental place he found was a Dollar. They had a black Jeep Grand Cherokee. T Bone produced his driving license which informed the young man behind the counter that he was dealing with a Mr Austin Riley from Cambridge, England.

"Are you here on business or pleasure?" asked the young man affably.

"Oh, pleasure," said Mr Riley. "I want to have a look around the area; go to the Hoover Dam, Red Rock Canyon, maybe check out Lake Mead. And, of course, do a bit of gambling, see some shows, have a few beers."

"Well, Sir, you can certainly do all of that here."

They both laughed.

The paperwork was completed. T Bone paid cash and then went to collect the SUV, a huge beast of a vehicle. Perfect for the job.

Mr Riley rented the car for four days.

T Bone then drove to the massive MGM Grand hotel with its six-thousand-eight-hundred-and-fifty-two rooms. He had already reserved a room and so he had no trouble in checking-in.

Once checked-in he was allowed to use the MGM's enormous seven storey parking garage at the rear of the hotel. T Bone drove around to the garage and parked the SUV, by a small miracle, on the ground floor. T Bone often attributed these glad chances of getting a really good parking space as being the help of The Parking Fairy, which at times became (as now) more important than Father Christmas or the Easter Bunny.

T Bone grabbed his one hold-all bag that was his only luggage, climbed out of the big vehicle, blipped the lock and alarm from his car keys and then, whistling a merry tune, made his way to the Luxor which was only a short walk away in the sunshine.

The whole group met in Frank's room.

Frank invited them all to sit and then passed beer bottles around.

He had a plan.

Of course he had a plan.

A daring plan.

Whether it was going to work or not was another matter.

*****

Ketcher came around again; back in the chair. This time he could not see out of his right eye; it had closed as the flesh around it had swollen and it felt to him as if it were on fire. Also, his right cheekbone hurt with bruising and his neck hurt even more.

"Hello again, Mister Ketcher. I expect you are in a lot of pain. Yes?"

Again, that mocking tone.

Because of the pain in his cheekbone and eye socket agent Ketcher could barely move his mouth to open it, so he grunted a reply.

"I'll take that as a yes. Now, my friend here…" He waved his left hand at the SiC who was in front of Ketcher again. "He likes to hurt people..."

Ketcher, as painful as it was to move his lower jaw, interrupted, "Y-Yuh…don't…shay?"

Al-Makira frowned. His eyes flicked to the torturer who reached out, grabbed a handful of Ketcher's hair in his left hand, and pulled it back. Ketcher's chin came up as he gasped and the man slapped his face with his free hand. Ketcher cried out and then his hair was released.

Al-Makira said, "That's what you get Mister Ketcher if you try to be clever, or interrupt me. Understand?"

No answer.

"Understand?"

No answer.

His torturer put his booted right heel onto the bare toes of Ketcher's right foot and ground down.

Ketcher screamed as three of his toes broke. His head slumped forward as he passed out again with his hair hanging in front of his eyes and spittle escaping in glutinous strands from his mouth.

Al-Makira took a deep breath and let it out slowly.

"Take the filthy pig away. We'll try again later."

*****

As a Knight of the Realm, Sir Michael Corrigan often received invitations to attend functions; these might be for a number of reasons, the commonest of which were charity fund-raising events. But sometimes they were to support an individual or company and, sometimes they were for just a damned good meal at a black-tie dinner-dance, simply for the hell of it.

These functions were not, and are not, compulsory. Indeed, some knights do not attend any of them. Sir Michael, however, did attend a few, because, as he often said to friends, "…if I have been given this honour, then the least I can do is turn up from time to time…".

One of Sir Michael's favourite events was an annual dinner-dance held in the function rooms above the offices of the Zoological Society's offices in Regent's Park in London. It was also one of his wife's favourite evenings out as well, and it gave Red the chance to buy a new dress with shoes and handbag to match, get her hair done (all of this on Sir Michael's credit card), and get to be called Lady Corrigan (the wife of a male Knight never gets to be called by her first name).

Sir Michael and Lady Corrigan arrived at the zoo at just after 6pm and were allowed to park in the car park in the grounds of the Zoological Society. Sir Michael had driven there with his wife in the passenger seat alongside him. Sir Michael was in a black dress-suit, white pleated dress shirt, black bow-tie. Red was in a close-fitting silver-grey dress that showed off her slim size 12 figure and complimented her long dyed bright-red hair that was piled up artistically on the top of her head and held in place with a narrow gold and diamond hair band. The dress had thin shoulder straps and a plunging neckline that showed off her admirable cleavage and it ended just above her knees. Beneath it she wore smokey black tights into silver-grey court shoes with three-inch heels, all of which accentuated her shapely calves.

Sir Michael's car was a black Range Rover with a 5-litre supercharged V8 petrol engine. However, Sir Michael would not be driving home, that would be in the hands of David James who was Sir Michael's bodyguard, and James was at present sitting in the back seat of the Range Rover behind Lady Corrigan.

James was an ex-Marine; a big broad-shouldered guy who stood at six-feet-five-inches tall with a close-cropped beard and black curly hair. He was dressed in black cargo trousers, black tee shirt and a black blouson jacket and he was armed with a Heckler and Koch 9mm USP semi-automatic pistol holding fifteen rounds that sat in a holster beside his left armpit.

He was husband to Anna who was the senior officer in charge of administration and finance in the SOU building. Some organisations might object to husbands and wives working for the same organisation, but Sir Michael was not in charge of a normal organisation and he liked to keep close-knit bonds; it ensured that the officers looked out for each other and gave the members a feeling of belonging.

James had slid in behind the steering wheel after Sir Michael had vacated his seat, and he sat there reading a Clive Cussler paperback and playing music on the car's stereo system until the dinner-dance was over. As Sir Michael came out of the building James was already out of the car with the rear doors open as his employer and Lady Corrigan approached. Red was gripping her new Gucci black patent clutch-bag under her left arm and with her right arm she was hanging onto Sir Michael's left elbow, and she was giggling in a tipsy fashion having drunk just enough Champagne to make her feel merry. A strand of her red hair had come loose and was dangling over her left eye.

It was now 11.30pm.

"Have you had a good evening, Sir?" asked James, smiling.

"Yes, thank you, Dave," answered Sir Michael as he helped his wife into the back right-hand side of the vehicle.

James waited until his boss had entered on the other side. Sir Michael and Lady Corrigan put their seat belts on and then James got behind the wheel. He locked all the doors from the inside, and started the car. As he started to move off Red said, in a somewhat loud voice, "Home James!"

How many times had he heard that one? He smiled as Red giggled into her fingers behind him. Then she puffed the errant lock of hair out of the way and giggled again.

James moved out to the entrance of the car park where he pulled up and waited for an on-coming vehicle to pass. He then pulled onto the road known as the Outer Circle which runs right around Regent's Park and turned left, going west. The greenery of the park was to their left and trees bordered the edge of the road to their right. With the trees in full leaf, they seemed to add to the darkness, a darkness that was punctuated only by the street lights.

A few hundred yards further on James signalled right and crossed the Macclesfield Bridge and came up to Prince Albert Road where he waited for their chance to cross the road. When it was all clear he went straight across into the tree-lined Avenue Road and kept going north towards Hampstead where Sir Michael and Lady Corrigan lived.

By the time they had reached Swiss Cottage Red was asleep with her head resting on Sir Michael's right shoulder.

They negotiated the busy thoroughfare of Swiss Cottage and then crossed the Finchley Road to enter Fitzjohn's Avenue, a long tree-lined avenue that runs south to north away from London. The avenue contains a mixture of large Georgian and Victorian double-fronted houses, some still in private ownership as the builders had intended and some have been converted into flats and apartments.

A large grey van fell in behind them, and got a bit too close to the Range Rover's rear bumper.

Dave James glanced into his rear-view mirror.

The man in the front passenger seat lifted his mobile phone to his face and spoke into it. The van was so close that the beams from its headlights were blocked by the back of the Range Rover and therefore could not completely dazzle James. That was the van driver's mistake as it allowed James to get a pretty good look at both the passenger and the driver. And the passenger, who was on the phone, kept looking at the driver and then at the Range Rover.

James, who was trained to pick up on these kinds of signals, felt uneasy. His eyes slid back to look at the road in front of the Range Rover's large bonnet.

A few yards further on and James once again glanced into his rear-view mirror.

"What's up Dave?" asked Sir Michael, quietly, so as not to disturb his sleepy wife.

James gave a wry smile. His boss never missed a trick.

"I think we're being followed, Sir."

Sir Michael did not turn around to look, he knew better than that. If James thought they were being followed then they probably were. Turning around would only alert the men following.

Sir Michael said, quite calmly, "Better do something about it then."

The procedure was now avoidance techniques, and the easiest technique of all was to keep moving – at speed.

"Hold tight, Sir." Dave James put his foot down and the supercharged V8 engine pulled them easily away from the van which made the driver of the van curse loudly.

The Range Rover was now just under half-way along Fitzjohn's Avenue and coming up fast to Nutley Terrace which crossed left to right. There was a short wheelbase flatbed truck with wooden sides over to their right waiting to come out of the turning and as the Range Rover approached at speed it suddenly shot out in front of them. James swung the wheel left, trying to go around the truck but it accelerated and James was forced to brake hard with the tyres screeching on the tarmac.

Red woke up with a start as she was flung forwards into her seatbelt. "What the..."

"Sorry, Lady Corrigan!" shouted James. "We have a bit of a problem developing!"

The skid had brought the Range Rover's front grill tight up to the left-hand door of the truck without hitting it, but it meant that the passenger in the truck could not get out, so they started to manually wind down the window. The passenger was a woman. She was winding with her left hand and bringing a pistol to bear with her right.

James hit the electric window button and the glass in the door beside him slid smoothly down faster than the woman could wind. As soon as James could get his arm out of the window he drew his gun and fired two shots at the passenger in quick succession. The hollow point rounds hit her in the face and her head jolted backwards so that she disappeared from view.

Having been left behind, the van was now coming up fast behind them.

In the back of the front seats of the Range Rover were small wooden panels which dropped down after pressing a catch. Sir Michael pressed his and the dropping panel revealed a compartment that held a 9mm Glock 17 semi-automatic law enforcement pistol. He grabbed the gun as his wife did the same to the panel in front of her. Red had rapidly sobered up.

Maria "Red" Corrigan knew full well what her husband did for a living, and she knew the risks that went with it. For that reason, she had agreed with her husband who had enrolled her for private shooting lessons at a military range. Here she had practiced regularly with a variety of handguns until she got good enough to have her own firearms license and join a gun club. Lady Corrigan may have been dressed in a tight dress and high heels but she was no timid female. And she was a bloody good shot.

At the same moment that James had shot the woman the truck driver had exited his side of the vehicle and was now coming around the tailgate. And as that was happening the grey van pulled up about thirty yards back and four men got out; two from the front and two from the rear end. They had seen the earlier gun flashes as James had shot the woman and they were now wary. Things were not going to plan. The driver of the Range Rover was supposed to have been shot dead and a frightened Sir Michael and Lady Corrigan were supposed to have been abducted. That wasn't happening. The men crept forwards leaving the van doors open.

James looked quickly into his rear-view and wing mirrors. "Four behind!" he called out.

The man coming around the truck's tailgate was carrying a shotgun and he called out something in a foreign language to the men from the van as they approached in a crouching run.

The driver from the van was nearly upon them and he was carrying some sort of assault rifle.

"Doors!" called Red as she undid her seat belt, and James hit the button that released the door locks.

Red flicked the door catch and then shoved the door with her right elbow. The van driver checked in his advance as the rear door wagged open. Moving fast, Red leaned forwards and twisted to her right putting her head and shoulders out of the car's interior. Holding the Glock in a double-handed grip she fired three times and one of the hollow point bullets struck the van driver in the top right of his chest. He dropped the rifle and fell to his knees just as James shot the man with the shotgun at the truck's tailgate. The man went backwards as he fired one of the chambers of the shotgun up into the air.

The other three men from the van scattered; the man who had been in the passenger seat went left and the other two went into the front garden of a house on the right.

"Hold tight folks!" shouted James. "Let's get out of here!"

Red slammed her door shut.

A police car siren could be heard somewhere in the distance. No doubt someone had called in the disturbance. Sir Michael would deal with the police later, if it was necessary. Right now they needed to get the hell away.

James pushed the gearstick into reverse and shoved his right foot down. The tyres squealed and smoked and then bit into the road and the Range Rover rocketed backwards.

The two men in the front garden broke cover and started running back towards their vehicle, but the man who had been the passenger had moved off to one side and he now stood on the pavement to the Range Rover's left and waited for the big black car to come level with him as it surged backwards.

Sir Michael had his own window down, and as the man lifted his pistol at him Sir Michael fired four times, pumping bullets to allow for the speed and motion of the car he was in. Two bullets went wide: one hit a tree, another cracked off a gatepost, but the third and fourth found their mark in the man's belly and upper right ribcage. He twisted on his heels before sprawling onto the pavement's surface.

Another siren joined the first.

Then another, with the wailing seeming to be coming from all directions.

Still accelerating backwards and rapidly approaching the front of the van, James swung the steering-wheel and hauled on the handbrake. The car turned 180 degrees in the road and its left side came around and alongside the van. Sir Michael was now looking out of his open window and directly at the van that was only about four feet away from him. He fired a couple of rounds at the van's rear tyre so that the bullets punctured it and it burst so that the vehicle collapsed at that corner.

James floored the accelerator again and they shot away from the van. He hauled the wheel again and they bore off right with the tyres squealing into Nutley Terrace. With Sir Michael and Red hanging on for grim death in the back of the car James kept his foot down and slewed the vehicle right and north into Masefield Gardens where he raced to the end of the road to turn right and east into Netherhall Gardens. He burned along this road and then slowed up at the top before turning sedately and left and north into Fitzjohn's Avenue. They had now gone around in a rough circle to the west of Fitzjohn's Avenue and had re-joined it beyond the carnage that they had caused only moments earlier.

A police squad car came towards them and passed them heading south towards the bodies in the road.

"Is everyone alright?" asked James as the car cruised along just under the speed limit as if nothing had happened. Red had only just managed to get her seat belt back on.

"Yes thanks, Dave. Well done!" said Sir Michael.

Red leaned forwards and ruffled Dave's hair. "Bonus in the pay packet this month I think."

Dave laughed. "Thank you, Lady Corrigan."

"And right now," said Sir Michael, "I think we could all use a stiff drink."

"Amen to that!" said Red. There was a pause, and then Red asked, "Shall I put my gun away now, dear?"

**

James pulled into the private drive. In front of the Range Rover was a five-bar gate that was made of steel but was textured and painted to resemble wood. As he approached the gate an automatic reader sensed the big car and the gate swung open. After he had driven through the gate swung shut behind them. A few more yards and then they were directly in front of Sir Michael and Lady Corrigan's double-fronted house that was on the west side of Hampstead Heath and near the Leg of Mutton pond. As they climbed out of the Range Rover a man in black military-style fatigues came out of the darkness.

Dave James had already phoned ahead from the hands-free system in the car and had put the house security on alert. The man in the black fatigues gave a quick salute to Sir Michael.

"Everything alright, Sir?"

"Yes thanks, Price. But I think we should get inside. We don't know if these people will try again."

Agent Price, a member of the SOU, escorted the couple to their front door whilst James put the car away in the detached double garage. Then he went over to the house to check on his charges. By the time James arrived at the front door agent Price had already melted away into the shrubbery of Sir Michael's large and extensive garden.

Sir Michael put a glass into James's hand as he came into the lounge, a glass with a large measure of single malt whiskey in it.

Sir Michael raised his own glass to James. "Thanks Dave. You saved our lives."

James simply nodded.

Red was sitting on the edge of a leather sofa with her own glass of Chairman's Reserve Caribbean rum on ice. She asked, "Who do you think they were?"

Sir Michael had been pondering that problem immediately after their escape. The man with the shotgun had called out to his team members in Arabic.

*****

Al-Makira gripped his mobile phone in his left hand. He was angry and his jaw was clenched as he listened to the report. The hit upon Sir Michael Corrigan had failed.

"You stupid fucking moron!" he snapped the Arabic into the phone. "Now he will be on the alert…What do you mean, what do you do now? Get another plan put together as fast as you can and try again…" Al-Makira stamped around in a circle waving his right arm about. "No, I don't need to know the details, just grab Corrigan or his fucking wife! And this time do not fail me!" He was breathing heavily. "Moron!" he shouted into the phone, then he hurled it at the nearest wall where it smashed to bits. Raising his hands into the air with his fists clenched he screamed, "Get me agent fucking Ketcher!"

**

Al-Makira, with his temper diffused and his self-control back in place, was once more sitting behind his table and he watched as Agent John Ketcher emerged out of his numbed blackness into pain again.

"Here we are again, Mister Ketcher."

The mocking tone again.

Agent Ketcher looked a mess; his nose was broken and his right eye was closed, swollen, bruised and weeping, and his right cheekbone was also heavily bruised. Spittle had dribbled out of his mouth and he probably had a broken or missing tooth in there somewhere, although his face was so numb he could not feel it. His right foot was swollen around his broken toes and the pain from those toes was indescribable.

"You look a mess, Mister Ketcher."

Ketcher discovered that he was no longer sitting naked in a chair but was instead sitting naked on the bare floor of the room with his ankles under his bottom. His hands were in front of him, not tied together by rope or a cable tie but fastened with steel handcuffs. He moved his hands and the cuffs rattled.

Ketcher peered with his one good eye at his hands. A rope was there; it was tied around the small chain that linked the cuffs together. It rose directly up into the air and disappeared above him.

Ketcher's head lifted to follow the rope. It went up to a metal pulley that was fixed into a substantial brown beam that was in the ceiling and then a length of the same rope hung free beside Ketcher's right shoulder.

Al-Makira nodded at the SiC who immediately reached out for the free end of the rope and hauled on it. Ketcher's hands came up and then his arms followed. The SiC kept hauling on the rope and Ketcher's hands were lifted above his head at full stretch of his arms. More hauling and he was forced to come off his knees and then to stand, and then to come up onto the balls of his feet which made his right foot a hotbed of agony.

His torturer tied the rope off on a cleat on the wall by the door. It left John Ketcher hanging like a meat carcass.

The SiC moved away from the rope and picked up the shaft of a pick-axe that had been leaning against the wall and from which the steel business end had been removed..

"So, Mister Ketcher," began al-Makira. "Where were we? Ah, yes...Are you a British agent? Yes?"

No answer.

His torturer stepped forwards and hit Ketcher in the stomach with end of the pick-axe shaft.

Ketcher cried out, spitting gobs of phlegm and blood, gasping to get air into his mouth, unable to breathe through his wrecked nose.

"I did not hear your answer, Mister Ketcher."

No answer.

The end of the pick-axe handle was rammed down onto the toes of Ketcher's other foot.

More screaming.

The Second-in-Command stepped forward and put his booted foot on Ketcher's newly broken toes. This was too much to bear.

"No more!" shouted Ketcher. "Pleash! No more!" Ketcher really could not take any more. He was not in the military. He was not a hardened soldier or a member of one of the elite forces that had gone through interrogation training. He was a field agent in MI6. He wasn't tough enough. Sod this.

"Are you a British agent?"

Ketcher was sobbing pitifully. "Yesh! Yesh. Yesh..." His voice trailed away.

Al-Makira looked up. A slow smile crossed his face. "And who do you work for?"

Ketcher took a deep breath. "I'm w-with...MI...Shix...Brit-ish...Intell-lingensh."

"Very good, Mister Ketcher. Or should I say, Agent Ketcher? Hmmm?"

"Yesh," Ketcher gasped. "Yesh."

Irfan, the torturer, did not look at all happy now. Ketcher was answering questions, and Irfan enjoyed his work.

"So, if you work for MI Six, you must know Frank Cross. Yes?"

Frank Cross? Frank Cross? Who the hell is Frank Cross?

"I'm waiting...Agent Ketcher."

"I...d-don't...know any...anyone...c-called...F-Frank Crosh."

"Really?" said al-Makira. "Then perhaps you know who Sir Michael Corrigan is? Yes?"

The pick-axe handle was lowered. The SiC tapped the end of the handle on the floorboards.

Ketcher groggily shook his head. "D-Don't know...the nnn-name."

The SiC swung the pick-axe handle upwards into Ketcher's testicles.

*****

THURSDAY 19TH JUNE

Sir Michael Corrigan lay in his bed on his right-hand side and stared at the face of the alarm clock that was about twelve inches away from him on the top of a built-in bedside cabinet. 4.15am.

His wife was fast asleep beside him with her long slender right arm on top of the duvet and her red hair fanned over her pillow.

Sir Michael was thinking. Putting it all together.

He put it all together.

Intiqam.

What were they going to attempt next? They had missed him once. What next?

He rolled over and pushed himself up onto his left elbow, looking at his wife. Then he rolled back, got up, and went downstairs to use the phone. He could have used the phone in his office, but that was upstairs and he did not want to disturb his wife.

Sir Michael called his office; the Specialist Operations Unit never slept, there were always staff on duty. A woman answered the phone.

"Ahh, Vicky," said Sir Michael. "I am going to need your help."

He outlined what he wanted Vicky to do and then ended the call. He went back upstairs and slid into bed, then he settled onto his back and went to sleep.

On her side of the bed, Red closed the one eye that she had opened.

*****

LONDON – LATER THAT SAME DAY

It was a beautiful clear and sunny morning and Sir Michael heard the whoomph of the exhaust of his wife's black Porsche 911 as it left the garage and headed away from the house. There was a pause as the five-bar gate scanned the reader device in the car and then opened, and then came another whoomph as she passed through the open gate and out onto the road beyond. Sir Michael checked his watch. 8.55am.

Red was not alone because David James was following her in a dark-grey short-wheelbase Land Rover that had a huge black bull-bar mounted on the front. Red was heading for her gym down near the Royal Free Hospital, south of Hampstead Heath. Sir Michael, not surprisingly, following the attempted kidnapping last night, had told his wife to be careful. She had kissed him and told him not to worry and that she would be fine. "And anyway, dear, I'll have Dave with me."

Sir Michael had relented and his wife had driven off, and he was just finishing his breakfast cup of coffee when the police arrived in two high visibility Vauxhall Astras on the road side of the five-bar gate.

The steel post that held the five-bar gate had a camera and a speaker system built into it, and Sir Michael had a number of mini screens situated around the house so that he could see who was at the entrance. One of these mini screens was set in the kitchen wall by an entrance door to the hall and Sir Michael could see the police cars in it. Sir Michael reached out and pressed a small black knob that was alongside the screen. The five-bar gate swung open and the police pulled onto Sir Michael's wide front driveway.

A woman stayed behind the wheel of the first car, but the passenger, dressed in a dark-blue two-piece suit, white shirt and plain grey tie, got out and stepped it out to Sir Michael's front door. The man in the suit was soon joined by another three police officers; these were in uniform, including caps on their heads – two men and one woman – from the other car.

Sir Michael opened the front door just seconds after the suit rang the doorbell.

"Sir Michael Corrigan?"

"Yes?"

"I'm Detective Inspector Cain of the Metropolitan Police. May we come in, Sir?"

"Yes, of course Inspector." Cain noted that Sir Michael had dropped the designation Detective from his title, but then just about everybody did that. Sir Michael led them through to the large kitchen at the rear of the house. "Would you like a coffee? It's pure Colombian, made from real Colombian beans."

"No, thank you, Sir." He would have loved a coffee.

Sir Michael, in an open-neck shirt and jeans, perched himself onto a high stool near a work surface that was in front of a large window that overlooked the garden. "How can I help you?"

"Where you in Fitzjohn's Avenue at around midnight last night?"

"Yes."

The Detective's eyebrows shot up in surprise. He had been expecting a denial. "You were?"

"Yes, Inspector. My wife and I had been to a dinner-dance at the Royal Zoological Gardens."

"Oh," said Cain. "Can I ask…where is your wife?" The DI looked around as if Lady Corrigan might materialise out of one of the walls.

"I'm afraid you've just missed her. She's gone to her gym near the Royal Free. I expect you passed her. She's driving a black Porsche 911."

"Oh. Yes. We saw that. Nice motor."

The three police officers standing behind DI Cain shifted their feet.

Sir Michael smiled warmly. "What's this about Inspector?"

"Well, Sir, there was a shooting in Fitzjohn's Avenue at around midnight last night."

"And you think I might have seen something?"

"Did you, Sir?"

Sir Michael Corrigan shook his head. "No. Can't say I did. Sorry. But I did see a police car hurrying south at about that time…Ahhh!" Sir Michael clicked his fingers. "One of your officers took a note of my number plate, and that's what's brought you here."

"Yes, Sir." *Christ, this bloke's sharp.*

"Now I understand."

There was an awkward pause, then the Detective Inspector asked, "Where is the Range Rover now, Sir?"

Completely unruffled, Sir Michael answered, "In the garage." He inclined his head in the direction of the garage building. "Would you like to see it?"

"If I may, Sir."

"Of course, you may."

The keys were on another kitchen work surface near the entrance door.

"Those are the keys there, Inspector. Just press the red button on the handset as you approach the garage and the doors will open automatically."

"Would you like to come with us, Sir?"

"Do I have to?"

"No, Sir."

"Then I'll wait here, if you don't mind."

Detective Inspector Cain turned and picked up the keys. He nodded at one of his men. "Sergeant. Wait here with Sir Michael. You two, come with me."

They left.

The Sergeant stood with his feet slightly apart and with his hands together in front of his stomach. He was staring around the kitchen and trying to avoid looking at Sir Michael.

"Sergeant?"

"Sir?"

"Would you like a coffee?"

The Sergeant sniffed a couple of times and looked at his feet. He looked up. "I can't really, Sir." He looked guiltily towards where his senior officer would be.

"Sergeant. I won't tell if you won't."

The Sergeant gave a small smile. "Well, I suppose just a small one, Sir."

Sir Michael poured the man a cup, and while the Sergeant drank and savoured his pure Colombian coffee (made from real Colombian beans) Detective Inspector Cain got into the garage and then into the Range Rover. The car was immaculate and there were no guns hidden anywhere. But, of course, Mr James had already dealt with that.

The guns that had been used by Sir Michael and Lady Corrigan and James were all untraceable – that was the nature of the Specialist Operations Unit. Therefore, it did not matter that the police forensic team had recovered bullets from a gate post, a tree and the bodies of the dead and would-be abductors, they would never be able to tie them to any weapon.

And the two men who had survived the abortive kidnapping had run for it and had disappeared. One of these men had been told that he was a moron by al-Makira.

After a thorough search of the car and the garage DI Cain and his officers returned to the kitchen. The Sergeant had finished his coffee and Sir Michael had washed the cup up and put it away. The Sergeant's face was a picture of innocence. He'd even remembered to wipe away the coffee moustache.

"All okay, Sergeant?" asked Cain.

"No problems, Sir."

The Detective inspected the Sergeant's face for a moment or two, but apart from blinking a couple of times the Sergeant's face betrayed no emotion. Satisfied, the DI then turned to Sir Michael. "Can I ask you what you do for a living, Sir Michael?"

Detective Inspector Cain had already checked up on Sir Michael Corrigan. The records showed a clean sheet regarding any law-breaking or misdemeanours. Not even a parking ticket. What the records had shown was that Sir Michael had worked for GCHQ, and that following his departure from that branch of the British Security Service, Sir Michael had dropped out of sight.

"I'm retired," answered Sir Michael.

Cain took in a deep breath then stood and looked around the kitchen. Finally, he said, "Well, thank you for your time, Sir Michael."

"Not at all, Detective Inspector." He gave Cain his full title back.

Sir Michael saw them all to the door and, after releasing the five-bar gate again, waved them away.

Back out on the main road Cain sat in silence next to his driver, Detective Sergeant Sheila Hastings, who turned to her boss and asked, "Nothing?"

"Nothing," answered Cain, frowning. "But then he's a bloody spook."

"Should we put him under observation?"

Cain shook his head. "We can't prove he's done anything wrong."

"But?"

"But, my gut says otherwise." He shifted uneasily in his seat.

"So, what do you want to do, boss?"

"Have him watched." Cain puffed out his cheeks. "But we need to be careful. If we get this wrong with a knight of the realm, they'll have our guts for garters."

*****

Unfortunately for Errol Moon he had not been allowed out of his room by Frank to experience the delights of either the Luxor hotel or Las Vegas, the self-styled entertainment capital of the world. Frank had explained that if, by some chance, Diana's kidnappers knew what he looked like and he was spotted by them then the mission might be jeopardised. It was conceivable that the bad guys might snatch Errol off the street as well and make the money demands of his wife, or they might even kill him.

Frank softened the blow by allowing Errol to watch as many in-house movies as he wanted and to have as much room service as he liked, but to rein in the consumption of alcohol. As a result, Frank discovered that Errol like pizza – lots of pizza.

And while Errol worked his way through the Italian food, either Frank, Tommo, Clonk or T Bone baby-sat him.

As it turned out, Errol was the perfect "captive" because, despite being worried for his daughter's safety, he never complained but kept them all entertained with his stories from the music business, so the hours passed by fairly easily and in mutual friendship. Which was just as well, because pretty soon things were going to get a whole lot more dangerous.

*

Tommo ended up doing more than his fair share of baby-sitting Errol. The reason for this was that Frank, Clonk and T Bone carried out a number of reconnoitres of the MGM's garage and surrounding area, both in broad daylight and at night. And although the members of the Shadows team were not known to the kidnappers, and although the kidnappers did not know they were there, Tommo, with his height and massive frame would have instantly attracted attention. Frank was wise enough to know that if the kidnappers kept seeing the same big guy hanging around the area where the money switch was to take place, they might get suspicious and call the exchange off – worse, they might panic and kill Diana. Therefore, Tommo stayed with Errol, and he also ate pizza.

*****

Agent Ketcher was back in the chair in what he had come to know as the torture chamber.

"Would you like some water?" asked al-Makira.

Ketcher had come to realise that he wasn't going to see a doctor any time soon, that this man with the velvety soft and deadly voice was probably going to kill him. And he was in such pain that he just wanted it all to stop, and he didn't care how. For that reason, Agent John Ketcher summoned the last of his small and dwindling reserves, formed his answer, took a breath, and said, "Fuck you."

Al-Makira held up a hand as Irfan stepped forwards to mete out more punishment. "No." Al-Makira lowered his hand and Irfan frowned at not being able to hurt Ketcher some more.

Al-Makira continued, "Put him back in his room. Give him no food or water, and tomorrow we'll give Mister Ketcher all the water he could possibly want."

*****

Lady Corrigan walked back into her house. "Hi Mike, I'm home!"
"I'm in the kitchen, love."
Red walked into the kitchen. She always moved in the liquid manner of a cat but with her head held high. She was dressed in black leggings that had a bright-pink squiggly design traced over them and a tight-fitting cropped vest top in the same matching design scheme. She was wearing an open tracksuit jacket over the top of the vest and white Nike trainers on her feet. Normally, Red liked to go to the gym ready changed and then get showered after her work-out, after which she would get changed into her baggy blue denim jeans and a dark-blue tee shirt. She kept this change of clothing, a hair brush and a small make-up bag, in her kit-bag which she was holding in her left hand.

That's what she would normally do. However, she and Sir Michael had agreed that today she must be seen and easily recognised – her red hair alone would not be enough – and so she had come home in what she had gone out in. She and Sir Michael wanted the would-be kidnappers to get a good look at her.

"Good workout, dear?" asked Sir Michael handing her a cup of coffee.
"Yes, thanks."
"Were you followed?"
"Yes." She sipped the coffee.
"Both there and back?"
Red nodded. "Yes."
"Were they police?"
She shook her head. "Dave says they were probably the same lot as last night."
"So, now they know the route."

"Yes."

"Where's Dave now?"

"He's gone to change his car and then he'll be back out on the main road, like you asked him."

Sir Michael nodded. He was standing with his back against the worktop that was below the garden window. He looked at his wife. "Red, are you sure that you want to go through with this?"

Without hesitation she said, "Absolutely." She went up onto her toes and kissed her husband's lips.

*****

Sensei Nakamura came out of his wash house. It was a beautiful warm morning with a clear blue sky above. The sensei was wearing a freshly laundered plain grey kimono and he placed his hands on his hips as he took in a deep breath and looked up at the sky.

He froze.

Something was not right.

He closed his eyes, which cut out all visible distractions, and allowed all of his other senses to heighten. Then, without moving, and with his body completely relaxed, he allowed his senses of smell and hearing to explore his surroundings.

Ever since Tandy had arrived the sensei had been picking up on small disturbances to his inner-self and his inner calmness. He was always self-aware and something kept intruding into his state of being, disrupting his *zanshin*; awareness.

He had also noticed other things; some small indentations in one area of the bed of moss, a pine branch pushed out of alignment in his deliberately manicured garden, crushed leaves amongst whole leaves, pine needles on one end of the engawa. He knew this had not been due to Tandy's movements because he had been both aware of her movements and had been watching her closely.

No. Someone was sneaking around Hagakure.

Someone was in his garden.

And that someone had been near or by in the last few minutes, while he had been having his wash.

Whoever it was, they were good.

But not good enough.

The sensei could smell the man's scent in the air. Someone who had not washed for days and who had been sitting in some mouldy earth.

The sensei knew this person was somewhere around. However, he could not hear or sense anyone nearby at the moment, so he opened his eyes and continued along the engawa towards the zen garden.

On passing through the door at the end of the engawa the sensei turned left and stopped. Tandy was sitting and looking at the big rock, but not how she had been positioned the first day that she had arrived. This time she was wearing her gi and sitting cross-legged with her back up straight, chin up, hands on knees, beathing regularly and deeply, and apart from her diaphragm moving her chest there was not a single other movement.

She was practicing *Zazen* - Concentrating on her beathing and emptying her mind of thought.

The sensei approached her, not making a sound.

Tandy did not move.

Back at Cannon Head Frank had taught Tandy how to use her senses – just as Sensei Nakamura had just done – the way that the sensei had once taught Frank. She and Frank would sit out on the villa's patio and she would close her eyes after having looked around for five seconds. With her eyes shut she would then tell Frank what it was she had seen; the shape of clouds in the sky, various birds and where they were, what sort of bug was sitting on a leaf, marks on the patio floor. Having completed this she would then keep her eyes closed and listen. She would then tell Frank what she could hear; had the sound of the waves in the sea altered? Was the wind blowing? How many cars were there on the coastal road outside the villa? Could she hear any voices on the wind? It was a skill she was constantly testing, improving and perfecting.

However, the listen-and-hear practice was not the same as Zazen. Never-the-less, she had discovered that the two disciplines could be combined so that she became even more aware of her surroundings.

Without moving a muscle other than her lips and tongue she said, "I know you're there, my sensei."

"Ve-ry go-od," said Sensei Nakamura.

*****

FRIDAY 20th JUNE

Another beautiful day. Sir Michael called out, "Have you got your mobile with you?" to Lady Corrigan as she opened the front door and stepped outside.

Her "Yes," floated back to him. "It's in the pocket of my fleece." She was wearing her white Nike trainers on bare feet, a black spandex sleeveless crop top and figure-hugging lycra leggings that were lurid purple with large pink spots. Between the waistband of her gaudy leggings and the hem of her crop top she had bare skin, because Red liked to show off her impressive abdominal muscles that she worked so hard at maintaining. She had a light-blue fleece over her right shoulder and her gym bag in her right hand. She went from the front door of the house to the garage and went inside.

From the upper branches of a tree that was just outside the perimeter wall of the Corrigan's extensive garden, and some one-hundred-and-fifty yards away, a man watched her through binoculars. He watched as Lady Corrigan entered the garage and he spoke into a mobile phone. He said two words in Arabic,

"Get ready."

Moments later Lady Corrigan's black Porsche came out of the garage and then pulled up at the five-bar gate. This time Lady Corrigan did not sit inside the car waiting for the gate to automatically open. Instead, she got out of the car and waited as the gate opened. She had put on the fleece and her long bright-red hair was loose about her shoulders and, as the gate swung open, she tossed her head, flinging her hair to one side. It was all being done deliberately to attract attention.

Red got back into the Porsche and turned right and out of the private road directly onto the A502 North End Way and Dave James pulled away from the opposite kerb to follow her. Mr James was behind the wheel of an old white 7 Series BMW. About a hundred yards back a silver Ford Mondeo also pulled out onto the road from the kerb-side. The Ford had Detective Inspector Cain inside with Detective Sergeant Hastings back in the driver's seat. The two police officers had no idea who James was or that he was following the Porsche. He was just another car on the road. As the convoy moved off, they were joined by a leather-clad girl with a full-face black crash helmet who was seated on a powerful Yamaha motorbike that had just come up behind them.

A few hundred yards further on the Porsche passed another parked vehicle, an old blue Ford Sierra, which pulled out sharply in front of James' BMW. As James eyed the Sierra with suspicion the offending car's passenger spoke into a mobile phone.

Red was heading south towards Hampstead. She passed the famous public house called Jack Straw's Castle on her right and went on into Heath Street, following yesterday's route to her gym.

"Keep up with them," growled Cain, and although Hastings had the car perfectly positioned, she touched the accelerator and moved nearer to James' rear bumper.

At the junction with East Heath Road Lady Corrigan turned left, and continued onwards for a few hundred yards. Behind her the passenger in the Sierra began chattering excitedly into his phone and behind the Sierra the BMW suddenly slammed on the brakes.

Detective Sergeant Hastings was just too near and the police Mondeo went straight into the back of the BMW and both cars came to a halt. Dave James had judged it perfectly. Lady Corrigan had agreed with her husband that she should not be followed by the police if the plan was to work. The police had to be stopped.

The motorbike rider saw the collision and swerved around the back of the Mondeo and accelerated away with a burble of exhaust.

James got out of his car as the Porsche, the Sierra, and the motorbike kept going. James walked over to the Mondeo and tapped on the driver's window. The window came down.

"Bit too near, weren't you?" said James as he bent down to look inside the car.

"Why did you stop?" demanded Detective Sergeant Hastings who was wearing a very peeved expression on her face.

"A cat ran out in front of me."

"A cat?"

"Yes, you know, a cat. About eighteen inches long, tabby colour, eats mice, goes miaow."

Hastings gave James a glare then flashed her warrant card at him.

With faked belligerence in his voice, James asked, "What's that supposed to prove?"

"We're police officers."

"So?"

In the passenger's seat Detective Inspector Cain exhaled heavily and watched as the Porsche and the Ford Sierra disappeared from view.

The Sierra moved nearer to Lady Corrigan with the motorbike hanging back. They were travelling along a narrow road with impressive houses behind high walls to their right and the undergrowth and woodland of Hampstead Heath immediately to their left. They passed Cannon Lane on their right, then Well Road and then Well Walk. They were coming up to Heathside, also on the right, and, from it, a small silver removal van pulled out in front of Lady Corrigan and stopped, blocking the road.

Red braked, stopped, and put the Porsche into neutral. Then she wound down her window and leaned her head out to shout at the driver. The Sierra had pulled up behind her and two men jumped out and ran forwards.

Fifty yards back the motorbike pulled up as one of the men grabbed the Porsche's door handle and yanked the door open. Then he grabbed Red at the shoulder by the material of her fleece and pulled. Red screamed as her upper body came out of her seat but the seatbelt brought her to a halt. The other man joined the first and together they wrestled with Red and her seatbelt.

On the other side of the removal van a car had pulled up and was sounding an impatient horn. The removal van driver made motions as if the van had stalled and that he was trying to get it to start.

The girl got off her motorbike and lifted her visor before she began to walk towards the Porsche.

The two from the Sierra now had Red out of the car and onto the road. At any moment a vehicle might come up behind them and then their plan would be wrecked. Red was screaming in fury and kicking and punching like a wild thing.

The girl on the motorbike stopped walking. She was now about twenty yards from the Porsche. "Hoy!" she yelled. "What are you doing?"

Ignoring her, one of the men hurriedly felt into his trousers pocket and produced a plastic bag with a pad of material inside and he pulled the pad out and shoved it into Red's face. A few more struggles and she collapsed as the chloroform knocked her out.

The motorbike girl took a few steps nearer. "Hoy! What's going on?"

The impatient driver on the other side of the van was still sounding his horn and was also now shouting obscenities out of his driver's window.

The man who had used the chloroform cursed and in his native Arabic said,

"Get her in our car! There's no time to shove her in the van! Quick!"

Red, Lady Maria Corrigan, was bundled off the road and dumped ignominiously onto the back seat of the Sierra. The removal van started up and both it and the Sierra headed east, disappearing into the London sprawl.

They left behind the black Porsche, sitting in the middle of the road with the driver's door hanging open, and a girl in black leathers had filmed it all on her mobile phone.

*****

Ketcher's left eye opened. He had known from the fractured shadows on the wall, formed by the sun coming through the slats of his window barrier, that when he had woken up some moments ago that it was sometime in the late morning. He had then been dragged off his bed and out of the door.

He had not been brought to the usual interrogation room. In actual fact he was in a room on the floor below the interrogation room. This room was on the ground floor, there being three floors to this building, built something like a tower. The room had no windows and had been adapted so that it resembled a wet-room, with a rubberised impervious membrane on the gently sloping floor. Any water landing on it ran off to a drainage hole in one corner. It was usually used by al-Makira and Irfan as their private shower room.

Ketcher had passed out again and when he came back to consciousness he found that he was now lying naked on his back and that there was something hard beneath him. The back of his head, his shoulder blades, hips, buttocks and heels told him it was probably something wooden.

He tried to sit up, but could not. He was bound to the twelve-inch-wide plank by stout ropes at his ankles, stomach and chest. His hands were tied in with the roping around his stomach.

"Back with us again, Agent Ketcher?" Al-Makira was bending over him, about eighteen inches away from his battered face. "Tell me what you know about Sir Michael Corrigan."

Ketcher now knew that a board was underneath him and that he could not get off it. He now knew damned-well what was coming and if he could have given this man chapter-and-verse on the SOU Director's life story he would have. He would have given Corrigan's address, car registration number, where he went for his holidays and his inside leg measurement. He would have gladly blabbed the lot. But he couldn't. He simply did not know.

"I-I can't..." gasped Ketcher, and then a rough beige-coloured towel went over his face and the board was tilted so that his head was lowered and his pain-filled feet went up.

Waterboarding is a form of torture that has been used world-wide through history; the Spanish Inquisition used it, as did the Japanese and Nazis during the Second World War. It was used by the American Central Intelligence Agency (CIA) up to January 2009 when President Barack Obama signed an Executive Order banning its use.

The world's terrorists still use it.

During waterboarding the victim is strapped to a board with the board at a slope of between ten to twenty degrees; head down, feet up. The person is face up and then a light material covering is placed over the face after which water is poured on, usually from a watering can, so as to control the flow. As the wet material presses down over the mouth and nostrils it produces an immediate gag reflex and gives the person the acute sensation of drowning. The water should be poured intermittently over the captive to prevent death.

Waterboarding causes extreme pain in the lungs and can permanently damage the lungs and brain due to oxygen starvation. Ketcher knew what was coming and from behind the towelling he screamed in terror.

The water was poured on.

**

One hour later al-Makira pointed at Agent Ketcher and said, "It's as I thought. He knows nothing. Untie him and put him in the chair. We'll make the film of him."

With a body as limp as a dead eel Ketcher was untied and released from his bonds and then unceremoniously dumped on the wet-room floor before being dragged away. His body left a slick wet mark across the floor as the last of the water dribbled down the drain.

*****

"Abducted?" said Sir Michael who was standing in the hallway of his house with his hands on his hips.

"Yes, Sir Michael. I'm very sorry." Detective Inspector Cain was standing on Sir Michael's front doorstep. He had both of his hands thrust down into his jacket pockets. He was feeling very awkward. He did not want to have to admit that he had been following Lady Corrigan, or that he had not had permission to do so. And he did not want to tell Sir Michael that, even if he had obtained the permission, he had lost her.

"When did this happen?" asked Sir Michael who knew exactly when it had happened, because David James had told him.

"About an hour and a half ago, Sir."

"Do we know who by, Detective Inspector?" Sir Michael believed he knew damned-well who had abducted his wife, but he wasn't going to tell the police officer that.

Cain looked at Sir Michael. *He's taking this very well.* "We don't know, Sir. We've traced the car of course."

"Of course," echoed Sir Michael without a shred of sarcasm in his voice.

The DI gave the knight a glance, then said, "If I may say, Sir Michael, you don't seem too disturbed by this news. Is there something you should be telling me?" The detective took his hands out of his pockets.

Sir Michael gave a slight shake of his head. "No, Detective Inspector. But I expect that you have already discovered that I used to work for GCHQ, and as a member of a branch of the British Security Services I got used to hearing bad, and often disturbing, news. I am, of course, most concerned about my wife, and I'm sure that you will do everything you can to trace her and get her back to me safely…as will I."

"Meaning?" The DI frowned.

"Meaning, that I still have contacts and friends in the Security Services." Sir Michael gave a half smile. "Now, Detective Inspector, about that car?"

There was a slight pause and then Cain said, "It's a blue Ford Sierra. It was found abandoned in a road in Kentish Town."

"I'll bet it was burned out." No fingerprints, no DNA, no evidence, no clues.

"Yes, Sir Michael."

"And you know it's the right car because…?"

Cain was not about to tell Sir Michael that they'd had the Sierra in their sights when then smashed into the back of a BMW, the driver of which had turned out to be a Mr David James who worked for Amalgamated Exchanges Co.Ltd. The detective did not know that company was, in fact, a fake, and was, in fact, the Specialist Operations Unit – but the DI was never going to find that out. All that DI Cain could find out was that Mr James' public record was as clean as polished glass.

"Actually," said Cain, "we had a stroke of luck. We've received a film, taken on a mobile phone, which clearly shows the abduction taking place."

"Ahh," said Sir Michael. "And this, no doubt, showed the Sierra's numberplate."

"Exactly. Sir."

Sir Michael crossed his arms over his chest and asked, "Do we know who owns the mobile?"

"Umm, actually, yes we do, Sir. It was a young lady on a motorbike. She witnessed the whole thing and decided to turn her film over to the police."

"How very public spirited of her," said Sir Michael.

"Yes, it was Sir. However, the young lady in question wishes to remain anonymous."

"I don't blame her."

"Quite, Sir."

"Do we know where the abductors went after they dumped the car?"

"No, Sir. It wasn't in an area covered by CCTV."

No surprises there thought Sir Michael. "So, they probably switched vehicles. That would suggest a certain amount of planning, wouldn't you say, Detective Inspector Cain?"

"Indeed, Sir." *This bloke really is bloody sharp.* "Have you had any contact at all from the abductors?"

Sir Michael shook his head. "No, not as yet."

"Could we wait, in case they call you?" asked Cain. He looked hopeful.

"You mean inside my house?"

"Well, yes."

"I'd rather you didn't," answered Sir Michael. "But I'll call you if they do."

Detective Inspector Cain pulled an unhappy face. Since the police could not force Sir Michael to allow them access to his house, just to wait for the phone to ring, there was not much the detective could do. However, Cain tried once more. "Really…it would be best if…"

"No, thank you, Detective Inspector." Sir Michael's face was firm, his voice was resolute and his arms remained folded across his chest.

And that was that.

Detective Inspector Cain nodded in a resigned manner, then he shrugged his shoulders and turned away from Sir Michael Corrigan to walk slowly back to where Detective Sergeant Hastings waited in a newly supplied car.

*****

NORFOLK

Shirley Gainsborough put the last of the several terracotta flowerpots that she had been cleaning onto a shelf in the greenhouse and wiped her forehead with the back of a wrist. She was wearing a pair of long pink rubber gloves on her hands and they left a dirty smudge above her right eyebrow. She puffed through her lips a couple of times and then bent down and picked up the bucket of warm water that she had been using to clean the pots. She walked out into the large garden and headed for the kitchen sink drain at the back of the house. The sun was out and there were only a few fluffy white clouds in the sky. Some house martins were wheeling high-up hunting for bugs that they picked out of the air and down on the ground the flower beds were in full bloom. Shirley was wearing an open-necked black-and-white checked shirt that she had tucked into the waistband of a pair of three-quarter-length light-blue denim jeans and had a pair of old green sandals on her bare feet.

Something was wrong. She tipped the filthy water down the drain and puffed again.

Larry should have phoned by now.

Oh, she knew damned-well that he was with Gail Wetton, and that they were having an affair, but he always called when he got back to England after one of his "business" trips. Shirley wasn't bothered that he was having an affair, after all, she was having one of her own.

He should have been back today.

He had not called.

She put down the bucket and walked through the open french windows into the lounge. The kids were at school so she had the house to herself.

Perhaps Larry had called his office?

She went over to a sideboard that sat along one wall and picked up the telephone. She dialled his office.

"No, sorry, Mrs Gainsborough," said the young male aide called Barry at the other end, "but Mister Gainsborough has not called in. He should be back by now and we don't know where he is. Do you think he's alright?"

"Yes," said Shirley, trying to sound positive. "I'm sure there's a simple explanation. (*He's probably bonking Gail somewhere*). Could I speak to Gail please?"

"I'm afraid she's not here either, Mrs Gainsborough. She took a couple of days leave…" (*I'll bet she did*) "…and we've not heard from her either. It's most irregular. There's a report to go in to committee, the PM wants it, and, well, I don't know…"

Shirley cut across him. "Yes, thank you, Barry. If Larry calls in, will you let me know please?"

"Of course, Mrs Gainsborough."

Shirley hung up. *I bet he's with Gail!* Shirley might know about her husband's bit-on-the-side but he was not going to rub her nose in it, and this was really rubbing it! *Now, where's her address?*

Shirley went upstairs and then up again by a purpose-built staircase that wound up onto a small landing. They'd had the roof space converted into an office for Larry some time ago. It was his office and inner sanctum.

Shirley grasped the door handle to the office, pushed, and stepped forwards at the same time. But instead of opening the door she walked smack into it. She stepped back and glared at the door. It was obviously locked.

Bloody locked! Now she got annoyed. She kicked the door. It didn't budge. Then, with her temper flaring she took a deep breath and kicked it harder. With a splintering of wood the lock broke free of the door surround and the door was flung open.

Shirley marched straight over to Larry's desk. He was just old-fashioned enough to have a leather-bound organiser diary and address book, which he kept on the top of his desk.

Still in a temper, she sat down and leafed through the pages of the address section, slapping the pages over, until she found Gail's name, address and telephone number. Angrily, she snatched up the extension phone on the desk top and dialled Gail's number. No answer.

Damn! She tore the page out of the organiser and marched out of the office.

She checked her watch. Her eldest son was aged sixteen. A good sensible boy who could be relied upon. The kids weren't due to finish school for about three hours so she sent her son a text telling him that she had to go out and would he take charge of the rest of the children until she got back. She added a couple of kisses to the text and ran down the staircases. At the bottom of the stairs she grabbed her keys off the hall table and tore out of the house. She ran to the garage and got into her car. She fired up the Ferrari F430 and roared out onto the road, heading for Epping, and Gail's flat.

*****

EPPING - ESSEX

Gail Wetton was not in, or at least she was not answering the doorbell.
Wetton owned a ground floor one-bedroom flat with a red front door and a cat flap. The door also had a letter flap which Shirley lifted to peer inside. No movement.
Shirley put her mouth to the letter hole and shouted, "Larry! Are you in there?"
No answer. No movement.
Shirley battered on the door with a fist.
A neighbouring door came open and an elderly man with a ring of white hair around his head and carpet slippers on his feet said, "Excuse me. Are you looking for someone?"
Shirley turned to the man and composed herself. "I'm looking for Miss Wetton. She works with my husband."
The man frowned and thought for a bit. Should he trust this woman? Why not? She had, after all, given the correct name of the absent occupier. "Well," he said, making a decision. "You've got the right address, but she's not in."
Politely, Shirley asked, "How do you know?"
"Because I have her key."
"Oh! Why's that?"
The old man looked at her and leaned sideways into the door surround. "Because I feed her cat when she goes away."
"Oh." Shirley looked at the cat flap. "Please. Do you know where she's gone?...Miss Wetton that is...not the cat."
"I believe she went to Venice."
Venice! How romantic! I'll kill him! "Ah. Okay. Right. Thank you." Shirley was turning to walk away when the man said,
"Funny thing is, she's supposed to be back by now, and I haven't heard from her. She always lets me know when she gets back from

189

abroad…because of the cat, you see."

"Ye-es, I see," said Shirley. "Thank you very much." She gave the man a smile and walked off.

Where the hell are they? Shirley's anger began to dissipate as a nagging worry began to settle in the back of her head.

*****

Ketcher came around again. Very slowly. When was this nightmare going to stop?

Why don't they just fucking kill me?

But Intiqam did not want him dead, yet. He had something he had to perform for them.

Someone slapped his face a couple of times. It was supposed to revive him, but after all of the punishment that he had endured it had no more of an effect than that of a pesky fly landing on him. It neither created more pain or increased what he already had. Ketcher's senses were simply shot.

He was back in the torture chamber and he was back in the tubular steel-framed chair. Once again, he was naked. His hands were tied behind the chair with wire and his ankles were likewise bound to the chair's two front legs.

"Agent Ketcher?" There was that voice again. That calm, terrifying voice.

With a supreme effort of will Ketcher lifted his head. His one good eye focussed on and then stared at al-Makira, who said,

"I appreciate that you do not like me. But I would like you to know that I am most impressed at your powers of endurance. Most men would be dead by now.

"I am also convinced that you do not know who the agent known as Frank Cross is, or who Sir Michael Corrigan is, or their where-abouts. If you had known, I am sure you would have told me."

Ketcher's muddled brain thought, *perhaps they're going to let me go?*

"However, despite not being able to help me with the information I require, there is something you can do for me…Bring her in." This last order was given to his Second-in-Command.

The SiC left the room for a few moments, when he returned it was with two other men who were dressed in the same army fatigues as al-Makira and the SiC. The two men dragged Gail Wetton between them into the room.

Gail and Larry had not spent long in their detention in Venice. In fact they were removed from it the following day.

They were kept separate and drugged unconscious, after which they were placed into black body-bags, the type used to transfer corpses, except these had small breathing holes along the sides. They were then taken by boat to one of the remote outlying islands of the Venetian lagoon where they were bundled into a stripped-out Airbus EC130 passenger helicopter. The helicopter took the body-bags to Treviso airport, because it is not as busy as Marco Polo, and there they were transferred, still in the body-bags, to a private jet that was owned by Intiqam but registered to a private company that did not exist.

From Treviso the Right Honourable Lawrence Gainsborough MP and Miss Gail Wetton were flown, still unconscious, to the city of Mosul in Northern Iraq. In Mosul they were administered more drugs to keep them under and then they were transferred to the Bell Huey that took them to the village of Qaryat Musawara where they had been placed in separate buildings.

Through all of this Larry knew nothing of the whereabouts of his girlfriend, because al-Makira did not want Larry to know. He needed Larry to remain compliant and the threat of physical violence to Wetton was doing just that. And that was because Lawrence Gainsborough MP was the prize, the bargaining chip, rather than Wetton.

Upon being brought into the room with Ketcher, Gail Wetton could barely stand. She was still in the pink dress that she had been wearing when she had arrived at Marco Polo airport with Larry, except that now it was filthy and about six inches of the stitching had come undone below her right armpit. Her jacket had been removed and thrown away some time ago. The belt she had been wearing around her waist was also gone as were her shoes so that she was barefoot and both her feet and lower legs were dirty. Her long blonde hair was tousled and filthy and she had dirty marks on her face and bare arms.

Wetton took one look at Agent Ketcher slumped naked, bound and beaten, in his chair and she screamed.

Gail's scream cut through Ketcher's muddled thoughts like a knife. His head came up and he stared at her through his one good eye. He did not know it but he had lost the sight in his other one and the skin around this blind eye was now massively swollen. His nose was so broken it had almost ceased to exist and his right cheek was blackened with bruising. In fact, his face was so beaten that he looked like something from a Victorian freak show. His hair was matted and in dis-array and his breath wheezed in and out of his mouth in which two teeth had been broken. But he had reacted to a woman's scream, and the chivalrous male that dwelt inside of him made him sit up straighter.

Al-Makira watched Ketcher's body-language and smiled with satisfaction. He approached Ketcher. "We are going to make a little film, you and I. Yes?"

Ketcher said nothing. *What's coming now?*

"If you co-operate no harm will come to this lovely creature." Al-Makira turned and waved his left hand at Gail. "If you do not co-operate, I will have her stripped and beaten and turned over to my men, and they can do what they like with her. I am sure they would like to take turns at such a nice, leggy, western blonde."

Gail gasped and wriggled in the grip of the two men that held her arms. "No!" she cried. "No! Please! No!"

Al-Makira walked over to her and produced a long knife from a sheath on the belt at his hip. He smiled at her then nodded to the two men. They pulled at her arms by her shoulders so that she came to stand upright on the balls of her feet with her chest pushing forwards. They were holding her pinned so tightly that she could not wriggle without inflicting pain into her shoulder joints, so she kept still as she stared with horror at al-Makira's knife.

Al-Makira put the tip of the blade at the top of Gail's cleavage and then cut down, being careful not to touch her skin, which was not easy as her chest was heaving in panic. The blade parted the material of her dress as if it were tissue paper. He kept the knife edge moving down until he had sliced through about twelve inches of material and then he took the knife away. The dress fell away each side of the cut revealing her upper chest and a pink lace bra.

"No!" she screamed. "Do what they want! Please do as he says! Please!"

Al-Makira looked at her bra and her heaving breasts beneath the lace and smiled. "Very nice," he said. The two men holding her were grinning lasciviously.

Gail's breath was coming out of her mouth in little gasps.

Al-Makira licked the tip of his index finger on his left hand and then ran it down Gail's cleavage. "Yes, very nice." He put the knife away.

"Please!" Despite the pain it gave to her shoulder joints Gail twisted in the men's arms. She cried out to Ketcher. "Do what he wants! Please!"

"So," said al-Makira as he turned away from her and back to Ketcher. "Shall we make our little film now?"

It was then that Ketcher became aware of the equipment in the room. A few feet in front of him, mounted on a tripod, was a Sony movie camera with a microphone mounted to the front of it. A man in the same terrorist army fatigues moved into position behind the camera. Either side of the camera were spotlights, also mounted on tripods although not yet turned on.

"Now, I am afraid you have a few lines to say." Al-Makira produced a sheet of folded paper from an inside pocket of his jacket. He waved the paper at Ketcher. "You do not have to learn them; you just have to read them out. I am sure you will give a good performance. Yes? Like a big Hollywood actor. Yes? Like Clint Eastwood, or Robert De Niro." He laughed.

Ketcher did not laugh.

"So, here are your lines Agent Ketcher. You will say your name and then you will say, "This message is for Sir Michael Corrigan. Intiqam is holding your wife here at Qaryat Musawara. We also have Lawrence Gainsborough MP and Miss Gail Wetton. Send Frank Cross here in exchange for them. We are also holding his girlfriend. If you do not send Cross to us by this time next week then the hostages will be filmed being publicly executed…"

Gail's cry interrupted al-Makira. "No!" she shouted. "No! Don't kill me! Please!"

Al-Makira ignored her and continued, "You will then hold the sheet of paper up to the camera. I have written today's date and time on it. You can do that, can't you. Easy. Yes? Have you got that?"

Al-Makira stared into Ketcher's face as Gail began to sob. Much against his will Agent Ketcher agreed with a nod of his head and said, "Okay."

"Good," said al-Makira. "Now, get her out of here." Gail was dragged out crying and pleading for her life.

"D-Don't…hu-rtt herrr," gasped Ketcher.

"Don't worry," said al-Makira. "She will come to no harm as long as you do what you are told." He rubbed his hands together. "Let us now make our movie. Yes?" Al-Makira loved making movies.

*****

In an old barn to the north of North Weald Bassett north of Epping, and to the west of Tyler's Green in the English county of Essex, Lady Corrigan was sitting in an old grey armchair. The chair had seen better days; it was grubby and some of the old horse-hair stuffing was coming out of the back of it. It was positioned in the middle of the barn.

Lady Corrigan had come around slowly from the chloroform feeling a little giddy. She had quickly closed her eyes and allowed herself to sleep off the rest of the effects. Now she was awake again and was surreptitiously taking stock of herself and surroundings.

She had all of her clothes on, the ones that she had been wearing when she left for the gym, and this included her fleece. But she was barefoot and had her ankles, knees and wrists tied together with stout white cord and she had a piece of grey duct tape over her mouth. She was also tied to the chair by the same type of cord that was wound around her wrist bindings and it went down to a cross-member between the two front chair legs. It meant that in the unlikely event that she could get her legs and ankles free and managed to make a run for it she'd be dragging the chair behind her. She gently moved her head left and then right. She could not see anyone, but she could hear voices somewhere behind her. She moved her head more freely as she looked around.

The barn was a large one with a cracked concrete floor and a peg-tiled roof. The roof was held up by a system of huge blackened cross beams that gave her the impression that she was inside the upturned hull of an ancient sailing ship or galleon. There were big cobwebs up there in the dingy darkness.

The lower parts of the walls were made of brick and within them were the same kind of black beams as the roof. These beams were set vertically every few feet and had horizontal woodwork nailed to them on the outside. There were no windows but she was facing a large double door that was a few yards in front of her and was pulled shut. She could see daylight through the gaps in the woodwork and around the edges of the door. Red decided that the barn must be a few hundred years old, and in other circumstances might even seem attractive. It was probably the kind of barn that got converted into trendy living accommodation, and probably had a preservation order on it.

She heard some movement behind her and then some footsteps. A few seconds later a man walked around in front of her and stood facing her with his hands folded across the belt buckle of his jeans. Smiling, he looked down at her.

A voice behind her called out, "How is she, Ali?"

First mistake thought Lady Corrigan. *Never let a hostage know your name.* The question had been asked in a heavily accented guttural voice. The owner of the voice was called Fazil, although Lady Corrigan did not know that of course. He was also the leader of the kidnap team.

"She is awake," said the man in front of her. He had the same kind of accent.

Lady Corrigan glowered at him.

"She does not seem to be very happy."

The man behind Red laughed. "No, my brother, I am sure she is not."

Red growled a curse at him from behind the duct tape.

The man called Ali put out his left hand and lifted some of her hair, letting it fall through his fingers as he smiled at her. "You have very beautiful hair, Lady Corrigan."

Red snatched her head to one side.

"Still as wild as when we grabbed you, eh? Well, you can be tamed. You will find that out."

Red growled again.

"Oh, and by the way," said the man. "We took your mobile phone out of your fleece. Just in case you decided to call someone…like your husband, Sir Michael." He produced the phone from a pocket in the back of his jeans and wiggled it at her. "And, if you think you can be tracked with it, we have turned it off." He grinned.

Lady Corrigan kept quiet.

The man behind her came and joined his partner and said to him, "You talk too much." Then he leaned forward and, without warning, he slapped Red's face. Tears sprang to her eyes, although not because it hurt. These were tears of anger and frustration; frustration at not being able to punch the man in the face.

"You behave, Lady fucking Corrigan," hissed Fazil, "or you will get worse than that." He rubbed the front of his crotch with his right hand to emphasis the point. Then, laughing, he walked away.

*****

LONDON – EARLY EVENING

"Well, where the hell is he?" demanded the British Prime Minister down the phone from Number Ten. "I need that report from Gainsborough. He's the one with all the bloody answers!"

"I'm very sorry, Prime Minister, but we can't trace him. He seems to have disappeared."

"Disappeared, Barry? Disappeared?"

"Sorry, Prime Minister."

"Find him, Barry. Find him!"

The PM hung up, leaving Barry staring at the handset.

Where on earth was Lawrence Gainsborough and Gail Wetton?

*****

Al-Makira was taking a call on a new mobile phone whilst pacing up and down the room he was in. He was being informed of the abduction of Lady Corrigan. Al-Makira was sure that by holding Lady Corrigan as a hostage Sir Michael would comply with whatever Intiqam demanded of the knight and director of the SOU.

However, once again, al-Makira was hearing that the operation had not gone smoothly.

"What do you mean," he growled, "someone filmed you?"

There was a short pause as Fazil hesitated. He swallowed, then said, "There was a girl. On a motorbike."

"And she filmed you?"

"Yes, al-Makira. On her phone. There was nothing we could do."

"Yes, there was, you fool!" snapped Al-Makira. "You could have killed her. It's called *getting rid of witnesses*, you stupid idiot!"

Swallowing this insult, Fazil said rather reluctantly, "There is something else, al-Makira."

"What?"

"The film is…well it's…now on the television."

Al-Makira's temper boiled and he only just stopped himself from throwing this second phone at the wall. "On television? You fucking idiot!"

"It was un-avoidable. We…"

"Never mind that now!" He was fed up of hearing this man's excuses. The next time he met him he would shoot him. "Have the British police traced the car you used?"

"Yes..." Fazil raced ahead before al-Makira could swear again. "...But we dumped the car, set fire to it and transferred to another."

"Has Lady Corrigan been harmed?"

"No..." The kidnapper went to speak further, to tell his commanding officer that she was anything but a passive victim, that she had fought like a wild thing, and that they had had to sedate her, but al-Makira cut him off.

"Good. See that she remains that way. Where is Lady Corrigan now?"

Fazil's voice became ingratiating. "We have her somewhere safe, al-Makira."

"Where?"

"We are in a barn in some countryside near the pick-up point. It's in North Weald. It's in Essex."

Al-Makira growled again. "I know where North Weald is, you fool!" He tightened a fist then continued, "It may take a couple of days to get some transport to you. We have a helicopter outside Paris that I can get to you. Can you look after Lady Corrigan for two days?"

"Yes. But..."

"Good. I'll get back to you...and no-one, like no-one, is to leave that barn. Do you understand?"

"What if the police should find us?"

"In that case shoot Lady Corrigan, and use suicide vests for yourselves."

The kidnap team leader swallowed awkwardly. He had just been given the death penalty if he screwed this up.

"Do you understand me?"

"Yes, al-Makira."

"Good." Al-Makira ended the call. He called in his Second-in-Command. "Irfan, is the television set still working?"

"Yes, my Brother."

"I want to see the world news." The SiC went off to retrieve the only TV set that they owned. However, before Irfan left the room al-Makira gave him another order,

"And I want the girlfriend of Frank Cross grabbed right away. No more fucking delays!"

*****

LAS VEGAS

As the British Prime Minister fretted so the world turned.

In Las Vegas Frank looked at his Shadows team. It was night-time and they were all assembled in Frank's hotel room. Apart from T Bone and Errol they were all dressed in black cargo trousers, black T shirts, lightweight black jackets, black socks and black trainers. T Bone and Errol were outfitted differently as part of Frank's plan was that they had to appear more casually dressed so as not to alert the kidnappers to their real purpose. To that end, T Bone was wearing an open-necked blue check short-sleeved shirt, brown cargo shorts, but with the same black ankle socks and black trainers. Errol was wearing brown open-toed sandals with long beige shorts, and a white T shirt under a red and white checked shirt which he wore with the buttons undone.

Frank ran his eyes over the team. "Right," he began. "Before we go, we leave our phones here." He did not want a mobile going off if they wanted to keep silent, and would sound shrill in the concrete confines of a parking lot. The phones were duly collected and placed in the drawer of Frank's bedside cabinet.

"Okay," said Frank. "You all know what you're doing?"

There was a chorus of "Yes, boss", Boss being Frank's designated title on any of their missions.

"Any last questions?"

"No, boss."

Weapons and equipment had been checked, double checked and then checked again. Each man carried a hold-all with his gear inside, except for Errol, who was carrying a briefcase.

"Right then. Let's go."

The Shadows left the room. They were going into action. They were going to try and rescue Diana Moon, and this was not going to be easy.

*****

JAPAN – 16 HOURS IN FRONT OF LAS VEGAS

Kimonos were what Tandy and Sensei Nakamura wore at breakfast, lunch and the evening meal, all of which were taken in the same room in Sensei's Hagakure, and he would not permit any of his students to come unchanged and unwashed to his meal times.

This was lunch time. Tandy had been practicing her kata all morning and once again they were sitting cross-legged opposite each other at the low dining table. Tandy had finished her traditional Japanese bowl of plain steamed rice, a bowl of miso soup, a bowl of grilled fish, and a cup of green tea. The bowls and the tea cup (with no handle) were all of hand-thrown pottery, coloured in pastel shades and bearing exquisite abstract designs and patterns. Tandy had learned from this that not only should a meal be pleasing but that the crockery and utensils should also give pleasure to the user. It did away with the western fashion of just chomping down a meal off a boring plain white china plate.

Nor were any of the meals too heavy, as Sensei Nakamura had adapted them to Tandy's appetite. However, because they were training hard, it was essential that Tandy consume foodstuffs that would give her a balanced diet for her body to use. It was true that the sight of the grilled fish had not exactly tempted her, but she did not want to offend the sensei who, so far, had prepared all of her meals, meals that they had taken together. However, once she started to eat the fish she discovered that it had been cooked to perfection and was delicious.

Tandy finished her meal and placed her chopsticks on the table alongside her empty bowls. There are certain rules to be observed when using chopsticks: you never, ever, stick them vertically into your bowl of food, because chopsticks are only ever placed this way in a bowl of rice at the altar at a funeral, and you must never use them to point with or to pass food to another pair of chopsticks. Chopstick-to-chopstick is only ever used to pass fragments of cremated bone into an urn.

Tandy looked across the low table to the sensei and said, "*Oishii.*" Delicious.

The sensei smiled. "Arigato."

There was a slight pause, and then Tandy said, "Sensei Nakamura?"

"Hai?"

"Will you teach me how to cook like you, please?"

The sensei's eyebrows lifted. "You want to cook Japanese?"

"Hai. *Onegai shimass.*" Yes. Please.

The sensei's eyebrows went higher. "Ohh. Onegai shimass?"

She nodded once and briskly. "Hai!"

The sensei frowned a little, so that Tandy thought he was going to refuse. But then he nodded. "Okay. We do cooking, after training. Hai?"

"Hai." Tandy smiled widely.

There was a pause, and then Tandy asked, "Sensei, is there a member of staff here with us at Hagakure? Someone extra in the grounds, maybe?"

"Ahh," breathed Sensei Nakamura, and he nodded sagely as he put down his chopsticks. "So, you sense it too? Ve-ry good…No staff member…We are being watched."

"What?" she blurted out with her face showing.

The sensei's eyebrows went up.

"Oh, I apologise my sensei. Watched. By whom?"

Sensei Nakamura shook his head. "Not know. But we find out soon."

"Really?"

"Hai. Person bound to show up. They are a bit crumbry."

Tandy frowned at "crumbry", and then got it. "Oh, you mean clumsy."

The sensei smiled at the correction. "Hai…Crumbry." He nodded briskly. "Right now, we ignore. They are of no consekw…consaqu…"

"Consequence?" Offered Tandy.

"Hai. Concretense. Now we get changed. We train. Hai?"

"Hai!"

They therefore stood, bowed, and did the washing up before getting changed into their gis before the next bout of training. Today, Tandy would be learning how to use the jo staff herself.

*****

T Bone entered the vast MGM Grand ground floor parking lot that fronted onto Tropicana Avenue; it was 9.30pm and 28 Centigrade. It was dark outside, although it never gets really dark on and around the Strip because of the huge amount of neon lighting that floods the city. However, there were strip lights on in the garage where large parking bays were laid out in multiple lines, bays that were taken up all around him by all types and models of vehicles. The floor was black tarmac under a white but grubby concrete ceiling that formed the floor to the deck above. There were the usual pipes and conduits common to this kind of structure running up and across the pillars and ceiling.

T Bone was carrying his own hold-all and he was humming loudly to himself. He went straight to his SUV where he'd left it after he had checked into the hotel. T Bone did not look around him, he simply walked up to the car, blipped it, and got in. It was parked between a white utility van on his left and a blue Ford Mustang on his right. The front of the SUV was facing the drive-lane. He dumped his hold-all into the passenger's foot-well; as this was an American car the passenger's side was to the right. T Bone leaned across and unzipped the hold-all. Inside it were his weapons, ammunition, a red plastic First Aid box and a road map, which he took out and made something of a play of studying. He left the hold-all unzipped.

T Bone was wearing an ear-piece that looked like an I-Pod and a throat-mike that had been designed to look like a silver Saint Christopher piece of jewellery. In fact all of the group would by now be wearing the same bits of technology instead of cheek-mikes and full-on ear-pieces which would have looked suspicious – especially to the kidnappers.

T Bone had hummed aloud to make it seem that he was humming along to a tune on the I-Pod. Now his lips moved as he spoke quietly with the mike picking up his vocals. On his way to the car, he had seen three men at various points around the garage and he was surreptitiously keeping an eye on their locations. He explained this to Frank who was walking slowly along Tropicana Avenue with Errol and heading towards the garage. Frank picked up the words in his own ear-piece.

"Roger Roger," said Frank quietly, but also using and punning T Bone's first name.

"Very funny," growled T Bone.

Frank grinned, stopped walking, and looked at Errol. "T Bone's in position."

T Bone would not speak again unless it was absolutely necessary. He wound down the driver's and the passenger's windows.

A few minutes later Frank and Errol came up to the entrance of the parking lot. It was 9.40pm.

They stopped walking and Frank turned to Errol.

"Right, Errol, tell me again what you have to do."

"Okay, Frank." Errol took a deep breath. "I let you go in and at nine fifty-five I go into the lot, stand in the middle of the lot and call out *I am Errol Moon, is anybody here?* Then I wait for the kidnappers and I ask to see

Diana."

"Very good," confirmed Frank. He put his hand on Errol's shoulder. "Remember, don't hand over the briefcase until you have Diana."

"Right." Errol, not surprisingly, sounded nervous.

Frank looked at the man. "Are you sure you still want to do this, Errol?"

Errol swallowed. "Yes, Frank. I want my daughter back."

"Okay, but also remember, she's probably not here, we are going to have to grab one of these guys to make them tell us where she is."

"Okay." Errol didn't sound OK.

"You'll be fine," said Frank. "Just remember to try and get beside or near a big vehicle like a van or a truck or a large SUV so that you can get behind some decent cover if the bullets start flying." It wasn't exactly the most encouraging of speeches, but it was at least the truth.

"Where will you be?" asked Errol.

"Don't worry about that," replied Frank. "I'll be able to see you, but you won't be able to see me." He patted Errol on a shoulder and smiled. "That's why we're called Shadows."

Errol nodded. This was scary. He tried to smile back, but he was so nervous that he was almost shaking.

While Frank had been talking to Errol, Tommo and Clonk had moved into their pre-planned positions: Tommo had walked along Tropicana Avenue some yards in front of Frank until he came to the corner of Tropicana and Koval Lane with the end of the garage block on his left. Here he turned left into Koval Lane and continued walking past the end of the garage block. When he was almost past the end of the garage he entered the parking lot through an archway, and then he hunkered down behind a big Toyota four-by-four. He put a finger the size of a large banana to his throat-mike and tapped it twice. The taps were a pre-arranged call sign and meant, "Tommo. I'm in."

Tommo heard two taps come back to him as Frank acknowledged him by tapping his own throat-mike.

Clonk had turned off Tropicana Ave and had walked into Audrie Street. He walked along Audrie Street and around the back of the parking garage which was flanked by tall palm trees. Further along the road on the left was the MGM Grand Conference Centre, however, Clonk did not need to walk that far because half-way along the parking-lot was another entrance into the building and he stepped inside and moved into the darkness behind the

parked cars. Clonk was three taps.
Tap-Tap-Tap.
Reply, Tap-Tap-Tap.
"Right." Frank checked his watch then turned to Errol. "Clonk and Tommo are in position. Time for me to go." He turned and clapped Errol once more on his shoulder. "You'll be fine."

Frank went in the front of the building on the Tropicana Avenue side. He walked purposely as if he were heading for a car. He approached some stairs that led up to his left through some broken shadows and suddenly he had disappeared.

*****

MI5 and MI6 were on full alert. It was late at night and the Prime Minister had called the heads of both security services in to see him for an emergency meeting at number 10, Downing Street. The Environment Secretary, the Right Honourable Lawrence Gainsborough MP was missing, as was his personal assistant Miss Gail Wetton. Gainsborough's wife had been contacted and she too was worried for her husband's safety.

The security services had started digging. Agents from MI5 had entered Wetton's flat and found a scribble pad with the details of the flight from the London Dockland airport she had booked, together with a note of the name of the hotel. It was confirmed when they hacked into her computer.

Where were they going?
The Hotel San Gallo. Venice.

*****

Tandy bowed to the sensei who returned the action. They were both holding a jo. Sensei Nakamura's jo was a deep red colour, whereas Tandy's was almost bone white. His was red oak and hers was white oak. The sensei was holding his staff half-way along its length in his right hand and vertical to the floor.

"Before fight with jo, must get used to it. Get used to weight. Get used to it in hand. Do not grip hard, grip soft. Hai?"

"Hai."

"Re-wax wrist. Move jo from wrist, not arm or erbow." He allowed the higher tip of the jo to move forward and to the right, then he allowed it to dip down, revolving and turning his wrist so that, what was the top the staff, now swung around to the left sweeping across and above the floor, which meant that the other end came up to his right. Keeping the movement going he turned his wrist some more and brought the end that was now nearest the floor up and around to the right before turning his wrist again to take the end of the jo down and around to the floor again.

"Observe," said the sensei as the jo made a pattern in the air. "Ends of jo traver in a figure of…a figure of…*hachi*…"

"Eight," said Tandy. "A figure of eight."

"Hai. Figure eight!" He nodded as he twirled the jo. "You copy. You try."

Tandy grasped the staff and held it out as the master had done.

"Remember Tandy, do not grip hard."

Tandy smiled and relaxed her grip. She thought of the word re-wax, and smiled some more. She started to move the jo, letting it almost roll in her palm and fingers.

Slowly she let the jo roll, allowing the balanced weight of it to take it down and around and back up, rolling her wrist, keeping it moving.

"Good. Keep jo moving, but do faster," said the sensei and he began to speed up.

Tandy followed him. The jo in the sensei's hand started to part the air with a sound similar to that of helicopter blades whumping. Tandy's began to do the same, and then suddenly her staff was spinning out of her hand and cartwheeling across the room to land with a loud clatter on the wooden dojo floor.

Sensei Nakamura kept his going. It was now making a deep roaring noise, like a great wind pouring through a cave. Tandy watched in astonishment as the jo became a complete blur, almost becoming invisible. If anyone had stepped in to grab the jo they almost certainly would have lost their fingers or had their arm shattered.

And, just like that, the sensei stopped.

"Wow!" said Tandy. She gave some small applause.

Sensei Nakamura bowed. "Is practice."

"I'm afraid I dropped mine."

"Ha. Grip went soft. Force of movement tear jo out of your hand. Get jo. Try again."

Tandy went and retrieved her staff and the morning was taken up with Tandy learning not only this whirling technique in her right hand but also her left. She was shown how to pass the moving staff from one hand to another, and when she had got the hang of all that the sensei started to show her how to block and strike with the weapon; because that's what a jo staff is – a very formidable weapon.

*****

Out on Tropicana Avenue Errol Moon rubbed his sweaty hands together, looked up at the clear black night sky and muttered a prayer. Then he checked his watch. 9.55pm.

He walked, with his heart thumping so hard in his chest he could hear it, into the parking-lot. He looked around. There was no sign of Frank or any of the others.

Oh God, please make this work!

He moved a few steps forward then stopped, blinking to adjust his eyes to the half-light of the parking-lot. It was as warm down here as it had been outside. Shafts of different coloured bright neon lighting came in from the street and were interrupted by the shapes of the various parked vehicles. Mixed with the garage's rather inefficient strip lights the outside neon caused two-dimensional angular shadows to be thrown in the semi-gloom across the walls and tarmac floor – and Errol realised why the kidnappers had chosen this place at this time of day – the bad lighting and shadows were confusing to the eye. A perfect place for an ambush – or robbery.

A car reversed out of a parking space a few yards in front of him and on his right. Errol felt like his heart was going to come into his mouth. He stopped walking.

Was this them?

Errol's mouth went dry.

The car pulled into the drive-lane area with its rear-end towards him. Then it pulled away with a slight squeal of its tyres and drove out of the lot at a far exit.

Errol hugged the briefcase to his chest and continued walking until he had gone a good distance into the parking area and stopped. Standing in the middle of the drive-lane he summoned up his courage.

"I'm Errol Moon! Is anybody here?"

The words echoed back from the concrete.

Silence.

"I'm Errol Moon, Diana's father!"

Silence.

This was not what Errol had expected. Were the kidnappers even here? Was this all just some sick joke?

Errol started to get annoyed.

"Listen, you bastards, I'm here like you asked!"

In the shadow of a stairwell, which was forward from Errol and on his left, Frank smiled to himself. *Go for it Errol!*

Frank now held his revolver in his right hand and his assault rifle was slung over his right shoulder. The suppressors had already been attached back in his hotel room.

Errol called out again. "If you're not here, I'm going to go!"

There was the sound of two car doors slamming shut. The noise came from the far end of the parking lot, away to Frank's left. Errol was still to Frank's right although Frank could not see him because the line of parked cars beside him was obstructing his view.

After the slamming doors came silence.

"Okay!" shouted Errol. "Fuck you then!"

Silence. Then...

"We hear you, Mister Moon."

Frank's head came up. That voice had an Arabic accent. But which direction had it come from? Left? Yes, left.

The car at the far end started up.

Then footsteps. One set of footsteps.

Was this one of the kidnappers or a car owner?

The footsteps kept coming.

If it was one of the kidnappers, where are the others? T Bone had reported that there were possibly three of them down here.

Frank heard the sound of someone running along the street behind him. They ran on in the direction of Tropicana Avenue, and the front entrance to the car-park.

The car that had started up drove out of the lot but away from where Errol was standing.

The footsteps kept coming from Frank's left, the foot-falls getting louder. Frank kept still. Then a figure, the man who was making the foot-falls, moved slowly from the left into Frank's field of vision. He was carrying a gun, a Glock, in his right hand, held down near his hip.

Definitely one of the kidnappers.

Where were the other two?

In the Jeep Grand Cherokee T Bone watched a second man move towards him from somewhere to the right of the black SUV and come forward. The man was in jeans and a black shirt and he crept slowly towards the front of the Jeep. Could this be one of the kidnappers? Or was it just an inquisitive by-stander who had heard all the shouting?

T Bone continued reading his map as the man came level with the front of the car. The man stopped and threw a glance at T Bone, who ignored him and continued to study the map in his hands.

The man moved on. He had a pistol in his right hand. OK, not an innocent by-stander.

T Bone took his suppressed Sig Sauer semi-automatic out of the hold-all and then eased the SUV's door open. He stepped down out of the big vehicle and hunkered down beside the front right-hand wheel of the white van leaving the SUV's door open behind him.

The man in front of Frank stopped. He was facing Errol from about twenty feet away.

The man that T Bone was following stopped and moved to the left.

The man in front of Frank, spoke up, "Is the money in the briefcase?" he demanded. Again, that Arabic accent.

Off to Frank's right Errol answered, "Yes. Where is my daughter?"

"She is safe."

"Where is she?"

"I told you, she is safe." The man sounded petulant.

The man took a step forward, it placed him under a light.

Bloody amateur, thought Frank. But it gave Frank the chance to have a good look at him. He was thin and angular and about thirty years old. About five-feet-six-inches tall, clean-shaven but swarthy with close-cropped jet-black hair.

"Give me the money!" the man demanded.

"Not until I see my daughter."

Frank had to hand it to Errol, he had balls.

"If you do not give me the money, I will have your daughter killed!"

Errol shouted, "She's not here is she? You bastard!" The parking-lot echoed with his anger. "She's not here! You're trying to double-cross me!"

"Give me the fucking money!" The gun came up in the man's hand. Errol Moon was about to be shot for a briefcase full of non-existent cash.

Frank sighted and fired; the suppressor closing down the bang so that it sounded like a loud thud, like a fist hitting a watermelon, with the sound echoing off all this concrete.

Frank's accuracy with a gun had earned him the reputation of being an exceptional marksman – if he could see a target, he could hit it. The hollow point 9mm bullet hit the kidnapper in the right side of his head just in front of his ear. It penetrated his skull and exited the left side of his head in a spray of blood, bone and brains.

At the sound of the suppressed gunshot Errol knew he had to get behind a car, but this was all happening so quickly and he was a musician, not a member of the Special Forces. He was still turning to hide as the man in front of T Bone saw his partner-in-crime, heard the suppressed shot and, at the same instant, saw his partner get kicked sideways by the impact of the bullet. This second man brought his gun up, his right arm straightening as he aimed it at Errol.

In one flowing movement T Bone stood up and brought his gun to bear on his target and fired; a double tap. Two rounds hit the man in the back and his chest pushed forwards as the bullets tore out of his frontal ribs. He went down in a dive to the floor and sprawled lifeless and face-down onto the tarmac.

Errol dived and landed heavily on his right side between two parked cars, dropping the briefcase which slid away from him but towards the far end of one of the parked cars.

Frank quickly checked his area then moved away, stealthily, getting behind a large white Chrysler hatch-back. He saw that Errol had taken cover.

T Bone ducked down and back into a space between two parked vehicles; gun up.

Where was that third kidnapper?

Suddenly, a figure came sprinting in from beyond the car where Errol was hiding, which put him to the right of Frank; this must have been the running man and he must have made his way around the outside of the garage to get him past Frank to put him in his current position. As T Bone stood up and stepped out onto the drive-path he brought his gun onto the running target. He got the impression that this guy was quite tall and broad-shouldered but before he could take the shot the man had made it to Errol and he ducked behind Errol's covering car, out of sight. The man bent down, grabbed one of his Errol's ankles, and heaved. With a cry of despair and fear Errol was being dragged out from his place of cover; he grabbed around the back of a tyre at the back-end of the car and hung on.

Still bending over, the man dropped Errol's legs, stared down at Errol and growled, "Where is the fucking money?" And then his eyes shifted and he spotted the briefcase lying on the floor just beyond the prone Mr Moon.

He stepped over Errol and grabbed the briefcase. He opened it and stared at the empty interior. His top lip curled but he made no noise; he simply turned towards Errol and aimed his gun at him.

Frank Cross fired once and the bullet whipped between the two cars that were either side of Errol and the kidnapper and hit the kidnapper in the side of his neck just below his right ear lobe. He cried out as his head pulled over and he went down.

Frank walked up to the end of the car and looked down at the man who was now lying on the floor on his back beside Errol in the dark space between the two vehicles that was sheltering them. Blood was beginning to pool under the dead man's head. Frank turned his attention to Errol who had let go of the tyre and was gaping up at Frank in astonishment.

"Wha...?" said Errol.

"Are you okay, Errol?"

Errol manoeuvred so that he was lying on the floor with his back against the car's hubcap. "Yeah...Yes...Is he?" He pointed at the body.

"Dead? Oh yes. He was going to kill you."

"I know...Jesus! But what a shot. It's so dark down here. How could you see?"

"I make sure that I eat all of my carrots," said Frank. He smiled. Then he squatted down and looked at Errol. "Well," said Frank. "I'm afraid that's torn it. Now that they're all dead. The plan was to take one of these guys alive and then persuade him to tell us. I didn't figure that they'd panic and start shooting so early. With them all dead we have no way of finding out now where your daughter is being held."

Errol sadly shook his head. How were they ever going to rescue his daughter now?

"Don't worry," said Frank, trying to sound positive. "Something's bound to turn up. It always does when you're chasing bad guys." But he knew in reality that they did not have a hope in hell, and that Diana Moon was going to die.

Frank turned around and called out, "Hey, T Bone!"

"Over here," came the answer. T Bone ambled towards them. "Nice shooting, boss."

"Thanks," said Frank. He looked down at the dead man again and then around at the other two. "We'd better clear this mess up before someone calls the police." He spoke into his throat-mike. "Clonk, do you copy?"

"Here!" James Cameron's Scottish brogue called to them from a few feet away. He was walking towards them with the assault rifle cradled in his arms. "So, not quite to plan, eh? What you might call a bit of a balls-up. Now we'll never find out where they've got the lassie."

"Oh," a deep voice came out of the far darkness. "I wouldn't exactly say that, man."

Frank, T Bone and Clonk turned towards Tommo whose dark face and form was almost invisible in the gloom of the garage. The top of his head seemed to be almost touching the ceiling of the garage, and he was dragging along behind him what looked like a bundle of clothing with a pair of white training-shoes attached at the far end. A large rag doll perhaps?

Tommo walked up to them with a huge smile across his face. He effortlessly held up the rag doll in his left hand so that it dangled in the air about a foot above the floor.

It turned out to be a slightly-built girl aged about eighteen or nineteen. She had long black hair that was now tousled about her head and shoulders. She wore a beige army-style jacket that had the left-hand sleeve missing where it had been completely torn away at the shoulder, and a blue denim shirt that was pulled untidily out of the waistband of her knee-length black skirt. Under the skirt she was wearing black leggings that were filthy and which had a large hole torn over her right knee revealing a grazed and bloody kneecap. Her ensemble was finished off by the pair of scuffed white trainers. Her hands had been fastened behind her with a plastic cable tie and she was continually opening and closing and flexing her fingers that had long fingernails painted with black nail polish that matched her black lipstick. Tommo was holding her by the scruff of her jacket at the back of her neck and she was glaring at them all through made-up dark eyes with long lashes.

Clonk gave the girl a once-over look, then asked, "Who is she, and where the hell did you find her?"

"She was behind the wheel of a van parked back there." He jerked his head towards the rear of the building.

"Get-away driver?" asked Frank.

"Reckon so," said Tommo. "She was sitting there holding a gun over the top of the steering wheel."

"Bit obvious," said Frank. The comment made the girl glare at him even harder.

T Bone asked, "How did she get in that state, Tommo?"

"After I dragged her out of the van she got away, an' I had to chase her through some bushes," answered the giant. "An' she put up quite a fight." In fact, she'd had quite a surprise when Tommo had pulled open the door beside her, batted the gun out of her hand, and then grabbed her arm to haul her out of her seat. Landing on her feet she had quickly recovered from the shock of being seized by a giant and had managed to pull her arm out of Tommo's grasp. Suddenly free, she had taken off in a sprint, with Tommo hard on her heels.

Frank laughed. He was imagining the tussle when they had finally come together; like an alley cat caught by a bear. "I think you can put her down now."

"Oh, no, boss." Tommo shook his huge bald head. "She's better off like this. She's a bit of a wild one." He lifted his heavily muscled left arm to look at her as she hung from his fist. She turned the glare on the big man. "Yessir, quite a wildcat."

Frank walked over to her. "You know these men, don't you?" He indicated the two bodies that were in plain sight on the garage floor.

For an answer she spat at him, so her slapped her face.

"I'll take that as a yes," said Frank as he wiped the spittle off his jaw with his hand and then rubbed it down the front of her jacket. "Now listen. You know where they are keeping the girl and you are going to take us to them."

She pulled her upper lips back from her teeth in a silent snarl.

In fluent Arabic Frank suddenly said, "If you do not take us to the girl, I will kill you. Understand?" and he was satisfied to note that a flash of recognition ignited in her eyes.

She had understood him. So, Frank had been right. These kidnappers were from the Middle East.

She continued to snarl at him.

Frank gave an understanding nod of his head then walked away from her and back to where Errol was sitting concealed from view on the floor behind the car. He bent down so that the girl could not see his face and said very quietly to Errol, "I'm going to pull this guy part way out and I want you to grab the tops of his trousers and waggle his legs about when I aim my gun at him, and stop waggling when I fire. Got that?"

Errol gave Frank a nervous thumbs-up with both hands.

Frank stood up, he was about fifteen feet away from Tommo and the girl and he turned to look at her. He spoke to her in Arabic. "If you do not tell me where the girl is, I will kill this man here." He bent down again and pulled the dead man's lower legs clear from the end of the car.

The snarl disappeared from the rag doll's face.

Tommo, T Bone and Clonk were staring at Frank.

"So," said Frank to the rag doll. "Where's the girl?"

No answer.

Again, in Arabic Frank said, "I'll count to four, and if by then you haven't answered my question, I'll shoot him. So, if he dies it'll be your fault…One…"

No answer.

"Two."

No answer.

"Three."

No answer.

"Four!"

Frank held his arm out and aimed the gun at the body and Errol immediately began to move the dead legs about. Frank pulled the trigger and the legs stopped their dancing as the sound of the shot reverberated around the car-park. The girl's mouth came open in shock. She had no idea that the owner of the legs was already dead, and she assumed that Frank had just executed one of her team. Which is exactly what Frank wanted her to believe.

Frank wasn't finished yet. He bent down and shoved the feet and legs out of sight with his own foot and then he grabbed the collar of the dead man. The shot that he had just fired had hit the dead man in the head and had blown half of his skull away. Frank heaved the man out into the open and dumped him like a sack of bloody garbage onto the garage driveway. In the shadowy surrounds of the car-park it was not a pretty sight.

The girl's wrists twisted in their plastic grips behind her, she was clearly in distress and wanted to put her hands to her face. She was making small mewling sounds.

Frank walked up to her and shoved the business end of his gun's suppressor into her right eye.

"Now," he growled in his perfect Arabic. "Tell me where the girl is, or I'll blow your fucking brains out!"

*****

Agent Ketcher stared through his good eye at the camera lens that was aimed at him, he was visibly shaking, but not from cold because it was not cold in the room. Far from it. Ketcher's body was running with sweat. The shaking was due to the torture, both mental and physical, that he had endured, and his mind and body were now close to complete breakdown. So, he struggled to listen to his tormentors. He tried to concentrate. He tried desperately to hold it together and to do what he was being told to do. To save the life of Gail Wetton and to save her from being raped and executed.

"Now," breathed al-Makira into his right ear. "Let's try that again, shall we? And let's try and get it right this time. Yes?" Al-Makira came around to stand in front of Ketcher, and as he did so he waved Irfan, his Second-in-Command forwards to stand to the left of the chair. Irfan was holding a curved scimitar down to his right-hand side by its hilt in both hands.

Al-Makira cupped the agent's chin in his hand. "Get this right…Or you know what will happen to Miss Wetton. Yes?"

Al-Makira felt Ketcher's head move as he nodded his agreement.

"Good," said al-Makira. "Then…Action!" and he stepped to one side.

Two lights, positioned either side of the camera, came on and shone into Ketcher's face. The light was on him because he as was sitting in the metal-framed chair in front of the open window and this placed him in silhouette. With the lights on and shining into Ketcher's face the silhouette was negated. He was being filmed from the knees up, so that the people who would view this would know what he had gone through, and that al-Makira was serious in his threats.

Ketcher managed to get all of the prepared speech out with only a couple of stumbles, which al-Makira was prepared to overlook as he felt it gave gravitas to Ketcher's performance. When he had finished, Ketcher held up the piece of paper with the day's date and time written in large black figures on it.

It did not matter to al-Makira that he did not actually have either Lady Corrigan or Tandy Trudeau as his prisoners at the moment as he had claimed on the film. He would get them, of that, he was sure. What mattered was that the film went out into the internet so that the hated British would hear his demands and deliver him Frank Cross. Al-Makira was fed up of wasting any more time, so he was playing this bluff that he was sure would go his way.

Al-Makira stood beside the camera and smiled, pleased with the agent's performance. "Very good, Mister Ketcher," he said. "You are now finished. I think you get the Oscar, yes?"

The lights beside the camera were still on as Ketcher dropped the piece of paper to the floor and slumped exhausted in his chair. But the camera was still filming.

Al-Makira came around behind the agent. He placed his left hand gently on Ketcher's left shoulder which made Ketcher flinch.

"Calm yourself," said al-Makira in his silky voice. "You are all done. Finished. You did well, Agent Ketcher." Al-Makira bent down so that his head was level with Ketcher's and removed his hand from Ketcher's left shoulder. As he did this, he looked over the agent's right shoulder, straight into the camera lens and said out loud, "I am al-Makira. Get me Frank Cross. If you do not comply with my demands…This is how the rest of the hostages will die." His right hand moved quickly and he removed a steel garotte from his jacket pocket, slipped it over Ketcher's head, and with both hands he pulled backwards.

Agent Ketcher of MI6 got his fingers to the steel wire but he was too weak to make any impression on the garotte as it sliced into his neck, cutting through flesh, cartilage and his wind-pipe. He briefly struggled and tried to cry out as the wire went deep, his feet and legs kicked about the filthy floor, he emptied his bladder and he coughed up blood and then died. And it all went onto the same piece of film.

Al-Makira continued to look at the camera from behind the bloody and filthy corpse of John Ketcher. The self-styled commander of the terrorist group held up his gory hands and posed for the camera lens and shouted, "I am al-Makira! I do this for Intiqam! For The Cause! For al-Qadia! Get me Frank Cross!"

*****

The girl was now in no doubt that Frank would kill her if she did not reveal where Diana Moon was being held captive.

"Okay! Okay!" she said in English but with a heavily accented voice. "I will tell you. Please, do not kill me. I was only supposed to drive the fucking van!" Frank had lowered his gun but lifted his gun towards her face again. Her eyes went wide. "Please! Please! Do not shoot me!"

Frank stared at her with a hard and brutal expression, then said in English, "Okay. I won't kill you, but only if you do exactly as I say. Understand?"

She nodded rapidly. "I understand. But will you do something?"

Frank was not feeling very disposed to helping her. Never-the-less he asked, "What is it?"

"Will you get *him*," she tossed her head at Tommo, "to put me down?"

A ghost of a smile flickered across Frank's face and he looked at Tommo who lowered her to the ground.

"Don't even think of running away," said Frank and he waved his gun at her.

"I will not," she said in a petulant voice, like a spoilt child who has been told that they can't have any more chocolate.

Frank beckoned to Errol who was now standing out on the open garage floor and he joined the group. Then Frank, Tommo, T Bone, Clonk, Errol and the girl made their way to the Grand Cherokee SUV with the sound of police sirens reaching their ears. The cavalry was on its way.

The rag doll looked at Errol as he joined them but she still did not realise who Errol was, and she still had not figured out that she had been duped into thinking that one of the gang members had been executed in front of her. They all climbed into the SUV with T Bone in the driving seat.

The interior of the Jeep was laid out with two bench seats either side of the vehicle. They put the girl in the back between Tommo and Errol, with Clonk sitting opposite her. Frank got into the passenger's seat beside T Bone.

Frank turned to the girl. "Where to?"

Again, in English she answered, "Do you know where route one-six-oh is?"

"Yes."

"Get there first, and then I will give you other directions."

Frank didn't thank her. He looked at T Bone who started up the SUV and headed out of the garage.

They exited out of the back of the garage and turned right. From here they went up to Kova Lane at the far end of the garage building, where they turned right which took them the few yards to the neon bedecked Tropicana Avenue. They turned right onto Tropicana and drove along to the equally garish Strip sitting in its ribbons of lights. This they crossed and came up to Highway 15. Here they turned left heading south, riding in silence, and passing the lit-up fairy-tale towers of the Excalibur hotel, and then the Pyramid of the Luxor hotel on their left with the laser beam on the apex of its roof aiming through the darkness at the stars of a clear desert night. The glowing upright slab of the Mandalay Bay hotel also slid past them. They crossed the junction for Highway 215 and came up to Highway 160 where they turned right, signed for the small town of Blue Diamond, and headed for the distant mountains which were now just a smear of darkness against a backdrop of the darker sky.

The road that they were now following was bordered either side by rocky and inhospitable desert - part of the Mojave Desert valley - and it was pitch black out there.

In the dark interior of the Jeep, that was lit only by the glow from the dials in the dashboard, Frank asked, "Where to now?"

The girl craned her neck around Tommo's bulk to look out of the windscreen. "About two miles ahead on the right there is a large bill-board advertising La Jolla Real Estate..."

"Real estate?" interrupted Clonk. "Bloody hell! Who'd want to live out here?"

Frank answered, "Someone who thinks that Vegas is going to expand even more perhaps?"

"Bloody hell," repeated Clonk.

"Go on," said Frank to the rag doll.

"Okay. Opposite the bill-board there is a turning, on the left, it is only a rough track and it leads for about half a mile to a shack. That is where the girl is."

Errol spoke up for the first time. He growled, "The girl, as you call her, has a name. She's called Diana Moon, and she's my daughter."

The girl turned and stared at Errol. "You are her father?"

"Yes. And if anything has happened to her, it won't be one of these guys that kills you, 'cause I'll do it myself!" He had lifted his hands as if he were about to reach out and strangle her.

The girl swallowed, staring at Errol, and she would have touched her hands to her throat if they had not still been tied behind her. Errol stared back at her with murder and vengeance in his eyes.

"Right," said Frank, taking back control of the situation. "How many men and women are at this shack?"

The girl tore her eyes away from Errol and hurriedly answered Frank, "Four men and one woman."

"Any look-outs?"

"No."

"You sure?"

"Yes."

Clonk spoke up, "You'd better be right." He had pulled his knife and was playing with it. It was a very large knife.

**

The shack was a basic square wooden structure whose sides each measured about twenty feet long. It had a shingle roof that sloped from high up the back to down at the front and the building was surrounded by beaten earth. There was an old battered filthy red Toyota Hilux truck parked along the left-hand side of the shack as you viewed it from the front.

There was a wooden door in the middle of the front of the shack that led into one large room and the door was flanked either side by a large window. There was one window on each of the sides of the building, and these looked in on the one room. Beyond the main room and on the left was a small room that housed a toilet and shower, and to the right of the main room was a single bedroom where Diana Moon was being held. The toilet had a small window in the back of the building and the bedroom had one window at the back, which was boarded-up.

In the front room, to the right of the front door, was a small sink and a two-burner gas hob that was fed by a large canister of liquid gas that sat under a crude wooden work-surface that served as the cooking preparation area. In the middle of the room was an old black pot-bellied stove whose chimney flue went straight up through the ceiling. The stove was not lit, because although the shack was in the desert, night-time temperatures around Las Vegas can drop to 4 degrees C in winter. However, being June, the night-time temperatures were between 21C and 25C.

Against the right-hand wall and under the window was a table that was big enough to seat four people. Two of the kidnappers, both men and both from Afghanistan, were playing cards and smoking. In the middle of the table were two opened packets of cheap cigarettes and a metal ashtray full of discarded cigarette butts; beside the ashtray was a brass Zippo lighter. The air around the card players was heavy with the smoke and the bad smell of the cigarettes.

There was a small television in the left-hand corner of the room formed by the front wall and the left-hand wall. Two more of the kidnappers were lounging in battered armchairs that had the old stuffing bursting out of the sides. These two men were watching an old black-and-white Humphrey Bogart movie on the TV. These two were from Iran.

The only woman in the group was pacing backwards and forwards in front of the stove. She, like her fellow kidnappers, was dressed in black combat fatigues. She was good-looking and tall with long black hair that fell to just below her shoulders. She came originally from Syria.

"Why do you not sit down?" said one of the card players. He spoke in Arabic.

She paused in her pacing and answered, "They are late. They should have been here by now." She checked her watch.

The card player shifted in his chair. "They probably got caught in traffic. Anyway, they would let us know if there is a problem. Stop worrying."

The woman turned to the door as if to step outside, but then thought better of it.

**

"Real estate sign coming up on our right," announced T Bone. The SUV's headlights picked out the bill-board.

"Here," said the rag doll and she made a nodding motion with her head. "Turn left here."

It meant that T Bone had to cross the carriageway, but that was ok as there was a turning point marked in the middle of the road. T Bone slowed up and pulled the SUV around and across the highway.

Having made the turn and crossed the road the SUV crunched onto a dirt track, just as the captive girl had said. At a signal from Frank, T Bone stopped the Jeep. He turned off all of the vehicle's lights. T Bone did not need to be told that they might alert the people in the shack. Stealth was now the order of things.

Frank turned to the girl again. "You said half a mile?"

"About that."

"What's the layout?"

There was a slight hesitation and Frank thought for a moment that she might not tell him. But, in her mind's eye, she saw the dead bodies in the MGM's garage and knew that these guys were not messing about. "There is one room at the front where we all eat and sit, and there is a bedroom and a shower and toilet at the back."

"Is the shower and toilet a combined room?"

"Yes."

"And which side are the toilet and bedroom on?"

"Facing the shack, the toilet is on the left and the bedroom is on the right."

"Is there a back door?"

"No."

Clonk gave a low grumble at that. It meant that the only main access was through the front door.

"Are there any windows?" asked Frank.

"Yes. Two at the front either side of the front door and one at either side of the front room. Then there are two more at the back; one for the toilet and one for the bedroom, but you cannot get in through the bedroom window because it is boarded up."

T Bone spoke up. "Presumably to stop Diana from trying to escape."

The rag doll looked guiltily down at the floor. "You will not get in that way. You would need a battering ram."

"Ahh," said Frank, "we don't need a battering ram, we have a Tommo."

T Bone and Clonk grinned. The girl frowned. "What is a Tommo?" she asked.

Frank just smiled at her. "I'm sorry about this."

"What?" she asked and then Clonk leaned forward and hit her in the neck with a hypodermic, and out she went.

"Sweet dreams," said Clonk. They had been carrying a pair of the needles in the First Aid box that T Bone had brought to the car in his kit-bag. The needles were there in case they might need to knock out Diana and then keep her under, because they did not know what condition she might be in. Clonk had decided to use one of them for a different reason. He looked at Frank for confirmation of his action.

"Needs must," he said.

"No problem," said Frank.

**

Frank's team headed up the track. Above them the inky black sky held a profusion of stars; something that you could not see if you lived in the actual city of Las Vegas, due to all of the light pollution. Either side of the track the desert ran away as a rock-strewn sandy wilderness whose terrain undulated like a petrified sea. There were no lights and again it was pitch black dark out there. They had left Errol back in the SUV with the second hypodermic that was loaded with the knock-out drug, and with the instructions that if the rag doll came around and tried to escape Errol was to stick it in her.

Moving silently through the darkness, the team approached the shack. There were no curtains at any of the windows that they could see and all of the lights in the place were on. Clearly the people inside were not expecting trouble. That was about to change.

"Check your throat-mikes and ear-pieces," whispered Frank.

One after another the men tapped their throat-mikes and received a nod from Frank that all was working. Still whispering, Frank said, "Okay, wait here while I recce the place." And with that he slipped away.

The team did not hear him go, and they could not hear him moving. A few years ago, when Frank Cross had been under Sensei Nakamura's tutelage, the sensei had instructed Frank in many of the ways of the ninja. One of these had been *shinobi-aruki*, the art of stealth-walking. It was a technique based on the way that the walker placed his, or her, feet down on a surface and allowed the walker to move over any surface without making a sound. Frank was employing the technique right now.

He approached the shack as silent as a ghost, keeping just outside of the small puddle of light that the interior of the shack threw out onto the desert floor.

Watching the interior of the shack intently from the darkness, and listening to the sounds within, Frank took a clockwise turn around the shack. Then he came back to the team. "Right," he whispered. "Tommo, you go around the back to the boarded-up bedroom window. T Bone the left-hand side window. Clonk to the right. I'm going in through the front door. When you're in place tap your throat-mikes twice. Immediately after the last tap I'll chuck in a couple of flashbangs and then we hit them all at the same time."

"Prisoners?" asked Clonk. T Bone threw him a glance.

"None," said Frank. "These are Arab mercenaries, and I think that they're using Diana to collect money for some greater cause. Probably terrorism." His mind whispered the word Intiqam. "And anyway, they would have shot Errol out of hand back at the MGM."

"Okay," said Clonk. His face was set grim. "Let's go get the bastards."

"And rescue the girl," reminded Frank.

Nearer to the shack the four men split up, moving with purpose with the barrels of their assault rifles pointing forwards and their fingers over their triggers. They moved into their designated positions as Frank stood in the darkness a few paces back from the entrance door. If anyone came out now, he would shoot them.

After a few seconds Frank heard three sets of double taps come into his ear-piece. After tapping their mikes, the three men stuck their fingers in their ears and turned their eyes away from the shack. Frank pulled two flashbangs out of a cargo pocket.

A flashbang is another name for a stun grenade. It is supposed to be a non-lethal explosive device used to temporarily disorientate the senses of an enemy. Although it is supposed to be non-lethal there have been cases where the explosion has been detonated so near to a person that they have died. However, usually the grenade gives off a flash that momentarily blinds the eye for about five seconds after which the target suffers impaired vision. A freight train at a distance of 15 metres creates about 80 decibels, a military jet taking-off with an afterburner creates about 130 decibels, and eardrums can rupture at 150 decibels. The bang that accompanies the flash is greater than 170 decibels, and that is what stuns.

The grenade has a ring that is pulled free and then the flashbang is thrown.

Frank faced the door, ran forwards, and kicked it open. He lobbed in the two grenades then shoved his fingertips into his ears and looked away as the flashbangs detonated.

A second after the flashbangs went off T Bone and Clonk smashed the barrels of their assault rifles in through the glass of the two side windows as

Tommo shoulder-barged into the boarded-up rear window and took it out as though it were only matchwood. Frank stepped into the room and shot the sole woman who was lying on her side just in front of the pot-bellied stove. Frank noticed that her nose was bleeding just before he put a single round into her head. T Bone got the two men who had been watching the TV; one had been sprawled over the arm of his armchair and holding his head, and the other was groping for an AK-47 rifle that had fallen with him to the floor. Clonk shot the two men who had been at the card table. One of the card players had been crawling towards Diana's bedroom door with a revolver in his right hand when Clonk's two shots hit him in the head, and the second card player got two rounds in the centre of his chest as he struggled to get up off the floor.

It was all over in just under five seconds. The table was now on its side and the cards, cigarette butts and the cigarettes from the packets were scattered about the floor of the room.

Diana Moon had been protected from the blast of explosive and bright light because her bedroom door was kept closed by her abductors. However, she screamed out as Tommo came crashing through the wall in a storm of splintered woodwork and shattered glass. Tommo looked down at her and in his deep bass voice he said,

"Hello Miss Moon. We're here to rescue you."

They would not need the hypodermic because Diana Moon feinted.

"Shucks," said Tommo as he looked down at her sprawled limp body.

Frank came into the room. He was carrying a ring of keys that he had found on the meal preparation surface. As quick as he could he worked his way through the set of keys until he had unlocked Diana's handcuffs from around her wrists and ankles and then he produced a knife and cut her free of the plastic binds.

Frank looked at Tommo. "Okay big fella, time to go."

Tommo bent down and lifted Diana off the bed as if she were as light as a feather-filled pillow. He put her over his left shoulder and ducked under the doorway as he left the room. Frank followed Tommo out of the bedroom and cast his eyes over the filthy floor of the shack. Besides the cigarette butts and playing cards there was also an empty ashtray and a Zippo lighter. Frank bent down and picked up the lighter. He opened it and flicked it. It lit, so he closed it and put it in one of his pockets. Then, just as they were about to leave the shack, Frank saw something else on the floor, something glinting beside the overturned table. It was a lady's watch. He picked it up. It was quite an expensive Tag Heuer and it was working.

"What's the betting this is Diana's?" said Frank.

"An' look, boss," said Tommo. "There's a good-looking leather shoulder-bag."

Frank picked that up as well and took a quick look inside it. Sure enough there was a purse containing Diana's credit cards and money inside. Frank dropped the watch into the bag and handed it to Tommo.

"Take this to the car, Tommo, I've got one more job to do."

Tommo ducked out of the front door and Frank walked over to the gas hob. Attached to it was a length of rubber pipe that went onto a fitment on the top of a very large liquid gas cylinder. Frank closed the cylinder's valve off and then lifted the cylinder.

Very heavy. Lots of gas inside.

Perfect.

He put the cylinder down onto the floor and dragged it in front of the door and towards the back of the shack. He bent down, and with his knife cut through the rubber tubing. Then he opened the valve in the top of the cylinder. Gas hissed out.

Frank picked up a grubby towel that was lying on the work surface and walked outside. He used his knife to tear a strip out of the towel and went to the Toyota and unscrewed the petrol cap. He poked the strip of towel into the petrol filler tube and then took it out. The end was soaked in petrol. He bent down and picked up a fist-sized rock and tied the strip around it and then went back to stand about thirty feet away from the front of the shack.

Frank counted to thirty, letting some of the gas build up inside even though the door was open and the side windows were smashed. He took the brass Zippo lighter out of his pocket, flicked the wheel to produce a flame, and touched it to the towel-wrapped rock. It caught light immediately and he threw it overarm and through the open door to land inside the shack beside the gas cylinder. As the rock with its burning material went through the door Frank ducked, turned, and ran for it.

The flames reacted instantly with the gas and ignited in a hissing booming fireball that rolled around the room and licked out of the broken windows. Moments later the remaining contents of the gas cylinder exploded like a bomb, blowing the walls apart and taking the roof off the shack.

By the time Frank had joined his team at the SUV what was left of the wooden shack was burning, with the flames flaring yellow and white and lighting up the night like a beacon.

Diana had come around and was being tearfully reunited with her father who kept hugging her and repeating his thanks to the team who were standing around the open end of the SUV.

"Here, Diana," said Tommo as he handed over the shoulder-bag. "I think this is yours."

Diana had not quite got over the shock of being saved by a giant, but she was overjoyed that she'd got her possessions back. After a few moments she looked up at Tommo as he towered over her and said, "Just how frickin' tall are you?"

"One hundred feet ma'am," came the low rumbling reply, and then he gave her a dazzling white smile and a deep chuckle.

Diana Moon laughed.

Frank smiled. "Well done everyone," he said. "Time to go."

"What about her?" asked Clonk.

They all turned to look at the rag doll who was still sitting inside the SUV. She had come around from the shot of anaesthetic that they had hit her with earlier and she was scowling at them, like a cat in a cage.

"Let her go," said Frank and he casually laid his assault rifle down onto the floor of the Jeep.

"You must be fucking bonkers!" said Clonk. "She's one of them. She's a terrorist!"

Frank faced his friend. "I said, let her go."

"But…" began Clonk.

T Bone spoke up. "Boss says let her go. So, we let her go." He pulled out a knife from a sheath on his belt and climbed into the SUV.

"This is stupid," protested Clonk. "We should slot her." He meant shoot her.

T Bone squatted beside the rag doll, turned her around, and cut through the plastic bindings around her wrists.

She brought her hands in front of her and rubbed her hands together as T Bone backed out of the vehicle. She got out of her seat and started to climb out of the back of the vehicle behind T Bone. She climbed over the rifle that Frank had laid down and got her feet onto the ground. As T Bone moved away from the SUV she took a step away from it then suddenly whipped around and grabbed the rifle, swinging it round to shoot the group who were clustered in a tight circle.

"For The Cause!" she screamed. "For Intiqam!"

But, before she could fire the weapon a gun went off, and she jerked backwards, hit between the eyes by a hollow-point round. Diana screamed. The rag doll went back and down, striking her now bloody and ruined head against the rear bumper of the SUV as she fell. She bounced off the bodywork and went sprawling onto the desert earth.

Like a rag doll.

Frank lowered his revolver. It had been a very fast draw.

"Je-sus, that was quick!" Clonk broke the silence. They all stared at Frank, and then down at the corpse.

"You knew," said T Bone. "You knew she'd try that, didn't you Frank?"

Frank put his gun away and nodded ruefully. "Yeah. But I gave her a chance. Stupid girl, she could have just walked away." But even as he said it Frank knew that she would never have walked away. She was a fanatic. She had yelled the word that had made Frank's blood run cold – Intiqam. It was confirmation of what Frank had suspected all along – Intiqam had been behind the abduction, the threats for money and the white envelopes. The terrorist organisation was back, if it had ever gone away.

"Fucking terrorists," murmured T Bone. "They're all bloody nutters."

"You're right there my man," agreed Tommo.

T Bone turned. "Let's get out of here." He climbed back behind the steering wheel and started up the car.

Diana had regained some composure, due mainly to a fatherly arm around her shoulders. She looked at Frank's stern face that was being lit rather monstrously by the flames of the burning shack. "You guys don't mess about, do you?"

"No, Miss Moon. We do not."

"Come on darlin'," said Errol. "Let's go. I want to tell your mother."

The last person to get into the Jeep was Tommo, who had picked up the dead girl's body up off the track and he had tossed it out of the way into the darkness of the desert so that they did not have to drive over it.

As they left the area the remains of the shack collapsed with a whoosh and a high spray of red sparks that went up into the night sky.

**

They got back to the MGM but could not park the Jeep back in the hotel's garage because it was now closed off as a police crime scene. Lines of blue and white plastic were hung all around it, so they drove to the Venetian where the parking was free. Having parked the car, they walked to Harrah's hotel and caught the monorail down to the MGM. Even though some of the team were dressed in black combat fatigues they were largely ignored; this was America, where you can wear what you like - they were just another group of tourists enjoying the sights.

Having disembarked from the monorail, T Bone said, "I don't know about you guys, but I need a beer."

"Good idea," agreed Frank. "But let's first dump our gear back at the Luxor." He turned to Diana. "And before that, young lady, you have to report back to your employers."

"What?" she gasped. "Looking like this?" She was grubby and dishevelled.

"Yes," grinned Frank. "Exactly like this. However, first I need your mobile phone."

Diana rooted about in her bag and produced it for him. He took it off her and punched the front of it so that it cracked.

"Hey!" she objected. "That wasn't cheap you know!"

"I'll get you a new one, I promise. Now listen…" Frank outlined a story for her.

**

Diana Moon and her father entered the MGM Grand hotel and went up to the night concierge who was an elderly straight-backed man in a grey suit with grey hair and a wonderful sweeping moustache. He was called Nick, and he recognised Diana immediately.

"Miss Moon! How lovely to see you!" The accent came from California. "But, my god, look at the state you're in! Where have you been?" He ran his eyes over her dishevelled appearance. "I know the management have been worried about you."

"Oh, thank you, Nick. I wonder, is Miss Levin here?"

"Oh, yes, Miss Moon." He leaned forward conspiratorially, "I sometimes think she's a vampire, because she never seems to sleep." He winked.

Diana smiled at his thinly veiled disrespect. "Can I see her, please?"

"I'll call her."

A few moments later Diana and Errol were in a lift and on their way to the office of Miss Levin. As they entered her large airy office Miss Levin stood up from behind her very large black-topped highly-polished desk. Behind her was a huge plate glass window, and because the MGM Grand is thirty floors high, and because Miss Levin had an office that was on one of the higher floors, she had a fabulous view in the daytime of northern Las Vegas and the desert and mountains beyond. At night the view was the myriad of lights that lit up the city. It gave her the perfect backdrop for framing her before she started grilling staff members.

Laura Levin was forty-two years old with a slightly angular, but very attractive face, a face with red lipstick to her cupid bow lips. She possessed piercing green eyes behind long false eyelashes and she had applied exactly the right delicate shade of green eyeshadow to compliment her eyes. The only flaw to this woman's good looks was her nose, which was just slightly hawk-like. She had long black hair that was pulled tight across her head into a ponytail, small ears with diamond stud ear-rings in the lobes, an elegant neck and a perfect body. She worked-out regularly at the gym and took tae-kwon-do classes twice a week. So, you might want to tangle with her in a bed, but not in a fight.

She was wearing high-heeled black patent court shoes, barely-black tights, a knee-length black pleated skirt and a black silk sleeveless shirt of which she had left the top two pearl buttons undone. If she had dyed her hair with a strip of white down one side she could have passed for Cruella de Vil.

She came around the desk in a somewhat strange easy-rolling movement, as if she were going to hunt Diana down, and then sat with her perfect bottom resting on the front edge of her desk. She crossed her legs at her ankles and then crossed her arms and placed her fingers with their long poppy-red painted nails (they matched her lipstick) around her biceps – she was proud of her biceps - then she ran her eyes over Diana. Then she ran her eyes over Errol, and then back over Diana. Her red lips were held in a rather sour pout.

"Won't you both please have a seat?" She was not altogether sure that she wanted Diana's dusty clothes on her furniture, but custom demanded good manners.

Diana and her father dropped into modern chrome and black leather armless chairs that were placed about five feet away from the front of Miss

Levin's desk.

"Well, my dear," began Levin without unfolding her arms. "You look as though you have been through the wars. Where on earth have you been?"

"I'm so sorry to have left you in the lurch," said Diana. "It was all so silly, really."

"What was?" The arms stayed folded in place. Her fingers played on her biceps, as if she were running them over the keys of a piano.

"I wanted to see some of the area around here on my day off, because I've never been here before."

"Yes?" The fingers moved again.

"And, well, I rented a car and drove out to Death Valley."

Miss Levin arched a perfectly-crafted eyebrow. "On your own?" Her voice hinted at the words, *You stupid girl*.

"I know it was very stupid of me, I know. And I got lost, and then the car broke down." Diana started to get tearful. It was the story that Frank had concocted for her and she was giving an award-winning performance.

Miss Levin softened a little - although the arms stayed crossed. "Try not to upset yourself, Diana."

"No, Miss Levin."

"Why didn't you phone for help?"

"I, I dropped my phone. See…" Diana produced the mobile that Frank had smashed.

"Oh. Yes. I see." The fingers came off the biceps and Levin relaxed her arms. "And I take it that you've been out there all this time?"

"Yes, Miss Levin.."

"Then how did this man find you? Is he a relative?"

"Oh, sorry, Miss Levin. This is my father, Errol Moon."

As Errol smiled at Miss Levin something clicked in the back of her mind. *Errol Moon.*

Errol said, "Diana told me she was going to drive to Death Valley, and I told her not to go, but she can be a very determined young lady…"

Diana interrupted, "When dad didn't hear from me, he came looking for me, and it was only by a stroke of luck that he found me…otherwise…I might have…Died!" She burst into tears and her father put an arm around her shoulders and hugged her.

Laura Levin could have asked Errol where he lived that he was so quickly able to race to his daughter's rescue. She might have asked where he found her. She might have wondered why Diana had gone to Death Valley dressed as though she were going to walk down a cat-walk. But she didn't. Her father's name had somehow distracted her.

Errol Moon?

Miss Levin had been in the music and entertainment business for most of her adult life, and she was sure that she had heard that name before. A frown flickered briefly across her brow before she said, "There there," and handed Diana two tissues from the highly expensive Japanese black lacquered tissue-box on her desk.

"Thank you, Miss Levin." Diana softly blew her nose.

As Diana dealt with the tissue and her nostrils Laura Levin had a lightbulb moment, but her face remained passive. "Did you say your father here is called Errol Moon?" She waved a hand at him.

Diana looked up. "Why, yes."

"Errol Moon, the Caribbean record producer?"

"That's me," said Errol rather proudly. "And Diana is both my daughter and my discovery."

Miss Laura Levin nearly said "Aha!" She had been in the entertainment business long enough to know now who Errol Moon was and why she had suddenly recalled him - Errol Moon was very successful at finding, recording and promoting talent. The accounting part of her very astute brain began making calculations. She leaned forward. "Mister Moon, I get a lot of talent here at the MGM; singers, bands, musicians…I wonder…if I became an agent for them and pushed them your way, could we perhaps work together?"

Errol looked levelly at Miss Levin's inscrutable face. "In what way, Miss Levin?"

"Oh, please call me Laura."

"Very well…And you must call me Errol…But again, in what way?"

"Well, let's say that if I spot a real talent, I could *introduce* them to you."

Errol nodded, with just the hint of a frown on his face. He was frowning so as to keep the smile from his face. "That sounds like a good idea to me…Laura. I take it that if you did *introduce* someone, and that *if* they were any good, you would take a percentage of their earnings?"

Levin shrugged and gave a small smile. "Say, twenty-percent?"

"Say five," countered Errol.

Levin's eyes narrowed slightly, the long black lashes and hooked nose now making her look slightly raptorish.

Diana's head moved from side-to-side, watching the two business-people as they locked horns.

Levin's eyes remained narrowed, although her smile widened. "How about fifteen?"

"Try, ten."

"Done." Levin's smile was even wider now and her eyes had opened. They both leaned forwards and shook hands.

"Excellent. I look forward to doing business with you, Laura."

"Thank you…Errol."

The frown had gone from Errol's brow and he was now smiling as broadly as his new business partner. "I'll get my solicitor to draw up the papers straight away." This deal meant that he could branch out from the Caribbean, an ambition he had often dreamed about. And his first branch would be to Vegas.

"Marvellous." Laura Levin looked at Diana. "So, my dear. Where are you singing at the moment?" Levin lifted her bottom and smoothed down her skirt. She walked back behind her desk with a certain swagger to her shoulders.

"In one of the lounges, Miss Levin."

"Ah yes, one of the lounges. Well," smiled Levin as she sat her perfect bottom down in her perfect chair and gave both Diana and her father a perfect smile. "Let's see if we can do better than that for you, shall we?"

And at that precise and perfect moment Diana Moon's career took off.

**

Frank and the Shadows team entered one of the bars in the Luxor. They sat, belly-up, on high stools at the long bar and waited for their beers to be served to them. In front of them and above the back of the bar were a line of huge TV screens; one was showing a baseball game, another an American Football game, and another was showing world news.

Frank had been served his beer and was just about to taste it when he froze with the edge of the glass almost at his lips. He could not hear what the presenter was saying but the screen had a highlighted strip along the bottom where words moved right to left. They were informing Frank that a kidnapping had taken place in London and that the person who had been snatched was Lady Corrigan. The news footage showed two men wrestling a woman with bright red hair out of the driver's seat of a black Porsche, the film clip having been taken by someone holding a mobile phone.

"My god," whispered Frank.

T Bone, who was sitting on Frank's right looked at him. "What's up, Frank?"

Frank kept his eyes on the screen as he answered, "That's Red, that's Lady Corrigan, Sir Michael Corrigan's wife."

Tommo, T Bone and Clonk had never met Sir Michael, although they knew who he was because Frank had mentioned him in the past.

The three men joined Frank in looking up at the screen.

"What do you want to do about it, Frank?" asked Tommo.

Frank took a couple of breaths then said, "Nothing." He knew that Sir Michael had enough agents working for him in the Specialist Operations Unit that he did not need a retired agent called Frank Cross.

"You sure, boss?" asked T Bone.

"Positive," said Frank, and he took a long pull at his beer.

*****

SATURDAY 21st JUNE

10 DOWNING STREET

"Shit!" exclaimed the British Prime Minister. The expletive was not a word that the fresh-complexioned round-faced man with short dark hair and almost school-boy looks often used, and certainly not in public. However, on his laptop, he had just been shown the film of Agent Ketcher. The film had been placed onto the internet and picked up by GCHQ. The laptop was sitting in the middle of the PM's desk. He ran his right hand through his dark hair and looked around at the three other men in the room with him.

The three men with the Prime Minister were: The Chief of the British Secret Intelligence Service, MI6; the Director General of the British Security Service, MI5; and the Metropolitan Police Commissioner. Three of the four men were in suits with white shirts and plain ties. The PM's own suit jacket was draped over the back of his chair. The Commissioner was in full police uniform and they were all seated in the PM's office.

The PM pointed at the laptop's screen. "I presume this is for real?"

The Chief of MI6 nodded. "Yes, I'm afraid it is, Prime Minister."

The PM shook his head. "Have we found Larry yet?" The PM was referring to Lawrence Gainsborough.

This time the Chief shook his head. "Unfortunately, no, Prime Minister. We know he arrived in Venice, and we know that he got as far as the hotel that he and Miss Wetton were booked into, but after that he seems to have disappeared."

"I think we can assume," put in the Police Commissioner as he waved a hand at the laptop, "that this threat is real and that this terrorist organisation, Intiqam, has got hold of them."

The PM frowned. "And Sir Michael's wife?"

The Director General leaned forward. "We're on it…However, I suspect that Lady Corrigan, as the film claims, has been abducted by the same group. There was also, of course, that film of her being abducted in the street"

The PM nodded thoughtfully. "Yes, of course." He had seen the film, taken by a witness in the street, of Lady Corrigan being forced out of her car and then dragged away. He stroked his chin then said, "Gainsborough, I get. He is, after all, an MP. I even get Wetton, since she was with him." He looked at each of the men in front of him individually, as if trying to read their faces. "However…Why Lady Corrigan? Why not Sir Michael Corrigan? And why him anyway? Why target him specifically on the film?"

When there was no answer the PM continued, "I mean, what's so special about Sir Michael? Does anybody know?"

Of the three men sitting facing the Prime Minister only the Director General of MI5 and the Chief of MI6 knew the answer to that. Only they knew that Sir Michael Corrigan was the Director of the Specialist Operations Unit – and they were not about to reveal that secret. After all, the SOU was not supposed to exist, and the PM certainly knew nothing about the organisation. If he had he would probably have had apoplexy. Therefore, the two men in charge of the British Security Services were going to make certain that the covert SOU stayed that way. So, they both shrugged. If they did not say anything then they could not lie – or be held accountable.

The Police Commissioner spoke up. "As far as we can establish, Sir Michael is the director of a number of companies and has holdings in a few more. I can only assume that this is some sort of kidnapping for money."

The PM looked at the policeman. "Except they haven't mentioned money. They only asked for this man Cross, whoever he is. Why is he so important to them? Do we know who he is?"

The Director General of MI5 and the Chief of MI6 wrinkled their chins and brows, shook their heads, and then said in chorus, "No, Prime Minister."

The PM settled his eyes on the Director General. "Would you make a few discreet enquiries into the background of our mysterious Mister Cross?"

"Certainly, Prime Minister," said the DG. *Not bloody likely!*

The Chief of MI6 smiled slightly.

The PM read the Chief's look. "What is it?" he asked.

The Chief appeared to consider his answer then said, "Perhaps Frank Cross has got nothing to do with this at all. Perhaps the name has been inserted by these terrorists to throw us off the scent, to get us doing exactly what we are doing now. Running around in circles."

"Ahh, yes, I see," nodded the PM. "You mean we concentrate on Cross when we should be concentrating on Lady Corrigan and Gainsborough?"

"Exactly, Prime Minister."

"And Trudeau?"

"Same thing, Prime Minister. A bit of extra bait on the hook."

The Prime Minister stroked his chin. "Yes. Yes, you could be right."

"I mean," oiled the Chief. "Who is the more important...Lawrence Gainsborough and Lady Corrigan, or some man we've never heard of before?" He almost scoffed at the idea, and he glanced at the Director General. The two of them certainly did not want this to go any further.

"And..." said the PM, frowning and looking at the Police Commissioner as a thought struck him, "Find out who this Trudeau woman is. If we can find her, then she might be able to fill in some of the blanks for us."

The Commissioner inclined his head. "Of course, Prime Minister." *Do you think I've just been sitting on my backside?*

"And..." the PM continued, "...can we find out if Lady Corrigan is still in this country, or if she is already abroad as these terrorists claim?"

The Commissioner cleared his throat. "Actually, I can confirm that the police are working closely with our colleagues." He caught himself, because it sounded as though he were about to make a speech, or a statement for the press. "At this point in time I can report that Lady Corrigan has not left the country through the normal channels. Unfortunately, however, a search thus far has not revealed a thing." He paused. "The fact is, Prime

Minister, we haven't a clue where she is."

The Prime Minister sat back in his chair and placed his hands on the edge of his desk. "Then she could be out of the country, and if she is then I pray to God that they haven't got her, because if this film is anything to go by, she's in deep shit."

There was silence in the room for a few moments and then the PM broke the tension, "Okay. We need to start considering options. We know where these terrorists are because they told us…"

"That could be a ruse, Prime Minister," interrupted the Chief of MI6. "It could even be a trap."

"How so, and for whom?"

"Well," continued the Chief, "they may want us to send a rescue mission into this Qaryat Musawara village so that they can ambush them. Why else would they announce the name of the village, unless they wanted to lure people in to kill them?"

The PM thought about that for a few seconds, and then said, "Yes, but, they haven't set a trap for a group of Special Forces on a rescue mission have they?…They've asked for this Cross character."

"You mean," began the Police Commissioner, "we should find Cross and give him to them in exchange for the hostages?" He didn't like the sound of this.

"Why not?" asked the PM.

"Well," said the Commissioner, "first, it would be giving in to the demands of terrorists; second, we have no guarantee that they would release the hostages, if indeed they have them, or have them at this village; third, do you want to watch Cross being the star of a similar film to the one you just watched? And. we've just agreed that we don't know who Cross is, or where he is."

"Hmmm," said the Prime Minister, and he drummed the fingers of his right hand on his desk top. Bad all round; ethically, morally, humanely…and politically. He looked at the Chief of MI6. "What do *you* suggest then? Could we use some of your agents?"

The Chief emphatically shook his head.

"Why not?"

"Because you're going to have to use more than just a few well-trained MI Six agents for this job, Prime Minister. If you're taking on a terrorist training camp, and that's what this village could be, then you are going to need a full-on Special Forces rescue mission."

"We could lose the hostages in the process," said the Commissioner.

The Chief continued, "Yes. If it goes wrong, or the hostages are somewhere else, then you can wave good-bye to them."

"Right then," said the Prime Minister, stiffening his resolve. "We are going to need a plan of action. I need to call in the members of the Chiefs of Staff Committee to discuss this."

The Chiefs of Staff Committee comprises: the Chief of the Defence Staff - who is the Chairman and is the professional Head of the British Armed Forces; the Vice-Chief of Defence Staff; the First Sea Lord; the Chief of General Staff (the Army), and the Chief of Air Staff.

The PM stood up. "Thank you, gentlemen. I will of course keep you all informed, and include you in any discussions."

The three men stood and gave their thanks.

The PM was already reaching for his telephone as the men filed out of the room. One thing was nagging at his mind; who the hell, really, was this man Frank Cross?

**

The three men left Number 10 and briefly shook hands in front of the famous, and now closed, black door before turning for their cars; the Commissioner in a Vauxhall Astra in its blue and yellow police livery, the Director General for a BMW 5 series in silver, and the Chief of the SIS for a white Audi A6. All of the cars had drivers and all of the cars were bullet-proof.

The DG and the Chief of MI6 appeared to be having a light conversation as the Police Commissioner moved away from them. They hesitated on the pavement with small smiles on their faces whilst the Police Commissioner got into the rear seats of his car, clicked on his seat belt and was driven away.

The theatrical smiles on the faces of the two men faded away as the Director General turned to the Chief and said under his breath, "It could take days for the Chiefs of Staff Committee to make a decision."

The Chief gave a wry smile but made no comment. Instead, he asked, "Do you know if Sir Michael has seen the film?"

"If he hasn't, it won't be long until he does."

"And then?"

The Director General shrugged. "Who knows? That would be a Unit problem, not ours."

The two men turned and got into their respective cars.

**

Sir Michael had, of course, received the film and he knew that the Prime Minister had. He knew this because Brian, his contact in MI6, had informed him of the fact, and shortly after the film had arrived the Chief of the Secret Intelligence Service had gone to a meeting with the PM at Downing Street.

Sir Michael knew what the PM would do next; he would call a meeting of the Chiefs of Staff Committee. However, that would take some time to get all the members into the same room, and once there they would discuss and debate the situation and what to do about it *ad nauseum*. Meanwhile, four people might be tortured, and then killed, and all because Intiqam wanted Frank Cross.

Of course, Sir Michael knew where Frank Cross was based, and he also knew that Frank's reaction to being asked to operate on behalf of the Unit would be to stick two fingers up in the air and tell him where to go. That, however, would be under normal circumstances, and these were not normal circumstances, because two of the people under threat by Intiqam were Sir Michael's wife, and Frank's girlfriend and partner, Tandy Trudeau.

The Director of the Specialist Operations Unit did not know the current whereabouts of Miss Trudeau, but he did know where Lady Corrigan was. The kidnappers did not know it, but Lady Corrigan had a tracking chip placed under her scalp. The chip was quite small, being no bigger than one of those round pieces of paper that get knocked out by a hole punch. It had been placed, quite painlessly, beneath Red's scalp a few weeks ago and the only way you would be able to find it would be to shave off all of her hair, and even then, you would have to know where to look in order to find it. It was a very efficient little chip and a satellite was following it. But for the satellite to be of any use you would need a tracking device - Sir Michael had a tracking device.

Rightly, or wrongly, Sir Michael had been talking about this tracking-chip innovation with his wife over their dinner table and had explained that they were inserted into the agent's scalps. Somewhat surprisingly, Lady Corrigan asked if she could have one. She knew the kind of business her husband was in and she convinced her husband that this was a good idea, for in the high-stakes games that Sir Michael was involved in, those nearest and dearest to him would always be under threat of being used as a bargaining piece – as had happened now.

These chips had also been inserted into the scalps of every SOU field agent. Along with the tracking upgrade there had been a thorough background check into all of the members of the Unit's staff. This had been as a direct consequence of the actions of the traitorous SOU Chief Officer, Simon Lancaster, and the Intiqam SOU infiltrator, Aarif El-Sayed. As the finding and eliminating of these two men had been down to the actions of Frank Cross and Tandy Trudeau, it had been Frank that had afterwards suggested to Sir Michael that, as the head of the SOU, he should instigate those checks. Those checks had been carried out and revealed that the Unit was clean. However, because Sir Michael often worked with the Director General of MI5 and the Chief of MI6, he had pointed out to them that it might be a good thing if they gave their ranks a similar shakedown.

The chips had turned out to be quite an innovation as they enabled the SOU to know exactly where their field agents were anywhere on the planet at any time of the day or night.

The chips meant that the staff tracking the agents on assignment no longer had to rely on the outmoded system of ear-pieces, hidden microphones, mobile phones and the use of a satellite passing over the heads of the agents at the right time, because the chips could be monitored by a specific satellite 24/7.

So, Sir Michael knew where Red was, and that information was going to stay with him, because he wanted Frank Cross on the case, because Frank Cross was the best there had ever been at exterminating rats and scumbags – and Intiqam fitted both of those descriptions. And now that Frank had Tandy with him those rats and scumbags would not stand a chance if the duo were turned loose on them.

As far as Sir Michael was concerned there were two problems: one was the fact that Frank Cross and Tandy Trudeau had left the service of the SOU before the chips were issued, and the other one was that the Prime Minister had now unwittingly turned this rescue mission into a race – a race to destroy Intiqam in its nest – and if the British Government went in too heavy-handed with a Special Forces strike then all of the hostages could be lost.

And Intiqam would win.

For al-Qadia.
For The Cause.
Sir Michael Corrigan needed Cross, and Trudeau.

**

That evening, the Prime Minister was signing some official documents at his desk in his office at Number Ten when his wife walked in with a cup of coffee for him. They had been talking earlier about the kidnappings and the PM had briefly mentioned the name, Frank Cross.
His wife put the coffee cup down on the desk and said, "Darling?"
"Hmmm?" said the PM, engrossed in the document in front of him. He muttered, "Bloody Treasury reports."
"Yes dear…You mentioned the name Frank Cross earlier."
"Hmmm. God, look at this. What a suggestion."
"Darling, wasn't he something to do with some Caribbean island or other?"
"Hmmm. Goddam bean counters."
"Isn't there a man by that name in charge of security on one of those islands?"
"Hmmm? Possibly, possibly. And, God, look at this." He crossed something through with his fountain pen and jotted something in the margin.
The PM's wife folded her arms across her chest, lifted her eyebrows slightly and made a small moue of her mouth. "Just thought I'd mention it, dear." She unfolded her arms, turned and walked to the door where she stopped and said over her shoulder, "We've got boiled mouse for dinner."
"Jolly good," said the PM without looking up.
His wife left the room and closed the door behind her.
"Thanks for the coffee," said the PM. He looked up. "Oh. She's gone. Now where was I?"

*****

Because Japan is six hours in front of Iraq it was early afternoon at Hagakure, and the man that had been hiding in the sensei's garden felt his mobile phone vibrate silently in the pocket of his combat trousers. He answered the call. It was a text and it told him to grab the girl.
He was not particularly happy with that as he had wanted to watch her

some more. He had even decided to try and take some more photographs of her on his mobile phone and hopefully he could get her either naked in the shower again, or perhaps, at least, undressing. No, he wasn't happy, but orders were orders – and al-Makira was giving those orders.

The man closed the text down and sent one of his own to the back-up team that were waiting in a rented flat two miles away from the sensei's large estate. The team comprised of eight men: two Syrians, one Pakistani, two Iranians, and three from Iraq. They were bored, short tempered and anxious, for they had been sitting around doing nothing ever since Tandy had arrived at Hagakure.

These men all held completely legal passports that had been issued by their own countries of origin. It allowed them to pass freely through borders - just like any other tourist. Except these were terrorists, not tourists.

The leader of the group, one of the Iraqis, took his orders directly from al-Makira, and it was al-Makira who had pulled these men together from around the world. They were all hard men and they all believed in the cause of Intiqam.

On getting the word to go they left the flat in a hurry and boarded a large black windowless Honda van and then drove quickly to the road outside Hagakure. They were all dressed in green combat dress with green boots and green full-face ski masks. Six of the men were carrying old German Heckler and Koch G36 assault rifles each with a thirty round detachable box magazine.

Outside Hagakure the six men with the assault rifles checked their weapons and then got out of the back of the vehicle.

In the front of the van a man remained behind the steering-wheel. Beside him, in the passenger seat, sat another man, one of the Iranians; he was cradling a Russian Lobaev sniper rifle. This bolt-action single-shot rifle is claimed to be the most accurate sniper rifle in the world – but that depends on who is handling it. The man in the passenger seat knew how to handle it. He climbed out of the vehicle, following the team of killers at a distance. He walked across to the torii gate and climbed the first few steps, then he moved off them and into the bushes and shrubs that lined the bottom of the hill that Hagakure was built on.

The team of killers continued up the steps leading to Hagakure, moving rapidly but stealthily to the top.

**

Sensei Nakamura and Tandy Trudeau were in the dojo. The sensei was holding Tandy's wrist and was twisting it one way whilst demonstrating a strike to the base of her throat with his fingers when he stopped. He went as still as a statue.

"Wha..." began Tandy.

"Shh!" warned the sensei. Then he whispered, "Can you hear it?"

Tandy closed her eyes.

No...Ahh...There...At a distance...Many running feet...Boots landing on stone...Coming closer...Coming up the steps from the tori gate.

Still with her eyes closed, Tandy said, "I hear them, my sensei." She opened her eyes. "Who..."

Sensei Nakamura held up a hand. Tandy fell silent.

"There are *roku*...How you say? Sis of them."

"Six," said Tandy. *How the hell can he tell that?*

"Hai! Sis."

"They could just be visitors," suggested Tandy.

"No visitors. Visitors no run."

"Perhaps it's the police come back," suggested Tandy.

"No porice. Porice arrive with siren. Make big noise."

Tandy and Sensei Nakamura exchanged glances.

All of the suspicions of the last few days came together in their heads: the disturbances in the garden, the movement of shrubbery out of the corner of the eye, small tell-tale signs left on the ground, Tandy's underwear that she thought had been moved. They had suspected that they were being spied upon. Was this as a result of that?

"They are nearing top of entrance steps," said the sensei. "We onry have a few moments."

"But..." Tandy hesitated. "It could just be a group of people coming to see you."

The sensei shook his head. "No invite anyone."

"Yes, but..."

Sensei Nakamura put his hand on Tandy's arm. "Okay. We check. But this never happen before."

Tandy began to suspect that she was somehow to blame, although she could not figure out why.

Sensei Nakamura, on the other hand, was absolutely sure that this was something to do with Tandy; after all, he had lived here for many years and, as he had said, it had never happened before.

The sensei hurried over to the rack of weapons and took from it Tandy's jo staff. He walked quickly back and handed it to her saying,

"Quick! Come with me."

As she grasped the jo, Tandy felt a sudden flutter of panic in her chest.

Sensei Nakamura turned to her, as if sensing her disquiet. "If this nothing, then, no probrem. If bad, then we are warriors. Samurai. No fear. You be rike Tomoe Gozen. Hai?" The Beautiful Samurai.

Tandy smiled and nodded. "Hai!" And, with the sensei's confidence in her, Tandy's fears melted away as they both dashed for the door of the dojo.

The men reached the top of the flight of steps, turned right at the bamboo grove and walked a few yards before halting. They could clearly see the sensei's big house from where they stood, regrouping, and waiting for the resident watcher to join them.

Outside the dojo Sensei Nakamura and Tandy turned towards the men. Although they were some distance away, they could clearly see them, and that they were armed. The men turned towards them and stared back, not moving, waiting for something, or someone, and definitely not here paying a social visit.

"My god," breathed Tandy.

"God not here," said the sensei. "Onry you and I."

Sensei Nakamura ran his keen eyes over the group, and he knew, beyond a doubt, that this was an undisciplined team, the members of which had probably never gone into action as a single unit before. This would be useful. Sensei Nakamura pointed towards the building where Tandy slept. "Hurry! You go there. Do not go in your bedroom. Go next room. Wait for attacker. Move fast and defend strong. Hai!"

"Hai! What about you, my sensei?"

"No worry about me. I give them big surprise!" He smiled. "Hai?"

Tandy smiled back. "Hai!" She had to trust him, because he was, of course, the deadliest martial artist on the planet.

They split up with Sensei Nakamura running towards his house and Tandy running for her bedroom.

The watcher ran up to the leader.

The leader nodded the watcher a greeting and asked, "Where have you been?" He spoke in a generic Arabic that all of the men could understand. They had all received their language lessons from a petite young lady with black hair in the Intiqam training camp in the hidden valley.

"I am sorry," said the watcher. "I had to find out where the girl went."

The leader pointed forwards with his assault rifle. "We have just seen the old man go into the main house. Unfortunately, he has seen us, so he has been alerted." But he wasn't worried about that. This was just an old man. "We have also just seen the girl." He waved the barrel of his assault rifle. "She went into that building, further along."

The watcher tried to keep the look of longing from off his face.

The leader turned and pointed at three men who were standing at the back of the assembled group. "You three will kill the old man...The rest of you, come with me." They all dropped into a crouch and then paced it out towards the main building.

Once into his house the sensei entered the formal room in the centre of the building. This was a room as yet unvisited by Tandy. It was a large room and used solely for entertaining guests and for personal contemplation. On the wall opposite the entrance shoji was a pair of matched samurai swords – a daisho – comprising of a long katana and a shorter wakizashi.

The swords, mounted horizontally on the wall, had been made by the renowned sword maker, Kanenobu, and they had been forged in the year 1689. The swords were extremely valuable, and extremely sharp. Sensei Nakamura took down the katana, and, with all due reverence, he grasped the tsuka, the hilt, the flat steel of which had a casing of two strips of bone that had coloured from white to a pale yellow over the centuries. The bone strips were held in place by two wooden pegs that were pushed tightly through holes in both the bone and the steel. The hilt was bound with flat bindings of scarlet silk. The bone had been decorated with superb miniature engravings of samurai warriors and mythical beasts and Sensei Nakamura curled his right hand around it as he removed the blade from its black lacquered saya - the scabbard - and then replaced the saya back on its mount. Then he went and stood in the middle of the room. Waiting.

Tandy, as instructed, went into the room next to hers. She saw the sense in this; if she had been watched – and she was sure now that she had been – then the attackers would come to her bedroom, and not this one.

The seven men arrived in a group beside the engawa of the main house where they split up, with four of them continuing on to Tandy.

At the main house one of the men approached the sliding entrance door and moved it aside. Warily, they crossed the entrance doma and slid back the white shoji screen in front of them. They were entering the room where Tandy and the sensei ate their breakfast.

Moving slowly forwards, with his companions covering him and acting as back-up, the first man stepped into the room. He was holding his rifle in both hands with his right one beside the trigger guard and his left one forwards on the barrel, with his left elbow sticking out to one side. To his immediate left was the white paper wall that separated this room from the formal room - where Sensei Nakamura stood waiting.

Now on bare feet, Sensei Nakamura took four silent paces forwards and stopped about two feet away from the paper wall. He slowly lifted the katana in the double-handed grip needed to control the blade. He brought the sword up into the vertical position, edge forward and in front of his right shoulder, and settled.

The sensei watched as a shadow spread across the translucent screen in front of him. The man's outline was being thrown onto the screen by the light that was coming through the open door. Sensei Nakamura could clearly make out the shape of the man's left arm and the assault rifle that it held.

The image was followed immediately by another as the second man entered through the door, and the two men moved further into the room. A stupid mistake, pressed close together like that.

Like a striking mantis, the sensei took a single fast step forward and swept the katana downwards in a fluid sweeping motion. The blade sliced through the paper screen and cut cleanly through the arm of the first man at the jutting elbow joint. Blood spurted out of the severed arm and splashed across the white paper screen as the man screamed in pain and pulled the trigger with his right index finger. The bullets sprayed across the far end of the room before the man collapsed, writhing and bleeding out on the tatami mats. The katana didn't stop moving; having cut down it now came back up in a scything arc that sliced sideways through the second man's left-side ribcage and halfway up his torso. It went through the material of his jacket and the bones of his ribs as if they weren't there and continued on without snagging to cut through his lungs and his heart before exiting out of his back with the sword point only just alongside his spine. The man dropped his assault rifle and grabbed at his side as he coughed up blood, but he was dead before he hit the floor where he joined the first man.

The third man fired on reflex, sending the rounds in the direction of the sensei, shredding through the paper wall into the next room. He stopped firing and tried not to stare down at the two bloody corpses on the mats. With his face pale with shock, he stood and faced the tattered wall and peered at it through the gun-smoke. Where had the old man gone? Where was he? Could he see movement on the other side? Surely no-one could have withstood his onslaught?

Sensei Nakamura knew how people's minds worked in an attack situation: when firing guns, people either fired at waist to head height, or too high. They never fired low.

Sensei Nakamura had struck the first two targets and then had simply sat down cross-legged on the floor. The third man's G36 rounds had gone clear over his head. Now the sensei sprang to his feet and, as he could now clearly see his target through the holes torn in the screen, he whipped the sword around from the side, slashing right to left.

Again, the paper of the shoji screen parted and off came the third man's head.

Over at Tandy's building the sound of the assault rifles reached the ears of both the four attackers and Tandy. Tandy frowned; had they killed her sensei?

The leader, however, was smiling inside his ski mask. The sensei was dead. Now for the girl.

Because of the gun-fire there was no need for further stealth, so the watcher – who wanted to be first in - shoved aside the shoji screen that gave access to Tandy's bedroom, expecting her to be perhaps cowering in a corner. But she wasn't there.

Suddenly she came ripping through the paper wall separating her bedroom from the next. She arrived into her bedroom barefoot and wearing her gi and with her face full of vengeful determination - and the jo in her hands began to move at speed. It smacked down across the watcher's wrist above the hand that was holding the Glock and smashed the bone. The man screamed in agony as he dropped the gun and Tandy kicked it to one side as she stepped lightly into the middle of the room with the other three men pushing past the injured watcher. They fanned out as they bundled in through the opened entrance.

If they had fired, they would have killed her, cutting her down like dry grass, but they didn't. They were too close together and were hampering each other and Tandy had the element of surprise on her side.

The watcher was crawling around on the floor, yelling and holding his smashed wrist. All of this caused a moment's delay in the group, and that small delay was all that Tandy needed. She brought one end of the jo down hard onto the barrel of the nearest assault rifle held by the leader of the attackers. The strike knocked the front of the gun down and almost out of the leader's hands. Tandy then lashed out with her right foot in a mae geri front kick to the man's testicles and he cried out and doubled over, going down onto his knees.

Tandy put her kicking foot down and spun 360 degrees to hit the third man who had entered the room on the right-hand-side of his head with the dragon's tail whip. He went over and to his left, crashing through the shoji screen that Tandy had just entered through. The jo now smashed down onto the crown of the fourth man's skull and he dropped his rifle before he staggered forwards onto his knees.

Tandy heard a noise behind her and spun around, as agile as the gymnast that she was. The watcher was holding his broken wrist to his chest but had snatched up the pistol with his other hand. Tandy took a sideways step towards him and, as the gun came around to point at her, she hit him with yoko geri kekomi, the side-thrusting-kick. She struck him full in the face with the side of her left foot that was tensed and as hard as a block of wood. The impact smashed his nose and took his head back so fast that it broke his neck before sending him into the side of the house so hard that he nearly went clean through the cedarwood panelling of the outside wall. He slid down the panelling and fell dead to the floor.

Another noise behind her, and Tandy spun again with the jo swinging out at full length. It hit the last man in through the door, the one she had hit over the head. He had managed to get off his knees and was standing up but swaying. This time the jo cracked into the side of his face by his right ear. The staff took the man's head over to one side. Tandy stepped in and jabbed the four fingers of her left hand into the base of his throat which crushed his windpipe and then, as he went backwards, she kicked him with mae geri so hard that she drove his ribs into his lungs before he crashed out of the entrance door.

Now the leader came back up, holding his crotch but bringing his assault rifle to bear. Too slow. The jo hummed and struck the gun to one side and then Tandy spun on one foot and hit the man with a spin kick, boshi geri. It was her heel that she deliberately smashed into his head. It fractured his skull and sent him backwards through what was left of the paper wall and into the guest bedroom where the tatami mats cushioned the fall of his dead body.

The man she had hit with the dragon's tail had witnessed this she-devil in action and did not want any more of it. *The hell with Intiqam, I'm outta here!* He suddenly leapt up off the floor of the guest bedroom with his right hand holding the side of his head and dived for the door, leaving his weapon behind. He scrambled over the body of his fellow attackers and ran outside. Tandy went after him.

He got as far as the koi carp pond where he stopped and looked along the path to the sensei's house. At that moment Sensei Nakamura came marching resolutely out of his house holding a long blood-stained sword at his side. The sensei saw him and hurried forwards.

"Shit!" the man cursed and turned back, only to see Tandy stepping over the dead body of the man in the doorway. It was now that the man realised that he had left his assault rifle behind. "Shit!" He turned again, but Sensei Nakamura was closing the gap, and was lifting that wicked-looking blade.

"Tandy called out to the sensei, "How many?"

"San." Three.

"All dead?"

"Hai! And one much shorter than when arrived."

The man clearly understood English. Horrified, he turned again, only to find that Tandy was now only about six feet away from him.

"Who sent you?" she asked. The jo staff was still in her right hand, although this time it was not moving. But the man had seen what she could do with it and was wary of it and her.

"I said, who sent you?"

The man did not answer.

Tandy could see the fear in his eyes, which were the only part of his face that was visible beneath his ski mask.

"Look," said Tandy. "Someone sent you. Now, we can do this the easy way where you just tell us, or, we can do it the hard way where the sensei here cuts bits off you until you come clean."

The man's eyes slid to the sword and then back to Tandy.

She smiled at him. "Do tell. I know that you can understand me."

There was a pause, and then the man said, "Intiqam."

Tandy suddenly felt as though something had breathed cold air into her chest.

Intiqam!

She had already fought and defeated them once. Now she'd had to do it again. *When will they learn? These bloody terrorists! Can nothing stop them? I've got to let Frank know.*

Tandy's face hardened. "Can you give me a name? Someone behind all of this?"

Sensei Nakamura might not be able to speak English fluently but he was managing to follow this conversation pretty well. He flicked the katana's blade down and to one side so that the surplus blood on it scattered across the floor at his feet.

The man watched the action and swallowed. He looked at Tandy.

Tremulously he said, "I can't. He'll kill me."

"Who will?" pressed Tandy. And then the man jerked to one side as his head was struck by a sniper's bullet and he went sideways and backwards with a welter of spray into the koi pond behind him.

"Down!" shouted Tandy, and she and the sensei dropped to the ground.

No further shots were taken, so, after a couple of minutes, they tentatively raised themselves up.

"Wait here," ordered Sensei Nakamura, and then, before Tandy could object or stop him, the old martial arts master was off towards the area where the shot had come from, brandishing his sword.

The sniper had stayed motionless in the spot that he had picked to watch the front of the minka. He had watched as the team split into two and approached their targets. He lay in his cover and felt rather like a spare part; what did they need a sniper for when they had a seven-man team moving in to kill an old man and a girl?

And then he heard the screams and the gun shots coming from both the main house and the guest house.

Seconds later, when the old man had emerged unscathed from the house carrying a katana dripping blood, the sniper knew what had happened, and who had been screaming – and it hadn't been the old man.

The sniper had begun to settle down, ready to line the old man up for a head shot when one of the team came charging out of the guest building as though the devil himself were after him. The devil turned out to be a young woman in a white karate gi and carrying a staff.

The sniper had been able to hear everything that the girl said to the team member, who was now standing in front of a pond, because the sniper spoke good English as well as his native Iranian. He soon realised that the team member was about to spill the beans on who had organised this hit, and so he swung the rifle sight away from the old man and had shot the team member in the head.

As soon as he had taken the shot the girl and the old man had dropped to the ground out of sight, so that the sniper could not get off another round. With the whole raid gone to hell the sniper broke cover and ran. He sprinted across to the steps and then ran and jumped down them two and three at a time, almost bowling over on a couple of occasions in his haste. On reaching the torii gate he dashed across to the van and crashed in beside the driver.

"Get the fuck out of here!"

The driver stared at him. "Where are the rest?"

"They're all fucking dead! Now start the van and get us the fuck out of here!"

The driver did as he was told, started the vehicle up, rammed it into gear and stamped down on the accelerator.

Sensei Nakamura disappeared into the undergrowth of his garden moving as stealthily as the trained ninja that he was. If the sniper was still here, he would be tracked down and killed.

Tandy went back to her room and checked the bodies. All dead. She searched them and was not surprised when she found nothing on any of them that could identify them. From the bodies she went to her belongings on the shelf and retrieved her phone and then went and sat cross-legged on the engawa of the big house.

Tandy speed-dialled Frank. She felt a thrill when she heard his deep voice at the other end,

"Hi Tandy, how are you?"

"Good question," she answered. "Sensei Nakamura and I have just fought off an attack."

Frank said jovially, "Hey! Really? You must really be enjoying the lessons then?"

Tandy breathed out heavily. "No, Frank, you don't understand. This was not a training session. This was for real. Real terrorists! Frank, it was Intiqam."

There was a pause at the other end of the line as Frank's blood ran cold and his tone changed from gentleness to high concern. "Are you alright?"
"Yes, we're okay. But it was nasty stuff."
"How many of them?"
"Seven in total, and a sniper outside who got away."
"Is Sensei Nakamura okay?"
"Yes, but I think he's annoyed at having a dead body in his fish pond."
Despite his concern, Frank stifled a laugh. "Right. Well, I think you had better come home." He meant to St Margaret. "They might try again."
"I guess you're right, Frank…Damn! And it was all going so well!"
"You enjoyed it then? The training?"
"It's been fantastic. The sensei is amazing. But I think it's my fault we've been targeted, and I don't want to place him in any more danger, so I agree with you that I should leave."
"When do you think you can get back?"
"Soon. I had better help him tidy this place up first though."
"Messy?" asked Frank.
"Real messy. The sensei took three of them out with his katana."
"Ahhh," said Frank, imagining the bloody carnage. "Okay. Give me a call when you leave, yes?"
"Will do. Love you."
"Love you too, darlin'." And with that the line closed.
Tandy looked up. Sensei Nakamura was coming back through some dwarf pine trees and from a different direction to the one he had left. He marched across his manicured moss carpet still holding the katana in his right hand. He walked up to Tandy who remained squatting on the engawa.
"He gone," he said. "Bastard!"
Tandy gave a small smile. It was the first time that she had heard him curse. She stood up and bowed. "Arigato, my sensei, for helping me."
"No probrem." He returned the bow. "However, you know that they came for you?"
Tandy nodded. "I'm sorry. Yes, it would seem so."
"No aporogise. Not your fort. These are scum. Rats. Need big chop chop!" He brandished his sword.
Tandy burst out laughing. "Yes! Need big chop chop!"
Sensei Nakamura threw back his head and joined in the laughter. Then he sobered.

"We must move bodies. Porice may come."

"Oh! Yes! Someone may have heard the gunshots. What shall we do, sensei?"

The sensei stroked his chin as Tandy thought to herself that not even Mrs Johnson (whoever she was) would be used to clearing up this sort of a mess.

Sensei Nakamura looked at Tandy. "We get wheebarrow and put them in wash-house for now. Hai?"

Wheebarrow? Tandy smiled. "Hai!" she said. The wash-house was as good a place as any, and hopefully the police, if they arrived, would not go there.

*****

Al-Makira was almost purple with rage. He shouted into his hand-set, "What do you mean…they missed them?"

The man who had been the sniper said something at his end to which al-Makira exploded, "I gave you all one simple job to do and you fucked it up!"

The man said something else, to which al-Makira replied, "I don't care if he was a martial arts master! You all had guns…you should have killed him! I mean, there were seven of them! Seven! Eight, including you. Surely one of you could have shot the old man?…I'm not interested in your excuses!…Where's the girl now?…The police?…Oh, really…No, don't try again. I'll think of something else. All we've done is warn Frank Cross!" And he cut the line. "Morons!"

He threw the handset at the wall.

*****

Tandy and the sensei could hear the police car siren coming nearer as it wound its way up the side of the hill. The wail died out as the driver pulled up and cut the ignition.

Tandy and Sensei Nakamura were sitting cross-legged on a plain black blanket in the sunshine in front of the sensei's house drinking green tea when the two police officers appeared. Tandy was in her pink kimono and Sensei Nakamura was in his grey one.

Tandy and the sensei had been moving quickly once the decision had been made to move the bodies. The sensei had produced a large wheelbarrow and they managed to get two of the bodies into it. The sensei then pushed the wheelbarrow over to the wash house whilst Tandy carried another of the team over her left shoulder in a fireman's lift. That moved three in one go, and a couple of quick journeys later and all seven bodies had been cleared away out of sight. Then the katana had been quickly wiped clean and was now back in its saya and mounted on the wall, and the blood had been quickly mopped from the surface of the house mats, although large areas of staining remained.

There was not much that they could do about repairing the destruction of the paper walls of both the big house and Tandy's bedroom, so they just ripped the paper away and shoved it into the trash bins. Nor was there much that they could do about removing the blood staining of the house mats, so Sensei Nakamura had dashed to his kitchen and come back with a bag of flour. This he sprinkled liberally over the blood staining – to the unknowing it resembled plaster dust. It would have to do.

The male police officers that arrived turned out to be fresh-faced and in their mid-twenties; shiny black well-polished shoes, spotless dark-blue uniforms with razor-like creases to their trousers, crisp white shirts, blue ties and blue caps on their heads. They walked business-like over to Tandy and the sensei and bowed. The sensei nodded back but did not get up. Tandy, however, came to her feet and bowed before sitting down again. This action by Tandy made the two policemen glance at each other. Then they looked at Tandy again, then at each other, and then back to Tandy, who smiled innocently up at them. One of the officers took out a pocket-notebook and a biro, cleared his throat, and, turning to Sensei Nakamura, he asked in Japanese,

"Mister Nakamura, isn't it?"

"Sensei, Nakamura, if you please," corrected the sensei, also speaking Japanese.

"Oh! So sorry." Both policemen bowed again. "Sensei Nakamura,"

"Hai." The sensei nodded again.

"And who is this lady?" The officer looked down at Tandy as she sipped tea from a delicate ceramic cup, and he was suddenly struck with a bolt of recognition. "Wait! You are…"

As Tandy could not follow the language Sensei Nakamura interrupted and replied for her. "This is Miss Tandy Trudeau. She is one of my students."

The policeman looked thoroughly confused. He looked at Tandy, and then at Sensei Nakamura, and then back at Tandy. Surely this was the beautiful Hollywood A lister…whose name he could not quite remember. "Ahh, right," he said. "Miss Trudeau, you say?"

Sensei Nakamura smiled benevolently at the young man. "That's right officer. Trudeau." The sensei looked at Tandy and said, "Please spell out your name for the officer."

Tandy smiled, then said, "T.R.U.D.E.A.U."

As neither police officer could write in English, let alone understand or speak it, they simply stared at her.

"Hadn't you better write that down?" asked the sensei, nodding towards the open notebook.

The policemen continued to stare at Tandy and Tandy smiled back at them. She had seen that look of recognition on people's faces before.

"Is there something wrong, officers?" asked the sensei.

"What?...Oh, yes." The officer with the open notebook bowed. "We've had a report…of gunfire…coming from here."

"Gunfire?"

"Hai. Gunfire. Do you own a gun?"

"No."

"Oh." A pause. "Can we see inside your house?"

"Yes, of course. However, you will, of course, have to take your shoes and socks off before you enter, and you must excuse the mess."

"Mess?"

"Yes. This is a very old house you know…"

"It is very beautiful," said the police officer with no notebook, although he was looking at Tandy and not the house.

"Thank you," said Sensei Nakamura, still speaking in Japanese. "However, the walls inside are shoji and are being removed and the wooden wall supports replaced or renovated." In a sudden flash of inspiration, the sensei said, "We have been using a nail gun. It is very loud. Perhaps that is what someone heard, and thought it was gunfire?" Sensei Nakamura smiled at the officer with the notebook. The sensei did not own a nail gun.

"Perhaps," agreed the officer. What he was thinking was *If the house is being renovated it must be very very messy inside.*

"I am afraid that there is much dust and dirt," said the sensei as he scrutinised the officers in their immaculate uniforms.

The two officers exchanged looks. *Boots and socks off, and dust and dirt?*

"And some cobwebs," added the sensei. "Big cobwebs. *Very* big cobwebs."

The one with the notebook folded it shut with a snap and placed it back in his pocket. "I, that is, we, are sure that, like you suggested, someone heard your nail gun and mistook it for gunfire. I'm sure that everything is in order, Sensei Nakamura. We are sorry to have disturbed you."

"Not at all, officer. You are just doing your job."

The two officers bowed formally and politely to Tandy and the sensei and then turned and left.

At the top of the steps that led down to the torii gate they stopped, hardly able to contain their excitement, and the one with the notebook said, "You know who the woman is, don't you?"

The officer struggled with the double L that formed the English pronunciation of the name. "Hai! Harry Berry!" and then added, wistfully, "She is beautiful."

"And very sexy!" said his partner. He demonstrated the outline of the curves of a woman in the air. "I remember her in the movie, *Swordfish*! Oh boy!"

The other officer giggled. "Hai! Ve-ry sexy!"

"And what about her in *X Men* as *Storm*? In that tight leather uniform?"

"Oh, yes! What a good film!"

"Hai! But did you also recognise the old man?"

"Of course. It was Sensei Nakamura."

"Are you sure?"

"Of course."

"Have you ever seen him before?"

"Well, no. Who else would it have been?"

"Pat Morita!"

His partner looked puzzled as they began to descend the flight of steps. "Who is Pat Morita?"

"You know? Pat Morita…Miyagi San…*Karate Kid* movie!"

"Ohh…Yes! Miyagi San!...Wow!"

**

Tandy turned to Sensei Nakamura. "Blimey, that was close."

The sensei smiled. "Is okay now. They not come back."

"Maybe so," Tandy frowned. "But we must get rid of the bodies." The image of Mrs Johnson driving a dumper truck came into her mind. She shook her head as the sensei said,

"No probrem. I have truck. We dump bodies in mud pots near fumarows. Mud pot goes grob-grob. Bodies go." He grinned evilly. The noise he had just made was his version of what a bubbling pool of boiling mud sounded like. "Hai, they soon disappear pretty good."

Tandy's face had taken on a slightly sickly look. "Do you mean glob glob?"

"Hai. Grob grob. Sound is very funny. Hai?" He laughed.

Tandy stared at him. The sensei had just said two amazing things: first, he had a truck and she never knew that he could drive, and second, he was going to dump the bodies in a pool of boiling mud near a fumarole. Still with her slightly disturbed face she said, "Mud pots…Fumaroles?"

"Hai. Kyushu is covered in fumarows and hot springs. Very hot mud. Goes grob-grob. Soon get rid of bodies."

Tandy pulled a face.

The island of Kyushu has fourteen active volcanoes and a number of these are in the Kirishima volcanic range, which is the nearest range to Hagakure. Around these various volcanoes are scattered vents and fissures in the earth's surface. Some of these contain hot boiling mud in what are called mud pots and some are called fumaroles: fumaroles are vents with deep white-hot cores that give off intense heat, steam and noxious gases. Other vents are geothermal springs, or hot springs, and they are full of superheated boiling water which comes up from deep underground where it has been heated by the hot magma of the volcanoes. This boiling water is often toxic and highly acidic. A body shoved into any one of these three types of openings would not exist for very long, being either burned to nothing by intense heat or stripped to the bone by the powerful baths of boiling acids depending of course on what sort of vent it is. Either way, they were extremely efficient at disposing of any kind of animal that fell in, and nothing would be left.

"Come Tandy. Time to get changed, and then put bodies in truck."

Tandy had come to realise that this man's title, given to him by Frank Cross, as the most dangerous man in the world, was absolutely correct. And it made Tandy wonder about this old man's history. If he could be so blasé about getting rid of seven bodies, what else had he done in his life – and for whom?

The truck turned out to be an old battered light-blue Honda with a flat-bed at the back and a basic cab at the front that contained two tatty plastic-covered seats. It was parked on a rough tree-shaded and almost overgrown service road that ran up from the main road – the one that the estate's steps led down to. The service road ended behind the building that sat along-side the area where the bonsai trees were situated. The building turned out to be a large garden shed that was stacked with tools and equipment – it had been where the wheelbarrow had come from.

Tandy got changed into clothing befitting the moving and dispatch of bodies at night; she wore a pair of black trainers, black cargo trousers and a black sweatshirt over a dark-blue tee shirt. The sensei was in a dark-grey kimono and, rather incongruously, bare feet in a pair of yellow Nike trainers.

Half-an-hour of wheelbarrow-work later, together with some lifting and shoving, and the bodies were in the back of the truck. With everyone on board a blue tarpaulin was tied over the top of the grisly cargo. The team's guns and ammunition were then collected up, with the rifles and pistols going into one potato sack and the ammunition into another. The sacks were then shoved under the tarpaulin with the bodies.

Sensei Nakamura then went into the shed and came out with a pair of long-handled bolt-cutters, a pair of heavy-duty gardening gloves, a padlock and two black rubber full-face masks with two large round lenses in the front to see through and with twin particle filters screwed in place below them.

The sensei looked at Tandy. "These hep you breathe. Fumarows and mud poows have much bad gas, and very stinky."

Bloody hell, thought Tandy.

Sensei Nakamura placed all of the items onto the floor of the cab so that Tandy would have to sit with them between her feet.

*****

It was oppressively hot in the room and Lawrence Gainsborough MP sat on his backside on the filthy floor with his legs splayed out in front of him and his back against the dirty plaster of the wall.

On arrival at Qaryat Musawara he had been pulled out of his body-bag and then dragged backwards with a rag tied over his eyes. When his abductors had taken the rag off he had found himself kneeling in front of a man who had introduced himself as al-Makira. When Gainsborough went to ask a question al-Makira had struck him hard across the face with the back of his hand and told him that he was western scum and that he was only to speak when he had to answer a question. He was then hauled away and taken to this room; a room with no windows, a bucket to relieve himself into, one door and no furniture. Since then he'd been given some food. The man who had given it to him had found an old can of dog food at the back of a shelf in what passed for a kitchen. He had opened the can and forked half of it onto a dirty plate and then, along with a plastic bottle of tepid water, he had then presented it to the MP with a flourish and a smile on his face, as if he were on a *Master Chef* TV programme. Gainsborough had stared at the brown mess on the plate, caught a whiff of the meat, and felt his guts heave. He threw up into the bucket. As a consequence, the room now smelled of stale vomit.

Gainsborough sat with his head hanging forward, his hair matted and in disarray, with the left-hand side of his face heavily bruised where he had been hit by al-Makira. He had two guards outside the one door, guards who, before he was thrown into the room, had kicked him until he had collapsed. They had then taken his shoes and socks away from him together with his jacket and the leather belt to his trousers. His shirt was open to the waist and was torn in several places. His trousers were filthy and a seam in the material beside his left knee had opened up. Whenever the door opened it was to admit his guards to feed him some more delicacies and they took a great delight in giving him a beating so that his legs, arms and ribs were sore.

There was no fight in Lawrence Gainsborough and so he stared at the floor between his legs and waited for the next terrifying ordeal.

He looked up suddenly as he heard a woman scream. The sound was followed by a couple of loud slaps and he rolled to his left towards the entrance door, as if he were about to get up and go to her aid.

But he could not.

He was to weak and too afraid to help Gail Wetton.

She screamed again.

"Don't hurt her!" he called. But the words were only in his head and not out loud. The British MP began to cry.

*****

Night came.

With Sensei Nakamura driving they bounced off down the track behind Hagakure and out onto the main hill road.

Ten twisting miles later the sensei pulled the truck off to the right of the main road and headed along what looked to be an old farm track. However, it did not lead to a farm; it led to a wide steel-frame chain-link gate set in a ten-feet-high chain-link fence that had razor wire along the top. On the front of the gate was a sign; red Japanese writing on a white background.

Tandy peered at it through the truck's windscreen.

"What does that say?" she asked.

"It say, danger, keep out," answered the sensei. Before Tandy could say anything else the sensei said, "Stay here." He retrieved the bolt-cutters and the gardening gloves from under Tandy's feet and climbed out of the cab.

With the driver's side door open Tandy could smell the rotten-egg stench of sulphur coming into the cab of the truck from outside; which is typical of volcanic activity.

The sensei walked up to the padlock on the gate, put on the gloves, and made short work of the lock with the cutters. Still with the gloves on, he pushed the gate wide open.

He retrieved the padlock, got back into the truck and drove through the gate. He got out of the truck again and, still wearing the gloves, he went back and pulled the gate closed. He then got back in the truck and they headed further along the track.

Another one-hundred-and-fifty yards and Sensei Nakamura stopped the truck, turned off the ignition, and turned the headlights and sidelights off.

Despite it being night-time, it wasn't dark outside. There were so many vents that were lit up from inside by their white-hot contents that the area was lit by their glow. If it had not been for the circumstances, Tandy would have found it to be quite beautiful.

"Where are the fumaroles and mud pots?" she asked.

"Many fumarows and mud pots here. They surround us," said Sensei Nakamura. He waved a hand around and smiled at Tandy.

Tandy smiled uncertainly back at him. "Won't it be too hot to get near a fumarole?"

"Ahh, we no go near fumarow. As you say, too hot." He turned and looked out into the night. "We use mud pot. Is much safer, and soon get rid of bodies."

"Lovely," muttered Tandy.

Sensei Nakamura turned back to her. "Tandy, no get upset about this. These men try to shoot us. These men are scum."

Tandy gave an emphatic nod at that. "Hai, my sensei. You are right. Forgive me."

"Nothing to forgive." He gave a small smile. "Now, pot we want is just over there." He stuck his right thumb towards his side window.

Tandy's eyes widened. "Shit!" she exclaimed. "You mean we're right on top of it?"

"No, no. We are beside it. Very safe. But watch where you tread."

"Why?"

"Ground very soft. Might corrapse."

"And this is your version of safe?"

Sensei Nakamura giggled. "Just be carefur. You be fine." And with that he picked up one of the rubber gas masks and climbed out of the truck. He turned and looked back into the cab at Tandy.

The sensei was right; the mud pot was alongside the truck and only a few feet away. Tandy could hear it bubbling, and it did indeed sound like glob glob as bubbles of superheated steam forced their way up from deep underground to burst with a glutinous pop on the surface of the hot mud pool.

Further away she could hear fumaroles huffing and puffing as they belched their sulphurous smoke into the air like so many asthmatic dragons, and all around there were vents that hissed like angry snakes as they spewed steam into the sulphurous air. Tandy could feel a monstrous heat through the open door.

"Can't stay rong," said the sensei. "Must act fast."

"Why? Because of the sulphur?"

"No. Because tyres of truck might mewt."

"Melt! Bloody hell!"

"Or truck might sink. Many bodies. Truck very heavy."

"Je-sus!"

Sensei Nakamura pulled the rubber gas mask on over his bald head and waved at Tandy to follow him.

Tandy grabbed the other mask and climbed out of the cab. As she pulled it on she could feel the subterranean heat coming up through the soles of her trainers. She could also feel the ground vibrating as the volcanic activity far below gave rise to small tremors. Even through the breather she could smell the sulphurous fumes and she was now even more aware of the hissing, puffing and mud-popping noises all around her. This whole area, she now knew, was one huge area of dangerous volcanic activity. It was why the chain-link and danger signs were up – the Japanese authorities did not want anyone coming in here - and dying.

On arriving beside the chosen mud pot for the first time Tandy had stared at it, but the heat from it near the edge was intense so that after only a short time she had to back away. However, she continued to stare at the mesmerising mud bubbles.

The pot was in fact formed by a deep gaping fissure in the ground, some fourteen feet long and eight feet wide, and shaped like a giant eye. It was surrounded by rocks that looked like they were made of melted chocolate because of the mud that was splashed over them. Beyond those rocks the surface of the ground was stained yellow from the dissolved sulphur that was coming up in the water all around them as steam from the bowels of the earth.

"Very hot," said Sensei Nakamura. Even though his voice was muffled by the gas mask his sudden appearance alongside Tandy made her jump.

She put her hand over her heart. "Je-sus! Don't do that!" She realised that she had to raise her voice to make herself heard. "I could have fallen in!"

"No, no. You safe. I save you, Tandy."

Tandy looked at the little man's eyes that were watching her from beyond the glass lenses and she smiled. "Hai, my sensei. I believe you would."

Sensei Nakamura had smiled back; the only indication of which was the crinkling of the corners of his eyes for Tandy could not obviously see all of his face. "Now," he said almost conversationally, "we chuck bodies in." And he turned and walked over to the truck with its ghastly cargo whilst Tandy stared open-mouthed beneath her face mask at his receding back.

Despite the perilous situations of the hot mud pots, the fumaroles, and the treacherous hot ground beneath their feet, the two of them set too and unloaded the bodies, one-at-a-time, from the back of the truck, and carried each one between them over to the mud pot.

Getting the corpses into the heaving, popping, boiling mud of the pot was the most horrific and disgusting thing that Tandy had ever done; it even beat her experiments on live sewer rats that she had carried out to discover how fast the deadly cone shell venom worked. This was the venom she had used to dispatch her targets when she had operated as the assassin known as The Scorpion.

Tandy and Sensei Nakamura had to hold each body – Tandy holding an arm and a leg on one side while the sensei held an arm and a leg on the other - and then slide them head-first into the bubbling liquid mud. Tandy and the sensei could not throw them in because they did not want to be splashed by the scalding mud; instead, it was a kind of gruesome launching ceremony, a description that seemed very fitting to Tandy as she watched the first of the bodies slide below the surface, a sight that was almost too horrible to witness. Sensei Nakamura, realising her discomfort, took her gently by the arm and told her to be strong, and she firmed her resolve and continued with the grisly task. The worst body, of course, was the one that had been decapitated by the sensei's sword, and he, like all the others, literally went in head-first, tossed into the heaving mud by the sensei who swung it in by its hair.

With the deed done in record time, Tandy and Sensei Nakamura hurried back to the truck, and quickly removed all of the guns and ammunition that the seven men had been carrying.

Sensei Nakamura instructed Tandy to wait in the truck whilst he carried the items in their potato sacks over to a fumarole some fifty yards away and whose hot smoking vent was about the size of a bath and whose sides were lined with sulphur. Further down into the vent was a red-hot opening with a white core at its centre, like the entrance to Hell.

The guns were thrown in first and from a safe distance, with the intense heat instantly incinerating the potato sack and then melting the components of the firearms as if they were toy guns made of plastic. The hot gaping maw seemed to suck the weapons down, and every time it did it belched foul smoking fumes, as if it were grateful for this strange feeding.

Finally, in went the sack containing the ammunition. This was a rather risky business and sensei Nakamura elected to dump it into the fumarole by standing well back and swinging it through the choking air into the smoking pit. And then he took to his heels and ran as fast as he could back to the truck.

Tandy was already in the truck as the sensei climbed in, started the ignition and shoved the gearstick into reverse. As he pulled away the ammunition began to detonate like firecrackers, with some of the rounds finding their way out of the fumarole to zip through the air. One of them struck the front wing of the truck and it whined away into the night.

"Blimey, sensei. That was close," said Tandy.

"Hai! Must get out of here!"

The sensei reversed at speed back down the track to the gate. Here he opened the gate with his gloves on and, when he had guided the vehicle through the gate, he closed it and secured it with the padlock he had brought with him. This last action made Tandy wonder if her sensei had done this disposal of bodies here before, and why. But she kept that thought to herself as she really did not want to find out what the answer was.

Tandy and Sensei Nakamura took off their gas masks revealing faces that were slick with sweat. The sensei removed his gloves and looked at Tandy. He frowned and nodded as he said, "Very good, Tandy.. Was not nice. But necessary. Hai?"

Tandy nodded back. "Hai." She paused, then asked, "My sensei, I know we have just dumped the bodies in a large mud pot, but…I mean…someone might find them."

"Ah," nodded the sensei. "Water and mud very acidic. Even now they are being dis…disso…dissorv…."

"Dissolved?" offered Tandy.

He lifted his hands off the steering wheel and spread his palms. "Hai. Disovered. Be gone by morning."

Tandy frowned. "Oh, yes, I see." *Yuk!*

The old man gripped the wheel and sat up. "Now we go home. Have nice hot cup of tea! Hai?"

*****

SUNDAY 22nd JUNE

LAS VEGAS

Frank opened his eyes and looked at the digital readout on the radio beside his king-size bed. 8.10am.

Wearing only his boxer shorts he kicked his legs out of bed and dropped to the floor and did fifty push-ups then fifty sit-ups. Then he went and had a shower. And then he had a shave.

He walked back into the bedroom with a fluffy white towelling bath-robe around his naked body; a bath-robe supplied courtesy of the Luxor hotel. His mind was running over the attack on Tandy and also the TV footage of Lady Corrigan's abduction. Were the two things connected? He pulled his kit-bag out from the bottom of the wardrobe and dumped it on the end of the bed. He pulled his change of clothing out of it and that was when his mobile phone went off on the built-in bedside table.

He did not recognise the number and was about to close it down when something nagged at him. Frank therefore opened the line and held the phone to his ear, but he said nothing.

A familiar voice said, "Frank. I know you're there and listening to me."

It was Sir Michael Corrigan.

Frank took a breath. He knew he was going to regret this. Just by acknowledging his ex-boss would be like asking a hypochondriac "How are you?".

"Hello, Sir Michael."

"Did you see the news?"

"Yes."

"You know why I'm calling."

"Yes." Frank sat down on the edge of the bed. "Lady Corrigan has been abducted."

"Will you help?"

Pause.

"No," said Frank.

"Please, Frank."

"Why should I?"

"Because you're the best."

Frank firmed his jaw. "Don't bullshit me."

There was another pause, this time from Sir Michael, and then Sir Michael said, "Yes. You're right. I'm sorry. But you *are* the best, and I really do need your help."

"Why? You've got other agents. Why me?"

"Frank…it's Intiqam."

Frank felt as if the temperature of the room had suddenly dropped to frost level.

There. There was the connection Frank had been searching for; Lady

Corrigan and Tandy had both been attacked by agents of Intiqam - the terror organisation was back. He guessed he'd known it the moment he'd seen the newsreel. However, he still needed confirmation. So he asked,

"How do you know that it's Intiqam?"

"They sent me a film."

Frank raised his eyebrows. "A film?"

"Yes...Incidentally, MI Five and MI Six have also seen it."

"*Incidentally*," said Frank. The word was loaded with sarcasm.

The sarcasm was, of course, noted by Sir Michael but he made no comment. Instead, he said, "Their copy went to their headquarters, mine was sent directly to my house."

Frank's training and experience brought him up to full alert. "So, they know where you live?"

"Apparently." Sir Michael seemed to be unruffled

"That's not good news." Despite himself, Frank felt himself being drawn in. And he knew that Sir Michael would know that too.

"Look," said Sir Michael. "Don't concern yourself with me. I'm more concerned about my wife."

"I appreciate that, but first, tell me about the film." Frank knew that if MI5 and MI6 had seen it, then the Prime Minister would have as well. "Who's in it? What's in it?" And with those questions being asked Sir Michael knew that he'd just recruited Frank Cross. He answered,

"It's an MI Six agent, reading a message. He'd obviously been beaten and tortured first, before he was killed."

"How?"

"Garotte."

"Poor bastard," said Frank. He shook his head at the thought of what the agent must have gone through. Frank took a long breath. "I take it that the message was a ransom demand?"

"Kind of."

"What do you mean *kind of?*"

"They don't want money or assets, or even the release of people who they might regard as political prisoners."

"So, what do they want?"

"You, Frank."

Frank was silent for a moment and then said, "I must have really pissed them off when Tandy and I terminated El-Sayed, Lancaster, and their hit squad."

"Yes," agreed Sir Michael, "although they do not know of Tandy's involvement. So that's why they are only wanting you." Sir Michael paused slightly then continued, "There's something else you should know."

"Yes?"

"The film was made by someone calling himself al-Makira."

"The Cunning," translated Frank. "So what?"

"Al-Makira's real name is Yousuf El-Sayed. He is Aarif's elder brother."

"Ahh," said Frank as another connection was made. "So, that's why he wants me. This is simple vengeance. He'll probably want to execute me on camera and show it to the world. A film to say "this is what happens to those who oppose me"."

"Just so," agreed Corrigan. There was another pause. "Frank, there's something else."

"Yes?"

"They say they've got Tandy."

To Sir Michael's astonishment Frank laughed.

"What's so funny, Frank?"

"Tandy's in Japan." No point in telling the Director of the SOU that Tandy had only recently beaten off her own kidnapping attempt.

Sir Michael sounded concerned. "Are you sure?"

"Positive."

"Well, that's a relief," said Sir Michael and Frank could hear that genuine relief in his voice. Sir Michael had been the man that had moulded Tandy into the international assassin known as The Scorpion, and he'd followed her life, career and progress ever since she had been a little girl. "In that case Al-Makira is obviously lying. Although it could be he's trying a bluff, although to what end I don't know. He can't know Tandy's real identity…Can he?"

"No chance," said Frank.

"Good." Sir Michael continued, "He also said that they've got the MP, Lawrence Gainsborough and his secretary, Gail Wetton."

"Has he?"

"Possibly. We know that Gainsborough and Wetton were abducted in Venice and haven't been seen or heard from since."

"Sounds like Intiqam is building up quite a collection of hostages."

"Trying to, but they are not holding my wife yet. Or, rather, they haven't

264

taken her out of the UK yet."

Frank's eyebrows went up then down as he registered surprise and then suspicion in a heartbeat. "How do you know she's still in the UK?"

"Because she has a tracking chip in her head."

"What?" Frank was aghast. "You've had a tracking device placed in your wife's head?"

"Actually, it's not actually in her head, it's under her scalp."

"Oh well," said Frank laying on the sarcasm. "That makes it alright then."

"Frank, it was my wife's idea."

"Pardon?"

"Red. She asked me to have it placed under her scalp."

"Why? No, don't tell me."

But Sir Michael did anyway. "It was done in case something like this happened."

"Jesus, what a way to carry on a marriage! You really are quite the romantic, aren't you Sir Michael? Most husbands buy jewellery or dresses."

"Yes, well, the thing is, Frank, we can track her…"

"We?" interrupted Frank.

"Yes. We. Come to England, Frank. I'll give you a device that will enable you to track her and find her, particularly if they get her out of the country."

"Where is she now?"

"Essex."

"If you know where she is, why don't you organise a rescue mission with the Special Forces guys?"

"What, and risk them going in all guns blazing and getting my wife killed? Come off it."

"Okay." Frank's mind whirled. Sir Michael was right. A Special Forces raid would be too risky. Frank stood up and paced about his bedroom in his bath-robe. "You said earlier that al-Makira wants me."

"Yes."

"Well, supposing he had managed to smuggle your wife out of the UK, and just supposing Intiqam had managed to grab Tandy, have you any idea of where am I to go to carry out the exchange?" *That's a joke*, thought Frank. *Once al-Makira has me, he'll kill every last one of us, and put it all on film.*

"Oh yes, we know that."

Frank stopped pacing. "We do?"

"Yes. It's been given to us, quite deliberately, in the message in the film.

In fact, Intiqam practically sent you a written invitation."

"And?"

"Qaryat Musawara."

"Jesus! I know where that is."

"I know you do."

Qaryat Musawara - Arabic for Walled Village - had been the village in Iraq where Frank had been sent some months ago by Simon Lancaster. Lancaster had arranged a mission for Frank to carry out on his own; Frank was supposed to have been killed. Lancaster had sent him on what he considered to be a suicide mission because he wanted him dead as part of the Intiqam plan to wreck the SOU, and thereafter MI5 and MI6 from the inside. However, Lancaster had not banked on Frank's extraordinary ability to survive and be able to execute his enemies as if they were just a bunch of flies whilst he had the biggest fly-swat.

The mission had been to enter the village at night and undetected and then to burst in on a meeting of some senior members of Intiqam, with the order to kill every last one of them.

The SOU had been informed of the meeting through an agent codenamed Mongoose who worked undercover for MI6. However, before Frank could get into the building holding the meeting, he had witnessed Mongoose shot dead by El-Sayed who was wielding a shotgun. Unbeknown to any of the Security Services was the fact that Mongoose was Frank's sister. Immediately following his sister's murder, a vengeful Frank had attacked the meeting and, by using hand-grenades and small-arms, Frank had killed everyone there, except El-Sayed, who had managed to get away.

Aarif El-Sayed may have escaped Frank's clutches, but the murder of Frank's sister had only enforced Frank's determination to track down the terrorist and kill him. Cross and Tandy had succeeded in tracking El-Sayed and Tandy had sent him to his death. And now al-Makira wanted Frank Cross, for vengeance.

Frank asked, "Are you sure that the filming was done at Musawara?"

"No, that's only what they've told us. They could be lying. But you might be able to confirm it."

"How so?"

"This al-Makira chap always films his executions in front of an open window. You might recognise the view."

Frank actually laughed. "Recognise the view? That's a bloody long shot."

"I know. But try anyway."

"Can you send me a copy of the film?"

"I'll do it straight away."

"Thanks. Send it to this phone. I'll get back to you to confirm the location, if I can."

"Good."

Frank made a puffing noise. "Okay," he said. "Looks like they're going to get me."

"So you're in?"

"Do I have any choice?"

"Sorry, Frank."

"No, you're not...And I have to do this, and you know it. They're not going to stop until they have me."

"Or until al-Makira and Intiqam are all dead," said Sir Michael.

Frank paced some more, then asked, "How far have MI Five and MI Six gone with this?"

Sir Michael answered, "The PM is calling a meeting tomorrow morning of the Chiefs of Staff Committee."

Frank knew that would mean that it would not be long before a Special Forces group would be sent out to Iraq on a rescue mission.

"How long have I got before the Special Forces boys go in?"

"I'd say about a week. Maybe less. Probably less. It depends on how fast the Chiefs shift their arses."

"Damn. It sounds like this might develop into a race. I don't want the Special Forces guys getting tangled up in my plans."

"I can try and delay them. Have a word in a few ears."

"That would be good."

"Can you still do it, Frank?" Corrigan sounded tense and he was mightily relieved when Frank answered,

"Yes, and I'll do it my way."

"No problem. I'll give you what support I can...except..."

Frank noted the hesitation. "Except what?"

"Well..."

Frank could imagine Sir Michael Corrigan puffing out his cheeks.

"Out with it, Sir Michael."

"It's just that if your rescue attempt goes wrong, I will not be able to get you out of the shit. You'll be labelled a mercenary and a murderer."

Frank Cross smiled to himself. This was the penalty for leaving the Specialist Operations Unit – even the unofficial had become unofficial.

"No contract. Is that it?"

"Yes, Frank. Exactly."

No contract meant the mission was not sanctioned. He was on his own. If the rescue mission failed there would be no-one back home to protect Cross and his Shadows team.

"Well then, Sir Michael, I had better make sure that the rescue does not go wrong."

"Fingers crossed," said Sir Michael, which seemed pretty weak and tame, given the circumstances.

"Okay, Sir Michael. I'm coming to England. I'll get a BA flight and I'll meet you in the arrivals hall of Heathrow airport. Stand in the line for the cab pick-ups and hold up a piece of cardboard with the name Harry Lowe written on it." At the other end of the line Sir Michael smiled. Harry Lowe had been one of many aliases that Frank Cross had used when he had worked for the Unit. That particular alias had been killed off, almost literally, by The Scorpion, acting under orders from Simon Lancaster. "And don't dress too smart," continued Frank. "You're supposed to be a cab driver remember, not a knight of the realm."

"I'll see you at Heathrow, Frank. And Frank…?"

"Yes?"

"Thank you."

"Yeah, right. Do me a favour though…if they get Red out of the country phone me and let me know immediately."

"Will do."

Frank cut the call and tossed the mobile onto his bed.

Frank shed his bath-robe and started to get dressed. A few seconds later his mobile went off, so he picked it up. It was the execution film. He watched it dispassionately, ignoring the terribly beaten man that was the focal point of the film and the way that he had been killed. Frank was able to zoom in on sections of the film so he zeroed-in on the view out of the window behind the wrecked victim; there were the ragged sticks and straw roof tops of the local buildings that he recognised, and in the far distance was the scree that lay at the bottom of a high cliff; a high cliff with a plateau on the top. He had once laid belly-down on the edge of that cliff and had scoped out the village.

Yes, it was Qaryat Musawara alright.

Frank closed down the film and began to dance his thumb over the phone's keypad. He confirmed the film's location to Sir Michael, as he said he would. Then he started the dance with his thumb again; time to get Shadows ready for their next op. With any luck T Bone would not have made it to the airport yet as he had to drop off the Grand Cherokee first.

**

T Bone had returned the SUV and had then hailed a cab for the airport. Sitting in the back seat of the cab his mobile went off and he answered it straight away as it was Frank.

"Yes, boss?"

"Don't go home," said Frank. "Go to the Pefkos City Hotel in Limassol, Cyprus, and I'll meet you there in a couple of days."

"Sure boss, but what's up?"

"Rescue mission." Frank then briefly explained the circumstances.

T Bone whistled. "Sounds hairy."

"I'll be relying on you guys to make it less hairy."

"Count on me, Frank. I'm on my way." With that, the call ended and Frank then phoned Clonk and Tommo and asked them to come to his room. As they were both in the hotel they were with Frank in a couple of minutes. Errol was no longer in the Luxor as he had been found a room in the MGM Grand. It was free-of-charge, thanks to Miss Levin, and anyway, Errol was not a member of Shadows, so his work was done.

Once Clonk and Tommo had joined Frank, he explained the situation and the mission. Like T Bone, Frank told them to go to the Pefkos City Hotel and wait for him.

Clonk, ever the practical Scotsman, asked, "What about weapons?"

"Leave that to me, but I assure you there'll be no shortage of them and they'll be top-of-the-range."

"Fair enough," said Clonk.

Frank turned to Tommo. "Any questions, my friend?"

"No, Frank. All good."

"Right then guys. See you in Cyprus." Frank shook hands with the two men and, when they had left, he used his phone again.

Sir Michael answered straight away. "Yes Frank. What can I do for you?"

"Top-of-the-range weapons and equipment," answered Frank. "I'll let you know exactly what I want when I see you."

"Very well. Where do you need them?"

"The RAF base at Akrotiri on Cyprus and my team is going to need the use of a Hercules transport aircraft for a multiple parachute drop."

Corrigan coughed at the end of the line then said in a rather strangled voice, "Bloody hell, Frank, that's going to take some doing!"

"Sir Michael," said Frank as formally as he could. And then his voice went cold. "If you want me to get your wife back, rescue an MP and any other civilians, and take out al-Makira and the rest of this Intiqam scum, you'll get me what I want."

Sir Michael was instantly contrite. "I didn't say I couldn't do it," he said. "But why a Hercules? And why Cyprus?"

"Firstly, because I've jumped out of one before." And he had when he was in the Special Air Service. "And second, because Cyprus is as near as we can get to Iraq whilst using a secure British air base." For the next ten minutes Frank told Sir Michael Corrigan the full details of his plan, then he ended the call. He made another call to President Nigel Ibraheem and told the President that his diplomatic bag was going to come back to him and to have it picked up at St Margaret's international airport, which was named after the President.

After all of that Frank sat down on the edge of his bed and called Tandy.

At 9.15am in Las Vegas it was 1.20am in Japan on the following day. Tandy had helped Sensei Nakamura clear up the wreckage from the attack as best she could. They had then had a meal and then Tandy had packed her bags.

It had been whilst she was packing that her phone went off and she received the call from Frank.

"Hi Frank."

"Where are you, m'dear?"

"Still with the sensei, but I'm packing to come home even as we speak."

"Good. But don't come home. When you get to Tokyo get a flight to Larnaca in Cyprus."

"Cyprus? Are we having a holiday?"

"Sorry love, far from it. We're on a rescue mission."

"Who are we rescuing?"

"Me."

**

After Frank had explained what was going on to Tandy, he asked her to get a large sheet of plain paper and one red and one black felt-tip pen when she got to Cyprus.

"What for?" she asked.

"So that I can draw a map," he answered. Then he told her that he loved her, ended the call, and went around the room with an antiseptic wipe and wiped down any surfaces that he might have touched. As Frank was a wary user of a hotel room when he was on assignment these objects and surfaces did not amount to much. After that, Frank picked up his two kit-bags, one contained his clothing and the other was the diplomatic bag. This second bag held the weapons they had used to rescue Diana Moon.

He then left the room, checked out of the hotel and hailed a cab for the airport. Once there the diplomatic bag went off to the Caribbean whilst Frank headed for the Mediterranean.

*****

Tandy had packed. She was now standing on the sensei's engawa. No longer in either her kimono or her gi she felt decidedly overdressed in her trainers, T shirt, jacket and jeans.

Sensei Nakamura approached her and bowed. Tandy, honoured by this simple act of respect for her, returned the bow. The sensei was holding a long narrow package in his hands. It was neatly wrapped in brown paper and was about twelve inches long, two inches wide, and two inches deep.

"This for you, Tandy." He held out the package with both hands and she took it from him with both hands, as was the custom. It felt like a long narrow box under the brown wrappings. Fancy, and highly expensive chopsticks perhaps?

Tandy arched an eyebrow and smiled. "Arigato, my sensei." She bowed again. "What is it?"

"Is surprise. You open at Haneda airport. Hai?"

"Hai. Yes, of course."

They stood for a moment, looking at each other in an awkward silence. The Tandy said, "Oh, sod this!" and she stepped forwards and hugged the old man. Slowly, while she held the embrace, he brought his own hands up and very gently placed them on Tandy's upper arms, his thumbs lightly resting on her biceps. She stepped back from him and looked, with slightly dewy eyes, into his face. The sensei remained holding her arms.

"You, ve-ry good student." He released her arms and bowed again.

"You," said Tandy. "Ve-ry good sensei." Their smiles turned into laughs.

There was the toot toot of a motor horn from down on the road.

"Cab's here," said Tandy.

"Hai. Must go now. You come back and see me. Hai?"

"Try and stop me." She quickly stepped forwards and planted a robust kiss on his right cheek. Then she stepped back, gave him a blinding smile, turned, and she was gone.

Sensei Nakamura made his way back along the engawa with the fingers of his right hand gently stroking his cheek where he had been kissed. As he stepped into his house he dropped his hand then lifted it again, and wiped away from his eye what might have been a tear.

**

It took a while for Tandy to get to Haneda airport, her journey being a reverse to the one that had brought her to Hagakure. Her flight was on time and she had a few minutes to wait in the departure lounge before she boarded. Seated, she took the sensei's present out of her carry-on bag and placed it on her knees. It wasn't heavy. She lifted it to her right ear and waggled it. It didn't rattle.

Tandy sat it back in her lap and tore the brown paper away. She looked down at a shiny black lacquered box. She lifted the top off and stared wide-eyed at the content: there, folded lengthways upon itself like a thin flattened snake, was a karate black belt.

"Wow!" she exclaimed.

And then, much louder, with a double fist-pump, so that people looked around at her, she cried out, "YES!"

*****

MONDAY 23rd JUNE

"Do you think he will come?" asked Irfan.

"He'll come," smiled al-Makira. "After receiving our film and our demands, the British Government and Sir Michael Corrigan will be shitting themselves."

"You really think this will work?"

"They'll have no choice but to send Cross to me. After all, we have their precious MP, and the MP's lovely girlfriend."

Irfan nodded and smiled. "Yes. And soon we will have this Lady Corrigan."

"Yes," nodded al-Makira. "Although none of them are of much consequence," said al-Makira waving his right hand. "They are but breadcrumbs." And he smiled at his little joke. But he really wished that he had Tandy in his clutches.

*****

Frank Cross came in on a British Airways flight and landed in the afternoon at London Heathrow for terminal 5. He had no need of the baggage reclaim hall as he was not travelling with check-in luggage, only a carry-on bag. Therefore, he cleared through to customs in double-quick time and arrived out onto the arrivals concourse. His eyes skimmed the row of men and women who were lined up the other side of the arrivals barrier and who were holding up various bits of paper and cardboard with the names of passengers written on them; some scrawled, some printed neatly.

Frank spotted the name Harry Lowe in large black letters and recognised the man who was holding it up. Frank nodded at Sir Michael Corrigan as he walked past him and Sir Michael scurried to catch up with Frank when he emerged from the end of the barriers. Sir Michael was wearing a dark-blue pair of cargo trousers, a dark-blue open-neck cotton shirt and a dark-blue blazer. He looked every inch a private-hire cab driver. They shook hands.

"My car is in the car-park, Sir," said Sir Michael. "Can I carry your luggage for you?"

Frank threw him a glance, smiled, and said, "No, that's okay."

"Fine, Sir. Then follow me." Corrigan struck off towards the multistorey car-park.

It was a fine warm day with a blue sky that had only a few small fluffy white clouds in it. The garage was stark and grey. The car turned out to be a large black Mercedes-Benz S Class with tinted windows all round.

"Nice car," commented Frank. "Yours?"

"Yes. Get in."

The two men slid into the leather seats, closed doors and fastened seatbelts. Sir Michael guided the big saloon out of the car-park and headed for the airport's Western Perimeter Road.

"Where to?" asked Sir Michael.

"Head for the Harrow area."

"I didn't know you lived in Harrow."

"I don't." He did, but he wasn't going to tell Sir Michael that. If Sir Michael wanted to know where Cross lived then he would have to find out for himself. And so far, any attempt to do that had failed, because Frank Cross was damn good at covering his tracks.

"What happens now, Frank?"

"You're going to arrange for that Hercules transport plane to be on the ground at RAF Akrotiri on Cyprus."

"I've already done that. Your lift is all arranged."

Frank was secretly impressed; it had not taken Sir Michael very long and he must have pulled in multiple favours. "Excellent," said Frank. "On board it will be our weapons. I have written it all down for you." He waved a sheet of A4 paper. "I want one Smith and Wesson model sixty-four revolver…"

"That'll be yours then," interrupted Sir Michael, who knew that Frank favoured that particular gun.

"Yes," confirmed Frank. "And I want it loaded with nine-millimetre hollow point bullets. I also want two loaded speedloaders for it as well as four Glock Nineteen's with suppressors, three Heckler and Koch MP Seven's, an Accuracy International L Ninety-Six A One – that's a sniper rifle to you – with a scope and a leather carry case, and all the guns must have spare ammunition, four magazines to each gun. Plus, four black double-edged tactical knives, four stun grenades and eight L109A1 fragmentation grenades."

There are various types of fragmentation grenade, but they basically all work the same way: the person holding the grenade to be thrown is also holding in place a lever, or "spoon". A cotter pin with a ring attached holds the spoon in place, and if this pin is removed the grenade is now "live". Once the grenade is thrown the spoon flies off, which causes an internal striker to detonate a primer. This, in turn, ignites a fuse which then detonates the explosive main charge. Depending on the type of grenade, the final detonation will have a delay from spoon fly to explosion from anywhere between two to six seconds, but all will have a kill zone radius of around sixteen feet and a casualty radius of around fifty feet. However, you can pull the pin and, provided you do not let the spoon fly off, the grenade will not detonate, even though it is now "live". With the lever still in place you can put the pin back in and make the grenade safe again. The British Army L109A1 grenade is 97mm long and 65mm in diameter. It is a deep bronze green colour with a rough surface similar in feel to sandpaper, which allows for a better grip on the weapon.

"Anything else? I mean, is that all?" Sir Michael's sarcasm was plain as he left the Perimeter Road and pulled onto a roundabout, from where he picked up the link road to the M25 motorway.

"No," said Frank, smiling. "I also want a detailed map of the area surrounding Musawara, a state-of-the-art monocular, about four square feet of very fine camouflage netting, five sets of night-vision goggles, five pairs of protective goggles to be worn in a parachute jump and four parachutes, one of which must be a tandem set-up. And I also want this kit." He took out another sheet of paper. On it was a set of figures, measurements for five tactical uniforms. "I want them in black and grey night camouflage," said Frank.

Contrary to what most people think, black is not a good colour for night stealth work; the black is just too black for night-time. The best night camouflage is black and dark grey cloud patching or stripes, which break up the human outline far more efficiently.

Frank gave both sheets to Sir Michael who took them in his left hand and gave them a quick glance as he drove. "I see Tandy's going with you." One of the uniforms was a lot smaller than the rest of the set and with just that glance Corrigan had spotted it. Frank was impressed.

"Yes," said Frank. "She's the one on the sniper rifle." There was a pause. "Well?" asked Frank. "Can you do it?"

Sir Michael Corrigan stuffed the papers into the inside pocket of his jacket as he stared out of the window at the road ahead and the traffic. "Of course, I can do it."

From the link road Sir Michael turned right onto the M25 heading clockwise. From here the Mercedes picked up the M4 at junction 4B and headed east to junction 3 and then north onto the A312, heading for Harrow.

Frank had a house in Whitmore Road, Harrow. It was an address that he used to live at full-time. It was also an address that the Specialist Operations Unit knew nothing about, even though the late Aarif El-Sayed had stumbled across it when he was trying to track-down Frank in order to have him killed. Fortunately, because El-Sayed had been operating without the approval of the SOU, he had not kept a record of where Frank lived. And, in any case, the house was not registered to him in his real name, instead it was another alias.

As they neared the outskirts of Harrow Frank asked for the tracking device that Sir Michael had mentioned on the phone.

"It's in the glove compartment."

Frank leaned forward and popped the catch on the compartment in front of him. He reached in and took out a small dark-grey plastic box about the size of two cigarette packets placed side-by-side. It looked like a large mobile phone. Most of the front of it was taken up by a screen with some small buttons underneath.

"Press the yellow button," said Sir Michael.

Frank did so and the screen lit up. What it showed resembled a car sat-nav. Frank was looking at a large green area with three diagrammatic buildings in white in the centre of the screen; two small buildings and one larger one. A red dot was flashing in the middle of the largest building.

"I take it," said Frank, peering at the screen, "that dot is Lady Corrigan?"

"Yes. And if you press the blue button, you'll pan out, and the green button zooms you back in again."

Frank turned in his seat towards his ex-director. "Aren't you worried for her, Sir Michael?"

Corrigan threw Frank a quick glance. "Of course I'm bloody worried!" he snapped. "That's why I sent for you for Christ's sake!"

Frank nodded at this out-of-character display of emotion by the Director of the SOU. "Yes," said Frank gently. "And now I'm here. And I promise I'll get her back."

There was a pause. Sir Michael massaged the steering wheel of the Mercedes with his fingers then said, "I'm sorry…Thank you, Frank…I really need you and your special skills set on this one."

Frank said nothing, giving Sir Michael enough time to compose himself.

After a few seconds Sir Michael resolutely lifted his chin and continued,

"Fortunately, as you can see from the tracker, she's still in the country. But you'll have to move fast to get her, because I'm sure that they're going to move her out of the country, and pretty soon."

"What makes you think that?" asked Frank.

"First, because they said in the film that they already have her, so they must be confident of getting her out of the UK, and second, because the building she's in is right next door to an airfield, outside North Weald Bassett. You can see the airfield if you pan out on the tracker."

Frank panned out.

There was North Weald airfield. Frank studied it for a few moments, then asked, "What do you know about it?"

Sir Michael gathered his thoughts for a moment then said, "Right. It's just outside of Epping, in Essex. I've already had a look at the plans for the airfield. It's got a fairly long runway, so you can land any size of jet in there, even the big international ones at a pinch, but I'm pretty sure our kidnappers will not be trying to smuggle Lady Corrigan out in one of those. No, it's probably either a light aircraft, a helicopter, or even a business jet."

"Hmmm," grumbled Frank. "A light aircraft or helicopter would not have the range to get Lady Corrigan all the way to Iraq, but a business jet would."

Sir Michael nodded. "You're right. But a business jet would have to land, run out, turn around, refuel and then line up and take off again. That would take too long and attract too much attention. My guess is a chopper. They'll just fly in, drop down, pick her up and leave before any official can do anything about it. They may even have a cover story ready."

"Yes," said Frank, nodding. "Like a mercy airlift, or something along those lines?"

"Exactly. Remember, we are dealing with an organisation that seems to have a lot of money behind it."

"From al-Qaeda and Isis?"

"Yes, but I think they are also raising their own capital."

"How?" asked Frank.

"I think they are behind these money-or-violence threats that have been turning up globally in little white envelopes."

Frank nodded. If Sir Michael believed that then there was a distinct possibility that he was right. You did not get to be the head of an alternative British Secret Service organisation without having your finger on the pulse of world criminal affairs.

"You mean," asked Frank, "these little white letters that have been delivered to the rich and famous?"

"Mostly the rich. Famous doesn't necessarily mean rich."

"Okay," said Frank. "But to get back to Lady Corrigan...Where do you think they'll take her? Across the Channel to Europe?"

"Yes, that would be the most likely. But, of course, we don't know where. It could be France, or Germany, Holland. Any number of landfalls."

"I guess, in that case, I had better stop her from getting airborne."

"That would be best." Sir Michael's face betrayed no emotion and Frank wondered how his former boss could keep his cool like this.

Frank said, "But if they do manage to get her airborne the tracker will tell us where she's going." He continued to stare at the tracker. "I think you're right about the chopper. Intiqam will want to be very low profile and be able to just drop in and out of any airport or airfield that they might use. If they bounce in and bounce out they might even get away with not carrying out all the normal formalities, depending on how desperate and daring they are."

"I'd say they are very desperate and very daring," said Sir Michael. "After all, they snatched Red in the middle of London at prime time."

Frank gave a sideways glance to the Director. That made sense. And, as Sir Michael had reasoned, by helicopter the kidnappers could take Lady Corrigan to any one of a number of European countries the other side of the North Sea or the English Channel. Hopefully Frank could get to Lady Corrigan before they moved her.

"Where do you want me to drop you off, Frank?"

"Northwick Park underground station please. Do you know it?"

"Yes, we'll be there in a few minutes."

**

Sir Michael pulled up outside Northwick Park tube station. This station is on the underground Metropolitan line which went west and branched to either Amersham, Chesham or Uxbridge, or east into central London. By dropping Frank here Sir Michael would not know in which direction Frank was going to travel - which was the whole point.

Still holding the tracker, Frank got out of the car leaving his door open. He then opened the rear door on his side of the car and retrieved his bag. He closed the rear door and then bent down by the front door and looked in at Sir Michael.

"Don't worry," said Frank. "I'll get your wife back safely and in one piece."

Corrigan leaned towards the open door and gave a small smile. "Thanks, Frank."

"Just make sure that I get the equipment I need and that there are no hitches in getting me and my outfit onto the RAF base."

"Will do."

"And keep the Special Ops boys out of my hair."

"I'll try."

"You won't," said Frank firmly. "You'll do it, or the shit will definitely hit the fan." With that he closed the door somewhat harder than he had intended, turned, and headed for the station.

After Sir Michael had driven off Frank re-appeared at the entrance of the station and looked around him. Sir Michael would not have been able to know which drop-off point Frank would want, but the car might have been bugged, and someone else in the SOU might have been listening in, or Sir Michael might have been followed. That would mean a tail. To avoid that, Frank crossed the road and spent fifteen minutes carrying out anti-tail manoeuvres before he arrived back at the station satisfied that he was not being followed.

He then used an Oyster pre-payment card to get him through the barriers. The card was registered in the false name of William Newport which was one of Frank's many aliases. He went down to the trains where he went east to central London. He got off two stops later at Wembley Park and then got back on a train heading west to West Harrow station. He was still anti-tailing.

At West Harrow he got off the train, exited the station and walked to his house which was not far away. On the way there he called into a small supermarket and bought two ready-made cheese sandwiches in their plastic throw-away boxes.

Having got to his house, he went indoors and took a shower and got changed into a pair of black cargo trousers, a long black leather zip-front jacket with zip-up pockets, black woollen shirt and black socks and black trainers. He put the tracking device into one of the deep pockets on the left thigh of his cargo trousers. He then went into the kitchen and made himself a cup of black coffee and ate the cheese sandwiches while standing up with his back to the sink.

Having finished the coffee and sandwiches, he washed up the cup and placed it upside-down on the draining board and put the sandwich wrappers outside in his wheelie-bin.

He then went up into the loft space via a drop-down step ladder that came out of a trapdoor above the top landing.

Frank's house was a semi-detached, and in the loft, against the wall that he shared with his next-door-neighbour, was a large grey steel cabinet - six feet high, six feet wide and twelve inches deep. The twin doors on the front were locked with a key pad. Frank punched in the code and opened the front to display an array of revolvers, semi-automatic pistols, assault rifles, knives, ammunition, speedloaders, and a number of holsters. In the bottom right-hand corner was a small black case.

Frank lifted out the black case, opened it, and took out the four passports and credit cards that it contained. He selected those for William Newport. He tucked the passport and credit card into an inside pocket on his jacket and returned the case to the cabinet.

Next, a supple black leather holster went onto the belt of Frank's trousers and at his right hip, after which Frank selected the model of handgun that he tended to favour: a Smith and Wesson Model 64 revolver with a four-inch barrel. He put one speedloader into each of his two jacket pockets.

Frank favoured a revolver over a semi-automatic pistol. A semi-automatic pistol, depending on the size of the magazine, can hold in excess of ten rounds. The bullets in the magazine are pushed up into the firing chamber by a plate pushed by a spring. These springs and plates can sometimes jam, rendering the gun useless. A revolver, however, only holds six rounds. This means that it has less firepower, the trade-off being that it does not jam. To get around this problem of a lack of rounds the speedloader has been developed. This gadget holds six bullets in a circular clip. By holding the points of the bullets over the empty chambers of the revolver, and by pressing a button on the top of the loader, all six bullets drop into the chambers. Frank had learned to do this rapid change so that he was now extremely fast at it, and this speed and dexterity had saved his life more than once.

With the speedloaders and the loaded revolver Frank now had eighteen rounds. These were hollow-point bullets. Hollow-point bullets have a greater killing force because they have a greater destructive power than a hard-point round. This is because the hollow-point spreads on impact with the human body, causes major damage to the internal organs and creates a bigger exit wound.

A tactical military-style dagger went into a sheath on his belt on his left hip and he was all set.

He locked the cabinet, came down out of the loft, closed it and went downstairs. Hanging on a hook on one of the walls in the entrance hall was a full-face black crash helmet. He lifted it off the hook and left the house.

Beside the house and built into the side of it was a single garage that fronted onto a driveway. Frank unlocked the up-and-over garage door and lifted it open. The garage housed Frank's immaculate black 1960 Jaguar saloon with a 3.4 litre engine, twin SU carburettors and four forward gears plus overdrive. Frank really loved this car and had given considerable thought about shipping it out to the Caribbean. In front of the Jaguar, and placed side-on to the front of the oval chrome radiator grill, was a powerful steel-grey Yamaha FJR 1300cc motorbike.

Frank had owned a 1300cc Yamaha motorbike before this one, but he had recently replaced it with this beast that had hardly been used and he was looking forward to giving it a real thrashing. It was just that he had not reckoned on having to thrash it for this present reason – the rescue of Lady Maria Corrigan.

Frank took the bike off its stands, wheeled it out onto the driveway and put it back on its stands. Then he went back and locked the garage.

He then got on the bike and looked up at the sky; somehow not as blue as earlier but it looked like it would stay dry. Frank put on his crash helmet, took the bike of its stands and hit the starter. The engine went first time and Frank gave it a couple of noisy revs to satisfy the neighbourhood curtain twitchers, and then he was off, accelerating with a harsh growl down the road and heading in the direction of the town of Epping.

*****

Sir Michael had made it home and he now sat hunched forwards with his elbows on a work desk and his hands clasped together in front of him in the small office in his house. He had a cup of black coffee beside his right elbow as he looked at a computer screen. His computer could also be used as a tracking device, and he controlled his breathing as he stared at the red dot that hovered over the building that Frank Cross was heading towards.

He lifted the cup and took a mouthful of coffee. This plan had better work. A failure would have a result too ghastly to contemplate.

*****

It takes about an hour by car to get from Harrow to Epping, but Frank was not in a car and he could get to the front of traffic queues and open up the bike in areas where a car cannot, although he made sure that he kept just below the speed limit because the last thing he wanted was to be pulled over by the police. He balanced the motorbike easily, threading it through the gaps in the various vehicles, watching for pits and bumps in the road as he shot over the tarmac.

He got onto the A409 and headed for the Borehamwood area and then, with the traffic so far being relatively light, cut across east to the A1. Once on the A1 he headed north to junction 23 of the M25 motorway and from here it was motorway and top speed to junction 27.

He reached junction 27 just before 6pm. Frank left the M25 and joined the M11, heading north and sped along this short stretch of road to junction 7. Here Frank left the motorway and went up the ramp and into a large roundabout that could take him to north to Harlow, around and back to the M11, or east onto the small A414. Frank negotiated the frantic traffic on the roundabout and swung onto the A414 which, in places, was little more than a wide country lane.

Frank went along this road for about two hundred yards then pulled over and checked the tracker. The red dot was still positioned over the building, so Lady Corrigan had not yet been moved. That was a bloody relief. He hoped that fact would make his job a damned sight easier. Frank put the tracker away and continued to follow the A414. There were wide fields and copses of trees beyond the hedgerows to Frank's left and somewhere over to his right, behind more hedgerows, was North Weald airfield. Suddenly, as if to illustrate the point, a small aircraft, a four-seater white piston-powered Cessna 182 Skylane, went through the air left-to-right two-hundred feet up and in front of him with the single propellor on the nose cone a whirring dark blur. The craft was obviously coming in to land as it came in low with its engine revs dropping and buzzing like an angry bee.

It dropped out of sight beyond a line of trees as Frank carried on along the road. He slowed up at a large roundabout where the road either continued onwards or right for the airfield. Frank ignored the turning and went forwards, slowing up again for another large roundabout that was a few hundred yards further on. The roundabout formed a crossroads; right for North Weald Bassett, straight on for Chipping Ongar, or left onto a small B road, called Weald Bridge Road, that wound off and away through the green summer countryside. Frank pulled over and waited just back from the roundabout and checked the tracker again. It indicated that he should turn left so he turned left onto the B road going north.

Frank passed some bungalows away to his left and then went through a small collection of houses either side of the road. Beyond these, and some one hundred yards further on, he pulled up again and once more pulled out the tracker; the red dot was further on and over to his left – that would mean only one thing: Lady Corrigan was nearby. Frank moved off slowly and watched for some kind of track or farm entrance that might lead through the fields to the building where Lady Corrigan was being held.

*****

As it turned out, Tommo, Clonk and T Bone caught the same flight out of McCarran airport, Las Vegas. Their Delta airlines flight did not fly direct to Cyprus, it landed at Paris, Charles de Gaulle airport. Here they transferred quickly to a Lufthansa flight out to the shared, although still disputed, Greek and Turkish island of Cyprus in the Mediterranean Sea, landing at Larnaca.

From Larnaca they all shared a cab from the airport to the Pefkos City Hotel where they awaited the arrival of their boss. They hadn't known it, but they were getting out of the cab in front of the Greek hotel as Frank was powering along the M11.

Tandy meanwhile, was waiting at Changi airport, Singapore, having arrived by British Airways and had then gone through transit to await her flight to Larnaca. She was sitting in the BA departure lounge and had just received word to go to the exit gate.

All the members of Shadows were travelling First Class, so at least that took some of the bumps out of the journeys.

*****

Al-Makira was back on his mobile. He was talking to Fazil in the barn. "We have a helicopter on its way to North Weald. It should be at the airfield in about an hour. Make sure that Lady Corrigan is ready for transport."

"Yes, al-Makira. It shall be done. But…"

"But what?" snapped al-Makira. "What is wrong?"

"Why cannot the helicopter land here, at the barn?"

"You idiot! Are you completely stupid? Look outside. Do you see trees? How is a helicopter supposed to land amongst all those trees?"

"Yes. Of course. I am sorry…"

"Shut up! And get Lady Corrigan ready…And don't harm her…and do not fuck this up. Do you understand, Fazil?"

"Yes,,al-M…" Fazil began to answer, but al-Makira had already ended the call and the kidnapper was left staring at his phone.

*****

Four hundred yards further on Frank found what he was looking for: a track. It had no gate across it so that it formed a narrow gap in the hedges and trees that lined either side of the road. The track was made of rough concrete that had baked dried mud spread liberally across the surface where farm vehicles - probably mostly tractors - had dropped the wet earth from their wheels whilst waiting to pull onto the road; there were smears of it curving onto the road. Beyond the gap in the trees, and to either side of the track, was an enormous field of rapeseed that stood some two to three feet high and which stirred in a slight breeze. The bright yellow flowers that seem to have an inner light that almost overwhelms the eye had already fallen as the plant blooms during April through to late May. Now Frank was faced by acres of leafy stems topped by pale ripening seed pods.

Frank pulled onto the concrete and raised his helmet's visor. He looked up. The sky was a light grey colour but there were no rain clouds and the early evening light was good; it would be light easily until at least 9pm. Frank cut the engine and wheeled the Yamaha up the track where he was able to hide it in amongst a tangle of convenient bushes and tall weeds.

Frank considered his rescue plan. It was quite a simple one: burst in on the scumbags, shoot any bastard who opposed him and grab Lady Corrigan.

Frank was not bothered about the noise his Smith and Wesson would make because the farming community allowed the shooting of pheasants out here, and, together with the bang of automatic bird scarers, the locals had got used to the sound of gunfire at all times of the day. The final part of the plan was to get back to the bike, and, with Red on board, get the hell out of there, just in case the police arrived.

With the Yamaha suitably hidden, Frank took off his helmet and placed it over the bike's handlebars. He scuttled over to the track, moving in a crouch and keeping low so that he would not be seen above the sea of whispering rapeseed that stretched out and away on either side.

The track rose slightly uphill and just before Frank came to the top of the rise he dropped onto his stomach and commando-crawled the rest of the way to the ridge. At the ridge another concrete track came from left to right, forming a T junction. Frank stuck his head out from the cover of the rapeseed.

At a good distance away to his left and right were lines of trees that bordered the sides of the huge field. In front of him, across the track that formed the T junction, was an ancient spreading oak tree and beyond it was more of the rapeseed crop. Beneath the heavy boughs of the oak the track ran to the right for about fifty yards towards a large barn with two smaller brick-built structures behind it and to the left. The roof of one of these had caved in.

The barn and the buildings behind it were old. Possibly even Tudor. All of the buildings were built in the same style: the lower three feet was built of brick with huge black beams set vertically into the ground and which held up a pitched roof made of red tiles.

To the right of the nearest barn, and at one end of it, a large white Ford Transit van was parked with the front facing him. The vehicle had the word AMBULANCE written in reverse above the windscreen.

Beyond the main barn Frank could see the top of another oak tree, and beyond that and to the left were two huge horse chestnut trees. Any kind of farmhouse was no-where in sight. No farmhouse meant no farm workers and Frank seemed to be alone in this field.

Frank checked the tracker again. It showed that Lady Corrigan was still in the building and, from the layout on the screen, she had to be in the nearest barn.

As Lady Corrigan had observed, above the brickwork the walls of the barn were made of horizontally placed feather-edged weather-board. These had been painted with so much creosote over the years that the outer layer was now black. The building had no windows in the side that Frank could see and he correctly assumed that the entrance was where the ambulance was parked. He would need to get nearer the barn to have a better look inside.

With that decision made he drew his Smith and Wesson, crouched down, and darted across the road where he hugged up behind the trunk of the oak tree. Then, after checking the area again, he broke cover.

This next part would be more difficult; he had decided to throw caution to the winds and make a run for the barn. He would be heading along the track in direct view of the barn; if someone came outside, they would easily see him. And if someone spotted him, he would shoot them and risk a full-on fire-fight.

One thing he was sure of – they would not kill Lady Corrigan. He reasoned that the kidnappers had not gone to all of these lengths to have to get rid of her. However, he did not know of al-Makira's instructions about what to do if they were discovered.

It took Frank only seconds to sprint along the track to the barn, keeping his eyes all the while on the barn and its surrounding area.

Frank made it to the barn without incident.

The concrete at the end of the track continued forwards and spread around the barn and the other buildings in a light-grey sheet. It was cracked in places and weeds and grass grew out of the cracks. In front of him, and about halfway along the length of the barn, an old harrow, that was slowly rusting away and resembled a giant steel hair-curler, was stood on end and propped up against the side of the barn's woodwork. In front of the harrow, and also alongside the barn, was an old Farmall tractor that should have belonged in an agricultural museum. Its original red paint was flaking off and its tyres were flat and a good crop of tall stinging nettles was growing up around it.

Frank slipped into the gap between the harrow and the tractor. He was a very fit man and the short run to the barn had hardly touched his breathing. Up close to the barn Frank could see that there were narrow gaps in some of the horizontal planks that made up the walls of the ancient building. The gaps had been formed where either nails had rusted away over the years and allowed some of the planks to slip apart, or where the top edges of the planks had simply rotted away.

Cautiously, Frank leaned towards one and peered through one of these gaps. To Frank's right, as he looked into the barn, was a pair of closed barn doors – clearly the entrance – and an old armchair was sitting in the middle of the floor with its back towards him. Over the right-hand arm of the chair he could see a slim human arm with a somewhat delicate hand that had bright red nail varnish on the fingernails – so definitely female. But was this Lady Corrigan? As if in answer to his unspoken question the woman moved and Frank got a glimpse of long bright-red hair. Yes. Definitely Lady Corrigan.

Frank continued his inspection. Apart from Lady Corrigan he counted four men; one was sitting in a white plastic patio chair and was facing Lady Corrigan. He was armed with a sawn-off side-by-side shotgun. The other three were to Frank's left and towards the back of the barn. They were also sitting in white plastic chairs. There was a table up against the end wall of the barn and Frank could see some sort of assault rifle lying on the table's top; although what make of weapon it was, he could not see.

Frank therefore assumed that they were all armed. And, from their body language, he could tell that they were all bored – and that meant that they would be jumpy. But Frank had to know if there were any more kidnappers, and if they were outside.

Frank came out from his cover and began a silent reconnaissance around the outside of the barn. As he moved, he continually moved his head this way and that, watching both the barn and the fields around him. Watching and listening. Seeing and Hearing. He checked the barn and the fields, and the white van. The van had the word AMBULANCE stencilled in black letters along its side. It was not the world's greatest example of signwriting and, up close, it looked rather crude. But from a distance, or on the move, it would fool most people.

Frank circled the van then continued moving and scanning the area; if these guys were any good then they would have placed a sentry out in the rapeseed where they could not be seen.

However, these guys turned out to be not so good. There were no sentries at all and, on his return to the tractor, Frank was almost disgusted at their failure to put out any kind of a watchman. But it did at least do him a big favour.

Frank circled the whole of the main barn and came back to the harrow again - and that was when he heard it; the distinctive airborne thump of an approaching helicopter.

He heard shouts from inside the barn and then he heard the barn doors being shoved open with a squeal of ancient hinges and the rasp of old wood going over the concrete floor.

It took Frank only a second to realise that the helicopter was what the kidnappers were waiting for, and that there were too many trees around for the chopper to land safely near the barn. No, they were not going to land here, they were going to get Lady Corrigan into the van in order to get her to North Weald Airfield, that's why it had AMBULANCE stencilled on the side. And he knew that if he did not stop them now and they managed to get Red to the airfield and the pick-up point, then she might be lost to him, and the rescue bid would have failed. Time to throw the idea of caution out the proverbial window.

The thudding of the helicopter's rotor blades became louder as the aircraft approached then suddenly it was roaring overhead; a dark-green Russian Kamov Ka-60. It was a big aircraft at fifty-one feet long and fifteen feet high. With a crew of two on board it could take a further fourteen passengers and push them through the air at a maximum speed of one-hundred-and-eighty-five miles-per-hour.

The helicopter was heading straight for North Weald as Frank came out of hiding and ran towards the front of the barn. As he rounded the corner of the old wooden building he heard a woman's voice screaming abuse, and he was just in time to catch a brief glimpse of some bright-red hair and to see some purple and pink legging-clad legs kicking frantically before she was bundled out of sight into the back of the Transit.

The man known as Fazil slammed the two rear doors shut and came to the driver's side of the van. He spotted Frank immediately and brought up the AK-74M assault rifle that he was holding.

Frank did not hesitate, he put two rounds into Fazil's head from a distance of twenty feet. The hollow point bullets spread Fazil's head along the side of the van as the driver crunched the gears and sent the van careering forwards towards Frank. Frank dived to one side and fired twice at the driver's side window as he went down. The window shattered and the driver yelled as one of the bullets creased his upper right arm, but the man kept driving.

Frank rolled up onto his feet, squatted and went to shoot at the rear left-hand tyre with his last two rounds, but then he put his gun up; if he missed

- which was unlikely but which might happen if the van hit a rut or a pothole in the concrete track and bounced or slewed - he might put the bullets in through the back of the van, and into Lady Corrigan.

Frank did not fancy having to explain to Sir Michael that he had shot his wife, so he opened the revolver's chamber, tipped out the remaining two rounds into his hand and stuffed them into a pocket of his jacket. Then he pulled out a speedloader and dropped the six bullets into the gun and closed it up. He then holstered the weapon and took to his heels, sprinting into the field of rapeseed plants and angling away from the van as it roared off along the track, heading for the left-hand turn and the opening for the road.

With the track forming a right-angle at the oak tree, Frank was now running in a line that formed the long side of an equilateral triangle. If he could get to the road opening in the field before the van, he might still be able to stop it and he put on an extra burst of speed. However, Frank was now trying to run through a field of tall plants with rough and uneven soil beneath his feet whilst the van was on flat but rough concrete.

On board the van, the man in the passenger seat beside the driver pulled out his mobile phone and called al-Makira. Al-Makira recognised the incoming call.

"What is it?" snapped the terrorist leader.

"Commander, we have a problem!"

Al-Makira could hear the panic in the man's voice. He took a breath and let it out through his teeth in a slow hiss before asking, "What kind of problem?"

"We have been discovered!"

Al-Makira gritted his teeth. *I am surrounded by incompetents.* "Who by?"

"We are in the van! We have Lady Corrigan with us!" The man was blurting out the sharp sentences as the van tore over the rough and irregular concrete beneath its wheels. "We have left the barn and we have a man chasing us! He shot Fazil!"

"Moron!" exploded al-Makira. "I told you what to do if you were discovered!"

"I know commander, but…"

"Why did you not use the suicide vests?"

"They…They are back in the barn, commander. We were just leaving in the van with Lady Corrigan when this man showed up. But..."

"Hold on," al-Makira interrupted him. "You said you have a man chasing you? One man? One fucking man! Fucking-well shoot him you idiot!"

"He is running. And…I…I have no weapon on me commander."

"You f…" began al-Makira, and then he stopped.

One man.

Just one man.

One man staging a rescue attempt.

Could this be Frank Cross?

It had to be Frank Cross.

It could not be anyone else.

Al-Makira's eyes narrowed. Al-Makira – The Cunning.

"Never mind," he said into his phone. "Allow him to get near to you, but don't let him catch you…and don't fucking shoot him! You hear me?"

The passenger's eyebrows had shot up at the sudden reversal of orders, but he was not about to argue with his commander. "Yes, Sir. I understand."

"Good…Don't fuck this up or I will personally feed your brain to the dogs!"

"Yes, Sir…How…" but his commander had rung off.

Al-Makira walked around in a tight circle. *He's coming. Frank Cross is coming!* And he smiled like a jackal. *My plan is working. He is following the breadcrumbs.*

Frank was racing towards the entrance of the field with the van closing in from his right when he realised that he wasn't going to make it. So, he stopped running and drew the revolver, took up the Weaver position with his right arm extended, his left hand cupping his right and his left elbow tucked towards his right arm. He tracked the van, moving his hands and arms smoothly right to left, and fired a double-tap.

The first 9mm bullet took out the passenger's window, whipped past the faces of both the passenger and the driver, and smashed out the driver's window. The second bullet struck the passenger in the side of his neck which blew the right-hand side of it away and jerked him over onto the driver.

Despite being splattered with blood and bits of bone the van driver did not stop and he pushed the body away from him with his left elbow. Seconds later the van tore through the gap in the hedges. It roared out onto the road, forcing a car coming towards them to swerve and bump up the edge of the road only narrowly avoiding crashing into the hedgerow.

Frank could only wonder about the way in which Lady Corrigan was being thrown around inside the van. But better a battered and bruised Lady

Corrigan than a dead one. In fact, she was face down on the floor of the van with Ali struggling to sit on her whilst trying to avoid being thrown about himself.

Frank reached his Yamaha and dragged it out of cover. He shoved on his helmet and leapt aboard. He started the bike up, skidded it around and tore out of the opening past a middle-aged man and his wife who were out of the car by the hedge and who stared at him in alarm as he roared away after the van.

Michael Green, stationed in the North Weald flight control tower, looked up from his console on which he had been tracking the flight of the incoming Ka-60 Helicopter. The airfield had been contacted a few hours ago by someone who introduced himself as an aide to Sultan Ahmed al-Nahyan, the president of an Arab Oil Company. The aide explained that the Sultan's wife had sustained a broken leg and fractured hip whilst riding one of her horses over estate ground owned by a good friend who owned a farm near to the airfield. The demand, couched as a polite request, was that the Sultan's wife was to be emergency airlifted to a private hospital in central London. She would be brought to the airfield by private ambulance – and there was to be no fuss and no press and no interference.

Green, being a particular kind of man, checked up on the Sultan's credentials and had them confirmed. Green had therefore called the aide back and had informed him that North Weald would do everything to see that the Sultan's wife would be transferred from the airfield as quickly, efficiently and as anonymously as possible.

The aide who had called was actually al-Makira, and the real Sultan would never know anything about the extraction of his wife, because at this moment he was soaping himself in a bath in a very expensive room at The Savoy hotel in London, while his wife was shopping in Oxford Street. Meanwhile, the part of the Sultan's wife was being played by Lady Corrigan, albeit under extreme duress.

The helicopter was now landing at the far northern end of the airfield a short distance away from some hangars located to the west of the airfield near the perimeter of the airfield's runway.

In a standard race from a line the Yamaha would have beaten the van hands down. But the van had a head-start on Frank. Fortunately, he knew the route the van would take and he therefore twisted the throttle and tore forwards, crouching below the raked-back windscreen, and easily balancing the bike beneath him.

He quickly came to the roundabout that he had turned left at earlier. The van had already taken the turn onto the A414 and was out of sight at the moment. In order to gain same distance on the fleeing vehicle Frank did not bother to go around the roundabout and simply cut right, heading for the right-hand exit and leaning the bike over, going the wrong way around the roundabout. A large high-sided removal van was coming towards him and Frank's waiving of the Highway Code meant that the removal van driver had to hit the brakes.

Frank shot past the front of the removal van and yelled "SORRY!" as the driver hurled abuse out of the window and listened to his packed load slide and smash behind him in the interior of the van.

Up ahead, the phoney ambulance was coming out of the next roundabout. The dead passenger slipped sideways into the driver who angrily shoved the body away from him again causing the van to swerve, so that Ali shouted at the driver to take it easy and slow down. A plea that was ignored.

Despite Ali's loud protests the driver floored it and bore off down Rayley Lane - the narrow road that led to the airfield where the helicopter had just settled down onto its tyres. The perimeter fence of the airfield was now running along beside the van on the right-hand side of the road and the van driver could see the big squat Ka-60 aircraft away over to his right and he gritted his teeth in determination to get to it.

The van flashed past the North Weald Golf Range on the left and raced up to another roundabout which he swerved around, cutting in front of a Mini as it came onto the roundabout from Vicarage Lane West on the left. The driver of the van hauled at the steering wheel in a desperate attempt at keeping the vehicle both going forwards and keeping all four tyres on the surface of the road.

A few hundred yards back Frank had his head down as he stared through his windscreen with determined eyes.

The van went into Merlin Way as Frank roared past the entrance to the golf range, forcing a car that was leaving the range to pull up hard to avoid a collision. More abuse followed Frank as he called out yet another useless and unheard "SORRY!".

The van driver spotted the entrance to the airfield over to his right. He also spotted the large red NO ENTRY sign that was posted alongside the road. Another square sign informed him that to get into the airfield he would have to drive up to the next roundabout and double back to come into the entrance further along the road.

The van driver ignored the instruction and slung the van to the right past the NO ENTRY sign and went in through the open gates of the airfield, where another sign in front of an office window told him that ALL VISITORS MUST BE CHECKED IN. This included ambulances.

A man behind a desk behind that office window leapt to his feet and waved frantically at the vehicle that had just shot past outside. "Hoy! Where d'you think you're going? HOY!"

The van kept going. However, instead of taking the service road that ran around the inside of the perimeter fence, it sped across the north to south runway where a small red and white Cirrus SR20 was just starting to make its descent and was coming in over the far perimeter fence. Fortunately, the pilot saw the van and pulled up in time to avoid a collision. The Cirrus swung away from the airfield and the control tower was treated to some fine old Anglo-Saxon expletives over the air from the enraged pilot. Having crossed the runway and having gained the far service road, the van driver floored it for the Ka-60 that was sitting off to one side at the far end of the airfield with its rotor blades chopping around - waiting. The pilot had received a hurried message over his radio that the package was on its way; a message that had come from the passenger before Frank had shot him dead.

There was a pilot and a co-pilot seated in the front of the Ka-60 and they both stared out of the cockpit window at the van that was tearing towards them as if all the devils in hell were after it. Moments later the devil from hell came roaring across the tarmac of the runway on a Yamaha motorbike.

The two helicopter pilots turned and looked at each other with puzzled expressions on their faces before turning again to watch the scene that was unfolding in front of them. This was supposed to be a simple pick-up.

On the western side of the runway, over to Frank's left as he approached the helicopter, was a large double hangar with a white four-seater Piper Cherokee light aircraft sitting inside, the front end of which was sticking out of the hangar by about three feet. Beside the end of the Piper's right-hand wing stood a tall elderly man with a neatly trimmed white beard and moustache below a completely bald head. He was wearing thick heavy-duty faded blue overalls over a dark-blue shirt and was wiping his oily hands on an oily rag, and he was staring at the amazing set of events that was being acted out only a few yards away from him. He could clearly see what he thought was an ambulance and which was only about fifty feet away. It had pulled up only a short distance from the front of the helicopter that had landed noisily only a few minutes ago.

The man watched, aghast, as the rear doors to the van crashed open at the same time as the driver jumped out of the cab. The driver ran around to the back of the van and then he and another man, who had appeared from inside the back of the vehicle, proceeded to hustle a lady with long bright-red hair out of the interior. Not only that, but she was wearing gym gear and was shouting abuse and kicking and screaming. And then a guy on a motorbike arrived, flashing past the end of the hangar where the old man was standing.

Frank had seen the van pull up and had also witnessed the back doors flying open. He also saw that they were getting a furious Lady Corrigan out of the back and that she was kicking and screaming and fighting like a wildcat. Frank skidded the bike to a halt some thirty feet away and sideways-on to the helicopter and tore off his helmet and tossed it onto the floor. He swiftly drew his Smith and Wesson revolver.

If Cross could see something he could hit it. But he dared not open fire as there was too much of a struggle going on and it would be too easy to accidentally hit Lady Corrigan as she was bucking and thrashing in the hands and arms of her abductors. And yet he had to do something to stop them getting away; he took aim at the base of the rotor blades. If he could punch a couple of rounds into the mechanism, he might be able to disable the chopper and might yet manage to rescue Lady Corrigan. But what if the rotor-blades wrecked and crashed into Red? They were damned long rotor-blades and would act like giant scythes if they flew loose.

Frank got off the bike and shouted towards the helicopter at the top of his voice, "Armed British Agent! Lay down your weapons and give yourselves up!" Then he aimed the Smith and Wesson and fired two shots over the top of the helicopter.

The old man in the overalls dropped the oily rag as his mouth came open in shock. What the hell was going on? He had clearly heard what Frank had shouted, and when Frank started shooting he ducked behind a large empty steel oil barrel that was up on end and just to his right. He crouched down so that just his head was showing over the top. He wasn't going to miss this!

Frank's rounds went over the top of the pilot's canopy which got the pilot's attention.

Back in the office the man who had waved at the van - and who had then witnessed Frank come roaring through the gates on a powerful motorbike – reached for a phone to call the police.

The side doors to the helicopter were now open with the two men trying to bundle Lady Corrigan inside where another man, a crew-member, was waiting to welcome her aboard. Lady Corrigan, although both of her wrists had been tied together, managed to punch this crew-member in the face with both of her fists as she was dragged over the sill of the aircraft.

The driver, who was still on the ground, then rounded on Frank and pulled a semi-automatic pistol out from behind the waistband of his jeans and popped off six of his own rounds.

"Shit!" gasped the old man as he flinched as the shots were fired, but he remained watching from behind his oil drum.

Four of the driver's hurried shots went into the tarmac of the service road, a fifth went up into the air and the sixth smacked into the black leather saddle of the Yamaha which Frank was now taking cover behind.

The rotor-blades of the helicopter began to beat faster.

Lady Corrigan, Ali and the van driver were now on board.

Michael Green was on his feet as were the other three staff of the control tower. He and the rest of the staff had just witnessed a gun battle take place between a motorcyclist and the Sultan's private helicopter. This was supposed to go quietly, with no fuss!

Green stood with his left hand holding a telephone to his left ear whilst his right hand was gripping the top of his head as if it might fall off. Sultan or no Sultan, private transfer or no private transfer, he was calling the police.

Frank stood and levelled his revolver at the front of the helicopter, shouting for them to cut the engine and surrender. And then the aircraft was lifting off.

The old man was coming out of his crouch and, still with his mouth open, was staring at both the helicopter and Frank in turn.

The terrorists were getting away.

Frank dashed over to the old mechanic.

"I'll pay you a thousand pounds if you'll fly me after those terrorists!"

The old man's white beetling eyebrows shot up in alarm. "Terrorists?"

"Yes! Terrorists! Do you really think that that is an ambulance?" Frank jabbed out his gun in the direction of the van whose back doors were wide open and clearly revealed the bare stripped-out interior of the vehicle. "Does that look like the inside of an ambulance to you?"

The old man stared at the van for just a couple of seconds, taking it all in. Then he said, "Bloody hell!"

"Exactly!" yelled Frank. "Did you see it? They've just kidnapped Lady Corrigan!" He jabbed out his gun again, this time in the direction of the departing helicopter.

The old man frowned. "Lady Corrigan?"

"Yes! Goddammit! Haven't you seen the news lately? Lady Corrigan has been kidnapped by terrorists, and that's them, right there!"

The man stared at the helicopter as it soared away from the airfield. "Bloody hell! Yeah. I remember, it made the news! Bloody hell!"

"Right! Well, that was her! You just saw her! And they're getting away! Can you help me?" They could still hear the whump-whump-whump of the helicopter's rotor-blades.

The old man turned to look Frank fully in the face. He frowned with suspicion. "And who are you, exactly?"

"I'm an agent with MI Six." It was close enough.

"MI Six?"

"Yes."

"So, you're a secret agent?"

"Yes. Look, I haven't got time to explain this. Can you help me rescue Lady Corrigan?"

"I take it you want me to chase after that helicopter in my aircraft?"

Bloody hell! "Yes! Please!" The helicopter was now a diminishing object in the sky.

"And how do you know where they are going? How are we supposed to follow them?"

"I have a tracking device." Frank had fished it out of his cargo trousers and he held it up.

The old mechanic peered at it then looked at Frank. "Terrorists, you say?"

"Yes! Terrorists!" *For God's sake....*

The old man's back straightened. "Fucking terrorists eh? Right! Let's see what we can do."

"You mean you'll help me?" Frank had been certain that his ludicrous suggestion was about to be refused, and that he'd spend the night in a police cell trying to explain all this whilst Lady Corrigan was spirited away.

"Of course, mate. Let's get you aboard!" All of a sudden the old man was all RAF efficiency.

"What's your name?" asked Frank.

"James. James Ward. People call me Jim."

"Good to meet you, Jim. I'm Frank." They shook hands, with Frank not bothered about the old mechanic's grimy paw.

"Let's get going," said Jim.

Frank turned and ran towards the Piper.

"No!" Jim shouted as he moved away from the Piper and headed around the aircraft, going for the other half of the hangar. "Don't get in there. She's not flying. Oil feed problem, see?"

Great! Frank ducked under the Piper's wing, moving towards the front of the aircraft. "What then?"

"This!" Jim jabbed out a hand and pointed.

Frank emerged out in front of the Piper and came to an abrupt halt as he stared at the next aircraft that inhabited the hangar; a beautiful Second World War Mk 9 Supermarine Spitfire.

"You've gotta be joking?"

"No, Sir," said Jim. "We use her for private flights."

The Spitfire, designated PV202, had been built at Castle Bromwich in 1944 and moved to No 84 Ground Support Unit at Thruxton, Hampshire in October of the same year. From there the aircraft was moved to Northern France where it saw action in twenty operational sorties before returning to Lasham in England in December of 1944. From Lasham the Spitfire was moved to Dunsfold and then out to Holland, eventually moving into Germany where it saw front-line action.

At the end of the Second World War the aircraft was flown to Ireland for the Irish Air Corps where it was used to train pilots who were to fly the Seafire aircraft, a version of the Spitfire that could operate from the deck of an aircraft carrier.

In December 1960 PV202 was bought for the use in the film *The Battle of Britain* and then it was sold on to a new owner who moved it to Cornwall. From here the old aircraft was sold again and what remained of the Spitfire was moved to a barn in Saffron Walden, which was not many miles from where she was now.

At Saffron Walden a complete restoration commenced, and then the old Spitfire was later moved to Sussex where restoration was completed as well as a conversion into a two-seater. The Spitfire then flew again in February 1990 and has been used ever since. Nowadays, as Jim had said, the fabulous aircraft, painted in a cloud pattern of green and grey, took people up into the sky for their bucket-list flights.

"Well, come on!" yelled Jim as he threw Frank a harness. "Get that on. We've got terrorists to hunt down!"

Frank caught the harness and shrugged into it as he ran forward. He should not have been smiling at this stage of the deadly chase, but he was. He was going to go up in a schoolboy dream. He was going up in a Spitfire!

"Will she catch the chopper?" shouted Frank, trying to control his excitement.

"Sure," answered Jim. "The Spit has a top speed of four-hundred-and-forty miles-per-hour and a range of four-hundred-and-twenty miles, so we'll easily catch that chopper, which will only be doing about one-hundred-and-seventy to eighty miles-per-hour."

However, what they did not know was the helicopter's destination: Le Bourget airport, north of Paris. In a straight-line flight from North Weald to Le Bourget the flying time at 180 MPH would be just over one hour – and the terrorists already had a head start.

Frank followed Jim up onto the famous elliptical wing of the Spitfire and then opened the rear bubble-shaped canopy before scrambling into the seat behind the pilot. On went the seat belts as Jim climbed nimbly into the pilot's seat.

Jim twisted around in his seat. "I'm afraid you're going to get a bit cold."

"Why's that?" asked Frank.

"Because we'll be flying at altitude, and there isn't any heating in a Spit...You're not exactly dressed for it."

Frank looked down at his body clad in his black motorbike gear. "I'll be okay, I was warm enough on my bike in this."

"Bikes can't fly son," said the old mechanic with a wry smile. He then pointed at his head. "Put your headset on."

Frank did as he was told. He was now wearing a contraption that comprised of black cushioned ear-pieces and a leather face mask. This was his communications set that linked him with the pilot.

With the canopies open Jim went through the series of start-up procedures, starting with pushing open the throttle and followed a few seconds later by pumping the fuel primer a half-a-dozen times. After a few more preliminary checks Jim simultaneously hit the starter and booster coils and the Rolls-Royce Merlin engine fired up with a series of loud rapid coughs that blew smoke and flame out of the exhaust ports either side of the fuselage, giving Frank a brief whiff of aviation fuel.

Over the combined roar of the engine and propellor Jim's command came over Frank's earphones. "Close your canopy."

Frank moved the bubble canopy into place and a few moments later, with the engine warmed up nicely, the oil, fuel and water pressures came to operating temperature and pressure. They began to move forward with Jim making contact with the airfield's control tower. But something was wrong.

In the control tower Green had put the phone down on its cradle and was reaching for his radio hand-set. He had no intention of granting the old warbird permission to take off whilst they were waiting for the police to arrive.

Damn! thought Frank as he listened to the conversation between Jim and the control tower. It looked like his desperate plan would fail just as he thought this might be his chance to get after the terrorists.

However, Jim had other plans and he just kept talking quietly, unhurried, moving the Spitfire forward, taxiing away from the hangar and heading for the north end of the north to south runway.

Meanwhile the Cirrus SR20 that had had its landing interrupted was coming around for another attempt to put down.

The control tower staff were now in a state of panic as they watched the Cirrus swing through the air whilst the Spitfire took its place at the end of the long strip of tarmac, getting ready for take-off, and the chatter built up between Green and Jim Ward.

Green, horrifyingly aware that the Cirrus was coming in to land, was still refusing to give Jim permission to take off – but Jim wasn't having any of it. As the control tower lectured Jim the Spitfire kept rolling forwards, fairly slowly at first but then rapidly building speed as the aircraft began to head down the runway. The end of that runway came towards them fast, and Frank wondered if they would make it. And then they were up, roaring up toward the sky.

"WOW!" exclaimed Frank. "WOW!"

Jim's laugh chuckled into Frank's headphones. "Everyone says that."

As they cleared the end of the runway the Cirrus touched down at the other end with the pilot bombarding the control tower with as many swear words as he could think of, but with the staff in the control tower giving a chorus of sighs of relief as Michael Green collapsed down into his chair.

The take-off in the Spitfire had been as smooth as any that Frank had ever been on, including the St Margaret Presidential Jet. They curved away from the airfield and were just in time to see three police cars arrive through the airfield's entrance gate complete with flashing blue lights. As the vehicles came through the gates a man came out of the office and pointed up at them. However, as a flying police car has not been invented Frank and Jim were up and away and escaping from the clutches of the law.

As they headed away over the patchwork of the Essex countryside Frank said into his microphone, "There's going to be hell to pay for this, Jim. You're going to be in a lot of trouble."

"I don't think so, Frank. If you're MI Six you'll be able to pull some strings…won't you?"

Frank blinked a couple of times. This old boy flying this old aircraft was obviously no slouch. Frank spoke into the mike again. "Absolutely," he confirmed. He would have to get Sir Michael to pull those strings.

Moments later North Weald airfield was far behind them as the Spitfire climbed elegantly up into the sky accompanied by the drum-beat thudding of the big Merlin engine. Jim levelled the Spitfire out at two thousand feet and his voice came over Frank's headset.

"Now, where do we go from here?"

Frank crushed down his schoolboy enthusiasm and concentrated on the job in hand. He looked at the screen on the tracking device. "Head due south. That's the direction the chopper is heading."

"Okay," Jim acknowledged. "Hopefully we'll spot it further ahead. But we've some cloud coming up, so it could be tricky."

"Okay, Jim. Just keep her going straight and we'll just have to do our best."

"Roger that."

I can't believe he just said Roger That. And I'm in a Spitfire! Wow! This is great!

Jim put the old aircraft into another steady climb and then levelled out at fifteen-thousand feet. They passed through some banks of mist that were forming the clouds that Jim had mentioned and moments later they spotted the helicopter and came up on it fast.

The flight ceiling of a Spitfire is high at just over thirty-six-thousand feet whilst the ceiling of a Ka-60 is just under nineteen-thousand feet. At the moment the Spitfire was way below her operational ceiling, whilst the helicopter was at ten-thousand feet.

"Can you force them down, Jim?" asked Frank.

"I doubt it," replied Jim. "But we can let them know we're here, and shake them up a bit."

"Do it," said Frank. Then a thought struck him. "Can I say Tally Ho?"

"Be my guest."

"Tally Ho!" yelled Frank.

Jim took the Spitfire into an easy slide downwards that never-the-less pushed Frank back into his seat with the G-Force. As the Spitfire swung through the air Frank gripped his knees with both hands and uttered *Jee-sus* as they flashed over the top of the helicopter with only some forty feet to spare over the top of the KA-60's rotor blades.

Panic broke out in the cockpit of the helicopter as the Spitfire roared overhead. And then they watched in horror as the old aircraft peeled away to their left and began a turn for a run back at them.

Lady Corrigan had been subdued by jabbing her with a hypodermic and she now lay on her back with her eyes closed and wrapped head to foot in a red blanket. She was strapped to a stretcher and she lay between Ali and the ambulance driver. There was a third man with them who was nursing a severely damaged nose where Lady Corrigan had struck him. All three men were wearing headsets with mouthpieces. The pilot spoke into his microphone, talking to the three men in the back of the helicopter. He was under orders to get Lady Corrigan - now referred to as "the package" – to Paris as fast as possible and there deliver her into other hands. He had not been told that he would be shot at by a motorcyclist or challenged in the skies by a Second World War Spitfire!

"We are under attack!" he snapped. "What should we do?"

As the leader of the ground group was lying dead beside a barn in Essex Ali took control. "Keep on this heading while I contact al-Makira." Ali pulled a mobile phone out of his pocket. *I hope phone reception is going to work up here.* He took his headset off, pushed the mobile against his left ear and stuck the index finger of his right hand into his other ear, trying to blot out the roar of the helicopter's engine and churning rotor-blades.

Al-Makira's mobile buzzed. He answered. "Yes?" As he listened his eyes widened and he had to stop himself from letting his lower jaw sag open.

Then his face hardened.

"Don't be stupid! How can it possibly be a British Spitfire? They're all in fucking museums!"

"Well, Sir," yelled Ali. "I can assure you this one isn't!"

As if on cue, the Spitfire tore past overhead and al-Makira clearly heard it. "Did you hear that?" Ali's voice held a trace of panic. "That was the Spitfire!"

There was a pause, and then al-Makira asked, "Why are you being chased by a Spitfire?"

Ali swallowed. He had hoped that his commander would not ask that question and therefore, in a loud but faltering voice, he answered, "We believe that it is the same man that discovered us at the barn!"

Cross! This is excellent! "How do you know that?" snapped al-Makira.

"He came after us on a motorbike!" shouted Ali. "He caught up with us at the airfield. He started shooting at the helicopter!"

The pleasure that al-Makira was now feeling allowed him to ignore Ali's panic. Cross was definitely following the breadcrumbs! He was being drawn into the web. Al-Makira asked, "How far away from Paris are you?"

"We have a good way to go yet, Sir!"

"Continue as you are, and maintain your height. The Spitfire will not shoot you down. Do you hear me?"

"Yes, Commander…Should we try and shoot them down?"

"No! Do not make any attempt to engage them. Just get to your destination. Understood?"

"Yes, Commander!"

"Good. I will have a crew standing by to take the package the moment you land at the destination." He ended the call.

Ali put the phone away, and then ducked involuntarily as the Spitfire swung close past their port side showing its undercarriage.

Frank hoped that whatever was in his stomach was going to stay there as they came out of the swooping pass on the chopper. He swallowed hard and said, "Jim…Do we have guns on board?"

Jim laughed, the noise crackling in Frank's earpieces. "Yes, Frank. We are fitted with the original spec for a Spitfire; four Browning machineguns on each wing. But no ammunition."

The ammunition would have been .303 cartridges, three-inches-long and made of brass.

"Probably just as well," said Frank. There would be no sense in riddling the helicopter with highly destructive bullets. But he thought that it might have been nice if they'd had them.

"I can keep pestering them," offered Jim.

"Go for it!"

The Spitfire dived again and Frank gripped his fingers even harder into his knees.

*****

Tandy was now en route to Cyprus, passing over the Bay of Bengal and was soon to cross into the Indian air space. She was relaxing in her seat and watching the film *Rush Hour* on the large screen set in the back of the seat in front of her. It was the film that starred Jackie Chan and Chris Tucker. Tandy laughed to herself at the antics of the two leading men, for she knew that the time for laughter would be ending soon enough.

*****

The Spitfire swept around the Ka-60. Jim kept the old aircraft corkscrewing and rolling around its prey, dogging it all the way down to the southern British coast and out over the English Channel. By the time the helicopter arrived into French airspace both the pilot's and co-pilot's nerves were shredded.

Still with the Spitfire in close attendance, the helicopter was now making contact with a Le Bouget flight controller who was a young lady called Simone and she had also picked up the old warbird on her tracking screen. The helicopter she had no problem with because Air Traffic Control had already been advised that it was carrying a very important, but unnamed, casualty that was to be transferred immediately it touched down to a waiting private jet, a silver-bodied Learjet 60, bound for Iraq. Once again, al-Makira had played the part of the Sultan's aide.

So, the helicopter was not a problem, but the Spitfire, on the other hand, was a total surprise, and Simone was concerned that it would compromise both the helicopter landing and the Learjet taking off. This could throw the Le Bourget airspace into dangerous confusion. She could see the Learjet from her console in the airfield's control tower.

Simone turned in her seat and waved to her senior officer, Roger Legrande. He hurried over to her. He was a tall lean man in his early fifties with a head of thinning dark hair, a thin moustache and high cheekbones. Having draped his jacket over the back of his own chair he was now wearing only the trousers to his two-piece suit and a white open-necked shirt.

Simone quickly filled him in on the situation. He listened and waved her to carry on doing what she was doing; she was a fine air traffic controller and Legrande had every confidence in her abilities.

On board the Learjet the lead pilot had been contacted by the lead pilot in the helicopter and, in his turn, the Learjet pilot had contacted al-Makira because the terrorist leader had issued an order that he was to be told the progress of the abduction of Lady Corrigan. Despite the earlier interference of Frank Cross, and also despite the interference of the Spitfire, it seemed to al-Makira that all was now continuing according to plan, and with a range of over nine thousand miles the Learjet did not have to land anywhere between Paris and Mosul, its destination in Iraq. They just had to get Lady Corrigan transferred on the ground and the Spitfire had yet to get permission to land. And Simone was not going to allow the latter; she was determined to get her control of the airspace back in tidy order.

However, Frank and Jim had suspected that this might happen and they had formulated a plan; as the Spitfire neared the airfield Jim got onto the radio,

"Hello Le Bourget. This is Spitfire PV two-oh-two. I am on a training flight and have an engine oil-pressure problem. This is an emergency. Request permission to land. Over."

Frank and Jim doubted that the terrorists would report the fact that they were being chased by a British Spitfire, because the question on the ground would be "Why?" No, they would be keeping quiet and pretending that nothing out of the ordinary was happening, even if the tracking screens told the air traffic controllers something different.

Simone immediately picked up on Jim's contact and now she had to treat the old aircraft's approach as an emergency landing. She glanced up at Legrande who was standing beside her and leaning forward, looking at her tracking screen. He gave her a slight nod of encouragement. It was going to be a close call if she was to avoid a collision between the helicopter and the Spitfire. Concentrating hard, she gave Jim her permission to land as the helicopter came in-field. The big KA-60 hovered over a tarmac landing zone that was off to one side of the main runway and not far from the private jet which was already firing up the engines that were situated towards the rear and either side of its long fuselage. The helicopter dropped as the Spitfire also came in-field.

Swooping down and coming in low, Jim waggled the wings of the aircraft to give the impression that he was struggling for control. The wheels touched with a screech of tyres onto the tarmac and the old aeroplane landed and rolled out. Not stopping, Jim left the runway, swung around and kept going, taxiing the aircraft to be as near to the Learjet as he dared, which defied all of the airfield's safety protocols, and which prompted Simone to ask Jim in awkward English just what the hell he was playing at.

The Spitfire pulled up about fifty yards from the helicopter which was about one-hundred feet from the Learjet. Frank immediately opened his canopy and scrambled out of his seat and onto the aircraft's wing as Jim kept the engine revs up. Frank jumped down onto the tarmac and drew his Smith and Wesson. He had reloaded the gun while he was in the air and he now ran towards the KA-60 as Jim began to turn the Spitfire around, getting ready to leave.

Legrande stared out of the control tower's windows with both hands on his head, and asked aloud, "What the hell is going on?"

Simone threw up her hands and said, "Paah!"

The doors to the helicopter came open and an unconscious Lady Corrigan, still strapped to the stretcher, was swiftly manhandled out of the interior by Ali and the man who had been the van driver. There was a man standing guard at the top of the steps that led up to the entrance of the private jet, and he was waving frantically at the two men, urging them to hurry and get Lady Corrigan on board as they jogged with her inert body across the space between the KA-60 and the Learjet.

As soon as Lady Corrigan was clear of the helicopter it began to wind up its engines ready to take off.

Frank checked away from the spinning blades of the helicopter and their downdraft and, crouching and running hard, he re-aligned his course onto the stretcher-bearers.

The control tower had already been informed that the stretcher transfer would happen and that the KA-60 would instantly take off after the transfer. But they could not have factored in the Spitfire that was dangerously close to the helicopter. Simone, not wanting to create a major diplomatic incident, granted the helicopter clearance to take off. It was with some relief that the pilot and co-pilot got the chopper into the air and away from the package delivery point.

Lady Corrigan's stretcher was lifted up the Learjet steps and hurried past the guard and into the body of the waiting aircraft.

Frank, still running in a crouch, ignored the KA-60 taking off as he dashed towards the Learjet.

The guard on the jet's steps saw Frank, spotted the revolver in his hand and recognised the threat. He turned inside the jet and, only a couple of seconds later, came back out holding a Kalashnikov assault rifle. He opened fire.

The control room went into panic.

"Call security! Get the police!" yelled Legrande.

Simone was way ahead of him. She'd been responsible for landing both the helicopter and the Spitfire and she was determined that this breach of security was not going to get further out of control on her watch.

The airport had two squad cars already outside the entrance doors to the main building and it took only a few moments for their crews to get around to the airfield where they hit the sirens and lights and went rocketing towards the Learjet.

Frank turned back to the Spitfire and made a big waving motion with his left arm, meaning "Get the hell out of here!"

Jim got the message and began to head the aircraft towards the runway, building up the revs of the engine.

"Now what the hell's going on!" yelled Legrande, now with his arms wide apart.

The police cars came nearer and had been joined by a fire truck and two dark-blue Citroen saloon cars that contained four security personnel in each car. They were all armed.

Simone instructed the Spitfire to stop and cut the engines.

Jim kept going. He still had ample fuel to make it back to England, probably to land at Biggin Hill in Kent where he knew there were other bucket-list Spitfires flying. At least, he reasoned, he would be among friends when the police finally caught up with him and arrested him.

Meanwhile, Frank had fired and winged the man at the top of the Learjet's entrance steps in the shoulder which had made the man stop shooting. Frank made a rush for the steps and had almost made them when he was rugby-tackled to the floor by one of the security guards who threw both arms around Frank's legs to bring him down and then began to fiercely hang on to his legs. Frank rolled onto his back and was about to punch the guard in the face when he realised it was a woman of about twenty-five years of age. He realised that if he were to hit her he would probably break her nose and he simply could not do it, so he allowed his fist to open.

Damn! Damn! Damn!

As Frank lay there the injured man in the Learjet pulled up the entrance steps and closed the door. A pair of well-shined shoes arrived beside Frank's head and he looked up along a length of trouser leg. A stern-faced policeman in a slightly rumpled uniform was looking down at him and holding a semi-automatic pistol which was pointed at Franks' face. The policeman gave a slight smile and, in French, said, "Monsieur, you are under arrest."

Frank knew what the man had said even though he could not hear him, for the private jet was now moving away from them with its engines screaming as they went up a pitch.

"You've got to stop that 'plane!" shouted Frank, raising his voice above the noise and pointing at the aircraft.

"I think not, Monsieur," the policeman shouted back. "It 'as been given special clearance."

"Why?" shouted Frank. But the policeman merely shrugged again. It would seem that the long tentacles of Intiqam had found their way around another problem, and Frank watched helplessly from his position on the floor as the sleek silver jet taxied away with Red on board.

He had failed.

Jim was now breaking a whole new set of safety protocols as the Spitfire ran out across the apron with one of the squad cars rolling alongside with an officer shouting and waving out of the open passenger's window.

Jim waved back cheerily at the officer and kept going until he was swinging the aircraft onto the end of the runway, then he opened the throttle.

The squad car managed to keep up with the Spitfire for about one-hundred yards and then it lost the race as the aircraft accelerated away and then took off into a darkening sky.

Frank managed to get himself disentangled from the young woman and then he handed over his revolver before he got up and dusted himself down.

His knife was removed from his hip and then, with his wrists in front of him, the hand-cuffs went on and he was led across to one of the squad cars where a hand was placed upon his head as he got into the back seat of the car. There was no point in fighting this. He would have to go with it and try and get Sir Michael to pull even more strings. As he settled down into his seat, he watched out of the car window as the sleek Learjet shot screaming over the top of them.

With the range to be able to fly direct to Iraq, and with the kind of power and airspeed that its engines could generate, the Learjet would be there in just over four hours. And it would be taking Lady Corrigan to a meeting with al-Makira.

*****

Frank was taken to the local police station and searched. They already had his gun his knife, and now they had his speedloaders, some spare bullets, his motorbike ignition keys, his house keys, his passport, his wallet, and his mobile phone. They were unable to access his mobile and Frank was not about to let them. The police also had the tracking device and this particular item was intriguing the officers.

Frank had hardly uttered a word since arriving at the police station. He only spoke when they asked him his name and address. He gave the false name of William Newport, which matched his passport, and a false address. After that Frank had been allowed to pee and then he had his leather belt removed from the waistband of his trousers and his trainers were taken away. Then he was taken to a secure square room that was all white walls with lights buried in the ceiling, and a table and two chairs that were all bolted to the floor - in case he decided to throw one of them at someone. He sat at the table and rested his elbows on it. A uniformed police officer was in the room with him and standing against one wall and with as much movement as a cardboard cut-out.

A detective came into the room. He was wearing a smart grey suit over a white shirt with a plain blue tie and he was holding the tracking device. He did not give his name but he sat down at the table opposite Frank and did not turn on the recording device that was built into one of the walls. They had already confirmed Frank's nationality from his passport; therefore, they knew he was British.

The detective sat back in his chair and folded his arms across his chest. He spoke passable English. "What are you doing 'ere…Mister Newport?"

Frank remained leaning forwards with his elbows on the table. He fixed the detective with a level gaze. "I am with the British Secret Service, and I was trying to apprehend a terrorist who was kidnapping Lady Corrigan."

The detective blinked. He processed the information then gave a small smile. He gave a sideways nod of his head then held up the tracker.

"What is this?"

"It's a tracking device."

"What is it tracking?"

"Lady Corrigan."

"Why?"

"I just told you, she's been kidnapped. Check the international news reports."

"I will." The detective did not move. "You say that this Lady Corrigan has been kidnapped?"

"Yes."

"Hmm...The air traffic controllers at the airport say that the person put on board on a stretcher was the wife of Sultan Ahmed al-Nahyan."

"That's not true. It was Lady Corrigan."

"So you say." The detective sat back in his chair and folded his arms.

Frank gave a small sigh and also sat back and folded his arms. "Okay. You don't believe me. Fine. But be it on your own head if you do not act on this information."

The detective made a small movement with his lips, as though he were rolling a small sweet around in his mouth. But he still did not move.

Frank gave a slight nod. "Okay. If we are going to play this game, I wish to make a telephone call."

"I am sure you do," smiled the detective. Again, he made no attempt to move.

Frank exhaled heavily then asked, "Can you at least answer me a question?"

"If I can."

"Where is the private jet going?"

The detective considered this for a moment. What harm would it do?

"I believe it is going to Mosul."

"That's in Iraq."

"I know."

"Lots of terrorists in Iraq," said Frank.

The detective pondered this thought then stood up. "Please wait 'ere."

"I'm not going anywhere."

"That is correct, Monsieur. You are not." And he left the room.

Frank interlinked his fingers on the table top and stared at his thumbs.

*****

CYPRUS

Tandy's flight touched down at Larnaca. She disembarked her aircraft and wafted through Passport Control and Customs, smiling profusely at everyone. Just another tourist. Outside it was late evening and starting to get dark. However, she picked up a cab with no trouble and went to the Pefkos City Hotel where she checked in and received the pass-key to her room. She did not bother to go to her room. Instead, she toted her baggage through to the bar area and met Tommo, Clonk and T Bone who were sitting in leather armchairs nursing beers.

Tandy plonked herself down in a vacant chair and looked at her comrades. "Where's Frank?"

All three men shook their heads and Clonk spoke up. "No word yet."

A frown momentarily flittered across Tandy's brow. Then she said, "I'm sure he'll contact us when he's ready…Another beer gentlemen?"

*****

FRANCE

At 9pm Frank was allowed his phone call. They gave him back his mobile and he rang Sir Michael and told him where he was. Sir Michael took a deep breath at the end of the line but said only three words, "Right. Sit tight."

"There's something else," said Frank.

This time Frank heard Sir Michael give a sigh at the other end. "Go on. What is it?" *Now what?*

"There's a guy called Jim, he's a pilot and he flies a Spitfire out of North Weald airfield…"

"A Spitfire, you say?" The tremor had gone and he now sounded intrigued.

"Yes," said Frank.

"A real Spitfire? As in Battle of Britain Spitfire?"

"Yes, Sir Michael."

"What of it?"

"It's what got me to France."

"What? Bloody hell, Frank…"

Frank interrupted, "Look, he, Jim that is, helped me track down Lady Corrigan."

There was a pause at the end of the line. "Oh, right…"

"It's probably landed him in a spot of bother…"

"A spot of bother!" spluttered Sir Michael. "Christ Frank!" and before he could go on Frank said,

"Yes! Listen, he did us both a very good turn. Please work your magic and get him out of any official trouble that he might now be in." Frank could picture Sir Michael shaking his head.

"Well, Frank, you've gone too far…"

"Please?" said Frank. "Pretty please?"

"Oh, bloody hell…I'll see what I can do." That was confirmation enough to Frank that Sir Michael Corrigan would fix it for Jim.

"Great! Thanks Sir Michael. I knew I could rely on you."

"Here!" began Sir Michael. "I never said…" But Frank had rung off.

While Sir Michael stared at his own phone Frank smiled grimly; he could hardly do anything else. He thanked the detective for the use of the phone, locked it against prying fingers and handed it over for their retention once again. After that he was taken to a cell where he sat on a bench that was fixed to a stark white brick wall which matched the other three. He waited.

One hour later a uniformed officer, who was in charge of the police station's administration, came to see him; he was an older man, tall and straight-backed and pushing retirement who had seen most things in his long career. But he had not come across anything like Frank before; because after Frank had made his one call things started to happen very fast. It was fairly obvious to the police officer that Frank was seriously connected with persons way above his own pay grade; so seriously connected that the chief officers in the building had started scurrying about like ants whose nest had been kicked.

The policeman had decided it was better to keep quiet and go with the flow and he entered Frank's cell with Frank's earlier, and none-to-friendly, detective in tow behind him. The uniform entered the room whilst the detective stood leaning against the door-jam with his head on one side. The detective looked at Frank with an amused expression on his face.

Frank remained seated on his bench. The uniform looked down at him and then said in a gruff voice, and in French, "Well, Mister William Newport...if that is your real name...you can go."

Frank smiled politely and thanked the officer in his own language, then he stood up and moved past the officer to the detective who came out of his lounge against the woodwork. Frank put out his right hand. "Thank you, Officer. It's been nice meeting you." The detective slowly lifted his own hand and then clasped Frank's.

"Likewise, I am sure," replied the detective in English. "Perhaps next time you come to France you will cause less...'ow you say...Aggro?" He let go of Frank's hand.

"I'll try." Frank returned the almost smile.

"Try very 'ard, Monsieur."

Frank was taken to a desk near the entrance door to the police station where he had his possessions returned, including the tracker, but with the exception of the Smith and Wesson, the speedloaders, the spare rounds and his knife. The uniformed officer had those in a brown cardboard box. "These will be returned to you via MI Six."

Oh well, that's the last I'll see of them, thought Frank, although he was not unduly concerned because he had others. In fact, he had a similar Smith and Wesson revolver in a left luggage locker in Charles de Gaulle airport.

The brown box was removed and the uniformed officer nodded towards the road outside. "Monsieur, we 'ave a car outside waiting to take you to Charles de Gaulle airport, where you will be expected to fly back to Britain."

"Expected?"

The Frenchman gave a shrug. "Personally...Monsieur Newport...I do not care where you go, as long as you get the 'ell out of France."

*****

The Learjet touched down at Mosul airport in northern Iraq where Lady Corrigan was once again transferred on a stretcher, in a sedated state, to a waiting helicopter - the olive-green Bell UH-1 that al-Makira used as his own private aircraft.

Al-Makira was not on board the helicopter. However, he was delighted to hear the news that Red was finally in Iraq and that she would soon be in his clutches. However, he was not so happy to learn that the man he believed to be Frank Cross had been arrested by the french police, when he might have been grabbed by his own men.

Furthermore, if it had been Cross, he now had to hope that he would continue to follow the trail of breadcrumbs to Qaryat Musawara.

Al-Makira felt that his plan was very slowly starting to become unglued, and he did not like it.

*****

Frank was taken to the airport by two uniformed and armed police officers who accompanied him all the way to a British Airways check-in desk. Once at the desk they stood either side of him.

The young lady behind the desk looked first at Frank, and then at the two policemen flanking him, and then back at Frank. Being the consummate professional, she said nothing, but Frank noticed her left eyebrow which arched momentarily.

Frank gave her a look of complete innocence, then asked, "Can I get a flight to Larnaca, in Cyprus?"

"Of course, Monsieur."

The two policemen shared a glance; not going to England then?

Frank looked left and right at the two officers. "I have friends in Cyprus."

They said nothing, but they both stared at him with fish-like eyes.

The girl behind the desk asked, "First Class, Monsieur?"

"Yes please."

"Oui, Monsieur." She tapped at a keyboard. "There is one flying out at twelve-fifteen tonight."

"Excellent," said Frank.

"Your name, Sir?"

"William Newport," said Frank and he produced his passport.

The policemen turned to go. Their job was done.

"What?" said Frank after them with an offended tone. "No kiss goodbye?"

One of the officers turned back, went to say something, thought better of it, and then they both turned on their heels and marched off. Frank swung back to the check-in lady and gave her a winning smile. She smiled back.

"'Ow are you paying, Monsieur Newport?"

Frank produced his William Newport credit card and handed it over. Moments later he was booked in, First Class, for the midnight flight to Larnaca.

*****

TUESDAY 24TH JUNE

Lady Corrigan had been brought before al-Makira. She had been removed from the helicopter that had landed just outside Qaryat Musawara and then stretchered into the town where she had been taken into a single-storey house and dumped off the stretcher and onto a filthy bed with her arms bound with rough rope at her wrists and her legs bound in the same way at her ankles. She was still wearing her purple leggings and black crop-top. But she had had her trainers taken from her, and then they had been "lost", so that she was barefoot. She was also minus her fleece; "lost" as well, presumably.

Lady Corrigan had been brought back to consciousness and given some water. The water had made her retch as it was the first drink that she had received for some hours and that delay, combined with the remains of the drug that she still carried in her body, had made her stomach heave.

However, Lady Corrigan, being made of stern stuff, quickly recovered her composure, and her spirit. Once she was feeling better she had swung her legs off the foul bed and had begun a campaign of staring malevolently at the two guards who were in the room with her.

When al-Makira decided that she was well enough to be moved her guards had released her from the ankle rope, but not the wrist bindings. This had been carried out carefully by one of the guards whilst the other one stood over Lady Corrigan with an AK-47 aimed at her head.

With the rope removed, Red was pulled off the bed and taken outside and across to the tower-house that al-Makira used as his headquarters. The entrance door to the house had been opened and Lady Corrigan had been roughly manhandled inside and then shoved through a second door on the ground floor.

Al-Makira was standing up and waiting for her. He was an imposing figure in his clean and pressed combat fatigues. To him she looked surprisingly clean, although her bright red hair was tousled and could do with a good brushing. Al-Makira noted her bare midriff and tight lycra leggings and the thought flickered through his mind, *How these western whores love to display themselves*. He also noted that her fingernails and toenails matched her hair colour. Now he knew why she was called Red.

Al-Makira smiled at her and affected a slight bow with his head. "Good day, Lady Corrigan," he said as politely as possible.

Lady Corrigan looked at him through narrow and hostile eyes. If she could have crossed her bare arms over her chest she would have done, but she was still tied at the wrists. "And just who, are you?" she asked.

Amazingly, she was managing to retain a large measure of self-assurance and also managed to inject a fair amount of malice into her five words. So much so, that al-Makira was, at first, rather taken aback.

His Second-in-Command, Irfan, who had come to stand behind Lady Corrigan, glowered at the back of her head and then glanced at his commander. "Shall I hit the bitch?" he asked in Arabic.

"No, my brother," al-Makira answered back in the same language. He waved his right hand as if nothing that was being said was of any consequence to him. "Not yet." He turned his attention back to Lady Corrigan.

"Welcome to my headquarters, Lady Corrigan. Or should I call you…Red?"

"You can call me *Lady* Corrigan," answered Lady Corrigan haughtily and hoping that it would annoy her captor.

However, her words and demeanour did not seem to annoy him. "Ahh, yes," he said, almost with a laugh. "You English, you so like your titles, don't you?"

"So, it would seem, do you…Al-Makira."

Al-Makira's humour vanished. He recognised insolence when he heard it and his eyes slid to his SiC, who got ready to slap her. "You know who I am then?"

"Of course. I've seen your ghastly propaganda films that you have starred in. But I must confess that I do not know the name of this rat that is skulking behind me."

The Second-in-Command nearly exploded and he drew back his hand to strike her.

"No!" ordered al-Makira, stopping him. "Leave us!"

"But…"

"I said leave us, my brother."

Irfan spun on his heels and stamped out of the room, swearing as he went.

Al-Makira looked into Lady Corrigan's eyes. "That was a stupid thing to do, *Lady* Corrigan. My Second-in-Command is not one to cross."

It had been a very clear warning and Lady Corrigan sucked in a large lungful of air before she asked,

"What do you want me for? Why have I been kidnapped and brought here?"

"Because, my dear Lady Corrigan, you are bait."

Red frowned at him. "Bait?" she asked.

"Yes. Bait. You are the cheese in the mousetrap." He grinned at his little joke, like a cat would grin at a mouse.

"And who is the mouse?" asked Red.

"Why, Frank Cross, of course."

Lady Corrigan frowned some more, her face registering puzzlement. "Who is this Frank Cross?"

"My dear Lady Corrigan, please do not play the innocent with me. He is an agent who works for your husband." Al-Makira did not know that Frank had left the Specialist Operations Unit.

"My husband?" Lady Corrigan looked at the floor and shook her head, causing her long red tresses to cascade untidily about her shoulders. She looked up. "So, this is what this is all about? You want my husband?"

"No!" Al-Makira spun away from her then turned back. His face was now tight with emotion. "No, Lady Corrigan, I do not want your husband. I told you…" and he ground the next words out between his teeth, "I want Frank Cross!"

"But why?"

"Because he murdered my brother!"

Red's mouth came open in astonishment. Then her head came up and her posture straightened. "Your brother?" she took a breath. "You mean to tell me that this is all about vengeance for your brother? Are you mad?"

Al-Makira's eyes flared in annoyance and his face hardened. "No, Lady Corrigan. I am not mad. It is as I said, it is because this Frank Cross murdered him."

"Murdered?" said Lady Corrigan. "Murdered? My god, but you're a fine one to talk! Look at all the shooting and killing you have done, the executions you've carried out. And why? I'll tell you why…"

Her voice cut off as al-Makira back-handed her across her face. Red let out a sharp cry as her face snapped around at the strike and she staggered to her left, but she remained standing and then swung back towards her attacker with both of her tied hands up to her face, feeling with her fingers at where he had struck her.

"Yes," she hissed at him. "That's about your limit! That sums you up. Does hitting a defenceless woman make you feel big?"

Al-Makira had his lips pulled back in a snarl. "Shut up, Lady Corrigan!"

"Why?" she snarled back. "What are you going to do? Hit me again? Shoot me?" She stared straight at the man who held her captive. "Well go ahead, you bastard!"

Al-Makira balled both of his fists at his sides, desperately wanting to pull a gun and shoot the whore. However, he knew that if he did that then he would lose a top-level hostage and one very big bargaining chip. He needed her alive – for the moment.

Barely able to control his temper, al-Makira bellowed for his Second-in-Command who appeared so quickly through the door that he must have been standing just outside.

"Irfan, my brother," growled al-Makira. "Take this bitch and throw her in with the other whore that we have captured."

Without a word, Irfan seized Red by an arm and hauled her out of the door. But Lady Corrigan had the last word as she was dragged out,

"I hope that Cross *does* come for you! And I hope he kills you!"

"Get her out of here!" yelled al-Makira.

Red Corrigan was hustled outside and across the rough surface of a village street in her bare feet to another house. Once inside and on the ground floor she was pushed face-first into a door whilst it was unlocked and then opened. She was then shoved inside with such a force that she landed sprawling on the hard earth floor. The door slammed behind her as she jumped to her feet and rushed to the door. She kicked it hard a couple of times and, although it rattled in its frame, she only succeeded in hurting her right foot.

Lady Corrigan took a couple of steps back and glared at the door as if doing so could make it dissolve.

A feeble and hesitant voice behind her said, "H-Hello. Who…are you?"

*****

Frank slept for most of the overnight flight, after all, yesterday had been a long, eventful, and tiring day and there was nothing that he could do above the clouds at thirty-thousand feet. When he woke up he had just enough time to have a cup of coffee before the aircraft began to make its descent into Cyprus airspace.

The jet touched down and Frank joined a queue of bleary-eyed travellers that led from the aircraft, through all of the usual airport procedures, to the arrivals hall. By the time he cleared the airport buildings it was just after six-o-clock in the morning. There was a slight early morning chill in the air but that same air held the promise of a warm day. Frank walked over to a taxi rank where a sleepy Greek man sat behind the wheel of an ancient silver Mercedes saloon that had the driver's window wound down and had the driver's hairy shirt-clad arm sticking out of it.

Frank tapped on the roof of the car and the driver came to with blinking eyes. Frank wished him a good morning. "Kalimera."

"Kalimera," grunted the driver as he came to his senses. He peered out at Frank, removed his arm from the open window, and then ran a hand over a day's growth of dark whisker stubble.

"Do you speak English?"

"Of course," answered the driver in his heavy Greek accent.

"Good," said Frank. "Do you know the way to the Pefkos City Hotel in Limassol?"

"Of course," answered the driver with confidence, although he quickly racked his brains to establish exactly where it was in Limassol. "Get in."

Frank did as he was told, dumping his bag on the spare leather seat beside him.

The Mercedes had obviously clocked up a whole lot of miles over the years, but the inside was clean and tidy and smelled of old leather and wood polish and not of old trainers, cigarettes or half-eaten food. The car pulled away and, as they drive on the left-hand side of the road in southern Cyprus, the driver hung his right arm out of the window again, steering with his left hand.

The driver glanced in his rear-view mirror at Frank who, despite his sleep on the aeroplane, looked a little haggard. "You okay, Sir?"

Frank smiled. "Yes, thank you. I'm just sleepy, that's all." The taxi driver's question made Frank realise just how tired he was. "How long will it take to get to the hotel?"

"It's just over forty miles, so about an hour." He twitched his right hand in the air outside the car. "Maybe less."

"That sounds good," said Frank. He stifled a yawn.

The driver smiled. "Okay, Sir," he said. "You just relax and I'll get you to your hotel, no problem."

"No problem," echoed Frank and he promptly fell asleep. It might not have been the wisest thing to do considering that he did not know anything about the taxi driver who could easily have been a member of Intiqam. However, despite his fatigue, Frank's self-preservation senses were not ringing any alarm bells and he had learned to trust those senses over the years.

*****

The owner of the voice introduced herself,

"I'm Gail Wetton... It looks like these people have k-kidnapped you too...Are y-you okay?"

Wetton was sitting on a chair at the same table that al-Makira had sat at earlier.

"Oh," said Lady Corrigan as she shook some tresses of hair from off the front of her face. "I'm Lady Maria Corrigan. You can call me Red; all of my friends do. I take it they have captured you as well?"

"Yes," sniffed Wetton. "We were g-grabbed in Venice. Then they drugged us...and brought us here."

"We?" asked Lady Corrigan as she approached the young woman in the tattered dress.

"Yes. My boyfriend and me."

"Your boyfriend?" Red looked around at the bare walls as if she were expecting someone, some man, some boyfriend, to materialise out of thin air.

"Yes, Larry."

"Larry?"

"Yes. Oh, b-but he's actually...the R-Right Honourable...Lawrence Gainsborough...He's an MP."

"Yes," said Lady Corrigan, her mind whirling. "I know of him...Not personally, you understand. But I thought he was married?"

Wetton looked at her dirty fingers that were clasped in front of her on the filthy tabletop. "He is...I mean...but...yes...but...Oh, bugger!"

"I see," said Red, now smiling in a kindly way, despite the terrible circumstances. "You're having an affair with…Larry?"

Gail's eyes came up to meet Red's. "It's not like that…He loves me."

Red nodded. "I'm sure he does. Look, it's not for me to judge you. And, right now, quite frankly, I don't give a shit."

Wetton's eyebrows shot up.

"Right now," continued Red, "we've got to think of a way of maybe getting out of here."

"No good," said Gail. "We're in some fly-blown village m-miles from anywhere and surrounded by desert. Even if we c-could escape, they would hunt us down in minutes. And even if we c-could avoid them, we'd probably die of thirst, or heat stroke, or snakes, or…" She trailed off miserably and looked at her fingers again.

"Hmm," said Lady Corrigan. "Doesn't sound too good does it? We'll just have to wait to be rescued then."

"Rescued?" said Gail looking up and with her eyes widening.

"Yes. If I know my husband there'll be a rescue mission underway, even as we speak."

*****

"We're here, Sir."

Frank came awake with a start. He glanced at his watch. 7.14 am. It had only seemed like thirty seconds ago that he had dropped off. "Oh, right. Great. Sure. Thank you. Efharisto." Frank rubbed a hand through his hair and then looked outside. It was daylight with early sunshine and an already clear blue sky. Across the dusty tarmac road sat the hotel.

The Pefkos City hotel is a stark white building made of concrete with seven stories and is set in an L shape behind a line of trees. There is an entrance to the left. Over to the right, and also in front of the building but shielded by those trees is a large swimming pool. To Frank it did not look like the place had the luxury of a five-star hotel but it did look somehow welcoming, even with its rather stark and angular lines.

Frank got out of the taxi with his bag in his hand. He glanced around before putting it down on the floor and he then pulled out his wallet. "I'm afraid I do not have Euros."

"No problem," smiled the driver. "English pounds will do perfect."

Frank handed over some paper money and said, "No problem. Efharisto poli." Thank you very much.

The driver took the cash, nodded, smiled and then drove off. Frank put away his wallet, picked up his bag and headed across the road towards the hotel.

**

The inside of the Pefkos City hotel was airy, cool, modern and welcoming, with white walls and light-grey marble floors. Frank stopped just inside the entrance doors and glanced around and noted that there were no CCT cameras that he could see. He headed towards the reception desk. A young dark-eyed elegant Greek girl with tresses of shoulder-length thick black hair was standing behind the desk. She was probably coming to the end of the night shift and was dressed in a flattering uniform of white shirt, burgundy-red waistcoat, matching skirt and black high heels, which must have been killing her after standing behind the desk for so long. She was wearing a plastic name-tag brooch over her left breast; it read Eleni. She smiled a warm and welcoming smile at Frank and bid him good morning and welcome. "Kalimera. Kalostone."

Frank returned the smile and said, "Kalimera, Eleni. I am William Newport, and I have reserved a room."

With her elegant hands with their long fingers and dark-pink painted nails the young lady tapped at a computer keyboard that was set below the level of the desktop. She frowned then smiled. "Ahh yes, Mister Newport. You are on the top floor." Her English was impeccable. "Your wife is already here."

"Great," answered Frank. *Tandy.* Frank smiled to himself, she'd used *Wife* and not *Partner* or *Girlfriend*.

Eleni smiled some more. "May I see your passport please?"

Frank produced the fake passport for William Newport. Eleni examined it and then tapped some information into the computer. She then returned the passport which Frank put into an inside pocket of his jacket and then she picked up a plastic card about the size of a credit card and swiped it through a machine beside the keyboard. She handed it to Frank. "Room seven-oh-two, Sir."

Frank took the card from her. "Thank you."

"You're welcome. Please enjoy your stay."

"Thank you." Frank smiled his most charming smile at her, then said, "I am actually part of a larger group."

"Oh?"

"Yes, they probably got here before me; a Mister Cameron, a Mister Collins and a Mister Davidson? You couldn't miss the last guy, he's about so big." Frank lifted his right hand into the air above his head and smiled at the receptionist.

"Oh, yes," she said. "I certainly remember him…and the other two gentlemen as well, of course." She checked the computer screen in front of her. "Mister Cameron and Mister Collins are in room seven-oh-seven, and Mister Davidson is in room…let me see…ah, yes, room seven-oh-six, just across the corridor." She smiled an efficient smile at Frank.

"Wonderful," said Frank. So, the boys were using their own names. Why not? It wasn't as if they were on the run from the law, and it was Frank who had to get them all onto the Akrotiri air base and past the officer in charge.

"Has it been explained to you," asked Frank, "that we are booked in for one week?"

Eleni checked the computer again. "Oh, yes, Mister Newport…and all paid for in advance."

"Excellent," said Frank. *I bet that hurt Sir Michael's credit card!* "However, I would like it known that we might not be in our rooms every night as we are here on a special seminar, at the air base."

"I see," said the receptionist. There was the slightest of frowns on her face.

"But don't worry," smiled Frank as charmingly as possible. "We won't be claiming any money back for non-use of the rooms, if that is what you are worried about."

The frown faded. "I'm sure everything will be perfectly in order, Mister Newport."

"Marvellous. Efharisto poli." Thank you very much.

Good, that was that dealt with. Now they just had to get to Qaryat Musawara, kill the terrorists, rescue the hostages and somehow get back home. Frank had not figured that last part out yet. Still, they had a week.

"Will there be anything else…Sir?"

"No. Efharisto. You have been very helpful."

Eleni looked at Frank and batted her long dark eyelashes.

Frank gave her another charming smile. "Could you point me in the direction of the lift?"

"Over there, Sir." She pointed over to her left.

Frank thanked her again and headed for the lift doors. He poked the lift call button and waited until the doors cranked open, then he stepped in and pressed the button for the seventh floor. Moments later he was stepping out onto a burgundy-red carpet spread over a white tiled floor.

He came to room 702 and swiped his entrance key-card and walked in by first pushing the door handle down with his right elbow and then pushing the door open with his shoulder. No fingerprints. He walked into the room and noted Tandy's bag on the floor over by the window. He dropped his own bag onto the double bed and fished out his mobile. He thumbed in a number then held the phone to his ear. Tandy answered. "Hi Frank."

"I'm here," said Frank.

"We're all in room seven-oh-seven."

"Excellent. I'm in seven-oh-two. I'll be with you in a few minutes."

"Okay, see yah."

"See yah." Frank put the phone back in his pocket, found the bathroom, had a pee then washed both his hands and his face. Then he headed for the entrance, stepped outside into the corridor and went to room 707 where he knocked quietly on the door.

Tandy opened the door, flung her arms around Frank's neck, went up on tip-toe and kissed him warmly on the lips.

"If you think I'm gonna do that laddie, you've got another think coming," growled Clonk from inside the room.

They all laughed. Tandy released Frank who then shook hands with the three male members of Shadows who were sitting around; Tommo and T Bone on the edge of the end of the bed and Clonk in one of two chairs. With the exception of Frank, who was still in his travelling clothes, they were all in shorts and T shirts with flip-flops on their feet. Tandy's T shirt was coloured fuchsia pink with ruffled sleeves.

"Any problems so far?" asked Frank who was relieved when he got a bunch of negatives back. "Good."

"When do we find out what this is all about boss?" asked T Bone.

"Yeah," said Tandy placing her left hand on her hip. "And when do we get the plan?"

Frank glanced from T Bone to Tandy. "Both are good questions. I'll fill you in very shortly. But first I need to speak to Corrigan." Frank took out his mobile again and called Sir Michael who answered straight away despite it being just after five-thirty in the morning back in the UK.

"Yes, Frank."

"I'm in Cyprus. Is everything in position."

"Yes, Frank. You're all set. Everything you asked for is at the base..."

Frank interrupted. "Everything?"

"Yes, everything."

Frank was impressed. "Well done, Sir."

"Yes, well, it took some doing I don't mind telling you, especially in so short a time."

"Do we know when the air transport can take-off?"

"Yes, but not 'til about one a.m. tomorrow morning."

"Hmmm," grumbled Frank. "I'd hoped to get out of here before that."

"Sorry, Frank. Best I could do."

"Okay, Sir. I know you've done your best. Thank you."

"That's okay. Now, when you get to the base ask for Group Captain Jonathan Baukham, the commanding officer. Mention my name."

Frank felt uneasy and he asked suspiciously, "Have you given him *my* real name by any chance?"

"No, Frank. Of course not. So far I haven't given him anyone's name who is in your team."

"Good."

"However, you will have to give a password to get past the gate security and another one to prove who you are to the commanding officer. This will get you and your team through the air base and onto your flight. The CO is expecting you and he knows that you are all travelling to the target incognito."

"Understood," said Frank. *Same old same old.* "What are the passwords?"

"To get you through the front gate it's *Athena*, and to confirm your group in front of the Group Captain it's *Aphrodite*."

"Got that," said Frank, although he did not repeat the words. "Well done, Sir Michael."

"Yes, Well...Never mind all that," grumbled Sir Michael Corrigan. "Just...Well...Well...good luck, Frank."

"Thank you, Sir Michael. Hopefully, the next time I speak to you we will have Lady Corrigan safe and sound." *Either that or we'll all be dead.* He closed the line and looked at his team. "Okay, it's like this..."

For the next twenty minutes Frank laid out for them what had happened so far, including the abduction of Lady Corrigan, the MP and his mistress; the attempt to kidnap Tandy in Japan; the film sent by al-Makira; the place where it was filmed and the links with Intiqam and why al-Makira wanted Frank. When he had finished Tandy whistled and sat back in the chair alongside Clonk.

"Blimey, Frank," she said. "When we knocked off Lancaster and El-Whassisname we really seriously got up their noses, didn't we?"

Frank grinned and continued with the briefing: He told them about Sir Michael asking him to help get his wife back and he explained the chase to North Weald, the helicopter and the chase by Spitfire to France. "You lucky bastard," said T Bone. "I've always wanted to go up in one of those."

"I'll see what I can arrange for you," said Frank, smiling. He finished the review by detailing the fact that in France he had been arrested and placed in a cell, where he would still be had it not been for the intervention of Sir Michael. At the end of it Frank turned to Tandy. "Do you have the paper and pens that I asked for?"

Tandy went over to the bedside cabinet and picked up two pens and a folded sheet of white paper. Opened out it was about the size of a tabloid newspaper. She opened it out.

"Will this do?"

"Excellent," said Frank. She gave him the paper and pens.

There was no table in the room so Frank knelt down on the tiled floor and spread out the paper. He looked up at his team then looked down at the sheet of paper and began to draw, making sweeping lines in red ink, and as he did so he said,

"This is a plan of the area surrounding the village in Iraq called Qaryat Musawara…that's Arabic for walled village. These lines are the escarpments that make the sides of the valley that the village sits in." He paused and looked around at them. They all looked steadily back at him. All of them had dealt with detailed maps before so they knew all about such things as escarpments, spot heights and contour lines.

He continued, "The edges of the escarpments are faced with very loose shale that runs down to the valley floor." He swopped pens for the black one and drew a large square shape between the red lines of the designated valley walls. The group craned their heads forward as they studied the map. Frank's Shadows knew that Fank had been to Qaryat Musawara, and they knew enough about their team leader to know that the sketch plan would be accurate in its detail, if not to scale.

As he drew, Frank said, "This is how the village is laid out...The village is surrounded by a wide and ancient but high wall that forms a square." As he spoke, he sketched in the details of the walls, entrances, buildings, narrow streets and alleyways. Having done that he then drew a line that came from the western end of the valley, came up to the village, went around the northern wall and headed off and away from Qaryat Musawara heading east. Frank said, "And this is the main access road. It comes right up to the walls. You can leave the road at various points to enter the village through the arches in the walls." He then used the pen to mark a cross in the middle of the sketch of the village. "I'm pretty sure that this is where they are holding the hostages, or, at least, I think it is the place where the execution of the MI Six agent took place."

"How do you know that?" asked the low rumble of thunder that was the voice of Tommo.

"Because," answered Frank, "it's the tallest building in the village with the best view out of a window, which means it is the best building from which to scan the area." He reminded them of the view that Sir Michael had sent to him on his mobile.

"Right," said Frank in an authoritative voice. "Here's what we do; questions and comments at the end please."

Frank went over the rescue mission, part of which involved a long-range accurate shot with a sniper rifle that was to be taken by Tandy. At the end of the plan there was complete silence from the group. They looked at one another and then at Frank. It was T Bone that spoke up,

"And that's your plan, is it?"

"Yes," said Frank.

"You must be out of your fucking mind," growled Clonk.

"It's madness," said T Bone.

Tommo said, "You mean that you are jus' going to walk in, and jus' give yourself up?"

"Yes."

"Why?" asked Tandy. She did not look happy.

"Because, if we attack the place straight on, they will surely kill the hostages out of hand...and probably film the executions."

"You're bonkers," said T Bone.

"Trust me," said Frank. "It'll work."

"Well, if it doesn't," growled Tommo, "you're gonna be a dead man." He looked at Tandy. She still did not look happy.

"It will work," said Frank. "We," he waved a finger around at the group, "will make it work."

No-one said a word.

"So, that's settled then," said Frank. "And Tandy takes the shot."

T Bone smiled at Tandy, and although she smiled right back, she was not exactly delighted with the prospect. With a long range shot there were too many variables: wind speed, wind shear, heat and even gravity on the speeding bullet. All would affect the round being fired and affect whether the shot hit…or missed. And if she missed, she could say good-bye to Frank and start making his funeral arrangements.

Frank nodded then looked around at the group again. "And I want the shot taken without a suppressor. I want these terrorists to hear the bang."

He watched their faces register surprise. Surely the loud report of a sniper rifle would alert the terrorists? He smiled at them. "Yes, I know that it will alert the terrorists, but it will also be your signal to come out of whatever cover you are in and go into action. Once Tandy takes her shot the place is going to go rapidly to hell."

"Damn right," growled Tommo. "Once that sniper rifle goes off the terrorists will be running around like ants."

"Agreed," said Frank as he looked around at them all. "However, our expertise should allow us to mop them all up pretty quick…Yes?"

They nodded. Although Frank would have liked a bit more enthusiasm.

Not getting it, Frank asked, "Anything else?"

"Yes," said T Bone. "You've said that I've got to take out the communications room."

"Yes," answered Frank. He looked questioningly at T Bone who asked,

"Do we know that these guys have a comms room? I mean, have you seen it."

"No, I haven't seen it," said Frank and then he held up his hand to stall T Bone's next question. "But they'll have one, you can depend on that."

"How so?" asked Tandy.

Frank turned to her. "Because they have been sending out videos of their executions, and that will take some technical expertise. And if they have such expertise you can bet they'll have a comms room."

"Makes sense," agreed Clonk, and there was much grunting and nodding of heads, except from Tandy, who asked,

"What if there's a guard on the comms room? Once the shot is taken by me, they'll be on the alert and T Bone might not be able to get in there before a call for help and reinforcements goes out."

As usual, with her flair for the finer detail, Tandy had spotted the flaw in the argument.

"Good point." T Bone wagged his finger at her. "A guard will have to be dealt with silently before Tandy's shot is taken, and with a knife in him, or her, they'll certainly struggle, and possibly scream, and that would warn the comms room people."

There was a long pause as they all considered this, and then Tandy said, "I might have something that will help."

She got up and left the room and re-appeared moments later holding a small soft plastic box about the size of a cigarette packet. Frank smiled because he immediately knew what this was. "Don't tell me you took that to Japan?"

"Of course," smiled Tandy. "A girl never leaves her sewing kit behind."

"A sewing kit?" said Clonk. "What do you want a fucking sewing kit for lassie?...Oh, excuse my language."

"Language excused," said Tandy graciously. "But this is not an ordinary sewing kit."

"You can say that again," muttered Frank.

Tandy refrained from actually repeating herself and she held out the kit towards T Bone. The soft plastic container was zipped around three sides so that when it was opened it flapped open along its fourth side like the spine of a book. Inside were a number of small spools of different coloured cotton threads, some safety pins, some eyed needles and a number of pins with large pink pearlescent heads to them. These last items were all individually enclosed in strips of cork that were held together by small tight ties of cotton thread.

T Bone took the kit from her.

"Go on," she said. "Open it."

"Carefully," offered Frank. "Very carefully."

T Bone looked at Frank and then at Tandy. He had the feeling that he was being sucked into a practical joke. Then, heeding Frank's warning, T Bone slowly opened the kit, half expecting something to jump out like a Jack-in-the-box.

He got the kit opened. Nothing happened.
He peered at the contents. "And just how is this supposed to get me to silence a guard?"
"Perhaps you sew his mouth shut," offered Clonk.
Tandy laughed then pointed at the kit. "You see those pins?"
T Bone went to touch one of them.
"I wouldn't touch them if I were you," said Frank.
Tandy smiled at him and then turned to T Bone who had frozen in the motion of almost touching the pins. "The points of them are covered in a venom extracted from a particularly poisonous sea shell. If you prick your finger with one of them you'll be dead in about three seconds...give or take a second."
"Shit!" said T Bone as he jerked the kit away from him, holding it at arm's length as if it were some deadly insect. "You're kidding me?"
"No," said Frank. "She's not. It's why she became known as The Scorpion. She carries a sting." He smiled at his girlfriend.
"Je-sus," breathed T Bone.
Clonk was sitting forwards. He peered at the pins in the kit held in T Bone's outstretched hand and then he looked at Tandy. "Do they really work that fast?"
"Oh yes," said Tandy in a matter-of-fact voice. "The venom becomes liquid the moment it enters the skin and then it instantly attacks the central nervous system and the brain. After that, your whole system shuts down and you die. It's very efficient." She smiled.
"Bloody hell," said T Bone. "Remind me never to annoy you."
Tandy laughed and then continued, "They're perfectly safe. You just have to be careful with them."
"And that," said Frank, "is how you take out a guard silently. You get right up to him and stick one of these in him."
"Oh," said T Bone sarcastically. "I just saunter up to him, say *excuse me*, and stick a pin in him?"
"Yes, something like that," said Frank. "I'm sure you'll think of something. I have every faith in you."
"Bloody hell," said T Bone again.
"Lassie," said Clonk. "How did you find out about all this venom stuff?"
"Oh," Tandy answered. "I experimented on sewer rats."
Not surprisingly there followed a long pause during which T Bone zipped

up the container and handed it back to Tandy. She tossed it onto the end of the bed and Tommo, T Bone and Clonk looked at it as though it were a lit stick of dynamite that was about to explode.

"Right," said Frank, diverting their attention. "Any more questions?"

The team looked at each other again. They knew that they were not going to move Frank Cross from his plan and so they decided to go with it – and the pins – no matter that it all seemed to be complete madness. What followed were a few minor questions about the distances involved, timings, the terrain and what it was like underfoot, and then Tandy asked,

"How do we get there?"

"Ahh," said Frank. He had been putting this part off. "We, umm, we go in by a Hercules transport aircraft."

"Sorry," said Tandy sitting up. "But how are we going to land a Hercules near the village, and without giving the game away?"

"We don't," said Frank, and Tandy realised that the other three men were grinning at her.

"Then…how do we…get there?"

"We jump," said Frank.

"Oh, no. No, no no! Oh no," Tandy wagged a finger at him. "I'm not jumping out of no bloody aeroplane! Anyway, I don't know how to!" She folded her arms across the front of her T shirt and gave him a look that said *Get out of that one, Buster!*

"You don't need to know how to jump," said Frank. He was smiling broadly. "You and I will go in tandem."

Tandy dropped her arms, sat up straighter and said, "What? We jump out of the plane on a bicycle?"

All except Frank laughed and she glared at them so that they rapidly shut up.

Frank lifted both hands and waved them. "No no no. Not that sort of a tandem." Frank said, "Jumping in tandem means that we jump together. You are strapped to the front of me, and I control the fall. Easy peasey."

"Oh, no. No. No. No." She looked around at the rest of the team, her eyes searching for support. But they just grinned at her until Tommo said, "This won't be a HALO jump then?"

Frank answered the big man, "No mate. Not a HALO jump."

"I know I'm going to regret asking this," began Tandy, "but what is a HALO jump?"

Frank rubbed the back of his neck before answering, "It stands for High Altitude Low Opening. Most Special Forces use it for getting into enemy territory undetected. The aircraft approaches the position for the drop at about thirty-thousand feet, you jump, wearing special kit so that you can breathe and not freeze to death on the way down, and then you deploy the parachute at about eight-hundred feet above the ground. In that way the aircraft you were in is so high it cannot be shot down, and the enemy don't see you drop."

"Have you done that?" she asked of her own personal hero.

"We all have."

"From thirty-thousand feet?"

"Yes."

"That's the height of a passenger aircraft."

"Yes."

Tandy looked around at the group; they smiled and nodded at her. She looked at Frank. "But you said we're not doing that. Right?"

"Right."

She thought a bit, then said, "Can't we fly in by helicopter?"

"Won't have the range," said Frank.

Tandy, not exactly keen on the idea of plunging through space, albeit that she would be attached to Frank Cross, had still not given up on the idea of an alternative means of transport for the intended invasion. "Okay," she said, hopefully. "By car then?"

"Too far," said Clonk.

"And a car would take too long to get there," said Tommo.

"And time is of the essence," said T Bone.

Tandy looked into each of their faces then put her hands on her hips. "Charming! Bloody charming! No support at all."

They were all smiling at her.

"Don't worry, Tandy," offered Frank. "The jumping is dead easy."

She raised an eyebrow. "I don't like the word *dead* in that sentence."

"Yeah," said Clonk. "The jumping is easy - it's the landing that's the real bastard."

Tandy stared at him.

Tommo laughed aloud. "Seriously Tandy. Jumping is like falling off a..."

"Aeroplane?" finished Tandy. "Look. I'm not at all happy about this."

"You'll do great," offered T Bone.

"Hmmm," said Tandy. "How high will we be jumping from if it's not thirty-thousand feet?"

"Not very high," said Frank.

"I don't trust you, Mister Francis Cross. How high is not high?"

Clonk answered, "About ten thousand feet." Frank gave him a withering look that said *Why don't you shut up!*

Tandy's mouth gaped open. "Ten thousand feet?" she squeaked.

Frank shrugged. "Yes. About that."

"That's as high as a bloody mountain!" she said plaintively.

"Oh, no," said Clonk. "Everest is just over twenty-nine-thousand feet."

"And Mount Kilimanjaro in Africa," put in T Bone, "is just over nineteen-thousand feet." He nodded at Clonk who nodded back.

Frank gently slapped his forehead. "Look, just shut up will you?"

"Just tryin' to be helpful boss," said T Bone, grinning from ear-to-ear.

"Well, you're not," said Frank.

"Jeez," said Tandy and she looked at the floor. Then she asked, "What happens if the parachute doesn't open?"

"Well," said Clonk in his broad Scotts accent, "They won't have to get a spade and bury you lassie, because you'll have done that job yourselves."

"Oh, Jeez," muttered Tandy.

Frank gave Clonk another withering look and the Scotsman decided to look intently at the wall by the door.

There was silence all round and the men stopped smiling and looked from one to another. If Tandy refused to do this jump, then Frank's plan would have to be scrapped and they would have to start again…and without her.

She looked up at them and asked, "Apart from HALOs, how many jumps have you guys done?"

There came a chorus of "Loads" "Lots" "Hundreds" "Tons" with the words accompanied by much nodding of heads.

"Well," she said. "I suppose the view at least will be amazing?"

"Umm," Frank hesitated. "We're actually going in the dark."

Tandy's eyes widened. "In the dark!" She stared at her partner. "Frank. You're joking, right?"

"No love…And we go tonight."

"Oh shit," said Tandy.

*****

Lady Corrigan had been seized by her arms, had a hessian bag pulled over her head, and then she was dragged out of the room she shared with Gail Wetton. She was taken to another room where she was forced to sit on the floor, still with the bag over her head. The bag had a musty damp smell to it, like the inside of an old church. Lady Corrigan wrinkled her nose.

Back in the other room Gail Wetton sat at a wooden table across from al-Makira. She was still in the dress that she had been wearing when she and Gainsborough had been snatched, and it was now filthy. She had her grubby elbows on the dirty table while al-Makira sat back in his chair with the back of his left hand placed delicately against his mouth and nose; Miss Wetton was beginning to smell. He took a small breath and asked,

"Has Lady Corrigan talked to you?"

Gail looked at him.

"I asked you a question."

Gail swallowed, then replied, "Yes." Despite her situation she smiled slightly, aware of why his hand was in front of his nostrils.

"And what was it that you talked about?" growled al-Makira.

Wetton looked at him. "She...She mentioned the idea of trying to escape."

"Ahh." Al-Makira smiled behind his fingers. "And what did you say to that?"

"I told her there was no chance."

"That's very good." He paused, then asked, "Has she mentioned Frank Cross at all?"

Gail Wetton frowned. "Who?"

"Frank Cross?"

"No...I don't think so..."

Al-Makira sat up. It was only a comparatively small movement but it seemed to generate physical violence. "You don't *think* so?"

"N-No. No. She didn't."

"You're sure?"

Gail clasped her hands together. "Yes...I'm sure."

Al-Makira scowled at her with his dark eyes glittering.

Gail Wetton rubbed her lips together. "How is Lawrence?" she asked.

Al-Makira's scowl lifted and he smiled as he considered the question. Finally, "He is...well."

Wetton sat forwards. "Can I see him?"

"No."

"Why not?"

"All in the fullness of time, my dear."

"Where is he?"

"He is near. You will see him again, when I have Frank Cross."

"W-What's so important about this Frank Cross?"

"You ask too many questions." Al-Makira stood up, pleased to be able to put some more distance between himself and the stink. However, he seemed to be thinking about her last question. He dropped his left hand and his handsome but hawk-like features stared down at her and he said to her in a cold voice, "He killed my brother."

Al-Makira turned and left the room. Outside the room al-Makira looked at his SiC. "Go and get the other western whore and bring her back with this one," he said, and he walked away.

*****

RAF BRIZE NORTON - OXFORDSHIRE

Captain Martin Buckley, an officer in B Group 22 SAS and based at the SAS headquarters at Stirling Lines, Credenhill, Herefordshire, had received his orders from his Commanding Officer - he was to select eight troopers and lead them on a rescue mission to Iraq. Buckley was five-feet-nine-inches tall with wide shoulders to match his wide chest. His jet-black hair was close-cropped and he had steel-blue eyes above a mis-shaped nose that otherwise spoiled a rather handsome face with its square jaw. He had been in Service for fifteen years and had a distinct military bearing.

Buckley had been hurriedly briefed on the nature of the mission and where it was. Speed and surprise, he was told, were of the essence. Buckley had then picked his troop – six men and two women – and they were then transported as fast as possible to RAF Brize Norton. Once at the RAF base they were hurried aboard a C-130 Hercules transport aircraft. The irony of that would not have been lost on either Captain Buckley or Frank Cross.

Even more ironic was the fact that Captain Buckley and his team would be flown into the Akrotiri RAF base on Cyprus. This was because the distance by air from Brize Norton to Mosul airport in Iraq is 2,350 miles and the range of the Hercules is 2,360 miles. With such a narrow margin of milage the Hercules would not be able to fly back to England and therefore it would have to land at Akrotiri to re-fuel, before delivering the team to its objective.

Like Frank's Shadows, the SAS would be flown in the Hercules from Akrotiri to the Drop Zone in Iraq. And, again like the Shadows, Captain Buckley's crew would jump from the transport aircraft in full kit with full equipment and attempt the rescue of the hostages held at Qaryat Musawara.

However, the SAS team would have been astounded, surprised and also a little worried if they had known that they were following in the wake of Frank's team.

*****

The Shadows team did not need to get changed at the hotel into the right combat gear that they would need for the parachute drop and their armed incursion because they simply did not have it. All of it, they hoped, was to be delivered to the Akrotiri air base.

After the discussion about the rescue mission Frank and Tandy went back to their room where they locked their door and Frank had a shower.

While Frank had his shower Tandy stripped off and got in there with him and he did not object. They had been apart for quite a while and they desperately needed each other, and so they lathered up and had some fun with the suds that a bar of soap produced.

After the shower Frank and Tandy caught up on some sleep. When they awoke it was lunch-time. But before they went down to the dining room Tandy produced her new black belt as she shouted out, "Tah-Dah!"

"Oh, well done, Tandy," congratulated Frank and he clasped her to him and kissed her with a passion.

Lunch was taken in the hotel's dining room along with the rest of the team. The meal consisted of Greek salad with Feta cheese on top and a side order of hunks of crusty bread. After this they were able to relax through the hot afternoon, sitting around a table beneath a sun umbrella by the hotel's pool; they were all wearing shorts and short-sleeved shirts.

Frank caught Tandy's eye and they both excused themselves. They went back to their room where they gave their bed some serious action; the bed creaked a bit but did not make too much noise given the strain that it was put under.

With their sexual appetites slated Frank and Tandy went back down to the pool area where Clonk, Tommo and T Bone where still sitting around the table. The three men looked up as Frank and Tandy appeared.

"Better?" asked Clonk with a huge smile on his face.

"Much better," smiled Tandy, and Tommo burst out laughing.

Frank and Tandy sat down at the table and together they fended off a series of ribald comments.

When the conversation had moved away from Frank and Tandy's love life Clonk produced a pack of cards from the back pocket of his shorts.

"Cards, anyone?" he asked.

"What, with you?" said T Bone.

"Who else?" said Clonk.

Tommo sat forwards. He only just fitted into the chair that he was sitting on. "Well, okay man. But no cheatin'"

"Who? Me?"

"Yes, you," said Tandy.

Clonk smiled. "I don't cheat. I just bend the rules."

"No," said Tommo. "You cheat."

"Frank," pleaded Clonk. "Help me out here, laddie."

"Not likely," answered Frank. He had picked up the pack of cards, had opened it, and was now inspecting the cards. "These seem well used." He continued his examination of the pack.

"Aye, well, so they are. What of it?" asked Clonk.

"Oh, nothing, nothing," smiled Frank.

"Give 'em here then." Clonk held out a large paw and Frank returned the cards.

"How about poker?" asked Clonk.

"How about rummy?" joked T Bone.

"Or patience?" suggested Tommo.

"He hasn't got any," said Frank.

"Oh, ha ha. You're all sassenach bastards!" growled Clonk.

"Hoy!" said Tandy. "Who are you calling a sassenach? My roots are African, not Great Britain."

"Me too, man." Tommo's voice was a deep boom.

"And," continued Tandy, "I'll have you know that my great-grandmother was a Zulu princess."

"My apologies, lassie." Clonk waved a gracious hand in her direction.

"What about me?" asked Tommo.

Clonk looked at the giant and asked, "Was your great-grandmother a Zulu princess as well."

"No."

"Then bollocks," said Clonk.

"If we play poker," said Frank, "what are we going to play for?"

"Oh, just for the hell of it," said Clonk. "Just for the hell of it."

"Then I'm in," said Frank.

"Me too," said Tommo.

"And me," said T Bone.

"Oh, I get it," said Clonk. "Now that there's no money involved, you lot want to play with me."

"Of course," said Frank. "Now it doesn't matter if you cheat because you've got nothing to cheat for."

"He'll still cheat," said T Bone.

"Bollocks," said Clonk.

"Deal the bloody cards," said Tandy.

**

Around seven-o-clock, with the card games finished (Frank won three games, Tandy two, Tommo two, T Bone two and Clonk only the one - despite cheating), Frank received another call on his mobile phone from Sir Michael. This call had not been expected and Frank got up and paced around the pool as he spoke into the phone. He stopped walking when Sir Michael informed him that a rescue team of British Special Forces, in this case the SAS, had been put together.

Frank was a little annoyed at this and his voice betrayed that annoyance as he said into his mobile, "Damn! You told me that it would take the British government longer than this to approve a rescue team."

"Yes," said Corrigan. "I must admit that I am surprised at their speed."

"Bloody hell, Sir Michael, this has just turned into a flaming race!"

"I'm sorry, Frank." Sir Michael sounded plaintive. "There wasn't anything I could do."

Frank took a breath. "No, I suppose there wasn't. Okay, there's nothing we can do about it now. We'll just have to avoid any delays and be right on it." He paused, then asked, "Have the Special Ops boys left the ground yet?"

"No, Frank."

"You're sure?"

"Positive."

"Well, at least we have a reasonable time frame to play with. But even so, it's going to be close."

"Just do your best," said Sir Michael.

"You know I always do," replied Frank. He gave a grim smile and ended the call. But he'd had a thought: *How are the Special Forces team going to get back out of Iraq?* Frank's mind ticked over and he gave a slight smile.

As Frank came back towards the team, Tandy sat back in her chair. She looked up at Frank. "Trouble?" she asked.

The rest of the team turned to look at their boss. Questions were forming, but no-one said anything.

Frank looked around at them all. He wasn't going to bullshit them. "There are some SAS people heading for where we're heading." He pronounced the SAS like a word - Sas.

Nods all round. No comments.

Frank said, "They shouldn't prove a problem as we'll be at the target before they are."

"That's alright then," came Clonk's deep Scottish brogue. "I'm gonna have a beer. Anyone else?"

Frank could not help smiling. Even with the threat of their plan being ruined, due to the SAS being on their tails, the members of the Shadows team took it all in their stride; if Frank wasn't worried then neither were they. And Frank reasoned that there was no point in being panicked into rushing headlong into this, because that was when mistakes were made. Now was the time for efficiency and cool thinking - and a good meal that evening would help. But right now a couple of beers would not hurt.

The beers were ordered and Clonk got up from the table and headed for the bar.

Clonk came back accompanied by a white-jacketed waiter bearing a circular tray on which were balanced bottles of Mythos beers – no glasses.

The beers were doled out and Tommo raised his bottle up into the air. "To success," he said and they all lifted their own bottles into the air.

"And happy landings," put in Clonk.

"Shut it," said Tandy.

After they had downed their beers, Frank suggested that they go to their rooms, have a quick freshen up and then meet in the hotel's restaurant. This was passed unanimously.

At just after 8.00pm they met in the restaurant. They all decided to go for the barbequed lamb chops with a side salad and washed it all down with Mythos beers. When they had finished, the meal was put onto Frank's tab and then they adjourned to the bar just before 9.30 where they sprawled into a variety of armchairs. However, no more alcohol was consumed, just coffee.

Frank looked at his team. Now would be the time when most soldiers would get their adrenalin rush, when the butterflies hit the stomach, as if they were performers about to go onto a stage in front of thousands of fans; but not this group. Tandy, Tommo and T Bone were chatting amicably and Clonk had actually fallen asleep and was making low grumbling noises that Frank took to be snoring.

Eventually, Frank checked his watch; it was 10.40. He looked up, "All set?" he asked. He was greeted with nods and grunts – except from Clonk who was still asleep. "Right, let's get going then." Frank shoved Clonk in his big muscley shoulder and he woke up with a start.

"Whassup?"

"Time to go, ugly," said Frank.

"Ohh, and I was just having a dream about a lovely lady who was…" He stopped and looked at Tandy.

"My my, Clonk," said Tandy. "You've gone a lovely shade of red."

"Bollocks," said Clonk and they all laughed as the Scotsman heaved himself out of his comfortable chair.

"Right," said Frank as they gathered at the entrance to the restaurant. "Go to your rooms. Check you've left nothing. Use the toilet. Have a wash if you need one, and then get back down here in the lobby for eleven-ten."

The team did as instructed, and were back in the lobby just before 11.10.

They strolled out of the hotel looking for all the world like a group of friends on a holiday who were going out to a bar for the night. They waved down a cab which took them to the front gates of the Akrotiri RAF base, home to 84 Squadron.

11.29pm.

The Akrotiri air base is huge. It occupies a peninsular in the south-east corner of Cyprus and is literally a complete town. Here, apart from the military buildings and the aircraft runway, there are houses for the base personnel, schools, shops, the Princess Mary's Hospital as well as sporting facilities and entertainment. It even has its own beaches.

The base is classed as a Sovereign Base Area and is under the Command of the Station Commander; in this case it was Group Captain Jonathan Baukham.

*****

The SAS team, led by Captain Buckley, hunkered down into the basic webbing seats of their own Hercules as the big aircraft made its way along the approach tarmac towards the end of the Brize Norton runway and the take-off point.

The team, dressed in dark camouflage-pattern battle dress, had already checked their weapons and equipment and were sitting in a line, with Captain Buckley sitting in the middle. The captain spoke up above the noise of the engines,

"Everyone okay?"

There were grunts and thumbs up as replies, and then the huge aeroplane was tearing down the runway, heading for take-off; heading for Cyprus.

The flight would take about six hours.

They were unwittingly racing towards Frank Cross and his team.

Ultimately heading for Iraq.

Heading for a fight.

*****

The Shadows team got out of the cab and strolled towards the barrier in front of the entrance gates which was lit up in a barrage of lights. A big man with a short regulation haircut and wearing camouflage fatigues came out of a small white building that was the guard-post and, in a business-like manner, he approached the barrier. He stopped his side of the barrier and placed his hands on his hips. He had the three stripes of a Sergeant at his shoulders and a pistol in a holster on his right hip. Frank watched the man run his suspicious eyes over them, although they stayed just a little longer on Tandy.

Frank and his team stopped on the civilian side of the barrier. Frank turned and looked at his team. He had to admit that they certainly looked an odd lot: Tommo, the bald-headed black Caribbean Islander at nearly seven feet tall and as solid as one of the monolithic stones at Stonehenge; T Bone, rugged and also tall at just under six feet with a fuzz of hair on his nearly bald head; Clonk, the shortest man in the group at five-feet-and-six-inches with a shock of untidy hair and a ZZ Top beard. He was shaped like a small boulder, and was just as hard; and finally, Tandy, the A-lister film star look-alike. If they had not all been wearing shorts and T shirts they would have looked like they had just walked off rehearsals from the back-lot of a Hollywood Super Hero film set. However, they all bore expressions that said they were deadly serious - apart from Tommo, who, although he had his mighty arms crossed in front of his huge chest, was smiling broadly and showing a perfect set of white teeth in his dark face. However, somehow his smile looked as threatening as the scowls on the other faces.

The sergeant finished his inspection and addressed Frank who was standing just forward of the rest of his team.

"I'm Sergeant Lock. Sir. Can I help you?" Best to put the word Sir in there as one never knew who you might be dealing with.

Frank knew that as a military man the sergeant would not want any padding as to why they were here. He just wanted the facts.

"Good evening Sergeant. We have an appointment with Group Captain Baukham," said Frank. "Sir Michael Corrigan has arranged it. He said to tell you…Athena." Frank had not mentioned his own name, and did not intend to. This was supposed to be a covert mission after all, and covert operatives did not bandy names around.

The sergeant held Frank's eyes with his own for a few long seconds. Then, still with his hands on his hips, the sergeant said, "Wait here, Sir."

"Certainly, sergeant."

The man turned abruptly and headed back into the white building. A few minutes later he came back out again, and this time the barrier went up and he walked up to Frank. Tandy knew that Frank was six-feet-three-inches of solid muscle; the sergeant was standing eyeball-to-eyeball with him.

11.41pm.

A slow smile crept across the sergeant's face. "Welcome…Sir. You and your team are to follow me." He blinked and then held Frank's gaze again and added succinctly, "Don't wander off."

Frank kept silent.

Frank, of course, had been here before when he had been given the mission to assassinate a group of Intiqam members in the same village to which they were now heading. Frank had been flown in on his own on a small passenger aircraft supplied by the Specialist Operations Unit. The flight had landed and he had been transferred immediately to a Hercules transport aircraft. Very few people had met him and no-one had seen his face because he had worn a ski mask the whole time; wearing it had been hot and stuffy but it had kept his anonymity. Therefore, no-one on this air base could possibly know that Frank Cross had been here before.

They were escorted onto the base by the sergeant and, after a few yards, they were taken into another white building, although this one was a lot larger than the guard-post. Inside, on the stark white walls, were some framed photographs of various aircraft in flight and a single framed picture of Queen Elizabeth ll. There was a desk before them with a door behind it which was closed. In front of the desk were five chairs. Frank guessed that the chairs had been hurriedly scrounged and arranged for them.

"Please be seated," said the sergeant, so they sat.

11.55pm.

All the members of Shadows had served in the British Army and were used to being moved about with no explanations or social niceties. However, although Tandy had served, she had never really got used to the taciturn orders and the continual bull. Frankly, Tandy found their treatment thus far to be bordering on rudeness. She was about to say something out loud to Frank when the door behind the desk opened and a tall straight-backed man in a well-pressed RAF uniform entered. Frank stood up and the rest of his team followed his example – except Tandy, who folded her bare arms across her bosom and crossed her legs above her knees.

The officer noted that, although all but one of the group had stood up, none of them had saluted. He ran his eyes over them. The sergeant was standing at the back watching the backs of their heads; hands on hips, feet apart. Balanced.

"I'm Group Captain Jonathan Baukham," said the officer in polished English. "I'm the Station Commander here. I believe you have a word for me."

"Aphrodite," said Frank. Athena, the Greek Goddess of Wisdom had been used to get onto the air base, and Aphrodite, the Greek Goddess of Love and Beauty, was being used to speak to the Station Commander. Without the help of the two Goddesses the Shadows team would not have got further than the entrance barrier.

The Station Commander gave Frank a long hard look, then said, "Please sit down." So Frank sat down again and the team copied him.

The sergeant at the back remained standing. Still with his hands on his hips, feet apart. Still balanced.

Frank's first impression of the Station Commander was not a good one. Frank thought that Group Captain Baukham was a bit of a stuffed shirt, had probably come into the Royal Air Force from a family with a military background, had been to university and was good at filing and bean counting.

Baukham was in his late thirties and stood at six-feet-and-four-inches tall. He had a clean-shaven and angular face with bright clear blue eyes, close-cropped brown hair and wide shoulders. Quite handsome actually.

Tandy watched him from under lowered eyelids and she had to admit that she liked the look of him. She was still sitting back in her chair with her long tanned legs crossed above her knees. She raised her left eyebrow.

Baukham's eyes flicked to Tandy's legs, then her face and then to Frank. The Group Captain cleared his throat. "Now," he said. "I have been given the co-ordinates for a DZ. These came to me from the British Security Service..." He paused and ran his eyes over the group again. *Who are these people?* "As I understand it, you want me to drop you into Iraq. Is that right?"

Frank said "Correct" as Tandy emitted a little groan.

The Group Captain zeroed-in on her noise. "What's wrong...Miss?"

Before Tandy could answer, Frank said, "She's never done a jump before."

"Ahh," said Baukham. "Hence the tandem rig that was ordered. I take it that therefore there are to be no HALO jumps then?"

"That's right," said Frank. *That was pretty sharp.* Frank began to revise his first impression of the officer as he avoided Tandy's eyes. "No HALO jumps."

Baukham nodded. "Very wise," he said. He looked at Tandy again. She reminded him of someone, but he could not place the memory. "And what about you guys?" The Group Captain waved a hand at Frank's team.

Frank decided to release some information. He needed the Group Captain on his side and he did not want to antagonise him.

"We're all Special Forces," said Frank. Actually, they were EX Special Forces, although Frank Cross was not about to admit that.

"Ahh." Baukham nodded, understanding. "I wondered who, or rather what, you were, when I received my orders." He lifted his chin and nodded again, and Frank was about to say something when Baukham pointed a finger at Tandy and said, "Including the lady?"

Frank gave one small nod. "Including the lady."

Wow! thought Tandy, *I'm now included! I'm one of them! I'm Special Forces!* She managed to keep her face straight.

"Forgive me," said Baukham, "but she doesn't look like Special Forces to me."

Tandy bridled. But before she could say something, Frank, without batting an eyelid, said, "She's my sniper."

Baukham's back straightened up just a little and he raised a surprised eyebrow. "Your sniper?"

"Yes."

"A sniper?"

"Yes."

"Oh. Is she any good?"

"She's the best," said Frank.

"Really?"

"Really."

"And she's sitting right here," said Tandy who was now frowning at the Group Captain. She uncrossed her legs, placed her hands in her lap and placed her knees and ankles together. She said, "And she is quite capable of answering questions."

The Group Captain smiled. It was quite an engaging smile. "I do apologise, Miss. I did not mean to offend. Most snipers I come across are male and as ugly as sin."

Tandy still did not smile. Ignoring the somewhat sexist remark, she said, "Well I'm not."

The Group Captain, realising that he had put both feet in it and then jumped up and down in it, raised the palms of his hands and said, "Yes. I am terribly sorry. I do apologise." He smiled.

Tandy did not smile back. There was a long pause, during which time the members of the Shadows team sat and looked at him as though they were hunters and he was potential prey. Eventually, Tandy said, "Apology accepted."

Baukham kept the smile on his face as he breathed out slowly and nodded. The tension in the room dispersed and Baukham stood up. "Right then," he said. "Time to go. Sergeant Lock here will take you to your transport aircraft. It's a C-One-Thirty Hercules. It's on the end of the runway and it's fuelled and ready to go. The flight plan has already been communicated to us, logged, and the DZ confirmed."

Frank nodded, and recognised the intervention of Sir Michael Corrigan in those details.

The Group Captain continued, "I would appreciate it if you would check the DZ once you get on board."

"Certainly, Group Captain," said Frank, who was getting the distinct feeling that he and his team were wanted off this airbase as fast as possible. "What about the arms, clothing and equipment we asked for?"

"It's all on board the Hercules. I'm afraid you'll have to get togged-up on the aircraft." The Group Captain looked at Tandy. "And we do not have separate changing rooms on board." The team would all have to get undressed and dressed in front of each other.

"Don't worry about that," said Frank, grinning, "we're a close-knit crew."

"Quite," said Baukham. He held out his right hand. "Well, good luck."

Frank shook the officer's hand. "Thank you, Sir." And then Frank actually snapped off a smart salute which brought another smile from the Group Captain.

Group Captain Baukham turned and left the room, glad to be getting away from them – the least amount of contact that he had with them meant the least he had to report if the shit hit the proverbial fan.

The sergeant led the team back outside into the warm night air.

Tandy hooked her left arm through Frank's right. "Frank?"

"Yes, m'dear."

"What's a DZ?"

"Drop Zone," answered Frank.

"Urhhh," said Tandy. "I wish I hadn't asked."

**

The sergeant struck off smartly towards a parked rugged sand-coloured military truck that had a hooped matching sand-coloured canvas cover over the back. The sergeant approached the cab and then turned to Frank and his team. "Get in." He waved the team into the back of the truck and then he climbed up into the cab, banging the door shut with a heavy clang.

12.14am.

The team climbed in and settled themselves onto the bench seats that lined either side of the truck.

"Not exactly friendly, are they?" growled Clonk.

"I expect their orders are to check us and then get us the hell off their base as quickly as possible," said Frank.

Clonk shrugged.

"Same old same old," commented T Bone and the truck started off with a jolt and a cough of grey exhaust smoke.

The buildings of the base sped past, but because there were no windows in the canvas roof the Shadows team could only watch out of the open back of the rattling truck.

After a couple of minutes the truck pulled up. They heard the cab door open and then close with the same noisy clang and then the sergeant appeared at the back. "We're here."

The team jumped down out of the truck and Tandy wished that this had been the highest that she would have to jump this night. As these thoughts went through her head she found herself standing on a road alongside the air base's runway. The wide strip of tarmac stretched away from her with the dark night lit through by the runway's landing lights and those of the many buildings and hangars. In some of the hangars she could make out the threatening shark-like shapes of the Eurofighter Typhoon aircraft that were based here. Her attention was drawn back to the sergeant who said,

"Your lift is over there."

They turned as the sergeant shoved out an arm and pointed. About one hundred feet away, sitting on the end of the runway, was the huge bulk of the C-130 Hercules transport aeroplane.

"Blimey!" said Tandy, and Frank grinned.

Introduced in December 1956 these aircraft have been carrying passengers and freight all over the world on peace missions and for battle support. The Hercules is just under one hundred feet long and just under forty feet high. It has a wingspan of one-hundred-and-thirty-two feet and those wings hold two Allison T56-A-15 turboprop engines, each one of which pushes out 4,590 shp (shaft horsepower), which is the amount of power that can be generated at the propeller shaft. There are four propellers to each engine, each one being thirteen-feet-six-inches in diameter.

The aircraft has a maximum speed of 370 mph at 20,000 ft, with a cruising speed of 336 mph. Its range is 2,360 miles and has a service ceiling of 33,000ft when empty. It has a crew of five: two pilots, one navigator, one flight engineer and a loadmaster.

Being a transport aircraft, its cargo hold is between forty feet to fifty-five feet long depending on the model of the Hercules. However, the holds of all of the models are nearly ten feet wide and nine feet high. It can carry 92 passengers, or 64 airborne troops, or 3 Humvees, or two M113 armoured personnel carriers, or 74 litter patients with their attending 5 medical crew. It has not been called the Hercules for nothing and the Shadows team were not exactly going to take up much space or prove a weight hazard to the giant aircraft.

Frank and the other three guys had been in one of these beasts before on a number of occasions, either in the 1 Parachute Special Forces Support Group or the SAS.

The long rear loading ramp had been lowered and the team made their way over to it and walked up inside where they were met by both the lead pilot, Alan Sampson, and the loadmaster, Dave Wright, who introduced themselves. They were both wearing regulation RAF one-piece olive-coloured flying suits. Tandy thought that they looked very military and was a little un-nerved.

Frank, Clonk, Tommo and T Bone lined up alongside each other and across the width of the loading ramp. They took up a stance: feet apart, backs straight, heads up, arms behind them with their hands clasped together. Tandy tagged onto the left-hand end of the line, stuck out her chest and copied them. Once again, they made an odd assortment, dressed as they were in shorts and T shirts.

Tandy let her eyes wander over the lit-up interior of the cavernous interior of the Hercules; the impression was that she was inside some giant beast's ribcage. The walls were steel grey and with curving steel ribs that formed the carcass - the air frame - of the aircraft. However, the walls and ceiling could not be described as spartan as they were festooned with trunking, cables, piping and steel boxes of various sizes that housed electrical devices. In front of this display of a seeming jumble of technical and engineering, and either side of the cargo area, sat a row of collapsible fold-up seats. The floor beneath Tandy's trainers was also steel, painted grey, and had a number of large removable panels and flat locking devices built into it.

Tandy's eyes came to rest on the pilot and loadmaster who were scrutinising the group, with their eyes checking only momentarily as they swept across Tandy's face. She noticed the check and realised that they were doing and thinking what hundreds of other people, male or female, had done in the past – they thought that they recognised her but could not place her. She kept a straight face, teeth clamped tight together, and looked business-like.

"Welcome aboard." Sampson addressed Frank; he was frowning and he did not move.

Frank smiled at him and offered him a handshake. Crews usually liked to know why they were flying and Frank correctly guessed that this crew had only been told of the Drop Zone.

Sampson shook the offered hand and his face softened a little.

"I'm sorry for all this cloak-and-dagger stuff," said Frank. "But I can tell you that we are on a rescue mission."

"In Iraq?" asked the loadmaster who also responded to an offered hand to shake.

"Yes."

"Must be pretty important people to warrant a night drop, and at such short notice," said Sampson.

Frank nodded. "Believe me, they are."

"Fair enough," said Sampson, who at least now knew why he was going to be flying in a very hazardous area. "How are you getting back out?"

Frank hadn't exactly figured that bit out but he knew that the Hercules would not be picking them up when the operation finished. So, he smiled and said, "Sorry. You know how it is. Need to know."

The pilot nodded. He had flown people into black ops before and knew that you never got to know everything when one of those was underway. "How high are you jumping from?"

"Ten thou'," answered Frank and he heard Tandy groan.

"Okay," said the pilot. He turned and pointed at some large green heavy-duty plastic boxes that were stacked against a bulkhead that separated the cargo from the rest of the Hercules. "Those are yours."

"Do you mind if we check them before we get rolling?"

"Go right ahead. Let me know when you're ready."

"Thank you…Guys?" Frank jerked his head towards the boxes as the pilot left them.

Having opened the boxes, the team laid out the contents in five piles; one for each of them. While this was going on the loadmaster stood with his muscular arms folded across his chest and watched the proceedings without saying a word. If there was something missing it would be up to him to source and supply it, so he was rather relieved when they confirmed that all that they needed had been delivered.

12.25am.

"Right guys," said Frank. "Let's get changed."

They began to strip off on the spot and Dave Wright was somewhat taken aback when Tandy peeled off her short shorts and T shirt. She was wearing light-blue silk high-leg knickers with a matching T shirt bra courtesy of Marks and Spencer, but he had to smile when she leaned forward and plucked at the waistband of Frank's black Calvin Klein briefs making it thwack against his bare skin.

"Hoy!" called Frank. "Behave!"

Tandy straightened up and saluted him. "Yessir! Anything I can assist you with, Sir!"

The other three Shadows started laughing, and pretty soon the ribald comments and jokes started up as they variously insulted one-another.

Dave Wright began to relax and he unfolded his arms; this team obviously knew each other very well and their stripped-down semi-nudity wasn't affecting any one of them; the girl, quite rightly, was just one of the team and not regarded as some object of desire.

Wright watched them as they replaced their tourist clothes with the black and grey tactical outfits that Frank had ordered, the jackets and cargo trousers of which had a multitude of pockets. The outfits came with soft-soled black trainers that were high at the ankle, black silk socks and black silk base layer vests. The tourist clothes would not be seen again; indeed, they would be destroyed when the aircraft got back to the air base, thus proving that the Shadows team had never been on board the aircraft, or anywhere near Captain Buckley…What Shadows team? Sorry, never heard of them.

"Right guys," called out Frank. "If you've got mobile phones on you, you can keep them, but make sure they are turned off." Frank did not want a phone ringing just as one of them was sneaking up on a guard – and Frank knew there would be guards.

Phones were duly produced and turned off.

With their new uniforms on, guns were stripped down, examined and rebuilt then loaded, and Wright stared open-mouthed as he watched Tandy take an Accuracy International L96A1 sniper rifle out of its case, take it to pieces, and then put it back together in a matter of seconds. *Wow!* thought Wright, *this is my kind of girl!*

Tandy put the long weapon into its leather slip and placed it on the floor near the seats with the rest of the checked assault rifles. The rest of the armaments and equipment that they would need remained in the plastic boxes.

Eventually Frank checked with his team. Were they all set? He got their positive replies and turned to the loadmaster.

"We're all set here," said Frank.

"Good," said Wright. "Let's get going then."

"'Scuse me laddie," said Clonk. "How long will it take to get there?"

Wright looked at the Scotsman. "Our cruising speed will be about three-hundred miles per hour, so it should take us about two hours."

Clonk turned to Frank and raised an eyebrow. Ideally, a covert incursion, that was to be used to take out as many armed and unknown personnel as possible, would be carried out at around 4.00am, this being when the body mechanism of a human is at its lowest ebb. But time was against them and they would have to adapt.

Wright saw the look that passed between Clonk and Frank; it was a look that said *Oh well, can't be helped. Never mind*, but he ignored it and continued, "If I were you, once we're up, I'd try and get some sleep."

"I don't suppose you've got a bar on board?" asked Clonk.

The loadmaster shook his head and smiled. "No. But I can get you some tea when we're airborne."

"Tea!" exclaimed Clonk in the same way that he would respond to the offer of a rat sandwich.

"Tea will do just fine," said Frank and he elbowed Clonk in the upper arm.

"What?" said Clonk. "What?"

The team chuckled.

"Now," said Wright. "If you'll all just take a seat and put on your seat belts, I'll tell the pilots to be on our way." And with that he left.

The Shadows took their places in a row along the left-hand side of the cargo bay with Tandy nearest the loading bay with the sniper rifle at her feet. Frank was beside her, then Clonk, T Bone and finally Tommo at the other end. With nothing else to do they watched as the loading ramp was hauled into place by the action of hydraulics. It closed with a low booming noise in the hollow area. Tandy was staring at it.

"Will we have to jump out of there?" She pointed at the ramp now settled securely into place.

"No love," said Frank, smiling. "There are two doors up near the bulkhead on either side. See them?" He pointed. They looked like a larger version of the type of escape doors you get on standard international aircraft. "We open them and...er..."

"Jump out," finished Tandy.

"Yes, exactly."

"How long will it take before we hit the ground?"

"Okay," said Frank, and he turned to her. "We'll be dropping at a rate of around two-hundred-feet-per-second."

Tandy's eyebrows shot up.

"Don't worry," calmed Frank. "You won't be aware of it. You won't get that swoop in your stomach like on a rollercoaster ride. In fact, you won't even have the feeling of falling...it's more like a feeling of floating."

"O-kay," said Tandy with a slight shake to her voice. Not entirely convinced.

"So," continued Frank, "in answer to your question *how long*, because we will be jumping from around ten thousand feet it will take under a minute until I have to deploy the chute."

"O-kay," repeated Tandy, still not sure. "And what do I do with the sniper rifle?"

"Oh, right. Look, tighten up the carry strap on the slipcase and put it around your neck so that you have the rifle across the front of your body. That way you won't have to hold onto it"

"It weighs twenty-seven pounds, and that's without the scope and ammunition," said Tandy. "This is a lot of weight for our 'chute to be carrying."

Frank shook his head. "It won't make much difference, dropping through the air."

"Hmmm," Tandy frowned. "It might make quite a difference when we land though."

"Don't worry, love, I'll deal with it."

"Don't worry Tandy," came Tommo's deep resonant voice. "If you want I'll jump first, so that I can catch you when I'm down."

"You'll have to catch both of us," said Frank, laughing. "'Cause we'll be jumping in tandem. Remember?"

"Oh yes. I forgot, boss."

"Tell you what though," offered Clonk.

"What's that?" asked Tandy sitting forwards so that she could see him along the line of the seats.

"Tommo can help pick up the bits!"

They all turned to look at the Scot. No-one was smiling at him.

"What?" said Clonk holding up his hands. "What?"

"Clonk," said Frank with a hard frown on his face. "Why don't you shut up?" It was not a question.

As much as a lump of hairy granite can register remorse or apology, Clonk's face was equally as responsive. However, he did start to say something, but the team never got to hear it because, at that moment, the engines of the Hercules fired up. This was followed by such a vibration within the aircraft that fittings and equipment started to rattle all around them.

To Tandy, who was only used to flying in comfortable passenger jets, it felt like she was sitting in the middle of an earthquake. *I don't like this!* she thought. *I really don't like this!* She turned and looked at Frank, who gave her a reassuring smile and a wink.

"Do they pressurise the aircraft, like they do with airliners?" she asked.

"Oh yes," replied Frank, anxious to keep Tandy calm and moderately happy. "You'll probably feel your ears pop as we gain altitude, just like a normal airliner. However, when we have to exit…"

"You mean jump out."

"Ummm, yes…When we have to jump out, they will have dropped in altitude and de-pressurised the aircraft. You won't notice a thing though." He smiled.

Tandy tried to smile back, but all that happened was an expression on her face like she had just sucked on a lemon.

"How are they back there?" asked Sampson who was settled into the pilot's seat.

"All set," answered Wright from the flight-deck's bulkhead doorway. 12.46am.

Sampson turned to his co-pilot seated alongside him. "Right then, let's get going."

Headsets went on and there was some brief radio communication between the aircraft and the control tower. Clearance was given and the huge aircraft started to move. Back in the cargo bay the seated Shadows team felt the beginnings of movement as a slight sideways jolt and Tandy reached out and gripped Frank's hand. Clonk saw the movement, but this time he kept his mouth shut, allowing himself only a small smile. He knew that Tandy was feeling out of her depth and extremely nervous at the coming drop and he decided that he had ribbed her enough. She was, in his opinion, one very gutsy lady.

The Hercules trundled out onto the end of the runway and took up position for take-off. To a casual observer it looks like an aircraft of this size should not, and could not, possibly, ever be able to take off.

Inside the cargo hold the Shadows team listened as the four engines built up in revolutions, and then suddenly they were again jolted sideways in their seats as the mighty aircraft surged forwards. The ground speed built up as the wheels hurtled over the tarmac, and then they were up.

Frank could tell the exact moment that they left the ground by the difference in sound. "We're up," he said to Tandy who squeezed his hand a little harder. Seconds later the team became aware of the tilt of the aircraft as it began to climb steadily.

After a few minutes the Hercules levelled-out at 20,000 feet, and a few moments after that the loadmaster came back into the cargo area. He smiled at them all.

"We've levelled-out now and we'll stop at this height until we near the DZ. I can get you that tea now."

"How high are we?" asked Tandy.

"Twenty-thousand-feet, Miss."

"Lovely," said Tandy. She pulled a face and swallowed. "I'll have a tea, please. Black with plenty of sugar."

Frank turned to her. "You don't take sugar in tea."

"I do now."

Frank laughed. Then said, "Black tea for me too please, but with no sugar." The rest of the team then chimed in with their orders.

Wright left them, feeling like a waiter and heading for the galley that was behind the flight deck. He reappeared a few minutes later with a tray full of the hot drinks. The team gratefully took their teas and sat with them cupped in their hands - they were at 20,000 feet and it was cold in the cargo hold.

With the teas drunk the team began to doze. Dave Wright came and collected the empty cups which woke them all up.

"Sorry guys," he said. "Just send someone forward if you want anything, but as we don't have any in-flight entertainment, then, like I said earlier, I suggest you try and get some sleep and I'll come and let you know when we are nearing the DZ."

"Thank you," said Frank. Tandy managed a smile, Tommo nodded and T Bone flicked off a salute. Clonk was already asleep.

**

Half-an-hour after Shadows took off from RAF Akrotiri Group Captain Baukham put the telephone back on its cradle on his desk. He rubbed his face and then looked up his sergeant who was standing in front of his office door.

"It would seem, sergeant, that we have another Special Ops group coming in."

"Sir?" Sergeant Lock twitched his left eyebrow.

Sergeants, the world over, are able to convey all sorts of questions, comments and answers to their commanding officers by the single use of the word *Sir* together with small movements of their facial muscles. Sergeant Lock was no different.

Baukham puffed out his cheeks then said, "That was the Air Chief Marshal, and before that I had the Secretary of State, and before *that* I had the Chief of General Staff on the line."

"Sir." (a small downward contraction of the lower lips)

The head of the Royal Air Force is the Air Chief Marshal who liaises with the Secretary of State, and the head of the British Army is the Chief of General Staff.

"The Special Ops are coming in by Hercules. They'll be here in about fifteen minutes. Get them off the aircraft and here to me while the Hercules refuels, and as soon as the aircraft is refuelled I want them off this base ASAP. Am I understood, sergeant?"

"Sir!" The sergeant saluted, spun on his heels and hurried out of the Station Commander's office.

Baukham sat back in his chair. *Now, what the hell is going on?*

**

The Hercules with the SAS on board landed with a loud rub of its tyres on the runway and came to a screaming halt just short of the end of the tarmac. The aircraft was guided to a position by a member of the ground crew - a man wearing what looked like a dayglo red boiler suit – to where the Special Ops team could disembark. After that it was moved to another area for refuelling while the team were trucked, at almost reckless speed, over to Group Captain Baukham's office. It was the same vehicle that had carried Frank and his team.

Once again, Sergeant Lock acted as escort. Captain Buckley and his team were ushered in front of the Station Commander's desk where chairs had once more been provided. None of the SAS team saluted the Station Commander when he entered, but they only sat down when he did.

Baukham stared at them. Then, rather hesitantly, he asked, "Can you tell me anything of your mission?"

Of course they could not.

"Yes, Sir. We are to be flown into Iraq."

Baukham raised both eyebrows as the captain gave out the restricted information, and then alarm bells began to ring in the Station Commander's head.

"Iraq."

"Yessir."

"Where no doubt you will drop in by parachute?"

"Yessir."

"Is this to be a rescue mission, Captain?"

Buckley had raised both eyebrows. "Why, yes, Sir."

Apart from the alarm bells in his head, Baukham felt something crawl inside his chest, but he kept his face passive as he turned to his sergeant who was standing beside him. "Sergeant Lock, please get me the co-ordinates of the DZ for the other Special Ops group."

"Yessir!" The sergeant left the room.

What's this all about? Thought Buckley. *What other Special Ops group?*

Group Captain Baukham cast his eyes over the group in front of him and said nothing – and they all stared straight back at him. They were all as hard as flint and Baukham had the feeling that he was on display, like some sort of stuffed animal in a glass case. The feeling remained until Sergeant Lock arrived back in the room somewhat breathless. He had obviously been running.

Sergeant Lock handed over a sheet of paper. Baukham glanced at what was printed there and then held it across his desk towards Captain Buckley.

"Captain. I have to know. Are these the same co-ordinates that you have for your DZ?"

Without taking the paper from Baukham's hand Captain Buckley scanned what was written there and then looked up at the Station Commander. "Near as dammit," he said.

Baukham's shoulders slumped.

"What the hell is going on here?" asked the SAS Captain.

Baukham straightened his back. "That's a damned good question, Captain. I wish I knew. All I can tell you is that another Special Ops group turned up here…and, under orders from the top brass, we are flying them out to Iraq, to those co-ordinates…on a rescue mission."

Captain Buckley's lips formed a thin line, his jaw hardened and his eyes took on a cold look. At that moment, Group Captain Baukham realised how hard this man in front of him was. He certainly wouldn't want to mess with him – or his team.

Buckley briefly mulled the problem around in his head, then said, "Makes no difference, Sir."

"It doesn't?"

"No, Sir. We have our orders, and we'll follow them. Simple as that."

"But it could be a waste of time on your part."

"Possibly, Sir. However, since we don't know what's happening at the Iraq end, we have to go with the mission on the understanding that we might now be getting into one helluva big fuck up. But at least we'll be forewarned of it."

Baukham ignored the swear word and sat forwards. "Forewarned is forearmed. Is that it?"

"Absolutely, Sir."

"Right. Well. There's nothing to be done at the moment while the Hercules you arrived in is being refuelled, so I suggest captain that you and your team have a cup of tea or coffee and we'll call you when it's ready to fly."

"Very well, Sir. Sounds like a good idea." The captain got up and his team rose to their feet with him.

Group Captain Baukham looked across to Sergeant Lock. "Sergeant."

"Sir."

"Escort these men…and ladies…to the canteen and see that they are fed and watered."

"Yessir." The sergeant saluted and then acted as a sheepdog to get this team of hardened soldiers out of the office and across to the canteen.

Not that long afterwards Captain Buckley and his SAS were climbing aboard the Hercules transport aircraft and Group Captain Baukham was more than happy that this shit storm was getting out of his hair and off his air base.

*****

WEDNESDAY 25TH JUNE

"Wakey wakey," said Dave Wright. It was just before 3.00am

There were a few groans as the members of Shadows were awoken from their various dream-states. All except Clonk who kept on snoring, until T Bone kicked his feet and he came awake with a snort that would have done a rhinoceros proud.

"Whas goin' on?" Asked Clonk, rubbing at his eyes.

"Man," said Tommo. "I swear you could sleep on top of an erupting volcano."

"Clear conscience laddie," said Clonk, smiling broadly.

"I can't think how," quipped T Bone.

Dave Wright intervened. "Okay guys," he said as he checked his watch. "We're descending to your drop height and we'll be over the DZ in ten minutes."

"Time to get ready to go," said Frank. He squeezed Tandy's hand that was still nestled in his own. He looked at her. "You okay?"

"Yes. Time to get this over with." She did not look as though she were looking forward to this next part of the operation one little bit.

"You'll be fine," said Frank. "Trust me."

"I do." And she leaned forward and kissed his stubbly cheek.

"Hey Tandy, will you kiss me too?" This from Clonk who was standing only a few feet away and who was starting to unpack their equipment boxes.

"Sure," smiled Tandy, "but only once we're down."

Clonk laughed. "I'll hold you to that, lassie."

"But no tongues," said Tandy, and they all laughed.

With the boxes unpacked, the rest of the team started their own equipment checks: the Glock pistols were placed into holsters; their suppressors went into jacket pockets and the H&K MP7 assault rifles were picked up off the deck of the aircraft and examined in case any particles of dirt had gotten into the workings. Knives were strapped on at hips and fragmentation and stun grenades, two of each to each of the men, were clipped onto webbing on the fronts of their jackets.

Sir Michael had managed to get Frank his favoured Smith and Wesson model 64 revolver with the 9mm hollow point bullets, and he had the two requested speed loaders to go with them. Frank put the revolver into its black leather holster on his hip. He pulled it out in a fast draw a couple of times and spun it cowboy fashion, showing off, before putting it back.

"Very nice, Boss," said Clonk. "Mind you don't shoot your foot off."

The team laughed, letting off some tension.

"Nearly time," said Wright and he moved to the aircraft's starboard door.

The team shouldered their parachute packs into place, secured the harness straps into place across their chests, and edged towards the door with the four men pulling the elasticated straps of plastic goggles over their heads; pulling the goggles onto their faces so as to protect their eyes.

Wright opened the exit door and instantly the outside air buffeted in, making the team sway as they stood to the right of the hatch, waiting for Frank to come to the head of the line. They were ready to file forwards to the opening and the ten-thousand-foot drop. All except Frank. He was talking to Tandy who had the long sniper rifle case balanced across her chest.

"Right, my dear. Listen up."

Tandy turned and looked at Frank with wide unblinking eyes and her lips in a tight line. She said nothing.

Frank put his hands onto her shoulders. "I am going to have you back into my chest and then I'll hook you up to me. When we get to the door stand with your feet inside mine. I will count to three and then I'll jump. The moment we are out I want you to starfish."

"Starfish?"

"Yes. Put your legs and arms out either side. I'll be doing the same thing. But one thing you must remember not to do is lift your head up. If you do, you will bring the back of your head into my face...and you don't want to knock me out, do you?"

"Oh," whimpered Tandy. "No way."

"Good. Remember that. Now, when I pull the 'chute you will feel a jerk, and then we will no longer be dropping face down. At that point you must stop starfishing and cross your arms across your chest. Okay?"

"Right. Got that. Cross my arms." She hoped that the rifle would not get in the way.

"Good. Now, as we near the ground just lift your feet so that only mine hit the floor. With any luck we'll have a nice controlled landing."

"*With any luck?*"

Frank smiled. "Trust me. It'll all be over before you realise it." He kissed her on her forehead. "Put your goggles on."

The goggles went on.

Frank pulled his own on.

Tandy turned around and snuggled back into Frank's body and he hooked her up to his tandem parachute harness. Tandy stood hugging her sniper rifle across her chest. Tandy now understood why Frank had made her have the strap of the sniper rifle's case so tight around her neck and chest; it meant that when she starfished she would be able to let go of it without it falling.

The team were looking at her, willing her to be brave as, with a strange stuck-together comedic walk, she and Frank shuffled the few paces over to the front of the queue and to the edge of the door. Frank was standing with his feet apart and Tandy placed her own inside Frank's as he had instructed.

Not wanting to look down into the void at her feet, Tandy looked up. The night sky was filled with stars, and ahead of her, towards the east a large half-moon cast a glow.

"Tandy, look down," came Frank's voice in her ear.

Tandy, against her better judgement, looked down. The starlight and moonlight was being reflected off the top surface of a layer of white fluffy clouds that stretched away into the distance like an enormous glowing duvet cover. As she gazed at the scene below her Tandy's fears were suddenly mixed with elation at the beauty of it. She wanted to tell Frank how wonderful it looked, but somehow her dry tongue got stuck behind her teeth.

A red light came on above the doorway.

"Time to go!" yelled Wright over the noise of the buffeting air.

Tandy swallowed and, as she swallowed, she heard Frank start to count to three,

"One…Two…" and he jumped.

What happened to three, you bugger? Tandy had barely let the thought come when she felt Frank's arms and legs go out and she instinctively copied him.

Starfish, starfish! Don't bring your head up…Don't bring your head up. She repeated the mantra in her head.

Terminal Velocity is the maximum speed that a body can reach when falling. The terminal velocity of a falling human is around 120 MPH and it takes about five seconds to get to this speed. With Tandy and Frank freefalling at around two-hundred-feet-per-second it would not take them very long to get to the ground – a fact that Tandy was now acutely aware of.

The rest of the team had jumped as well and were falling through the night sky behind and above them. However, Tandy could not see them. She was aware of her heart thumping in her chest and the sound of the rushing of wind past her ears. She could feel her cheeks buffeting as though the air she was passing through was trying to force her to grin, so she grinned and the air pushed her lips away from her teeth and into a wide manic smile. Then, suddenly, they were into the clouds; she could feel their wetness as if she were falling through a thick fog. And then, just as suddenly as they entered, they were out of the clouds and Tandy was struck by a strange feeling of euphoria as she saw the ground below her; a lightness of shadow amongst other deeper shadows. At first it seemed as though she were just hovering in the air, not falling, and then the illusion was shattered and the ground appeared to be coming up at her really fast which, of course, was another illusion, because she was dropping towards it.

Spreadeagled along Tandy's back, Frank brought in his right wrist and checked the altimeter that was strapped there. A bit bigger than a watch it gave him his height above the ground and it was rapidly changing as they plummeted earthward. He was watching for the right moment to pull the toggle on his rip-cord to deploy the parachute.

Tandy had felt Frank as he moved on her.

I hope he's alright.

And there below was the rock-hard and rock-strewn ground rushing up towards her.

I hope he's alright!

No sooner had the thought gone through her head than she was jerked upright as Frank pulled the toggle that released the rectangular black silk parachute from its pack with a loud fluttering noise, like the sound of a ship's sail catching the wind. With her feet going down and with the feeling that the ground was tugging at her legs Tandy glanced upwards and was relieved to find that the chute was open and she could see Frank's hands gripping the parachute chords to guide it on an approach. She could also see Tommo's rectangular 'chute up and to her left but she could not see the rest of the team.

Tandy looked down past her black trainers and was somewhat shocked to see the ground only a few feet away and coming up at her at an alarming rate and she gave a little squeal. At the last second she remembered to lift her feet as Frank expertly guided them in at an angle to the ground and then Frank's feet had hit the floor and he was taking a few hurried steps, staggering under the weight of Tandy and all the equipment that they carried.

He stopped.

Tandy put her feet onto the desert floor as the 'chute collapsed with a ruffling sound behind them.

They were down!

Tandy was amazed to find that she was standing upright and not sprawled in the dirt as she thought she would be.

They were in the dark with the clouds that they had dropped through obscuring the stars. But they were down.

"There," came Frank's deep soft voice as he took off his goggles and tossed them onto the floor. "That wasn't so bad, was it?"

He released her from the harness and she immediately turned to him so that he had to steer the long sniper rifle case out of the way.

After removing her own goggles and ignoring all the equipment and deadly weaponry that was strapped to the front of them Tandy flung her arms around Frank's neck and kissed him as hard as she could and then broke away, holding his hands.

"Bloody hell Frank! That was fantastic! It was almost as good as sex!"

Frank laughed. "Yes, and like sex, you can keep repeating it!"

They were still holding hands when the rest of the team came up to them out of the night; they had all shed their parachutes and had them bundled under their arms and they were all carrying their goggles in their hands.

Clonk stepped forward. He looked most concerned. "Well, lassie," he said. "How was it for you?"

Tandy grabbed him by the front of his jacket, hauled him in close and planted a fulsome kiss on his lips.

She pulled away. "Does that answer your question?" she asked.

"Ha ha…Aye, I'd say so lassie, I'd say so!"

"I hope there were no tongues," said Frank and they all burst out laughing. T Bone also stepped forwards, but he did not kiss her, electing instead to shake Tandy's hand and he was followed by Tommo who bent down and gave her a light peck on the cheek. "Good job, girl," he said.

Tandy had been initiated into their band of parachutists; she hadn't lost her nerve; she hadn't backed out. She'd made it.

Frank checked his watch.

3.12am.

He addressed the team. "Right guys, we've come here to do a job and the clock is ticking. So, let's camo-up and hide the chutes and the goggles. Let's get a move on; we've got some ground to cover." To Frank it felt like déjà vu; he had been in this situation before at virtually the same DZ when he had been dropped in to assassinate the Intiqam leaders, one of whom had been Aarif El-Sayed.

Frank produced a tin of black greasepaint, the kind of makeup used by actors. This was handed around and all of the team smeared their faces with the stuff. Even Tandy and Tommo added it to the surface of their dark Caribbean skin because it cut down any skin shine and broke up the outline of their faces.

When they had finished with the camo paint all of them had it smeared randomly about their faces, except T Bone, who had applied horizontal streaks of the black make-up to his face so that he looked like a movie version of an Apache brave in warpaint.

The team now pulled on their night-vision goggles. Gaps were now appearing in the cloud cover, which allowed starlight to get through, and this greatly improved the efficiency of the eye-wear. The breaking cloud cover also made it easier for Frank to be able to work out and confirm north with the aid of his compass and contour map that he was carrying.

Off to his left, and about half a mile away, was a long wall of rock that Frank had avoided crashing into when he had been dropped here previously. He knew that he had to follow the line of the rock face and continue onward and eastwards in a straight line.

Then, like the well-drilled team that they were, the team collected the 'chutes and protective goggles together and, after first making sure that nothing deadly was sleeping or hiding in ambush under them, placed them under some rocks along with Frank's wrist altimeter. Then they kicked some sand and loose stones from the desert floor over the rocks and re-united again, standing in a group. Frank looked at his team.

"Everyone set?"

They all gave him the affirmative.

Frank checked his watch.

3.25am.

"No talking now unless you absolutely have to," said Frank. "Let's go." And he set off at a fast jog with the team fanning out either side of him like a pack of wolves.

The four men had run with night-vision goggles on before on a number of covert operations – but Tandy hadn't, and she was running with the heavy Accuracy International rifle now slung across her back, so it took her a few stumbles in the dark before she got used to it. Fortunately, her innate sense of balance kept her on her feet. Before they had set off both Frank and Clonk had gallantly volunteered to carry the rifle for her, but she declined, not wanting to appear weak and feeble in front of the team. So far, she was being able to keep up with the rest of the team and it gave her a sense of immense pride, after all, these men were all ex-Special Forces.

As they ran on, the clouds had begun to melt away until they had almost disappeared, which meant that the team could see better with the blessing of the stars and the moon, and the goggles worked even more efficiently, although there was not enough light yet to allow them to remove the goggles completely.

*

The walled village of Qaryat Musawara was about five miles from the Drop Zone. Running in a group, at night and over rough terrain, it took the five of them an hour and twenty minutes to reach the edge of the plateau that overlooked the valley in which the village lay.

As they came up to the edge of the plateau the team went belly down and crawled towards it, eventually lying prone on the rough ground.

In front of them was the village of Qaryat Musawara laid out in a square, just as Frank had sketched it back at the hotel. The Shadows team lay in a line overlooking the cliff with Tommo on the far left, then T Bone with Clonk next to him. Beside Clonk was Frank, then Tandy. Frank checked his watch, then in a quiet voice, he said, "Heads up everybody. I make it four forty-five."

The rest of the group synchronised their watches to Frank then began scanning the area through their night-vision goggles. Except for Tommo, who, following a pre-arranged plan, took up a position twenty-five feet away from them where he lay down amongst some rocks and acted as a perimeter guard. As Tommo was doing this Frank had removed his goggles and was checking the village through the supplied high-powered monocular, starting with the village's encircling wall.

The wall that held the arched entrances was probably the reason why this place had been picked as an Intiqam headquarters – it was easily defendable, and the flat top of the high walls made for ideal observation posts.

The wall itself was about ten feet thick with those arched entrances built into it. There were two main entrances one to the west, to Frank's left, and the other to the east. A single road ran from the west through the valley and ran around the northern edge of the village before heading off to the east. There was another smaller entrance in the wall nearest to them to the south and a couple more in the wall furthest away in the north.

The village buildings were all inside the wall with the half-a-dozen goat pens being just outside around the perimeter. Also, there were dogs which roamed freely around the outside of the walls, and which made any stealthy approach difficult, as the dogs would start barking and then the goats would start bleating. They made a pretty good low-tech alarm system.

The buildings were nearly all single storey, although there were three that were three storeys high, being ground, first and second floors. However, all of the village buildings were of rough mud and brick walls covered in white plaster, most of which was falling off. The houses had flat roofs made of sticks, straw and corrugated sheets of rusted steel, all of which had been badly patched over the years. The messy coverings would be useless at keeping rain out, but, as rain hardly ever fell here, it did not really matter.

Off to the left, and just beyond the village, was an olive-green Bell UH-1 Iroquois helicopter that was sitting silently in the dark. The team did not know it, but this was the aircraft that had been used to transport Lady Corrigan, Lawrence Gainsborough and Gail Wetton from Mosul Airport to the village. Frank noted the absence of rocket launchers and machine guns, however the Huey still looked menacing.

As Frank looked at the chopper a rough escape plan formed in his head. He gently wagged his right index finger just above the surface of the ground towards the aircraft; movement was to be kept to the minimum. He whispered, "There's our lift out of here."

They all looked at the Huey and then resumed their inspection of the village below them.

After a while Clonk's low Scottish rumble vocalised what they were all thinking. "Quiet, isn't it?"

"Yes," whispered Frank. "But don't let that fool you. There may be guards out here patrolling. And, do you see the two guards lying down on the top of the nearest wall?"

"Actually," said T Bone, "there are two more guards; one at each of the main entrance arches."

In a lowered voice as he stared through the monocular Frank said, "Actually, there's another one in the shadows by the goat pen. That makes five in total."

"Six," corrected Tandy. "There's another just inside the nearest entrance arch."

Frank moved the monocular to check. "Oh, well done, Tandy," he said. "I missed that one."

"Should've gone to Specsavers," she quipped, quoting the famous TV ad for spectacles.

There was some light sniggering as T Bone and Clonk overheard the joke.

Frank shushed at them and then said softly, "Okay…T Bone?"

"Yes, Boss?"

"Have you ID'd the comms building?"

"Well," whispered T Bone, "I reckon that it might be the building over to the right that has all those aerials and satellite dishes sticking up out of the roof…It's just a guess mind."

Clonk sniggered again.

"Everyone's a bloody comedian," muttered Frank. But he was smiling beneath his own black smears. "T Bone. Have you got our sewing kit with you?"

"Yes, Boss." He patted the front of his jacket pocket.

"Damn," said Clonk. "And I've forgotten my knitting."

"Shut it," growled Frank, but he was still smiling as he rolled onto his right side and checked his watch again. Then he came up onto his knees and handed over his Smith and Wesson revolver and the two speed-loaders to Clonk. Clonk nodded his understanding at Frank. Back in the hotel Frank had explained that he would have to get rid of his weaponry before he entered the village for his meeting with al-Makira.

Frank whispered, "Give them back to me later, when the fun starts."

"Fair enough," answered Clonk, and he tucked the revolver and spare ammunition inside his jacket. Frank then doled out his grenades and his knife; T Bone and Clonk took one fragmentation grenade each, Tommo came back from guard duty and took Frank's stun grenade, and Tandy took Frank's knife and his Glock 19. Frank had kept his weapons on himself in case they had been needed on the run to the cliff top. But now, if Intiqam discovered a weapon on him, they might very well shoot him as he stood.

Tandy listened and watched what was going on and was not in the least bit happy.

Frank gave a whispered order, "T Bone, Clonk, go now and take up your positions, and remember…if you have to take someone out, try and do it quietly."

The two men both gave thumbs up signs.

Clonk was to get as near as possible to the west entrance arch and T Bone was to get to the east entrance – near to where the comms room was situated.

Frank said, "I'll wait here for an hour until five forty-five, and then I'll move off."

T Bone and Clonk would be moving under the cover of darkness but Frank was going to have to wait for an hour because Frank wanted to approach the village in the light. With a 4.00am strike now out of the question he had decided to go in as dawn was breaking so as to provide some light, so that he could be easily identified by the guards as he approached them; he did not want to be shot out of hand by some trigger-happy look-out, thereby ruining his rescue plan and forfeiting the lives of the hostages. Also, a lower light level would give his team cover, and it would also give them the ability to generate maximum confusion, coming out of the shadows and half-light when the fight started.

The next hour would be crucial because there could well be roaming bands of guards who might stumble upon them and raise the alarm, and then, again, the plan would be ruined. That was why Frank had asked for silence; if they met any Intiqam guards the knives would come out.

T Bone and Clonk gave each other and Frank another thumbs up and then they disappeared over the edge of the cliff. The only way off this cliff was by going over that edge. And the only way down to the valley floor was down the steep bank of shale and broken rock that lay in an acute slope along the face of the cliff. Frank gave a brief satisfied smile as he noted that he could not hear the two men moving.

As Tommo returned to his guard duty Tandy turned and, crouching, busied herself with laying the sniper rifle out on the ground, ready for use with the barrel supported by its integrated bi-pod that was up near the muzzle of the gun's barrel. Satisfied, she pulled some fine camouflage netting out of one of her pockets. This netting was a mixture of spun green and brown nylon so that it looked like Spanish Moss, the kind of straggly growth that hangs from the trees in the Deep South of America. She wrapped the netting carefully around the barrel and up as far as the telescopic sight; it effectively broke up the outline of the weapon from the front and would look like some low-growing plant-life through any binoculars or telescopic sight that might be aimed in her direction.

Tandy got belly-down onto the ground, wriggled to get as comfortable as she could, and brought her shoulder into the stock of the rifle, trying out the position for comfort whilst staring into the 'scope. She nodded in satisfaction and turned her head towards Frank.

Frank had noted Tandy's nod and he rolled back onto his stomach and continued to scan the village, very much aware that Tandy was staring at the back of his head. It was as if she were trying to communicate with him telepathically. He knew what it was that she wanted to say, but right now was not the time for it.

Tandy gave up staring at Frank's head and took another look through the rifle's 'scope.

Almost in the centre of the village, and directly in front of them, was one of the three storey houses. It was one of two houses in the village with a large satellite TV disc sitting on an unusually well-kept and solid wooden roof, the other roof being that of the communications building that T Bone had remarked on earlier. The house in front of them, Frank correctly surmised, was the Intiqam headquarters, and the place where agent Ketcher had been killed.

Frank, still lying belly down in the dirt, nudged Tandy with his elbow and then discretely pointed. "That's the window in question." He handed her the monocular. Leaning on her elbows, Tandy peered through the lens at an open window that was facing her and which was set in the side of the tall Intiqam HQ building.

She handed the monocular back and then sighted through the 'scope at the centre of the far window; this was to be her target. From her high vantage point on the cliff-top she would be shooting downwards, which would make her task easier. However, she would have to come up onto her elbows to raise her chest and shoulders up off the ground to allow for the bi-pod at the front of the rifle which lifted its barrel, but that was no problem for her. She took her time adjusting the rifle's telescopic sight and studying the window opening and then she rolled onto her side and looked at Frank. "Shouldn't be a problem."

"You're sure?" asked Frank. *Silly question.*

"Sure I'm sure." She sounded quite abrupt.

Frank gave a slight hesitation before saying, "Good." He then rolled into a squatting position and then scuttled off towards Tommo. He came up to the big man and hunkered down beside him. "Tommo, come with me."

They went back to the edge of the cliff and got back down on the ground. Frank carefully pointed with his left hand. "Tommo, how long do you think it will take you to get to that withered tree on the other side of the village?"

Tommo looked at it in the slowly gathering light. Sun-up would be in about twenty minutes time. The big man made a shrugging motion with his lips as he thought about that, then said, "About ten minutes, Boss. But what's all that other stuff with it?" There was a jumble of objects surrounding the tree that had lost all of their recognition in the bad light.

The big man took off his night-vision goggles as Frank handed across the monocular. Tommo held it up to his eyes.

Frank said, "I checked that area out earlier. Looks like stacks of old tyres and a number of oil drums. What do you make of it?"

"Yes," Tommo agreed. "I'd say that it's the town dump."

"It's also good cover."

"Yeah, and I'll be able to see the whole of the north side of the village from there, includin' that chopper." He swung the monocular to scan the helicopter.

Frank clapped his friend on the shoulder. "Good."

Tommo handed back the monocular.

"Okay," said Frank. "Set off now. Don't bother to signal. We'll all just assume that you are there in ten minutes time. When you get there keep an eye on the Huey. It's our taxi ride out of here. When the firefight starts head for the chopper and secure it."

"Okay boss. Got that."

"Good. Off you go."

Tommo gave a small nod. "What if I come across someone?" he asked.

"If it's a child or a woman knock them out. If it's a man…kill them. We have to assume that every man is a terrorist."

Tommo looked hard at Frank. "What if they're not?"

Tommo. Protecting the innocent.

Frank paused.

"Okay. Use your discretion, but don't leave them conscious. But if they're armed…Kill them."

Tommo nodded again, then he grunted and moved off, going over the cliff edge as T Bone and Clonk had done. Despite his size Tommo could move as silently as a leopard and neither Frank nor Tandy heard him go.

Frank waited for another fifteen minutes then he got up onto his knees. Still kneeling, he looked at Tandy. "Time to go love," he said.

"I don't like this, Frank." It's what she had wanted to say when she had been staring at the back of his head.

"I know you don't. But I'll be okay. Just keep focussed and play your part, and we'll all come out of this alive."

Tandy shook her head. "Al-Makira wants to kill you and you're going to walk in there completely unarmed. There's so much that can go wrong, and you're saying you'll be okay?"

Frank reached out to Tandy and touched her face. He'd had other women in his life before. He'd even dated a couple of top international models, but they had only ever been random affairs or rolls in a bed. None of them had ever come close to the feelings that he had for Tandy, the only woman that he had ever truly loved, which, he had to admit was odd, because when they first met she'd had a contract out on him and, as the international assassin known as The Scorpion, she had been trying to kill him. Frank smiled at her. "I will come back to you. I promise."

"Yes, but in how many pieces?" A tear formed along her lower right eyelid.

"Now, now, Tandy. No tears. Givvus a kiss."

Tandy lifted herself up off the rocky uneven floor and knelt in front of Frank. They held hands and kissed, his firm mouth on her trembling lips.
They broke apart and Frank smiled. "Make sure you don't miss."
"I won't."
He said, "I'm banking on it."
"I know."
Frank got up onto his feet, went into a crouching run and was gone.
Tandy wiped the tear away before lying prone again. She pulled the sniper rifle towards her, snuggled the stock into her right shoulder, and gave another preliminary sighting through the 'scope.
It was now only minutes before dawn and the pre-dawn light was beginning to filter over the edge of the earth away to Tandy's right. With the illumination came the colours of the valley with its surrounding cliffs and plateau. The floor of the valley began to transform from a dark purple to a deep pink with the many rocks scattered over its surface casting long purple shadows. As she watched, the pink blush swept up the sides of the cliff and then turned to a rust red. The rocks in the valley then began to change colour to the same red and within moments the ground around Tandy took on the same ruddy hue. Even the village was transformed: from being a threatening dark shape with the walls and towers like some Robber-Baron's mysterious medieval stronghold to almost those of a fairy-tale castle.
But Tandy knew that this was no fairy-tale. It was more like a horror story, and her Frank was going in to meet the monster.
5.48am.

Tommo had made it to the bottom of the cliff, angling away eastwards and away from the village. To get to the other side of the village he therefore had the furthest distance to travel. But as he had an exceptionally tall body with a muscular frame and very long legs he could run like a machine. Indeed, in his early military career when he had to run with the rest of the recruits he was always up at the front and always the first one home. But he never broke into a sprint; he didn't need to; he just stretched out those long powerful lower limbs and ate up the ground in his long stride pattern.
Going fast through the dawn light he sped away from the bottom of the cliff and skirted the village from about two-hundred yards away.
Suddenly a shadowy form rose up from the ground in front of him but with his back towards Tommo.

Tommo did not stop. He barrelled into the shape and knocked it down and only then did he stop running to look at the man on the floor.

Dressed in a dark grey djellaba the man lay spreadeagled on the sandy earth. He was unconscious because he had gone down hard and hit his forehead on the uneven floor of the desert. But he was coming around.

Tommo swiftly approached the man and dropped down beside him. A quick inspection showed that this man was armed, or at least he had been; his AK47 assault rifle lay on the floor a couple of feet away where he had dropped it when Tommo had barged into him. This man was clearly one of the terrorist guards.

Tommo reached down a huge hand and clamped it over the man's mouth and lower face. The man's eyes opened in fright and widened as Tommo put his other hand at the back of the man's skull. The guard tried to cry out, to raise the alarm, but it was the last thing that he attempted before Tommo twisted the man's head and broke his neck.

Tommo remained beside the body and looked around. Had the man been alone? Why had he been sitting out here on the floor? Tommo could see no-one else and he could hear nothing. However, Tommo could not remain there for very long; he only had the remainder of ten minutes to get into position. He stood up, easily lifted the body over his left shoulder, and began to run again.

Clonk had been heading towards the western side of the village. He jogged along, holding his rifle in his left hand and hardly making any noise in his soft-soled trainers. He was to take up a position near the western arched entrance in the village's wall, and there he would keep watch for Frank when he entered the village, and then move in to help in the extraction of the hostages.

The Scotsman stopped running as he got nearer to the wall and began to approach it with stealth. There had to be dogs. He took his night-vision goggles off and slung them along his left arm by his bicep.

Still no dogs.

Where are the fucking dogs?

There was a large goat-pen to his right made of a variety of short rickety wooden posts to which thin sticks of sun-bleached wood had been nailed horizontally. The pen was a square shape with only three of the sides made of the badly-built wooden fence. The fourth side was formed by the wall of the village which had a large corrugated iron shelter for the goats built up against the crumbling ancient brickwork. The pen sat between himself and the arch that he was zeroing in on.

There were a lot of goats, but no dogs.

Clonk stopped his approach, and that's when he heard the low growl.

He turned to his left just in time to see a long rangy black shape launch itself off the floor towards his head. It was all wild eyes and fangs. Clonk continued turning and brought his huge right fist around to meet the animal. He caught it with a fist like a small rock directly under its lower jaw and the dog changed direction in the air from the force of the blow. Clonk had not got his nick-name for nothing and the dog went rolling into the dust, completely unconscious. The goats gave some small muttered bleats, but that was all; they were used to reacting to a barking dog, and the dog had not had the chance to.

Scarcely acknowledging the beast as it lay in a heap, Clonk continued forwards.

Clonk could smell the livestock inside the pen, which made his nostrils flare, and as he came up to the pen a goat bleated out loud. Clonk immediately dropped onto his knees, crouching with his assault rifle up and his finger over the trigger. What had made the goat bleat? Had it been him, or someone else? Then he remembered Frank's request for silence and he quietly slung the rifle across his back and pulled his knife. It was a knife with a matt-black blade so that it would not reflect light. The goat bleated once more and Clonk crouched even lower, and then he heard a noise, a human sound, a human clearing its throat. It was only a few feet away and on the other side of the goat-pen. That was when he saw the glowing tip of a cigarette, the smell of which had been disguised by the stink of the goat-pen.

Clonk was no longer operating in the dark, with the world around him beginning to lighten up in a pre-dawn glow he knew that he might be seen at any second by the smoker of the cigarette. He slowly edged forward, coming around the badly built fence, until he could see the man who was sitting with his back against the wall. His AK47 lay on the ground beside him. The man was probably in his mid-forties. Thin; he was bearded with a scruffy salt-and-pepper beard and was dressed in a dirty grey djellaba with a piece of rag tied around his head.

Clonk waited.

The man put his cigarette to his lips and inhaled deeply and as he did so he closed his eyes in the enjoyment of the tobacco – that was his big mistake.

Clonk was on him in an instant. He drove the palm of his left hand up and under the guard's coarsely bearded chin so that his mouth clamped shut thereby stopping him from crying out, and his head went hard back against the wall. Clonk's knife slid into the man's throat. Blood poured out as the man began to wriggle, but Clonk was a powerfully built man and this skinny individual was no match for him. The man's legs began to kick so Clonk sat on them until, only moments later, the man went limp.

Clonk thought about rearranging the body to make it look as though he were asleep but decided that if someone found him it would only be seconds before they found out that he was dead, and then they would raise the alarm. Clonk wiped the blade of his knife clean on the man's clothing and then put it away. Then he reached down and lifted the man and lowered him into the goat-pen. One of the goats bleated again and then a couple more joined in. It gave Clonk an idea; he climbed over the fence, grabbed the body by the shoulders, and dragged it out into the middle of the goat pen. Goats almost instinctively like standing on anything higher than their surrounding terrain, so that the moment that Clonk released his grip on the man's shoulders the goats came over the body and climbed up on it, effectively screening it.

Clonk then went over to the goat shelter and stooped inside the entrance. The floor was covered in damp straw that smelled of goat pee. Clonk gathered up a large armful of it and went and spread it over the dead man's body amongst the standing goats before going back inside the shelter. He sat down in what was left of the damp straw, knowing that the little round brown balls that lay about him on the floor were not aniseed. Even so, despite the shit, the goat shelter was never-the-less the ideal hiding place. He hunkered down and waited.

T Bone had made it to the eastern side of Qaryat Musawara and was slowly closing in on the main eastern arch entrance. He was no longer wearing his night-vision goggles as his eyes had accustomed themselves to the lightening gloom. Like Clonk, his goggles were now around his left bicep. He had come bent double in a long loping run and he made it to the wall's entrance without discovery. Warily, he edged into the shadows of the arch with his knife in his right hand. From in front of him he heard a laugh and he froze, flattening against the dirty brickwork of the inside of the arch. Two men with automatic rifles slung over their shoulders sauntered past a few feet away.

T Bone waited.

One of the men laughed again. His companion was clearly relating an amusing story. They kept moving and T Bone listened carefully as they walked away.

T Bone crept forward. He came out of the protection of the cover of the arch and was standing beside the street that ran around the inside perimeter of the village. He checked both ways then darted across the road, getting into more shadows. He paused for a moment and checked the map that he had in his head, the map that Frank had drawn. He hoped it was accurate. Then he moved to his left and came across a small street, no more than an alley. It went in the direction that he wanted and he ducked into it and jogged forwards. The alley ran for about forty feet and then came to a crossroads with another alley.

Shit, thought T Bone. *This place is like a bloody rabbit warren!*

He would need to orientate himself to his target – the comms room.

His eyes fell on an old wooden ladder that was propped against the wall of one of the buildings on the corner of the crossroads. He moved over to it, tested it for strength and then, satisfied that it would just about hold his weight, he climbed up it as fast as he dared.

He was relieved to find that from the top he could see most of the roofs of the village – and he could see the roof of the comms room with its aerials and satellite dish. It was to one side of one of the alleys that formed the crossroads.

He heard another laugh.

Bugger it, it's those two jokers back again.

T Bone climbed off the ladder and onto the roof which was made of a patchwork of corrugated iron sheets. They creaked rustily beneath his weight.

In the room below the sheeting an elderly woman lay on a bed. She rolled onto her back and looked at the ceiling. "I'll bet it's those bloody goats again," she muttered. She would have a word with their owners in the morning. She rolled over and went back to sleep and began to snore.

Beneath his trainers the roof creaked some more.

This is all I need! I'll probably fall through this fucking roof at any second!

The two guards passed right below him and T Bone watched them as they wandered off as if they were on a Sunday morning stroll.

Fucking amateurs. But he was glad that they were and he managed to climb back off the roof and down the ladder without alerting them or having the ceiling cave in.

He moved off in the direction of the comms room. He found that it was also a corner building at the end of another small alleyway. T Bone stopped at the corner of the building that was diagonally opposite the comms room and edged his head forwards, ready to dart back if he thought he had been spotted. He was in luck; although there was a guard sitting outside the only door to the comms room, he was asleep. The guard was dressed in a voluminous light-brown djellaba and he was sitting on the floor with his back against the door. His knees were pulled up and his head was resting on his knees. His AK47 was leaning against the wall beside him with the wooden stock resting on the floor by his right elbow.

T Bone watched the man for a few seconds and when he did not move the Shadow member pulled back behind the building he was standing beside. He was forming a plan in his head, but first he needed some cover. He eased away from the corner of the building and came up to its front door. He had noticed earlier that the door was ajar…so was the building occupied or derelict? T Bone kept facing the corner of the building whilst he tentatively knocked lightly on the door with his left hand, hoping that it would not waken the guard around the corner. He reasoned that if someone answered the knock then he would simply apologise in Arabic and then quickly formulate a plan B – whatever the hell that would be.

No-one answered the knock.

He knocked again.

No answer.

He opened his left hand and gently pushed the door. It came open with only a slight creak. There was a step down into the room that held a dusty table and one broken stick-back chair. T Bone took a pace into the room and swept his Glock through the air.

Nothing but dust and a few dirty cobwebs.

No-one at home then.

T Bone pushed the door closed. He took the night-vision goggles off his arm and dropped them onto the floor – he would not be needing them again.

With his place of cover secured T Bone decided to try out one of Tandy's pins. Even though he'd heard the lecture from Tandy he still did not quite believe that they were as fast acting and deadly as she claimed. However, he thought he would give it a go. So, standing just inside the front door, he pulled the sewing kit out of his breast pocket and, feeling a little foolish, he opened it and carefully removed one of the cork-wrapped pins. He put the kit away and then opened the door. He carefully checked outside and then stepped out into the alleyway. He pulled the door almost shut and edged towards the corner of the building again. He stuck his head around the corner; the guard was still asleep. T Bone took a breath and stepped forwards. He managed to get right up to the sleeping guard when he opened his eyes and looked straight at T Bone. T Bone jabbed out with the pin and stuck it into the man's neck as he opened his mouth to shout.

The cry of alarm died in his throat. His mouth continued to fall open as his eyeballs rolled up into his head and then he appeared to feint away with his head lolling to one side and his body sliding sideways. It was such a strange reaction that it reminded T Bone of someone doing some corny acting, as if they were in a Carry On film.

T Bone put out a hand and joggled the man's right shoulder. He was as dead as a doornail.

T Bone looked at the pearlescent end of the pin that was sticking out of the man's neck and whispered, "Bloody hell."

T Bone pulled the body back into its sitting position. The man stank. And being dead did not help either as his bodily fluids began to drain out of him. But the dead man would seem to be fast asleep to all but the most scrutinising of observers.

T Bone glanced at the door of the comms room. He could easily shove the door open and toss two fragmentation grenades inside, and, as tempting as that was, yet he could not. The mad plan that Frank Cross had outlined earlier back in the hotel room relied on the members of Shadows following the plan to the letter. No noisy offensive action was to be taken against the terrorists until Tandy had taken her shot. That shot was to be the signal for the team to go instantly into action, and the only exception to that rule was - as silently as possible - the removal of the various guards that were patrolling.

With this in mind, T Bone moved away from the door. Now he had to move quickly; there was no cover around in which to hide, so he scuttled away from the dead guard and around the corner where he re-entered the deserted house and settled down for a very uncomfortable, and filthy, wait.

However, as uncomfortable as T Bone's present situation was, he would have been happier if he had only known that his team-mate was sitting in a pile of goat shit somewhere else in the village of Qaryat Musawara.

Tommo had made it to the dead tree and the tyre dump without further mishap. On reaching his objective Tommo tossed the body he was carrying further into the stacked collection of tyres. The dump was some three-hundred-and-fifty yards away from the walls of the village, a distance Tommo could easily cover quickly in his giant strides. His job was to wait until all hell broke loose - and all hell would break loose - and then he was to come a-running. The tree hardly gave any cover because Tommo was built like a tank and the tree was only a foot wide at the widest part of its dead bark-peeled trunk. However, all around it were the stacks of old worn black tyres; car tyres, truck tyres, bike tyres. Many worn down to the underlying steel mesh. The desert landscape was not kind to tyres.

Amongst the tyres were big rusty oil drums, the kind you cut in half to make a barbeque. Some were on their sides and some were standing up.

Tommo had learned from Frank that humans often could not spot humans if the human trying to hide took on a different shape. Tommo therefore sat down between two upright drums and hunched over. Now, from a distance, he was just a large dark shape amongst the discarded junk – A shadow? A torn tyre? A crushed oil drum maybe? But not a man. He had effectively disappeared.

**

Ali, the man who had aided in the abduction of Lady Corrigan, was brought into the room by al-Makira's SiC. Ali did not look too comfortable, as his eyes fell upon his commanding officer, who was sitting behind a rough wooden table with a cup of tea at his right elbow and a brown leather shoulder holster with a gun inside it by his left.

"This is Ali," said Irfan. He propelled Ali forwards by pushing into the middle of Ali's back.

"Ahh," breathed al-Makira. "Irfan tells me that it was you who was largely instrumental in getting Lady Corrigan out of England. Is that true?"

Ali nodded, trying to make it not look like a subservient gesture. "That is so, my commander."

Al-Makira picked up his tea cup, pressed it to his lips and drained it. He set the cup back down on the table which was stained with the rings of many past damp cups. "You did well, Ali. In fact, I understand that it was you who saved the abduction from being a complete fuck up."

Ali said nothing.

"I note your silence. Humility is a good quality to have and I appreciate humility as well as effort and loyalty," said al-Makira. "In fact, I need men like you; men who can make their own decisions as well as follow orders." He looked steadily at Ali's face. "Do you think that you are such a man?"

There was a pause, then Ali answered, "Yes, my commander."

Al-Makira stood up and came around the table to face Ali. He reached out and picked up the shoulder holster and removed the gun - a small dark-green snub-nosed Glock 26 semi-automatic pistol. He pointed it at Ali.

Ali swallowed. Was this to be his reward for getting Lady Corrigan safely out of England and into the clutches of this terrorist commander? Was he to be shot so that he would not be able to talk about what he knew?

Al-Makira smiled, then he turned the gun around and handed it to Ali. "Do you know how to use it?"

Ali took the weapon and looked at it. "I take it you flick the safety, point it and pull the trigger."

Al-Makira smiled at the brief succinct summary. "Yes," confirmed the terrorist commander. "It really is that simple. So, if you wanted to, you could shoot me right now…couldn't you?" Al-Makira smiled.

Ali smiled as well and he held out the gun for al-Makira to take back. "Why would I want to do such a thing, my brother?"

Al-Makira's smile widened and he looked over Ali's shoulder where Irfan was holding a Glock 19 pistol to Ali's head without him knowing. Irfan lowered his gun.

"Keep the gun, Ali." Al-Makira handed him the shoulder holster as well. "As I said, I need men like you. I need them around me. Would you like that, Ali?"

"I would be honoured, my commander." Ali checked the safety catch on the Glock then tucked the gun into the holster.

"Very good. Tell me, where did you live, before you joined us?" This sudden change of tack caught Ali by surprise, but the subtlety of the question did not go undetected; it meant that in an instant Ali's life had just changed. He was now a fully initiated member of Intiqam. He answered,

"In Manchester, my commander."

"You do not have a Manchester accent," observed al-Makira.

"No, Sir. I was born in Camden, in London."

"I know where Camden is," said al-Makira testily. He gathered himself and continued in a kindly voice, "How did you end up in Manchester?"

"My wife comes from Manchester. I moved there to be near her."

"Very commendable," said al-Makira. He waved a hand in a gracious manner. "Did you work in Manchester?"

Ali noted the past tense of the question. "Yes, Sir. I was a hospital porter."

Al-Makira noted the word *was*. "Well, no longer," said al-Makira and he turned away from Ali. With his back to Ali al-Makira asked, "Do you have any children?"

"Yes, Sir. Two. A boy and a girl."

"How old are they?"

"My son is twelve, and my daughter is nine."

Al-Makira asked the next question as he turned back to face Ali, "And your wife, is she pretty?" The Intiqam leader sounded oily and Ali suddenly did not like where this conversation was going.

"Yes, Sir, I think so."

"Yes, I'm sure you do." *We might be able to use the boy. The wife and daughter might come in useful too – especially if they are pretty.*

Al-Makira put his right hand onto Ali's left shoulder, almost as if he were conveying a blessing. "I have enjoyed our little chat, Ali. Go now and get something to eat and drink. Irfan will instruct you in your duties and then you will come back to me, where you will be around me…as a shadow, yes?"

"Very well, my commander."

Al-Makira removed his hand and flicked his fingers in a gesture of dismissal and Ali was led out of the room.

Habib pushed open the door to the room in which Lady Corrigan and Gail Wetton were being held captive. He pushed it shut behind him and the two women looked at him whilst someone outside locked the door.

Gail was sitting on the only chair in the room and Lady Corrigan was sitting cross-legged on the floor with her back against the drab wall opposite the door. There was a large hole in her leggings, about the size of a saucer, just to the right of her right knee.

Habib was dressed in a white cotton shirt that was open halfway down his chest, stone-washed Levi jeans with a brown leather hand-tooled belt around his middle and brown leather handmade shoes. He had a pair of Gucci sunglasses pushed into the black locks of his wavy hair and he would not have looked out of place on the deck of a millionaire's yacht.

Lady Corrigan looked up at him. "Who do you think you are? One of the Bee Gees?"

Habib did not know who or what the Bee Gees were, but he could hear the derision in Red's voice.

Rather than rising to the bait, he feigned disinterest and forced a charming smile, and said, "Hello ladies."

"Come to look at your pets?" asked Lady Corrigan.

Habib nodded his head slightly to one side. "Something like that. I wanted to know what a couple of western whores looked like."

"Not much unlike your eastern whores I should think," said Lady Corrigan. She was still sitting with her legs crossed and had spoken back to him as if she were having a polite conversation in an English tea room. "Are you married?"

The two sentences strung together by Lady Corrigan did not lose their meaning or insult on Habib. His eyes suddenly went flinty hard.

"Be very careful, Lady Corrigan. Remember, you are in my power, and I can do what I like with you and your blonde friend here."

"Your power?" questioned Lady Corrigan. "I thought al-Makira was running this rat hole."

Habib hesitated before he smiled. "And so he is," he agreed. "But I have certain…shall we say…privileges?"

"You mean that if you want to beat us up and rape us al-Makira will do nothing to stop you."

Gail whimpered.

Habib's eyes slid from Lady Corrigan to Gail and then back again. "I see you understand your situation, Lady Corrigan."

"Oh, I understand all right. But I'll tell you this…you come for me and you'll have a fight on your hands…and that's despite me being a western whore."

Habib did not answer. He simply gave her that charming smile again and turned to the door, but inside he was seething with rage. How dare she talk to him like that? It was all he could do to stop himself from walking over to her and kicking her in the face.

He knocked casually on the door which was unlocked and he stepped out of the room.

When the door closed Lady Corrigan looked at Gail who looked as though she were about to feint.

"What a piece if shit," said Red.

"Do you think you should have annoyed him like that?" Gail was chewing at her bottom lip in anguish.

"Damned right I should."

"But what if he comes back for you…and…what if…" The sentence trailed off.

"If he comes for me, Gail, I'll have his balls off him!"

**

Frank Cross made his way down the shale that covered the front of the cliff. He moved quickly, quietly and lightly so as not to disturb the loose surface and make a noise. On reaching the base of the cliff he headed out towards the strip of tarmac that served as a road in from the western approach to the village. He was coming in from this side because he wanted the rising sun to illuminate him; if he came in from the east, the sun would be behind him and he would present as a big threatening silhouette – a big threatening silhouette that some jumpy guard might take a shot at.

Frank had to control this situation if he were to get himself, his team, and the hostages out alive. And walking in like some kind of Rambo would not be the way to get things done.

He made it to the road and turned towards the village as the first rays of the day's sunlight broke over the end of valley. He was some three-hundred yards away from the walls and a giant shadow, that of the walled village, was cast towards him; a dark shape, like a huge stain on the ground around and in front of him, a shape that was slowly shrinking, retreating back towards the village as the sun gradually rose higher in the cloudless dawn sky. At any other time, watching the sun come up and the dawn break like this in this place might have been quite a beautiful sight. But not now, for this dawn carried the threat of violence and death with it.

Frank started walking towards the wall; not too fast, not too slow. A nice, even, confident pace. He started to go over his plan for rescuing the hostages: his team had made it quite clear to him that they thought the plan was insane, suicidal. It was based around al-Makira's ego, and his inflated opinion of himself. Frank wanted, needed, to get himself placed, as fast as possible, into the execution chair. And to do that he had to inflame al-Makira's temper to the point where the terrorist commander simply wanted to kill Frank rather than torture him. Once in the chair, Frank then had to get al-Makira near enough to the chair, and thereby the window, for Tandy to shoot him. But if he was hauled away for torture then the whole plan would go down the toilet…and the hostages would die.

Should he have come up with a better, more secure, less suicidal plan? Probably. However, it was too late now to change it. The maniac that was al-Makira wanted Frank Cross – and Frank was going to make sure that he got Frank Cross.

Frank was fifty yards out from the wall when a man came out from under the entrance arch and started walking towards him. The man was dressed in a creased and filthy red and white striped djellaba. He wore a strip of identical red and white cotton material wound around his head and he was carrying a Kalashnikov AK47 rifle, casually held across his hips and which he turned towards Frank as the distance between them decreased.

"Who are you?" demanded the man in Arabic when he was easily within hailing distance.

Frank stopped walking. He answered back in the same Arabic, "I am Frank Cross. I am here to speak with al-Makira."

Of course, the man had heard of Frank Cross; he and the rest of the guards had all been briefed by al-Makira, and the man knew what his commander wanted him for. He should have simply escorted Frank to the man they called The Cunning, but he wanted to make a name for himself, to show how he, and he alone, had captured this Frank Cross – a feared assassin. So, he walked forward and got within an arm's length before he suddenly brought up the butt of the rifle and shoved it at Frank's head.

The blow never landed. Frank jerked his head out of the way and then drove his right fist into the man's left ribcage. Frank could deliver a karate punch that would smash a one-inch-thick wooden board. The man gave a gasp as his ribs broke and he began to double over. Frank tore the AK47 out of the man's grip, reversed it, and slammed the butt into the man's head as he went down. The man hit the floor and lay there without moving. Frank held the rifle by the end of its barrel and swung it at the surface of the road.

He smashed the rifle and then tossed it away to one side, onto the desert floor.

He looked up.

Another man was walking towards him.

This one was in camouflaged fatigues and was wearing a green beret at an angle on his head.

Frank straightened up as he turned to face the new arrival. "I am Frank Cross, and I have come to speak with al-Makira." Again, in Arabic.

The man stopped some fifteen feet away and covered Frank with his own AK47. This one had witnessed what had happened to the first guard and was a lot more wary.

"I will take you. Put your hands behind your head and walk in front of me."

"What about your friend here?"

"He is a fool." No love lost there then.

Frank complied. He walked past the guard who had moved aside, stepping off the pitted surface of the tarmac for the rock and sand surface of the valley floor.

The guard followed at a safe distance with his rifle pointed at Frank's back. They were heading for the main western arch of the wall and, as they neared it, Frank noticed the goat pen on his right. Frank's eyes suddenly widened a little as he spotted what he thought was a body partially covered in straw and lying face down amongst the goats.

Clonk had been here, that was for sure.

Frank's escort did not appear to have noticed the body, but then the light was still not that strong and the goat pen was in shadow from the wall.

Frank, moving only his eyes, glanced around the goat pen and his eyes finally came to rest on the corrugated iron sheeting of the goat shelter and, in that instant, Frank knew where Clonk was hiding, and Frank also knew that Clonk would remain in cover until he was needed.

However, there was still the danger that the body might be discovered as the light was increasing with every second. So, to distract his escort from the goat pen Frank turned his head over his left shoulder to ask a question. This would mean that the guard would instinctively look at Frank's face, and would therefore look to his left, and away from the goat pen.

Frank, in the local tongue, asked, "Where are they keeping the hostages?"

Of course he knew that the man would not tell him, but the man fell for

Frank's ruse and looked at Frank's face as he answered, "That is not for you to know, unless al-Makira commands it."

"Are you taking me straight to al-Makira?"

"Yes of course. Now be silent!"

With those last three words they had left the main road, passed the goat pen, and were now moving under the archway.

They emerged the other side of the arch where three other guards hurried forwards. They were also dressed in camouflage and they were also armed with AK47's, but they made no move to harass Frank. They simply surrounded him at a safe distance. Frank gave a thin smile. Their actions obviously showed that they had heard of Frank's reputation of being a most successful and deadly assassin, and, even though he appeared to be unarmed, they were not taking any chances.

The five-man group, with Frank in the middle, headed further into the village. And, as they walked, they attracted more and more guards to them, like bees around a honey pot.

Bloody amateurs, thought Frank. *They should be staying at their posts, not mobbing me like I'm some sort of rock star.* But it showed Frank how disorganised and undisciplined these troops were.

As they walked, some of the guards began chanting *Al-Makira! Al-Makira!* and waving their guns in the air, and pretty soon they were all chanting it. However, Frank also noticed that a large number of the doors, and the shutters on windows of the houses on the streets they traversed, remained closed. A great many of Qaryat Musawara's residents obviously lived in fear of the occupying force, and Frank wondered what atrocities these guards had carried out on the local population.

The group finally arrived in front of the door of the tall house that Frank had identified as the Intiqam headquarters and it opened without anyone having to knock, showing that news of his capture had obviously spread rapidly.

The chanting mob fell silent and moved away as Frank's captor shoved him in the back, and towards the open door. The door led directly into a downstairs room. Ducking under the doorframe Frank found himself looking at a small group of men in camouflage battledress; one of whom stood out - Irfan.

With a sneer, Irfan said, "So, you are the great Frank Cross." He spat on the floor.

"Yes," answered Frank. He lifted his chin. "And who are you?"

Quick as a flash the man slapped Frank around the face. "We ask the questions here, not you."

Frank would have liked to have grabbed the man by his throat and punched his face in, but he did not. Part of his SAS training had been about capture and interrogation – his own capture and interrogation. And the underlying principle was not to give the enemy any excuse to beat, maim or kill you. So, Frank stood and looked through passive eyes at his attacker, not giving him a reason to inflict further violence.

Irfan, however, was annoyed at Frank's lack of response; he wanted an excuse to beat the hell out of Frank, and so he lifted his hand to strike Frank's face again.

"Irfan!" The SiC's name was barked out and the open palm halted in mid strike. A bigger man, also dressed in combat fatigues, ducked into the room from a far door. "Leave him alone, my brother."

The palm was reluctantly dropped with its owner glaring at Frank.

"So," said al-Makira. "You are Frank Cross."

"And you must be the one known as al-Makira."

Al-Makira nodded graciously. Then he asked, "Where is your back-up team?"

"Back-up team?" replied Frank, raising an eyebrow.

"Yes, you're back-up team…Other special services, black ops people."

"Oh," said Frank, dismissively. "I came alone. That's what you wanted, wasn't it?"

"I do not believe you," snarled al-Makira. "Where are they? Tell me!"

Frank gave a small smile and shook his head.

Irfan slapped Frank across the face again.

Frank looked at Irfan then said to al-Makira, "Your boys don't go in for much imagination in their questioning techniques, do they? Do they just try to beat a response out of everyone they question?"

Irfan lifted his hand, but al-Makira stilled him with his own raised hand. The commander then turned and singled out one of the men who stood nearby,

"You, go and put the troops on alert!"

"At once, al-Makira!" said the man, and he scurried off to carry out his orders.

That's going to take some time thought Frank. *This lot's so bloody*

disorganised. But that, he knew, was to his advantage.

Al-Makira looked back at Frank and then said, "I note that no-one has seen fit to tie your hands."

Frank shrugged.

"I suppose that also means that no-one has searched you?"

Frank gave another slight smile, but did not answer.

"Who brought him in?" asked al- Makira. There was an edge to his voice.

"I did." Frank's escort pushed to Frank's right-hand side. The man nodded obsequiously towards his commander – delighted that he was to be recognised as the man who had captured Frank Cross.

"And did you not think to search him or tie his hands?" Al-Makira put his own hands behind his back.

The man looked at Frank's hands, then at al-Makira, then back to Frank's hands and then around the room, then back at al-Makira whose hands had re-appeared holding a black Ruger GP100 .38 Special revolver. He levelled the stubby barrel of the gun at the man whose eyes widened in terror.

The noise of the gun blast was very loud in the room.

The man screamed and grabbed his stomach where the bullet had hit him. He collapsed onto his knees where he clutched at his stomach, gasping and groaning in agony, with his head dropping nearer the floor, almost as if he were praying. Al-Makira, looked down at the hapless victim, and then, quite dispassionately, shot him in the head and watched the body topple forwards.

"Now," said al-Makira in barely disguised fury. "Perhaps one of you idiots would like to tie our guest's wrists!"

There was instant pandemonium as at least four men leapt to carry out al-Makira's orders lest they be the next one to get a bullet.

Some gaffer tape was found and wrapped around Frank's wrists while he just stood and looked at them all with a disinterested and dispassionate look on his face.

When Frank had been secured to al-Makira's satisfaction the commander turned to Irfan.

"Irfan," said al-Makira. "Please search our Mister Cross."

Frank received a very professional pat-down, and then the SiC said, almost reluctantly, "He is not carrying any weapon." If he had found one it would have given Irfan the excuse to hit Frank again.

"Good. Now, Mister Cross, please come with me." Al-Makira looked around him at his soldiers, pointed at the body that was still lying on the floor, and growled, "And get this piece of worthless shit out of here!"

Al-Makira turned and stomped out of the room followed by Frank and then Irfan who pointed a pistol at Frank's back. Al-Makira crossed to another door and was about to push it open when Frank said,

"Aren't we going to go to your execution room? You know...the one where you murder your victims? Or are you just going to beat me up first?"

Al-Makira turned and looked at Frank and then his dark eyes flickered over to Irfan. Those eyes came back to rest on Frank.

"I won't scream you know," said Frank, almost conversationally. "And you won't get me to tell you anything."

Again, those dark eyes flickered. "Perhaps," said al-Makira with a slight but cruel smile, "I should show you our film studio." He moved away from the door and began to climb a steep set of wooden stairs. Grinning, Irfan prodded Frank in the back with his pistol again and they followed al-Makira to the top floor of the building.

They came to a small landing with three doors leading off it and al-Makira opened one of the doors. He stepped into what he had referred to as his film studio – the place where he executed his victims on video. A man in camouflage fatigues was adjusting the tilt and angle of a large Canon camera set on a tall tripod stand; it was aimed at a vacant chair in front of an open window. Frank recognised the view out of the window, it was the same one that Sir Michael had sent through to Frank's mobile phone.

Frank's plan was working...so far. He had hoped that he would not be shot dead the moment al-Makira set eyes on him, and that had not happened. But Frank suspected that al-Makira wanted to make Frank suffer before he died, before he crushed him like a cockroach. However, Frank knew that what he had to get al-Makira to do was get Frank into the execution chair, and he therefore had to think up some ruse, or insult, that would get him seated in it instead of being dragged away and tortured.

Frank glanced at the gun that al-Makira was still holding and then at the chair in front of the open window.

Al-Makira saw where Frank was looking and smiled. How amusing it would be to have Frank Cross sit there, to threaten him with torture and degradation and death before causing him terrible pain. Perhaps he should have Cross skinned alive before placing him back in the chair and killing him in front of the camera? Yes. Yes. Yes.

Al-Makira waved a hand at the execution chair. "Please sit down, Mister

Cross."

Frank's body checked just for a second, and he almost laughed out loud. But he controlled that check and his face betrayed nothing as he turned towards the chair, and, just for a split-second, his eyes moved to the cliff in the distance. That cliff looked to be a long way away. It was where Tandy lay in the red dirt with a sniper rifle. So far away. So very far away. In fact, from this distance, the shot at the target did not seem possible to achieve. Had he really made a very big mistake?

Frank sat down.

From her place on the edge of the cliff Tandy caught the flicker of movement in the room through her telescopic rifle sight. She snuggled the stock of her rifle more firmly into her right shoulder.

Al-Makira turned to a man standing just inside the door. "Ali, bring me the MP."

Ali, who was now wearing the gifted gun from al-Makira in a holster over his left shoulder, saluted. Al-Makira smiled as Ali dropped the salute and hurried away.

The door to Lawrence Gainsborough's room was pushed open and Ali walked in. "Get up, and come with me."

"Please," pleaded Gainsborough, not getting up off the floor where he was sitting with his legs tucked underneath him. "Don't kill me. Please…"

"Shut up, and get up." Ali pulled out his newly acquired Glock pistol. "I said, get up…or I will shoot you where you are." It was only a threat because Ali dare not shoot a hostage without al-Makira's permission. Not unless he wanted to be summarily executed himself.

The Right Honourable Lawrence Gainsborough struggled to his feet. He looked a mess. His hair was unkempt and matted, his eyes were sunken, his clothes were torn and dirty, his feet were bare where some of the guards had stolen his shoes and socks, and his face, hands and arms could be best described as filthy.

Ali jerked the gun towards the door. "Come with me."

"Where…where are we going?"

"Shut up."

Gainsborough was pushed out of the door. He was then led across one of the small village streets, down an alley and in through another door at the back of a building. He was then shoved up some flights of wooden stairs and into a room that had a couple of chairs and a camera and some lights set on tripod stands.

There were four other men in the room; three terrorists standing and dressed in camouflage-pattern clothing and a big guy in a black and grey tactical uniform who was sitting in a tubular steel chair with his back to an open window.

One of the terrorists was watching Gainsborough through hawk-like eyes; the second one was holding a gun in one hand and a scimitar, a long curved shining steel sword, in the other. The man with the sword was pointing the gun at the man in the chair; the third terrorist was busying around the camera that was aimed at the man in the chair. The man in the chair, despite the surroundings, seemed quite relaxed. He was sitting back with his legs out in front of him and crossed at the ankles, and he was holding his hands loosely in his lap, even though his wrists were securely bound together by the grey tape that was wrapped around them.

Frank smiled at Gainsborough.

Tandy had stared though the scope as she watched Frank back up to a chair to sit down with his broad back and shoulders towards the window.

She had just snuggled the butt of the rifle further into her right shoulder, getting ready to take the vital shot, when she heard a noise behind her. *What was that? Jeez, no distractions now! Please! Not now!*

A guard had found her and he was standing about twelve inches away from the soles of her black trainers. He was wearing dark camouflage battledress and desert boots and had a black and white checked shemagh wound around his head of wild black hair and bearded face - a desert-tanned face with a large hooked nose. He was carrying an AK47 - and he looked like trouble.

The man with the hawk-like eyes was al-Makira. "Good," he said as Lawrence staggered into the room. "Welcome, Mister Gainsborough. I am al-Makira." The welcome was delivered with the same courtesy he might have extended to someone attending a dinner party in a millionaire's villa. The only things that spoiled the image were the surrounding room with its bare floorboards and plaster-peeling walls and Lawrence Gainsborough hanging in filthy rags. "Please, stand over there."

Al-Makira indicated the far wall with a gentle sweep of his hand and Lawrence moved that way.

"Ali, my brother," al-Makira turned to the man. "Go and tell Habib to bring the ladies here…Oh, and tell him to have them hooded."

Ali nodded and left the room.

The guard was staring down at Tandy, pointing the barrel of the gun at her back. He had been put on alert and he should have radioed his discovery in to his central control in the village below – but he didn't. Instead, he said in Arabic, "Leave the gun alone and get up."

Oh, shit! thought Tandy. *This is all I fucking need.*

The guard kicked at Tandy's heels. "Get up!" *When he rolls over, I will shoot him,* thought the guard. *But I want to see the fear in his eyes before he dies.* He grinned.

Because Tandy's hairstyle was a black spikey mop, and because she was staring down the barrel of a sniper rifle, and also because her black tactical uniform was baggy, the guard had no idea that it was a woman that was lying on the ground in front of him.

A few moments later Ali came back into the room. He nodded, almost a half-bow to his commander. "Habib is on his way."

"Excellent, Ali. Now please stand to the left of the chair." Al-Makira waved a hand, indicating where he wanted Ali to position himself.

Ali did as he was bid, standing to the left of the execution chair, which put him beside Frank's left arm, with both his and Frank's back to the open window.

"You." Al-Makira pointed a finger at the cameraman. "You. Tie his arms to the chair!"

The man looked at Frank's hands and then at his commander. "But, al-Makira. They are already bound together."

Al-Makira almost exploded with rage. "Well, fucking-well untie them! Must I do everything myself? Untie his hands, then re-tie them to the arms of the chair, you moron!"

The hapless cameraman cast about him, desperately trying to see something with which to tie Frank's forearms. His eyes settled on his own dirty trainers. Hurriedly, he bent down and began to wrestle the grubby laces out of his trainers whilst al-Makira huffed and puffed, shuffled his feet

noisily on the floorboards and glowered at him.
"Come on! Come on!"
"Yes, yes, al-Makira."

Tandy heard the guard but she had no idea what he had just said. She could, however, read the menace in his voice. She was still sighting through the rifle's scope. There was a flicker of movement beyond Frank, further inside the room.

Eventually, having preformed a strange kind of hopping dance as he removed the two sets of laces, the cameraman moved towards Frank's arms. He leaned forwards with his face only about a foot away from Frank's.
"BOO!" said Frank, and the cameraman jumped back.
If it had not been for the fact that al-Makira wanted Frank's arms tied to the chair he would have shot the cameraman there and then. "Stop clowning about you fool!" yelled al-Makira.
"Yes,yes!" said the man. "But…I…I have nothing to remove his tape."
Ali, standing beside Frank's left arm, felt into his own trousers for his clasp knife. However, Irfan beat him to it. The SiC stepped forwards and from out of a pocket in his fatigue trousers he produced a flick-knife. He touched a button on the side of the knife and the blade sprang open and, without a word, he handed it to the cameraman who took it and then knelt down in front of Frank and clumsily slashed through the gaffer-tape around Frank's wrists. He nicked Frank's skin and a spot of blood showed.
"Careful," said Frank. "We don't want any bloodshed, do we? Not yet anyway."
The cameraman looked up at Irfan who snarled, "Get on with it!"
The cameraman turned back to Frank and looked into his face as he fumbled quickly at the knots and tied Frank's wrists to the arms of the chair. With the task finished the cameraman stood and went to give the knife back, blade first.
"The other way, idiot!" snapped Irfan.
The man reversed the knife and handed it over. Irfan closed the blade and dropped the knife back in his pocket.
"Good," said al-Makira, barely reining in his temper. He shoved his gun into the waistband at the back of his trousers. He glowered at the cameraman and then jerked a thumb towards the camera and lights. "Now, get back

behind the fucking camera and let's get on with this."
"Is it show time?" asked Frank. He smiled.

The guard kicked Tandy's heels again. "Get up!"
Shit! This isn't going to work! I can't take the shot! Frank's going to die!

Habib entered the room that the two ladies were in; he had two black hessian sacks tucked into the front of his trousers belt and was carrying two lengths of plastic ties in his left hand and a Sig Sauer semi-automatic pistol in his right.
"You." He waved the pistol at Lady Corrigan. "Get up and come here." It was not the kind of request you would refuse.
Red got up and walked resolutely over to Habib.
"Turn around."
Red did as she was ordered.
"Put your hands behind your back."
Again, she complied and just before Habib secured her wrists with one of the plastic ties he stole a look at the curve of her bottom. Lady Corrigan had a very nice bottom; indeed, she was very proud of her bottom. She had spent a lot of time and effort in the gym getting her bottom into a nice shape.
"Seen enough?" asked Lady Corrigan.
Habib actually coloured slightly at being discovered. As a response he removed one of the sacks from his belt and pulled it aggressively over Lady Corrigan's mass of red hair, but she never made a sound.
"Stay there." ordered Habib.
"Well," came Lady Corrigan's muted voice from inside the black hood, "I can hardly run away wearing this, now can I?"
Habib ground his teeth. He would have loved to be able to beat the hell out of this stuck-up imperious woman. But he kept quiet and walked over to Gail.
"Come here."
Gail got up from her chair and approached Habib.
Lady Corrigan heard him say, "Turn around."
"What are you going to do to us?" whimpered Gail.
"You'll find out soon enough," answered Habib and he pulled his other sack over her head. Then he holstered his Sig Saur and seized Lady Corrigan and Gail Wetton by their upper arms and hustled the two women over to the

door and knocked on it. The door was opened and the two women were pushed outside.

With their hands behind their backs, they were hustled some more out onto a street, and then, after a few moments, they were led into another building where they were pushed up some wooden stairs. At one point on the stairs Gail fell onto her knees with a cry and she was hauled back onto her feet by Habib.

Struggling to keep her resolve, Tandy breathed out heavily and lowered her head and eyes away from the scope. She rolled slowly onto her back and stared up at the man.

The guard's eyes widened in surprise as he found he was looking at a beautiful tanned face whose cheek bones were streaked with black camo cream above full lips, and he began to smile a wolfish smile.

I can have some fun with this one he thought.

Inside the room, where the filming of Frank's execution was to take place, they heard a knock on the door and then Red and Gail Wetton were shoved, still wearing their hoods, into the room. Habib nodded towards al-Makira and then left, closing the door behind him.

Gainsborough recognised Gail's dress. "Gail!" he called out. "Are you all right?"

Still with the hood over her head, Gail turned to the sound of Gainsborough's voice, her movements jerky, like that of a blind person unused to their surroundings. "Oh Larry, is that you? I'm okay, are you?"

"Yes, but…"

"Shut up!" snapped Irfan and Gail and Lawrence both shrank away from the barked order.

Al-Makira stepped forwards and pushed the two women against the wall that was opposite the window. Then he grabbed Gainsborough by the front of his filthy shirt and pushed him against the same wall and to Lady Corrigan's right-hand side so that she was now in between Lawrence and Gail. Al-Makira took a couple of steps back, and for one moment Frank was seized with a dread; was al-Makira about to shoot them in front of him? However, with one swift motion, instead of shooting them he reached out both hands and tore the hoods from off the women's heads, which left them both blinking.

Al-Makira ran his dark eyes over them. "Stand there and keep silent, or I will have Irfan shoot you."

The guard really should have radioed in his discovery. But he hadn't – and that was his big mistake.

Suddenly Tandy moved. Her left foot swept up and caught the guard in the side of his right knee joint with enough impact to make his leg give way and with enough force to knock him sideways and to his left. He put out his hands to break his fall – and dropped the rifle.

Tandy was instantly on her feet, moving in on the guard with the intent of either knocking him out or killing him, depending on how he reacted.

Both ladies stood with their backs to the wall and their hands behind them; Lady Corrigan was tall and upright whilst Gail was standing meekly with her head down and her shoulders sagging.

Red looked around the room and her gaze fell on Cross.

"Hello, Lady Corrigan," said Frank as cheerfully as possible.

The guard did not react quite as she had expected. Frank had taught her to expect the unexpected and she'd missed it completely, because the guard went down onto his left shoulder, rolled, and came up onto his booted feet. He cast a glance at the rifle, realised that he would not be able to reach it before Tandy and he therefore pulled a long double-bladed knife from a sheath at his side. He dropped into a fighting stance.

Shit! thought Tandy. She was well aware that Frank was now sitting in the execution chair, and that if she did not get back to her sniper rifle in time it would be the end for Frank. She brought her hands up into her own fighting stance.

The guard grinned. He knew he could easily beat this bitch.

Lady Corrigan looked across to Frank and politely asked, "Who are you?"

"I'm Frank Cross," he answered her. "I'm here to rescue you."

Frank had seen Lady Corrigan only once before. It had been after he and Tandy had rid the world of two traitors, one of which had been al-Makira's brother. Cross had needed to get to Sir Michael Corrigan and inform him of the assassinations, and to do that he had entered Sir Michael's house via the back door and the kitchen, a kitchen where Lady Corrigan had been preparing omelettes as a supper for herself and her husband. Red had not seen Frank Cross as he had passed behind her, but he had seen her.

"As you can see," put in al-Makira, smirking. "He has failed."

Frank looked at al-Makira. "I'm not dead yet."

"Don't tempt me," hissed Irfan, who stepped nearer to Frank so that he was standing beside Frank's chair and by his right shoulder.

Frank ignored Irfan and spoke directly to al-Makira. "Can't you keep your little pets under control?" he asked.

Irfan leaned forwards and growled, "Keep pushing, and I'll take your head off." He lifted the scimitar and waved the razor-sharp blade across Frank's throat.

The guard was standing with his feet apart, his body crouched forward and his head up. Balanced. He had obviously done this before, so he was obviously a knife fighter.

He rapidly closed in on Tandy and flicked the tip of the knife towards her stomach. Schooled by Frank, he had taught her to always look at the knife if such a weapon was being used against her. She could hear Frank's words in her head; *It's no good looking at his baby-blue eyes if he has a knife in his hand – his eyes won't hurt you, but the knife will - so watch the knife, and don't take your eyes off it.*

Ignoring the first flick as just a feint Tandy stepped to her left. This meant that if he struck again it would be with an awkward outward jab. Unless of course he turned to his right.

He turned to his right.

With the scimitar hovering half-an-inch from his throat Frank kept his head perfectly still, but he moved his eyes from al-Makira and looked levelly at his tormentor.

"Irfan!" barked al-Makira. "He's mine!"

The SiC reluctantly stood back and lowered the wicked blade.

The guard thrust his knife at Tandy again, but this time with more force; a deliberate stab. Tandy twisted her torso in tai-sabaki, body shifting, so that the knife passed harmlessly in front of her stomach. She stepped away from the attack and lifted both hands up in front of her face.

The guard's eyes followed them and he extended his right arm, holding the knife out towards her. He did not know it but he had just fallen for a distraction technique – his attention had gone to her raised hands. That small distraction was all that Tandy needed; she thrust her right hip towards him and brought up a lightning-fast yoko geri keage, a sideways snapping kick, driving it up so that the top of her foot smacked into the man's outstretched arm at the bottom of his humerus bone by his right elbow. The impact of the kick crushed his ulner nerve so that a lance of pain went up his arm and he cried out. This pain was immediately followed by numbness in his little finger and ring finger so that he let go of the knife which spun from his hand.

Tandy's kicking foot landed on the floor, but she had to duck and spin away from him as he turned and swung a left hook at her face.

Al-Makira stared at Irfan. "You don't touch him." It was almost a snarl. "You understand? I've got him at last!"

"If you've got me," asked Frank, "why do you need these three?" He meant Lady Corrigan, Gainsborough and Wetton.

Al-Makira's lips curled. "For insurance…And for fun," he said.

Jerking away from the hooked punch, Tandy then stepped quickly to her right and kicked him hard with a front mae geri kick, driving it into his lower abdomen. The force of the kick buckled him in the middle and sent him backwards so that he fell onto his backside – right beside his fallen rifle. He grabbed it and got the fingers of his left hand around it as Tandy jumped forwards and landed her right foot onto the gun, stamping down hard, ramming the weapon down onto the rocky ground.

There was a cracking sound as two of his fingers that were around the weapon broke. He cried out again and, on instinctive reaction, swung his right arm at her and caught her behind her legs. Tandy went down to his left, falling onto her front. The guard scrabbled up onto his feet with his left hand clenched in a painful fist. He had somehow managed to pick the rifle up with his busted hand and had transferred it to his right – and, even though his hand was still numb, he was bringing the rifle to bear on her.

"For fun?" repeated Frank. "Man, you must be really sick." He did not want to say out loud what he knew must be true – that after this maniac had killed him he would turn his attention to the man and the two women…and god knows what sort of film he would make of the women before he slaughtered them.

"You know," continued Frank. "I think you are quite mad. I think that you want me so much that your mind has gone."

Irfan cast a glance at his commander, a commander that had stopped at nothing just to get this man here.

"Yeah," continued Frank. "You're mad sure enough...Al-Makira, the Cunning..." Frank laughed. "More like al-Ahmaq, the Arse Hole."

Al-Makira clamped his teeth together in rage. He drew in a deep breath and lifted both of his hands like claws. Then he took a small faltering step towards Frank. Frank was hoping that Tandy was, right now, staring down the 'scope of her sniper rifle.

In fact, he was banking on it.

Tandy had rolled onto her back as the guard moved towards her with anger and hate now pushing him on. He was nearly upon her, with his right index finger feathering the trigger, when Tandy moved.

She threw herself to her left and kicked out with her right foot. His balls seemed to explode in pain as Tandy's foot lashed up and smashed into his manhood. He let out a strange strangled cry and his face screwed up in agony as Tandy quickly rolled over to avoid the bullet that must surely come. It didn't. Instead, the barrel of the AK47 swung down to point at the floor as the guard reached for his crotch with his broken left hand. He staggered away from her and to her left with his agonised face looking up to the sky.

Tandy sprang to her feet, readying herself to finish him off, but he turned, sweeping the rifle around, bringing the rifle to bear on her again. He was only about eight feet away from Tandy, and if he fired the weapon two things would happen: first, the terrorists would be alerted, and second, the bullets would cut Tandy in half. And if Tandy died then Frank would die. And if Frank died then the hostages would die.

In desperation, Tandy took two long fast steps forward. With the speed of a striking snake she went into the technique taught to her by Sensei Nakamura – the Dragon's Tail Whip.

Her right foot swept through the air and her instep struck the left side of the barrel of the gun knocking it out of the guard's right hand so that it spun away to land on the ground as her whip-kick continued; her right foot landed on the desert floor and instantly she was spinning on that same foot and with her left foot leaving the floor as her body delivered a full fast 360-degree turn. The now kicking left foot whirled up and around through the air at head height so that her left heel smashed into the left-hand side of the guard's head.

There was a crack as his skull was fractured and his neck jerked over at an impossible angle. The force of the impact pitched the man over to his right where he landed heavily like so much discarded baggage on the rocky and stony ground.

Tandy kicked the man hard in the ribs and, getting no response, she crossed quickly to the guard's rifle, picked it up and threw it some yards away. Then she scrabbled back to her prone shooting position. *Jesus, I hope Frank's still alive!*

Al-Makira was trembling with a barely controlled murderous rage at Frank's insults. "You western scum! You dare to insult me! You will pay for that!" He took another pace towards Frank, but he was still about four feet away.

Come on, thought Frank. *Come nearer. Much nearer.*

Tandy was struggling; the fight with the guard had made her breathe heavily and had increased her heart beat; even the thud of her heart would transfer into the rifle and put the aim and shot off. Looking through the rifle's scope she could see Frank's head and shoulders through the scope's cross-hairs, and she could see movement just beyond him in the room, but she could not hold the rifle steady and the image kept wobbling. A long range shot like the one she was about to take could be thrown off target by the smallest of her body movements. As she hugged the butt of the rifle into her right shoulder even her pulse could translate to a minute variation; one half of a degree off-centre would translate into a bigger deviation when the bullet landed after crossing the distance involved.

But was Frank alive, or had they killed him while she was fighting the guard? Was that his dead body sitting in the chair? Tandy looked away from the 'scope, blinked heavily once, and then looked back again.

As she refocussed her eye through the tube of the 'scope Frank turned his head to his right to look at someone beside him. Tandy saw the movement. *Frank's alive!*

Tandy was almost ecstatic with relief, but that only made things worse in her body because it made her tremble, and that made Frank's image keep jarring slightly through the crosshairs of the 'scope.

Damn! How the hell am I supposed to hit the fucking target while I am waving this all over the place? Damn!

In fact she wasn't waving the rifle all over the place at all; she was just expert enough to know that her smallest of movements would ruin the shot, and might get Frank killed if the bullet hit him rather than the real target – al-Makira.

Now Tandy had to get her breathing back to normal as she would have to have her body under complete control when she squeezed the trigger.

The Accuracy International L96A1 sniper rifle fires a 7.62 x 51mm bullet with a muzzle velocity of 2,790 feet-per-second. With a range of 3,608 feet (or 1,100 meters) it meant that a bullet leaving the rifle would arrive at its target at the full extent of the range in just over one second. As Tandy's target was much nearer than that it would mean that the bullet would strike in less time than it took to blink twice.

Tandy pursed her lips and frowned.

And then the realisation struck her. How many times had Frank instructed her in controlling her breathing when they had first got together and he had begun to teach her his martial art of karate? It must have been easily a dozen. And surely Sensei Nakamura's zen teaching was for just such a moment as this?

Zen.

Open mindedness.

Calmness.

Be in the moment.

Concentrate. Be calm. Think only of the now, not what might happen in the future.

With the stock of the rifle nestled against her right cheek Tandy actually smiled. "*Rook at rock,*" she heard the Sensei's voice in her head. *Look at the rock.*

Still lying prone, Tandy closed her eyes and took a deep breath, held it, and then exhaled slowly, allowing her body to relax as she let the air out of her lungs. She did this twice more, for she knew from past experience that she need only do this three times to get her pulse, breathing, and blood pressure back to normal. She let her body relax, while, at the same time, her mind remained alert and focussed as well as calm. Just as both Frank and Sensei

Nakamura had instilled in her.

Zen.

Tandy opened her eyes and looked through the 'scope. She watched as a figure dressed in camouflage fatigues approached her partner and loomed over him.

This was it.

She allowed the crook of her right index finger to hook around the trigger of the rifle.

Al-Makira stood and looked at Frank. The terrorist's fists were balled tight and his following words were loaded with hate and malice, "Personally, I would have liked to have had you for a few days so that I could have given you a proper welcome…I might yet change my mind."

"Oh," said Frank. "You mean stripped and beaten and tortured? Like you did with agent Ketcher?"

"Yes," hissed al-Makira. "Just like agent Ketcher."

"And you're going to film me being executed, like him?"

"Yes," said Al-Makira.

Frank looked at al-Makira with hardened eyes. "Well, I've seen your sick little films, and, quite frankly, they're not that good…Quite amateurish in fact. And typical of you, you cowardly piece of shit."

Al-Makira seethed with anger, but still he did not move nearer. He stared at his victim. "My films have served their purpose. And as you said earlier, you are not dead yet. I might still have you out of that chair and passed into the hands of my brother here." Al-Makira nodded towards Irfan who smiled with delight, like a jackal sensing prey. "Perhaps," said al-Makira, lowering his face nearer to Frank's, "I might inflict more pain on you than you can possibly bear, and I will still make a sick little film of you as you gag and scream…and finally die. And your stuck up imperious Lady Corrigan," al-Makira waved a hand towards the woman in question, "she can add in the background music as she watches you, and screams and cries."

Frank looked into al-Makira's mad blazing eyes. *Come closer.* "You really are quite insane, aren't you?"

Al-Makira's lips twitched and he took another step forward before reaching out to put his hands on both of Frank's tied wrists, leaning heavily upon them. "You killed my brother, Mister Frank Cross…"

"Killed?" interrupted Frank. "You mean *exterminated*, don't you? Like you would a rat?" *Lean in some more, you bastard.*

Al-Makira's eyes widened as his top lips drew back, showing his teeth. That final insult from Frank is what did it; it pushed al-Makira over the edge. He would not, could not, wait any longer. All thoughts of torturing his captive flashed away as a red mist of rage flooded his brain. He turned his head towards the cameraman and ground out the words, "Are you ready?"

"Yes, al-Makira."

"Then start filming!"

The cameraman bent down to the back of the camera which was aimed at Frank. But before the man could touch the button to start the recording al-Makira shouted at him, "Not him, you fool! Aim it at me! Get me in the shot first, you maggot!"

"Yes, yes, al-Makira," garbled the man.

Al-Makira turned back to Frank; he was still leaning on Frank's wrists. He started to smile.

The cameraman started to fiddle with the equipment so as to take the camera off lock and to turn it in its mount, but his fear of al-Makira was making him all fingers and thumbs.

Al-Makira, now believing that he was being filmed, leaned forwards. His one thought now was not about torture, or beatings. His one thought was to kill Frank Cross and he hissed out the next words from between clenched teeth, "Well, you say you exterminated my brother…Now I am going to exterminate *you*, Mister Cross. I am after vengeance, and I am going to execute you, right now, in front of the world. I am going to show them that I can do what I like to you." He sneered. "Because, you see, I have you right where I want you."

Frank looked quite calmly into al-Makira's face.

The desert air was still.

Tandy took in a breath.

"Actually," said Frank, "I have *you* right where I want you."

Al-Makira frowned.

Al-Makira lifted his eyes towards the open window. In his mind the germ of a warning began to take shape.

He stared out towards where Tandy lay with her rifle.

Tandy could see him through the rifle's scope; he seemed to be looking straight at her – but that was impossible…wasn't it?

Tandy blinked.

She waited for that instant between heartbeats; between the pushes of her pulse.

Realisation struck al-Makira.

The time was now.

Tandy squeezed the trigger.

BANG

The hollow point bullet crossed the space between the cliff edge and the tall building so fast that the report of the gun came after the bullet had passed through the window opening and into the room.

Tandy had aimed to hit al-Makira right between the eyes.

But the shot was off.

"Damn!" breathed Tandy.

But it did not matter. If al-Makira had been looking straight at Frank the downward trajectory of the bullet from Tandy's place of concealment on the cliff-top would have meant that the round would have hit the terrorist commander in the top of the head. Instead, he was looking up.

The round hit al-Makira just above his right eyebrow and took the top right-hand side of his head away in a sudden eruption of bone, blood and brains that sprayed over the cameraman behind him who screamed in panic, and who, by sheer coincidence, captured it all on digital film.

Gail Wetton screamed.

The impact of the high-velocity bullet threw al-Makira's head back, and his body was also thrown backwards, pitching away from Frank as his hands left Frank's wrists, his arms opening out either side of him as he fell. He crashed into the camera and the lights tripods. The camera came off its fixing, and they all fell onto the cameraman in a chaotic tangle. Al-Makira's body collapsed onto its back on the floor alongside the cameraman who pulled away from the corpse and started gibbering with his hands to his mouth.

Having taken the kill-shot, Tandy immediately chambered another round into the breech of the rifle. She quickly adjusted very slightly to the right and fired again.

The hollow-point bullet hit Irfan in the left-hand side of his ribcage and opened out into a jagged mushroom shape. Deflected by the rib that it had just passed through the bullet tore through his left lung, ripped through his heart then tore through his right lung before exiting out of his right shoulder blade, shattering the bone.

The impact of the hit took Irfan over sideways and he had dropped both his gun and his scimitar before he toppled dead onto the dusty wooden boards of the filthy floor where he joined his dead leader.

Blood was already pooling around al-Makira's wrecked head and Irfan's soon joined it, and together the mix began to work its way down through the cracks in the room's floorboards.

At the moment that al-Makira was shot, Ali had ducked down to squat beside Frank's chair and he now produced a clasp knife and pulled out his Glock.

In the room downstairs Habib was eating a sandwich when he heard a shot from outside. However, he could tell that the gun's report had been a long way off and he ignored it; al-Makira's undisciplined men were always randomly firing off their weapons - and then came the sound of a body heavily hitting the floor above him and he grinned. Al-Makira and Irfan must be giving Cross a real working over. He took two quick bites and finished his sandwich. He decided to go up and watch the fun.

To Tommo, T Bone and Clonk that first bang of Tandy's sniper rifle was the signal for them to move into action and to carry out the rest of Frank's desperate plan. Before Tandy's second shot was even fired they were up and moving: Tommo out of his wall of tyres; T Bone out of his empty house, and Clonk out of the smelly goat pen.

Tommo began running hard towards the helicopter, arms and legs pumping.

Ali came to his feet, making sure to keep within the cover of the room's walls so that Tandy could not see him. He stared down at Frank, holding his knife in one hand and his gun in the other.

T Bone leapt out of the door of his cover house and ran around the corner and up to the front door of the communications room. He tore the door open, tossed in two fragmentation grenades, slammed shut the door and then dived onto the floor of the street with his fingers in his ears.

The explosion blew the door off its weak hinges so that it sailed over T Bone's head and smashed into the wall of the building opposite. Somewhere a woman screamed. T Bone took his fingers out of his ears. Dogs were barking all over the village and he could hear people shouting. He got up and checked the interior of the comms room; there were two ragged corpses inside and the electronic equipment was now just mangled wreckage. T Bone tossed another grenade up onto the roof and ducked away as the grenade exploded and brought down the aerials and the two satellite dishes that were up there. The explosion also brought down the feeble roof which crashed into the remains of the comms room and then caught fire. Dust and the first tendrils of smoke billowed out into the street from the open doorway as T Bone took to his heels and legged it away down the street. He came to the corner and went to turn right towards the Intiqam HQ building. Three men wearing camouflage uniforms and carrying AK47's were running towards him. He lifted his MP7 and took them all out with a quick burst. The men spun away from him, taken off their feet to land dead in the dust.

Gail Wetton took a step forwards, towards the ruined head of al-Makira. She brought her hands from behind her back – they had never been secured - and she snatched Irfan's gun from off the floor at her feet where it had come to rest after he had dropped it. She lifted the weapon and pointed it – pointing it at Frank.

In the room downstairs a puzzled look crossed Habib's face. There was blood dripping down through the cracks in the floorboards. A lot of blood.
Too much blood for one man.
Habib wiped his mouth, grabbed his Sig Sauer pistol off the only table in the room and dashed for the door.

Gail's hands and arms were up in the isosceles firing position; hands together in front of her chest with the arms forming the sides of the isosceles triangle, a shooting position only a trained marksman would take up. Her finger tightened on the trigger and she screamed "For Intiqam! For The Cause!" just as Lady Corrigan kicked out and connected with the underside of Wetton's right wrist. At the same time Ali slashed with his open clasp knife and swept the blade through the shoelaces binding Frank's left wrist to the metal arm of his chair. Frank dived out of the chair and to his right and Wetton's ruined shot went high over the top of the chair and out the window.
Ali fired two shots at Gail with his gift from al-Makira; two shots in rapid

succession, a double tap; one went into her stomach and the other struck her in the top of her chest just below the base of her throat. The heavy thump of the bullets sent her backwards into the wall and back alongside Lady Corrigan.

"What the hell..." began Frank.

"I'm MI Six!" yelled Ali. "I'm an undercover agent! It's all been a set-up! Wetton's al-Makira's fucking girlfriend!"

"Bloody hell!" said Frank as he struggled with the laces on his right wrist. He heard a gurgling cough and his head snapped around to look at Gail Wetton who was still on her feet but supported by the wall behind her back. Her eyes were bulging and blood was spilling out of her mouth but she was still standing. She had her feet apart and she still had hold of her gun. She had started to lift it.

Habib had heard Gail shouting, followed by the gun shots, and he was now charging up the stairs to the filming room.

Wetton was staring hard at Frank as the air gurgled out of her throat. Blood spilled out over her lower lip as her weapon came up.

Lady Corrigan realised what was going to happen and she kicked out again, knocking Wetton's arm upwards and with enough force to make Gail lose her grip on the gun which fell to the floor and skidded away on the floorboards. Red's kicking foot landed on the floor and she rounded on Wetton and kicked her again with her right foot and hard into the stomach. Wetton doubled over, coughed up more blood and collapsed forwards onto the floor.

Lady Corrigan looked down at Gail Wetton. "Shitbag," she said. She tossed her hair back from her face and turned to Frank. "Looks like I'm rescuing *you*, Mister Cross."

"Where did you learn to kick like that?" asked Frank. He'd taken Ali's knife off him and had managed to free his right wrist. He swiftly crossed the room to Lady Corrigan. and he now used the knife to cut the plastic binds on Red's wrists.

"Private kick-boxing lessons in the gym," she replied as she massaged her lower arms.

Frank barked an ironic laugh, then said, "Right. Let's get out of here." He turned, closed the knife, and tossed it across the room to Ali who deftly caught it in his left hand.

Lady Corrigan had seen the gun that Wetton had dropped on the floorboards and was in the action of bending down to pick it up when Habib kicked the door open.

Everyone in the room froze.

But instead of stepping into the room Habib stopped outside.

And Frank knew then that they would not be getting away just yet.

And they did not know it, but the camera, which was now upside-down on the floor was still on and filming everything.

Clonk jumped the rickety fence that enclosed the goat pen and dashed under the entrance arch. As he emerged at a run two guards were coming at him, one left and one right. The guard to his right opened up with his AK47 but, because he was running, the shots went wild.

Clonk dropped to one knee and fired off one shot from his suppressed Glock. It hit the running guard in the chest and dropped him so that he carried out a strange backward somersault with his legs going up in the air as the back of his neck hit the floor.

The other guard, seeing his partner taken out with one shot, stopped moving and brought his AK up to his face. Clonk threw himself to his right, rolling at full stretch over the earth floor and dry dust with his arms outstretched and his hands clasped around the butt of the gun. He fired two shots, placing the bullets into the man's chest. With a grunt of pain, the man pitched over and the AK was dropped.

Clonk got up and moved off, entering the maze of streets that formed the interior of the village and heading for the Intiqam HQ.

Showing extreme caution, Habib checked the room. The door had gone back against the wall of the room giving him a clear unobstructed view; in front of him, on the floor, lay his Commanding Officer, the Second-in-Command, and just to his right was the cameraman. He took a step to the right which gave him an angled view of the room; to his left stood Lawrence Gainsborough who looked terrified and who had his hands up to his chest. Alongside him was Lady Corrigan, who was crouching down but had nothing in her hands. Seeing that those two were unarmed and therefore no threat he took his attention off them. To Lady Corrigan's left Gail Wetton lay face down on the floor with a red pool beginning to bloom on the woodwork beneath her. Her gun was lying on the floor about three feet in front of her.

Lady Corrigan looked at Habib, she had not managed to get to the gun before Habib had appeared, and if she went for it now she knew he would kill her out of hand. She glanced across to someone else in the room.

On seeing Lady Corrigan's glance, Habib quickly stepped left and checked out the right-hand side of the room; the cameraman was now kneeling away from the wall that the door was up against. He had his hands up to his face and was gibbering like someone from a Victorian lunatic asylum; he was spattered with blood. Beside him were the mangled tripods with their smashed lights and on the other side of the room lay the camera. Further to his right was the open window with Frank Cross crouching beside the chair in front of it. Habib could see that Frank was unarmed – so who had shot these three bodies? There must be someone else. Someone he could not see from the angle where he stood. Someone near the window? Someone beside the chair?

Habib raised his pistol and stepped into the room, arcing the gun around towards the window, fingering the trigger for a reflex shot.

The pilot of the Bell Huey helicopter was sitting in the pilot's seat reading an old tattered copy of Playboy magazine with his flying helmet nestled in his lap. His co-pilot had gone into the village about an hour ago and had not yet come back, probably seeing a woman.

The pilot was used to staying with his aircraft because al-Makira tended to use it as his own personal means of transportation; it was rather like being a chauffeur, so he had to remain with the vehicle in case al-Makira wanted to fly at a moment's notice. He'd heard some shooting, but that was nothing unusual because these undisciplined terrorists were always firing their weapons up into the air.

The pilot put down the magazine and closed his eyes. If al-Makira wanted him he would get a call from him, or Irfan, on his mobile. He did not know that both of those men were now dead. His head lolled forwards and he quickly dropped off to sleep with the magazine dropping at his feet into the footwell of the helicopter.

Habib fired, reacting to Ali, just as Ali levelled his own gun and pulled the trigger. Both men were moving, so both shots missed their deadly mark although Habib's shot creased Ali's arm right arm by his bicep.

Ali cried out with the pain.

"Traitor!" yelled Habib and he pointed the Sig at Ali again, holding out the weapon in a professional double-handed grip.

Tandy had heard the shooting that was clearly coming from Frank's room. She still had the rifle trained on the open window and she tried to see what was happening through the 'scope. She couldn't make out anything and so she had to hope that Frank was still alive.

With Habib's gun pointing at Ali Frank saw his chance and took it. Uncoiling like a spring he launched himself at Habib. Frank's rammed his head forwards aiming for Habib's upper chest while he got his arms around both of Habib's arms at the elbows, pressing them into the side of the terrorist's body. Habib fired, but the shot went into the frail plaster of the wall by the window as the two men staggered backwards into the wreckage of the camera tripod and light stands, and then onwards into the cowering camera-man. With his arms pinned, Habib dropped the gun, and all three men went down thrashing and scrabbling at each other.

A guard in a dark grey djellaba came running along the top of the wall towards Clonk who was out in the open and about to turn into the first small side street. As the guard was above Clonk it meant that Clonk did not see him.

Tandy spotted him, moved the rifle and fired as the guard raised his weapon to shoot Clonk. Tandy's shot kicked the guard off the top of the ancient structure. He somersaulted through the air and landed only a few feet behind Clonk to lay like a bundle of dirty washing.

Clonk turned and looked at the man and then realised what had just happened. He turned again to look towards the cliff and lifted a hand to wave at Tandy. "You're welcome," muttered Tandy as Clonk moved into the side street.

Tandy moved the rifle, scanning through the rifle's 'scope for her next victim. A man came up through a hatch onto the roof of a house with an AK47 in his hands. It wasn't T Bone and Tandy knew where Tommo and Clonk were, so she picked this man off with a head shot.

Frank and Habib were now lying on top of the cameraman who was kicking and screaming. They rolled off him, locked together like wrestlers.

Amir Darwish, the Intiqam accountant, was in a state of panic; there were gun shots, explosions and screaming going on outside the small ramshackle house that he occupied. *What is going on? It must be the British or the Americans! These stupid terrorists! I knew it would all go wrong!* There came a scream from just outside and someone slammed against his fragile front door that was not much more than a vertical set of old wooden planks held together by horizontal bits of wood and rusty nails. Darwish recoiled from it. *I must get out of here! I'm not a fighting man. I'm a bloody accountant! Bugger this...I'm getting out of here!* He grabbed his laptop and two large ledgers from off the rough wooden table that he had been working at and made for the door. He got the door open and nearly fell over the body that was lying there at the threshold. Darwish stared down into the man's sightless eyes for a second, then he stepped over him and dashed away down the narrow street. *Where is that bloody helicopter?*

The two men finished rolling, with Habib coming up on top. He managed to get an arm free and he drove a punch at Frank's head, but Frank jerked his head to one side and Habib's fist smashed into the rough wood of a floorboard. Habib cursed aloud as Frank got his right hand free and swung a haito-uchi, ridge-hand strike, at Habib's head, which connected along his left upper jaw and ear and which snapped Habib's head to one side and knocked the man over so that he fell off Frank.

With the wrestling holds broken, both men were up onto their feet in an instant, their bodies swaying as they looked for a weakness in their opponent and an opportunity to attack. The two men were only about six feet apart with Habib rubbing at his left ear.

The cameraman was still down on the floor, lying on his back with his hands just in front of his chest, with his feet pulled up near his backside. Ali had been trying to get a shot at Habib. But there was too much movement and confusion, and now Frank was standing in front of him, blocking his aim at Habib.

Out of the corner of her left eye Tandy saw a movement and swung the sniper rifle towards it. A man in a djellaba had just run out of one of the village's narrow streets and had crossed under the arch that Clonk had used for his entry into Qaryat Musawara. The man was heading west out of the village, running in sandals which made his gait look awkward, but never-the-less, he was running as if all the hounds of hell were after him. He was holding up the hem of his djellaba with one hand whilst he held what looked like large books and a laptop under his other arm.

Tandy almost shot him, but those books, laptop and those sandals checked her – not a soldier type; not a terrorist - and she looked over the top of the rifle's 'scope. She could see Tommo running hard towards the helicopter and then realised that the man with the books was heading there as well.

Tandy smiled. *I don't rate your chances if Tommo gets hold of you.*

Habib glanced around the floor of the room. There it was. His Sig Sauer semi-automatic was underneath the chair that Frank had been sitting in.

Frank saw the glance and said in Arabic, "You won't get the chance to use it."

"Then I will have to kill you with my bare hands," snarled Habib and he took a fast step forward and launched a powerful right foot mae geri, front kick, off his back leg, to Frank's stomach. Frank easily palmed it away with his left hand and snapped out a uraken, back fist, to Habib's head with his right.

Habib ducked, but even so, Frank's fist caught him just above his forehead. It jarred Habib and he took a step backwards, but then unleashed a right foot mawashi geri, roundhouse kick, to Frank's head. Frank ducked under the kick which went to his right and rammed a right gyaku tsuki, reverse punch, into the back of Habib's exposed right rib cage. Habib grunted but he did not go down. Instead, he stepped away from Frank, turning and watching his opponent.

The two men stood and looked at each other.

Once again, Frank was blocking Ali's aim.

Red had been helplessly watching the fight and she had seen Ali and had realised what he was trying to do. Her eyes fell again on the gun that Gail had dropped.

Frank looked into Habib's eyes. "Not quite the push-over you expected?" said Frank.

"My compliments," returned Habib. "Where did you learn your martial arts? In some squalid back-street gym, no doubt."

"Actually, I studied under Sensei Nakamura, in Japan." And Frank saw the glimmer of recognition at the name, followed by a shadow of fear that briefly crossed Habib's face just before he attacked again.

Red picked up the gun.

Habib came in with another right foot mawashi geri. However, this time the kick came in low to Frank's left knee, but it was a feint as Habib then whipped the same kick upwards to try to catch Frank in the side of his head. It was an old free-fighting trick, and Frank wasn't about to be caught by it. He shrugged backwards to avoid the kick and then spun on his left foot going into boshi geri, the spinning back-kick.

Habib turned his head slightly to the right so as to watch and react to the kick, but the kick was so fast that Habib did not manage to completely avoid it, so that Frank's right heel smashed into the assassin's face, broke his nose, and rammed him backwards as blood gushed out of his nostrils and over his moustache and beard. As Habib fell backwards, he caught his feet on the squirming legs of the cameraman and went headlong into the wall behind him, dislodging some plaster. Even with a broken and bloody nose, Habib began to struggle to his feet. Frank got ready for him, readying himself to give a final fast and deadly punch, when Lady Corrigan stepped forwards and aimed the gun that she was now holding.

"Okay," she said aloud. "Enough of this shit!" and she pulled the trigger and put two bullets into Habib's chest.

Habib collapsed with his legs straddling the body of the still gibbering cameraman.

"Well," said Frank, dropping his fists. "That's one way of settling it." He looked at Lady Corrigan. "It seems that, apart from martial arts, you know how to use that." He pointed at the Glock semi-automatic pistol that she was holding.

"I, am a member of a gun club," she said. She made the announcement in an imperious voice in the same manner that one might say *I am the President of the local branch of the Women's Institute*. "Actually, I'm quite a good shot."

Frank gave a wry smile. "You don't say?" *Is there no end to this woman's skills? Sir Michael must be very proud of her.*

"I do say, Mister Cross. Now, shall we get out of here?"

"My thoughts exactly, Lady Corrigan." He looked across to Lawrence Gainsborough who was watching all of this with his mouth open in horror and astonishment. "And, Mister Gainsborough, let's see if we can't get you home as well."

Gainsborough closed his mouth. "Thank you, Mister Cross, I wish you would."

"Well, Sir, that's what I'm here for."

Tommo reached the helicopter before the accountant did. He dragged the door open and grabbed the still sleeping pilot by his flight jacket and hauled him out of his seat. He threw the pilot on the ground who rolled in the dirt and then came up onto one knee as he went for a sidearm in a leather holster at his right hip. But as he pulled the gun clear he realised how big Tommo was and his mouth fell open.

That hesitation saved Tommo's life because it allowed Tommo the fraction of a second that it took for him to react and shoot the man with his MP7.

The accountant came to a staggering halt some ten feet away and then stood there looking from first the pilot and then up at Tommo. Breathing hard and finding his voice the accountant said, in perfect English, and with only a slight accent, "Please, I am not a soldier…I am just an accountant! I must get away!"

"Are you armed?" rumbled Tommo, in a voice like distant thunder.

"Armed?"

"Yes, armed," he demanded. "Are you carrying a weapon?"

"No, no. Just my laptop and ledgers." The items were under his left armpit and he patted them nervously with his right hand. He watched Tommo's face with suspicion, half expecting the big man to take them from him. But Tommo was not concerned with ledgers. Keeping the MP7 in his left hand and aimed at the accountant Tommo patted the little man down with his right hand. Satisfied that he wasn't armed, he indicated the helicopter behind him with a jerk of his big thumb.

"Okay," said Tommo. "Get in the Huey and keep still. I'll be right behind you, an' if you try anythin', I'll smash your head like a walnut."

The accountant, who did not want his head smashed like a walnut, or any other sort of nut, complied with the order and moved past Tommo who was scowling at him.

Tommo helped the man get into the Huey where he scrambled into a corner and squatted on the floor. The giant man looked from the little man to the dead pilot. *Frank's not going to like this. Who's gonna fly the damned chopper?* Tommo turned and got into the belly of the helicopter where he sat just inside the door cradling his MP7 in his arms, waiting for his team and scowling some more.

Frank heard Tandy take another two shots, with their report muffled by distance.

Good girl. Two more down, thought Frank. He now had to get the hostages out of the building that they were in as a matter of urgency for he did not want to get surrounded and boxed in.

Lawrence Gainsborough turned to look down at Wetton's body. "Gail." He said her name in a plaintive voice. "I never knew. I never knew…"

Frank took him by the elbow. "It's called a honey trap, Sir."

"I never knew." He had tears in his dark tired eyes.

"No, Sir. I know. Now, let's go shall we?"

"Should I have a gun?" asked Gainsborough in the voice of a small and terrified boy.

Frank had no intention of giving the Member of Parliament a gun; he might panic and shoot one of Frank's team with it.

"No, Sir. You just leave all the shooting to me, Ali, and Annie Oakley here."

Red Corrigan could not help but smile.

Frank retrieved Habib's Sig Sauer from under the execution chair. He checked it and, satisfied, said, "Okay. Let's go. Ali, you lead the way. Lady Corrigan, you next, then you, Sir."

Ali opened the door, stepped outside and started down the stairs. A terrorist appeared at the bottom of the stairs so Ali shot him before the man realised that Ali had effectively changed sides.

Red and Larry followed Ali down and just before Frank left the room he hesitated and looked down at the cameraman who was sprawled on his back. Why had he stopped gibbering?

The cameraman was now looking hard at Frank, whose eyes zeroed in on the man's left arm. It was tucked alongside his body with the forearm moving, as though he were trying to reach something beneath him with his left hand. Frank put his foot down on the man's lower abdomen between his hip bones and pushed down hard. The cameraman cried out and he jerked his hand free; a Glock 19 Compact pistol slipped out of his back pocket onto the floor.

The man's lips curled back and he cursed Frank roundly in Arabic.

"So," said Frank in the same language. "Not the little coward that you were acting to be." He shot the man once in the head.

Frank turned to the door and was about to leave when he suddenly thought *Cameraman!*

There should be a camera. It would have filmed him.

It would know what he looked like.

His gaze swept the room and settled on the camera. He quickly stepped over the bodies of the cameraman, al-Makira and Irfan and crossed the room. He picked up the camera and removed the SanDisk from inside which would have held any photos and film that might have been taken. Frank put this in a pocket and then he smashed the camera onto the floor. He then stamped on it until it was completely wrecked. He kicked the bits about and then he turned and left the room.

T Bone, having destroyed the terrorist's communications centre, was now heading towards the building that Frank had been taken to, and from which he was now escaping.

The members of Intiqam, who did not know that their leader had been killed, were in disarray because they were receiving no orders to tell them what to do. There had been gunfire, although they did not know which direction it was coming from, or who was responsible for it, and there had been three explosions. Dogs were still barking and a few feminine screams had been heard in direct response to the various gun-shots. What the hell was going on? Where was al-Makira? Where was Irfan?

Some of the terrorists had discovered the devastated comms room but they had no idea who had caused it or where the attacker had gone. The soldiers of Intiqam where scurrying around in disorganised undisciplined groups who, every now and then, ran into either T Bone or Clonk and were duly dispatched with a bullet in the chest or head.

Since Qaryat Musawara was a maze of tiny alleyways, it was not difficult for T Bone and Clonk, being the highly skilled and experienced soldiers that they were, to keep one jump ahead of the armed rabble, and they soon converged on the main HQ building.

T Bone got there first and arrived just as Frank emerged from what was supposed to have been his place of torture and ultimate death. In front of Frank, and heading a ragged queue, was Ali, followed by Lady Corrigan and

Gainsborough. Ali lifted his gun as T Bone came towards him.

"Don't shoot!" yelled Frank. "He's with me."

T Bone approached the group as Clonk came racing around the corner of a nearby building. He suddenly stopped, whirled around and fired his MP7 back down the small side street that he had emerged from. There were a few screams and then Clonk came at a run towards Frank's group.

Ali swung the gun again.

"Don't!" yelled Frank. Ali's gun was lowered.

"My," said T Bone as he scowled at Ali, "but he's keen aint he?"

"Yeah, but he's on our side."

"Could've fooled me."

Ali shrugged his shoulders. "Sorry."

"Okay," said T Bone. "But just be careful."

"We'd best get a move on," said Clonk as he came to a halt beside the group and regained his breath. "These terrorists are coming out of houses like fleas off a drowning dog's arse."

"Very descriptive," said Frank.

"Christ!" said T Bone, looking at Clonk and holding a black gloved hand to his face. "You stink."

Lady Corrigan looked at Clonk with an offended expression on her features, as if she had just stepped into a main sewer. She waved a regal hand backwards and forwards in front of her nose.

Clonk grinned. "Don't blame me if bloody goats are not toilet trained."

"Oh," said T Bone, "It's the goats. I thought it was you."

"Okay, okay," said Frank, trying to remain serious. "Listen to me." He looked at Ali, Red and Larry. "We are now going to get moving. So, if I shout Down, do not, I repeat, do not, drop flat; it takes too long to get back up again and the delay could get you killed. Instead, you drop down onto one knee and crouch, and when I say go, you go. Got that?" Ali, Red and Larry nodded affirmation. "Good."

"Your gun," said Clonk. He handed over Frank's Smith and Wesson and the two speed-loaders.

"Thanks mate." Frank checked the revolver's chambers, pocketed the speed-loaders, then looked up. "Okay people. Let's go. And at the double!" And, with full daylight now upon them, they began to run.

Back in the filming room Gail Wetton groaned, moved her head, and slowly opened her eyes, and with the opening of her eyes came the overwhelming pain from the two gunshot wounds. With a huge effort of will she put out her right hand and pushed herself over, off of her chest and onto her back, crying out and coughing up blood as she did so. Wheezing, and through filmy eyes, she looked up at the grimy ceiling and then put a shaking hand to her stomach. Her dress was soaking wet down there, and she was appalled and horrified when she brought that trembling hand in front of her eyes and saw the amount of blood that covered it. The same hand then went to her upper chest, but an inspection of that hand told her nothing because of the blood that was already on her palm and fingers, slick and congealing.

She knew she was dying, but with another huge effort of will she rolled onto her left side. She coughed up more blood. The coughing pulled at her stomach muscles and a massive wave of pain swept through her. She let the blood from her mouth dribble to the filthy floor. She moved her head and looked around the room and her gaze fell on her lover – al-Makira. She moaned and then coughed more blood, bringing her knees into the foetal position at the agony that the coughing spasm created.

And now she was angry. Gail Wetton knew that she was going to die and that she did not have long for this world, and the reason for her death was Frank Cross. It did not matter to her that it had been the traitorous Ali that had shot her. No, it was all the fault of that bastard Cross. All of al-Makira's carefully laid plans had gone wrong. And it was all the fault of Frank Cross.

She put her right hand onto her stomach and pressed down, keening at the pain but trying to stop the blood flow. She used her left hand to push herself upright and then she crawled on her knees across the few feet of floor to al-Makira.

With gritted teeth, and breathing heavily because of the shot to her upper chest, she made it to her lost lover and put out a bloody hand to caress the hair on what was left of his head. She felt like weeping, and then she had a moment of lucidity – Frank Cross was not in the room, which meant that he must still be alive; he had to die.

Wetton knew what to do.

It wasn't over yet.

She patted the front of al-Makira's battledress jacket and found his mobile phone.

Getting weaker by the second the clutched the device and went to speed-dial. All of this effort was almost too much for her and she collapsed onto the floor beside al-Makira's body. She rallied and found the number she was after and pushed at it with her thumb.

The number rang and in only a few seconds a man answered:

"Hello, my son."

Gail coughed up more blood before she said in a hoarse voice, "This is not your son...This is Gail..." She coughed. Her pain raged in her guts and chest.

"Gail?" said the voice. "Gail who?"

"Gail...Gail Wetton..."

Recognition clicked in. *My son's Western whore.* "Oh, yes. Gail..."

Wetton interrupted him. She had to get this out fast. She knew she was going. "Listen...Your son is dead...Your son is dead."

"Dead?" said the voice. Then, more angrily, "If this is some kind of a joke!"

"It's no joke...We've been shot...he is dead..."

"How?" roared the man at the other end.

"Frank Cross," gasped Wetton with the last vestiges of life ebbing out of her. The room was starting to come apart and blacken in front of her eyes. "Frank Cross," she muttered. "It was F-Frank Crossss..." and the last letters of his name came out like a snake's hiss as she dropped the phone and collapsed, lying beside her lover, their blood mixing and dripping through the rough floorboards to the room below.

"Hello?" said the voice on the phone. "Hello? Miss Wetton?"

But Gail Wetton was very dead.

The Shadows team ran in a tight line with Clonk taking point up front with T Bone at the rear. Frank ran in the middle with Ali in front of him and Red and Larry behind him. Their fastest route out of the village was by heading due West in a straight line down a long narrow central street, a street that led to the village's encircling street that lay within the perimeter of the outside wall, and thence through the western entrance arch.

The journey was not without drama; they were running with a background noise of barking dogs, shouting people and random rifle fire as the ill-disciplined terrorists fired at shadows, and probably at each other. Frank's group had not gone far when Clonk dropped to a knee and Frank ordered "DOWN!"

417

Two men in camouflage uniforms had just stepped out of a doorway in front of them. They were not expecting to see Frank's group and were caught completely unawares. Clonk shot them both in the head. It was a dispassionate and brutal scene that neither Red, nor Larry, and probably not even Ali, had ever witnessed before; an efficient soldier taking out the enemy with a complete absence of feeling for them. And, despite Red having killed Habib, both she and Larry looked away.

"MOVE!" cried Frank and the line got up and ran on. As they came past the bodies by the open doorway that the men had come out of T Bone called out "Clonk! Pass me a grenade!" He had used all of his up in dealing with the comms room.

Clonk unhooked one of his fragmentation grenades from off his tactical jacket and tossed it backwards to T Bone who caught it, pulled the pin, and tossed it inside the house as he ran past. A few seconds later the grenade exploded, wrecked the house, and killed the other two soldiers inside that T Bone had spotted through the open door.

And then something else happened.

Paper.

Paper billowed out of the wrecked doorway and out through the shattered window.

"Hey Frank!" called T Bone. "Look at this!"

Frank turned, saw the fluttering paper and stopped the running column. He ordered them all down then went back to T Bone who had turned back to gather a large fistful of the paper. Frank stared at it; good quality sheets of blank white paper and white envelopes were being held in T Bone's grasp. Some of the envelopes were sealed and had addresses on them. Frank took one; it was to an address somewhere in Nice, Southern France.

"Well, I'll be damned," muttered Frank. "So, this is where these start out from."

"Sorry?" asked a bewildered T Bone, not knowing that they had stumbled on the source of the world-wide white threatening letters.

"I'll explain later," said Frank. "Right now make sure this lot burns."

"No trouble there," smiled T Bone. "Take a look."

Already grey smoke was beginning to coil upwards through the ruined blasted roof and they could hear the woosh and crackle of the fire inside.

"Good," nodded Frank. "Then throw those inside and then collect as much of this paper that's strewn around and get it in there as well."

T Bone raised an eyebrow. "What's with the anti-litter campaign?" he asked.

"Like I said, I'll tell you later."

"Okay boss." And with that T Bone tossed his handful of papers into the conflagration.

Frank got the group back on their feet. "Come on everyone!" he yelled. "Let's get going!" and he got them running again while T Bone scrabbled about in the narrow street like some demented litter-picker. But the group had not travelled very far when a group of three men, drawn to them by the sound of the grenade exploding, appeared from a side alley forward from them and on their left. The men took one look at Frank and his team and started screaming "Intiqam" and "Al-Qadia".

"DOWN!"

Clonk and Frank levelled their weapons and fired. All three men went down, this time screaming in pain.

"MOVE!"

They ran on and T Bone caught them up, having carried out his bonfire duties.

Four times, as they hurried along, they heard the distinctive report of Tandy's Accuracy International sniper rifle, and each time they heard the bang a body had pitched off a roof to fall on the beaten red earth; on one occasion one of those bodies landed on the street in front of them. They all jumped over the corpse and it was at that point that Lady Corrigan turned to Frank and, still running, pointed upwards and asked,

"Who's doing all the sniping?"

"Oh," said Frank, not breaking stride, "that's Tandy."

"Who is Tandy?"

"My partner."

"Your *partner?*"

"Yes. Kind of like, my girlfriend."

"Jesus!" gasped Lady Corrigan. "Your girlfriend! Just don't ever piss her off, will you!"

They made it to the western archway where Tandy picked off another terrorist who had climbed up onto the top of the wall. The man made a spectacular silent dive through the air, arms outstretched, to land on the rickety wooden fence of the goat pen that had afforded Clonk his smelly cover. With the fencing smashed the goats saw their chance for freedom and took it. Bleating and jumping they ran away from the village with its sporadic and noisy small-arms fire as fast as their legs could carry them.

Frank could see the Huey in the distance a few hundred yards away. He turned towards where Tandy lay hidden up on the plateau. He waved at her and then pointed at the helicopter. Moments later he saw her stand up and start to move towards the edge of the cliff.

Frank led his group under the arch and drew them towards him in a cluster, like a teacher with a group of kids on a school trip. Clonk and T Bone immediately moved outwards to either end of the arch and covered the surrounding area with their assault rifles; T Bone facing West, and Clonk facing East into the village.

"Okay," said Frank to the group. "We have to make a run for the chopper. It's our taxi ride out of here. But it's out in the open, so no hanging about because we might come under fire. When we get there we might come under more fire, and we've still got to wait for Tandy to get to us. Clonk, T Bone, I want you to take up a defensive position a few yards out from the chopper so that any hostiles will be kept out of range of it. Then, when I call you in, you come at a run. Understood?"

"Yes Boss." They chorused without turning towards him.

"Right. Let's get going."

"Ummm," said Ali. He was looking towards the Bell Huey. "It looks like we might have company."

Frank followed Ali's gaze.

Beyond the helicopter, strung out in a line from left to right, and coming straight towards them at a fast jog, were nine members of the SAS, in full camouflage gear and armed to the teeth.

Captain Buckley and his Special Operations team had arrived.

**

Two of Buckley's team dropped off at the helicopter in case they needed to secure it, because Captain Buckley had also realised it's importance as an extraction vehicle. One of the men had a communications pack strapped to his back and he and his partner approached the Huey where they were rather surprised to come across Tommo. But then Tommo had that effect on most people the first time that they met him.

The rest of the SAS squad jogged up to Frank's group who were still taking cover under the arch and waiting for them. Frank had no intention of meeting them out in the open where they would make a good group target.

The SAS were all in camouflage battle dress with helmets, small backpacks, and with webbing on their chests from which were hung fragmentation grenades. They wore Glock 17 standard issue semi-automatic pistols at their hips and on their waist belts they had pockets containing extra ammunition clips for both the pistols and their L119A1 assault rifles which they carried across both arms and hugged to their chests.

The L119A1 C8 carbine is the standard issue assault rifle for the SAS and these had the shorter ten-inch barrel. They held 30 rounds of 5.56 x 45 mm NATO calibre bullets in a magazine.

All but one man carried the carbines. The odd-man-out was a young trooper who was carrying an Accuracy International L96A1 rifle, the same type of weapon that Tandy used. He was clearly this group's designated sniper.

Standing facing Frank, Buckley did not salute – so neither did Frank.

"Who are you?" asked Buckley, with a slight touch of aggression in his clean well-bred voice. His right hand hovered over his pistol.

Frank noted that right hand. "Frank Cross," he answered as politely as possible. He held out a hand.

Buckley's left eyebrow gave a small twitch and the skin around his eyes wrinkled slightly for a second. He looked at Frank's offered hand, then shook it.

"I've heard of you, Cross. You used to be in the Regiment as well."

So, that confirmed who these guys were. SAS. Frank inclined his head and gave the captain a ghost of a smile. "And you are?"

"Captain Martin Buckley. I'm in charge of this team."

"SAS," said Frank.

"Very astute."

"Takes one to know one."

"Quite," agreed Buckley. "Why are you here?" Very direct. Not wasting time.

A bullet struck the brickwork of the arch just above their heads and they all ducked involuntarily as some bits of ancient brick scattered down.

Frank turned his head slightly. "Clonk," he called. "See where that came from, and shoot the bastard will you?"

"It's a sniper!" shouted Clonk. "Givvus a bloody chance will you?"

421

Frank turned back to Buckley. "In answer to your question, I run a search and rescue team. We've just rescued these two." He pointed at Red and Larry.

Another bullet cracked off the brickwork.

"CLONK!" yelled Frank.

"Aye, boss, I'm working on it!"

Captain Buckley turned to the rescued. "Lady Corrigan, I presume? And Lawrence Gainsborough, MP?"

"Yes, Captain," said Lady Corrigan, answering for both of them.

"I was sent to rescue you, Lady Corrigan, and you, Sir." He nodded at Gainsborough. "Seems that Mister Cross here has beaten me to it." He turned then to Frank. "And al-Makira?"

"Dead," said Frank. "Along with his SIC."

"Thank God," said Gainsborough who lowered his head and stared at the ground.

Buckley nodded. He looked at the ragged figure of the MP and gave him a grim smile of understanding; this man had been through hell and even now that he was rescued, *although* he had been rescued, his shattered nerves might not hold out for much longer.

BANG

"Got the bastard!"

Without looking round at his team-mate, Frank called out, "Well done Clonk!"

At that moment four terrorists in grey djellabas came at a run around the corner of a building behind Frank's group. There were four shots and all four running men were taken out by Clonk before any of the SAS team could get a round off.

"Very impressive," said Buckley who had started to draw his Glock 17. He looked away from the destruction and, without fully holstering his weapon, let his eyes settle on Ali. "Who's this? One of your team?"

"My name is Ali," answered Ali. "I'm not one of Frank's team, I'm with MI Six."

"Bloody hell," said Buckley, smiling. "A spook!" He turned to Gainsborough and the smile disappeared. "Aren't you supposed to be with someone, Sir? A Miss Wetton?"

In answer to Buckley's question Gainsborough mutely shook his head. He had realised, back in the execution room, that Gail had set him up, had deliberately lured him into a trap. A honey trap as Frank had put it. And he had fallen for it, hook, line and sexy sinker. He felt like a complete fool and there was going to be hell to pay for this – not least from Mrs Gainsborough.

Frank answered for him. "Turns out, Wetton was one of the terrorists. She pulled Mister Gainsborough into a trap…Quite clever really."

Gainsborough threw Frank a glance.

"Where is she now?" asked Buckley.

"Dead," said Lady Corrigan. "And good riddance…Now, can we get out of here…Please?" The last few words were directed at Frank.

"Well," said Captain Buckley, also directing his speech to Frank. "Seems you've done a good job of getting them this far…would you like to run the rest of the show?"

It was quite an offer. Captain Buckley had heard all about Frank Cross and his exploits in the SAS, because Cross was a legend in their circles; the man who could always hit what he shot at and who always brought all of his team home, unscathed, from the toughest of missions. A man to take command, not to be given commands. And so, Buckley was not too proud to defer to the more experienced and better man.

"Very kind of you, Captain." Frank nodded and smiled. "But let's work together. How did you get here, and have you got an extraction plan?"

"We dropped in by 'chute," answered Buckley. "And we had hoped to get back out by Hercules." The Hercules transport aircraft is an amazing vehicle, capable of a take-off and landing on almost any surface and along a very short runway. The valley floor would have been perfect, had it not been for the profusion of rocks that were scattered over its entire surface.

"I don't think that's going to work Captain, some of this ground is treacherous," Frank waved a hand at the desert floor, "and also this could be a very hot extraction for them." As if to illustrate the point another bullet cracked past them.

"What do you suggest?" The captain deferred to Frank's experience again.

"Get on the radio and call off the Hercules. Then get your team into the chopper and we can then get the hell out of here."

Buckley smiled and nodded. "Right guys!" he shouted to his troops. "Get to the Huey!"

And they all began to run again.

As they ran towards the helicopter, Captain Buckley saw Tandy sprinting towards them from an oblique angle over to their left. Buckley waved towards her. "Incoming hostile!" he shouted.

Two of the SAS team on the group's left flank dropped to their knees and sighted their carbines on Tandy.

"She's friendly!" yelled Frank. "She's one of mine!"

The two SAS members lifted their weapons up.

"One of yours?" asked Buckley.

"She's my sniper!"

"Any good?"

"Top shot!" answered Frank.

As they ran, the team fell into a practiced defensive strategy: two members of the SAS team dropped back and went down onto one knee with rifles up towards the target. Then, a few feet further on, two more of the team dropped out and took up the same defensive strategy whilst the original two got up and ran back beyond the second pair. This deadly game of leapfrog was played over and over until the team reached their objective, and possible safety. The only member of the group who did not take part in this was the sniper, as his job was to be the calm and measured long range single shot.

Tandy came running and bounding at full stretch towards them, leaping over rocks and scrubby bushes like a young gazelle. As she approached, the two SAS troopers, one male and one female, at the front of the defensive strategy levelled their weapons towards the village. A group of twelve terrorists were running out onto the valley floor from underneath the arch that Frank and his teams had just abandoned. The ragged group was yelling and screaming and waving their AK47's in the air, and they fanned out as they got nearer.

Still down on one knee the two SAS troopers opened fire; short controlled bursts that drilled into the screaming men and sent them whirling and spinning onto the earth. After the initial first barrage of shots only three men were left standing and they turned and fled back to the village – they'd had enough, but the two troopers remained where they were and on the alert.

Tandy came up alongside Frank, who was standing underneath the drooping stationary blades of the helicopter. A member of the SAS was squatting on the floor and talking into his radio set, he was calling up the Hercules to cancel the extraction. Beside him a body lay in the dust. Tandy nodded towards it. "Who's that?" she gasped, getting her breath.

"The pilot," said Frank. He looked at the corpse and hoped that T Bone could fly the helicopter. If he couldn't they were stuffed.

"Oh…Blimey." Said Tandy, realising the implication. She looked around. "And who are our new friends?"

"SAS," said Frank.

"Blimey," said Tandy again. "Where did they come from?"

"Herefordshire, I should think," said Frank with a smile.

"Oh, ha bloody ha. Very funny."

Frank put out a hand and gently touched the side of Tandy's head; a gesture that was not lost on Captain Buckley, who was looking at Tandy, convinced that he had seen her somewhere before.

The trooper with the radio handset looked up. "Hercules cancelled."

"Right," said Captain Buckley. "Time to get on board and get the fuck out of here."

By now, the three terrorists who had made it back alive to the safety of the village, were shouting for their comrades. Their leaders had been found dead and, in the normal order of things, they had started to stop being an ill-disciplined rabble and were becoming slightly more organised, and therefore infinitely more dangerous. A tall man, with a large black beard and wearing a dirty white djellaba, was rallying the last of the terrorists outside the door to the Intiqam HQ by simply shouting at them all. They clustered around him, acknowledging him as their new leader of the hyena pack.

The new leader waved his AK47 in the direction of the helicopter and shouted, "Kill them, my brothers! For Intiqam! For al-Makira! For al-Qadia! Kill them! Kill them all!"

The crowd of some twenty men, in a mixture of djellabas and camouflaged uniforms, turned as one, and, screaming oaths, began to run through the village towards Frank's Shadows and the SAS.

The Bell Huey Iroquois can carry fourteen troops. There were eighteen in the rescue party and leaving someone behind was not an option, so the helicopter was going to have to work hard at getting off the ground and escaping.

Excepting Tommo, Clonk was the first in, where he discovered the accountant cowering behind the co-pilot's seat. Clonk stayed by the entrance hatch and, with Tommo, handed people into the aircraft while Frank directed operations from the ground beside the belly of the helicopter. T Bone clambered into the pilot's seat and tried to pull on the pilot's helmet.

It would not fit, so T Bone slung it out of the chopper. He tried the co-pilot's, which was even smaller, so that went the same way as the first one. He began to run his eyes over the controls.

Frank had watched the helmets being jettisoned. "T Bone!" Frank's shout came from outside. "Can you fly this thing?"

T Bone looked around at Frank and shouted back, "I'll let you know once we've taken off!"

Captain Buckley turned to Frank and was about to say something when he thought better of it and climbed into the aircraft.

As the rest of the group began to clamber into the Huey the hyena pack of terrorists emerged outside the western archway. Here they paused and screamed their insults. Then the tall man shouted something and they began to run the few hundred yards across the broken ground towards the Huey.

"Get this thing off the ground!" yelled Frank, and T Bone reached for the controls, his hands dancing over switches.

The engine fired up.

T Bone smiled and then rubbed his hands together.

Frank looked at Buckley. "Shame this chopper has no attack capability."

Buckley nodded grimly; they could have done with some extra firepower.

The two SAS troopers fired some rounds at the advancing terrorists then came out of their defensive kneels and ran for the chopper. As its rotor blades began to turn the engine began its curious screaming wheezing noise as it wound up.

The blades flogged the air faster and faster, sending up clouds of red dust as the pack came tearing towards them.

Frank and the two defending troopers were the last ones to get on board and they immediately turned in the doorway to open fire as the Iroquois lifted off the ground. The bullets took their toll with the tall man being the last to fall, the rounds thudding into his chest as he screamed a final defiance.

At first the take-off seemed ponderous; the blades churned the air and threw up clouds of sand and dust that swirled into the interior of the helicopter making the occupants cough and spit, and the big helicopter seemed to hang heavily in space as if it did not want to leave the desert floor. Then, suddenly, as if the aircraft had changed its mind, the blades bit into the air and the Huey surged forwards and then up, leaving Qaryat Musawara to its remaining shocked population of simple folk and goat herders. It was some time before the small population came slowly out of their houses to take stock of the bodies and damage.

And to give thanks that their oppressors had been removed.

**

"Right," shouted Frank over the sound of the rotor blades as the Huey headed away from the village. "Let's get these doors closed."

The doors to the open sides of the Huey were hauled back into place and instantly the stiff breeze that had been invading the crowded cabin was gone. However, the noise of the rotor blades had not diminished.

Frank turned to Tommo and asked loudly, "Who's this?" He was pointing at Amir Darwish.

The big man shouted back, "He says he's an accountant."

Bloody hell! thought Frank. *We'll be giving lifts to librarians next!* He looked at the little man, who stared at Frank with wide eyes and asked, in pretty good English, "Where are you taking me?"

"Good question," answered Frank in fluent Arabic, which had the effect of raising the accountant's eyebrows. And then, in English, "Where is the Intiqam training ground?"

Captain Buckley looked at Frank and gave a small nod of approval; the action wasn't over yet.

"Excuse me," yelled lady Corrigan as she pushed a trooper's filthy booted foot off her leg in its grubby leggings. "But I thought we were going home."

Frank gave her an engaging smile which did not remove the frown from off Lady Corrigan's face. "We will be…But not yet."

"Why not?"

"Well, you see, if we don't wipe out all traces of these vermin, they will simply come back at us. You might well be abducted again." He did not want to tell her that the Bell Huey did not have the flying range to get them back to Akrotiri and certainly nowhere near that destination with all of this weight on board. "So, we have to go to their lair and destroy them."

"Yes," shouted Lady Corrigan as she swept some of her red hair out of her face. "I see that. However, this terrorist organisation may have roots buried elsewhere."

"A good point," answered Frank. "But let us at least exterminate those that we know of."

Lady Corrigan nodded her understanding.

"And," continued Frank at the top of his voice, "I'm pretty sure that your husband will be going to do some rock lifting to see what crawls out, if he isn't doing that already. By the way…" Frank turned to Captain Buckley, cupping his left hand to the side of his mouth so that he could shout more effectively at the captain. "Would you send a message, to let the powers-that-be know that we have Lady Corrigan and Mister Gainsborough."

"Will do," Buckley shouted back. "As soon as we get on the ground." He stabbed his index finger downwards twice.

"Good…Now…" Frank turned to the accountant and again asked, "Where is the Intiqam training camp?"

The little man answered Frank with a shrug of his shoulders, "I don't know…I told you, I'm just the accountant."

"Okay," said Frank. "Clonk, take his laptop and ledgers off him and throw him out the door,"

"Oh, it'll be a pleasure," growled the Scotsman who was crushed up against the accountant in the limited space. He leered his best evil leer at the man. Coming through Clonk's mass of facial hair it had quite an effect.

"No! No! Please. I'm just…"

"The accountant," finished Frank. "Yes, I heard that. Now. Where's the training ground?"

The little man paused, but when Clonk hunched his wide shoulders and put out his big hands the man said,

"Alright! Alright! It's at a place called Wadi Talatah Ma!"

"Good," nodded Frank. "Where is it?"

"I…I don't know…I'm not a pilot…I don't know! I just get ferried backwards and forwards!"

Frank tended to believe him. This man was not a fighter. That much was true. But they needed to get to the camp fast and they needed to get there now. T Bone was doing a great job of flying the helicopter but, although he knew he was heading north-west by the helicopter's compass, he had no idea in which direction he *ought* to be flying. T Bone's job had been to get them up and away from danger and he had done just that, but he had no clue as to where he was or where to fly to.

Frank looked about him and shouted, "Heads up people! See if you can find any maps!"

There followed what resembled some sort of strange game of Twister with the members of Shadows and the SAS scrambling about inside the Huey.

After a few long moments Tandy shouted, "Hey! What's this?"

In a plastic see-thru folder in a pocket in the back of the co-pilot's seat was a set of maps.

"Let's see!" yelled Frank. "Give me some room here."

The troopers pushed back out of the way so that Frank could get onto his knees and put the collection of maps on the steel floor of the helicopter. There were five of them, each about the size of a daily newspaper.

Frank rejected the first three and then cried, "This is it!" He jabbed a finger onto the map. Qaryat Musawara was clearly marked and to the north of that village a blue circle had been drawn in felt-tip pen around a valley. Inside the circle was the name Wadi Talatah Ma. Frank turned to T Bone. "What's our heading?"

"North-west, Boss."

Frank checked the map again. He traced his finger north-west from Qaryat Musawara across the map. "T Bone, take us due north."

T Bone gave a thumbs up and, moments later, the helicopter veered to its new course.

Frank then climbed into the vacant co-pilot's seat, and then he began to intently compare the terrain that he could see below him out of the cockpit window and the large observation glass bubbles in the footwell that was forward of his feet with the map that he had on his lap. Frank Cross had had to rely many times in his various careers in the army, the police force and as an agent of the Specialist Operations Unit on the ability to read a map and check it against real geographical and topographical features, and he was doing that now.

Tandy leaned forwards over the back of Frank's seat and put her mouth beside his ear. "Frank," she said. "Do you actually know where we are and where we are going?"

Without taking his attention off the map or the various valleys, gullies, mounds, hills and outcroppings that were racing past underneath them Frank said in his best Rocky Balboa voice, "Absolutely, absolutely."

Tandy giggled at the accurate impersonation and then asked, "Where?"

Frank put his right index finger on a spot on the map. "I'm pretty sure we're here."

"*Pretty* sure?"

"Very pretty," said Frank as he turned and looked into Tandy's eyes; she really did have the most beautiful eyes.

"How long 'til landing?" shouted Captain Buckley from behind him. Frank checked his Rolex and shouted back. "About ten minutes." Buckley turned to look around the crowded cabin. "Check your weapons!" he ordered.

**

The Iroquois came in low and from the north through the narrow canyon that led into the Wadi Talatah Ma with the terrorist camp not suspecting a thing. After all, they had not received any emergency contact from Qaryat Musawara, nor would they since the comms room was a smoking ruin. And this Huey was often used by al-Makira and his Second-in-Command on their unannounced lightening visits. Once again Frank regretted the lack of firepower from the helicopter as it could have reduced the terrorist camp to a torn and shattered wreck within a matter of seconds.

The Huey had already made one quick drop-off to the south of the valley on the plateau that overlooked the camp. Tandy and the SAS sniper had scrambled quickly out of the body of the Huey along with Lady Corrigan, Gainsborough and Ali. These last three were instructed to keep well back from the edge of the cliffs that rimmed the valley whilst Tandy and the SAS sniper crawled into a position on the very edge of the cliff above the southern canyon. Here they lay down their bellies side-by-side and only about four feet apart. From their position they could look down on the whole of the training camp some one hundred feet below.

Men and women were already up and about in the camp and Tandy could hear orders being barked at the groups of fanatical volunteers who were being groomed to take their hate to the Western world. But none were taking any notice of the Huey.

The SAS sniper was quite enjoying being near to Tandy. He reckoned that she was quite a looker. Without turning his head as he watched through the rifle's 'scope he said,

"D'you know…you look like that film star? What's her name…?"

"Sofia Loren," said Tandy as she sighted through her own rifle's 'scope at the camp.

Tandy, of course, had heard it all before as she was often mistaken for the beautiful actress, Halle Berry. The trooper had used an opening line that she's been hit with a good few times in the past, except by Frank. He had never been that cheesy or predictable.

"What?" said the trooper, shaking his helmeted head. "No, no…It's…Ummm…"

Tandy moved her rifle to pick out targets without actually pulling the trigger. She and the SAS trooper were having to wait for the main attack to happen as a shot from them would put the camp on instant alert.

"What's *your* name?" asked Tandy.

There was a long pause. Then he said, almost apologetically, "Desmond."

Tandy made a sort of spluttering sound through her lips then said, "Desmond?"

"Yeah. Desmond Trubshaw."

"Blimey," said Tandy.

Hurriedly, Desmond said, "But my mates call me Buzz."

"Why?" Tandy didn't look round. "Do you keep bees?" She smiled to herself.

"Ay? Oh, no…Oh, I get it. Joke…No, it's cos of my face and my haircut."

Desmond Trubshaw did indeed have a very severe buzz cut which, when his helmet was removed, made him look as though he had a blonde scrubbing brush attached to the top of his head. But the addition of the word *face* that he had used in the sentence piqued Tandy's curiosity.

"Your face?"

"Yeah. They reckon I look like Buzz Lightyear…You know…From Toy Story."

Tandy turned her head and looked at Desmond. He was facing her. He did indeed look like the character from the hit film; his face was rectangular in shape with blue eyes above slightly prominent rosy cheek bones, and he had a well-shaped nose and a wide mouth, which was smiling at her.

"See what I mean?"

Tandy smiled back. "Okay, yes, I see what you mean." She smiled some more. "Buzz it is. I'm Tandy." And she turned to sight through her rifle 'scope again, but still with an amused smile playing about her lips.

The Huey touched down in a cloud of swirling dust which made it difficult for those on board to see the camp laid out in front of them, but it also meant that the terrorists could not see into the Huey either. But the Huey was such a frequent visitor that no-one in the camp paid it much heed as it landed a few yards away from a Chinook.

Frank pointed at this other helicopter and shouted. "That's our lift home!"

"Just a minute," said Lady Corrigan. "I thought you said *this* was our lift home?" She meant the Huey.

"No," put in Captain Buckley. "This Huey doesn't have the range to get us back to Cyprus…But that baby does."

Lady Corrigan looked at Frank who gave a gallic shrug.

Lady Corrigan's lips twitched in a half-smile. She realised that Frank had known that there was no way that the Huey was going to get them anywhere near getting home, and that he had not been about to tell her. She was beginning to understand this man – tough and resourceful, but also sensitive and thoughtful.

The moment the skids of the Huey bumped down onto the bare earth the Shadows and the SAS team were out, scattering in a wide arc in front of the helicopter and facing the camp. Only the accountant stayed on board, cowering in a corner, with his fingers jammed in his ears and with his ledgers and laptop still shoved up under his right armpit.

By hand signals alone Captain Buckley efficiently deployed his troops. Because Frank and his men had all served in the British Army, they knew these hand signals off by heart and they fell into a well-practiced manoeuvre: two of the SAS, a man and a woman, went straight to the Chinook with orders to shoot anyone they found there, secure it, check it for fuel, and empty it of any cargo so that they had room for the passengers for the flight back to Cyprus. The rest of the team, including Frank's men, split into four groups of two. At a run, two SAS men with T Bone and Clonk struck the first row of the tents to their left on the eastern side of the wadi, bursting in through the tent flaps and shooting anyone they found in there before moving swiftly on. While that was happening, Frank went with Tommo, and Captain Buckley went with his other female trooper, to move left and right respectively in a running advance on the parade ground and shooting range.

With the SAS and Shadows rifles now firing, and with the first of the terrorists screaming as they were shot dead, the rest of the camp erupted into life. Men and women began to spill out of other tents not yet reached by the men who had come to destroy them.

Chaos reigned amongst the terrorists. The assault rifles of the striking teams clattered; grenades were tossed into tents. Explosions tore the air, bullets flew, terrorists yelled and screamed. Fires broke out and smoke began to drift across the valley floor.

From her position high above the valley floor Tandy zeroed in on a man who was standing and aiming a rifle at T Bone, placing the man in the 'scope's cross-hairs.

BANG

Down he went. Tandy moved her rifle again.

BANG

Another terrorist went down.

BANG

And again, another hit.

Alongside Tandy Buzz had watched as Tandy had dropped all three of her targets. "Man," he said. "Who taught you to shoot like that?"

"Same as you," she answered, not taking her eye away from the rifle's 'scope. "The British army." And then added, "And Frank Cross."

Buzz sighted down his own 'scope. "Is Frank your boyfriend?"

Tandy smiled slightly to herself at the other sniper's interest. "Yes," she answered. "He's my boyfriend…In fact, he's more than just a boyfriend."

She fired again. Another terrorist went down.

"Oh," said Buzz. "I see." Buzz fired. Another one went down. He fired once more. A terrorist collapsed beside a Landrover.

Tandy fired again.

Buzz fired twice. The terrorists were going down like ducks in a fairground shooting gallery – except this was messier as the large rounds that they were firing punched into and through people, sending them flying as their blood sprayed from exit wounds.

Frank, Tommo, Buckley and the SAS soldier converged on the group of terrorists who were supposed to be taking target practice but who were now bunched up and entering into a state of panic.

"Turn around!" screamed their instructor. "Turn around! Shoot them!" He went down to a head shot from Buzz. The terrorists turned, bringing their guns up. Frank and his death squad wiped them out in short order so that within seconds the parade ground and target shooting range were littered with bodies. Captain Buckley instructed his SAS trooper to go amongst them to ensure they were dead whilst he and Frank and Tommo sprinted across to the southernmost and nearest row of tents and began to work their way through them, to join up with T Bone and Clonk and the rest of the SAS squad.

Tandy and Buzz had been taking out the defenders in a deadly efficient manner. Tandy picked up on a woman who dashed out of a tent and who began running for the northern defile. It was the teacher. She was carrying an AK47 and she ran past the front of a large collection of red oil drums that were off to the left-hand side of the compound. Tandy shot her in the back so that the big bullet tore through her and out of her chest. She went off her feet and went sprawling face first into the ground to land beside one of the oil drums.

Tandy dispassionately moved her rifle to seek out another victim.

And suddenly it was all over.

It had taken only five minutes.

Frank stood outside a tent and looked around. The wadi looked like a battlefield – which indeed it had been, albeit rather one-sided. Dead terrorists were everywhere; sprawled in the entrances of tents, up against the sides of vehicles and laying like broken dolls on the rocky beaten ground. They were laying amongst the heaps of tyres and slung in front of the ranks of oil drums. And the SAS and Frank's team had come away from the massacre without a single scratch.

"Right," called Frank. "Comms man to me! Explosives people place your charges! The rest of you collect as much intelligence as you can…" Frank was about to say more when a trooper called out to him and Captain Buckley and waved an arm. "Hey! You'd better see this!"

Frank and Buckley ran over to the trooper who pointed inside the tent that he was standing in front of.

Inside the tent were stacks of C-4 plastic explosive. They stood in an orderly display like slabs of nougat bars in a sweet shop. There were twenty slabs across the bottom, ten high and two deep, giving four hundred slabs of the deadly material, each in its own plastic wrapping. Beside them in cardboard boxes were the detonators used to set them off.

The captain whistled.

"Looks like we might have averted a disaster that was due to take place somewhere," said Frank. He looked at Buckley. "Can you blow this lot up?"

"Bloody right we can," answered the captain.

Frank glanced at his watch. "You've got ten minutes until wheels up!"

"Okay," said Buckley, and he turned to run and find his explosives experts.

Tommo had joined Frank who looked up at the big man and said, "get some men together and torch the other tents, and then head for the Chinook."

Frank turned and jogged over to the big helicopter as the explosives experts were heading for targets whilst the rest of the team disappeared inside the tents grabbing laptops, mobile phones, note books, papers, maps, anything that might give someone an insight into Intiqam and what they might do next – if they ever recovered from this.

Frank and Captain Buckley stood beside Chinook with the trooper with the communications pack.

"Right, mate," said Frank. "Inform whoever you need to that we have the hostages safe and well, and that we are coming into Akrotiri on Cyprus by captured Chinook."

The man nodded and grinned and fell to his task. It took a few moments to establish contact with Akrotiri; when he had finished the ten minutes were up and the training camp was burning. Those tents that had not been burning already were set light to and went up like dry tinder in the hot air; vehicle petrol tanks were exploding and the heaps of tyres were churning out thick black smoke that rose into the blue sky; it would not be long before the oil drums went up as well, helped on their way by the expertly placed C-4.

"Let's go!" Shouted Frank and he waved an arm at Tommo. "Tommo!"

"Yes Boss?" The big man came jogging towards him.

"Get the accountant and his books out of the Huey and into the Chinook and destroy the Huey."

"Yes Boss." And he jogged away through the clouds of acrid billowing smoke.

Captain Buckley looked at Frank. "Good job, Mister Cross."

They shook hands.

Up on the plateau Tandy stood up and looked down at Buzz.

"Time to go, Mister Lightyear."

Buzz rolled onto his left side. "Sure thing, Miss Berry."

They burst out laughing.

**

The Chinook had turned out to be fully fuelled, which saved the teams a lot of time. It took off with T Bone at the controls and it went straight up and out of the wadi churning its way through the broiling smoke-laden air and without having to bother going through the canyon again. The huge helicopter made the one stop on the plateau to pick up Tandy, Buzz, Lady Corrigan, Lawrence and Ali and then angled away from the valley.

Moments later a trooper, sitting uncomfortably inside the belly of the huge helicopter, pressed a button on a small hand-held black plastic box. This detonated the C-4 explosives they had placed, which ruptured the oil drums and turned their contents into a furnace. The same trooper then pressed another button and detonated the stacks of C-4 that they had discovered, which promoted a huge deafening blast and a massive fireball that totally consumed the Wadi Talatah Ma and wiped out nearly every trace of the training base. By the time all of that happened the Chinook was heading at top speed for the Akrotiri air-base on Cyprus.

**

Group Captain Baukham touched the fingers of his left hand to his forehead and groaned as the stolen Chinook came in to land at Akrotiri. He called for his sergeant and told him to get the teams out of the aircraft as fast as possible and to then lose the aircraft.

With its human cargo disembarked, the Chinook was somehow requisitioned by the British Royal Air Force and placed in a hangar. The hangar doors were pushed shut and, over the next few days, the helicopter was stripped down and apart for spares. It effectively disappeared. Chinook? What Chinook?

The Shadows and SAS, with Lady Corrigan, Lawrence Gainsborough, Ali and the accountant in tow, were hurried away from the helicopter and across to the office of the highly agitated Group Captain. Baukham told them all that he wanted them turned around and into the body of a Hercules transport aircraft…Now!

However, he had not reckoned on Lady Corrigan who, on arrival in the Group Captain's office, sat with her arms folded over her chest and, after Baukham had finished his tirade, demanded a shower, a change of clothes, and a meal for herself and anyone else of the rescue party that wanted them. She stared at Baukham and tapped a dirty bare foot on the floor to emphasise her requests.

Needless to say, Lady Corrigan got her demands met, including a very good meal for them all, courtesy of the Group Captain's chef.

After the meal, the Shadows team headed back to their hotel where they quickly showered and changed, with jeans, tee shirts, a variety of jackets, and trainers becoming the *de rigueur* dress code. Except for Tandy, who wore knee-high black high-heel boots over her skinny fit jeans. She was also wearing a black cotton shirt under a black leather zip-front bomber jacket that was tight-fitting around her waist. Then they grabbed their luggage, collectively smiled at the female receptionist, and checked out.

The receptionist watched them leave the hotel. She arched an eyebrow, tapped her pencil on the top of the reception desk, wondered what the hell they had all been up to, and then decided that it was best to forget all about them.

Outside the hotel a silver Mercedes taxi was waiting for Tommo, T Bone and Clonk. Their luggage went into the cavernous boot of the car and then the team said their goodbyes. The three men would be going to their separate homes via international passenger jets, whilst Tandy and Frank would be transported by the RAF because Frank wanted to make sure that the accountant and Ali got back to England.

As the Mercedes pulled away, Tandy and Frank turned with their own aircraft carry-on bags and hurried back to the RAF base.

While Frank and his team were off the air base, Baukham managed to persuade Lady Corrigan to reveal to a female staff member her vital statistics. Red was then duly issued with some blue and lacy underwear which Red wore under a pink shirt and a rather snug-fitting RAF issue tracksuit. Other members of the Baukham staff donated clothing to fit Ali, who ended up in black trousers, a blue and yellow checked shirt, a light-brown puffer jacket and a battered pair of blue trainers. Even the accountant was tidied up; he had to sit under guard in borrowed underpants while his djellaba and his own underpants were laundered and pressed in double-quick time. And while that happened, he was relieved of his laptop and ledgers which were placed with the other items that had been grabbed out of the line of tents by both of the teams. All these items were turned over to the SAS who placed them in a very large brown cardboard box that they had scrounged. The box bore the red trademark for Kellogg's Cornflakes and the troopers took turns to guard the box because it would probably now contain vital and important information rather than a breakfast cereal. The British Secret Services would have a field day with this little lot when Frank got it back to them.

Eventually, with everyone fed, watered and washed as bright as a new pin, and wearing clean clothes, the rescued and the rescue party, which included all the members of the SAS, were placed back on board the Hercules. As it headed along the runway, Group Captain Baukham watched it go and breathed out a sigh of relief.

"Sergeant Lock, get me an aspirin, will you?"

"Sir."

As the massive aircraft lifted off, thundering into the Greek air-space, Tandy moaned, "I know they did what they could for us, but, never-the-less, they couldn't wait to get rid of us."

"Happens all the time, m'dear," said Buckley. "We rescue people and are called heroes, but when we actually meet other human beings, they act as if we've got the plague."

"Well," said Tandy, pouting. "It's not fair."

"Neither's a black horse," said Frank, and she punched him in the arm.

**

The Hercules levelled out at twenty-five-thousand feet, and at that point the rescuers and rescued were allowed out of their webbing seats that were ranged along both the vibrating port and starboard walls of the vast empty cavern that was the body of the aircraft. They were no longer encumbered by weaponry or grenades as these had been stowed into heavy-duty lockable dark green plastic boxes which were placed up against the bulkhead that separated them from the flight-deck. Because of this freedom from equipment Tandy and Frank, the SAS, Lady Corrigan, Lawrence Gainsborough and Ali gathered in a loose standing group within the body of the Hercules.

There followed something of a party atmosphere because they were all going home. All except Amir Darwish, the little accountant, who sat on a webbing seat, off to one side like a timid mouse. He watched as the group celebrated a successful rescue mission; al-Makira and his Second-in-Command had been killed, a terrorist training camp had been wiped out, valuable intelligence had been recovered, a village had been freed from the fear of the terrorist tyranny, and new friends had been made. The party atmosphere was further enhanced because the SAS squad had carried out their own Special Ops on the Akrotiri air base and had managed to procure a crate full of bottles of Mythos beers, as well as three bottles of Metaxa brandy, each holding a litre of alcohol.

Fifteen minutes after the first beer cap popped Frank felt his mobile phone buzz in his dark-blue blazer hip pocket. Frank left the frivolity and went and sat down in one of the webbing seats that was just in front of the bulkhead door on the port side of the aircraft, a door that led through to the flight-deck. He held the mobile to his ear. He listened for a few moments and then said, "Okay", and hung up. He looked around at the party members. The group stood about, joking and laughing as they swayed and joggled to the aerial movements of the Hercules, and Tandy had discovered that high-heel boots were not the best form of footwear for moving about inside a military aircraft. The Hercules is not built for comfort like a passenger jet, and keeping on the move in one is much easier than trying to stand still – but not in high-heel boots.

Tandy had been watching Frank, and she knew enough of his facial expressions by now to know that something was wrong. She extricated herself from the combined attentions of three young male SAS troopers and turned towards her partner. She tottered over to Frank and sat down next to him. She had given up trying to look fashionable and she started to pull her boots off. She turned to Frank and asked, "What's up?" Now, with her right leg bootless, she began to massage her right foot through her thin nylon flesh-coloured pop-sock.

Frank's head swivelled towards her and he quietly asked, "Is Ali still carrying his gun?"

Tandy had to put her head near to Frank's head to hear him because of the background noise of roaring engines, clanks, rattles and partying people.

"Yes," she answered, equally as quietly. "I noticed that he didn't hand it in, but then you didn't hand yours in either." She got her other boot off.

"Neither did you," said Frank.

Frank was wearing his Smith and Wesson revolver in a shoulder holster by his left armpit and underneath his blazer. Tandy was carrying a compact Beretta Nano, a small easily concealed 9mm semi-automatic pistol. It was the same model of gun that she had used to execute Aarif El-Sayed in his London flat. She had it in a large zipped inside pocket of her bomber jacket. As civilians they were not obliged to turn in their weapons after a mission.

Tandy asked, "Why are you asking?"

"Because he's not who he says he is."

"Who is he then?" she whispered.

"Well, he's not MI Six."

"How do you know?"

"Without him knowing, I took a photo of him on my phone when we were on the air base and sent it to Sir Michael. He's just confirmed that MI Six do not recognise him as one of theirs, and they don't know who he is."

Keeping her voice down, Tandy said again, "Who is he then?" Tandy knew enough about covert surveillance to avoid turning to look at Ali.

Frank hissed, "He could well be a terrorist."

"A terrorist? But that doesn't make sense. He shot Wetton when she tried to shoot you."

"Yes, but was that to keep his cover story?"

Tandy considered this, then said, "I see what you mean, Frank."

"And if he is a terrorist, that makes him a terrorist with a gun."

"Jeez," breathed Tandy.

Frank asked, "Where's he carrying it?"

"It's tucked in a holster by his left arm-pit, under his jacket." Tandy frowned as she considered something else. "What if he isn't a terrorist?"

"Fair point," said Frank, nodding. "But we can't risk assuming he isn't. He's got to be suppressed; in case he is."

"Suppressed," said Tandy. "You mean killed."

"If it comes to that…yes. And we've got to act now."

The aircraft suddenly lurched and the party members staggered then gave a raucous cheer as beer bottles were waved in the air; trying to stand up whilst drinking in the shuddering aircraft had become a game.

Tandy kept her face towards Frank. She pursed her lips, then urgently asked, "Where is he, Frank?"

"He's standing away from the group on the opposite side of the cabin, in front of the exit door…Oh, damn!" hissed Frank.

"What?"

"He's standing beside on of the boxes we put the spare grenades into…and the lid's loose. I watched them being locked down."

"But that doesn't mean that he's actually been able to grab one."

"Agreed," said Frank. "But, if he's the terrorist we think he is, or might be, can we take that risk?"

They both knew that a single grenade exploding inside the Hercules would not cause enough material damage to bring the huge aircraft down – but it would kill a good number of the SAS. And it would probably kill or maim both Tandy and Frank as well as Lady Corrigan and Lawrence Gainsborough. And if Ali started shooting before he let the grenade explode, he would probably kill them all.

Tandy and Frank had to act fast.

"So," said Tandy, "we must assume he's used this party as a handy distraction to help himself to a grenade. Is he holding it?"

"Could be," said Frank. "He's got his left hand in his jacket pocket." In truth, Ali was still wearing the baggy second-hand puffer jacket and there was ample room in a side pocket to conceal his left hand and a fragmentation grenade. It was the reason that neither Frank nor Tandy could just pull their guns and shoot him, for, if he was holding a live grenade, then the moment the bullets hit him his dying action would be to release the spoon which would detonate the device.

Tandy looked down at her feet and frowned. When she looked up, she said, "Do you think he's actually holding a live grenade?"

"I don't know. If he managed to pick one up without anyone seeing it then he might have also been able to pull the pin undetected."

Tandy frowned some more. She knew from the knowledge she had gained from Frank on the flight out to Iraq that the cabin they were in was pressurised. She also knew that any explosion could blow a large gaping hole in the fuselage of the Hercules, a hole that would suddenly drop the pressure of the cabin and might cause anyone inside, and near the hole, to be sucked out. But if the aircraft could drop to ten thousand feet that would not happen. And Tandy knew that the cabin pressure would be safe at ten thousand feet because that was the height that she had jumped from with Frank. She looked at him and said,

"I've got an idea. Go and tell the pilot to drop to ten thousand feet."

He raised an eyebrow. "And then what?"

"No time to explain…Just leave the rest to me." With that she put her hand in the waist pocket of her jacket. She brought out her small travelling plastic sewing box with its pins and cotton and needles and looked at Frank who whispered,

"Surely not? Do you always carry that thing around with you?"

"A girl never knows when she's going to need her sewing kit." And before Frank could reply she said, "Get going Frank, Ali could start shooting and drop that grenade at any moment."

In the absence of any real plan of his own, and placing his trust in this very capable lady, Frank got up and headed for the door that led through to the flight-deck of the aircraft to get the pilot to descend.

Tandy kept her back towards Ali, unzipped her leather jacket almost to her waist and then unbuttoned the top three buttons of her shirt. She took hold of the top button, yanked it off, and put it in the hip pocket of her jeans. Then she turned and looked over at Ali, caught his eye, and gave him a winning smile. He gave her a rather weak one back.

She now had to try and pacify Ali as much as possible and weaken any resolve that he might have before she made any attempt at a move to disarm him. She had therefore decided to blatantly use her sexuality. Still in her pop-socks, Tandy moved across the cold hard steel floor of the cabin. She skirted around the jostling party and approached Ali in the somewhat fluid manner of a leopard stalking its prey; her almost bare feet were moving as if she were walking along a cat-walk instead of the floor of a Hercules transport aircraft and her hips took on a slight roll as if her waist had turned to molten wax. It was an outrageous display of sexual temptation. She arrived in front of Ali and put her left hand on her hip, transferring her weight into her left leg and pushing out her chest.

Tandy was a very beautiful woman, and here she was, displaying herself. Ali's eyes widened, his pulse quickened, and his throat constricted.

Frank went through to the flight-deck and the pilot looked around. "Hello," he said. "What's going on back there? It sounds like a party."

"It is," said Frank. "However, we have a problem." And he outlined what it was.

The air-crew's facial expressions went from alarm to grim determination.

"What do you want me to do?" asked the pilot.

"We have a plan to solve the situation. Will you please drop to ten thousand feet as gently as possible so that the terrorist does not suspect that we are descending?"

"Will do," said the pilot. "And then I'll radio both Brize Norton and the nearest landing site, in case we need an emergency touch-down."

Frank nodded at the sensible precautions. The flight engineer spoke up, "Do you need any help back there?"

"What, with a cabin full of SAS troopers? I shouldn't think so. One mistake by this terrorist and they'll have him for dinner as well as breakfast!"

"Okay," agreed the pilot. He looked across to his co-pilot, "Let's do this nice and easy." He immediately began to organise a slow descent.

The aircraft bumped and Tandy used it to sway just a little. She was holding her plastic sewing kit box in her right hand. Ali took his eyes away from the unbuttoned open gap at the top of Tandy's shirt, where he could see the beginnings of her cleavage, and he glanced at the box. It was open, revealing the pins and needles and small bolts of different coloured cottons, but it was obviously not a weapon, so he ignored it. Women, as far as he knew, carried all sorts of things like this on their persons or in their handbags. Perhaps she was going to sew a button onto something, or patch something up.

"How are you doing, Ali?" she asked. She actually batted her eyelashes a couple of times. "Have you ever been up in one of these aircraft before?"

"No," answered Ali rather abruptly. His smile had faded from his face.

Tandy lifted the open box and peered inside it, as if to select a pin or cotton. "I've lost a button on my shirt." She fingered the top of her shirt just a little too much with her free left hand. She looked up from the box, shifted her hips and continued to smile at Ali. The aircraft shuddered again and Tandy shifted her hips at the motion, then moved her shoulders and chest as if her back was somehow uncomfortable. "They move about a bit, don't they?" She arched her left eyebrow because she'd referred to the Hercules but, with her chest pushing forwards, she'd broadly hinted at something else.

No-one was looking their way. Ali was standing with his feet spread apart and his back to the cabin wall, the exit door was just to his right and the other bulkhead door leading through to the flight-deck was just beyond that. He had never been presented with such an erotic display right in front of him ever before in his life and, although Tandy had the most beautiful eyes, his own eyes kept glancing down at her chest. He fought with his emotions – for The Cause.

"Tandy," said Ali and almost choking on the name. He took a side-step away from her. "I know what you are up to." He took a breath. "I just saw you talking to your boyfriend. You're thinking of taking my gun off me, aren't you? Isn't that right, Tandy?"

Tandy just stood and looked at him as innocently as she could, as if she did not know what he was talking about.

Ali had some small beads of sweat forming at each of his temples. His voice hardened. "And where is your boyfriend? I saw him head forwards. Is he going to try and sneak up on me?"

"He went to the toilet," she answered and blinked heavily a couple of times.

"Yeah, right," sneered Ali. "Let's drop the pretence, shall we?"

Tandy took a breath and moved her spine and hips in a sinuous movement. "Don't you like me, Ali?" If any of the male members of the on-going party had noticed Tandy's small bodily contortion the testosterone levels would have soared. But, again, none of them noticed.

Ali slid his right hand into his jacket, near to his gun. "Don't give me that shit!" His eyes flared with anger and Tandy realised that the temptation moment had passed and that her ruse was not going to work. She was standing in front of him but too far away as yet to be able to grab him if he managed to seize his weapon. Tandy was now going to have to improvise, to try and get nearer and also give Frank time to get the pilot to lower the gigantic aircraft down through the sky without Ali putting two-and-two together and realising what was really going on.

"Okay," she said, lifting her chin and dropping the charade. "You've sussed me. So, just who the hell are you?"

Ali stiffened before he visibly relaxed and then smiled, as if this were all some terribly amusing game. Tandy felt like slapping the smile off his face. Instead, she answered her own question, "Frank and I think you're a terrorist."

Ali knew then that in his turn he had also been found out and his smile turned from amused through to sly. "I don't suppose that admitting that now can do any harm, especially since I am holding a grenade in my hand." He moved his left hand in his pocket, but he had not said the words *live grenade*, so was he holding a grenade with the pin still in it?

"And what do you intend to do with your grenade?" asked Tandy. "If you pull the pin, you will kill not only these people, but also yourself."

"I," said Ali, "am prepared to die for The Cause."

Despite the subliminal prompt she had given him, Ali did not pick up on what she had hoped for. *Damn! He didn't mention the pin.* Had he pulled it, or hadn't he?

"The cause?" she asked.

"Yes. Vengeance on the Western world. The Cause."

"Oh fuck off," scoffed Tandy. "What do you think your cause really is? The destruction of the Western World? Don't make me laugh." The aircraft gave another of its shudders and Tandy used this to take, what appeared to be, an unbalanced step towards the terrorist. It was faked. This was, after all, a lady whose balance was so good that she could stand on one leg on the ridge tile of a roof. She had, however, been able to move nearer to him.

Due to the shudder Ali had also momentarily lost his balance, and to regain it he briefly glanced down at the floor, and in that short time he had not noticed her movement. When he looked up he noticed that Tandy had lifted the sewing kit to her chest level where she hugged it against her right breast.

"There's always a money trail," continued Tandy. "Some fat cat sitting in a palace making money out of these so-called causes. Who is it that supplies you with weapons and equipment? And at what exorbitant rate are they selling all of that to you for? That's what all these causes are really about…Money, and power over the little guys. Guys like you. Wake up Ali, you're just a pawn in a much bigger game and you're also cannon fodder. Can't you see? You've been used!"

That last word was like a slap in the face to Ali and, as an angry reaction, with his right hand he pulled his gun from the holster - his gun that was his much-valued present from al-Makira. He levelled it at Tandy's stomach.

At that moment, Captain Buckley happened to glance over to the pair of them and he saw the gun come out. "Hold it right there!" he shouted. It was a perfect piece of mis-timing. Like bad news arriving at a wedding reception where the band goes quiet just before the guests start to falter into silence, the on-board party came to a halt and all faces turned towards Ali.

Shit! thought Tandy. In an instant she had lost what small control she had of the situation. *Anything might happen now!* She'd made a big mistake. She should have struck earlier when she had the chance. When Ali had looked down. Tandy could have stamped her foot in annoyance.

Ali looked at them all as they stared uncomprehendingly back at him, then he spoke up. "Captain Buckley, do not be a fool. I know you are not armed, and neither are your men. But, as you can see, I am. So, tell your men not to move," he ordered. "Tell them, or I will shoot this girl and then drop the grenade that I am holding." There were some small movements made by the personnel of the two teams – personnel readying themselves for action. Ali looked at them, prodded the gun towards Tandy's navel, and said, "Do it captain!"

Buckley hesitated then gave the command, and the SAS, although weaponless, squared up to the terrorist, who smiled a cunning smile at them.

Again, Ali gave an order. "Tell your men to sit on the floor, and then join them."

At the captain's direction, the troopers reluctantly sat down cross-legged or kneeling on the cabin floor. Amir Darwish did the same.

Captain Buckley then copied them by going down onto his knees. However, Lady Corrigan and Lawrence Gainsborough remained on their feet and Tandy could feel the almost electric crackle of reined-in action pulsating through the air as the seated teams glowered up at Ali.

Ali nodded towards Lady Corrigan and Lawrence Gainsborough who were standing almost in the centre of the seated group. "You as well."

They sat.

Ali looked at Tandy. She had not sat down and she had dropped the display of her sexual allure. Ali watched her. He had noticed the change in her, from soft to ice hard, and was about to tell her to back off when she asked,

"What's your real name? I bet it's not Ali."

"What do you care?"

"Well, if I'm going to be shot or blown up, I would at least like to know who's going to do it."

Ali considered his answer then said, "Very well, my real name is Nadeem al-Hadid." Proudly he said, "It means Virtue, and Iron."

"Hah!" spat Tandy as she put her left hand back onto her hip. "That's a laugh. It should be idiot and dick head!"

Ali's face and eyes hardened at the insults and his lips drew back slightly from his teeth. He was about to say something when the aircraft bumped again. Ali swayed a little and adjusted his stance, but Tandy remained rock-solid and balanced.

Frank, by now, had finished what he needed to do on the flight-deck. With the giant aircraft already slowly descending he had then made for the starboard side bulkhead door and pressed his ear against it. He could clearly hear the conversation between Tandy and Ali on the other side of the door, but he did not know that Ali had a gun pointed at Tandy's stomach and he was waiting for some sort of signal from her. He knew that the exit door was not very far inside the cabin from where he was standing. Would he be able to grab Ali, open the door and throw him out? He did not know, but if it came to it that is what he would try and do.

Frank put his hand onto the bulkhead door's latch and gripped it.

"So," said Tandy. "All of that seeming to help us rescue Gainsborough, and Lady Corrigan, was a smoke screen?"

"Yes," Ali smiled his sly smile. "I knew that if I acted against you, you would kill me, so I pretended to be on your side and that way I might have been able to get to Sir Michael Corrigan. I even saved Frank's life to add credence to my idea…Where is Cross?" Ali frowned and suddenly looked a little nervous. "He seems to be a long time in the toilet…" He glanced towards the front of the joggling aircraft.

"And by shooting Gail Wetton," Tandy interrupted Ali's thoughts, "you got rid of someone who could give you away…Very clever…Except that plan has now gone to crap."

"Perhaps." Ali's lips twitched as his attention came back to the girl in front of him. "I might not now be able to get to Corrigan, but I can still kill you, and Cross, and this lot." He inclined his head to indicate the seated personnel and then smiled some more at Tandy. "I had hoped to kill Cross not long after he had murdered al-Makira, but there were too many people around me who were handy with a gun for me to do that. Therefore, I simply bided my time…And look where it's got me. I have you both in the same place at the same time. The great Frank Cross, and his precious girlfriend." He sneered at her. "Together with a British MP, Lady Corrigan, and an SAS squad. You are all at my mercy, and I get to finish what al-Makira started…Vengeance!" His head turned and he waved his gun at the seated teams. And that small moment of foolish pride, that split-second of egotism, was all that Tandy needed. Her right hand whipped across her body to her pins and she pulled a naked one out of its bed. With the pearlescent end of the pin safe between the tips of her thumb and forefinger she lunged with it at Ali's exposed throat like a fencer delivering the final scoring thrust with an epee.

As the pin went into the skin of his neck Ali reacted first by jerking his gun up and firing and, simultaneously, his left hand came out of his pocket to snatch at the dress-maker's pin, and with it came the grenade which left Ali's fingers and dropped onto the floor.

"Grenade!" shouted Buckley and the seated passengers threw themselves flat and in a ragged heap as the gun's bullet went high. Captain Buckley threw himself onto Lady Corrigan in an effort to protect her from any explosion as the bullet loudly struck a steel cross beam in the roof of the aircraft, after which it then ricocheted dangerously around the cabin before coming to rest with a rattling clatter in a corner.

At the sound of the gun firing Frank had twisted the door latch and then rammed open the door with his left shoulder. He leapt into the cabin not quite knowing what to expect, but ready to lay down his life for Tandy and his brothers-in-arms.

Ali had felt the pin-prick like the hot sting of a wasp. His body had overreacted by firing his gun and dropping the grenade, and in the milliseconds that it took for the neuro-toxin to invade his body and tear through his nervous system he tried to cry out. He tried to turn to Tandy. But all he saw was blackness as his heart stopped, his lungs stopped and his brain and all of his bodily functions shut down. The cabin went black, his knees gave way, his hand holding the gun dropped as his arm collapsed, and he fell heavily face down and full length, smashing his forehead and nose onto the steel floor.

All eyes fell on the grenade that was rolling about beside the corpse.

The spoon was still in place.

Frank bent down and picked up the device.

He rubbed his left shoulder then tossed the grenade from one hand to the other, as if he were about to juggle with it.

"All safe," he called out.

There was a pause and then the seated team cheered. They would have thrown hats up into the air if they had been wearing any.

Captain Buckley and Lady Corrigan got to their feet as everyone else got to theirs. "Captain," said Lady Corrigan as imperiously as possible. "Will you stop pawing me? I appreciate that you are trying to dust me off, but it's like being mauled by a bear."

Buckley took his hands away from Lady Corrigan's exquisitely sculptured body and looked suitably chastised. However, Lady Corrigan smiled at him and put out a hand to regally touch the side of his face. She softly patted his cheek.

The SAS now crowded around Tandy who had retrieved her deadly pin and replaced it into its plastic container after which she had moved a couple of paces away from the body. Frank was standing beside her, holding her hand.

Lady Corrigan took a few uneven swaying steps, pushed her way into the admiring line of men, and stood directly in front of Frank. "Well, it seems that you have saved my life once again, Mister Cross."

"All part of the service, ma'am," smiled Frank and was caught unawares when Red went up onto her toes and kissed his mouth. There were cheers of approval from the SAS squad. She broke the embrace, smiled into his eyes and then she looked at Tandy, who was frowning.

"I owe him that one, my dear," said Red and so Tandy nodded and smiled. Red then looked down at Ali. She took her eyes away from the dead body and muttered "Jesus." Her eyes came to rest on Tandy's face which was still smiling serenely.

Tandy was standing in her pop-socks and swaying gently to the movement of the Hercules, standing as if nothing had just happened. Standing as if it was all perfectly normal to be standing with your boots off in a military aircraft full of SAS troopers with a corpse at your feet. A corpse that had been made that way via a lethal injection.

"Jesus," said Lady Corrigan again. She looked back down at the body. "I wouldn't have believed it if I hadn't just seen it."

"Scary, isn't she?" said Frank, and he softly squeezed Tandy's hand.

*****

On arriving back at RAF Brize Norton, the Hercules was minus the body of Nadeem al-Hadid as it had been flung unceremoniously out of the aircraft's starboard exit door somewhere over the Mediterranean Sea. If there was no body then there could be no inquest. Body? What body? Terrorist? No idea what you're talking about. Frank had then informed the pilot that the Hercules could climb to a higher altitude and had also informed him and the rest of the aircrew of the events that had taken place on board. Not surprisingly the crew were somewhat shocked; all of this drama had been acted out literally behind their backs.

"How do I explain the terrorist being ejected from my aircraft?" asked the pilot. It was a fair question.

"You don't," answered Frank.

"I don't?" The pilot raised an eyebrow.

"Do you have a passenger list?" asked Frank, grinning.

"Of course not. This is a Special Ops flight...Oh."

Frank continued grinning. "Exactly."

"Fair enough," said the pilot.

"There we are then. All's well that ends well. I'm going back to the party, before they drink all the beer."

After landing, Frank had telephoned Sir Michael Corrigan to inform him of his wife's safe arrival. Sir Michael was generous with his thanks and clearly delighted and relieved that the rescue mission had worked. He wanted to be reunited with his wife as soon as possible and Frank informed the Knight of the Realm that he and Tandy would accompany Red and make sure she got back to her home safely.

"Didn't you say you had this character, Ali, with you?" asked Sir Michael.

"Oh, him," said Frank. "No, he got off the Hercules and went for a dip in the Med on the way back."

"Good at high diving, was he?" enquired Sir Michael, who entirely got the picture.

"Olympic standard," answered Frank, and he ended the call.

Lady Corrigan ordered a cab.

**

The cab that Lady Corrigan ordered left Brize Norton and rolled up outside her house just off North End Way near to Hampstead Heath, North London. It was just after eight-o-clock in the evening and getting dark, and to Tandy, Frank and Lady Corrigan it had been a long day, a *very* long day.

Lady Corrigan got out of the cab, still dressed in her rather close-fitting RAF tracksuit, and was accompanied up to the front door of her house by Frank and Tandy. Frank and Tandy were still in their respective blazer and bomber jackets and jeans, and Tandy was now wearing her high-heel boots again.

Red almost skipped up to the front door of her house where she rang the doorbell and, a heartbeat later, the door opened and Sir Michael flung his arms around his wife, kissed her and all but wrestled her inside into the bright hallway, calling, "Come in Tandy, Frank, come in, come in!"

They went into the large room to the left of the front door. It was lit by two standard lamps that were placed in the front and rear far corners of the room; they gave the room a soft and restful glow. The room had a large plain dark-blue carpet on the floor and plain apple-white walls. The wall opposite the entrance door had a set of shelves that housed books and curios. The room also had a large flat screen television, a small round-topped table, a three-piece-suite in dark leather, a small wooden cabinet set beneath the set of shelves, and a Giant Schnauzer, named Cromwell, who lay in a basket in the far corner of the room and lazily lifted one eyelid. Through that one open eye the dog regarded Frank and Tandy and went back to sleep. If it was acting as a guard dog, it had just failed.

"Champagne!" cried Sir Michael and he went to the small round-topped table that held some champagne flutes and a bottle of Bollinger that was chilling in a Georgian silver ice bucket. He handed the flutes out.

The happy chatting group stood in a square in the middle of the floor with Lady Corrigan standing with her back to the door, Frank on her left, Tandy on her right and Sir Michael facing her. Sir Michael popped the cork, they all cheered, and Sir Michael poured the champagne into outstretched glasses.

"Now," said Sir Michael. "What shall we drink to?...How about a successful mission?"

They raised their glasses and chorused, "To a successful mission."

Frank's head then moved slightly to his right and then back again; he had noticed that someone had just turned the light off in the hall outside the room, and that hall was now in darkness.

Tandy had seen Frank's eyes swivel and she had followed his glance. Her eyes went back to Frank's and she gave the smallest of movements with her left eyebrow. That eyebrow twitch said *I saw it as well.*

Someone was out in the hall.

"Sir Michael," began Tandy, as casually as she could. "Do you keep an agent in the house with you? Like a bodyguard?"

"No," smiled Sir Michael. "The bodyguards are out in the grounds. Why?"

"Oh, I just wondered. That's all." She returned his smile and moved her champagne glass from her right hand to her left so that she could get to her Beretta Nano in quick timing.

Frank took a mouthful of champagne and noted Tandy's hand movement. Frank's ability to fast draw a gun from either a hip holster or shoulder holster and fire and hit a target was legendary. He copied Tandy, moving his champagne glass into his left hand before undoing the buttons on his blazer so that both sides of the jacket hung loose.

Cromwell then lifted his head and opened both eyes. He got out of his basket, stretched and then ambled over to Sir Michael. The big dog then looked up at Sir Michael who smiled and produced a dog biscuit from a trouser pocket for the dog to enjoy. Two chomps of the dog's jaws and the biscuit was gone; it was like giving an elephant a strawberry.

Cromwell sat down on his haunches, continuing to look pleadingly at Sir Michael, pretending that it had not eaten for weeks.

"Soppy old thing," said Sir Michael who scratched at the dog's head then asked, "More champagne anyone?" He looked around the group.

"Why not?" said Frank, holding out an empty glass. He smiled broadly at Sir Michael and said, "And then, you can tell me who this lady is." He diverted his glass from Sir Michael and moved it towards Lady Corrigan.

"What?" said Tandy as she, instead of Frank, received a top-up of more champagne into her glass from Sir Michael. She pointed with her free right hand at Red and was about to say something when Frank interrupted her,

"No Tandy." Frank shook his head. "This is not Lady Corrigan. Granted she's the same height, build and approximate age, and she has red hair, but she is not Lady Corrigan."

Lady Corrigan stared at Frank Cross as if he had gone mad. "Really, Mister Cross…" began Red.

"Really, Frank…" Sir Michael began to protest.

"Really, Michael," said Lady Corrigan as she stepped from the darkened hallway into the room. "I think you've been found out, my dear. And I think Miss Trudeau…" She nodded to Tandy who was standing with her mouth open in shock, "and Mister Cross, deserve an explanation…don't you dear?...May I have some champagne please?"

"Wha…?" began Tandy, but no other words would come out.

Frank chuckled.

Lady Corrigan's lustrous locks of flaming red hair were tumbled about her shoulders over the top of her black silk shirt that was tucked into the waistband of a pair of skinny-fit black designer jeans. Her bare feet were in a pair of kitten-heeled mules that had blush-pink feathers over the foot strap. She wore bright red nail varnish on her toenails and fingernails which matched her hair colour. Then, as she stood before them, she put her right hand on her hip and gave a hair toss that would have given Rita Hayworth in the 1946 film *Gilda* a run for her money. At that moment, Frank thought that, apart from Tandy, Red Corrigan was one of the sexiest women that he had ever seen.

Sir Michael went to the wooden cabinet to get another glass. Having retrieved one he handed it to the real Lady Corrigan and then poured her some bubbly.

"Cheers!" said Lady Corrigan. She waved the glass around the group, and took a sip.

"Cheers!" they all chorused – all except Tandy, who was still standing with her mouth open.

"When did you find out?" asked Sir Michael.

Frank answered, "As soon as she was pushed into the Intiqam headquarters room where I was and had her hood removed."

"But...But...But..." stammered Tandy.

Frank turned to Tandy. "You have a question?" he asked.

A bewildered Tandy said, "But...*how* did you know she wasn't the real Lady Corrigan?"

"Easy really," answered Frank, smiling. He turned from Tandy to face Sir Michael who was back to scratching Cromwell's head again. The dog was sitting with its eyes shut and was wearing a silly grin. "You see, I've met Lady Corrigan before...only she doesn't know that."

Lady Corrigan blinked. "Really? When?"

"The night that I came to see Sir Michael, after Tandy and I had rid the world of Simon Lancaster and Aarif El-Sayed."

The real Red shook her head, rippling the waves of her hair. "I don't..."

"You don't remember," grinned Frank. "Of course you don't. You didn't see me, but I saw you. You were in the kitchen, making an omelette, as I recall."

"Hang on," said Sir Michael. "I had thought about that. And I realised that if you were passing behind Maria, you would not know what her face looks like."

"Ahh but," said Frank, smiling and getting his empty glass refilled. "You have a glass-fronted wall cupboard directly above the worktop. I could quite clearly see her reflexion."

"Well, I'll be damned," said Sir Michael.

"But," said Red, waving her champagne flute. "How come I didn't see you?"

"Simple," answered Frank, still smiling at their confusion. "Your head was up, but your eyes were looking down at the worktop. You have a very upright stance Lady Corrigan, and to get that you hold your head up. You hold your head up but you look down with only your eyes...it's become a physical habit for you. So, I could see your face, but you didn't see me."

"Well, I'll be damned," repeated Sir Michael. He knew only too well what Frank meant, for Sir Michael had always admired his wife's imperious presentation. She always stood, and walked, as if she owned everything in sight.

"And, also," continued Frank, "I didn't want you to see me, so you didn't." *It's his bloody ninja skills again*, thought Tandy. "Okay," she said. "But then who's this?" and she nodded towards the bogus Lady Corrigan.

"Oh, sorry," said Sir Michael. "Let me introduce Miss Victoria Hart." Victoria – Vicky – gently waved her glass and gave a small curtsey.

Frank nodded. "And she is, I suspect, one of your agents."

"That's right," beamed Sir Michael. "Although Vicky has not been with us for very long…"

"How long?" interrupted Frank.

"Oh, about six months. Isn't that right Vicky?"

"Five," she corrected.

"Five," repeated Sir Michael. "However, she has shown great promise, and when I asked her if she would like to take on this job, well, she jumped at the chance."

Frank gave Vicky a charming smile and said, "You must be mad." He was secretly aghast at the idea that Sir Michael had taken someone, with not much experience, and shoved them into the line of fire. But it had been her decision, and, as Frank often said, life is full of choices.

"Well," continued Frank, "you certainly played the part to perfection Vicky, and you knew how to handle yourself when the chips were down."

"But why?" asked Tandy. "Why use Lady Corrigan?"

"Call me Red," said Red.

"Bait," said Frank, and his smile turned to a scowl as he looked at Sir Michael.

"Bait?" queried Tandy.

"Yes," admitted Sir Michael. "I'm afraid Frank is, ahh, right. You see I needed Frank, or you, to kill al-Makira. Frank had already made it clear that he did not want to work for me, or the SOU, again, so, I had to devise some method of getting him, and his Shadows team, to do the job…"

"…Therefore," interrupted Frank. "You set me up by setting up the kidnapping and by substituting Vicky here for Red." He turned to Tandy. "…And at a distance I could not see that Vicky was not Lady Corrigan. It was, as I said, only when I saw her in close-up that I realised that this lady here was not Lady Corrigan." His attention went back to Sir Michael. "But how did you know that Intiqam would try and snatch her?"

"Because," answered the knight, "they had already tried to grab both of us earlier on our return from a dinner date at Regent's Park. They failed, but I knew they would try again, and then I discovered that they had this house under surveillance…although they didn't know that I knew that. They really were not very good at it. I mean, fancy sitting up a tree in full view of the front door with a pair of binoculars. Stupid buggers."

Lady Corrigan joined in. "Mike suggested that we use a look-alike instead of me to get snatched. We just needed someone, at very short notice…a member of the SOU…who was prepared to take the risk and who is the same height and build as me, also with long hair." She proudly ran a hand through her own.

"Enter Vicky," said Sir Michael. He bowed graciously to her and she nodded back at her boss who continued, "Obviously, Vicky had to dye her own blonde hair the same colour as my wife's glamorous locks…"

"Took me bloody ages," interrupted Vicky, "and I had to rush over here at some ungodly early hour of the morning in order to use Lady Corrigan's hair dye."

"But it all worked out very well. Don't you think?"

"You bloody conned us!" snapped Tandy as she glared at the Director of the SOU. "Your bloody tricks could have got us all killed!"

Sir Michael straightened. "True. But I also wanted the only people on the planet who I knew could absolutely get the job done." He poked his index finger at Tandy and Frank. "In effect…you two."

"Well, I'm not happy!" said Tandy.

"Neither are six of the seven dwarves," quipped Sir Michael and, despite the bad joke, and despite herself, Tandy had to smile.

"But what about Ali?" asked Tandy. "You bloodywell missed him, didn't you."

Sir Michael nodded. "Actually, we missed Wetton as well. We had known for a while, through our intelligence network, that al-Makira had a non-Arabic, possibly European, girlfriend or lover, but we had no idea who she was, or where she was." His brow furrowed. "God knows what information Wetton passed to Intiqam, or if there are any more like her out there. I can see I'm going to have to get MI Five to give the staff of the MP's a shake-down." He nodded again at his own thoughts, then said, "I have to admit that Wetton played her role really well."

"Nearly too well," put in Frank. "She nearly killed me. Probably would have if Ali hadn't shot her to save his own neck."

Tandy came in here, "Ah, but Ali – Nadeem – he nearly slipped through the net as well, didn't he?" She sounded quite smug, trying to score another one over Sir Michael.

"Actually...No," said Frank.

"No?" chorused Red, Tandy and Vicky.

"No," said Frank. "I didn't trust him as far as I could throw him. I did not believe that he was MI Five because I had, after all, witnessed him bundling Lady Corrigan...Vicky...into both a van and a helicopter."

"And they knocked me out by sticking sodding needles into me!" added Vicky. "Which bloodywell hurt!" She took a mouthful of champagne and chucked it back down her throat, as if that emphasised her point.

Frank made no comment but Lady Corrigan put out an empathetic hand towards her.

Frank continued, "So, when we landed at Akrotiri, in the general organised confusion I managed to get a few photos of Ali on my mobile. I would have liked to have taken his gun off him but that would have aroused his suspicions and he might have done a runner and disappeared. I wanted to know what he knew, to see how far this Intiqam organisation has spread." Sir Michael nodded in agreement at this as Frank went on, "I was going to tackle him on the 'plane. It would have been fairly easy for me to get his gun off him, but then that all went to crap."

Tandy raised an arched eyebrow. She knew that if Frank wanted to take a gun off someone who was within touching distance, then they would not stand a chance – he was that fast, that skilled, that good. But the grenade threat had made even Frank's remarkable skills redundant.

Sir Michael said, "Frank sent me the photos and I checked with both MI Five and MI Six, and no-one had anything on Ali, so he certainly wasn't one of theirs. Therefore, he had to be a member of Intiqam, although he then seemed to be working to his own agenda."

"Which, of course, he was. He had lost his leader but he was still a member of Intiqam, so he formulated a plan and tried to execute it."

"He very nearly executed you," said Lady Corrigan.

"Anyway," said Sir Michael as he tried to inject a positive note. "You all got the job done, so well done!"

"Hang on," said Tandy. "I'm still not happy...and don't give me any of that jokey fairy-tale crap either! As Red here just said...You could have easily got us all killed!"

Sir Michael inclined his head with a small regretful smile playing about his lips. "Yes, Tandy, you are right," he admitted. "I should apologise for risking your neck, but how else was I to get the hostages rescued? If we had left it to the SAS they would have gone in as an attack force, mopping up only the foot soldiers, which would have given al-Makira time to escape with the hostages. Either that or he would have executed the hostages. The SAS might have been able to rescue Wetton, but, knowing now what we do about her, what would that have achieved? Her subterfuge would not have been discovered and she would have gone on working inside the government, operating and spying for Intiqam and al-Makira."

Tandy had to admit that what Sir Michael had just said made sense. She allowed a small smile to flicker across her face before she nodded as Sir Michael continued, "And don't forget, it wasn't until al-Makira was killed that we did actually find out about Gail Wetton. And if it had not been for the fact that Frank actually entered the lion's den, I doubt that we would have got al-Makira, Wetton, Irfan and Habib, al-Makira's pet assassin. And your team went on to wipe out all the rest of them in both their headquarters and their training camp. Incidentally, I must congratulate you Tandy on such fine shooting. The captain in charge of the SAS team was most impressed. Apparently, you downed more terrorists than his own sniper?"

Tandy smiled. She recalled the deadly shooting she had carried out alongside Buzz.

"And," continued Sir Michael, "I believe it was you that took out al-Makira with just one shot?"

"Bloody hell," said Red, and her mouth fell open. She turned full face and stared at Tandy.

"And her second shot took out his second-in-command," put in Frank.

"What was the distance?" asked Sir Michael.

Rather subdued, Tandy answered, "About eight hundred yards…give or take."

"Bloody hell," said Vicky. "That's about half a mile!" She also turned full face to stare at Tandy.

"And into an unlit room through an open window," said Frank proudly.

"Yes, damned good shooting," praised Sir Michael.

"Well…" Tandy poked the toe of her boot into the carpet and struggled to keep the smile off her face. "Thank you," she muttered, trying to keep an air of humility but secretly pleased at the praise.

"What about Gainsborough?" asked Frank.

"Oh, him…" began Sir Michael.

"Fucking idiot," said Red in an out-of-character burst of abuse.

Sir Michael glanced at his wife. "Yes, well," he said. "In private he'll get a bollocking from both his wife and the PM, and I suspect that the wife's will be far worse than the PM's. And in public he'll have his part in the hostage rescue blown out of all proportion and probably get a knighthood."

"Needs a good kick up the arse," said Lady Corrigan.

Sir Michael sighed. "Yes, m'dear, but he's a politician."

There was a pause in the conversation, and then Tandy said, "I wonder what will happen to the little accountant."

Sir Michael looked at her. "Oh, he'll be grilled by possibly MI five, possibly six, possibly both."

Tandy nodded thoughtfully then asked, "And then what?"

Sir Michael shrugged his shoulders. "More champagne?"

Tandy had her glass refilled. She knew that her questioning of Sir Michael would go no further. Perhaps he did not know the answer to her question. Perhaps he did.

There was another pause in the room as they all considered the repercussions of their various actions. Once again, Sir Michael Corrigan, the Director in charge of the Specialist Operations Unit, had played a consummate hand. Yes, he had set up both Frank and Tandy, but they really had been his best bet for getting al-Makira and the rest of the Intiqam members wiped off the map, and the exercise would have set back Intiqam for years, if indeed it had not wiped out Intiqam completely. On that last point they were, however, unsure - and that was because they did not know how far, and how deep, the Intiqam tentacles reached, or had reached.

Vicky had proved herself as a very good field agent, and she did not know it then, but she was going to get sent on other high-risk missions after further weapons training – something she had always dreamed about since joining the company that did not exist.

Lady Maria 'Red' Corrigan had got to take part in one of her husband's schemes and, she had to admit, had quite enjoyed the thrill and machinations of it all.

And Tandy and Frank had proved to Sir Michael the usefulness of their Shadows team – something they were not too sure was such a good idea.

"Now," said Lady Corrigan, breaking the spell. "Who likes Chinese food? My treat. Mike and I know a great little restaurant just down the road, in

Hampstead. We'll go in the Range Rover. Dave can drive." She looked at her husband. "Would you call him, please darling?"

Sir Michael Corrigan did as he was bid and a short while later Dave James arrived and went to get the Range Rover out of the garage.

As they headed for the front door Cromwell went back to his bed, grumbled quietly, and went back to sleep.

**

Lawrence Gainsborough MP never got the knighthood that Sir Michael had hinted at. He was met at Brize Norton by men in dark suits who put him in a dark car and took him directly to Number 10 Downing Street. Here he received a severe dressing down from the Prime Minister who, in the comfort of his private office, called Gainsborough every abusive name that he could think of and told him to "Keep it in your trousers from this point on!" and then promptly appeared in front of the cameras with his arm around Larry's shoulders as he was welcomed back into the fold after his much-publicised terrifying ordeal. Gail Wetton was only briefly referred to, and then only with much sadness and regret. She was praised for her service to her employer and no mention was ever made of her between-the-sheets gymnastics that she had been having with the Member of Parliament, or al-Makira.

After Downing Street, and after the TV interviewers had finished with him, Larry walked into his house where his wife hit him full in the face with the bottom of a frying pan. He spent the evening at the local hospital in Accident and Emergency, then he went home with his bandaged head and black eyes to sleep in a separate bedroom to his wife.

Two weeks later, Gainsborough resigned from his cabinet office and became a back-bencher. Two weeks after that he had a nervous breakdown and gave up being an MP to grow petunias and sweet peas at home in his large garden.

His wife never divorced him, but she kept her lover and her Ferrari.

**

Because the accountant was now on British soil some more men in dark suits had come from MI5 to Brize Norton. The accountant was taken away.

With him went the cardboard Kellogg's Cornflakes box with his laptop and ledgers and all the other items that had been acquired from the Intiqam training camp.

The accountant was taken to a small grey room in the basement of a large grey building somewhere in central London. The room had bare white walls, a concrete floor and a white ceiling with a single strip-light set in it.

He was placed in a chair in front of a steel-framed table with a white plastic top. Both the chair and the table were bolted to the floor. Across the table from him were two MI5 agents: a man and a woman. Both in dark suits. He had black hair and she had blonde hair. No names were given out. They sat and stared at Amir Darwish for a good ten minutes without saying anything.

During this time the accountant's eyes flickered left to right and back again as he watched the impassive faces of the two agents. Amir Darwish had no intention of having information pressed out of him by either intense questioning, or by downright torture. However, he did have enough intelligence to know that, if he was to talk, he might be able to cut himself a deal. He would want protection and a new identity. Because he knew that if Intiqam discovered that he had talked, then he would not live for very long.

But the two MI5 agents did not ask him any questions. They just sat and looked at him.

Eventually the accountant asked,

"Can I have a solicitor present?"

"No." This from the woman.

"Why not? I thought…"

"You thought wrong."

There was a long pause and then Darwish tried again, "I thought I was allowed to have a solicitor."

"Have you got one?"

"No…"

The MI5 agent shrugged her shoulders but made no comment. Her partner had remained sitting as still as a boulder. They resumed their stony silent gaze on the little man.

Strangely, by not actually asking the accountant any questions, he began to talk. In fact, he sang like a bird.

As a result MI5 contacted MI6.

This was Big, and getting bigger by the minute.

Over the next few days Amir Darwish revealed names and dates and accounts, and all of this was checked against his ledgers and laptop that he had been so keen to rescue and keep safe, as well as the information and intelligence that had been gathered by the Shadows team and the SAS.

Darwish had been a very efficient accountant. It was what he was good at, and he had kept immaculate records which al-Makira – had he been alive – would have viewed with horror. Because every single dealing, big or small, had been noted in great detail in the accountant's laptop, and backed up as a paper hard copy in his ledgers.

It was all on display; details of equipment, weapons, ammunition, vehicles and uniforms. Even cooking utensils, food and drink were listed. Even the mundane was listed; pens, pencils, paper; even drawing pins and toilet paper were accounted for. Every item in and every item out. Every profit and loss.

The interrogators could not believe their luck; here was Intiqam laid bare.

There was even a file that had a record of a list of people world-wide who had been sent a letter; a letter demanding money with menaces. It became known as the White Envelope List.

There was even a list of the banks that the money resided in. Cash and cheques had been presented by a variety of couriers into a variety of international banks and from those accounts the monies had been laundered and transferred around the world. However, the accountant had followed it all and had meticulously noted where it all was. And what this revealed was that Intiqam had been bank-rolled mainly by al-Qaeda and ISIS, with additional funding obtained from the White Envelope List. It seemed that both al-Qaeda and ISIS were supplying all of the arms and ammunition. But who had supplied those arms and ammunition?

For all of the exquisite accuracy of the accounts there was no mention of a supplier. It was certainly not Russia or China, who were the usual arms suppliers. There was no mention of any other nation either. So where were the aeroplanes, helicopters, trucks, cars, guns and ammunition coming from? Could it be from a company? Or possibly a private individual? If it was a private individual, he, or she, would have to be extremely wealthy. And powerful. And careful.

So maybe it *was* a country? However, the identity of that country, company or individual had been deliberately left off from the Intiqam accounts by the devious Amir Darwish.

So, Darwish knew who was funding Intiqam. However, he wasn't saying who was supplying the arms, or who or where Intiqam's world-wide-web of agents were placed. In actual fact, Darwish had no idea who or where the agents were. And, as he wanted to wake up one morning with his head still attached to his body, he certainly would not have told the Security Services that information anyway.

Never-the-less, all of the valuable information obtained from the little accountant allowed the Security Services to cut Darwish his deal, and, true to their word, they arranged for the accountant's disappearance. The timid little man was given a new name and a new identity and he was given a nice modern fully furnished three-bedroom flat in the county of Norfolk. Overlooking the River Bure, the flat was in Wroxham in the area of Norfolk known as The Broads.

Amir Darwish never moved into his Wroxham flat because Amir Darwish had revealed a great deal but he had not divulged *everything* he knew. He had not revealed the fact that over his period of forced employment with Intiqam he had, unbeknown to his employers, moved little unnoticed bits and pieces of Intiqam funds into a number of banks that were not used by Intiqam. These bits and pieces were *not* in the files and ledgers that he carried and were therefore completely untraceable. The missing money added up to two-and-a-half million Pounds Sterling.

Amir Darwish was taken by car to his Wroxham flat where he was escorted to his new front door by a different man and a woman wearing dark suits. He was given the keys to his flat and then the dark suits left him there outside. They got back in the car and it drove off. When the vehicle had disappeared out of sight Amir turned on his heel and walked away - and neither he, nor his wife and two children, were ever seen or heard of again.

**

The Director General of MI5 and the Chief of MI6 had been invited to a London club for lunch in the area known as Mayfair.

Mayfair, named after the May Fair. Its origins go back to around 1560 when it was known as Saint James's Fayer and based at Westminster. In 1686 it moved to another site where Curzon Street and Shepherd Market now stand and operated there until 1764.

Mayfair is now an affluent area of London. It sits to the eastern edge of

Hyde Park and is bordered by Oxford Street in the north, east by Regent Street, west by Park Lane and south by Piccadilly.

The heads of the two security services had been invited to the club by Sir Michael Corrigan and, after a couple of glasses of very decent single malt whiskey and some conversation that pointedly avoided shop talk, they dined in a large wood-panelled room that had original oil paintings of various British monarchs hung around the walls. The eyes of those monarchs looked down onto wooden tables that were covered in white tablecloths and antique plates, cutlery, wine glasses and decorative silverware.

They had a beautiful meal, ordered and paid for by Sir Michael, of seared scallops followed by crispy-skinned sea bass on a bed of crushed potatoes, cooked beetroot and samphire. For dessert they had a tangy lemon cheesecake with whipped cream and all was washed down with a good chilled Chardonnay, drunk from those antique glasses.

They moved from the dining room to the club's lounge where they sat in high-backed leather armchairs the colour of cigars and around a low walnut table. Brandy was served in large balloon glasses and then Sir Michael leaned forwards and asked,

"What are you going to do with all that money that you have recovered from Intiqam?"

There was a moment when you could hear the tall long-case clock that was standing in the corner of the room ticking like a heartbeat, and then the two heads glanced sideways at each other. The Chief of MI6 recovered first and asked cautiously, "Mike. Do you know something that we do not?"

Sir Michael gave a slow smile. "I *always* know some things that you do not. However...Be that as it may...I believe that you know the whereabouts of some very large amounts of money? Although you may have lost the accountant who dealt with it all."

The Director and the Chief held blank expressions on their faces whilst their minds whirled. How did Sir Michael know? And where was the leak?

"No?" asked Sir Michael, still smiling like a benign grandfather. "Let me assist your memories...This money was recovered from Intiqam." Sir Michael avoided the use of the word Terrorist out loud. "Money which you..." he wagged his index finger at both of them. "...discovered by interrogating a certain accountant."

The Director's face twitched like a gambler's tell.

"Oh yes," said Sir Michael as he noted the twitch. "I know all about the accountant because, you see, it was my agents that extracted him and brought him home." It was not strictly true, but the two heads would not know that.

The Director said, "I understand that it was the SAS that carried out the rescue?"

"You can believe that if you want to," said Sir Michael.

The two men glanced at each other again. The Specialist Operations Unit must have been involved. How else would Sir Michael know about both the rescue operation and the accountant?

The Director General of MI5 said, "The SAS never reported being helped…by anyone."

"Well," smiled Sir Michael. "They wouldn't, would they?"

The Director finished his brandy and put the glass gently down onto the table in front of him. "No," he agreed. "The Regiment tends to keep its own secrets."

Sir Michael sat back into the leather of his armchair. "This money is not yours, neither is it government money, and therefore it should be returned to the rightful owners. Don't you think?"

Somehow, the money that had been recovered had not been reported, as yet, to the Treasury Department.

"Well gentlemen," said Sir Michael. "I have enjoyed our lunch together. We must do it again some time. Yes?" And with that He stood up. He knew that neither of the men in front of him could report him, because his department did not officially exist.

Seeing Sir Michael standing, the two heads took the hint, stood, shook hands with Sir Michael, thanked him for the lunch and left.

Outside in the street the Director General of MI5 turned to the Chief of MI6 and asked,

"Well, what do you think?"

"I don't know."

"You do understand what the SOU does, don't you?"

The Chief nervously adjusted his tie and said, "Of course I do."

"Well then."

"Well then."

The two men looked at each other.

"It don't suppose that it would hurt…Do you?" said the Chief.

"No. I don't suppose it would."

"After all, it was a successful rescue mission. Good publicity for the government. Sabre rattling and all that."

"Yes," agreed the Director. "And only we know about the accountant."

"Best to hang on to the report then."

"Yes. Best."

"Okay. I'll see you...later, then."

The two men shook hands and headed off in opposite directions along the wet pavements of the nation's capital.

Inside the club Sir Michael Corrigan had sat back down in his chair with a slight smile on his face. He knew, as sure as night followed day, what would happen next and he ordered another brandy.

**

Three days later, Jim, the pilot of Supermarine Spitfire PV202, was back at North Weald with the old warbird. He stood outside his hangar and smiled lovingly at the once deadly machine, and wondered how the hell he had gotten away with breaking nearly every rule in the Civil Aviation Authority's book of rules. He'd even had a couple of new passengers registered with him for a flight in the aircraft – a certain Mr James Cameron, and a Mr Roger Collins.

One week later, Rick Duncan picked up his morning post. Amongst it was a plain brown narrow envelope. The envelope bore his printed name and address but had no stamp and no franking mark, so he did not know where it had come from, and thus there was no clue as to who might have sent it. He moved to his hall table and picked up a letter opener and slit the paper.

Inside was a suitably vague letter on government headed notepaper informing him that the circumstances surrounding his loss of recent money had been investigated by the authorities and that they were pleased to reimburse him. The notepaper mentioned no department, did not explain who had investigated his loss, did not tell him which authorities, and did not tell him who "they" were.

With the vague letter was a cheque for the full amount of money that he had paid out to Intiqam as money to avoid menaces. Rick rushed into the kitchen, grabbed his wife who had just stood up from the breakfast table, and spun her around, whooping and hollering. His wife, laughing with him and not knowing yet the reason for his joy, yelled, "Put me down, Rick! Put me down!"

Denise Anderson had been under the doctor for depression ever since the first white Intiqam threatening letter had arrived and after her art gallery had been burned down. The loss of her gallery had nearly broken her both mentally and financially.

But this morning she was smiling. In her hand she held an almost identical letter to that issued to Mr Duncan and a cheque for the amount of money that she had lost with the destruction of the gallery. It was enough to pay for a new gallery and then some. She held the cheque up to her mouth, kissed it and said aloud,

"There is a Father Christmas!"

Then she danced.

And danced.

Josephine Havers-Whyte burst into tears in the middle of the stable yard as she read her letter, and then went out and bought two new thoroughbred Arab horses with her cheque.

Duncan, Anderson and Havers-Whyte were only three of the people affected by the ripple effect of the money that had been recovered from Intiqam. And Sir Michael Corrigan, Knight of the realm, hearing of this ripple effect, was more than pleased with himself. Not bad for a department that did not exist.

*****

FOUR WEEKS LATER - THURSDAY 24th JULY

Frank and Tandy were laid out on comfortable plump sun loungers beside the swimming pool outside Cannon Head. The material of the loungers had broad stripes in poppy-red and white along their length and the frames of the loungers were touching distance apart with a small white plastic table set between them. On the table was a glass of *cuba libre* made with some of St Margaret's finest rum, and an opened bottle of the local beer.

Tandy was wearing a very brief bikini, consisting of what looked like small black triangles and bits of black string, and Frank was in a pair of bright red swimming briefs; they were as brief as Tandy would allow because she had warned him against wearing budgie smugglers, insisting that they were "disgusting".

They had arrived back on St Margaret, courtesy of British Airways, after staying on in London for two weeks, and had then headed directly back to Cannon Head in one of the island's shell-pink taxis. They had delayed leaving London because they had finally decided to sell both Frank's house in West Harrow to the west of London and Tandy's flat in Islington. As a result, they had stopped in Tandy's flat whilst they viewed property in London's developed Canary Wharf and Docklands area.

The Docklands area falls within the London Boroughs of Southwark, Tower Hamlets, Lewisham, Newham and Greenwich. London has had docks and small quays since Roman times. However, this area of low-lying marshes had been a breeding ground for thieves as it was insecure and overcrowded with shipping that fought for moorings. After a great many years of general disorganisation, the Port of London was started in 1696, with the building of the Howland Great Dock in Rotherhithe on the south side of the Thames. This was an area that was large enough to take vast amounts of shipping and was also secure. This was so successful that it led to the development of the Surrey Commercial Docks which in turn led, in the Georgian period, to the development of the West India Dock in 1802 and the East India Dock and the London Dock in 1805. There followed the Surrey Dock, the Regent's Canal, St Katharine's Docks and the West India South.

In the Victorian era were opened the Royal Victoria Dock, the Millwall Dock, and the Royal Albert in 1880. The King George V Dock came along later in 1921.

All of these docks had specific purposes. For instance: the Surrey took timber, the Millwall took grain and St Katharine's took wool and sugar. However, with other ports opening up around the British coast the London Docks began to lose shipping and thereby trade, until finally they became unviable and the area became both derelict and poverty-ridden. And it stayed that way for many years until the Docklands regeneration began after the 1980's.

Now the area has been transformed into a modern bustling scene of ultra-modern shops, office blocks, high-rise flats and apartments. There are high-end sailing and motor yachts moored where commercial shipping used to tie-up and the area has taken on the street café scene amongst the latest in modern architecture, as well as green open spaces bedecked with flowers, trees and shrubs.

Tandy and Frank had viewed a number of apartments; some with silly laughable millionaire price tags attached to them. However, some, although the prices being asked were still at the top end, were more affordable to them. They settled on a two-bedroom apartment on the top floor of a block at Selsdon Way, and it came with a subterranean garage. It was near Canary Wharf on the Isle of Dogs and overlooked the tranquil waters of the Millwall Outer Dock. There was no chain of buyers and Tandy and Frank had enough money between them to pay for the apartment outright with no loans or mortgages. And, once paid for, the combined sales of his house and her flat would easily recoup the costs involved, and they had already received several good offers on these properties.

From their sun loungers, Tandy and Frank began to lightly discuss the flat that they had bought, its colour scheme, its furnishings. Tandy lifted the glass of *cuba libre* and took a pull at it. Still holding the glass, she said,

"You know, we ought to get a lady-who-does in to keep the place tidy once we have finished decorating and furnishing it."

"Agreed," said Frank as he raised the bottle of beer to his lips. "Someone like Mrs Johnson."

"Yes," said Tandy. Then she plonked her glass down onto the table. "But Frank...Just who the hell *is* Mrs Johnson?"

THE END

*****

EPILOGUE

A large black S Class Mercedes Sedan with smoke-tinted windows rolled to a halt outside the western arch in the wall of the village of Qaryat Musawara. The Mercedes was one of a convoy of three like-bodied cars, and after they had pulled up on the beaten surface of the sand-covered road three men got out of each car leaving only the drivers inside.

It was mid-day and hot below a cloudless achingly blue sky and the men seemed wrongly dressed for the baking heat in their dark-blue tactical jackets and cargo trousers. But there was one man who was not dressed in this fashion. This particular man had emerged from the middle car of the convoy line; he was a tall, six-foot, blonde-haired, wide-shouldered Austrian, wearing a dark-grey well-tailored suit and had a pair of Gucci aviator style sunglasses on his shaved broad face. His name was Carl Mayer and he stood in the sunshine and looked at the ancient crumbling wall that surrounded the village. There were no goats and no dogs to greet him. Likewise, there were no people either.

With the withdrawal of the SAS and the Shadows teams the villagers had set about the few remaining Intiqam soldiers with old rifles, broom handles and a variety of sharp agricultural instruments. The soldiers, who were lacking any kind of leadership or organisation, were either summarily killed by the villagers - who were exacting a revenge for the brutal dictatorship that they had been living under with Intiqam - or they had simply run for it.

The villagers had then gathered up all of their worldly goods and moved out, they had had enough, and they left the dead fanatics where they lay, rotting in the sun and the desert heat.

With a nod from Mayer the eight men under his command drew semi-automatic pistols from underneath their jackets and moved off towards the entrance arch. They left a driver in each of the cars, armed for security reasons. Even from outside of the village the stink of death hit Mayer and his men. Indeed, a large Egyptian vulture was perched on the top of the entrance arch. One of Mayer's men took a shot at it and missed. The big scruffy-looking bird unwound its grizzled neck and flapped lazily away, moving as if in contempt of the shooter.

As they passed under the arch and entered the village Mayer took point. They advanced past the bodies that were strewn around; some were bloated with internal gasses, but some had been torn at, partially eaten by the rats, wild dogs, and carrion birds.

. The Austrian paused, wrinkling his face with disgust, and then he split his team into four groups of two, with himself in charge of one of them.

With guns up the groups moved off. Mayer went straight up the narrow street that cut the village in two and which was the same street that Frank Cross had used to get the hostages to safety. They passed the burnt-out smoked and gutted house where T Bone had thrown a grenade inside, and where the white letters and envelopes were now just so much grey ash. They then passed across the end of a side street and saw the devastation of the communications house with the ravaged blackened bodies of the communications team still inside.

Mayer took his mobile phone out of his jacket pocket and hit speed-dial and, when a voice at the other end answered, he reported that the village was empty of its inhabitants. Then he rang off.

Mayer carried on until he reached the tall building that had been used as the Intiqam HQ. Mayer and his two team members entered quietly, stepping over a body in the entrance doorway and another at the foot of the stairs. They went up.

They came to the execution room where Mayer crossed immediately to the body of al-Makira. The corpse lay on his back in a blackened pool of dried blood with a blonde-haired woman face-down beside him. She had her right arm flung across the dead leader's chest.

Mayer pulled her roughly to one side and looked at her as her dead pale face turned towards him. She had, at one time, been a pretty thing, but death was robbing her of that attractiveness. Mayer gave a slight twitch of his head and lips as if to acknowledge this, then he pulled his mobile phone from his pocket again and once more hit speed-dial. Almost immediately the same voice as before answered,

"Yes?"

Mayer said simply, "We have found your son, Sir."

"Is he…"

"Dead?…Yes, Sir."

There was a pause while the man at the other end of the call struggled with an internal turmoil. Then he said, "And Irfan?"

Mayer looked at the body of the Second-in-Command. "Dead as well, Sir."

Another pause. "And the girl?"

"Also dead."

"Very well, Mayer…" Another pause for the man to collect himself. "Please make arrangements to bring my son and Irfan home."

"And the girl?"

"Leave her. She is of no consequence."

"Yes, Sir."

"Mayer."

"Yes, Sir?"

"When you have finished, burn the village to the ground."

Mayer smiled. "Yes, Sir."

Later, as the village burned and the smoke curled up into the blue cloudless sky a man sat and plotted the death of Frank Cross. He believed that vengeance was needed for the killing of his two sons.

*****

AUTHOR'S NOTE

One of the trickiest problems that I faced when writing this story was moving the story around the multiple time zones of London, Italy, Cyprus, Iraq, Japan, the Caribbean and the USA (the Continental USA having 4 time zones of its own).

If, therefore, I have slipped up by a few minutes here and there I do apologise, and I hope that it has not spoiled the story for you.

Also – Having trained with a number of Japanese Sensei, and spent time with the Japanese people, I am aware of the way in which they pronounce the English language.

I have therefore, in this story, attempted to write how that pronunciation comes across to the Western ear, and it is not meant to make a mockery of the proud and honourable Japanese race. Neither is any embarrassment of them intended.

LOOK OUT FOR THE THIRD STORY IN THE VENGEANCE SERIES:

IN DARK CORNERS.

JAPANESE PRONUNCIATION – A Short Guide

Vowels are pronounced in the following way:
A – as in the a in "rat"
E – as in the e in "set"
I – as in the I in "police"
O – as in the o in "pot"
U – as in the u in "put"

Consonants are pronounced:
G – as in "got"
J – as in "just"
Ch – as in "church"
Z – as in "zoo"

The Japanese word for Punch can be spelt in English in two ways – *Tsuki* and *Zuki*. The correct way of writing the word is *Tsuki*. When saying the word, the T and S should be pronounced as the ts in "itself".
The word *Uchi* means Strike, with the U being pronounced as the examples given above.
The Japanese word for Kick is *Geri*, with the G being pronounced again as in the examples given above, and not like a J as in the English name Gerald.

When speaking Japanese every syllable is pronounced separately. For example:
Arigato - A-ri-ga-to – Thank you
Katana - Ka-ta-na – a type of Japanese sword
Sushi - Su-shi – Raw fish

*****

Printed in Great Britain
by Amazon